THE WAR BE DAMNED ... SHE WOULD HAVE HER MAN

She was so vividly alive as she stood there, her eyes wide, her breasts swelling against the soft material of her dress, her hand white and fragile on his sleeve. "I came to see you. I'm a fool to tell you, but I did. I missed you. I just couldn't stand it." She began to cry softly. "And you're sending me away." She raised a hand to her face. The wind ruffled her cape, fanned it out gently to show the slimness of her waist, the generous rounding of a breast.

He cried, "Ah—la pauvre!" and all the loneliness, all the yearning of the unnatural, womanless months spoke through his tones. "I have been stupid. I have been cruel. The words have always been in my heart and I have been too imbecile to say them."

His brain whirled as he felt the soft fur trimming of her bonnet brush his face, saw her parted lips turn upward toward his. Her arms were warm about his neck, her soft body pressed against his. She murmured something broken and undistinguishable in his ear, then clung closer, the hoops of her skirt cutting into his leg. He whispered, "Ah, ma cherisette, how blind I have been. How blind! The glint of your eyes and the wave of your wonderful hair. Your smile. Ah—there is so much—I have always wanted to kiss that hollow at the base of your throat—" She laughed softly and tilted her chin back with a happy shudder.

A little later she said breathlessly, "And we'll live in your lovely chateau at Loudéac?"

Other Pinnacle Books by Bruce Lancaster:

BLIND JOURNEY
TRUMPET TO ARMS
PHANTOM FORTRESS
THE SECRET ROAD
GUNS OF BURGOYNE
THE SCARLET PATCH

WRITE FOR OUR FREE CATALOG

If there is a Pinnacle Book you want but can't find locally, it is available from us—simply send the title and price plus 25¢ to cover mailing and handling costs to:

PINNACLE BOOKS
275 Madison Avenue
New York, New York 10016

_Check here if you want to receive our catalog regularly.

_Check here if you wish to know when the next_____will be published.

THE SCARLET PATCH
Bruce Lancaster

PINNACLE BOOKS　　　　　NEW YORK CITY

This is a work of fiction. All the characters and events portrayed in this book are fictional, and any resemblance to real people or incidents is purely coincidental.

THE SCARLET PATCH

Copyright © 1947 by Bruce Lancaster

All rights reserved, including the right to reproduce this book or portions thereof in any form.

A Pinnacle Books edition, published by special arrangement with Little Brown and Company in association with The Atlantic Monthly Press

ISBN: 0-523-40-045-9

First printing, April 1977
Cover illustration by Bruce Minney

Printed in the United States of America

PINNACLE BOOKS, INC.
275 Madison Avenue
New York, N.Y. 10016

TO MY WIFE
Jessie Payne Lancaster

FOREWORD

The Rochambeau Rifles appear in no roster of the Union armies. Their veterans published no regimental history, founded no G.A.R. posts. The unit is, of course, fictitious. Yet, in substance it was duplicated scores of times in the years between 1861 and 1865 by the foreign-born who flocked to the colors in seemingly endless thousands.

In the main, these foreign-born were refugees from the futile liberal revolutions that wracked Europe from the 1830's on. From the first call to the final surge at Appomattox, they fought for the Union which had harbored them and which they had adopted, finding in it the same urge that had sent them to the barricades and the battlefields of the Continent. They enlisted in groups to form units that were miniature national blocs; they dropped old ties and served as individuals and were submerged in native-born regiments.

There was among them the usual percentage of charlatans, adventurers, soldiers of fortune, and downright scoundrels. But the great bulk, so far as the records may be traced, fought on through sheer conviction, believing that in so fighting they were carrying on the old liberal struggle that they had regretfully abandoned in their homelands. In no sense of the word can they be identified with the glib, false legend that Abraham Lincoln's government bought them abroad like cattle on the hoof to fight the battles of the native-born. A man from Dresden might die in the wheat fields of Gettysburg or a man from Bordeaux might fall at Cold Harbor. But they fell as soldiers of the Union, not as mercenaries. Often placing their old flags on the battle line beside the flag of the Union, often using their own tongue within the limits of their units, often preserving old customs (like the beer wagons that followed certain Wisconsin Germans) nonetheless they emerge from the war years as American as Plymouth Rock or the Overland Trail.

It is perhaps owing to their basic Americanization that alien origins have been overlooked and forgotten. In the cold tables of army records a number and a state reveal nothing of a given unit, save possibly the most important fact that it existed, and existed for the Union. Yet as one goes back to the beginnings of such formations, numbers and states are pushed aside. The 55th New York hides the French "Gardes LaFayette" commanded by Colonel Régis de Trobriand. The 37th Ohio begins life as the 2nd German Regiment under Colonel Siber, and the 32nd Indiana is revealed as the 1st German Regiment of that state, led by Colonel Willich, whom readers of Carl Schurz's memoirs have met in the Germany of 1848 as a leader of German Republican troops.

So the roster goes—von Steinwehr and the 1st Astor Regiment; Dieckel's Mounted Rifles and the Italian Count di Cesnola; the de Kalb Rifles and von Gilsa; the 1st New York German Rifles and the Hungarian von Stahel. Sometimes the character of a regiment is indicated only by the man who raised it or helped raise it. There are Wladimir Krzyzanowski and the 58th New York; August Kautz and the 6th Pennsylvania Cavalry; the 69th Pennsylvania and its German-Swiss Tschudy, who fell at Gettysburg.

Other foreigners appear in native-born units. The former French hussar officer, Alfred Napoleon Duffié, transforms the 1st Rhode Island Cavalry into a first-class fighting unit. Colonel John Turchin (born Ivan Turchaninoff), a former officer of the Czar, leads Ohio troops from 1861 until a sunstroke incapacitates him on the threshold of Sherman's invasion of Georgia.

And the Irish? Their story is well known and perpetuated, unlike the stories of the French and the Germans and the Poles and the Spaniards, which have had little notice. By regiments, by brigades, almost by corps, they served throughout the war, leaving a trail of familiar names spotted through nearly every engagement of the Union armies—possibly through every one—

Shields, Sweeney, Lawler, Connor, Smyth, Patrick Jones, Meagher, Corcoran. Together with the native-born of Irish stock, they followed the Irish-American pattern that may be traced through our military history from Bunker Hill on to the Civil War and from there to Guadalcanal, Anzio, Bastogne, and Iwo Jima.

Germans, French, Irish, Poles, Italians, Spanish—men from almost every nation of the Western World, they made the Union theirs. Under the lens of history, there is no difference between a sincere allegiance that dawns in 1850 and one that dates back to 1620. And kin of these same men, born in Europe like them, took up the cause of the South, fought for it, died for it. To them and their conviction must salute be rendered as well.

The casualty lists of foreign-born and native-born represent a hideous bleeding away of the strength of this country. And the very presence of the foreign-born, whether they lived or died, is token of a bloodletting in Europe. This drain Germany felt most severely, perhaps even fatally. In the tens of thousands of Germans who came to this country, discouraged by the failure of the Republic and sickened at the dominance of Junkerism, by the Middle Ages lying close under a veneer of progress, was the cream of all Germany—the liberals, the progressives, represented by the high-born, the solid middle-class, and steady German mechanic or farmer. Here the German sang his *lieder,* formed his *Turnverein,* founded his German language press. But he became American. Had that stock stayed in Germany, it is possible that there could have been no Kaiserism. But it left and there was no liberal force remaining that was strong enough to check autocracy. Had it stayed, there surely could have been no Hitler. One cannot conceive of Carl Schurz and the countless thousands of men like him being subdued by concentration camps, Gestapo, censorship of thought and deed. Nor could Schurz and his like have been dazzled by the tawdry, lying doctrine of race purity and Aryanism.

The fictional Rochambeau Rifles, then, have solid fact on which to stand. While drawn from no one regiment they are remotely based on the 55th New York—the Gardes LaFayette—as our chief character, Jean de Mérac, stems (with many liberties taken) from the colonel of the 55th, Baron (later Count) Régis de Trobriand, American citizen as of 1861. Outside of Pelham's brigade and the Rifles, few fictional characters have been necessary and no fictitious units. In action, battlefields have been enlarged to include our imaginary commands. The only nonfactual engagement is that of Pingree's Store, where the ambush is partially based on an exploit of Michigan cavalry in 1864.

Students of Gettysburg may wonder at the reconnaissance-in-force by Berdan's Sharpshooters (1st United States Sharpshooters), supported by the Rifles, on the second day of Gettysburg. Such a coup took place. It is usually dismissed, when noticed at all, as of little importance. However, eyewitness accounts and testimony by Southern officers after the war suggest so strongly that Berdan's men at least played a large part in delaying Longstreet's attack on the Union left that fictional use of this coup and its possible results is thought justifiable. Men are arguing to this day about just what did happen during those precious hours of July 2, 1863. Perhaps part of the answer lies in Berdan's action.

As to the course of Philip Kearny's career had he not been killed at Chantilly, no one may speak surely today. Stanton is quoted as saying that he was to be given a corps at least. But there are enough contemporary hints and speculations to justify the fictional assumption that he was to have been given supreme command in the East.

General Dudley Pelham is fictitious. Unfortunately, there is far too much fact to base him on. The type of mind which actively hates all that does not conform to its own prejudices is timeless. It did not begin with the bigoted Know-Nothing Party. It did not die with it. That such prejudice can be unleashed in time of war as well as in time of peace needs no proof. The scapegoat history of the largely foreign-born XIth Corps; Hooker's hatred of Schurz, which culminated in a court-martial clearing the great German-American; the enmity that hampered Franz Sigel—these were all manifestations of which

Dudley Pelham would have coldly approved. As to the machinery against de Mérac set up by Pelham, it is based very generally on the railroading of General Charles P. Stone in 1861.

Various expressions which may strike the reader as modern if not actually current as of today will be found in this text. Each of them has been found in letters and diaries of the times or of even earlier times.

I wish here to acknowledge the debt that I owe my wife, who, as in our six other books, has worked with me, tireless, constructive, perceptive and encouraging. Without her aid and presence, each task would have seemed insurmountable.

Nor can I think back over this book without a feeling of gratitude for the editorial guidance, the ever-helpful and ever-friendly comment and advice, that have been so freely given by Edward A. Weeks, Jr., editor of the *Atlantic Monthly*.

In the same bracket, Mrs. Jeannette Cloud of the Atlantic Monthly Press has worked cheerfully and indefatigably with me. To her keen eye and clear thought I am greatly indebted.

My brother, Southworth Lancaster, has provided a wealth of detail from his great knowledge of military affairs and of transportation of the nineteenth century.

As always, the librarians and the staff of the Harvard College Library were immensely helpful. And with my thanks to them I must include no less thanks to the Public Libraries of Lexington, Massachusetts, and of Beverly, Massachusetts.

B. L.

Contents

	Foreword	vii
I	Return of a Traveler	1
II	The Rochambeau Rifles	16
III	The Potomac	44
IV	Under Way	58
V	General Dudley Pelham	79
VI	In Full Swing	107
VII	The James	137
VIII	Kearny's Men	171
IX	The Hospital	199
X	Defeat	228
XI	The Old *Kébir*	252
XII	Pursuit	281
XIII	The Rappahannock	303
XIV	The Stone Wall	341
XV	*Lettre de Cachet*	369
XVI	*Civis Americanus Sum*	391
XVII	The Turn of the Tide	422
XVIII	Gettysburg	445
	Epilogue—Washington, May 23, 1865	512
	Addenda	522

THE SCARLET PATCH

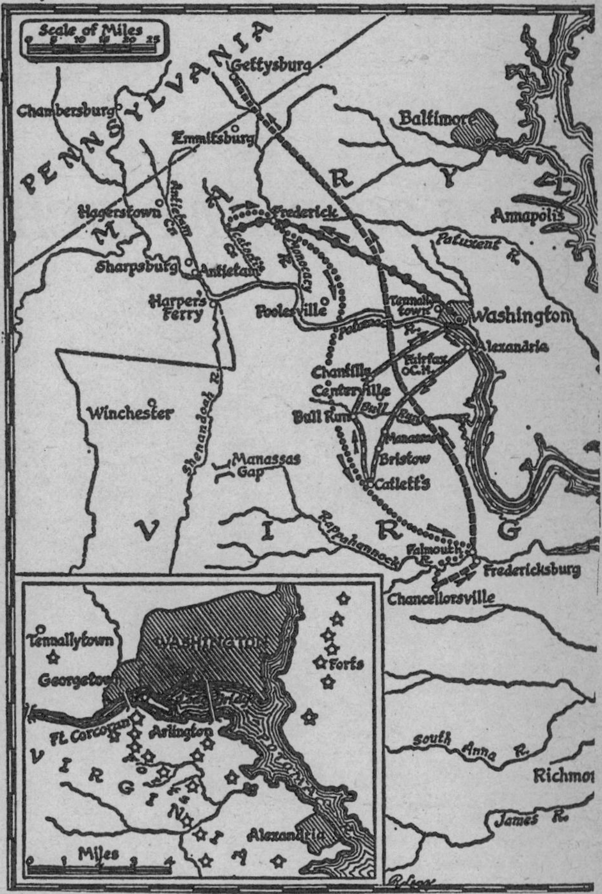

Scale of Miles
0 5 10 15 20 25
PENNSYLVANIA
Gettysburg
Chambersburg
Emmitsburg
Baltimore
MARYLAND
Hagerstown
Antietam Cr.
Catoctin Cr.
Frederick
Monocacy R.
Annapolis
Patuxent R.
Sharpsburg
Antietam
Harper's Ferry
Poolesville
Tennallytown
Washington
Potomac R.
Alexandria
Fairfax C.H.
Chantilly
Centerville
Winchester
Bull Run
Manassas
Bristow
Shenandoah R.
Manassas Gap
Catlett's
VIRGINIA
Rappahannock R.
Falmouth
Fredericksburg
Chancellorsville
South Anna R.
Richmond
James R.
Tennallytown
WASHINGTON
Forts
Georgetown
Ft. Corcoran
Arlington
VIRGINIA
Alexandria
Miles
0 1 2 3 4

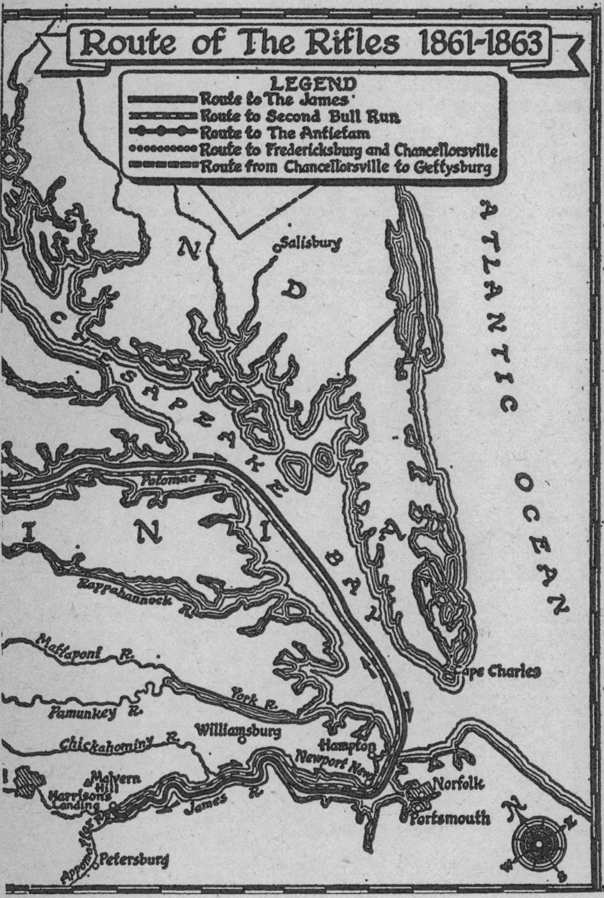

Route of The Rifles 1861-1863
LEGEND
Route to The James
Route to Second Bull Run
Route to The Antietam
Route to Fredericksburg and Chancellorsville
Route from Chancellorsville to Gettysburg
ATLANTIC OCEAN
Salisbury
Potomac R.
Rappahannock R.
Mattaponi R.
Pamunkey R.
York R.
Chickahominy R.
Williamsburg
Hampton
Newport News
Norfolk
Portsmouth
Cape Charles
Malvern Hill
Harrison's Landing
James R.
Appomattox R.
Petersburg

I

Return of a Traveler

THE waiting room of the Twenty-seventh Street station was crowded and its oil lamps flickered to a confused beat of voices. At the ticket windows pot-hatted civilians, Regular Army officers in feathered, steeple-crowned felts, men in Zouave fezzes, in kepis, in curved shakos, elbowed and argued. Among the benches, women in wide skirts waited by piles of luggage or called shrilly to straying, weary-faced children. A sergeant, broad, down-pointing chevrons on his sleeves, bawled, "Recruits for Governors Island! Get 'em the hell over here!" Newsboys whipped through the mass screeching, "*New York Herald! New York Times!* Extry! 6th Massachusetts gets to Washington! Extry! Jeff Davis calls for 30,000 men! Extry! Virginia sure to secede! Extry!"

A voice boomed sonorously, "Get your places on the Stamford local! Seven-twenty from Boston coming in!" There was a sudden rush for the wide-spaced cars out on the roofless tracks and hurrying passengers looked up the line to see swaying lights draw nearer and nearer. One by one the cars of the Boston express appeared, each drawn by slow-stepping horses that had trundled them away from the chuffing locomotive at Forty-second Street and on down the Fourth Avenue Tunnel. Men shouted orders, and as each car halted, its span of horses was unhitched and led over to the Stamford local.

Travelers from the Boston train dropped to the platform, clinging to valises and carpetbags or loading them gratefully on eager porters. Apart from the hurrying ruck and last to leave the forward coach, a tall young man with a topcoat over his arm followed at a leisurely, self-assured pace, his bags shouldered by a grinning Negro.

When he entered the waiting room, people glanced at him, settled back to their own concerns, screwed around to stare again. There was no one detail about him to stir their interest and yet they sensed something a little strange. Perhaps his clothes were cut rather full, perhaps the beaver hat flared slightly more than most. It may have been the coat of sleek English cloth over his arm or the solid luggage that the Negro carried proudly. But that was all, except that the chestnut hair was cut quite short and the broad, square chin and lean cheeks were clean-shaven, conspicuous features in a world of rich beards and curving side whiskers. Or was it the trim mustache? Then a door leading to the street swung after him and snapped the slender thread of interest that he had aroused.

Out on the sidewalk in the soft April evening the porter stacked the luggage carefully into an open carriage while the driver, a querulous, gray-whiskered Negro, watched irritably. "Whar'm I totin' all that?" he quavered.

The porter said scornfully, "Whar you think? Mah gennleman, he's gwine to th' Fif' Avenue Ho-tel. Yes-*suh!*" He gave a final shove to a leather case on the front seat. The light of an oil lamp shone down on black lettering—"J. de Mérac."

De Mérac paid the porter and climbed into the carriage, staring at a long line of men, headed by fifes and drums, who tramped east along Twenty-sixth Street. They sang "The Wearing of the Green" and marched under a flag whose gold harp was bright against emerald folds. Illuminated signs, held high, proclaimed "Death to Traitors! Join Cochrane and the 69th New York!"

The driver gentled his horse and then sent the carriage rolling on toward Fifth Avenue. De Mérac leaned back against the cushions, pulling thoughtfully at his mustache. "*Au fond*," he thought, "this perplexes one enough to split the skull!" He cast back in his mind, trying to sift out impressions gleaned from his earlier visit to America. Then he thought of what he had seen and heard in Boston, where he had landed not two weeks ago. Uniforms, flags, mass meetings, and men roaring a song that had moved him strangely, a beating, driving hymn about a man named John Brown whose soul went marching on. Fort Sumter had been attacked, had fallen; men of the 6th Massachusetts had died in a Baltimore street; Federal officers were deserting the Union. Yet so many people were convinced that there would be no war, that there could be no permanent rift in the Union.

As the carriage came nearer to the flaring gaslights of Fifth Avenue, de Mérac heard a growing buzz of voices over the grind of the wheels. The horse shied at the sharp blast of bugles and the driver reined in quickly. People ran out of brownstone houses, mixed with a thickening swarm that blocked off the Avenue. A woman cried, "Here they come!"

De Mérac stood up in the carriage and looked over the close-packed heads. The bugles blared again and he could make out the steady rhythm of marching feet. He caught his breath. Up the Avenue, red kepis aslant, marched eight buglers, their long *clarions* balanced on their hips, red legs swinging in cadence. Suddenly ten bugles flashed high in the air, spun above vizored heads in the old French bugle drill, were brought down in unison to send a quick-step ripping through the air. After them came a solid company, squad on squad of infantrymen in the same red kepis, blue coats, red trousers, and short white gaiters. Bayonets were rigidly aligned and the dress across squads was faultless. Another company, its fanion fluttering, a third. The bugle march rang on. Now the files were singing, cocking their heads to the infectious rhythm:

> *Ce chic ex-quis, Par les Turcos ac-qui*
> *Ils le doivent à qui? À Bourba-ki!*

De Mérac leaned forward. The sergeant on the nearest flank wore the Algerian and Crimean medals. In the ranks, other coats showed a glitter of ribbon and metal. The regiment might have been in Paris! Then he uncovered quickly. The color guard was passing, the American flag riding high over heads that might have charged shouting under the African sun. Far up ahead the bugles raved on and the ranks thundered out a song of the Boulevards, *"Rien N'est Sacré à Un Sapeur!"*

The last files swung north under the gaslights and the crowd broke up slowly or ran cheering after the twinkle of red legs and white gaiters. *"Vingt dieux!"* muttered de Mérac. *"Qu'est-ce que c'est que s'agit, enfin?"* He touched the driver's arm. "What regiment was that?" The short English sentence came smoothly, though with a noticeable accent.

"Them, boss? They's what folks calls the LaFayette Guards. French foreigners, I reckon. G'up, Dan!"

There were other bands blaring somewhere out of sight as the carriage rolled down the Avenue. The house fronts were alive with swaying flags. A slim officer, holding a sword close to his side, ran up brownstone steps to a door that swung open for him. De Mérac caught a woman's pleasant voice, "How did the drill go, Penn?" Then the door closed.

De Mérac smoothed his mustache and thought of the red kepis surging up the Avenue. Those red-epauletted shoulders, the Breton faces, the Gascon faces, Alsatian and Limousin faces! The regiment seemed a bit of transplanted France, if one overlooked the occasional unmistakable Yankee heads under the bright kepis.

Madison Square opened ahead and the driver worked carefully through a welter of omnibuses, heavy drays, and water carts. In the Square itself orators shouted from torchlit platforms. Crowds overflowed to the sidewalks, climbed lampposts, swarmed up trees, and even perched on the roofs of the large birdhouses that the city had built for the newly imported English sparrows. The

Negro pointed helplessly to an omnibus between him and the front of the Fifth Avenue Hotel. Its progress was blocked by a line of men who carried torches and coils of rope as they shouted: "Avenge *Sum-ter!* Hang Jeff *Davis!*" in wild unison. The jam was hopeless.

De Mérac told the driver to swing around to the West Twenty-third Street entrance, bring the luggage in, and collect his fare at the desk. Then he got out of the carriage, worked past the omnibus, and found himself struggling across the thick-packed sidewalk. He managed to squeeze through the door, his mind on the uncrowded ease of the lobby, only to be bumped and shoved into a still tighter jam inside. People were pressing painfully toward the big sign marked ELEVATOR. He clutched at his hat, tried to push on towards the distant desk, and was pinned fast. Men and women were shouting unintelligibly. Bonnets, beavers, steeple-crowns, kepis, shakos, swayed and bobbed. A thin-faced streetwalker caught in the jam wriggled provocatively against de Mérac but her made-up eyes were staring ahead. A man cried, high and whinnying, "Here he comes! Slid in through the side door!" There was a scuffle far down the lobby. A fat man near de Mérac jumped up and down screaming senselessly. People began to sing, "Bob Anderson, my beau, Bob!"

De Mérac gasped. "*'Cré nom de Dieu!* What's this?" The fat man yelled louder and tried to point. The scuffle died away suddenly.

A big man in a rumpled blue uniform, his clean-shaven face lined with care, was being boosted onto a bench by main force. A kepi was awry on his graying head. The crowd exploded. "Bob Anderson! Three cheers for the hero of Sumter. Yeeeaaah! Bob Anderson!"

Anderson raised his arms as though trying to beat down the din. A tense hush fell over the lobby, broken only by the creak and wheeze of the elevator. Anderson spoke slowly, his voice marked by a Southern accent. "Fellow citizens! There's no need for this. I'm just a soldier. At Sumter I tried to do my duty to my country as I've tried to do it since I left West Point."

Bedlam shook the crowd, shattered Major Anderson's

words. De Mérac stretched to his full height, looking for freer space.

Then he caught sight of a tall man erect and motionless on a landing not far away. He was striking enough with graying hair above a keen hawklike face, with his cavalry mustache and imperial. But even at a distance his deep-set eyes seemed to burn and stab over the heads of the crowd with a repressed intensity that was startling.

The crowd yelled louder, swayed and pushed. De Mérac lost sight of the rigid man, then was carried closer to him in the blind pulsation of the packed bodies. His eyes widened in surprise. On the gray lapel the red ribbon of the Legion of Honor showed bright, and an empty left sleeve was tucked into a side pocket. A compatriot! No doubt a retired colonel of hussars or *chasseurs à cheval* traveling in America, old memories now stirred by the acclaim accorded another soldier, one who had stood by his flag. And yet there was almost accusation in the hot, steady eyes.

The shouting died abruptly. Anderson was speaking again. "I swore at the Point to honor and protect the flag of my country and there weren't any if's or but's in that oath. So long as I've got a breath to draw, I stand by that oath. That's nothing to cheer about. It's only what I expect of myself and what you, as my fellow citizens, have got a right to expect from me." He dropped from his perch and de Mérac could no longer see him. People yelled, "Leave him out! Leave the major out!" Flat blue police caps loomed between Anderson and the crowd. Someone yelled, "Let's follow him! He's going out the side door."

The mob eddied off to the left. De Mérac braced himself against it and at last stood clear. He would have liked another glimpse of Anderson, whose few simple words he had found sincere and moving. But the frenzied push toward the doors was too thick.

He drew a deep breath, settled his cravat, and started toward the desk. Almost unconsciously he glanced toward the landing. The hawk-faced man was coming slowly down into the lobby. De Mérac eyed him, saw that the rosette was the military award—not the civil—of the Legion of Honor. They met at the foot of the stairs. De Mérac raised his hand to the brim of his hat, motioned the one-armed man to go ahead, saying, *"C'est déjà quelque chose, ce qu'on vient de voir."*

For an instant the eyes that met his were a-smolder with hot feeling, boring through him as though he did not exist. Then a smile spread quick warmth over the fine-drawn face. *"Je vous crois, monsieur, c'est vraiment quelque chose."*

The words were French but the accent was American. De Mérac masked his surprise and said in English, "Please excuse my mistake. Seeing the rosette of the Legion, I thought you French."

The graying head inclined courteously. "Very natural, of course. No need to apologize. You've just landed?"

"I came in this evening from Boston."

"This evening? Then perhaps, in honor of your arrival, you'll join me in the bar. It'll be empty, I guess, with everyone chasing off after Bob Anderson. My name, by the way, is Kearny—Philip Kearny. We spell it 'Kear' but pronounce it 'Kar'!"

"I am Jean de Mérac and shall be very happy to join you."

"De Mérac? Breton, eh? Lovely country, Brittany. Do you mind my remarking on your excellent English?"

De Mérac laughed. "I wish I might claim credit for it. In my family, it has always been insisted on. I began to speak it as soon as French. I fear, with such experience, it should be far better."

The bar was broad and airy and lit by shaded gas jets. A white-coated Negro showed his teeth in a grin. "Evenin', Major, suh. Got yo' pleasure right here!" He slid a bottle of cognac onto the bar, pushed up two glasses. "An' th' other gennleman?"

De Mérac ordered *marc de Bourgogne* and, while the Negro filled the glasses in majestic ritual, tried to place the name of his host. He was sure it was connected with the old patroon and manor families. Yet there was some other association hovering just out of reach in the back of his mind. And there was the matter of the rosette, the empty sleeve, the fluent French.

Kearny raised his glass. "*'Santé, monsieur.*"

"À *la vôtre,*" responded de Mérac.

"And," Kearny went on, "please tell me how I can be of service to you while you're here." The warm smile and the level eyes made the words a simple offer rather than a veiled request for information.

De Mérac inclined his head. "You are most kind to a stranger, sir."

"No Frenchman is a stranger to me in view of all the courtesies I've met in your country."

De Mérac said slowly, "I feel, perhaps, a little diffident—"

Kearny shook his head. "You mustn't. Not at all."

"Then I should be truly grateful for your opinion of the idea which brought me back here."

"So this isn't your first trip? I rather thought not," smiled Kearny. "By all means let's have your idea. I hope I can help."

De Mérac made careful circles on the bar with the bottom of his glass. "Perhaps it does not explain itself easily. I came here for the first time in 1857. Frankly, I came at a venture. From here I might go to Canada, even on across the Pacific to Japan, which your Perry has so kindly opened to the world."

Kearny raised his eyebrows. "You stayed on, instead?"

"Until last summer when family matters called me to France," he answered. "Such affairs move slowly, you understand, and I was not free to return until quite recently."

Kearny looked at him curiously. "I'd like to know what held you here and what brought you back."

De Mérac smiled in half apology. "It is hard to explain without sounding pedantic. *En somme,* I found, almost from the first, that I was witnessing the boldest experiment in democratic living that the world has ever known. Here it was, if I had wit to see it."

Kearny's eyes snapped. "That's it! That's everything! And you saw it! Go on."

"There is little more to tell. I traveled where I could.

By luck I found new friends in many parts of your country. I came to know that, *au fond,* the basic beliefs under which you live were much like those which I myself had been trying to formulate. I did not, of course, run about at all times with notebook and pencil like a German botanist. Friends were kind and it was easy to amuse oneself while watching. Nonetheless, I think that I was neither blind nor deaf and I felt a profound shock that I, supposedly an educated European, should have been so utterly ignorant of this world of yours, and with the shock came an idea. De Tocqueville's *Démocratie en Amérique,* while sound, does not go beyond the 1830's. Why should not I, as best I might, bring his work up to date? Such, Mr. Kearny, is my plan."

"Excellent! Capital! If I can help you in any way, I'd be very proud to." He studied the keen brown eyes under the level brows. "You're young to have thought out an idea like that."

De Mérac signaled the Negro to refill the glasses. "I am just past twenty-six, an age that approaches profound antiquity. But even at twenty-six one may marvel at your Union."

Kearny leaned forward. "You say 'Union'—not 'America.' Why?"

"But the Union, it is America," cried de Mérac. "Without it—*mais enfin—*" He completed his sentence with a shrug.

Kearny stiffened. "You see that! Right here in New York are people who've spent their lives in the Union and are so damned blind—oh, you must have heard them talk—here and in other places!" The stump of his arm twitched. The angry heat back of his eyes blazed into full fire, seemed to throw out an energy of its own until his body quivered like the housing of a powerful engine. "You saw that mob in the lobby. What did you think of it?"

"A remarkable, spontaneous demonstration."

"Is that all you think? That mob was yelling because Anderson simply sat in a fort he was ordered to hold. When he could surrender with honor, he hauled down his flag. No more than that. But because hundreds of other officers, even men like Robert Lee and Joe Johnston, desert the Union, Anderson is a hero for being passive. That'll give you some idea of what may happen to the Union."

"Still, from what one reads, Anderson must have found it difficult to know what to do."

The hawklike face flushed. "Knowing what to do? There was only one thing." He swept out his arm. "He ought to have fired first and he ought to have kept firing so long as he had a single gun on its carriage and one pair of hands left to serve it. Why—look at the warning he had!" Swiftly he traced out the tragedy of Fort Sumter.

De Mérac listened with deep interest. Then, in the midst of a sentence, the full light of recollection flashed over him. Kearny! Major Philip Kearny. The French press had been full of his story, had wrung the last flutter of panache from it. Half-forgotten tags ran through his mind as the major talked on. Commissioned from civil life to the United States Dragoons—a course of instruction at the French Cavalry School at Saumur—a volunteer with Marshal Vallée's army in North Africa—the passage of the Iron Gates, action at Metidjah, at the Mousaia. "*Triple sot* that I am," thought de Mérac. "I should have known at the first glance." There was more, much more. Service for the Union in Mexico and a shattered arm. Then 1859 and back to the French Army and the Chasseurs d'Afrique. "And I had forgotten that! Charging the Austrian center with his reins in his teeth! How the newspapers loved that!" Bonaparte had given Kearny the Legion of Honor and had offered him command of the famous Foreign Legion! "*Triple sot* again, that I should not have known at once this Don Quixote, this sane, Yankee Don Quixote!"

Kearny was finishing his exposé, crying vehemently: "Aren't we ever going to learn that to win we've got to hit first, hit hard, and keep on hitting? This is war, I tell you, and every second we waste'll bring the end of the Union nearer. My God, can't people see it? Can't they see what'll happen? We'll have two discordant countries side by side. They won't be strong enough to stand alone and they'll have to make alliances in Europe. Then you'll see European quarrels spreading over here, quarrels about who backs whom. You'll end up with five or six little nations that'll be continually fought over and partitioned and split up. That's not what this country was built for."

De Mérac frowned. "But surely it couldn't—"

Kearny cut in. "You just said that the Union is America! But there's more than that!" He pointed a rigid finger. "This goes beyond America. All over Europe people are watching this 'experiment' you talked about. If the experiment lives, then it'll keep hope alive in every liberal brain in Europe. If we let it fail; then the world as we know it'll take the road to autocracy straight back to the Middle Ages. All your revolutions in Europe will have been for nothing. So will ours. This whole business is just as important to a man in the Rue Vaugirard as to a man on Broadway. It touches Warsaw and Nashville, Stuttgart and Chicago. Are we all going mad? I've been living in Paris—Avenue Matignon—you know, near the Arc de Triomphe. The city was full of Americans working against the Union. I fought them until I was sure an explosion was coming over here. I thought—well, I thought perhaps I could be of some service." The blaze of his eyes died to a hopeless smolder and his face was suddenly haggard. "They won't have me," he said in a curious, flat voice.

De Mérac started. "*Vingt dieux!* You tell me—"

Kearny nodded bleakly. "Rejected."

De Mérac tried to keep his eyes off the empty sleeve but Kearny seemed to read his thoughts. "It's not my arm—unless they can't think of anything else. The Regular Army? I'm not West Point. New York State won't have me, although I was born at No. 1 Broadway. They have a new reason each time I go to Albany." The old fire flared again. "I've told them I'd go as a second lieutenant. I'd go as a private except that you need two arms to handle a musket."

De Mérac expostulated. "*Mais c'est tout à fait incroyable!*"

Kearny said wearily, "You have the expression *mal vu*

11

par les politiques, and with us, too, it seems more important how a man has noted than how he can handle a squadron of cavalry." He turned to the bar, swallowed the last of his cognac. When he faced de Mérac, his eyes expressed courteous contrition. "I've been talking too much. Please excuse it. But to you, as a Frenchman and particularly as a Frenchman who sees the Union as I do—you understand?" He looked at his watch. "I'm afraid I must be going. Please keep in touch with me. I have a room here to use when I'm in town. They'll always be able to tell you at the desk whether I'm here or in Newark." He raised his hand in the French salute, turned on his heel, and strode out of the bar, shoulders back and head high.

De Mérac felt the spell of Kearny strong on him as he rode the rumbling jerky elevator to his room on the fourth floor. Such a depth of sincerity and purpose underlay the undoubted panache that had caught the imagination of the French press. Kearny was a Murat with convictions, and all those convictions centered on the Union which had rejected him. It was actually painful to recall the angry heat of the eyes that had glared at Anderson, painful to remember their heavy smoldering as he told of the rejected offer of his experience and skill, not to mention his remaining arm and his life.

In the corner room overlooking Madison Square de Mérac found his bags neatly stowed by the foot of his bed. A gas jet burned cheerily over the mantel, lighting up the gay, fresh wallpaper. He tossed his coat and hat onto a chair and threw open the window that looked out on Fifth Avenue. Bands and crowds and orators were gone and a light breeze stirred the trees in the park where flocks of English sparrows chittered sleepily. He drew a deep breath. There was a smell to a New York spring as individual as the lemon-yellow light that filled the Place de la Concorde in winter twilights or the lavender tints that hung over the Charles River at Boston. It was good to be back. He would stay for two or three days before going down to Washington where he was to be the guest of Stoeckl, the Russian Minister. There were calls to be made. Pretty, dark Betty Barclay lived just over there on Murray Hill. Sara Trimble, a beautiful waltzer he remembered, was at her father's house on Washington Square, North. Then, to be sure, there was the ash-blond Louise Duane whom he had met last summer on the Normandy coast, traveling with her parents. East Fourteenth Street, just off Fifth Avenue, she had told him. Perhaps he could spend a week in New York. Stoeckl, an old friend of his family, would be glad to receive him at any time. He began to whistle *"Le Joli Carnet de Marie"* and rang for a brandy to help him through his unpacking.

Frowning over his bags, he found that Kearny and the echo of his intense words crowded out his first lighter thoughts. The Union was in danger, in grave danger, no matter how many people tried to shrug the matter away. He hung up a coat carefully, slid an empty valise into the closet. Beyond compromise and discussion lay war. Compromise had failed. Kearny was right. It was war. And the outcome of that war, said Kearny, would vitally affect the lives of men in countries who had never heard the word "Union," who, perhaps, had not heard of America. Then, logically, it could be the fight of a man in Tours as well as of a man in Brooklyn. He finished his brandy, lit a cigarette, and stared down at the gaslights on Fifth Avenue.

When de Mérac took off his coat, paper rustled in an inner pocket. He drew out a long envelope from which the wreathed head of Napoleon III stared icily at the fragile letters of the address: *"Au Baron Jean de Mérac, au soins du Parker House, Boston, dans le Massachusetts, États-Unis d'Amérique du Nord."* He had asked his uncle and guardian not to use the title which aroused embarrassing interest in democratic America. It was the old man's sense of fitness which had insisted on it. He drew out the thin sheets. Below the crest, the same fragile hand had written, *"Au Château de Loudéac, près de Carentour, Morbihan, France, Très-cher neveu—"*

After a few lines of local Breton gossip, his uncle swung into his main theme. "I did not oppose you when you first went to that species of wilderness. In effect, I approved for it leapt to the eye that your liaison with the German Baroness was becoming troublesome—" De Mérac's lips formed an "O" and he breathed out lightly. His uncle's word *gênante* exactly fitted Lisa von Horstmar, once his mistress. "—nor do I reproach you this time, you conceive. It is only that I do not understand your deep interest in a country so far from France. Do, my dear Jean, abandon your wanderings in a land that is utterly alien to you as a Frenchman and as a de Mérac. You are an orphan. You have ample means of your own. One day, as I do not need to tell you, you will inherit from me Loudéac and the added title of Comte de Tréguier. You are a graduate of St. Cyr and are, I may remind you, the first of our name who has not followed the profession of arms since 1385. Have you the right to bury all this among the redskins of the New York? This much for yourself.

"May an old man who has always held you in the deepest affection permit himself to speak selfishly? You are all I have, for collateral relations I do not count. Not for long shall I be here. Jean, it would sweeten my last glimpses of our Breton moors to see you riding across them on your English hunter, to know that each morning—but enough. Now I shall pass through the *salle d'armes* to the dining room where the tall chair in which you last sat will be vacant by my elbow. May I hope, Jean—not vacant long?"

De Mérac slipped the letter back into its envelope. There was much justice in the plea of the old Comte de Tréguier who had brought up the ward and nephew after the death of the father, at Sidi Brahim in '45, and of the mother soon after. Would it be well to go back until the issue between the States was settled and then return at a time when events were not moving too swiftly to be captured? The pleasure and comfort which his uncle would derive would be immeasurable. True, an act of proscription had been issued by Bonaparte against one Jean de Mérac for refusing to take oath to the Empire after graduating from the military college of St. Cyr. But the act had been, with seeming intent, vaguely worded, almost nominal. There had been no trouble about temporary admission on family business the summer before.

Acceptance of the Bonaparte regime, as nominal as the act of exile, would, no doubt, clear him for all time. So, it would be easy for him to re-enter France.

Yes. It could be done. Go back to Loudéac until the issue between the States was settled—that sectional issue of a country that was not his. He lit another cigarette and stepped to the window. A sectional issue? It was the Union and the Union abolished geography by touching every living soul. And if the soul believed in the free man on whom the Union was based, then that soul was touched and touched hotly, at Loudéac as well as in Albany.

Yet the fight for the free man and for the Union with all its implications might be carried on from Loudéac or Paris.

He drew an armchair to the window and sat there smoking as he looked down onto the Avenue. He could see ten gaslights stabbing the well of darkness below— two more, he told himself, than the number of seceding States up to that moment. A bent man toiled along the sidewalk dragging a long pole. He reached it up to the first light, turned off the jet. Slowly eight lights went out, then nine, ten. The bent man was out of sight and the dim glow of other unseen lights faded, leaving the Avenue in hard gloom. De Mérac shivered and lit another cigarette.

II

The Rochambeau Rifles

THE house looked out onto the south side of East Twenty-fourth Street. Its broad door was open to the May Day dusk and soft lamps in the hall glinted on brass numbers—"67"—and on the name plate "Willett Force." It was a house that people cared for, would come back to eagerly at the end of a day or of a year. The hall was wide with apple-green walls and the floor was thick with Chinese rugs of unbelievable yellows and rusts. Over the delicate Georgian table hung a painting of a clipper ship, vibrant against a sunset sea, tacking into the harbor of Hong Kong. Opposite, a long Chinese scroll, delicate and feathery, spread a narrow vista of falling water and bamboo-shaded rocks. On either side of the hall, broad doors gave glimpses of white woodwork, carved teak, and silk-smooth mahogany. Shallow stairs curved to a landing where a dull gold Buddha stared down benignly. From the drawing room at the right, a woman's voice called gently, "Willett! George hasn't *gone*, has he?"

A shadow fell on the landing, blurred against the wall, and Willett Force walked past the Buddha, absently touching its capped head, and came briskly down the stairs. The light from a hanging bronze lamp fell on grizzled hair, steady blue eyes, and weather-beaten cheeks. Trimmed whiskers joined a thick mustache and carefully parted beard. He said, "What is it, Ella?"

She came out of the drawing room, an oddly young face under a sweep of white hair so fine that the light behind it gave it a soft glow from nape to temple. She stepped quickly to her husband. In her wide lavender skirts and bodice she looked absurdly small and frail against his tall frame. He bent and kissed her. "You look like a Dresden marquise, Ella. What were you saying about George?"

She tapped a Chinese gold piece that hung from his watch chain. "Will—he hasn't gone, has he?"

"Gone? No, he's still up in his room. What made you think he'd gone?"

Her face looked suddenly pinched. "He—he might have slipped out after dinner." She went on quickly. "I shouldn't have blamed him. He hates a fuss." She smiled up at her husband. "I'm going to fool him, Will. No fuss." Her chin twitched as the night wind brought a tag of ghostly band music into the house.

Willett Force laughed. "George knows that, darling."

"He could wait till morning, couldn't he?"

"You saw the way he kept hitching his jaw at dinner. Just like your father. He's got his head down and he's going to charge." He shifted uneasily. "Oh—meant to tell you at dinner. The Government's buying the *Morning Star* and the *Amoy*. Of course, I don't feel like claiming anything beyond cost. And we'll write depreciation off that figure, too. H'm. They want us to keep the *Kowloon* and *Ningpo* and *Foochow* in the trade. Oh Lord. When this is over, you and I'll ship on the *Ningpo* and—"

A sudden buzz upstairs resolved itself into a deep young bass and a girl's light tones. Husband and wife glanced at each other, separated, and stood casually on either side of the hall, he straightening a stick in a blue china holder and she leveling the portrait of a wise-eyed old mandarin. The deep voice called, "Mother? Dad? I'm casting off!"

George Force, taller and broader than his father, came lightly past the Buddha, absently touching its head as the older man had done. In contrast to Willett Force's weather-beaten face, the son had the clear, high-colored skin of a farm boy on a cold day and his hair, carefully parted on the left, was the color of straw. His gray eyes danced with an excitement that overlay a deep seriousness. Behind him a pretty, brown-haired girl kept pace with him, one hand on his shoulder.

Ella Force looked up at them. "I was just going to call you, George. Aren't you afraid you'll be late?"

He threw an arm about her. "Would have been if I hadn't shut Marion up. Those questions! 'What's a battalion?' 'Who's higher, a lieutenant or a lieutenant colonel?' How'd I know? I'm no soldier. Where's the bag?"

"Over in the corner." She smoothed his lapel. "George dear—do you have to wear such dreadful clothes?"

Willett Force protested. "Have you forgotten that that suit was the admiration of the Columbia campus in George's sophomore year? The blue coat's not so shiny and those lovely fawn breeches will hold together for at least another week."

Marion said gently, "Let us know as soon as you can, George."

He picked up a leather-bound canvas bag. "Trust me!" he said, kissing his mother.

She said evenly, "Good-bye, dear."

"Sure you don't want me to do anything?" asked his father.

"Thanks, Dad. I'll go on with this."

"If you've made up your mind—why, that's all I want to know. Good luck, George—and—ah—well—oh, confound it!" He pulled four cigars out of his pocket. "Better stow those somewhere. May need 'em. And—well good luck and get back as soon as you can."

George grinned. "Sure will. 'Bye, Sis." He waved and was gone.

Marion slipped quietly upstairs. Mrs. Force wandered into the drawing room, her husband following aimlessly, hands behind his back and eyes shifting uncertainly about the room.

George Force strode along Twenty-fourth Street. With each step a feeling of unreality spread over him. It increased as he skirted the torchlit hubbub of Madison Square and the scene flicked through to his consciousness, sharp but remote, like something from a remembered dream. Broadway swept him along its noisy current and his mind seemed to hang off, to watch him, as he worked his way south. Then he climbed into an omnibus that rolled him farther and farther downtown while the din beat against his ears like a sound heard under water.

He dropped off at Chambers Street. Halfway down the block he saw an illumination across the front of a shabby building and walked quickly toward it, his head lowered. Then he glanced up at huge letters on the transparency. *"Français de New York! Formez Vos Bataillons! Les Fusiliers Rochambeau Vous Attendent!* Enlist in the Rochambeau Rifles! Rbt. Dalbiac, Col."

As he mounted the scarred stairs, his mind cleared for an instant. He grinned. The place had once been a more than questionable dance hall and he had come to it a few times during his senior year at Columbia. Then the shuffle of feet and the buzz of voices drew the haze of the present over him. A string of men lined the upper stairs and those nearest him were big and blond-bearded with the black-red-gold button of the ill-fated German Republic in their lapels. He heard guttural Rhenish, the soft blur of Irish brogues, the swift flow of French. Sight and sound washed about him without touching him.

He was at the head of the stairs where the line of men split and trailed away toward two tables set in a wide lobby. There were crossed French and American flags behind the tables, a placard on the wall threatening all French officers or graduates of St. Cyr on inactive status with permanent disbarment from the Imperial armies if they joined North or South. It was signed by the Marquis de Montholon, French Consul General in New York.

Voices back of the tables barked in quick French or strongly accented English to the slow-moving lines.

George stared at two seated men. The nearer was lean and dark, with a bony face and tightly waxed mustache. The other had piercing blue eyes, a ruddy face that was hidden by a square-cut red beard through which a scar curved white. Each wore medals on the left breast and the metal disks clicked against the tables as the men bent to dip their pens. They were in identical uniforms—blue kepis heavily piped with yellow, dark blue coats with broad yellow chevrons, thick fringed yellow epaulettes, light blue trousers, yellow-piped like kepi and coat, and short white gaiters.

He started as a voice snapped, "Well—recruit?" The line had moved on without his realizing it and he stood before the dark, saturnine sergeant, who rasped, "Name and forename, *alors?* Where born?" He heard his own voice giving thick answers which the sergeant wrote down with needle-pointed pen. As the questions rolled on, George glanced across at the red-beard who was leaning back in his chair and looking with rather sardonic appraisal at a tall, handsome man who spoke in slangy French. George could not catch the drift of the words but gathered that the tall man's name was Carrigan, and wondered how the Irishman came to speak French so well. Then the dark sergeant thrust a paper at him, snapping, "Into the next room, recruit, where the *toubib* will thump you. *Allons, filez!*"

In the blur that had wrapped him since he had left home, he undressed in a coatroom of the old dance hall. Naked, sweaty bodies jostled past him as he hung his clothes on bent hooks. Halfway down the room, a uniformed doctor, green epaulettes livid under the gaslights, was bawling: "Five-eight! One-four-seven pounds! No rupture! Bend over!" By the door a sweating clerk wrote feverishly, gasping in the reek of old and new sweat. The doctor butted toward George, pulled his mouth open, and stared into his eyes. "No teeth missing. No rupture. Get on the scales. Even six foot. One-nine-one pounds. Bend over—"

He was dressing again, his skin feeling sore and itching in the reek of the room. Hunching into his shirt he saw Carrigan arguing with the clerk, the former good-humored and tolerant, the latter sharp and high-pitched. The clerk covertly slid Carrigan's papers to the bottom of the pile, insuring delay in his examination. George instinctively called a warning, but a side door opened and the red-beard shouted, "The finished ones! Into here, *'cré nom de Dieu!*"

George stepped from the dressing room into the old dance hall. Through the open door he could see Carrigan, stripped down to fine linen underwear, like Brooks Brothers' English importations. The doctor was snarling at him. "Jesus! Looks like hell to see a big feller like you in women's drawers! Why'n't you tack lace onto 'em? One of the boys is apt to make a mistake, seein' you in them whorehouse pants. Stand up. Don't suck in your guts. For Chris' sake, you ought to have more belly than that. Where you been feeding? Up to Sing Sing?" Then the door closed.

The old hall was ghostly and smelled of dust and sweat. The tawdry paint was chipped and faded and the floor deeply scarred. Some twenty men huddled on long benches by the walls. George stood guard over his bag and wondered what would happen next. His mind, still floating above him, could form no connection between himself and the rows of French, Irish, German, and Yankee faces on the benches.

The door opened and Carrigan came in. He smiled as his eyes met George's. "And now?" he asked.

The hazy globe about George thinned a little. He answered, "Don't know. Say, I saw that damned clerk switch your papers. You ought to have cuffed him."

Carrigan shrugged philosophically. "The poor clerk? Ah—for my part I should not find it pleasant to sit like him, stewing all evening in a casserole of naked sweating bodies."

"Maybe you're right." George found himself wondering about the man's accent. "Look here, you ain't Irish, are you? I thought they called you Carrigan. My name's Force, George Force."

The other's handshake was solid and unreserved. "Not Carrigan, but very like it. It is Kérédern—Jean Kérédern." He looked about him coolly. "It is meant that

21

we sleep in this magnificence? Ah—here is the Alsatian, Sergeant Rapp."

Red beard a-bristle, Rapp marched into the room, followed by the other sergeant. He shouted—"Attention, recruits!" George looked about, startled. Along the bench a few men snapped to their feet as though a string had been pulled. Others rose, grinning in uncertainty. Then he noticed that Kérédern was standing like a statue beside him. Rapp bellowed. "Form yourselves into two ranks! No, *espèce d'imbécile!* Two!"

The men who had frozen at Rapp's first words clicked swiftly into place. George felt Kérédern's hand on his elbow, heard his voice. "Stand so. Heels together, toes apart. A silly posture, but one which is demanded."

Two lines were formed somehow. Rapp roared, "You will listen to me while I speak. In a moment there will enter Captain Allard, commander of this company—H Company. While he is here, you will not speak. You will not stir. In effect, you will try not to sicken him, nor sicken us who are your sergeants." He faced about.

To George, everything was still unreal—the hall and the echoing footsteps and the tall, overweight man who swung in through the door. His uniform repeated the blue and yellow of the sergeants', but there was gold on his kepi and great double arabesques of gold braid looped and twirled high up his leeves. His left hand clutched awkwardly at a scabbard.

George thought vaguely, "French again. Hope I can understand him."

Captain Allard surveyed the ranks through small, cunning eyes. Then he threw back his head and George started. Allard spoke the purest New York. "Glad to see you, boys. We've mighty near got a full company now and we're going to start work. Just remember one thing—I'm here as your friend. Most of us are out of the same Assembly District and that'll make a lot of things easy. If you get bothered by anything, come to me and I guess I know the right places to go to get things fixed up. Tell your folks that. Now we got a lot of orders and things and we want to get 'em right. I talk French like a

22

horse eats fish so I'll let Sergeant Rapp and Sergeant Cahusac pass 'em on to you. That's all. Good night, boys."

Rapp's face was impassive as he saluted the departing Allard. Then he turned to the ranks, clasped his hands behind him, and rocked back on his heels. Cahusac watched sardonically, twirling his mustaches. Rapp grated, "This company, it is American and like Americans it will talk. Those who do not understand English will be well advised to learn. You have taken the oath and from now are under orders at all times. Until we shall have cots, you sleep at your homes. You will report here at eight o'clock tomorrow morning. Dis—missed. *Rompez les rangs!*"

As though by tacit agreement, George and Kérédern made their way together up Broadway. Noisy life had ebbed from the great street and they walked on nearly vacant pavements. Now and then bars of light from windows fell across George's broad forehead and high-bridged nose, on Kérédern's square shoulders. The Frenchman said suddenly, "*Au fond*—a thing once done is so simple."

George took off his hat and ran his hand over his straw-colored hair. "Maybe that's what I've been trying to figure out. I've felt damn funny ever since I started this. I'll feel funnier, too, when I lug this bag home. I thought maybe we'd get rushed right off to Washington. The whole evening's been like one of those things I had when I was a kid—a big cardboard cylinder with slits along the sides. You know—a zoetrope. You stick in a picture of a line of dolphins and give the cylinder a spin and the damn fish seem to swim."

Kérédern smoothed his mustache. "Yes. That is the feeling, *précisément*—a sort of false life that does not touch one." He shook his head. "Ah, but it does touch one, that life we entered just now. It is a terribly real one. So real that I am tempted to ask how you, who are of this city, chose the Rochambeau Rifles."

"I tried LeGal's LaFayette Guards, but they're full up."

"And I tried them. But still I ask you, since both regiments are largely French."

George frowned. "Maybe I'm wrong. Most of my friends are in the New York 7th. But you see, we've got no one with any military experience—or very few—anywhere. I knew there'd be a lot of old soldiers in any French or German outfit. I speak French a little, so I chose the Rifles. With a bunch of old soldiers, I'll learn faster and be safer learning."

"But one could learn as an officer, perhaps?"

"And get a lot of people killed while learning? No! This isn't anything to fool with. It may be damned serious, and if it is, I want to be where I can do the most good. A lot of Dad's friends want to get me a commission but I don't see it that way. If I learn and if I'm any good as a soldier, that'll take care of itself. You feel the same way or you wouldn't have been there tonight."

Kérédern said, "Something must be done."

George looked curiously at him in the dimness. He wanted to ask, "But why by you, unless you're naturalized, and I don't think you are?" He was silent, however, as Kérédern's manner did not seem to invite questions. An omnibus clattered up Broadway. George said, "Why don't we hail it?"

Kérédern made a face. "I would walk to Central Park to get the smell of that hall out of my nostrils."

"It was kind of a mink's den, wasn't it? Just the same, I'd better get home as quick as I can or my family'll have turned in for the night." He waved to the driver, who began a slow swing to the curb.

Kérédern said, "Till tomorrow, then. May I say that I am glad that we find ourselves in the same company?"

"Oh, sure. So am I." He hitched his square chin diffidently. "Besides—well, anyway, it makes me feel good, seeing your people joining up like this. You—you kind of helped get the Union started and now a whole lot of you are helping us hold it together." The omnibus halted. George shook hands quickly and climbed in. As it lurched off, he peered through the blurred windows. Kérédern, head up and back straight, was striding up Broadway.

It was midnight and aproned porters were sweeping

out the echoing lobby of the Fifth Avenue Hotel. From time to time they glanced impatiently into a small parlor where a tall man sat writing busily in a cloud of cigarette smoke. He was oblivious of the hour and his pen scratched on steadily. By his elbow lay sealed envelopes. The uppermost was addressed to Baron von Stoeckl at the Russian Legation, Washington.

At last he dropped his pen and picked up the final sheet of a long letter, humming to himself as he reread it. "—and so, my dear uncle, this step I took tonight. If you will consider my reasoning as I outlined it, I am sure that you will see that good logic dictated my actions rather than the fever of the times. That I enrolled myself for three years may seem startling, yet the implication is that should the emergency settle itself in less time (as it surely must) we shall all be released.

"You may wonder, if wonder remains to you, why I bury myself in the ranks. No doubt by calling on friends here I could seize a lieutenancy at least on the strength of my St. Cyr training. But that training, as I reasoned to myself, fitted me to command conscripts in France, not volunteers in America. I do not feel that I should accept anything beyond what I may earn for myself in this strange new army of the Union. In fact, I speak of my step to few people and, to avoid recognition and the curiosity that all good Americans show in our little titles, I have enrolled myself as simple citizen, using a name which you bestowed upon me at baptism in the little chapel at Ploërmel. That is to say, I march as plain Jean Kérédern. May I ask, my dear uncle, that you address me as such in your letters, which should be sent in the care of our good friend, von Stoeckl?

"Yes, the cork is drawn and may not be replaced. I confess that I feel a little lost as I think of you and of Loudéac. But it may be soon that I greet you once more for none may say if this gale blow long or short—and it may well be the latter. But in any event, please know that I shall carry, wherever I go, the warmest affection for you. At least, one may now say that the last de Mérac follows the family pattern by taking up the profession of arms."

He lit another cigarette, frowned, then signed "Jean" on the final inch of the sheet. "*Vingt dieux!*" he muttered. " I hope he may not be too greatly shocked. *N'importe*. Ah—that Allard puzzles me, that one. I must ask George Force about him tomorrow."

For a time de Mérac's daily life presented too strong a series of contrasts to help his perspective. On most mornings he met George Force on a Broadway omnibus and rode down to the moldy quarters on Chambers Street where, in newly issued blue and yellow of the Rifles, they and some sixty others tramped through the dull elements of foot drill. In the afternoons they all struggled with the manual of arms, using an incredible collection of rusty, pitted muskets from the arsenals of Spain, Sicily, Baden, and Belgium. The green men worked under the eye of the sardonic, tight-buttoned Cahusac, while the rest suffered under the biting tongue of the red-bearded Rapp, who now wore a first sergeant's lozenge above the bend of his wide chevrons.

The work was too easy to absorb de Mérac's mind, for drill and manual were based on French patterns. He began to worry about the company, which seemed a bit of driftwood, unattached and unnoticed. He knew that other units of the regiment were scattered about the lower island in abandoned buildings, and old warehouses, but their existence did not touch H Company. He saw the name of the colonel, Robert Dalbiac, on a few papers and discovered that a Major Craig Wilson was second-in-command.

Captain Allard rarely appeared. On his few visits he was accompanied by sharp-looking civilians. Once a smooth, florid man, whom Allard addressed with great deference as Mr. Cusler, arbitrarily halted the drill and spoke with bland warmth to some of the men. One rainy afternoon, two lieutenants, confident and glib, watched the drill. They took no part in the work but, like Cusler, made a point of singling out certain privates for confidential mutterings. Their names, de Mérac learned, were Magnan and O'Keefe, but the knowledge did him little good as the pair rarely appeared in the hall where Rapp and Cahusac reigned supreme.

To George Force the period was less unsettling as he had a new life and a new vocabulary to learn. Little by little drill and manual came to him, aided by Kérédern's deft coaching. This help was given unobtrusively and tactfully. "Ah, but the second squad marches badly because the men all lean forward—just a little—between Rapp's 'Forward' and 'March.' A small thing, but important. . . . It is a pleasure to see the big Graf come to left-shoulder shift. No doubt you have noticed the placing of his hand on the butt." So the association of the first night grew steadily and George turned more and more to the Frenchman, not only for the instruction that he gave but for the companionship that had nothing to do with the echoing dusty hall.

As his skill grew, the company took shape in George's mind. The men ceased to be blue and yellow figures and stood out as individuals with pasts, futures, plans, hopes, and dreams. The fierce Melchior Rapp, George discovered, owned a prosperous paper shop on Hudson Street and sold high-grade sheets to the downtown lawyers. Cahusac had only recently closed a shooting gallery and fencing school near Barnum's Museum on Broadway. A beak-nosed man whom he had privately christened the Grand Duke turned out to be a Pell Street barber; a lean man who looked like a French duelist was revealed as a Staten Island farmer who interpreted life in strict terms of the Old Testament.

Among the Germans were tutors from Jena, Bonn chemists now employed by the Gas Company, waiters, laborers, skilled mechanics, and artists. Almost to a man they had fled the troubles of '48 and now, full-fledged American citizens, had voted for Abraham Lincoln.

The Irish embraced their full share of laborers and with them mingled schoolteachers, a few who had been studying for the priesthood when trouble drove them from Ireland, musicians and boss teamsters.

The French had known Limoges or Arles or Besançon or Laon or Dijon before their convictions—anti-Orléans, anti-Bourbon, anti-Bonaparte—had brought them to New

York. They were waiters, architects, dancing masters, textile workers, lawyers, importers, cooks, and laboratory workers.

The half-real days, balancing between the grim hall and the ease of civilian life, came to an abrupt end with the arrival of cots and gray-blue blankets marked with a black "U.S." That night, instead of taking Kérédern home to dinner as he had planned, George mounted guard at the head of the stairs with an anarchist from the Midi and was relieved at midnight by a mild-mannered editor from the Pas-de-Calais. As he stumbled into his cot, after carefully racking his pitted Charleville musket, he felt as though the very act of guard duty had put a new purpose into his life, was a real step in advance.

One night George woke from a dream of being jammed in a dense mob. He pushed at a woolly mass that pressed against him. Something wet slapped across his face and he gurgled, "What in God's name?" He lit a candle and saw a shaggy head, lop-eared and eager, panting hopefully. George groaned. "He'll be alive with fleas. Down, sir, down!" The dog wagged an unkempt tail joyously, then slumped to the floor. George blew out the candle. With a scuffle, the woolly mass landed with a thud back of his knees. He gave up the struggle. Sleep was too precious to waste brawling with a mongrel.

The next day, the dog tagged endlessly at his heels. He expostulated, "Why does he choose *me?*"

Leary, of the next squad, nodded wisely. " 'Twas Jerry Mulvehill as brought it in, him that greased off to join the 14th Brooklyn. It's like Mulvehill ye smell, else the dog'd not be after ye."

"God!" said George, remembering the dingy Mr. Mulvehill. "He better find someone else—"

"And the name's Mr. McArdle," prompted Leary. "Jerry'd strip to any man that forgot the 'Mister.' "

The shaggy head bumped against George's knee and the dog looked up soulfully at him. "Huh! We'll get him a collar. Then we'll tie him up with the rest of the company pups and keep him off my cot."

Leary winked at ex-chemist Reiff. Without his realizing it, George's fingers were scratching Mr. McArdle's rather tattered ears.

De Mérac was gratefully aware of the mellow quiet of the Force house as he sat at his hostess's right in the dining room. Candles, set in writhing dragon holders of black iron, threw a soft glow over the Chinese tapestry on the opposite wall. Above the mantel, a fine canvas of the Palisades gave out warm, autumnal tints. The room, like the whole house, seemed a changeless, timeless refuge.

Yet there was tension over the mahogany table. He knew that it underlay Willett Force's easy, courteous conversation. Mrs. Force, her young face alight with interest under its soft crown of white hair, was serene and composed, but de Mérac sensed her struggle against the impulse to touch the hand of her son, who sat close by her, his corn-colored hair set off by the blue and yellow of the Rifles. Pretty, brown-haired Marion at de Mérac's right was charmingly deferential to the foreign guest whom her brother had brought home. But there was an eternal question at the back of her eyes as they rested on George. Even Gretta, the prim German maid who supervised the activities of a younger waitress, was affected by the outwardly ignored strain and her eyes were fixed on her young *Herr* as though a kobold might spirit him out of his high-backed chair.

The undercurrents disturbed de Mérac. They broke the continuity of a family life whose charm he had felt at once. He tried to shut out the present and listened as Willett Force talked of the Pagoda Anchorage below Canton, invoking the old days of the China trade until de Mérac could see the clipper's slim bows sliding past the high-sterned government boats, the flower boats, the beggar boats that shot out from a jade-green shore.

Talk trailed away into silence as it had so often during the afternoon and evening. Under the table, close to George's boots, Mr. McArdle snored and snuffled, furnishing a bass for the treble squeak of the maid's shoes as she served an ice.

Mrs. Force said calmly to their guest, "It does seem as

though you were getting somewhere now, doesn't it, Mr. Kérédern? I mean, now that you actually live at the hall."

Tension eased about the table. She had boldly brought into the light the root of unspoken worry. The others looked relieved. De Mérac smiled under his mustache. "We have taken a step up the Matterhorn, at least."

George said quickly, "Two steps for you, John." He nodded at the broad corporal's stripes that slashed de Mérac's sleeves.

"*Ah, ça, par exemple!*" shrugged de Mérac. Two days before, Allard had appeared and read out a list of promotions. Nearly all the men with whom Cusler and other civilians had whispered had been made full sergeants, most of them patently unfit. He himself had been the last on the list of corporals. Capable and experienced men, such as a former sergeant major of Her Majesty's 39th Foot, had been coldly left out.

George went on. "You know, Mother, I was in a sweat when Allard read out the names. I was scared John'd get passed up, too."

"But me, I had no claim, not being citizen. Now you, George. You could be sergeant as well as any in the company. Consider Young and DuPuis and Reilly and Klotz."

George frowned. "I don't say I liked being left out. But I know I'm not ready to be anything more than a high private in the rear rank. I don't know enough. Just because Allard shoves up a lot of ignorant plug-uglies doesn't mean he ought to jump me, too. He ought to have named you and DuCharme and Mike Boyle as sergeants."

His father sipped wine slowly. "Things like that will happen. I looked up Allard. He's a ward hanger-on and naturally he's going to take care of his boys. You say Jack Cusler's been there? Well, he wouldn't bother with anything less than commissions." He inclined his head toward de Mérac. "That's something you ought to have, Mr. Kérédern. You've had military training, haven't you?"

De Mérac spread out his hands. "As has nearly every European, sir. Over there, peace is only a short gap between two wars."

Marion said, "I think it's perfectly fine of you to come to us, Mr. Kérédern."

He met her frank gaze. American girls had always charmed him with their natural ease and straightforwardness. He said lightly, "Perhaps it is too early to judge me. This all may be the excitement of the times."

She shook her head. "You've got the same look that George has." She caught her mother's eye. "Do you mind if I slip upstairs without waiting for coffee? Dora Chase is coming for me and I want to change before we go over to Trinity."

George pulled down the corners of his mouth. "Oh-oh! Dear Dora!"

Marion rose. "You don't have to do a thing about her."

"That'll be a change. John, when I was at college, I was martyrized more times, chaperoning Marion and that skinny little Dora over to the skating at Murray Hill on Saturday afternoons."

Mrs. Force raised her eyebrows as Marion left the room. "Dora's changed a lot in two years, George."

Willett Force chuckled. "A girl who has Jonas Chase for a father ought to be changed any way she wants. Now, my dear, coffee and brandy in my study, I think."

Later Mrs. Force and George went upstairs to overhaul some things that he wanted to take to Chambers Street. De Mérac sat in a leather chair in the study, where paneled walls were broken by rows of fine bindings, unexpected niches where carved ivories and glowing Sung vases were touched by lamplight. He sipped a mellow brandy and answered his host's question by saying that, in his opinion, the recent transfer of the Southern capital from Montgomery in Alabama to Richmond might have been politically necessary but was a military mistake. "Now we may threaten their capital as they threaten ours," he concluded.

"Our capital," said the other slowly. "I like to hear you say that, Mr. Kérédern. I hope you won't mind the question, but just why did you come with us?"

31

De Mérac tapped ash from his cigarette into a brass bowl. "You have every right to ask. My presence here is partly due to my interest in America. Of that I spoke at dinner. To that interest was added a chance meeting with a man who showed me that your Union and its survival were not merely an American affair. I will not repeat all that he said, but to me he made it clear that if there is collapse, then the pattern of the world as we know it will be set for another century or more. That pattern will not be a pretty one, Mr. Force."

Willett Force rose and paced up and down the Bokhara rug. "That's exactly it. I wish like the devil you could get the whole argument onto paper. It's the longest view I've met of what we're getting into a war over. Yes! It *does* cross the ocean. That's the biggest reason of all." His voice quickened. "I try not to blow off steam like a cruiser at anchor. That's the end of clear thinking, but—Oh Lord!—how can respectable, intelligent people back that damned Fernando Wood in his howl that New York ought to secede and become a neutral free port? I hear plenty of talk like that—even at the Century Club. I hear talk like that and then I see units like the Steuben Rangers or the LaFayette Guards or d'Epineul's Zouaves, d'Utassy's men or the Count di Cesnola's— French and Irish had Germans and Poles in uniform. It makes me wonder if perhaps the old stock hasn't gone to seed."

De Mérac said quietly, "You have also seen your own 7th on its way to Washington. You saw the 12th Massachusetts. When next a regiment passes through the city, study the faces of those young Yankee volunteers. You will find them in full flower and not going to seed."

The older man smiled suddenly. "You're right. It'll last. The old stock and the new'll save the Union yet. By the way, who was the man who clarified your ideas for you? I say 'clarified' because I'm sure the genesis was in your mind already."

"His name was Kearny—Major Philip Kearny."

"Good Lord! Not Phil Kearny? A one-armed man? Why, I've known his family for years. Poor devil. I hear Albany won't give him anything."

"I assure you that the refusal does not amuse him," said de Mérac dryly.

"I should think not! He's got the politicians against him, for one thing. For another, he's very wealthy—better than a millionaire, I'd say. And then—this is not gossip; it's perfectly well known—he married a Bullitt from Kentucky. He left her for another woman whom he took to Paris. There was a divorce at last and only recently has he been able to marry his second choice. The whole thing set badly with a lot of people. I'm afraid he's got a long way to go before New York will do anything for him. Well, that's his battle." He looked at his watch. "I wonder what's keeping George."

On the landing by the Buddha George paused, a bundle of battered treasures under his arm, relics of bygone camping days in the Catskills. Marion's voice came softly to him through the closed door of her room. "Do stop in the drawing room and tell Dora I'll be right down."

"All right," he said resignedly as he came on down the stairs and shouldered past the half-closed door. "Good evening," he said politely. "Marion says—" He stopped, frankly staring.

The girl who rose from the chair by the fire was tall and slim. The lamplight showed masses of dark hair under a little bonnet, wide-spaced eyes and a generous mouth that quirked at the corners. She had a light gray cape about her shoulders and her wide-skirted dress was blue with bright slashes. She looked inquiringly at George. "Don't worry, George. You don't have to look after Marion and me this time. Aunt Page is outside in the carriage. Marion's coming right down, isn't she?"

He managed to say, "Uh—yes—coming right away. That's what she said. Right away."

Dora Chase laughed up at him. "Thanks for the message. Oh, there she is, on the stairs. Good night, George. You know, that uniform is really very becoming." She floated out past him, easy and smiling. Then he heard Marion's voice and the outer door slammed. George ran his hand over his hair and stared out into the hall. "Well!—So that's Dora—I'll—I'll be damned!"

When George and de Mérac reached Chambers Street, they found the long hall a bedlam. Visitors had littered the floor with baskets and bottles. Two men sprawled unconscious on cots in a thick whiskey reek. On de Mérac's bunk three elderly Irishwomen crooned over young Leary. Beyond, heavy-footed Germans, men and women, danced to the wail of an accordion. Frenchmen pounded the floor and bawled:

> *Le capitaine est un légume.*
> *Il baise, il boit, il chique, il fume.*
> *Il ne peut même lire son nom.*
> *Il est bête comme un cochon!*

The company mongrels raced about in yelping frenzy.

"Home, sweet home," growled George in disgust.

"Of what do Rapp and Cahusac think, allowing this *tohu-bohu?*" muttered de Mérac.

Then an ex-mechanic of the New York and Harlem Railroad called to George, "Was looking for you when the red ball went up this morning. Thought you'd maybe go over with me and two-three others and watch the Brooklyn Atlantics play the Philadelphia Athletics."

A former Heidelberg tutor bowed formally to de Mérac and hoped, in bad French, that his *camarade* had passed a pleasant holiday. Leary left the old women and pushed a wallet into de Mérac's hand. "'Twas on the blankets ye left it and there'll be light-fingered folk about, likely. Ye'd best count what's in it."

De Mérac answered quickly, "Why, since I receive it from you?"

Suddenly disorder changed to joyous chaos as the company welcomed de Mérac and George, claimed them as its own. Remembering St. Cyr days, de Mérac clapped his hands and organized a mock court-martial which proceeded to try Captain Allard, in the person of Mr. McArdle, for conduct unbecoming a politician. The German accordions swept higher and higher over the laughter as an Irish corporal showed unexpected talent as the prisoner's counsel. Out of the corner of his eye, de

Mérac saw George whirling arm in arm with a red-cheeked Bavarian girl. The French sang on in ecstatic disrespect, *"Le colonel est un légume—"*

There was a sudden shout from the door. *"Dix heures et demie! Videz la boîte, 'cré nom de Dieu!"* Rapp stalked in, beard bristling. De Mérac, who had left the court-martial to waltz with a slim Hamburg Jewess, felt deep resentment of the Alsatian's tyranny.

When the last visitor had been herded from the room, Rapp pointed a scarred finger at de Mérac. "You, *bleu!*" The first sergeant used the ancient derisive term for raw recruit. "You, *bleu*, wil take ten men with brooms to see to it that this floor gleams like a ballroom at the Tuileries." He tapped de Mérac's chevrons. "See to it well. These pretty things may come off more easily than they are put on." The holiday was over.

May slipped into June and the banks of the Potomac began to stir with activity. Union forces stumbled across the river and occupied Arlington and the Virginia heights. Far upstream, Southern units unexpectedly evacuated the ruined arsenal at Harpers Ferry which they had held since mid-April. The wall-eyed, equivocal General Butler, ex-bobbin-boy, ex-lawyer, and eternal politician, blundered out from Fortress Monroe, collided blindly with a Southern force near Big Bethel and fell back. A youngish West Pointer, who had studied military science abroad, was named by Lincoln to command in northeastern Virginia. His name was Irvin McDowell and in their camps the Union troops cheered their first commander as he rode through, troubled and wondering as he surveyed his task. At sea, Confederate raiders began a slow, deadly nibbling at Northern commerce.

Little of this was apparent to the Rifles as they sweltered through drills and fatigues in their dusty halls or were taken on cautious marches through the quieter streets of New York, their new canteens clanking against bayonet sheaths and their new cartridge pouches and packs creaking. Allard and his lieutenants were inconspicuous as ever and the company was commanded, *de facto*, by the red-bearded Rapp and his tight-buttoned junior, Cahusac.

Marching with their squads, de Mérac and George sometimes caught glimpses of other blue and yellow companies, sole sign that their unit actually belonged to a larger body. In the ranks, the men got drunk, gambled, fought, joked, and stole from each other. A few deserted, either back to civilian life or to other regiments that seemed to promise greater chances for advancement, action, or leisure. So new a company could have been a rabble. Yet the thick leavening of trained men and above all the hard, competent grip of Rapp and Cahusac somehow brought about the beginnings of solidarity, efficiency, and company pride.

De Mérac formed the habit of getting up each morning well before the first notes of the company's bugles. He loved the feel of the June mornings, the glow of light that crept over tile roofs and chimney pots, the smell of wet pavement and the scent of fresh leaves that opened softly on the lone ailanthus tree in the court behind the hall. More, he had discovered a pump built into the wall where he could blow and splash in solitary comfort, unelbowed by other early risers who crowded about the well or the rickety three-seated privy.

One morning, as he sluiced a bucket of cold water over head and shoulders, a voice blared behind him in harsh Alsatian French, "*Bleu!*" Rapp's beard bristled with indignation. "Is your ignorance so unfathomable that you imagine that this pump may serve you? The well for the *bleu* of whatever rank, the pump for the trusted *sous-off*, and for *Messieurs les Officiers* the *lavabo* of the *bordel* in which they may awake."

De Mérac shrugged and drew water from the well, brackish and tepid. Rapp exposed to the climbing sun a torso that was marked with purple saber slashes and the starred puckers of gunshot wounds. He splashed violently and talked on, seemingly in a fine humor. "The pot simmers, *bleu*, the pot simmers," he said through a mask of lather.

"No doubt, then, the papers tell you more than they do me, Chef."

"Who may say no, since you are but a *bleu*. But it is not to the journals that I refer. Me, I am an old soldier and may sniff the air for news. The pot simmers stronger, as I remarked this morning to the sergeant Cahusac, who agreed. Thus I felt on the morning before the action at Tlemçen. I shall hold the company indoors till noon at least. Have your squad make up its packs and look well to its *asti-quage!*" He stalked back into the building.

Other men began to trickle out in the court, yawning, coughing, spitting, and scratching. There was a crisp patter of feet, a joyous whuff, and Mr. McArdle bounded out, followed by George Force, whose well-muscled shoulders caught the new sun. "Hi, John. What a day!" He filled his lungs, then began to scrub vigorously. "I could climb rivers and swim mountains. What the hell do we loaf around here for? I could bring back Jeff Davis's goatbeard all by myself."

De Mérac wiped his razor. "Rapp thinks something is going to happen."

Force looked up eagerly. "He does? By God, that may mean a lot. He's a wise old coot. What do you think?"

De Mérac shrugged. "Anything may happen. To a camp on Staten Island, perhaps. There is much talk of it."

"That all?" Force was disappointed.

De Mérac said dryly, "Would you care to patrol the Potomac at night, under Allard and Sergeant Young? Wait and see. It will be the Island."

There was no drill after mess. Rapp and Cahusac watched grimly as packs were rolled and the hall swept and scrubbed until it shone. Then they vanished, leaving the company to its sergeants and corporals. The day wore on. At noon they fell in and tramped down to the dirty Bel Air for badly cooked and badly served food, tramped back again.

De Mérac sat on the end of his bare cot and watched Force fit the new leash which the little Breton, Scoarnec, had cunningly braided out of rawhide, to Mr. McArdle's tousled neck. He tossed a cigarette stub into a tin, lit another, tried to keep his foot from tapping on the floor.

The double doors crashed open and Rapp and Cahusac roared: "Attention!" Rapp's hard eyes snapped and he broke out into a torrent of English and French, spattered with slang of the African army. . . . "See to your packs and blanket rolls. They must be tight as an Arab wench's thighs. The floor. It must be swept again, *klimbim!* You sergeants—see that your platoons are *complets, tout à fait complets! Vite! Vite! Dans une demi-heure! Rassemblement! Sacs à dos!*"

De Mérac stood transfixed. George whacked his shoulder. "It's come! John, we're going south. I tell you it's south!"

De Mérac shook himself. "*Vingt dieux!* No! We are not ready!"

Reiff, methodically testing the straps of his pack, grunted. "*Ja.* It is so. To the camp of Staten's Island we go." Then Leary caught the German about the shoulders and whirled him down the floor in a mad dance. "It's to the war, ye thick-headed Dutchy! The war and the Irish to the front av all. Glory be to God, we'll be smelling powder!"

De Mérac raised his voice above the growing din and shouted to his squad, "Scoarnec! Védi! *Les sacs. Vites!* Grady! Schmidt! The brooms! Garnier! Take the canteens of the squad to the pump and fill them. The pump, not the well!"

The brooms were still whisking and the men testing straps and adjusting belts when Cahusac stalked in. He ran a skilled eye over the hall, then snapped, "Fall in. *Sacs à dos!* Full equipment!"

An American voice said uneasily, "Hey, Sarge, where we going? Ain't had a chance to tell the folks."

Cahusac's eyes never moved. "Note that man's name! Attention! *Par file à gauche! En avant!*"

De Mérac, in a daze, moved with the stream of men that slid in a shuffling clatter toward the door. Then he was in the street, the sun warm on his face and the company in column, headed north. On the sidewalk Rapp stood at attention before the puffy Allard, who was laden with expensive haversacks, field glasses, and stiff new holster. Behind him, the gaunt Magnan and the stoop-shouldered O'Keefe were similarly equipped.

The ranks were silent, motionless. A Crimean veteran beyond de Mérac muttered disgustedly, "No doubt we go to line the streets while *bleus* from the Vermont make their departure." De Mérac said out of the corner of his mouth, "Staten Island."

Then he glanced toward Broadway. People were suddenly running along the sidewalks, shouting and waving. Three flat-capped policemen with long clubs kept the mouth of Chambers Street open. Someone in the rank behind de Mérac said, "Ah!" as though a pin had stuck him. Faint but clear, a blast of music echoed along Broadway. De Mérac's spine tingled. He glanced down the column, caught George's eye, bright with excitement. Allard bawled, "Attention!" and sent the company up the street, halting the leading squad at the corner.

The music came nearer and nearer. Heads craned along the sidewalk. De Mérac's heart pounded harder as he caught the tune that grew louder each instant—"*Le Chant des Girondins*," played full-throatedly and expertly. Suddenly there was flashing brass on Broadway. Bugles shot into the air, flourished, and blared out in unison. Some one cried, "The kepis! They are ours!"

The wild song of the Girondins thundered on, as more and more blue and yellow drifted by under the wide mouths of horns. French drums roared and echoed. De Mérac knew that his palms were moist against the barrel of his old musket. His throat ached with the shouts that he stifled. After the band came the bright fezzes of a Zouave company, bright fezzes over braided jackets, then rank on rank of kepis, moving steadily under the glint of bayonets. On the sidewalks men and women waved and cheered.

Two squads below de Mérac, George stretched to his full height and stared through misting eyes. There was strong color flaring high and the sun struck on the folds of the American flag. Beside it, the tricolor of France snapped and fluttered. The wind tossed it out straight to show the gold words: *Honneur et Patrie. Les Françaises de New York aux Fusiliers Rochambeau.* Rapp roared

"Present—*arms!*" and bayonets bristled high. George knew that his own point was wavering, knew that his knuckles were white with the strength of his grip. Something butted against him and Mr. McArdle, yelping shrilly, leapt against his chest, tugged at the new leash which George had looped through his own belt.

The two flags were gone. Musket butts clattered to the ground at Rapp's command. George knew that he was shaking violently and gripped his piece harder, furtively ran a hand over Mr. McArdle's shaggy head. Then his musket was on his shoulder and he was stumbling forward up the street. He set his muscles savagely, caught the rhythm of the squad in front. The dog, head up and tail floating, trotted resolutely beside him. Sound beat at his ears as he turned south down Broadway where the Rifles were marching between a thick hedge of beaver hats and tossing handkerchiefs. A small boy, racing along the column, shrieked, "It's the French! Here come the French!" By a crossing a bent old man leaned on a stick and caught at the swinging hands that passed him. His face was wet and he quavered, "The Union, boys! Keep it safe and God bless you!"

Sounds were vague yet insistent. From a lamppost a bearded man bellowed, "On to Richmond! The Union forever!" George set his jaw. He looked along the squad and carefully aligned his musket with that of the man beside him. Far ahead the two flags sailed on, side by side, and the old march of the Revolution thundered on. There were the flags, there was the regiment at last. The old feeling of isolation, of lack of purpose, was gone, trampled into shreds by the marching feet of ten companies.

Two ranks ahead of George, de Mérac marched, carefully watching the guide of his squad. Like his friend, he felt suddenly numbed and yet exalted. His trained eye told him, from the brief snatches that he had seen, that there was a regiment, regardless of handicaps, that a man could be proud to march with. He held his head higher. Then on the steps of an office building on the right his eye caught a tall, solitary figure, bareheaded in the sun that struck on graying hair, bony face, mustache, and imperial. There was a touch of color in the man's left lapel and his left sleeve was empty. Rigid he stood, as though taking the salute of a conquering army, and his hat was by his side. Beyond de Mérac the wiry Milhaud shouted, *"Holà! La Légion d'Honneur!"* and, discipline forgotten, pointed at the erect figure. Others took up the shout. De Mérac's free arm swept up in a gesture that was half salute, half greeting. On the steps Kearny threw his head back. He swung his hat above his head and his voice sailed high above the music. *"En avant!"*

Then he was left behind, and the blue and yellow river flowed endlessly on, frost-touched by bayonets.

From the railing by Trinity Church a girl's voice shrilled, "Here he is! It's the colonel!" De Mérac's head turned involuntarily. So there was a colonel after all! He heard the clack of hoofs over the steady clunk of boots. Then he went tense with surprise as the leading horsemen came into sight. Colonel Dalbiac was a tall, full-whiskered man with prominent eyes and a pleasant, slack mouth. He clutched the reins of his horse tightly, but the bridle was held by a private who walked by the mount's head, slowing its gait to a shuffle. The colonel's eyes flickered and blinked and his knees were uncertain against the saddlecloth. Once he tried to lift his broad-brimmed hat in answer to the cheers, but quickly clapped his hand back on the reins.

"Sang de dieu," muttered de Mérac as the led horse passed carefully up the column. "What next?" His eyes narrowed as another rider came on wearing the uniform of the Rifles as though he had been born to it. De Mérac had a fleeting glimpse of a jauntily cocked kepi, an impassive face much like Kearny's in structure, a spare body that gave to every motion of the horse. Gold leaves on the jacket identified him as Major Craig Wilson. De Mérac turned his attention to his squad.

Salt air was in George's nostrils. Over the bobbing heads he saw the Bowling Green open before him, then the Battery. He was intoxicated by the rhythmic swing of hundreds of arms, the lift and fall of white-gaitered feet. The Rifles shifted from columns into line, backs to the ferry sheds and wharves where moored craft chuffed and smoked.

Colonel Dalbiac shouted "Halt!" then "At ease!" and somehow had his horse maneuvered to face the ranks. He swept off his hat and his voice rang out surprisingly clear and firm. "Men of the Rochambeau Rifles! It will be my privilege some day to lead you in battle!" The men stared, coldly curious for the most part. The fine voice went on, saying a good deal but meaning very little, winding up with a graceful tribute to LaFayette and Rochambeau and Yorktown. When he ended, there were no cheers. The wooden-faced private helped him from the saddle and, amazingly, the colonel climbed into a waiting carriage and rolled north up Broadway.

Standing at ease, George watched the officers who gathered in front of the regiment. One of them, the Major Wilson who had ridden beyond Dalbiac, he thought he had seen in civilian days. He was about average height, trim and sparely built and moved with quick, light steps. His face was tight-muscled and bony, with a good nose and chin. It was a typically American face, George decided, and one that inspired confidence. One or two of the others were like Allard, but the rest were self-assured, obviously trained men. Several wore medals, notably the captain of the Zouave company, whose chest glittered.

The captains broke away from Wilson and doubled back to their commands. Orders snapped along the front, the companies wheeled, and the smell of salt and tar and smoke grew stronger as George heard the hollow planks of ferry slip echo under his feet. Then he was on board, crowded on a narrow deck as he piled his equipment with the rest. He caught de Mérac's eye, "Staten Island in a half hour, John!"

De Mérac nodded. "Ah—in camp this regiment will knit itself into something. It—" His head went back with a jerk as his glance caught the wheelhouse of the craft. Bright in the sun, gold letters glowed "Jersey City Ferry." At Jersey City was the railroad that led on to Philadelphia, to Baltimore, and to Washington! He braced himself to meet this shock. The raw regiment was being sent south and the discovery froze him in cold alarm. Others saw the sign and voices wailed: *"Ma mère!* She does not know!" ... "They can't do this to me! God damn it, I'll swim!"

De Mérac snapped, "Steady in ranks! Did you expect to be sent to the forts of Boston Harbor?" The murmuring died away. The ferry shuddered, turned in the stream, and headed for the Jersey shore. George threw out his arms. "John! We're off! I wouldn't trade places with God!"

De Mérac forced a smile. "I believe you, *mon vieux.*" He dropped his voice. "Some take it badly. Try to help them."

George called, "Schmalz! Where's your accordion? Védi! Get out your flute. We're on our way!"

Uncertainly instruments appeared. Védi and Schmalz looked vaguely about. De Mérac, his back to them, hummed softly. Men caught up the air, long forbidden in France and in many German states. The instruments joined in. The old chords echoed along the deck, were snatched up by companies above and below. Verses took shape, verses that could be as true on a red Virginia road as ever they were on the white highway that ran from Marseilles to the barricades of Paris, would be true wherever free men sang them. Higher and higher the voices swept:

> *Aux armes, citoyens!*
> *Formez vos bataillons!*

The ferry chugged on, its paddles churning inexorably toward the Jersey shore.

De Mérac urged the men about him to sing louder, swung his arms in time to the swell of the song. His eye caught Major Wilson by the rail of the deck above, looking keenly down at him and leaning forward as though about to speak. De Mérac stepped closer, a hand raised to his ear, but someone called to Wilson and he stepped out of sight.

III

The Potomac

Two days later, under a blistering afternoon sun, the Rochambeau Rifles toiled on out of Washington toward the heights of Georgetown and the spreading lands beyond. Softened by inactive weeks in New York, cramped by slow hours in trains and stations, the men leaned forward as they marched, mouths half-open from fatigue and eyes straining. Reddish dust lifted sluggishly to shoulder level and the slanting rays struck under the vizors of kepis. Sometimes woods gave brief stretches of relief that ended maddeningly in fresh heat-soaked miles.

From camps on each side of the road, men came to stare at the newcomers. Gray-coated troopers from Wisconsin waved; Minnesota Germans shouted in thick tones to blond-bearded men in blue and yellow. Minnesota gave way to Maine and Maine to New Jersey, Connecticut, Massachusetts, Ohio. And still the march went on.

In the ranks of H Company, George Force, his kepi a sweat-sodden mass, tried to cluck encouragingly to Mr. McArdle, who padded resolutely on beside him. "Come on, boy! Almost there." He smeared his sleeve over his steaming face and muttered, "God, isn't there any end to this damn road?"

In the squad ahead, de Mérac panted on, miserable in the heat that pressed down on his damp shoulders. Sweat burned his eyes and ran down his wrists. His socks felt hot and clammy and the tops of his gaiters chafed him. The heat and dust seemed to be drawing all the strength from his body. Another half hour? Another hour?

As last he saw the Zouaves, fezzes dejected and sodden, turn suddenly off the road into a field at the left toward the river, the other companies trailing after them. He stared unbelievingly. The field was newly mown and on the gentle slope stood row after row of Sibley tents—a whole empty camp. He muttered incredulously to himself, stared harder as he saw fires, men in white aprons by trestle tables. Beyond the tents a long, one-story gray stone building, deep-porched, stood in a pine grove.

Bugles wailed again and the regiment, wondering, swung into line, halted. Wheels rattled on the road and two carriages bowled on after the last company, stopped and disgorged a half-dozen officers, among them Allard, Magnan, and O'Keefe. The men of H Company muttered indignantly, as, dustless and cool, the three officers took their place in the front.

In its own street H Company was finally dismissed. De Mérac said to his squad, "Listen for the mess call. But before you eat, go to the canal by the river. Soak your feet and put on clean socks." He leaned wearily on his musket as the men slouched away. George, his face a mask of dust, puffed, "Let's get a soak, John. I want to find some water for Mr. McArdle, too. God, what a tramp. I came mighty near riding the damn pup." He ruffled the dusty ears of the panting dog. "Come on. I poured the rest of my canteen down his throat at that last halt. We'd—oh-oh, here comes Rapp with that mean look in his eyes. Too late to duck."

The Alsatian held a paper in his hand. "*Bleu*, you are to be corporal of the guard which I, myself, shall post at sundown. Sergeant Gerlasch of the Zouaves will have his eye on you. Make haste with your soup, *'cré nom de Dieu*, and then report for your work in which you will be able to make blunders of a depth unfathomable. You, too, *bleu*." He fixed George with his hard eye. *"Dans un quart d'heure!"*

George rubbed his forehead. "Stay up all night after that march! By God—" he laughed dryly. "Well, no one made me come here after all. What'll guard be like, John?"

After posting the ten-to-twelve shift that formed a wide-spaced chain about the camp, de Mérac took a lantern from a scar-faced Prussian corporal. "Sergeant Gerlasch, I go to make a tour of the posts." Gerlasch, baggy Zouave breeches dark with sweat, grunted approval as he studied a blistered heel. De Mérac, shivering in sodden clothes, moved on through the soft night. His relief was composed of men from half a dozen companies, most of them strangers to him. Post by post he was challenged and halted: *"Wer da?" "Qui vive?"* or "Halt! Who goes there?" Close by the canal and river he found George Force, tired but alert, with Mr. McArdle tied to a clump of bushes close by. The post after George's challenged smartly, and the next. Then, by the river he made out a gaunt shape leaning on a musket and staring out over the water. De Mérac said sharply, "You were told to challenge."

The guard straightened up. "Know I was. Honest to God, I ain't heard you. Them pinkletinks was hollering in the sump like hell-for-tanbark."

"The what?"

"Them pinkletinks. They—Jesus! 'Nother light coming." His challenge rang out, bravely unsteady. A deep voice answered, "Major Wilson." Under de Mérac's whispered prompting, the major was advanced and recognized. He asked the guard a few perfunctory questions, then turned his lantern full on de Mérac. "What are you doing here, Corporal?"

"Tour of inspection, sir."

"H'm—what's your name and company?"

"Kérédern of H, sir."

There was a pause and the light still shone on him. The major asked, "When are you relieved?"

"At midnight, sir."

Wilson pointed to a distant light. "My quarters are in that stone hunting lodge. Report to me when you're relieved."

When he had gathered up his relief, de Mérac freshened himself as best he could and wearily made his way to the lodge where a big Limousin sergeant eyed him cynically by the light of a lantern. "Enter, *'tit nom de Dieu*, that the *gros légumes* inside may remove your hide—as they no doubt plan."

The main room of the lodge was crowded with rustic furniture and its walls were hung with skins and antlers. At the long central table sat Wilson, trim as ever. Five captains were with him, three unmistakable Frenchmen, a heavy-set German, and a hulking Irishman whose nose began high over his eyes. Wilson nodded pleasantly. "Sit down, Baron de Mérac," he said.

De Mérac flushed. "Corporal Kérédern reporting, sir."

Wilson's lean face was unchanged. "Call yourself what you like. It's no business of ours." He lit a thin cigar, turned piercing eyes on de Mérac. "But it is our business that you're a graduate of St. Cyr. Really, I'd be glad if you'd sit down."

De Mérac shrugged. "As you please," and drew up a chair that was rough with bark.

Wilson said courteously to the other officers, "You want me to do the talking?"

The dark Zouave captain nodded. "You will have the goodness, please?"

Wilson folded strong brown hands on the table. "You haven't had a chance to know these gentlemen so I'll make the introductions." Each captain inclined his head as his name was mentioned—Corvisart of the Zouave Company, spare, dark, and needle-mustached; DuBosc of B, brown-bearded and alert as a fox terrier; LeNoir of G, hot-eyed and rough; Hein of D, a heavy, blond-bearded German, and Shea of E. The major went on, "I'm Craig Wilson. In civil life I'm an international lawyer, specializing in French cases. More recently, I've been very

47

busy with these gentlemen—and others of the regiment—plotting a palace revolution. Is that clear?"

De Mérac liked the major's direct look, his efficient spareness, and his surprisingly warm smile. "The statement is clear. I may not say the same for the purpose."

Wilson leaned his elbows on the table. "I'm risking a court-martial in telling you that the revolt is aimed at Colonel Dalbiac."

Corvisart flushed. *"C'est un vieux légume."*

"Et même pire," growled the swarthy LeNoir.

"Hell roast him" muttered Shea, rubbing his long nose.

Wilson went on. "You can't know much about this regiment, Baron, split up as it's been. We were formed to take the overflow of LeGal's Gardes LaFayette. Dalbiac has spent most of his life and more money than I like to think about trying in vain to get elected to something. Now the political boys have rewarded him at last by getting him appointed our colonel. They were glad to, since they held options on the cloth for our uniforms, equipment, muskets, and so on."

"Options?" asked de Mérac.

"Well, you see, they could grab the stuff when they wanted it and here was a nice new regiment to buy it. They turned a quick profit. Oh, it's not unheard of, I regret to say." He sighed. "I suppose such things couldn't happen in France."

Corvisart looked deeply shocked. "By no means. One would, instead, have had to seduce the mistress of one of Bonaparte's ministers."

Wilson smiled. "But to get back to the Rifles, you can see the state they're in. Few companies have their quota of officers or noncoms. Vacancies are being held for Dalbiac's friends—or the friends of those who use him. That's bad enough." His face hardened. "But, worse than that, he looks on the regiment as a toy. Take our move down here. We weren't ready to go and he knew it. But his connections brought such pressure to bear that we had to go, with almost no warning and ahead of regiments in far better shape. We didn't have tents. Influence fixed that and very likely some outfit is sleeping in the open because we have their canvas. We had no mess organization. He hired civilian caterers. So here we are, near the seat of action, simply to enable him, as he goes about New York, to refer to 'my regiment at the front, which I shall join shortly.' And he's kept the band up there to play at his dinners."

Shea's chairs creaked as he heaved himself forward. "You'll tell him the rest? About what we haven't got?"

Wilson nodded. "I'm coming to that. We have no lieutenant colonel, no surgeons, no chaplain, no quartermaster. We're simply ten companies wearing the same uniform—and that is not a regiment. Nor have we wagons and we can't get them, can't really get a thing from the Federal Government because we're still state troops. We haven't been mustered yet. Of course, it's against all law and custom, our being here at all. But here we are."

Hein stroked his fan-shaped beard. "Now to the point we come, yes?"

Wilson looked at de Mérac. "One of our vacancies has just been filled. I did not mention that we also lacked an adjutant. Now we have one."

"Yes?" said de Mérac. He was still puzzled at this extraordinarily frank talk. He felt sticky and dirty, the more so as he looked at Wilson's trim jacket with the triple loops of gold braid that curled high up the sleeves.

"Yes," said Wilson. "Yourself!"

De Mérac's scuffed boots grated on the floor. "*Quoi?*"

"*C'est nécessaire,*" muttered Corvisart. "*Tout à fait nécessaire.*" The others nodded, save LeNoir, who kept his hot eyes on de Mérac.

De Mérac burst out, "*Mais, enfin, c'est foudroyant.* You—you do not know me, you others. You do not—"

"We know enough," said Wilson.

"But, *vingt dieux*—why not look about among the five captains who are here?"

Wilson shook his head. "We've been all over that. When we found out about you and your training, we made up our minds quickly."

De Mérac passed his hand over his eyes. "Impossible. Why not try—"

Wilson's brown hand slapped the table. "Damn it,

what are you afraid of? You enlisted when there was no call on you."

"I felt there was necessary work to be done."

"Good! Work that you believed in. But you're like a trained architect carrying a hod. Good God, don't you realize that we're not a military nation? You ought to know that any man who can drill a platoon can walk into almost any regiment we've got and choose his own place." There was a brief silence. Then Wilson remarked to the rafters, "Of course, being adjutant to Dalbiac wouldn't be the easiest job in the world."

De Mérac said, "Easier, perhaps, than to get me a commission at Albany."

Shea laughed and Wilson said blandly, "I can play politics myself when I have to. I went to Albany a few days ago and got a blank commission out of the Governor. I'd made up my mind to get someone, you see. I'll just fill in your name."

De Mérac said wearily, "I find it hard to think, after these two days. Do I understand that all agree upon me?"

Wilson glanced at LeNoir. "Anything to say, Captain?"

LeNoir, arms folded across his chest, spoke heavily. "It may be well to repeat." He turned his hostile gaze on de Mérac. "I am a man of frankness. I am of the barricades. I do not, willingly, see an *aristo* like yourself given rank in a people's army. I've fought your kind all my life. I helped drive out Charles X and Louis Philippe. I tried to drive out Bonaparte when he betrayed the Republic. Now I have found a country that suits me not too badly. No. I do not welcome you."

"Then you reject me, Captain?"

LeNoir shook his head. "We have voted. I bow to the majority, as is only right. But I warned them, these others, that soon there will ride into camp the Comte de this and the Marquis de that and the younger son of a Vicomte, hungry for posts. In the end, *aristo* always sides with *aristo*."

De Mérac shaded his eyes against the light. "I respect your frankness. Major, I accept."

Wilson cried, "Good! You fellows are all satisfied—with LeNoir's reservations, of course."

"*Parfaitement*," said DuBosc.

When the captains had gone, Wilson rubbed his hands briskly. "That's settled. Tomorrow you'd better see about a uniform and a mount. For all practical purposes, you see, you command the regiment."

"Command it? I?"

Wilson nodded gravely. "What else? The adjutant issues orders in the name of the colonel. When Dalbiac's here, you've got to make him stand by and watch. When he isn't, I assure you that I'll accept and back up any order you issue. Good Lord, the idea's not new. I know a worse colonel than Dalbiac. His regiment's down here, commanded by a Swiss who isn't even in the army. The colonel pays him while he himself stays in New York and has his portrait painted against a lovely background of cavalry charges and smashed caissons or whatever you call them." He smothered a yawn. "Wish I could have left this business until tomorrow when we'd all had some sleep, but I didn't dare. Just had to get it settled. Now I'll stop talking. You must have a lot of questions you want to ask."

"Later—many. But for the moment I'd be glad to know how you had my name."

Wilson grinned. "About two years ago, up in Stockbridge, the Wardwells from Boston had guests and took them through a neighbor's rose garden."

"Stockbridge—Wardwell—yes, it recalls itself."

"You were among the guests but were so absorbed in a girl from Hartford that you didn't know whether you were looking at roses or garlic." He chuckled. "That garden happened to be mine. That night I dined at the Wardwells' where you had that same girl as partner. She happens to be my favorite niece, so I had quite a good look at you."

De Mérac said quickly, "Ah—yes. Miss Rosa Bailey. A charming girl. Later I had an announcement of her wedding to a young professor at Princeton."

"Yes, she's Mrs. Dexter now. Well, then the other day I happened to catch sight of you on the Jersey ferry and tried to call to you but someone hoicked me away. I saw you again in Philadelphia and was sure of you—of who you were. But I didn't get a chance to nab you until just now. As to your biography, I had that from Anne Wardwell. Guess that's enough for tonight, unless you've got more questions."

De Mérac thought for a moment. Then he said, "Just one, Major."

Wilson raised his eyebrows politely. "And that is—?"

"What," asked de Mérac, "is a pinkletink?"

"Good God!" snorted Wilson.

As de Mérac made his way back to the guard tent he met the unsleeping Rapp. "*Bleu!* At eight tomorrow morning this guard will find itself relieved. You, then, will supervise the digging of latrines."

De Mérac smothered a laugh. "*Parfaitement, mon sergent.* Ah—also, before eight o'clock, you will remove the stripes of a first sergeant." Rapp's face looked apoplectic in the lantern light. De Mérac went on. "You will replace them with the stripes of regimental sergeant major, the order being signed by myself as captain and adjutant."

The old soldier calmly accepted this new turn of the wheel. "*Entendu, mon capitaine.*"

Outside the guard tent de Mérac found George seated against a tree. "Sleep while you can, George," he cautioned.

George groaned. "Never thought I'd be too tired to sleep. Am, though. And then when I try to drop off, Mr. McArdle crowds against me. He's got hiccups from drinking too much water and damn near shakes me out of my blankets. Where've you been? Any news?"

De Mérac squatted beside him. "All that there is of the most important, George. I have just learned, my friend, that young spring frogs are sometimes described as pinkletinks."

"Earth-shaking," George said wearily. "Better send word to General Scott."

"And more. I find myself conscripted as regimental adjutant."

"Adjutant? That's great! Lord, I've wondered how long it would take them to find you out."

"I'm serious."

"So'm I. Known about you for weeks."

"The devil!"

"Sure. You know the Duanes in New York. Louise Duane told Marion. I figured it was your business and just didn't say anything. Adjutant! I thought maybe they'd end up by giving you a company, but this is great. Good luck, John, and don't forget us humbler forms of life." He straightened up. "And another thing—though I know I don't need to say it to you—militarily speaking you don't know me. Don't try to push me or pad things for me. You've got to build a regiment."

As de Mérac came down the hill, heading for the last time toward the tent that housed his squad and his few possessions, the endless stubble of canvas peaks, ghostly in the faint moonlight, swayed before his eyes. Under those brownish cones slept hundreds of other Frenchmen. With them were Germans, Irish, Americans, with a scattering of Spaniards, Italians, and Poles. No longer could he lose himself in those grassy streets. The sleeping mass was something he would have to mold. He had faith in the material of the companies, but ten good companies do not make a good regiment. Here, a good or bad adjutant could well personify Fate for the Rochambeau Rifles.

He drew a deep breath as a wind sprang up from the river and flowed over the short grass. On the far bank of the Potomac black trees stood out against a blacker sky. Far beyond those trees lay the advanced elements of the Union Army. "And beyond them?" he wondered. The wind grew brisker and hummed through guy ropes of the tents. Faint as snapping twigs, scattered shots sounded beyond the tossing trees, beyond the unseen outposts. Then they died away as though the wind had swallowed them up.

Early the next morning de Mérac sat in the cool main room of the hunting lodge while Wilson showed him a carefully drawn up list of matters that needed immediate attention. Outside, carpenters hammered up partitions on the deep porch that Rapp would use as his own particular office. Undisturbed by plane or hammer, an Italian tailor whom Rapp had combed out of the ranks squatted among shavings and loose boards as he sewed double loops on gold braid onto a new jacket for de Mérac.

Drinking coffee and smoking innumerable cigarettes, de Mérac listened, asked questions. He was carefully shaved and brushed but the fatigue of the past days lay heavy on him like a damp, tepid cloth. At last he pushed back his chair and flapped his hand wearily on Wilson's sheets. "This is all necessary. Of course. But I do not see a move that we can make until we are Federalized, until we are—what is the word?—mustered."

Wilson gnawed the end of a pencil. "I was afraid of that. What the devil can we do?"

De Mérac drew a fresh sheet toward him. "We can make schedules of drill. The guard posts can be shortened. There are sanitary matters. Then there is the matter of muskets. We have, from your figures, no less than seven different calibers in the regiment, each needing special ammunition. We must have the Springfield musket throughout." He pushed the paper away. "But, *dieu de dieu*—there again, they must come from the Federal Government. Major, we must be mustered—and without delay. I ask you, as a lawyer, how that can be done. What do we need?"

Wilson ruffled his graying hair. "That's the devil of it. Not until we've got the minimum number of officers."

"Go to New York and get them," said de Mérac.

"Not as easy as that."

"Why not? We are still of the state, you tell me."

"Yes. But—Ha! I've got it. By God, I've got it. Under law state troops can elect their own officers."

De Mérac's eyes snapped. "Here? Now?"

"Of course. Any time."

De Mérac shouted, "Sergeant Major Rapp." The Alsatian stalked through the door, new chevrons bright on his sleeves. "Rapp—send out word to assemble the companies for—for election of officers—is that right, Major?

Officers in doubt of procedure should consult Major Wilson. At once, Rapp." The veteran looked shocked at the idea of electing officers, but saluted smartly and doubled out of the room. "Now we move," said de Mérac. "We fill the vacancies. Then I shall go to the War Department myself and make application. We also—"

"Hold on," said Wilson. "Have you thought that some of the choices may not be the best? In fact, a lot are apt to be terrible."

De Mérac said grimly, "You gave me a free hand, you know. Leave the bad ones to me." His eyes narrowed. "There is one more thing, Major. You assure me that all this is strictly legal. Good. Thus we block such appointments as Dalbiac may make in New York."

"Damn it! I hadn't thought of that. Of course we do. He's scupered." Wilson chuckled. "The law's with us. Well, now we're moving."

Just before noon, de Mérac looked up as Rapp thundered, "*Bleu!* Do you then imagine—"

George bounded past Rapp into the room, shouting, "John—by God, they elected me! *First* lieutenant!"

De Mérac sprang up, "*Épatant*. Splendid! Major, the first fruits of the elections. Lieutenant Force of H Company! *Ah, ça!* This delights me, George." Wilson shook hands with George. "Willett Force's son, aren't you? Guess he'll be mighty pleased."

George stammered. "I don't know what to think about it yet. Never expected anything like it. Cahusac nominated me."

De Mérac said, "It was bound to happen, George. You couldn't bury yourself in the ranks."

"Ho! I said the same thing to a corporal last night." Wilson looked keenly at George. "You've got damned hard work ahead of you, young man."

George toyed nervously with the strap of his kepi. "Guess so. After all, I didn't come here for a vacation."

"How did Allard like the election?" asked de Mérac suddenly.

George set his chin. "All right. I—I guess he wanted Young but—anyway, part of my job's making Allard satisfied with me." He broke into a quick, excited smile. "Oh, I'm lucky. By God, I'm lucky."

Wilson's promise of a free hand to de Mérac was no empty gesture. When the Frenchman made his first tentative moves to bring order to the Rifles, the Major nodded gravely. "Anything you want. Just explain it to me first—not for my approval, you know—just so I'll understand." In one great sweep, de Mérac reshuffled the companies, forming six that were entirely French, one entirely German, one Irish, and two that held chiefly Americans. Other nationalities he distributed where he thought best. "There are objections, you conceive," he pointed out to Wilson. "First, the men rarely serve under the officers they elected. Second, I am open to charges of favoritism. Germans will say that the French companies are given easy work. Irish will say that the Germans do nothing but sleep. Americans will look upon Irish as my pets. The French will curse everyone. But it cannot be helped. The language problem is solved and the companies will gain in solidarity, which, for the moment, is important."

"I think you're sound," said Wilson crisply. "Go ahead."

The question of equipping himself was easily met. Houses in Washington, Philadelphia, New York, and even Boston, sent agents to the camps. To the gullible they sold fearsome devices—bullet-proof vests, metal gaiters against snakebite, filters connected to long rubber tubes through which, the soldier was assured, he might suck up pure water from the filthiest hog wallow. They sold dirks, bowie knives, short derringer pistols, portable ice-cream freezers, portable stoves.

De Mérac waved away the charlatans and bought a pair of heavy Colt revolvers, a plain cavalry saber, compact haversacks. From a string of horses he picked out a heavy-shouldered roan that showed fine bursts of speed and seemed powerful enough to carry his weight. For personal servant he found a sad-faced, rather mousy private named Louvel, who had been a waiter at Delmonico's and before that a valet. For groom he chose a scarred, swarthy ex-Chasseur d'Afrique, DuChesne, who eagerly adopted the new horse, christening it "Torpille" from its darting speed.

Watching the regiment march into camp behind its clanging bugles, Wilson glowed with pleasure. "You're doing something, I tell you, de Mérac. Look at that guide across squads! We're a lot better right now than those Regulars we saw yesterday."

De Mérac was not comforted. To him, the Rifles seemed almost as purposeless and isolated as they had in New York. They were a single regiment, comfortably camped by a river, not part of any army. More than anything, their equipment, particularly their obsolete muskets, troubled him.

Three times he rode into Washington to the War Department, DuChesne trotting erect and swarthy behind him on a bony sorrel. His sense of isolation increased as he passed the camps of a dozen states, saw signal flags flapping and dipping from the high ground by Arlington, to be answered by a quick flutter from the mysterious Virginia shore. In the city itself, batteries of artillery rumbled and clanked. Aides galloped through dusty streets, long lines of mule wagons were driven with contemptuous skill by lean, tobacco-chewing men. And none of the feverish stir touched him or his regiment. In the breathless corridors of the War Department he was jostled by shifty-eyed contractors, weary colonels, brisk, dry captains, and harassed clerks. In every bureau he was told courteously, sharply, indifferently, that his regiment had no business being in the Washington area, that until it was Federalized the Department would ignore its existence, would reach out no hand.

IV

Under Way

ONE hot afternoon de Mérac was frowning over a neat schedule that Rapp had prepared—"Assembly of buglers: 5 A.M.; Assembly, 5.15; Reveille. 5.29; Mess Call, 5.35—" He looked up. A carriage stopped by the door. A civilian in cool white linen jumped out and walked toward the camp. From the other side, Colonel Dalbiac descended importantly, strode up the steps, and entered the main room. De Mérac rose. "Good afternoon, Colonel."

Dalbiac's prominent eyes turned toward him and a hesitant smile played over the slack mouth. "Afternoon. New here, aren't you?" He fanned himself with a broad-brimmed hat.

"I am adjutant, sir. Captain John de Mérac."

The other sat down heavily. "Hot, isn't it? Nothing as bad as New York, though." He stared at the stacks of papers. "What's all that stuff?"

"Routine, sir," said de Mérac cautiously. "Matters for your attention. Of course, in your absence I have issued orders in your name. You care to look at these?"

Dalbiac tugged at his whiskers. "All that? Look here, can't someone do that for me? I haven't got the time."

De Mérac ventured, "The adjutant, as you know, sir, issues orders in the colonel's name. My authorization is here—signed by Major Wilson. If you merely add your own signature—"

Dalbiac snatched at a pen. "You can do all this for me now? Not bother me with it?" He signed below Wilson's name, then eyed de Mérac keenly. "Think I heard about you before I left New York. Someone told me you're a baron. That so?"

De Mérac shrugged. "Here—I am captain and adjutant."

Dalbiac nodded approvingly. "That's the talk. Well, this is fine. You run things the way you want. I haven't got the time for it. What sort of regiment have we got?"

"It can be a fine one," said de Mérac.

Dalbiac grunted. "Guess that's up to you and Wilson, isn't it? Anyway, what'll keep it from being good? God knows we've spent enough money on it."

De Mérac felt a greater confidence creeping over him. For the moment, this loose-mouthed man was not going to interfere. He said, "There are several matters that must be arranged. We are not yet mustered. The War Department will not move until we have all our field and staff officers." He watched Dalbiac carefully. "We have enough company officers—recently elected, under law."

Dalbiac showed no surprise over the elections. He pursed his full lips and said, "Field officers? What are they? What do we need?"

"There is no lieutenant colonel. No quartermaster. We have no surgeons. No chaplain—though the latter is optional under your regulations."

Dalbiac jerked at his sword belt. "Sure you've got 'em. Saw the Governor about 'em myself. Charley Brady and a couple of doctors and a priest. Guess they've been too busy to get here. Mustering, though. That means the Government begins paying for everything, doesn't it? Why haven't you and Wilson seen to it?"

De Mérac said smoothly, "No doubt because we could not reach the right quarters, Colonel."

Dalbiac puffed importantly. "I'm sure you did your

best, though. H'm. I'm dining with two Senators tonight at Willard's. Don't worry. They'll set things moving." He got up. "Going to take a walk around the camp. No, don't bother to come with me. You've got enough to do right here. Don't mind saying I'm damn glad I found you, Captain. We'll make a real show of the Rifles. Just send word to me at Willard's whenever I can help you. I'll be there when I'm in Washington. One word of advice. This war won't last forever and all these boys have got votes. Don't forget it." He shook hands cordially and tramped out of the office.

De Mérac stared after him, deep in thought. Unless there was a radical change, he felt sure that he could handle Dalbiac. He returned to his work. One by one, other companies of the regiment marched back into camp from bayonet drill, from route marches, from close-order drill, and bugles began to flare among the tents.

Then outside he heard a confident voice. "Captain de Mérac in there, Sergeant Major?" A figure in white civilian clothes stood in the doorway, smiling pleasantly. De Mérac, with a start, recognized the bland Mr. Cusler who had looked in at drill with Allard, back in Chambers Street.

Cusler's smile became more benign. "I'm ready for you now, Captain," he said.

De Mérac was puzzled. "At a later time it would give me much pleasure—you find me rather occupied."

Cusler's smooth-shaven pink face expressed approval. "Quite right. But I'm afraid that stuff on your desk'll have to wait. This is rather important."

De Mérac bowed politely. "This evening perhaps. These are regimental matters—"

Cusler laid a fine panama on the desk and drew out some papers.

"So are these. Look over this list, please. We've got to take care of these men and I've marked down the least we feel should be done."

De Mérac said, "May I ask who is included in the 'we'?"

"You might say, 'we, the people of New York County.'"

De Mérac glanced at the list and slow alarm crept over him. He set his jaw. "You won't think me rude if I make a comment or two? In confidence of course. These men! McGinnis of E be made sergeant? He is rarely sober and one of the dirtiest men in the regiment. Schmalz, next on the list, is too stupid and lazy to be of use even as private. Ah—Delahanty—I may not make him corporal since only yesterday he became first sergeant of I. But—*dieu*—these others! Grenier is absent without leave. Bartlett is always in the guardhouse." He handed the sheet back to Cusler. "Frankly I tell you that all this is as far beyond my powers as it is beyond my wishes."

Cusler's smile became even blander. "It may be hard for you to understand, but there are considerations—"

"Which lie, I am sure, outside civil influence."

"Hardly. Hardly. Read our history, Captain. You'll find that we've never allowed the military to dominate the civilian. Mind, I'm not finding fault with your attitude—only with your background." He began to chuckle. "And I'm not saying a word about the slick way you staged the elections. No hard feelings, although it upset a good many plans. But now—well—I'll just leave that paper with you." He rose, held out his hand. "Been a real pleasure. Heard a good deal about you and find myself agreeing with the high opinions I've heard expressed." From the door, he said pleasantly, "Of course I shall expect to learn that all those promotions are carried out."

When he was gone, de Mérac stared at the sheet. "But he was serious. Or was he? I think that he was making a test of me, for these are too small fish to linger in the memory of a Cusler." He tapped a long forefinger on the desk, frowning. The frown changed to a happy grin. He folded the sheet, slipped it into an envelope which he carefully addressed to Baron Vladimir Panoff, The Vendramin Palace, Venice.

Bugles were blowing more insistently outside as the last of the companies trailed back into camp. Wilson entered the lodge with his quick, light step and scaled his kepi onto a set of antlers. "They looked better today, John. What's for tomorrow morning—more regimental drill? Oh—I see you've got the schedule posted here. Very neat indeed. What's been happening?"

De Mérac lit a cigarette. "You are overwhelmed, Craig, at missing a visit from your colonel."

Wilson settled his well-cut jacket. "Oh, Lord! Is he going to bother us now?"

De Mérac handed him the paper that Dalbiac had signed. "Not unless there is a flaw in this."

Wilson chuckled. "Seeing that I drew the damn thing up for my own signature, there isn't likely to be. So Dalbiac signed it, did he? Kick up a fuss about it?"

"He seemed principally concerned in returning to the hazards of outpost duty at Willard's Hotel and barely glanced at it."

"Then your military power of attorney's complete." He waved the paper away. "All you've got to do is to keep Dalbiac malleable and ductile."

"Then the bland Mr. Cusler invaded us, demanding that we make sergeants out of the worst of our defaulters." He drew out the list.

Wilson looked very grave as he read the names. "Honest Jack Cusler? Damn it, we'll have to do something about this, you know."

De Mérac took the sheet from Wilson and returned it to the envelope, which he tossed into a carpetbag marked "Outgoing Mail," showing the address to Wilson first. "There—let it puzzle my old friend Panoff as much as any reference to it in future will puzzle me."

Wilson laughed, but his eyes were still grave. "Just hope you don't get into any trouble over that."

"No fear," said de Mérac. "Cusler is not of the military."

"Maybe," said Wilson doubtfully.

Dalbiac must have spoken persuasively to his senatorial friends, for two days later he bowled into camp with a regular army major. The latter, looking very lemonish about it, wandered from street to street where the companies were drawn up and then dully ruffled through the muster roles as company commanders called off the names: "Colette — Collas — Collé, S. — Collé, Z. — Colletet . . . Halezinsky — Hartleben — Hartmann — Hartzenbusch — Heuer . . . Delahanty — Delaney — Doyle — Eugan — Evers . . . Adams — Albright — Ames — Armstrong — Ashby —"

When the last man had been accounted for and the last oath administered, the regular major said sourly to Dalbiac, "That's all. You're part of the American army now." Under his breath he growled: "Steindorf! Loustalot! Mladnick! *American* army! Christ Almighty!"

"Just so, Major Buhler," said Wilson blandly.

The July sun drew a blanket of stifling haze over the grassy amphitheater where the brownish tents of the Rifles lay. George Force regretfully buckled his sword belt and hooked the heavy clasp where the letters "R.R." were interlocked. Then he picked up a leash and whistled for Mr. McArdle, who lay sprawled in a pool of dust that crawled with heat, his tongue lolling and his jaws languidly snapping at the gnats that hovered in a grayish cloud above his head. The dog shambled into the shade of the tent and George fastened the leash to his collar. "Come on. Going up to headquarters. God damn it. I've stood Allard's monkeyings just about long enough." He shook the leash and started up the slope to the lodge, Mr. McArdle whuffing disdainfully at a few unleashed mongrels.

George growled on, half to himself, half to the dog. "Damn Allard. He's always in Washington and I have to keep discipline. Then he comes back and upsets everything I've done. Stinks of rotten whiskey and scent out of a whorehouse most of the time. Let those three men out of guardhouse after I'd chucked 'em there for talking back to me! Tries to make a corporal out of Geranium Jones, the dirtiest man in the whole outfit!"

Then the life of the camp caught him up and his anger ebbed. It was noon and the men lay in the shade of their tents after an extended regimental drill. Smoke rose from the cookhouses, established to take the place of the now-departed caterers—breezy board shacks haunted by tough, cynical cats that openly sneered at the camp pets. Down by the canal that paralleled the river, brass flashes and discordant wailings echoed as the veteran sergeant bugler trained new musicians. Lines of mules were being led out to water below the carefully parked wagons. A few scattered Negroes hung about mule lines and cookshacks, eager to work for a chance of rations. Refugee blacks were more plentiful, it was said, across the Potomac. It seemed grotesque to him that slavery, the real root of all the trouble, should still flourish with the sanction of law in the District of Columbia. From the shady depths of officers' tents, a few voices hailed him—young Schoch of Hein's German Company, Mulcahey of Shea's, and the dark wiry Basque, Bordagaray of the Zouaves. He whistled to Mr. McArdle, who was beginning to lag. "Good regiment, boy! Just the same, I'm going to start things blowing about Allard."

There were a few new faces about the porch of the lodge, staff officers who had come down after mobilization. Captain Brady, the stubby, jovial Irish quartermaster; Dr. Wayne, a surgeon, a grayish, broken-looking man who kept to his tent and rarely spoke. No chaplain had yet been assigned despite de Mérac's requests. George nodded to the new pair and looked in at the clapboard office where Rapp kept a stern blue eye on his clerks. "Captain de Mérac in?"

Rapp saluted punctiliously. "Just now, sir, he prepares himself to go to New York." There was a hint of surprise in Rapp's voice as though he expected him to know of the trip.

"New York? Now?" He entered the lodge, crossed the main office to the narrow room where de Mérac had set up a Spartan cot. The door was open and he could see de Mérac settling the shoulders of a heavily braided jacket. On the cot lay a box marked "Brooks Brothers. New York."

George said, "So the camp isn't good enough for you, John?"

De Mérac looked around as he hooked his collar. "May I remind you that the train leaves in two hours from Washington?"

George sat on the cot and Mr. McArdle hopped up beside him.

"Don't worry," said George. "I had a few trifling company matters but I won't waste your time with them. Off to New York? Frankly, I think you'll have a rotten time. It'll be hot as the hold of a tea ship. And that coat's a disgrace. The epaulettes are tinsel, not bullion. And another thing. You're slighting your rank. You ought to have an aide. An aide named Force."

De Mérac said a little impatiently, "The train leaves in two hours, I repeat. You plan to go like that?"

"Go? What do you mean?"

De Mérac buckled his belt. "My note. I told you the time."

"Look here, John, I came up here with a real complaint, not to stage a minstrel show. I didn't get any note."

De Mérac drew a new kepi from a box and put it on. "I sent one, saying to be ready to go with me. I need you."

George stared. "Last note I had from you was about siting latrines."

Hard glints showed in de Mérac's eyes. "Then pack at once. We shall be gone three or four days. Hurry."

George said, "Three or four days! I—" But de Mérac had strode into the outer office, shouting for Rapp. George thought, "Damned if he doesn't mean it!" He jerked Mr. McArdle to his feet. "Come on! New York!"

As he left the lodge he saw de Mérac blazing at Allard in cold fury, his voice cutting like a saber slash. "Company commanders may not interfere with orders which I give. I need Lieutenant Force. If this happens again, I shall place you under arrest. If you bring political pressure to bear I shall see to it that the true story appears in all important papers. I am not unknown to some of the newspaper owners—"

George ran down the slope toward his tent. "Whew! John can lay it on when he wants to. New York! Gosh, though—wonder how he dares, with all the stuff in the papers!"

Half an hour later he and de Mérac were in a carriage, bowling past the long lines of camps toward Washington, with Mr. McArdle curled up at their feet. George rubbed his nose dubiously. "Hope this is all right, John. 'Course, it's wonderful to get a few days up there, but—" He pointed to a heavy column of Pennsylvania infantry in marching order heading toward the city with a long string of wagons in its rear. "McDowell's been moving a lot of troops across there, you know, and the Rebs are supposed to be somewhere around Centerville. You can almost see it from the heights."

De Mérac shook his head. "Wilson and I talked the matter over. McDowell is moving men undoubtedly. But he is not yet ready to fight. He will not be for some weeks. For one thing—if this were more than a transfer of troops, would he announce his every move in the press? No, George, that is for Rebel eyes—and so boldly done it cannot fool them. Myself, I feel quite safe in leaving the Rifles. My friend Colonel Labanieff—the Russian military attaché—agrees."

"Maybe you're right about the papers. Hope so. What are we going to do in New York? Go shopping at Lord and Taylor's?"

De Mérac smiled. "Precisely. We shop, though not in the usual stores. It was all explained in my note which Allard intercepted. That will not happen again. We need officers, trained if possible. Some of the three-months regiments have gone home, notably your New York 7th. You know many of them. I want at least six to come to us. It can be arranged. Wilson saw to that at the War Department. For myself I wish to find a Frenchman named Alfred Duffié who now trains the Harris Light Cavalry at White Plains but is not yet regularly attached. He is an officer of much service and gave up his commission with the 3rd Imperial Chasseurs to join the North. I learned of him through Stoeckl."

George burst out laughing. "This is the craziest war ever! The papers say McDowell's going to move on Richmond and we go off to buy a few assorted lieutenants. We don't know whom we belong to, even." He stirred Mr. McArdle with his foot. "Damn it, there's nothing solid about the whole thing. We're in an army and I've never seen anyone above the rank of colonel. I've only seen three or four generals' names in the paper—McDowell and Banks and Patterson and Scott. You know in some ways I feel less a part of something than I did in Chambers Street. I don't like it."

De Mérac shrugged. "You can't build an army overnight." The carriage jolted into the city. There were more and more troops in the streets—columns of red-legged Zouaves, Minnesota infantry in gray, rumbling batteries of artillery. De Mérac waved at them. "McDowell underrates the Confederate spies. Never will they believe in a threat that is carried out in broad daylight, even without the newspapers' aid."

Washington station was a bedlam and the northbound trains were crowded with beaver hats, straw hats, and gold-braided blue. As George jumped out by the train shed a swarm of newsboys swooped down through the crowd bawling an extra. De Mérac seized a smeared sheet and waved it. "Here may be the answer to McDowell's moves!" He pointed to huge headlines. "Great Union Victory! Peagram Surrenders to McClellan! West Virginia in Our Hands!"

George stared at the blinding letters. "God! That means the war's about over?"

De Mérac shook his head. "It means that it has scarcely begun. McDowell's moves must have been to mask McClellan's and to amuse the South. Now we may work in New York without too much haste—and even amuse ourselves a little with clear consciences. There's our train. *Allons-y*."

The Sanitary Commission was holding a great ball and bazaar under the hissing gas chandeliers of the Fifth Avenue Hotel ballroom. The floor below was a shifting pattern of epaulettes, of bare white shoulders that dipped and swayed to music of the Rifles' band, still held in New York by Dalbiac's orders. Around the edge of the hall booths were hung with bright bunting that set off bold signs: "Auxiliary of the 79th Highlanders." "For the Boys of the 14th Brooklyn." "*Louis Blenker und der 8ge Neu York Infanterie.*"

By the booth of the Duryea Zouaves, Dora Chase laughed up at George Force. "But this is the *fifth* waltz you've asked me for! You're spoiling your little sister's friend."

"Spoiling myself," said George. "John says we've got to go back tomorrow and I want to remember you in that pink stuff—what do you call it?"

Dora shook her dark hair. "It's called pink stuff, George."

"There's so much about you that I don't want to forget." He caught the eye of Dubiel, the bandmaster on the cannon-flanked platform, and nodded. The band struck up a waltz and George guided Dora expertly between a small Massachusetts gunner who manfully piloted a billowy matron, and a hollow-cheeked civilian who wove toward the bar with vague amiability. The band was superb and Dora gave herself to the rhythm of the waltz. It was nice of George to make such a fuss over her, even if he'd always think of her just as Marion's friend. She felt very happy and elated, a little the way she felt when regiments marched down Broadway and massed bands blared "Rally 'round the flag, boys." Not only was George devoting himself to her. It was more than that. The blue and yellow was part of the uniform of her country and the man who wore it had, a few days ago, been in a camp along the Potomac, making sure that the slaveowners didn't seize the Capital. Somehow it made her feel that it was *her* Capital. The music died in a slow sweep. She stepped back smiling. "That was lovely, George."

He smoothed out his white gloves. "But not the last. Oh yes, I know that you've got the next with Joey Brevoort but the ball isn't over yet. Look—here are John and Louise Duane, right beside us."

Louise cried, "What a pretty dress, Dora. Come along with us. We're going to have an ice at the d'Utassy regiment booth."

Dora hung back as Louise and de Mérac made their way toward the booth. George said, "Don't worry about Joey. This is intermission. You don't know it, but you'd love an ice—a nice pistachio one."

Dora said doubtfully, "All right—but I wish it were someone else than Louise. She's such a hard little snip. See the way she's got Captain de Mérac's arm! Trying to make everyone think she owns him."

"Don't worry about John. Anyway, he saw quite a lot of her and her family in Europe last summer. Here we go."

In the crowd about the booth, de Mérac felt gayer and more carefree than he had at any time since his enlistment. He waved to George and Dora across the bald head of an artillery colonel and turned back to Louise. *Ciel,* but she had grown far prettier since the summer before. She was, he thought, the prettiest girl on the floor with her ash-blond hair and startlingly dark eyes and dark lashes. She was small and looked rather slim, but the slimness was highly deceptive as the low-cut dress revealed. Her white shoulders were delicately rounded; no shadow appeared below the collarbones, and her breasts, it was obvious, were high and cuplike. He looked down at her as she daintily ate a raspberry ice that just matched the red dress. These American girls, so gayly frank and unspoiled. Louise's air of camaraderie, so natural and straightforward, would have seemed almost brazen on the part of one of his compatriots. But here in New York, anywhere in America, it was delightfully unstudied. He took her plate from her and slid it back to the booth. The crowd increased and they stood very close together, a propinquity that she seemed to accept with unconscious innocence.

Voices rose higher and he had to bend toward her to catch what she was saying. "*Baste!*" he muttered to himself. "This may be all very well for *her*, but me, I find this disturbing." He tried to keep his eyes from the silk sheen of bare shoulders and arms. She was saying, "—and when the music starts again, please ask the bandmaster—Ouch!"

A tendril of soft hair had caught on the third button of his jacket. She twisted slightly, looked up at him in mute appeal. Gently he freed the button while her lifted hands restored the lock to its place. Her breasts stirred to the motion. The corners of her mouth quirked and she looked up, aslant, from under half-lowered lids. In Paris, that look would have been direct invitation. Here, of course—

Beyond the booth a door banged and men surged about it shouting. Louise's dark eyes widened. "What? What *is* it?" Then a tall girl close by the door clapped her hands to her mouth and cried, "No!" She looked about as though startled by the sound of her own voice. She cried again, "No! Harry's there!" and swayed, eyes tight shut.

The news swept down the hall like a striking snake. "They're in Washington! Burning it!" ... "At Bull Run! Fifty thousand killed." ... "Army? God damn it, we haven't got an army any more!" ... "Beauregard! Close to Philadelphia! Cavalry's over the Jersey line."

De Mérac felt cold and hollow and his mind froze in quick paralysis. He knew that Louise was clutching at his sleeve, looking up at him in bewilderment. He recovered himself and urged her gently on to George and Dora. He said quickly, "To Mrs. Duane's box. I'll join you there." He glided away through the crowd that stood stunned and motionless. Somewhere across the hall a woman was sobbing quietly.

Louise turned to George. "What *is* it? Why did he go?"

George said tersely, "This way. Hurry, please."

Dora said, "Is it something bad, George?"

"The army. Now do hurry, please. McDowell *did* move. It'll kill John. He was so sure it was all a feint. Oh, my God—*if* they sent the Rifles in and we weren't there! Allard's useless!"

The Duanes' box was empty and George quickly seated the two girls. The hush over the hall was ghastly—broken just by the shuffle of feet and the choking sobs of one woman. Louise shook his arm. "Do find out something. Don't just stand there!"

He said obstinately, "John told me to wait. I'll—here he comes now—past the bandstand."

A cold fear gnawing at his heart, de Mérac wove on through the groups on the floor. Faces about him looked sick, hopeless. Then he saw Dubiel looking down at him from the platform with its useless cannon and sheaves of bayonets. He waved to him. "Dubiel! In the name of God, *play!*" The leader, in his yellow-frogged coat, fumbled through some sheets. "No! It must be of the country. That march you had from the 12th Massachusetts! 'John Brown!'—*Le Corps de Jean le Brun!*' Play till you split yourself!"

He hurried on to the box. Behind him, Dubiel swept up his baton and the band thundered out. People looked up, startled. Then new life came to their faces as the heavy chords slammed against the walls. At the edge of the floor a girl ablaze in orange flung out her arms and her clear contralto rang out: "Glory, glory, Hallelujah! His soul goes marching on!" Other voices joined in. Dubiel bent double as he whipped his men into a frenzy.

"*Va!*" muttered de Mérac. "That may help!" He waved abruptly to George as he neared the box. The latter stepped quickly to meet him. De Mérac said in a tense voice, "I saw a major of Regulars. It is true. A rout! We make our adieux at once."

George burst out, "Of course. Let's get going!" In his mind he saw the blue and yellow ranks of his company, mishandled by Allard—or deserted by him—being shot down, helpless, in a woody run. He barely heard Dora's answer as he said, "We're going, Dora. It's true."

She raised her voice. "You *must*. What can I do?"

"Tell Dad and Mother when they come back to the box."

Beyond him Louise was saying, "But John, there's no train until morning!"

De Mérac said, "We will ride a freight car if we must."

"But it may be all over, John. You can't do anything!"

Unsmiling he said, "Please present my apologies to your mother, George!" Before she could catch her breath the two blue backs were lost in the milling crowd. Then her mouth set in a thin line. "They've forgotten all about *us!*"

Dora's lips quivered. "No! They're thinking about—every one of us!"

The carriage rattled on toward the ferry through

streets that shrieked with fear and despair. Men bawled, "God damn it! It ain't over! We'll hit 'em till they quit." ... "Blame that baboon in the White House—playing county politics!" ... "Ah—it was all fixed beforehand. You wait. Lincoln and Davis damn well thimble-rigged it, I tell you."

In the carriage de Mérac swore fluently while George held tight to the leash of Mr. McArdle, rescued from the ignominy of the cloakroom. Once he said, "Forget it, John. You used your best judgment!"

"Judgment! I looked on the papers as I would on European papers. The move was in the air and I was blind to it. If anything has happened to the Rifles I—I am responsible. I should have told Dalbiac this recruiting could wait." As he swung his arm impatiently a faint trace of scent rose from the blue cloth. He waved it angrily away as though it were something that must be brushed off, something alien.

George repeated doggedly, "You can't be blamed."

"Who says not? And what do we show for our absence? You found three officers. I failed even to interest Duffié. I've made a blind, blundering waste of everything."

"Write it off as bad luck. What do we do about a train?"

"We go south on anything that moves. We keep on until we find the Rifles, wherever they are."

The next noon the two climbed feverishly from their train into the sullen heat of the Washington station. The place reeked of panic. Civilians, men in uniform, jammed the cars of a waiting north-bound train. From another track a newly arrived Connecticut regiment shuffled to the platform, the men white-faced and breathing heavily through parted lips, the officers running hopelessly around in search of someone in authority to tell them where to go.

George looked about bewildered, choking in the acrid smoke of the locomotives. "God's teeth! This place stinks of ruin." He stepped aside numbly as two unshaven, bandaged men cannoned past him, wild-eyed.

De Mérac hitched his sword belt. "Wait here, George," he said and ran to a Regular captain standing cold and unruffled by a pillar. "The Rochambeau Rifles! *Nom de dieu,* where are they?"

The captain barely turned his head. "Never heard of 'em."

De Mérac spun away from him, found a limping gunner who croaked in answer, "What? Rifles? Sure. Got chucked in by the stone bridge. Cut to hell. Or maybe it was a German bunch. I—"

George folded his arms in an effort to look calm. He watched de Mérac's flat-topped kepi dart among steeple-crowns, past wide felts, among slant-topped kepis. At his feet Mr. McArdle whimpered. Then a pretty, dark-haired woman swept up to him. Her voice broke in a gasp of relief. "You must be from the Rifles. Can—oh—can you tell me *any*thing?"

He whipped off his cap and tried to smile confidently into eyes that were heavy with fatigue and worry. "The Rochambeau Rifles, madam. May I help you?"

She set her chin with a visible effort. "Just tell me where they are. The newspapers! They're dreadful!" Her head went back. "Excuse me. I'm a little worried, you see. I'm Claire Wilson—Mrs. Craig Wilson. My husband telegraphed me to come down because he'd found a house near Georgetown." She managed a smile. "I think I know who you are. You're George Force and that's your dog. Craig's written about you two. And I know your family. You look like your father." She was completely calm now. "What should I do? We've been waiting here for hours but no one could tell us anything at all."

He said reassuringly, "Wait with me. John de Mérac's over there. We just got in from New York and we're going to take you right out to camp." He wondered privately what they would find at that camp.

She shook cinders from her narrow-hooped brown traveling skirt. "Oh—Captain de Mérac. Craig thinks a lot of him. I won't be in the way?" She turned and called, "Janet, dear."

A four-year-old mite, dressed like her mother save for

a hint of lace pantalette, trotted solemnly across the tracks. After her came a tall, gray-haired Negro, laden with bags, who crooned anxiously, "Jes' you watch out, little miss. Rest yo'se'f right by yo' ma." He snatched off a well-brushed hat as he bowed to Mrs. Wilson.

"Can you wait long enough to help get out bags in the carriage?" she asked.

His prominent watery eyes looked pleadingly at her. "You gwine out to this yere Freedom Army, ma'am? I come 'cross the river las' night with the Lincum sojers. Don't aim to go back."

Claire Wilson looked questioningly at George. He said, "You didn't bring him from New York?"

"No. I told you we got off the train early this morning and he helped us with our bags. I knew I could trust him as soon as I saw him. And he's been lovely with Janet. Can't he come with us, if he wants to?"

"Don't see why not. He looks like a gem and you'll need servants." He turned to the old man in his clean, threadbare clothes. "What's your name?"

The Negro stepped forward. "Thomas, suh. I'm—I'm right used to little gals, suh."

"You'd like to work for Mrs. Wilson?"

The yearning face, was suddenly slashed with ivory. "Yes, *suh!*"

"You won't want to go back over the river?"

The ivory vanished. "No, suh. Good folks own me. Den hard times come. Dey sell my woman. Dey sell my Sam and my Lou. Dat's five year gone and I ain't seed none of my own since."

George handed him a few coins. "See if you can hire a cart for the baggage."

Thomas took the money. "Fetch one d'rectly, suh." He padded off.

"One problem solved, Mrs. Wilson," said George. He caught sight of de Mérac as the latter stepped over a row of empty stretchers. His face was set like a mask and his eyes seemed to have sunk back into his head. George called, "John! Over here! I've found Mrs. Craig Wilson."

Concern was wiped from de Mérac's face and his hurried stride became an easy stroll. "How delightful!" he said, bowing. "May we take you to camp?"

"Mr. Force says we won't be in the way. Can you tell me what you found out?"

"That your husband and I will soon shudder over a mass of paper work."

She threw back her head. "Captain de Mérac, if Craig could turn into a soldier at his age. I can turn into a soldier's wife! What has happened?"

He said gravely, "I can find out nothing—except, of course, that the Virginia news is—" he broke into French—"*tout à fait écrasant.*"

Thomas returned, aglow. He had found a cart and a carriage, but they must hurry. He gathered up the bags, added George's and de Mérac's to them. De Mérac perched Janet on his shoulder. She crowed, "My daddy's a soldier and I'm going to see him."

De Mérac laughed. "A ride through the country and then you see your daddy, *hein?* What a *fête champêtre!*" His eye caught George's. Both were wondering what the streets of Washington would look like. Neither dared think as far as the grassy amphitheater near Tennallytown.

Pennsylvania Avenue was fairly cleared and patrolled by squads of cavalry. But the sidewalks swarmed with furtive, shaken men in soiled uniforms, side streets hummed with sullen voices. George cried, "Look, Mrs. Wilson. There's an omen!" He pointed to the dome of the Capitol where a derrick swung a heavy beam into place, adding to the soft curve.

"*Épatant,*" muttered de Mérac. Out of the corner of his eye he had seen the hospital stewards across the street dragging a limp body from a fence corner. The head was a tangle of soiled bandages and the face like yellow clay. But there was much that they could not hide from Claire Wilson: a drunken colonel reeling in his saddle; a line of blue-coated men, muddy, hopeless, unarmed, stumbling away under cavalry escort; an officer in Confederate gray, weaponless but unguarded, viewing the wide street with contempt; a stretcher at the mouth of an alley beyond Willard's, abandoned, an uncovered corpse turning a blue face to the sky. When they passed the War Department, George jerked his head at the brick walls. "Want to try for news in there, John?"

"What use?" asked de Mérac dryly.

They drove on in silence. De Mérac tried to sit quietly and study every street and every face that they passed. The Rebels had not crossed the Potomac. At least, not yet. That puzzled him. The Union Army—*his* army— seemed shattered, and a very small hostile force could probably have swept over Long Bridge in perfect safety.

Beyond Georgetown he lifted his head suddenly. The big white flag, red-centered, at the Signal Corps station was dipping and flapping against the sky. He stood up and stared at the Virginia shore and his heart leaped. Small but clear came an answering flutter. The Union still held the right bank. Then Mr. McArdle yelped as George lurched forward, pointing and shouting.

On the road ahead boots drummed in unison. Over the crest of the hill rode a group of officers in slouch hats and after them marched squad on squad of solid men in blue, the national colors, flanked by the buffalo flag of Indiana standing sharp against the ragged clouds. George cried, "Look at 'em. Those aren't beaten troops!"

Claire Wilson caught Janet's hand. The men marched beautifully, even to her untrained eye. But—they were not the Rochambeau Rifles.

De Mérac pulled at his mustache and wondered with her. Would the carriage roll into an empty camp? Or find a shattered, skeleton regiment?

Then over the beat of the hoofs and the grind of wheels a new sound, hoarse, steady, and rhythmical, throbbed through the air. Claire Wilson said quickly, "What's that?"

De Mérac snapped, *"Nom d'un nom d'un nom d'un nom—"*. He swung clear of the wheels and ran ahead of the horses. He topped a rise and a full-throated chorus swept up to meet him:

> *Le sergent est un légume.*
> *Il baise, il boit, il chique, il fume.*

*Il ne peut même lire son nom.
Il est bête comme un cochon.*

He saw, marching to the west, a thick rope of blue and yellow coiling along the twisting road. Halfway down, the flags of France and America floated side by side over ten full companies, with the red fezzes of Corvisart's Zouaves just swinging out of sight into a wooded stretch.

The carriage, whipped to a smart trot, overtook him, slowed down enough to let him swing into the seat, rattled on. George was standing up, waving his kepi and cheering. Claire Wilson stood beside him, her bright eyes wet and her lips half parted. Behind the carriage the wagon rumbled on, bearing Thomas to his Freedom Army.

The column grew more distinct as the carriage overtook it. Men began to shout and wave. George sprang wildly out and took his place by the flank of H Company, commanded only by the old Regular, Bates. The carriage went on, past the scowling LeNoir, past Chanel. Then toward the head of the column a spare-built horseman turned in the saddle, froze, whirled his mount about, and galloped back, a diminutive bugler pounding after him. Claire Wilson put her hand to her throat. "He's safe! They're all safe. Dear God, keep my voice steady!"

De Mérac vaulted from the opposite side of the carriage just in time to hear her call, clear and assured, "Here we are, dear. A little late but all right. Have you worried? Janet was a perfect lamb and I was lucky enough to meet George Force and Captain de Mérac at the station."

De Mérac kept along the column, then was swallowed up by a wave of company officers as Wilson's bugler sounded a halt. They were hot-eyed and resentful. "No one sent for us, God damn it!" . . . "*Lieber Hauptmann,* like *Dummkopfs* we the whole day sit!" . . . "Five of my little devils—five I put under arrest who tried to make their way to the Virginia!" . . . "*B'en oui!* It was pitiful. We hear firing, even. The men, they weep, and Lousteau, a good Zouave, breaks his musket over a stump."

... "My God, sir, it was plain hell. We could have done something if they'd just let us go!"

"Praise God they didn't," said de Mérac.

In H Company George was receiving a budget of news from First Sergeant Bates, who rumbled on, running the back of his hand over the short whiskers that curled under his chin. "I been looking after the boys since the loot'nant left, sir. Cap'n Allard, he's got himself into a Bureau to the Department—detached service. Loot'nant O'Keefe, he's got shifted for good to the 14th Brooklyn. Sure, the boys look pretty good, like you was sayin'. But they'll do better for you, sir. Always they takes it better out'n an officer."

George said, "Then I command H?"

"Looks like it."

He drew a deep breath. "We'll have to make this the best damn company in the regiment."

Bates shifted his quid. "Got a chance to now, sir."

"See me in my quarters after retreat tonight." He studied the men as they leaned on their muskets. Some of the sergeants would find themselves with less authority. A private here and there would hunt up the company tailor to have stripes sewn on his sleeves. Others would mend their ways, even if he had to resort to bucking and gagging. H Company must outstrip even Corvisart's élite Zouaves.

The bugles flared up and down the column. Commands snapped out and the Rifles took the road back to their camp. At the head, Wilson, bridle over his arm, talked earnestly with de Mérac. In the rear, Claire Wilson, her arm around Janet, smiled happily as she watched the swing and sweep of hundreds of arms. For the moment her husband, her regiment, and her country were safe. The men began to sing again:

Le lieutenant est un légume.
Il baise, il boit, il chique, il fume ...

V

General Dudley Pelham

A WEEK before his trip to New York, de Mérac had established an officers' mess, housing it in a portable building which was sent out from Washington in sections and bolted together by mechanics borrowed largely from Force's and Bolton's companies. Cooks were no problem in a regiment so heavily French and he installed an ex-Delmonico chef with three skilled assistants in the kitchen. Waiters had been difficult to find until he turned to Mrs. Wilson's worshiping Thomas, who produced a bowing butler and several competent underlings. To this mess he invited all officers of the regiment. Many came but others, like George Force, thought it better policy to mess closer to their men and appeared only occasionally.

Under the skilled hand of the chef, Vernet, who had gladly exchanged his kepi for a white chef's cap, the fame of the mess grew. To it, a few days after de Mérac's return, came the stocky, bearded Labanieff in full hussar's kit. He talked expansively about what he had seen at Bull Run as observer on McDowell's staff.

The officers, assembled for the occasion, listened attentively, rows of American faces, Irish faces, French faces, German faces, intent under the smoke-wreathed lamps.

The Russian, smiling placidly over his thick cigarette and his glass of old brandy, lectured on like an indulgent professor, largely ruling out personalities and treating the whole action as one more military problem. De Mérac had already begun to guess some of the story. The armies had blundered together. Regiments on both sides had broken in panic. Others had driven ahead aggressively. A Wisconsin regiment, unluckily wearing gray, had been fired upon by the New York 69th and badly shaken. A Union battery of Regulars at a vital point had held its fire while a heavy blue column bore down on its flank. The bluecoats turned out to be Virginia militia and the battery was largely wiped out. "So it went, my friends," purred Labanieff, "like our Russian game of *gorelka*—" he tilted his hand like a seesaw. "For raw levies, neither side was very bad. I have yet to learn who gave the Union order for retreat. It began slowly. There was no panic at first save among those troops not engaged, and in the wagon trains." He raised his eyebrows tolerantly. "One has seen it happen before. I may cite the French panic at the end of Waterloo, in 1815. No doubt had the order been given on the Southern side the result would have been the same."

"Were our generals at fault, Colonel?" asked Wilson quietly.

Labanieff spread out his hands. "I think not. On paper it was well planned. Neither side, however, had the skill or experience to move large bodies where they wanted them when they wanted them. There was delay—everywhere. For parallel I may cite the delay of Marshal Soubise in 1757. Or that of Emmanuel Philibert after the fall of St. Quentin in 1557." Other questions poured in on the Russian and he talked on in amiable pedantry.

When he got up to take his leave, Wilson ventured, "At least, Colonel, we've now got a lot of regiments who've been under fire. That's something to build on."

Labanieff settled his high green collar. "My dear Major—you *had*. Many are of the three months' levy and will now go home. You must build again."

In the back of the room George cried impatiently, "Start all over again? Good God, when are we going to get this thing over and get back to work?"

Labanieff smiled blandly. He must remember to write his brother in Cracow of the young American who looked on the great science of war as a mere interruption of work. He said gently, "You must build from the bottom—as must the South in great part. But—" he shrugged—"I do not think you will be idle. A battle has been lost and hence you will have a new commander. In the old days one shot the loser. Now one replaces him. I wish all of you gentlemen good luck under General McClellan, who surely will be appointed. And he will be given much that the beaten McDowell asked for and never had. It is always so."

Labanieff's warning proved as accurate as his earlier forecast of the summer's military operations had been faulty. George McClellan, riding on the wave of his conquest of Peagram in West Virginia, took command of the Army of the Potomac. With a staff and retinue that seemed both unwieldy and showy, he rode through the camps that lined both sides of the river. De Mérac watched him keenly as the cavalcade cantered past the Rifles, drawn up in rigid lines. He saw a small man with piercing eyes, a bushy mustache, and the chest and shoulders of a prize fighter. "Looks as though he's waiting to go on the stage at the Laura Keene," grunted George when the brief review broke up.

"That is unimportant," said de Mérac. "He rode fast but one could see his eyes travel to the right things—the men's boots, the cleanliness of the streets, the siting of the latrines and cookhouses." Privately, he thought the man decidely theatrical, as though always posing to himself as a fragment of a battle picture—the military frown, the fist resting against the small of his back and clutching ever-ready field glasses. None of this would matter if the new general would build an army out of the swarming regiments.

Theatrical or not, McClellan asked for and received

the wide powers that Labanieff had foretold, and started a whirl of activity that reached down to the Rifles in their sloping camp. Aides galloped up to the lodge with orders, paper work increased until even Rapp looked hollow-cheeked and red-eyed and the scar through his beard looked more livid than ever. Colonel Dalbiac reluctantly came down from New York, bringing his treasured band with him, and established himself permanently at the Willard.

Two days after the colonel's return to Washington, de Mérac mounted Torpille, her glossy flanks shining in the sun, and took the reins from the swarthy DuChesne. As he trotted toward the road a carriage halted and he touched his kepi to Claire Wilson and the grave-eyed Janet. The mother called, "Don't bother about us. We're just going to drive about the camp. We met the regiment down the road and Craig said it was all right and George Force wants us to give Mr. McArdle a run. Dinner with us at seven tonight."

"I look forward to it. While in the camp, I should value your opinion of Vernet's kitchen."

Claire Wilson's eyes widened. "Trespass in the mess! My dear Captain, I'd as soon invade the Union Club. I'll come and act as hostess for the regiment, though. I expect you'll be having shoals of young ladies as guests before long."

"Washington is still empty, Mrs. Wilson. I know no one here."

"Don't worry. People'll be pouring in, with Congress in session and all sorts of new things started. If you don't know any girls I'll find a dozen for you."

She waved and the carriage slid on to the camp. De Mérac trotted off, frowning. It was true that he and most of the officers of the Rifles had been working so hard that the camp—from their standpoint at least—had resembled that of a band of militant monks. "A fact," he said to himself, "that I find surprising and one that some others would find incredible. *Dieu de dieu.* I should like this night to go to a ball like that at the Fifth Avenue. I should like, too, to watch Louise Duane when she laughs. I should like—I should like to know where I may find Springfields for the regiment. I should like to know for what I meet the warlike Dalbiac this morning."

DuChesne trotting behind him, he sighted the stone house mentioned in Dalbiac's order—a high-shouldered, pillared affair on a rise to the left and commanding a fine view of the Potomac. There was a carriage tethered at the end of the drive, a cluster of saddle horses with orderlies standing by. An immaculate cavalry sergeant at the head of a trim squad halted him. He gave his name and was passed on respectfully. "The Cap'n'll find Colonel Dalbiac in the big room at the right."

De Mérac felt cheered. The guard was well turned out and flawlessly military. Then he saw a red flag wih a single star floating over the door. "*Alors!* A brigadier?" He gave his reins to DuChesne and entered the house.

The big room at the right was bare of furniture save for a blackboard and a few plain chairs. Dalbiac stood in a deep window, talking with two other colonels. He smiled pleasantly as de Mérac entered and said in an undertone that carried perfectly, "This is the French baron I got working for me." Then, louder, "Colonel Clay, Colonel Pride, my adjutant, Baron de Mérac."

Clay was a lean, ascetic-faced man with a cold eye and a distant manner. His slant-topped kepi bore the letters "N.J." in a gold wreath. De Mérac guessed that his real roots lay far up the Hudson on one of the great feudal estates that dated back to earliest Dutch days and embraced a whole county at least. Pride, whose eagles could not change his farmer's stoop, was brown-bearded with a solid chin and steady direct eyes that de Mérac liked at once. "Guess you wouldn't know my part of the country, just coming from abroad," said Pride. "Indiana. Come from near Terre Haute, but I guess that'd just be a name to you."

"It is near the Wabash, perhaps? I have been shooting there."

Pride's face lighted. "Have you now? Lordy, don't I miss it! Fall coming before long. Give a sight to be trailing through the marshes with my gun and two-three dogs ahead of me. Did you have luck?"

The door opened and the four men looked around,

each with the question in his mind: "Is *this* the one?" Then de Mérac saw major's gold leaves on the officer's shoulders, read deference to eagles on the square, clean-shaven, heavily muscled face. The major said, "General Pelham will be here immediately. Ah, I think it would be well for him to find you standing when he enters." The door closed. Spurred boots rattled on a bare floor somewhere outside and the door was pushed open—not violently, just firmly, thoroughly under control of the tall thin man who entered.

His grizzled hair was close-trimmed, his forehead broad, and his eyebrows made a straight line over hard eyes that held hot, repressed light. There was a trace of whisker by each ear but the rest of the grim face was shaven to the quick. De Mérac eyed the beaky nose, the tight-pressed lips and outslanting chin, held well back over a high stock. He thought the man would have looked perfectly at home as one of Cromwell's Ironsides or as one of the broad-hatted, grim-faced men whose portraits he had seen in Boston homes.

The shaven lips parted slightly and the brigadier said, "Be seated, gentlemen." His voice was cold and precise. He turned unwavering eyes on the group. "I am General Pelham, General Dudley Pelham of the Regular Army." His mouth barely moved as he spoke. "Your regiments have been assigned to my brigade. I understand that you are all from civil life." He pronounced the last two words with icy disdain. "In Mexico I saw civilian troops in the field. Their performance there does not encourage me to hope for much from your commands. Tomorrow, I shall inspect your camps, beginning with Colonel Dalbiac's. Colonel Clay will be next and then Colonel Pride. Your records must also be available to me. It is, I presume, too much to hope that there are any former officers serving under you."

Dalbiac said eagerly, "A lot of my captains served in the French Army. Got a German or two along with 'em I guess."

"I did not refer to foreigners," said Pelham coldly. "I see that we must count on civilians. With that in view I have prepared a brief lecture which will be followed by others. I shall not accept excuses for nonattendance or nonassimilation." He took a step toward the blackboard, put his hands behind his back, and rocked on his heels. "We are an infantry command. What, gentlemen, is the role of infantry?" He frowned and looked from face to face. Colonel Pride flushed as he said slowly, "To get there and shoot, I'd say."

There was a silence. Pelham's mouth set harder and his glance was like a cold blade. "When I require civilian comment I shall call for it. The role of infantry, gentlemen—" He talked on, clearly and concisely, turning every now and then to make quick sketches on the blackboard. As he wrote, the edges of his stiff white cuffs scratched on the surface. De Mérac leaned forward with keen interest. Here was a real soldier, real perhaps as the ember-eyed Philip Kearny. He knew his trade thoroughly and, what was as important, knew how to talk about it. Disdainful eye and cutting voice were forgotten. Under such a brigadier, the Rifles could develop to the fullest. When the last sketch had been drawn and the last, bitter, humorless comment made, Pelham laid down his chalk. "You will report here tomorrow afternoon at the conclusion of my inspections. Colonel Dalbiac, what is the exact strength of your regiment?"

Dalbiac said cheerily, "About ten companies."

Pelham's words sliced out viciously. "I—asked—you—the—exact strength. As of your morning reports of today."

Dalbiac reddened. "Why—my adjutant knows about things like that."

"In future, you will know about them. Is that captain behind you your adjutant? Well, Captain. Speak up. I assume, perhaps wrongly, that you've been listening."

De Mérac said, "Seven hundred seventy-four present for duty, sir."

Pelham's mouth contracted. "Be sure that your records show that tomorrow. How many sick?" His questions poured on. How many absent without leave? What percentage of foreign-made muskets? As he answered, de Mérac blessed the hours that he had spent over Rapp's

85

meticulous reports. His confidence in Pelham grew with each quick inquiry. The brigadier was obviously intent on finding out the last essential detail of his new command.

Pelham turned abruptly to Clay and then to Pride. De Mérac was surprised to find that the aloof Clay knew little of his regiment, whereas Pride's rather slow but tenacious mind seemed to have inventoried his, to know it as a careful farmer knows his tools and his stock. At last they were dismissed, Pelham adding, "And—Dalbiac—one moment."

De Mérac stepped out on the porch but the dry rasp followed him. "For one thing, Colonel, when I send for you—" he accentuated the verb witheringly—"it is you whom I wish to see—not your adjutant or your armorer or your hospital stewards. More important, it has come to my knowledge that you are seldom with your regiment. Now that I will not tolerate any—"

De Mérac stepped out of earshot and watched a troop of Rush's lancers galloping about an open field, their lance points glinting and their red pennons fluttering. "Real pretty sight, isn't it?" said Pride, drawing on a pair of worn gauntlets.

"Very. But the lance does not seem American to me, Colonel. Ah—I thought your definition of the role of infantry was excellent."

Pride flushed. "Pelham didn't seem to take to it, did he? Say, look here, you seem to know a lot of soldiering. What do you think of him?"

"He's a soldier, Colonel. He knows his trade. We are lucky to have him."

"Guess that's what counts—knowing how. Seems to me—of course, I'm new as paint to this—seems to me that this business is like farming. You can't make mistakes without losing your crop." He gestured awkwardly toward the far bank of the Potomac. "We've got to plant a mighty important crop over there and, far's I see, we can't afford to think of another danged thing till it's up, reaped, and in the barn. The most important crop since Moses led the tribes to the Promised Land. If it spoils, God help what we've all lived for. I get scared, looking at my boys—mostly from Terre Haute way—and thinking it's up to me, a practical farmer, to show 'em how to get that crop in. Farming's in my blood, Captain, but if I'd seen this coming I'd have gone to West Point and made myself into the best soldier my brains'd have let me. Now I got to learn a brand-new kind of farming." He heaved his ponderous shoulders. "Well, if other folks can learn, guess I can, too."

De Mérac looked gravely at him. "You will, Colonel. By the way, what is your adjutant's name?"

"Ralph Hargrove. He's a mighty smart Terre Haute lawyer, too."

"I should be most happy to meet him. You do not object if I call on him?"

"Oh Lord no! But look here. I'll send him over to see you, if that's all right with you. I'd sort of like to have him get a look at the way you do things."

"At any time, sir."

"That's mighty kind. Maybe I'll come over myself and listen. Great way to learn—just listening."

De Mérac watched him ride down the river, feeling that he had found a very sound man in the Indiana colonel. Then the door opened on Dalbiac's irritated voice. "I'll write my Senator about this."

Icy and level came the response. "Write the whole damned Congress if you wish. That is all. Good day."

Dalbiac flounced out, flushed and angry. When he saw de Mérac he grinned sheepishly. "Thinks he can tell me what to do, just because someone busted an egg on his shoulders. He'll find out."

"You return to camp, now, sir?"

"No. You're doing all right." He got into his carriage and rolled away.

In the stone house, General Dudley Pelham strode into the room that he used for both sleeping quarters and office. He tossed his wide brimmed hat, gold-corded, onto his desk and shouted, "Major Dunn! Come here!"

The square-faced Dunn stepped silently in. Pelham said curtly, "In future when you send orders summoning regimental commanders to me, kindly draft them so they will not bring with them a lot of busted Hungarian drill sergeants."

Dunn said, "I think my orders were clear, sir."

"They were not clear or else that fool Dalbiac wouldn't have had that chattering French monkey with him. We'll inspect that regiment first. I want you and every aide who comes with me to keep a damned sharp eye out. We'll find a lot that's rotten there. These damn foreigners!"

"Very good, sir. But I'm afraid we'll have to depend on that Captain de Mérac when we inspect the Rifles. He's been pretty well running the outfit in Dalbiac's absence and I hear he's doing a good job."

Pelham brought his hand down on the table in a stinging slap. "No! You'll keep him in the background. Shut him out!" He caught up his hat, flung it down again. "But—Jesus Christ, why couldn't he have been born a white man? He's a soldier and I'd have pushed him till he had a brigade of his own!"

Dudley Pelham's inspection of the Rifles, carried out under a blistering coppery sky, far exceeded in bitterness his reception of his three colonels. The regiment stood drawn up on level ground where the sun beat mercilessly. The brigadier, closely buttoned but seemingly impervious to heat and insects, stalked up and down the open ranks, followed by Dunn and a knot of aides with busy pencils and notebooks. He did not permit a single favorable observation to escape him. He stared at Corvisart's medals—the Turkish Order of Medjidie, the African medal, the Crimean, the Legion of Honor—and snapped, "In future you will refrain from wearing that trash. It is not regulation!" With equal disdain he banned the service medals and decorations of other veterans, left no doubt of his disbelief in de Mérac's figures on desertions and arrests, and finally turned to Dalbiac. "You will receive my comments in writing Colonel. That is all." He clattered off with his retinue.

Pent-up wrath burst out in the portable house that held the officers' mess. Dalbiac gulped iced champagne and shouted, "He can't talk to me the way he did this morning. Wait till I get up to Capitol Hill!"

Wilson frowned over a long julep. "What the devil will happen to us under a brigadier like that?"

De Mérac shrugged. "Happen? Why, we shall become an excellent regiment, I think. I could wish that his manner were different, but, *en somme*, I find that manner unimportant. My grandfather served without too much difficulty under our Vandamme, who was of a ferocity to make Pelham seem a mild, country *abbé*. No, we are lucky to find in our brigadier a highly competent soldier."

"*C'est vrai*," said Corvisart. "His judgments were not gentle, perhaps, but as a military man I may only find them correct." The bearded Hein nodded in reluctant aquiescence.

George set down his glass with a thud. "Maybe he is a good soldier, but he's not the only one in the army. Why do *we* have to get him? Hell, there are so many brigadiers in town that every time they sweep out the bar at Willard's a dozen of them come scuttling out of the dark corners like cockroaches. They—" he groaned—"Oh, Lord, here's that Major Dunn coming back with more woe. Guess he wants you, John."

De Mérac stepped out onto the porch. "This is a pleasure, Major Dunn. A glass of champagne? Some whiskey?"

Dunn shook his head. "No, thanks. Actually I'm not supposed to be here. I just gave the old man the slip and came back. Look here, de Mérac, it's bad luck for your outfit to be under *him*."

"Bad luck to be under a competent brigadier?"

Dunn looked at him curiously. "Glad you can take it that way. But there's more than just his manner. I ought to keep my mouth shut but I can't. You seem to know a lot about this country. Ever hear of the Know-Nothing Party?"

"Ah—I have heard—yes. They are anti-Catholic. Some of them smashed a stone that the Pope had sent to be built into the Washington Monument."

"That's the crowd. But they're antiforeign, too. They

wanted to kill all immigration from Europe. Pelham left the army after the Mexican War to work with them, but even they found him too radical. The party's dead now, of course—but Pelham isn't."

"I appreciate your confidence," said de Mérac.

Dunn hunched his shoulders. "Oh, that's all right. You've got the makings of a good outfit here, a damn good one. We can't afford to waste it. But *you'll* get no credit for what it does well and you'll get jumped on for every last mistake, no matter who makes it."

"No doubt. Does the general object to my unofficial command under Dalbiac?"

"Hates it like hell. But he won't say anything so long as he doesn't have to recognize it officially. Damn it, man, he knows perfectly well what would happen if Dalbiac had to run it alone."

Crockery clattered inside the mess. Negro waiters brought in platters of cold meat and salads. De Mérac suggested, "Better stay and lunch with us, Major."

Dunn's eyes roved wistfully through the window. "I'd like to, but the old man'll be yelling for me." The wistful look deepened. He reached through the window and caught up a stuffed egg in a crisp nest of lettuce. "Thanks for the invitation. I'll give you any hints I can. Good luck to you and the Rifles." He strode off, the egg bulging out his shaven cheek.

De Mérac came thoughtfully into the mess. The rush of preparation for the review had shown him that he could not act as adjutant and colonel at the same time. He surveyed the blue shoulders about the table. Then he saw the dark, heavy, Jewish features of Moses Greenbaum, lieutenant to the huge-shouldered Bolton. There was his man and the matter must be arranged at once, much as he hated to take Greenbaum away from his company, where he had shown real ability in handling men.

Late that day, when Greenbaum had been installed with Rapp in the orderly room, a heavy mail was delivered. The letters had stamps from Baden and Schleswig-Holstein, from France and Spain and Italy and the British Isles. There was a large stack addressed to

George Force in assorted young and highly feminine hands. There were also several for himself.

The Chemical Bank of New York advised that funds had been deposited to his credit by Barclay's of London. The next letter set him smoothing his mustache, his eyes bright with pleasure. Mrs. Duane wrote that her husband was going to devote his entire time to the newly formed Sanitary Commission, which was to look after the welfare of the armies of the Union. In the fall the family would move to Washington and hoped that he would know himself welcome at their new home. "Bravo!" he muttered. "That I find so charming that I make a *pied de nez* to Pelham."

From Loudéac his uncle wrote the usual Breton gossip that sent his mind scurrying back to the long moors dotted with Druid dolmens and menhirs, to narrow valleys where slate ribs jutted like the bones of half-buried monsters. "All Loudéac is charmed that you find yourself soldier at last. Ah, Jean, my youth returns as I think of you riding the prairies about New York and we all watch for your letters. This day I had sent to you the saber of honor which the Emperor himself presented to your Uncle Égide after Austerlitz. It is right that you, as the only member of the family now in the field, should have it."

De Mérac looked up in distaste as Rohde, Bolton's other lieutenant, entered the office quietly. Rohde was squat with a broad face that looked as if it had been pushed together from brow to chin. He had an irritating habit of dropping his voice to an intense, hissing whisper, furtive and conspiratorial. His whispers usually dealt with the shortcomings of other officers. On duty, and in the presence of superiors, he was more intense than ever, ostentatiously alert and quick to whip out a notebook with a bright, "Ready, sir." Now, meeting de Mérac's reluctant eye, he edged nearer. "I heard our Dr. Wayne has got a fresh case of whiskey," he hissed. "That's our third in ten days. Oh, it's all right. I didn't mean that." He bent lower over the table. "Of course, you knew what you were doing, bringing Greenbaum in here. But he's a Jew. I wouldn't trust him too far."

91

De Mérac got up quickly. "If I want comments from you on Greenbaum or any other officer, I shall request them in writing."

Rohde bubbled, "Glad to, sir. Glad to. Any time."

When Rohde had gone de Mérac lit a cigarette and thought over the day's happenings. The Rifles would soon be launched into the true stream of the Army of the Potomac. Washington would fill up after its summer of quiet and there would be houses where he could call. The Duanes', for instance. Repeated calls there and at other homes would not be taken as declarations of intentions as they surely would have been in Europe.

The slow-turning wheels of the Army of the Potomac caught up the Rifles, and moved them across Long Bridge. By dusk they had pitched their camp to the west of Fort Corcoran where the black snouts of heavy guns shone dully in the wet. Shielded by a rubber poncho, de Mérac walked through the new streets. Brady's wagons were unloading firewood at the cook tents. At the head of cach company line hung carpetbags under rude shelters with signs: *"Postes militaires," "Feld Post,"* or "Mail." The rain-darkened canvas hummed with voices contented, quarrelsome, excited, as the men sank down into their new quarters. In Hein's street a German nursed a stubborn fire, crooning:

Ich weiss nicht, was soll es bedeuten,
Das ich so traurig bin —

At the far end of the camp, mules brayed and lashed each other's ribs with hollow-sounding kicks. Bugles blew mess call and the acrid tang of wood smoke drifted through the rain. The move had been made expertly, as Dunn had assured de Mérac. The major's praise pleased him, yet the presence of the regiment on the other bank of the Potomac filled him with faint apprehension. It was as though he and the Rifles now stood on the last rung of their long ladder. The first rung had been Chambers Street, then the camp by Tennallytown. From this, the very last, there was only one direction in which they could go—south. He felt that his men were by no means ready for combat. He shivered when he thought of their armament. "*Enfin,* one could stock a museum with our muskets," he thought. "From Charleville, from arsenals in Baden, in Spain, in Italy. No doubt some of them date back to the Aztecs."

He walked slowly back to the portable house set up for the mess, where the sky-blue and yellow legs clustered about the bar. George, Wilson, and Corvisart were arguing amicably at one end. Quartermaster Brady shouted jovially to Hein across a glass of deeply amber rye. De Mérac ordered a vermouth-cassis. Wilson waved to him and held up a sodden *Richmond Examiner.* "Look here, didn't you tell me you'd met Phil Kearny?"

De Mérac nodded eagerly. "What of him?"

Wilson waved the paper. "This Reb rag says he's been given a brigade!"

De Mérac said incredulously. "No! Not Kearny! He has never joined the South."

"Devil a bit. He's been given command of a full New Jersey brigade. The Reb press calls him a slimy traitor because he's been entertained in the South and hence—"

De Mérac slapped the bar. "You have political influence, Craig. Use it now. We must serve under him!"

Wilson rubbed his square, clean-shaven chin. "Why, I offered to see what I could do about Pelham but you said no."

"Pelham is a fine soldier. In his place we might be assigned an amiable dummy. But Kearny—ah, *ça!* That is different."

Wilson shook his head. "Too late. New York turned him down, you know. Then someone in Jersey remembered Kearny owned a lot of property there and grabbed him for that state. No—we, as a New York outfit, couldn't shift like that."

De Mérac turned away and stared out into the rain. He remembered the tall, erect figure, the bony face with its graying mustache and imperial, the eyes that seemed to smolder. "*Quand même,*" he thought, "even with Pelham we must go on to the end—*jusqu'au bout.*"

Maneuvers became more and more complicated, involving pontoons thrown over swift streams by orange-piped engineers, the defense of batteries loaned to the small brigade for the purpose, simulated attacks where one regiment operated against the remaining two. De Mérac felt that the regiment was growing more solid in his grasp, although he could not always congratulate himself. Once he missed a rendezvous by taking the wrong road. Again, he brought his lines triumphantly over a crest, expecting to find himself abreast of the plodding Pride. To his horror he saw that by misjudging important contours his men sloped away at right angles to the position he was supposed to hold. He could only bite his lip in angry silence at Pelham's bitter comment, "You see, Major Dunn, that is the sort of thing we've got to expect from these mercenary troops. They've been posted so they can throw down their arms or go over to the enemy, depending on the situation." Then, raising his voice, "You will, as usual, receive my written comments on the day's work. That is all, gentlemen!"

Barring Pelham, de Mérac was well enough content in his new life. He found that he was developing a real, a very deep affection for George Force and for Craig Wilson, not merely as competent officers but true friends such as he had scarcely known before, men on whom he could rely, in whom he could confide, who seemed to rely on him and confide in him. It was as though the elder Wilson had somehow taken the place of his long-dead father, while George Force assumed that of the brother he had never had. Then, too, riding through the camps he sometimes came upon friends whom he had met in his previous stay—men from Wisconsin and Minnesota, from the New England states and New York and Ohio and Pennsylvania. Sometimes they were privates, like a group of young men from feudal Hudson River estates who had enlisted in a body in a cavalry troop and whose stable sergeant owned a dozen saddle horses in the shadow of the Helderbergs. Or they might be young officers like Charles Russell Lowell of Harvard and Boston who had shown such a flair for war that the Regular Army had welcomed him and was pushing him up, grade by grade, through the 6th United States Cavalry. New acquaintances hailed him from Ohio camps, from Delaware, New Hampshire, and Maryland camps.

Their reception of him, whether in their own establishments or in the mess of the Rifles, set de Mérac pondering. Would they have received him as cordially had he entered one of their own, native-born units? Had other Europeans fallen afoul of a Pelham? He called on the flamboyant German, Blenker, now in command of a full brigade. He had no trouble in gathering that all was well with Ludwig Blenker. From that camp he passed on to Colonel Weber, late of the Baden army, to von Gilsa, for whom '48 had ended a promising career in the Prussian forces.

He crossed the river and found the old LaFayette Guards, now the 55th New York, commanded by a striking-looking fellow Breton, Baron Régis de Trobriand. Then there was young Frederick Cavada, a hot-eyed Cuban on General Graham's staff, and Colonel Mahler, a Badener, at the head of the 75th Pennsylvania. He found the Pole, Wladimir Krzyanowski, and the Spaniard, Eduardo Ferrero, a French gunner named de Gresse and a Prussian, Hubert Dilger, who was on his way to take over an Ohio battery. On Long Bridge he ran into the young ex-officer of Chasseurs, Alfred Duffié, whom he had tried to secure for the Rifles and who now led a glittering bodyguard which followed General McDowell.

Most of these talks calmed his mind. In the first place, not one found himself hampered by a Pelham. In fact von Gilsa confessed that he felt the reliance and trust placed on him, due to his European training, to be almost embarrassing, while de Gresse complained laughingly that his experience was appealed to on all matters from the weather to the behavior of the stock market. Pelham, de Mérac decided, was a sort of military sport and by no means representative of the native stock. He was further satisfied by another point. He had talked with Germans from every state and principality, with Frenchmen, Poles, Cubans, Italians, Spaniards. Among them were a few mountebanks but the bulk seemed to him to wear the Union colors through sheer conviction.

Many of the '48ers told him that they felt they were carrying on the fight that had failed in Europe. Others, like Duffié, de Trobriand, and the English Sir Percy Wyndham, who commanded New Jersey cavalry, had nothing material to gain and possibly a great deal to lose, including their lives. That fact, he thought, would make the position of every foreign-born soldier much simpler. Pelham was not a problem for the army, but for himself alone. De Mérac could throw himself back into his work with a certain amount of relief.

October clothed the valley of the Potomac in shining gold, touched here and there with a red that set New Englanders and New Yorkers pining for the blazing glories of the Berkshires and the Catskills. Along both banks, in glowing groves and in yellowing fields, the Union Army strained gently at its bonds as a moored ship, waiting for flood tide, tugs at its hawsers. Great piles of supplies grew and mounted. Engines hooted endlessly as they trundled blue-laden trains into Washington. By the Lee house in Arlington, observation balloons rose lazily, swaying the cables that bound them to the earth.

Through the rumble and clatter of the force that McClellan was carefully and skillfully building, de Mérac rode in clear fall sunlight, Torpille's hoofs clock-clocking on the timbers of Long Bridge. He edged past mule teams, past jolting batteries of bronze Napoleons, blunt-muzzled Parrotts and Dahlgrens. High in the air the balloons were golden globes in the sun, shimmering against a milk-blue sky. What could the watchers up in the *nacelles* see, he wondered. No doubt they looked down at the Confederate main base near Centerville, probably as astir as the Union area.

He tugged at his mustache as he cantered on, running over figures in his mind. His never-ending quest for Springfields had been in vain but there was another matter that he had solved most pleasantly. Long ago he had learned that rations were issued to the individual soldier on a cash basis. Now, the flour issued to each man, and pooled for baking by the company cooks, produced far more bread than eighty men could eat. His mind had gone beyond that point. Why not draw, say six hundred single rations, ample to feed the eight hundred-odd men of the regiment when pooled, and claim the difference in cash? The cool-voiced major at the War Department not only said that he might, but showed him figures hard to believe, but official and tested. The cash difference between the flour *authorized* and the flour actually *issued* would amount to over four hundred dollars a month, which would be paid to the regimental fund and could be used in many ways to benefit the men. The baseball equipment that Force and Bolton wanted, for instance, or musical instruments, or socks of better quality than those supplied by the Department. Among the French and German companies he could find a wealth of skilled bakers. The ovens could be built by the Yankee mechanics. All in all, he was pleased with his trip.

He wound Torpille along the flanks of a regiment all in green, the men carrying deadly looking rifles, some mounted with telescopic sights, and wearing a wreathed "USSS" on their green kepis. De Mérac knew the unit—Hiram Berdan's 1st United States Sharpshooters, a rigidly picked lot from no one state but containing New York Swiss, Vermont hunters, and Minnesota woodsmen. That, he thought, was the way regiments should be recruited, breaking down state lines and state jealousies.

Then he was among the camps themselves, each stamped with the personality of its commander, camps where sentries slouched and stared, where sentries saluted smartly. At his own picket line he turned Torpille over to DuChesne and the swarm of Negroes who had attached themselves to the old Chasseur, and walked to his quarters rubbing his hands at the thought of the regimental fund. Rapp, his red beard bristling with mystery, intercepted him. "In your tent, *mon capitaine*, there waits a lady."

"A lady? In my tent? Who placed her there?"

"She herself effected the placing."

"*Diable!* No doubt she makes an error."

"No doubt, *mon capitaine*. But not on this occasion."

De Mérac shrugged and walked on to his canvas office, where a fly had been drawn across the front. As he was about to pull it aside, a faint whiff of scent, disturbingly familiar, reached him, a scent that suggested lilac and yet which was somehow lusher, headier. His jaw tightened and hard glints showed in his eyes. Then he shook himself and stepped into the tent. His face showed only calm politeness as he bowed to Lisa von Horstmar, who smiled lazily at him from a camp chair.

Her lashes drooped and her full eyes crinkled with amusement. "You are about to say that you are charmed to see me, Jean?" she said in her German-accented French.

He kissed her hand with elaborate courtesy. "Dear Lisa, you charm any eyes that fall upon you. Even my brave Rapp is no doubt sighing in his tent." He stepped back and surveyed her coolly. Four years had only ripened, made showier, Lisa's sensuous good looks. Her skin was flawless, her hair still softly gold, and there was no coarsening of her superb figure. She moved her shoulders and her firm breasts stirred under the blue silk of her dress. "Yes, charming, always. Louvel shall bring wine and cakes." He rang a bell on his neat desk.

She watched him curiously. "You seem strange, Jean. You do not even trouble to ask how I find myself in Washington."

"My brother officers say that this is a free country." De Mérac lit a cigarette. "And, no doubt it has escaped your notice, but I have hardly had time to ask even that most obvious question."

"And you didn't kiss me when you saw me sitting here."

He waved airily. "The effects of military discipline, dear Baroness. The tent, it is now open to the world. What would my men think, they who have no such delightful presence in their quarters, should they see me embracing one who must seem to them a Rhine goddess?"

Her smiled deepened. "But the tent may be easily closed, Jean."

He sat by his desk, idly twirling his cigarette between his long fingers. "An act of unfathomable ease, as you say," he answered, but made no move toward the fly.

The shadowy Louvel slipped in, set wine and cakes on a small table, effaced himself. Lisa tapped her foot on the board floor of the tent. "I took great pains to find you here. I have not forgotten that you fled to this absurd country, that first time, to avoid me."

De Mérac's eyes widened. "Fled? To avoid you? My dear Lisa, it is true that I came here, but, in coming, I could scarcely ask you to share my cabin, delirious as the prospect might be."

She leaned forward. "Then you have not forgotten—"

"But surely, I have forgotten much, in the pleasure of seeing you. My manners, for example. I have not inquired about your husband, the Baron."

Her full lips curled. "He enjoys his customary ill-health and the pursuit of unripe peasant girls." She made a quick gesture. "I push him away. It is about us that I wish to talk."

"And what else? Here we neglect our glasses which Louvel filled so carefully. *A tes beaux yeux*, Lisa."

She sipped mechanically. De Mérac knew that he was more and more aware each instant of her physical presence that set old memories racing hotly through his mind. He forced himself to smile blandly as, when she set down her glass, the smooth hollow between her breasts showed deep. She turned her eyes full on him, and her gaze, languorous and intimate, set his mind spinning faster. He lit another cigarette. "And still, dear Lisa, you do not tell me how you come to be here."

She said in a low voice, "Does it matter, since I am here?"

"But to me, of course it matters. It can only be of concern when one's friends appear out of the sky like this." He shook his head. "How can you think me not interested?"

She frowned. "It took you long enough to ask. Anyhow, I came through a whim."

He laughed. "*Épatant!* As I did. May I hope the country pleases you as it does me. But go on."

She bit her lip. "There was a time when you would not have talked like this to me. But no matter—for the present. You remember my cousin Dagmar? Her husband has been transferred from Dresden to Washington where he serves the Prussian minister, von Gerolt. I decided to come with them." Her eyes slid toward him. "You see—I had heard in Baden-Baden that you were here."

He smiled and bowed. "And from the steamer you come straight to me? Ah, Lisa, I am flattered."

"*Quatsch!* I do not like to be trifled with like this! No! I have stayed some weeks with Dagmar. Today, I drive across with the von Kollnitzes, who call on von Steinwehr, a colonel of your ridiculous army." Her eyes were suddenly full of a lazy light. "But I think I do not stay with Dagmar long. I think I shall rent a house. I think I shall make a long visit here. I shall find it amusing."

"No doubt, dear Lisa."

"And it is you who will show me Washington."

His forehead wrinkled with regret. "Ah—had you come sooner! Then we were closer to the city. But now—" he spread out his hands—"the Potomac is a very wide river."

"Jean, I am sure that, when I have my house, you will find the Potomac a mere brook. I shall expect to see you often—as I saw you in old times."

"It is I who am miserable, Lisa. My duties! They are unimaginable."

She sat back in her chair, a smile deepening about the corners of her mouth. "They, like the river, will shrink, my poor Jean. You will come to me."

Voices sounded outside the tent. De Mérac rose and strolled to the entrance. Then he turned to Lisa, assuming a doleful expression. "*Ma chère*, I am desolated. In the hot sun there waits a carriage with the Prussian arms on the panel, and even now a groom asks the way to this tent of Monsieur Ray Abbot, sergeant of the guard." He sighed. "You are far too kindhearted to keep Herr and Frau von Kollnitz sitting like onions in a *marmite*."

A crease showed between her eyes, faded. She rose slowly. "All happened today as I had foreseen. So will our future meetings." Her eyes snapped. "You thought to dismiss me, when you first came to America." Her

100

knuckles rapped on the table. "I tell you, it is I who dismiss—when I am ready. I tell you too, *mon ami*, that when I call to you, as I shall call, you will come."

He bowed and offered her his arm. "Not even Ulysses's men with wax-filled ears could resist such a call. May I escort you to the carriage?"

She stamped her foot. Then she threw back her head, took his arm, and stepped out onto the grass, throwing dazzling smiles at de Mérac and at all men with eyeshot.

Corvisart stepped up quickly and opened the door of the carriage. Shea, flushed to the tip of his long nose, muttered to himself as he took off his kepi. From the doorway of the orderly tent, Rapp stared in rapturous hypnosis. Out of company streets men walked with elaborate unconcern and drifted toward the carriage. Lisa dropped her parasol and the hissing Rohde jostled Quartermaster Brady to snatch it up. Lisa slid gracefully into her seat, smiled regally to the crowding men, and bowled off with a fluttering wave of her hand.

De Mérac walked slowly back to his tent and stood by the desk. "*Vingt dieux!* She is still the same. But am I?" He knew that he never wanted to see Lisa von Horstmar again. Yet every inflection of her rich voice, every movement of hand or body, recalled pictures out of the past, suggested intimacies the more vivid for being unspoken. And she would be in Washington, just across the river. He flung away a cigarette butt. "*Bordel de dieu!* Let her be in Washington or Stockholm or Trebizond! I am stronger than she."

There was a quick, light step outside and Wilson swung jauntily in, a cigar between his fingers. "Well, well! Cakes and wine, eh? Sorry I wasn't here to meet your guests."

De Mérac shrugged. "There were no guests."

Wilson tossed his kepi onto the table. "I'm disappointed in you. I thought that woman came out of here. Did you see her in the carriage? Whew! The boys were jammed around her six deep as it went out of camp."

"She was here, Craig. She was not a guest. She is not even a woman. She's a devil. In the fullest sense of the word, she has coldly ruined at least three men whom I know. She seduced her sister's husband not long after the marriage. The results were not pretty."

"Trying to bother you, is she?"

"She has tried. She will not succeed."

Wilson chuckled. "I'll bet on you. But I can see how she could play the devil with a man."

"This man will be quite too busy," said de Mérac dryly, seating himself at his desk. He looked out of the window, mind already whirling through the details of the regimental ovens. The step was one that he ought to take at once. Nonetheless, he felt that each rider from Pelham's headquarters might bring the order which would sweep the Rifles out of their permanent camp and hurl them among the brush-choked valleys and rolling hills to the south. Winter, with its snows and rains, would soon turn the whole of Virginia into a roadless, trackless morass where even small bodies of men would bog down hopelessly. Another six weeks at the most. Ah, McClellan knew the value of time. See how supplies piled up. Yes, orders might come any day. The Rifles must settle into their camp as though for a decade and yet be ready to move at the briefest notice.

George's tent, impersonal as a packing box at first, had taken on something of himself. A pair of worn boxing gloves hung over a shelf that held a row of battered books: N. P. Willis's *The Tent Pitch'd*, a copy of *Pickwick*, Yonge's *Heir of Redclyffe*, *The Petroleum V. Nasby Letters*, and Gautier's *Le Capitaine Fracasse*. Photographs of his family stood on an up-ended hardtack box, crowded by his neatly placed shaving gear and a stack of tied-up letters. On the floor, Mr. McArdle luxuriated on a rag rug by the narrow cot.

George dropped into a chair with his chin on his chest and an open letter in his hand. He scowled at the feminine handwriting on the sheets, then, with an obvious effort, stuffed them into his pocket and forced his mind to company matters. There was much that did not satisfy him. The old Regular, Bates, seemed unable to adjust from the little peacetime army to the sprawling volunteer mass that surrounded him. One or two appointments of noncoms were not working out well. To crown his troubles, a new second lieutenant had been assigned to him a few days before, a man who had done his three months' service with the 1st New York and had seen action at Big Bethel. Mason Randol was capable enough but seemed to think of himself as end man in a perpetual minstrel show. He bubbled from reveille to taps, singing scraps of song, cutting buck-and-wing steps, twisting his words this way and that, punning horribly, and greeting his own efforts with a high, quacking laugh. He came into the mess rubbing his hands and shouting, "Good evening, gentlemen. You too, Mr. Force!"

Now, into George's discontent, Randol came stamping and whistling, his prominent eyes and rubbery, thick-lipped mouth ready to greet his own wit. "What's new, George? No, I don't mean New York!" He slapped his hands and quacked gleefully. "What's orders?"

"Drill, if it doesn't rain."

Randol stuck his head out of the tent. "Rain? Ask me! 'Mackerel sky, not long wet, not long dry.' One squint and you get a prediction and a poem. Pelham going to pell 'em—I mean pile 'em out?"

George said, "No. I'm going to. Full-pack, including you. Route march. Tell Bates to get ready for it."

Randol whooped and clogged a few steps. "Yow! That Bates the Dutch, ain't it? You going?"

George caught up a red-bound book. "Got to see de Mérac. Take them out the Great Falls road and I'll catch up if I'm late." He hooked a leash to Mr. McArdle's collar. "Come on, pup."

Randol howled. "Look at that! Taking hindquarters to headquarters."

George ducked out of the tent, Randol's laugh tearing at his ears. He set his teeth. "I'll go crazy with that man around. Hell! Wonder if John'll listen to me."

Under the soft gray of the sky the camp stirred lazily in its brief leisure. In F Company a man was scouring a kettle and singing in a wailing minor:

> *Mon mari, il est parti*
> *A la pêche d'Islande.*

Il m'a laissé sans le sou—

When George entered de Mérac's quarters the latter looked up with pleasure. "*Ah—te voilà!* You're bringing back Eugène Sue? Ah, *Les Mystères de Paris!*"

George set the book on the table. "It's fine, I guess. Oh, sure, I liked it a lot." He planted his hands on the table and burst out, "Damn it, John, what's the chance of getting a pass?"

De Mérac's face went grave. "Ordinarily, excellent, since you ask for so few—and a day in the city would do you good. But I don't dare. Many officers are absent with those passes signed by the Secretary of War that even Pelham can't revoke. The rest suffer from—what do you call them—the play-offs, the shirkers."

George sat down heavily, heedless of Mr. McArdle, who laid his head across one ankle. "I didn't mean Washington—New York."

De Mérac crushed a cigarette in an ash tray, sighing, "I know it's lonely for you here, George. Of course, you want to see your family."

He shook his head. "No. Dora Chase," he muttered.

De Mérac stared. "*Mais enfin*, you have spoken more often of the Barclay girl or Miss Ledyard—"

George shoved his hands into his pockets. It seemed to him that Dora had had three stages of existence for him—the gangling and annoying friend of his sister; the pretty girl who had startled him in his mother's drawing room; then the delightful partner, no longer a stranger, with whom he had waltzed so often the night of Bull Run and who now wrote him friendly, amusing letters. He said, "Known her all my life but I guess I never really looked at her until last spring. I saw her a few times after that and then at the ball. It's—it's been like a snowball rolling downhill."

De Mérac said gently, "I am sorry, George. Truly, I did not know. But passes may be easier later, perhaps. She will still be in New York."

George jumped up. "That's it! Will she? Damn it, May Blackstock writes that Dora's as good as engaged to that fat Verplanck. I got the letter today. He's a quartermaster major in New York and doesn't know a keg of beef from a trunnion." He walked up and down, pulling at his chin. "Just about engaged! If I could only talk to her—just for a minute. Writing's no good. I won't quit without a fight. I'd tell her—"

De Mérac rose and laid a hand on his shoulder. "George, if I could find the least bit of regimental business that could reasonably take you to New York, you should go tonight. But there is none."

He turned quickly. "It wouldn't take long—one day, barring travel time."

De Mérac looked thoughtfully at him. "Yes, George," he said slowly. "It would take little time, I agree. But, *mon ami*, do you recall how little time it required for the news of Bull Run to reach the ballroom of the Fifth Avenue? Do you recall it took you and me more than a little time to rejoin the Rifles on hearing the news? *Ah, ça.* Such a thing could happen again."

George snatched off his kepi, jammed it onto his head again. "But look, John—oh, damn it, you're right."

"I am. It does not matter a sou to the Union Army who is engaged and who is not. You are part of that army. Believe me, I am sorry."

George managed a smile. "I know you are, John. Thanks. I'll get right back to work." He clucked to Mr. McArdle.

Two miles beyond the camp, sweating under his heavy pack and haversack, he caught sight of his company. The men marched at ease, muskets under their arms, hanging by slings, held like yokes across the backs of their necks. A haze of pipe smoke floated thin and blue above them. He quickened his pace, his steps falling into cadence with the song that poured out.

The Union forever,
Hurrah, boys, hurrah!
Down with the traitor and up with the stars!
So we'll rally round the flag, boys,
We'll rally once again,
Shouting the battle-cry of freedom.

The Union. It was all that mattered. Until it was secure, it was the be-all and end-all. George joined in the song as Mr. McArdle, his leash slipped, raced in vast circles through the fields.

VI

In Full Swing

NOVEMBER brought on days of sullen beating rain. The men of the Rifles were penned in dank, leaky tents where the floors were ankle deep in mud. Then army wagons dumped loads of lumber through all the camps and almost overnight, on both banks of the river, wood huts sprang up, tight, well-built huts with the old tents serving for roofs and cat-and-clay chimneys of tar-barrel chimneys thrusting up to the streaming skies. De Mérac tapped the regimental fund for extra lumber that put solid floors and heavy doors into the Rifles' huts. Péguy's company found a bank of white clay and turned their street into a replica of an Arab village. When Pelham, on a tour of inspection, ordered the white-domed buildings to be ripped down, the whole company gave vent to its feelings by getting roaring drunk, a demonstration which de Mérac did nothing to stop.

The tight-jawed brigadier, present or absent, never let himself be forgotten by the Rifles. Brady's wagons at the supply dumps had to wait to draw rations until both Pride's quartermaster and Clay's had been satisfied, with the result that the Rifles were given the leavings of all issues. This slight was explained, reluctantly, by Major Dunn as being due to seniority. He could only shrug helplessly when de Mérac pointed out to him that other brigades drew in rotation or on a first-come, first-served basis.

Pelham's inspections of the Rifles were more frequent and more searching than those to which the other regiments submitted. Owing largely, as de Mérac pointed out to Wilson, to the priceless leavening of seasoned officers and noncoms, the brigadier could rarely criticize. Sometimes he even seemed on the point of grudging praise, but on each occasion some alien note jarred him back into his cold disapproval. He might see one Zouave turning like a dancer to wind himself into his wide red sash, the other end being held by a comrade or tied to a tree. Or barrels of issue wine for the French companies, a lager wagon with beer for Hein's Germans, drew his anger. Twirling brass of the French bugle drill, a foreign decoration, a corporal shouting "*Au jus*" at morning mess, a sentry challenging, "*Wer da?*"—all served to choke back the smallest nod of praise.

On a rain-lashed afternoon, de Mérac stood in deep mud while Pelham, seemingly impervious to wind and water, spoke with biting terseness of the reports forwarded to brigade headquarters. With form and content he could not quarrel, but Rapp's crossed sevens and flowing nines were seized upon for stinging rebuke. De Mérac, when finally dismissed, tramped back to his quarters weary and discouraged. He sat by the stove in deep thought. Horses plashed on through the mud outside. He turned his head idly. A rider had just dismounted and de Mérac saw, as a horse turned slowly, tail to the storm, a saddlecloth with a single star. De Mérac's head jerked angrily. "*Bordel de dieu!* Again a brigadier?"

The door snapped open and a tall figure showed vaguely against the lowering gray of the outer world. De Mérac got to his feet quickly. In the dim light he could only make out a rakish red kepi, rain-smeared, and a long, frogged cloak trimmed with astrakhan that swirled out a flare of red lining as its wearer turned to close the door. A strong quick voice spoke as the man faced about. "It took me some time to trace my friend of the Fifth Avenue Hotel. My compliments on your camp. I took the liberty of riding through it."

Louvel crept into the room with a lamp and de Mérac's heart gave a sudden leap as he recognized his caller. "You are welcome, General Kearny. May I offer whiskey, sir? Brandy? Some coffee?"

Kearny stretched out a hard hand and gripped de Mérac's. "No ceremony, Captain. This call is unofficial. A drink? Ah—French coffee, strong French coffee with a good lacing of cognac. Let's pull up chairs by this stove. Damnable weather." Louvel took de Mérac's order and slipped out, returned with two smoking cups. Kearny raised his. "*Santé.*"

"*A la vôtre*," said de Mérac. Now that the lamplight was full on the general's face, de Mérac was amazed to see how it had changed. The lined forehead, the deep scores that ran from each corner of the nose, were still there. But the eyes no longer smoldered. They were young, alive, and burning with a clear, healthy light, gay and exultant. The mouth under the trim mustache was firm and eager.

Kearny sipped. "Ah—like being in France again. Yes, your camp is excellent. Understand that you've pretty well built up this regiment. Good! Your guards are alert even when it's raining blue beans like this." He set down his cup and turned his keen eyes on de Mérac. "Hear you don't exactly find favor in Pelham's eyes? That so? In confidence of course."

De Mérac held out a box of French cigarettes to Kearny, who took one appreciatively. He answered slowly. "It is my impression that General Pelham feels that he could work more effectively with native-born troops."

Kearny gave a quick smile as he lit his cigarette. "I see. Pity the regiment's from New York." He leaned forward and the light threw his strong features into relief. "I've got the 1st, 2nd, 3rd, and 4th New Jersey and Hexamer's 1st New Jersey Battery. We're in front of Arlington. My headquarters are at the Episcopal Seminary, just as close to the Rebs as I can get." His mouth hardened. "McClellan wanted to pull me back; says I'll annoy the Rebs. I told him that was what I was there for—and I'm still there. I wish to God I could steal your whole regiment from Pelham and add it to my brigade, but that's not possible."

"Between states—I understand," said de Mérac.

Kearny set his cup down with a clatter and sprang to his feet. "You're a captain. You're apt to stay a captain for a long time with the Rifles." He suddenly pointed a long finger at de Mérac. "I can get you—as an individual—out of here in twenty-four hours. I'll guarantee you the rank of major—on my own staff. You'll have the freest hand I can give you. You'll get credit for what you do. You'll answer to me—right up to the hilt—for any failures."

De Mérac felt as though a tight cord about his chest had been cut, a tight cord that galled and chafed with every tug that Pelham cared to give. He rose unsteadily. "On your staff, sir?"

Kearny jerked his sword belt straight. "Or in one of my regiments. Suit yourself. I can clear the tracks for you in twenty-four hours. I don't want your answer now. It'll be a pull to leave the men you've trained and I don't want you if one foot's back here with your Rifles. Write me in two days—yes or no. And whatever your answer is, remember this—we're all going hell-for-leather into a fight we've *got* to win. We're going in and all hell's flying artillery can't stop us."

De Mérac walked to the door with him. Kearny nodded toward Rapp, who stood rigid in the rain outside. "I stopped to speak to your sergeant major. He reminded me of an old *maréchal des logis* in the Chasseurs d'Afrique. A rare type. But how does he get on, adapting himself to this army?"

De Mérac pulled at his mustache. "He works magnificently. But at times he gives me concern, since he lives mentally in African days. For example, he always refers, even in writing, to the Rebel forces as 'the Arabs.' The old argot still clings to him. A recruit is a *bleu*, a doctor a *toubib*, equipment and quarters must be made *klim-bim*, a teamster a *tringlo*."

"Yes," said Kearny. "The point seems small but it could be mighty important."

The stable sergeant of a near-by cavalry unit strode past through the rain and waved to Rapp. "Hi, Mel. What's stirring in your shebang?"

Rapp answered calmly, "'Allo. Oats. Presently one routs out the beats and the jonahs who wish to skedaddle from their work."

"That's the stuff, Mel. Give 'em hell," said Oats.

Kearny chuckled. "Don't worry about old Rapp. He's getting on all right." He swung himself into the saddle and swept off in a flutter of red and blue.

Rapp looked after the galloping rider, awe in his hard blue eyes. "Ah, *mon capitaine,* there is one whom the desert tribes would call 'the old chieftain'—*le vieux kébir.*"

"I believe you, Sergeant Major. *Kébir* he is." He went back into the orderly room to reason out Kearny's offer. He felt that he could not slip from the Rifles simply to get out of Pelham's grasp. Then what? Would he be more useful on Kearny's staff or in one of his regiments? And what about the Rifles? Wilson was learning very fast and most of the company commanders were good. Corvisart could turn the Zouaves over to young Bordagaray and move up as Wilson's second-in-command. The Jew, Greenbaum, had surpassed all expectations as regimental adjutant and could be put up to a captaincy if he himself left. And—most important—throughout the regiment there was a solid core of experienced officers and noncoms. Surely, so far as the Rifles were concerned, he could join Kearny with a clear conscience. He wished, though, that Craig Wilson were in camp. The ex-lawyer's sound advice and unwavering friendship would be valuable. But the Major had gone to Washington, suffering from a slight sore throat, to help Claire and Thomas settle the house that had been found close to LaFayette Park.

Sometime close to midnight, de Mérac was awakened by Louvel, who held out an envelope and lighted candle. De Mérac blinked sleepily. Through a blur he made out feminine handwriting. He thought, "*Val* Can this be a joke of the von Horstmar?" His eyes cleared. The letter was from Claire Wilson. Craig had been seized with a quinsy, a rather severe case and one that would keep him confined for at least a week.

He sat up in bed. "*Diable!* A quinsy can be a bad affair. I shall ride over as soon—" His mind pulled him up short. Such an emergency might occur again. Lacking Wilson and himself, command would devolve on Corvisart—for Dalbiac could be forgotten—and the Zouave had studiously kept clear of regimental matters. Real action would come one day. How would the ten blue and yellow companies face it with no true commander? Whatever aspect he considered, every line of thought bent straight back to himself. He said dully to Louvel, "Send me the orderly on duty." Then he huddled into his yellow-lined cape and sat at his field desk. He set his chin. "How shall I express my regrets to General Kearny?"

The following noon a kepied aide delivered a note to de Mérac. It consisted of one line only: "I honor your decision as deeply as I regret it. Faithfully yours, P. KEARNY."

Often in the succeeding weeks, men of the Rifles looked up from the march, from camp duties, to see a hawk-faced, one-armed general watching them with a sort of fierce intensity, an envious longing. They came to know his name, but rarely used it. Instead, recognizing him as he sat his horse by a muddy road, they swung their kepis and hailed him as Rapp had hailed him. "*Voilà—c'est le vieux Kébir!*" Once Kearny joined de Mérac. "If you knew how much I wanted those men! Someday I'm going to send an aide over at night and have him bend those N.Y.'s on your collars into N.J.'s. Then I'll have the lot of you so fast that the regimental teeth will rattle."

"Have your aide see young Cordier in C Company," de Mérac replied. "He is most deft with metals."

Rains pelted harder and heavier and Virginia roads swam in a deep scum of mud. It was increasingly obvious that there could be no major moves until spring. De

Mérac's great problem was to fight the monotony of inaction. He started schools of instruction in all companies, bought sets of boxing gloves and had minstrel shows organized. But for all his efforts there were desertions, fights, and a marked increase in drunkenness, especially among the Irish and the Americans. Then he found a new weapon to combat fatigue through an unexpected order from General McDowell, to whose command the brigade had just been assigned. He rubbed his hands and sent an orderly for George Force.

The latter arrived with mud thick on his boots and rain skidding from his poncho. De Mérac asked blandly, "How are affairs in H, George?"

"Fine—for Mr. McArdle. Three bitches from the Ohio camp came over to make appointments for spring. For the rest of us, rotten. Randol's got a new side-splitter. He sees you walking along and yells at you. When you stop he says, 'How far away would you have been if I hadn't yelled at you?' Then he belches in glee and whacks your shoulder."

"*Epatant.* I shall try it on Pelham—when you get back from New York." De Mérac handed him a slip of paper. "McDowell's orders. I send one hundred men on leave each week. You are the first for the reason that you deserve to be."

George's brows contracted. Then he exploded. "Oh—by God! You don't know what this means. I'll get a chance to talk to Dora." He whirled toward the door. "Well, I'll say thanks later. Got to get the six-twenty!"

George stood uneasily by the window in the Chases' drawing room which faced on East Eighteenth Street. The pale winter sun shone on the funereal, dark furniture, on heavy red curtains discreetly looped back, on a fireplace of black marble that stifled a small coal fire. Over the mantel was one bright spot, the portrait of a strikingly beautiful woman with sad, grave eyes and a gentle mouth. Dora's mother. She had been an invalid for years but the few elders who saw her said that she had changed little. "Wish she were around instead of that damned Father Jonas!" George said to himself.

He caught sight of himself in a mirror of French gilt and became even more acutely self-conscious. He was in the full dress of the Rifles. The fringed epaulettes with the single silver bar, the loops of gold braid high on the dark blue sleeves, the bright buckle of his sword belt, the shining scabbard, and the broad gold stripe down the sides of his sky-blue trousers renewed his confidence a little. Dark blue, light blue, gold and yellow brought out strikingly his clear skin and smooth, straw-colored hair. His kepi, sunken top bright with more gold braid, lay on the stiff sofa where he had flung it. He slid it nervously along a window sill until it was hidden by a tall rubber plant. Then he coughed and ran his finger inside his collar. His kepi, insecurely balanced, fell to the floor with a soft plop. He gulped and dove after it, fingers clawing about the carved base of the rubber plant stand.

There was a ripple of laughter from the door. "George! What on earth are you doing?"

He straightened up and a fold of curtain swept hair across his eyes. He shook it back, reddening, and held out the offending cap. "It—it was just this."

"Oh—it had rolled off? Just drop it on that chair. George, it's so nice your coming around like this. I didn't even know you were back in New York. Do sit down." She settled herself on the sofa in a rustle of light gray skirts. George perched on a small chair, his sword clanking against its frail legs. He smiled uncertainly at her. Her dark hair fell in ringlets about her pretty face and her mouth quirked at the corners. George twisted the sword knot. "I'm just here for three days, Dora. My first real leave."

She folded her hands in her lap. "I'm glad you thought to look in. Of course you've seen Betty Barclay and Jane Ledyard."

He tried desperately to think of some easy, clever reply. It came out as, "No. I haven't," and he fell silent.

Dora's small feet stirred under her wide skirt. "Oh, well, you will, of course. Ah—where's Mr. McArdle?"

"I left him at home. Didn't want him bouncing on your sofas and things." He rose suddenly. "Listen, Dora. I came just to ask you—is it true?"

She looked up at him, clear eyes puzzled. "Is what true, George?"

"I—I heard about it. About Stacy Verplanck."

"Stacy? What do you mean?"

He bent toward her, words tumbling out. "Are you engaged to him? I heard you were. And I just want to tell you, if you are, you've got to think a long time about it—and then you're going to change your mind."

She got up slowly, firm little chin on high. "George Force—are you warning me against him?"

"No!" he said. "No! Not against him. It's just—" To keep from seizing her hands he jammed his own deep in his pockets. "Oh, confound it—"

She broke in, a wondering note in her voice. "Would you mind if I were?"

"What do you think I'm trying to say? I—I'm saying you're not getting engaged to anyone—unless—oh, the devil. I thought it'd be easier saying than writing."

"I'm not engaged to anyone, George," she said gently.

His hands flew from his pockets and he swept her into his arms. "Yes you are. To me."

She gasped, braced her hands against him, and looked up at him wide-eyed. "George! Please! No. Wait. You've never said anything like this before. You've never written—"

"I have written, time and again."

"But nothing about this. It's been about the camp and Captain de Mérac and Mr. McArdle and Geranium Jones and Randol and—"

He shook her arms gently. "Then I was a fool. But how could I know that you'd want to hear any more than that? I—well, maybe I'd have said something more at that ball, only I had to go, you remember. If I'd had any sense, I'd have asked you that first time I saw you at our house. I haven't been able to think of anything else since then. And when I heard that yarn about Verplanck—"

She said in a rather shaky voice, "George, you—mean this?"

"Mean it? Of course I do. When I first heard that yarn

115

I nearly mutinied because John wouldn't give me a pass to come and find out."

She gave a low laugh. Then she reached up and ran her fingers through his hair. "I've always wanted to rumple your hair, George. Just as long as I can remember." He stared at her, incredulously. She whispered, "Everything's all right, darling—if that's really the way you feel about me."

"Feel about you! Dora!" His arms were about her. "Dearest, I wish you could know how much you've been in my mind. You keep popping up—the way you smile and the way you cock your head when you're puzzled, and the lilt of your voice. You must know all that!"

Her hair was dark against the gold of his epaulettes. "I do know, George. Maybe I oughtn't to say so, but I do." She laughed again. "For one thing, I have heard some of the older girls say that you—well, you were most accomplished. George, dear, I do love the way you stuttered and stormed. It wasn't accomplished and I loved it."

He whispered, "Are you happy as I am?"

"Happy—so happy." She tilted her chin upward as he bent down. She went on: "You've always been sort of a hero to me, George, way back in the days when I used to see you coasting down Murray Hill with the other boys. I used to brag about you when you went to Columbia, brag about the Columbia freshman I knew. I was proud of you when you went right into the Rifles and didn't wait for something easy. I can tell you this, you see, because you didn't know I was alive, even. Then when I saw you in your uniform that time and you acted as if you thought I was someone else—I kept pretending to myself that I was someone else because you looked at me as you never had before."

"And I kept on looking at you, didn't I? Didn't I come to see you as often as I could? Didn't I steal every waltz I could with you at the ball? Didn't that tell you anything, even if I was too mizzle-witted to say anything?"

"I thought you were just being nice—and, oh George, you don't know how nice you can be without trying! Oh, the girls that are going to hate me!"

He stroked her hair. "Stop pretending to be humble. If you feel the way I do, you'll end by kicking the spire off Trinity. Look, Dora—we'll be married—really soon?"

She nodded like a grave child. "As soon as ever we can. We'll see Father and—"

"He'll be for us, of course?"

"Of course. He'll be coming in almost any minute now." A key rattled faintly in the outer door. "Heavens! There he is now." She kissed him quickly, then slid to the French mirror, her hands to her hair. "Do I look a fright?"

George settled his coat, hitched his sword belt as Dora called, "Father! In the drawing room. George Force is home on leave!"

The door popped open and Jonas Chase padded into the room. He was a short, dumpy man, nearly bald, with hamlike, clean-shaven face, and a petulant mouth. He made straight for Dora, kissed her affectionately and fussed about her. "Well, well. So my little girl's got a caller!" His voice was rather high and squeaky. "Growing into quite a belle—that's the word—a belle. Won't have time for her old father, soon." He padded over to George and held out a flabby hand. "On leave, eh? Do they pay you when you're on leave? Goodness gracious. Heard in Wall Street today how much it was costing us, keeping all you fellows down there."

George grinned. "Maybe it'd be cheaper to bring us back and buy off the Rebs."

Chase raised his plump hands. "We shouldn't be doing any of this. Ruining business. Why don't we back Fernando Wood and declare New York a free port? It's bad everywhere. Had a letter through the blockade from my friend Peyton Garth in Richmond. Says it's the same there. Davis wants to seize cotton for his government. Outrageous! That's the word—outrageous. Now, daughter darling, you better run upstairs. Mother'll have had her nap and she'll want you there when she wakes. Been a pleasure to see you, George. Remember me to your father and mother." He held out his limp hand.

George drew a deep breath. "Just one thing, sir." Dora slid quietly to his side. Jonas Chase's lobster eyes bulged farther. George went on: "I can't tell you anything about myself, sir, that you don't know already. So I merely say that Dora and I deeply hope for your consent to our marriage."

Mr. Chase plumped down into a small chair that was thick with tassels. He planted his hands on his knees and stared. "Goodness gracious! What's this? Consent? *Marriage?*" His hands flew into the air. "Oh, impossible. Impossible! You don't know what you're asking. Dora's our only child. I—I don't know what I'd do without her. Oh, bless my soul. She's too young. Her mother'd die without her. Just think of me, coming home and not finding Dora here."

Dora gave George's arm a warning squeeze. "Perhaps it's rather sudden for you, Dad. Let's just say we're engaged. We want to announce that much, as soon as we can."

Her father bounced up and padded about the room, arms behind his back. "Engaged? Oh, no! No! No! I can't even think about it."

She said gently, "The Gwathmey girls are both younger than I and they were married last month."

"That's it. Proves my point. Take those Gwathmeys, now. Rattlebrains. That's the word, rattlebrains. I tell you that their grandfather, old Horatio Gwathmey, had so little sense that he *actually dipped into his principal*, once. Now that wild blood's showing again. No. That's my last word."

Force set his chin. "Not mine, sir. I think I've a right to be heard."

Chase goggled at him. "Right? Right? Now I shall settle this matter once for all. Dora, you will go up to your mother, at once."

George saw her head go back defiantly. Then she squeezed his arm once more. "Come over tomorrow, dearest. I'll send a note." She stood on tiptoe, kissed him, and slipped from the room.

George faced Jonas Chase. "Do you object to me, personally, sir?"

"Gracious, no! But Dora's just a child. She's—"

"A lot of girls marry younger, sir. And Dora knows her own mind."

"Nonsense. Carried away by this fool war. Turns all the young ones selfish, that's what it does. Why—I am nonplused at you two talking about marriage and never giving a thought to *me!*"

"We have the right to think of ourselves a little, sir."

"But you don't think of Dora. Look here, George, you're in a damned shaky business that may blow up. Good God, why did they send du Chaillu to Africa to get a gorilla when we've got one right here in the White House? And more than that—you're in a damnably dangerous business. You may not get through it, you know."

"We both know that, sir."

"Then how in the name of common sense can you, a grown man, consider the risk of making my daughter a widow? No. That is all. You will not write Dora again. You will not see her again."

George picked up his kepi. "That, sir, will rest entirely with Dora." He bowed to the little man. "Good evening, Mr. Chase." Out in the hall, where a soft gas lamp burned at the foot of the long stairs, George looked wistfully up. His heart jumped as he saw Dora, leaning over the upper railing, the light soft on the smooth slope of her neck. She blew him a kiss and called in a low voice, "Don't worry, George. Wait till Mother has a word with him."

George waved his kepi. "My love to your mother, dearest. See you tomorrow." He swung out of the house, chuckling deep in his throat and swinging his arms. He hailed a cab, drove down to Fourteenth Street, and sent a huge basket of flowers to Dora. Then he walked home, hitting a pace that would have wrecked his company. He alternately chuckled and whistled as he pictured his family's reception of his news. His parents would be delighted. Marion would chaff him good-naturedly and Mr. McArdle would make the whole neighborhood hideous with wild yelps. He snapped his fingers at the thought of Jonas Chase. There would be some way of working him around. George began to whistle louder, pealing out a song that he had heard Negroes singing on Long Bridge:

> *Fo' it must be now dat de kingdom's comin'—*
> *It's de year ob Jubilo!*

Back at the camp on the banks of the Potomac Colonel Pride had formed the habit of dropping in at the orderly room or the mess of the Rifles. Sometimes he came alone, sometimes he brought with him a young captain or two, pleasant-mannered young lawyers from the Wabash or serious-eyed farmers like himself. Before hailing de Mérac, Pride always peered wistfully into Vernet's rich-smelling kitchen. The usually irascible chef exclaimed in delight and brought forth choice tarts stuffed with preserved strawberries, melting *baba au rhum* or jam-covered delicacies which he called *beignets* and which Pride stubbornly identified as fritters. This gastronomic ritual amused de Mérac and Wilson, who racked their brains to discover the link that brought out Vernet's explosive *"Bon jour, Monsieur le Colonel!"*

Pride was present when the mail wagon brought de Mérac not only news that the Duanes were about to move into a house on I Street near the so-called Minnesota Row, but also the Austerlitz saber of honor from Loudéac. De Mérac unpacked in the presence of the Indiana colonel, Wilson, and George. He watched the three heads bend over the rosewood box, one shaggy and bearlike, one fine-drawn and keen as greyhound's, one clear-featured and eager. Pride rumbled, "That's mighty pretty, now. Nice to have something from your folks." Wilson muttered: "If there *are* ghosts, John, I guess the man who first carried that'll be riding right with you." "Sure is something to have," whispered George, reverently. He slowly read the inscription as de Mérac drew out the heavy, curved blade topped by its open, Turkish hilt. *"Napoléon ler ... Empereur des Français ... Chef d'Escadron Egide de Kérédern de Mérac ... Austerlitz ... 2 décembre, 1805.* So that's where you got the name Kérédern." There was another package, small and light. To de Mérac's surprise there fell out a vizor of Florentine tortoise-shell work. He muttered, "My father's." He could vaguely recall the scarlet-topped kepi with its rich vizor lying on a carved chair in the great hall in Loudéac. Pride smoothed the shell with his rough fingers. "He send it to you?"

"He was killed when I was a boy. At the massacre of Sidi Brahim in '45 where four hundred and fifty French stood off three thousand Arabs. Rapp can tell you about it. He was a young corporal in the relieving force that arrived too late."

Pride nodded in complete understanding. "Just like some of our Indian fights. Some of my name got slaughtered near Fort Wayne under St. Clair in 1791."

De Mérac sent the saber to the chief armorer for polishing and the vizor to Sansone, the best tailor in the regiment, to be attached to his choicest French-style kepi. George said enviously, "You'll make us all look like damn dull birds, John. It didn't matter so much before, but now with the town filling up! I'm going to creep through back alleys."

The town was indeed filling up, almost to overflowing, with the return of Congress and the whirl of war. Big houses and small, that had stood shuttered, now showed glowing windows along LaFayette Park, on Connecticut Avenue, and out toward Georgetown and Silver Spring. The mud that engulfed the camps turned the broad streets of the Capital into hopeless quagmires where, on mild days, pigs wallowed in grunting joy. Women poised on curbs, hunting for a place to cross while they fiddled with a complicated arrangement of cords and springs that lifted their outer skirts clear of the mud. At every corner ragged boys knelt with brushes and scrapers, removing the muck gathered on boots, skirts, and trousers at each crossing. Bars sprang up wherever a roof and wall could be found. In curtained houses, sleek-headed croupiers chanted, *"Faites vos jeux, 'sieurs—'dames. Rien ne va plus!"* Some of these curtained houses held more than poker and faro tables and even Continental eyes bulged at the daring of bright dresses. Corvisart reported to Bolton, *"Décolletage?* Ah, *pensez-vous!* It was enough to make blush a captain of cuirassiers. Although," he added in strict fairness, "I have known captains of cuirassiers who were of a pudicity unfathomable."

De Mérac called on the Duanes and found Louise more sparkling than ever, stirred to a high pitch of excitement by the vibrant war capital. She seemed genuinely delighted to see him, greeted him with gay frankness when she caught sight of him at other houses. One or two girls openly set their caps for him, especially a radiant wisp of a girl in Baltimore where he went occasionally. These he avoided, for of course there could be no entanglements for a man who would repatriate himself at the end of the war. But Louise was different, with her gay, unaffected, almost boyish air of friendliness.

Yet Louise often disturbed him. There were glints in her dark eyes that were not at all boyish. With apparent unconsciousness she revealed, in her low-cut dresses, the curves that were startling in a figure seemingly so slim. In the quick turnings of a waltz, her skirts swept out and up to show fine ankles and a hint of gracefully tapering legs. Watching her across a ballroom, chatting with her over an ice, he sometimes found himself aware of a suggestion of the same appeal with which Lisa von Horstmar was so amply endowed.

Through von Stoeckl he secured cards for the Duanes to legation receptions and was amused to see how Louise adapted herself to the swarms of poised young attachés. There could, however, be no mistaking, from her attitude, to whom she owed her presence at such gatherings.

Before Christmas, de Mérac sent George on leave to New York again. The petulant Mr. Chase had capitulated to the extent of allowing the young people to meet—though not too often—and to write most discreetly.

De Mérac watched George and Mr. McArdle bowl riotously off in a carriage. Then he sent for Vernet. The Rifles would give a Christmas Eve party in the officers' mess for those held in Washington. The chef, moody at first since he himself had not thought of the plan, melted as de Mérac spoke of *potage crème d'orge à la royale,* of *le rostbif a l'anglais garni de croquettes de pomme de terre et de hâtelets sauce Chablis.* They also discussed the relative merits of Mersault and Château d'Yquem and Montrachet and Vouvray.

Then invitations were sent out, to be followed by a deluge of acceptances. Of the higher officers only Pelham refused, in a curt note which Dunn had obviously toned down and mellowed as much as possible.

The dinner was a vast success. De Mérac looked down the table that boasted stars as well as eagles. McDowell spoke fluent French to Baron de Trobriand. Colonel of the 55th New York. Kearny, his hawk face aglow and his keen eyes matching the glitter of his cross of the Legion of Honor, was courtly and attentive to Claire Wilson. Handsome Joe Hooker and white-haired General Sumner amiably shared Louise Duane's bright sparkle and ringing laugh.

There were other guests whom de Mérac watched attentively, notably General Ripley of the Ordnance Department. Later in the evening the general, well warmed with wine, might listen with practical sympathy to his host's need of Springfield muskets.

There was thick snow outside and the guests fell silent as the broad doors opened and a German choir, uniforms dotted with snow, sang *"Stille Nacht, heilige Nacht—"*

An orchestra, picked from the band, played for dancing, and Louise waltzed delightedly with Colonel Labanieff, magnificent in gold braid, tight raspberry breeches, and gold-tasseled Hessian boots. "Such fun, John," she cried when he claimed the next dance. "Oh—we came in through a snow tunnel and there were all those lovely Zouaves holding torches and the Germans have a big Christmas tree in their street. We could see everything—two pet raccoons and an opossum. And tomorrow you're going to take me to that darling old de Trobriand's camp? This is just like being in Europe. Oh—and I know all about Madame de Trobriand. Her father was that Mr. Jones, head of the Chemical Bank, and she's been lady in waiting to the Duchesse de Berri in Venice." She gave a little wriggle of delight. "I can never thank you enough for all this."

"You put us all in your debt by being here," de Mérac replied.

The guests left early in the morning to the jingle of sleigh bells. For some days de Mérac watched for an order from Washington, giving the Rifles their long-wanted Springfields. Then Greenbaum brought him three official envelopes. "Thought you'd want to look at these yourself."

De Mérac ripped them open, swore violently. "Name of a filthy camel! Look for yourself!"

Greenbaum stared at the sheets. "Well—I'll be damned," he muttered. The three orders said nothing about Springfields. Instead they officially transferred Vernet, Lestoq, and Moreau, the prize cooks of the mess, to higher quarters. De Mérac suddenly burst out laughing. "It is justice, my friend. Appreciating our cooks, the high gods insure their lives by transferring them to deep, deep safety."

"Doesn't get us those Springfields, though," growled Greenbaum.

Two days later de Mérac, sipping tea with Louise at the British Legation, looked up with a start to see Lisa von Horstmar bearing down on him. He stiffened, reluctantly introduced Louise. Lisa spoke pleasantly. "I saw Mademoiselle across the room yesterday at Madame Greer's and admired her. My child, how well that solferino becomes you." She chatted on amiably, to de Mérac's amazement. ("As though she were the pious friend of my aunt Élodie!") She left with a smile for Louise and an easy nod to him.

Louise puckered her mouth into a red button and her eyes were round. "Ooooh! Isn't she pretty?"

"Not in my opinion," de Mérac answered.

She set down her cup. "You know, you're absolutely right! First you think she's pretty and then you see she isn't—quite."

De Mérac nodded absently as he saw Lisa laughing up into the eyes of a tall young captain from Pelham's staff. "Now what the devil is she up to?" he wondered. "May I hope to be permanently assigned to the safe rank of old and valued friend!" He collected himself, realizing that Louise was speaking to him.

"John, what were you laughing about with Laura Kirke a little while ago?"

"With Miss Kirke? Ah—that must have been when I informed her that New York Central was down to 62¼."

Louise pouted and then said archly, "Yes, that's the sort of thing men always tell poor dear Laura. No—it was something else. I heard the name 'Springfield.'"

"Ah—I told her of my base plot to buy arms for the Rifles with that Christmas Eve dinner."

Her eyes widened. "You meant Springfield muskets? You really want them?"

"Militarily—more than anything in the world."

Louise looked puzzled. Then she looked past de Mérac, calling, "Joey! Joey Chilton! Do come here a second."

A good-looking young civilian hobbled over on a clubfoot and was introduced to de Mérac. Louise smiled at him. "Joey, you're in Ordnance. Why can't Captain de Mérac get Springfields for his men?"

Chilton raised his eyebrows. "You haven't got any, Captain? Still carrying the old rust-traps? I'll see about that." He pulled out a notebook and jotted down a few lines. De Mérac murmured his thanks, omitting to say that General Ripley himself had been powerless in the matter. Mr. Chilton he dismissed from his mind.

From the legation he went on with the Wilsons to a dinner given by a couple from Buffalo. He found himself growing irritated, although he liked his hosts, who set a fine table. He was rather disturbed to realize that he was missing Louise's gay talk, the play of light across her hair, the appeal of her dark, vivid eyes. "*Allons*," he thought. "As a friend she is charming, but, I assure myself, by no means indispensable."

When George came back from New York, he stamped into the orderly room cursing some army wagons that had blocked his carriage at the entrance to the camp. "It was a nasty jam, John. I sent old Rapp to tear into the damn drivers."

Almost immediately Rapp lunged into the office, his rigid calm gone for once and his eyes bulging. He shouted, "*Regardez-moi ça, mon capitaine!*" In his scarred hands he held a brand-new Springfield, still coated with the grease in which it had been packed. "But there are cases, veritable cases of muskets!"

De Mérac sprang from his chair. "They are ours?"

Rapp set down the musket and produced a grease-spattered form. It was from the Ordnance Bureau and was signed "Jos. E. Chilton." De Mérac cried, "*Mille tonnerres des cent mille dieux!* They are for us!"

George stared. "How in hell did you get them?"

"At the British Legation! From Louise Duane. She smiled on a chief clerk and our troubles ended. Now we shall not fight as cripples!"

As the New Year broke over the still immobilized armies, de Mérac began a slow tightening of the reins of the regiment against the day when bugles would send the blue columns out of their camps for the last time. In one way, his work had been made easier. Without warning, Pelham had removed Dalbiac from command of the Rifles and attached him to his staff, where the unhappy colonel trotted dejected and unnoticed in the wake of the brigadier, close chained to headquarters. The move left Wilson in actual command, but he insisted that de Mérac continue. The major himself assumed charge of the five left companies of the regiment and Corvisart, as senior captain, took over the right five, leaving the capable Bordagaray in command of the Zouave company. Now there was no need to maintain the fiction of any command other than de Mérac's, and Wilson backed him loyally in every move.

De Mérac, looking to the future, began to think a little of himself as well as of the regiment. To spell Torpille, he bought a second horse, a quick-footed black that DuChesne christened "Cigale." He gave up the practice of detailing a different bugler for his own use each day and hunted about for a musician who would be with him permanently. He accidentally fell upon a round-eyed, round-cheeked boy named Castex, a Burgundian from Beaune who, early orphaned, had sold newspapers from Union Square to the Battery. The fourteen-year-old had been badly deviled by older men in Péguy's company and joyfully welcomed the transfer. When de Mérac bought the boy a stocky, nimble-footed pony, the little bugler's doglike devotion changed to sheer worship.

One January day, when a northeaster was blowing hard lines of sleet across the camp, a squad of men from the provost guard, tough, hard-bitten cavalrymen, rode up to de Mérac's quarters. A blue and yellow figure with its arms bound stumbled beside them and a sergeant from Bolton's company walked grimly in the rear, carrying a rifle. The horsemen trotted off and the sergeant tramped in, saluting as he pushed the now unbound prisoner ahead of him. De Mérac spoke sharply. "*Eh bien*, Sergeant, this is not regulation."

Sergeant Cole said, "Captain Bolton's compliments. Said he thought you'd want to see this deserter yourself."

De Mérac pushed back from the table and stared at the dripping figure. The man was spare-boned, a good infantryman's build. The face turned defiantly toward him had a strong chin, a thin-lipped mouth, and heavily muscled jaws. The eyes were almost frightening. They were like splinters of ice, unwavering, cold, asking nothing and telling nothing. De Mérac asked. "Where was he caught? Long Bridge?"

Cole said, "That's what's funny, sir. They got him down to a place called Dutcher's Run, fifteen, twenty mile south. It was patrols as caught him, sir. Not regular provost."

De Mérac stared, "Dutcher's Run. But that is almost within the Rebel lines. Was he trying to desert to them?"

"Says he ain't, sir. This here gun's his. Five rounds missing out his pouch."

De Mérac drummed his fingers on the table, frowning.

At length he said, "Very good, Sergeant. I shall talk with him. You need not wait."

Cole withdrew, saluting. De Mérac leaned his elbows on the table. "You are the first deserter from I Company, my friend. I find your choice of direction odd. So odd that I wish to hear more of it before I act. What is your name?"

The thin lips stirred. "Gerritt Dekdebrun, sir."

"Ah—yes. You came in the last lot of recruits. But you knew that leaving your command meant deserting."

"Didn't care."

"Why, then, did you go south?"

"Kill." The answer was bitten off.

De Mérac studied the cold, unwinking eyes. Something of their expression he had seen in the older men, but never with such intensity, never so implacable—the look, the expression, of a killer. "You went, without orders, to fire on enemy outposts? There'll be enough of that later."

Dekdebrun said, "No!" and his eyes froze deeper.

"Couldn't you wait until the whole regiment should move?"

"Waited too long now."

De Mérac pulled at his mustache. The boy could hardly be nineteen, save for the ageless expression. What was the key to the cold brain? The name—Gerritt—ah—Gerritt Smith, the upstate abolitionist.

He said, "You hold a grudge, then?"

"Father and uncle. One brother. Killed. Burned in Kansas by slavers."

"You are from New York. What did they do in Kansas?"

"Went out there with a party. To vote Kansas free."

De Mérac looked at the rifle that the sergeant had left standing against the wall. It was fitted with a telescopic sight, like those carried by some of Berdan's green-clad sharpshooters. "Your own?"

"Why I was late enlisting. Worked till I could buy it."

De Mérac clasped his hands behind his head. "Listen, my friend. Under law, you have deserted. I could have you sent to the prison at the Dry Tortugas. It is not a pleasant place. Equally could I have you shot."

"Hear what you say." There was no impertinence in the reply, just a glacial disregard for anything beyond the man's obsession.

"You would do well to understand it. You wish to kill the men who, as you see it, murdered your father and uncle. If you desert again you will undoubtedly meet one of the two fates which I mentioned. In either case you could do little damage to the Rebels." A plan began slowly to form in his mind. "Can you ride?"

"Anything."

"You can handle revolvers?"

"Dead with them. Dead with this." He nodded toward the rifle.

"Good. Then attend to me. This charge I shall drop. You will leave your company and be attached to me. Someday, we go into action. It will be your duty to cover me at all times. If your horse, which I shall provide for you, is shot, you will keep up on foot as best you may. If mine is shot, you must cover me more closely than ever. Wherever I go, you follow. That is clear?"

"Clear."

De Mérac asked suddenly, in French, *"Votre nom—Dekdebrun—vous êtes belge?"*

The answer came in English. "Father from Belgium. Bruges. I'm American. Talk French. Talk Flemish. Don't like to."

"Talk as you please, so long as you follow my orders. From today you march with me, and if you slip off I shall treat you as deserter. You will have to work hard. There is much more to soldiering than killing."

"No," said Dekdebrun.

De Mérac sent him back to Bolton with a short note. As the door slammed de Mérac felt a shudder as he recalled the cold stare and sparse words of his new bodyguard. Here was a new factor to consider. He had known men like Wilson and Clay who had stepped forward at once at the threat of their country. Hein and Corvisart and Péguy and the others had, without urging,

129

answered the call of a land which they had made utterly their own. The impulse, while personal, was perhaps abstract. Now he saw the concrete impulse in the Belgian abolitionist, Gerritt Dekdebrun, frozen into a cold blood-lust because the forces which he regarded as evil had struck down those closest to him.

There were stirrings out in the West as the winter dragged on. A General Grant, a mere name to de Mérac and most of his colleagues, suddenly took Fort Donelson and Fort Henry on the Tennessee River and the Confederates evacuated Nashville. In the East, the good-looking, affable Burnside made a sudden and successful landing at Roanoke Island in North Carolina. Heavy mists, rains, and sleet still blanketed the Potomac and de Mérac, reading of the distant news, was reminded of muffled drums in the wings just before the great curtain at the *Opéra* rolled slowly up.

Yet the curtain remained motionless and tedium hung heavy over the sodden land that surrounded the massive ramparts and casemates of Fort Corcoran. Men, hitherto clean-shaven, blossomed out in thick beards that fell below the collar and vied with each other in style and cut. George Force emerged as a deep-chested young Viking with a fan-shaped blond growth, neatly parted in the middle. Dalbiac, who had managed to persuade himself that his transfer to the staff was a merited promotion, flourished whiskers that would have done credit to a Russian grenadier, and the mouselike chin of de Mérac's orderly, Louvel, sprouted fiercely. De Mérac and Wilson did not join in the rivalry, but the daily struggle with razor and soap served the same purpose as cultivating a beard—it helped pass the time.

As though to match ghastly weather and deep ennui, Jonas Chase suddenly turned even less tractable and wrote that, for reasons best known to himself, he saw fit to withdraw permission for George and Dora to correspond or meet. George shrugged bitterly and drove himself and his company harder and harder. De Mérac and Wilson watched him carefully. "Damn it," said the major, "the boy'll work himself sick."

De Mérac rubbed his eyes wearily. "He won't rest. How long, Craig, since he dined with you and Claire?"

"Must be about two weeks. For a while we were able to get him about every time you gave him a Washington pass. Claire's mighty fond of him and so am I."

"Insist on his going with you tonight. Claire will make him talk, may even find a solution. I assure you, *mon vieux*, that although I feel he sets some store by me, he will say nothing." That very night the major bore George off to Washington.

Two days later, as he returned to the brick house near LaFayette Park, Claire met him in the hall. "Craig, dear, could you and Janet look after Thomas for a few days?"

He smiled as he slipped out of his yellow-lined cape. "Not with any pleasure to Thomas. Why?"

"I'm going to New York. Tomorrow."

He stopped in the act of lighting a cigar. "Tomorrow? But, darling, that is the night of the dinner at the Montgomery Blairs'. You're going to chaperon Louise Duane and John."

"That can wait. I'm going up to call on Alice Chase. She's got to persuade Jonas—I don't know how, but she's got to—to let Dora come and stay with us."

"For how long?"

Her lips quivered. "We know, you and I, what's going to happen when spring comes. But at least, we're together now. Dora'll stay until—well, until there's no reason for her to stay."

He nodded gravely. "With my full blessing, darling."

Spring suns set the cauldron of war seething faster. There was a Union victory at Pea Ridge in far-off Arkansas. Then the valley of the Potomac shook to the cough of heavy guns as the Confederate ironclad *Merrimac* wrecked the wooden Union fleet, then fell back sullenly before the weird and unexpected *Monitor*. Off by Centerville the Confederate General Johnston suddenly abandoned that base whose supposed strength had been a great factor in keeping McClellan immobile. Reconnaissance showed that the stronghold could easily have been taken, as its defenses were weak and included wooden guns. There was a wave of indignation and McClellan was demoted from supreme command in the East, although still retaining the Army of the Potomac.

Down in the Shenandoah, Stonewall Jackson began to stir and the North saw a threat to its capital. The Union forces, no longer under a single head, were shuffled and reshuffled. The Rifles were assigned, detached, assigned again, were at last loosely attached, with the rest of the brigade, to the defenses of Washington.

George Force watched the changes, which seemed to take him farther and farther from active duty, with hot resentment that was tempered by one fact. Across the Potomac Dora Chase had been most surprisingly installed for an indefinite stay with the Wilsons, and every free moment found him riding a borrowed horse across Long Bridge or watching by the sallyport of Fort Corcoran for a carriage on whose box rode the beaming Thomas.

On a warm day in late March, George cantered along a grassy trail that led over the hills to spired Arlington and the river. Dora, in feathered hat and smart brown habit, sat a small-boned bay by his side. Ahead of them Claire Wilson paced along, a few yards behind Louise Duane and de Mérac. George smiled at Dora as he pointed toward Claire Wilson with his crop. "Ever tell you how she did it, honey?"

Dora cocked her head. "As soon as she told me about that awful beard of yours, I just picked up some scissors and started for Washington—it didn't matter *what* she did. Ugh! You look so much better with it off." She spoke lightly but she knew that her mother had drawn heavily on her frail strength, pleading, arguing with her father. Even to George she wouldn't speak of that. She reached out and linked her brown arm through his blue one. "Darling. Two more whole weeks before I have to go back! Oh—Louise and John have stopped on the skyline. They're waving to us."

De Mérac and Louise had reined in and were staring down into the hidden land beyond. Claire Wilson joined them and Mr. McArdle, his brown, black, and white coat dust covered, was barking frantically. Louise called, "George! Dora! Hurry!"

"Come on," said Dora, and the two trotted smartly up. Then Dora reined in abruptly, her eyes wide and her pretty face darkly intense. The land fell away before her, fell to the south bank, the broad, coffee-colored sweep of the river and the crowded Washington shore. Long blue columns streamed down to wharves, to rickety landings, to broad-beamed lighters. On they came, endless masses from all the New England states, endless masses from Ohio and Minnesota, from Illinois and Indiana. Pennons fluttered clear and red as Rush's Pennsylvania lancers filed off toward the river boats. Gun wheels echoed on hollow decks, red-trousered Zouaves swarmed onto barges and steamers. Steep below, almost at Dora's feet, drums slammed out and a full brigade of Wisconsin infantry wound down the road that hugged the south bank. North and South, from every state they came, and high over each column fluttered the national colors.

George rubbed his fist across his forehead as he stared. Dora laid a hand on his cuff. "Don't feel badly about it, George," she said softly.

He thumped the pommel of his saddle. "I'd go as a private in any of those regiments. Even the 14th Brooklyn!" Across the river, four batteries of horse artillery came on with a jingle, bump, and clank, the cannoneers galloping behind the brass pieces. Beyond them wound a thick red rope, a rope woven of the kepis of de Trobriand's 55th New York. He cried again. "Look at all that! And we're left rotting here!"

She closed her eyes and her small, even teeth set between parted lips. "Keep him here. Dear God, keep him here." She shook away her own thoughts and slipped her arm through George's again. "Had you rather go back to camp, dear?"

He looked down at her clear, candid eyes. "You're a swell girl, Dora. No—let's watch. Some day the Rifles'll be going that same way. Or maybe down into the Shenandoah after Jackson. That's what John thinks. Here comes the 69th New York. See the Irish flags?"

A few paces away, Claire Wilson held her reins tightly in her gloved hands as she watched the long columns. "I don't care! Craig's here—now—with me! I'll make up to him for every smidge of disappointment in getting left out. I will. He belongs with me. God, God! I don't know what I'm saying. I just want him here. That's all. The poor boy! I'm weak, I'm rotten weak. I hope he goes. I hope he goes tomorrow. I can face it—until after he's gone!"

Bright-eyed beside de Mérac, her delicate face upturned to the river breeze, Louise Duane waved her hand over the vast panorama where loaded steamers pulled out into the current. "I wouldn't have missed this for anything, John. You always think of the nicest things to do. Look—there are the d'Epineul Zouaves and their Indians. And right down below us—that battery! Its men have got on chain-mail epaulettes. I can see the glint from here. Oh, this is such fun! You know, you'd look awfully well in one of those artillery jackets. You're so tall."

He looked down at her, thinking, "I could kiss you now. I've seen that look before. But an American girl— she would take it as a declaration. No, it is better— *toujours en camarade*." Then his eyes turned back to the crowded river and the undying disappointment crept over him again, the bitter disappointment at being left watching on the bank while the Army of the Potomac embarked its thousands for the assault on the Yorktown Peninsula.

Late that afternoon, in the cool orderly room, Craig Wilson had just finished reading an order of de Mérac's that stripped the regiment down to the barest possessions. Thomas stood before him respectfully, turning his cockaded hat in his gnarled hands. Wilson stamped out a cigar. "I think that Mrs. Wilson told you, Thomas, that when the army showed signs of moving, she would go back to New York with Janet."

Thomas bobbed his gray wool appreciatively. "Ah knows New York fine, suh. My folks used to go to Saratoga. Ah'll look after Mis' Wilson an' Mis' Janet. Don' you fret 'bout dat."

Wilson's eyes widened in surprise. "But you see, Thomas, we've got our own servants up there. I told you that. Now, when we go you'll be able to choose between a dozen first-rate houses that want you. Mrs. Delancey Wayne, for one. Then the Cammann Davis family and the—"

For the first time in his life, Thomas sat down in the presence of a master. His old knees buckled and he slid down jerkily onto a camp chair, his long arms dangling between his knees. Two thick tears clouded his eyes and zig-zagged down his seamed black cheeks. "Mean you don' want me, suh?" he quavered.

Wilson stared at him in surprise. "Want you? Of course we do. You've been fine, Thomas, and I've written some letters about you. But—well—you see how it is. Now Mrs. Delancey Wayne—"

Arms still dangling, Thomas peered at Wilson incredulously. "But—Ah don' want to work fo' Mis' Wayne. Who look after Mis' Janet? Who bresh you' coats and fold 'em way you like 'em?"

Wilson said in a kindly tone, "Don't worry about us, Thomas. Mrs. Wilson'll be in New York and I'll be in the field. If you don't like Mrs. Wayne, there's Mrs. Pervere or—"

Thomas leaned forward pleadingly, his face a mask of woe. "Major—is *dis* freedom? All mah life I dream 'bout freedom. You tells me I'm free an'—an' you tells me I c'n work fo' Mis' Wayne 'cause you-all goin' somewhars else. You and Mis' Wilson and Mis' Janet—you'se my folks—an' you leaves me, leaves dis ol' nigger dat found you." He smeared a cuff across his eyes. "If dis yere's freedom, lemme stay slave till de Chariot of de Lamb come take me to Jordan's shore."

Wilson got up quickly, took a few sharp steps about the room. Then he plunged his hand into a drawer and drew out a white packet. "Thomas—here are your letters—look at them!" Thomas raised his head blindly. Wilson tore the packet in two, dropped the pieces into the wastebasket. "There. Guess we'll manage somehow.

When you drive Mrs. Wilson and Miss Chase home tonight, start packing up the civilian clothes I brought. Don't let Mrs. Wilson know what you're doing. Just pack them, because I think—well it'll be soon. Get them ready to ship to New York. When you get there, brush them and put them away from the moths."

Thomas looked wonderingly at him. "Mean Ah stay with Mis' Wilson and Mis' Janet?"

"Long as you want to."

Thomas drew himself up. "Ah don' never aim to leave mah folks, suh." His teeth suddenly showed. "Reckon dis is freedom suh. Ah chooses you an' you chooses me." He bowed. "Maybe I'd better mosey 'long an' git the carriage ready fo' Mis' Wilson and Mis' Dora, suh."

Wilson looked after the loose-limbed figure as Thomas headed for the picket lines. He recalled a comment of de Mérac's as a stream of black refugees poured past the camp. "This war, it is all very well—but what will become of those others, Craig, about whom, *au fond*, we fight?" He smoothed his graying mustache. "God, that's a question we'll be asking ourselves fifty years from now."

VII

The James

THE Rifles still lay about Fort Corcoran, and de Mérac set out to prepare them for any call that might come. Sets of orders were drawn up by Greenbaum and Rapp to cover every predictable contingency. Then they were filed, ready to hand. Officers and men lived out of their packs and haversacks. It was exacting work but de Mérac had the satisfaction of knowing that within a few minutes of the receipt of an order to move, the appropriate plan would be in operation, with each man knowing exactly what he must do.

In the Shenandoah, Banks and Frémont and Franklin fumbled vaguely after Jackson, three disconnected forces feeling for a single, united foe. On the Peninsula, McClellan lurched inland, slow and ponderous. He wasted time on a useless siege, trundled ahead again, calling wildly for more men, more heavy guns. He was past Williamsburg, he was on the Pamunkey; his maneuvers, hesitant though they were, looked well in the papers, which stressed the fact that McClellan was drawing closer and closer to Richmond. They did not call attention to the more important fact that the Southern forces, now commanded by a Robert Edward Lee, one-time colonel of the 2nd United States Cavalry, were still intact. But at Williamsburg, at Fair Oaks, a single figure had blazed forth and de Mérac heard his files cheering each new exploit of General Kearny, the old *kébir*, now commanding a full division though still ranking as brigadier.

Then Jackson slipped out of the Shenandoah and began a swift march toward Richmond and Lee's forces. McClellan, fearful of this threat to his right flank, acted quickly and began to shift his base from White House on the Pamunkey south toward the James. His hesitation gone, he moved surely and with great skill.

Under a hot June sun, the New Jersey pitcher, a bearded man with blacksmith's shoulders, scowled at the Rifles' batter. The catcher moved still farther back of home plate, ready to take the ball on the first bound. The two runners edged away from their bases, balancing like tightrope walkers.

The dense masses of blue hedging the diamond were suddenly still. The pitcher took a ten-foot run through the box and drove the ball at the batter. There was a sharp crack and the ball shot into left field. The runners raced around the bases, crossed the plate, and the batter pulled up at second base in a storm of yelping cheers.

George Force, chewing a blade of grass, leaned forward in his camp chair behind the first base and banged his hands. Greenbaum, beside him, made two marks on the board across his knees, shouting, "We're catching up; 17-14. Deery's up. Used to play for the Philadelphia Athletics. Listen to the boys hollering!" The volume was actually rather thin, since few of the foreign-born cared for baseball and the Rifles' supporters and team were largely drawn from H and I Companies.

Deery, a slim blond Irishman, stepped to the plate confidently, tossing his bat from hand to hand. The field was still again. George raised his head, listening. Through the New Jersey camp behind the diamond, hoofs beat. A guard called, thin and clear, "Hey, orderly, what's to pay?" The reply rattled crisply. "Hell's to pay. Where's your old man?"

George gripped the arms of his chair and saw Greenbaum's questioning glance. The orderly had ridden clear of the camp and dismounted where de Mérac and Wilson sat behind home plate. "Something's up," snapped the Jew. De Mérac had run out onto the field, waving to Colonel Clay. There was a brief parley. A bugler raised his trumpet and the crowd howled in protest, swarmed over him and sent a twisted bugle sailing high in air. By the plate, Deery leaned patiently on his bat, waiting for the game to go on. George shot from his chair. "Moe, he's breaking up the game. Something's bust!"

Greenbaum tossed away his scoreboard. "About time. I'm hitting back to the office." He raced off toward the Rifles' camp, a mile away.

Bugles were blowing on all sides. George shouted, "H Company. Fall in."

In the center of the diamond, de Mérac turned quickly from Clay and met Wilson's taut, keen glance. De Mérac nodded. "Right away. Embark at Alexandria in five hours. Heavy marching order."

Wilson threw back his lean head, tense with excitement and relief. "Thank God we're ready!"

De Mérac said quickly, "Yes. Will you take the regiment back to camp? I go to the orderly room. And Craig—" The Major checked himself as he turned. "You can send Castex to Washington. Claire can be at the wharf in ample time. Our ship is the *Aspetuck*."

Wilson shook de Mérac's arm hastily. "Thanks, John. I'd thought of that, too. No, I don't want Castex. Claire's a pretty good girl and I guess I'll spare her the sight of a ship's wake heading down the river." He ran off shouting, "Fall in, the Rifles!"

In packed river boats Pelham's whole brigade moved down the Potomac, anchored off Fortress Monroe, and then swung slowly up the James River. There was a disembarkation by lantern light, cold, terse orders from the Brigadier, and the Rifles led the way inland through the night.

Soon the roads were jammed with exhausted men, with battery after battery of dust-caked guns, long lines of transport wagons and ambulances—all moving in the opposite directions. Slow, uncounted miles from the river, hoarse voices of guides swung the Rifles at right angles to the line of march, sent them off on tangled tracks where herds of cattle struggled on under the goads of uniformed herders.

At last there was a halt in a grassy field hedged by trees on three sides. De Mérac wearily ordered a guard posted and watched while the rest of the regiment pitched tents or fell in their tracks, too spent to unroll their blankets. Then he lit a cigarette and considered his position.

He could make nothing of the steady drift toward the James while his line of march had led him away from it. Nor could he understand where the rest of the brigade had gone after the sharp turn from the original road. He shrugged. He had followed authorized guides, had halted where they had indicated. There was nothing to do but wait for daylight and fresh orders from Pelham. He cocked an ear to the night air. Far off on the main road he could catch the steady grind of traffic heading on toward the James. But no shots, no distant salvos of artillery jarred the air. He tossed away his cigarette and called for Louvel and his blankets.

The sun was sending down long drilling rays as he limped to the picket line to inspect Torpille and Cigale. The two horses, munching each other's manes in amity, looked quite glossy and fresh and de Mérac envied them. He himself had scarcely slept. His face felt pinched and sore. Hips and shoulders ached and his feet were swollen, for he had walked much of the way, bridle over his arm, during the night march over the sandy roads.

Torpille left off her browsing and gently butted de Mérac's arm. Something in the push of the soft muzzle, the liquid questioning of the big eyes, reached out to him. Torpille stood out as a true comrade, a living being to carry him surely and trustingly to meet whatever lay beyond the swaying belts of locust trees that hedged his vision. He gentled the sleek head and muttered, "What can be done for you, *mon amie*, I shall do."

DuChesne, red-eyed but alert, trotted up, two or three grinning Negroes at his heels. In answer to de Mérac's question he reported that both mounts were "*pimpantes, tout-à-fait pimpantes.*" The Negroes chuckled at the French words. One of them nudged his neighbor. "Sho do tickle mah ribs, hearing 'at boom-a-boom talk. What she mean, huh?"

DuChesne suddenly cocked his head to the west, muttered, "*Alors?*"

Far away a single heavy echo died, was caught up by fresh sound and carried like a dull blanket over the hot edge of the sky.

De Mérac turned quickly, whipped out his field glasses, and focused them on the distant treetops. Faint, almost indiscernible, a whitish-yellow haze rose stickily, thickened, as the faraway guns thudded on.

All over the sandy field men were struggling to their feet among stacked muskets to stare and mutter. Wilson, red-eyed but newly shaven, ran to de Mérac balancing a half-finished cup of coffee. Dekdebrun slipped into view, his cold eyes alight with a question. Wilson called, "Shall we put them under arms, John?"

De Mérac shook his head. "I think not. The guns are far. Let them rest." The light died from Dekdebrun's eyes and he squatted patiently on the ground, fondling his rifle. De Mérac leaned one elbow against Torpille's withers and watched the western sky. Wilson stood silently by him, sipping coffee and puffing nervously at a cigar.

The morning wore on. No word came down from Pelham. De Mérac and Wilson, forcing calm on themselves, strolled among the sprawling companies. In front of H, George Force stood with his carefully combed hair exposed to the sun. "Damn it, John, are we just going to sit here?"

De Mérac muttered, "*Diantre!* Does Pelham forget us?"

"No chance," said Wilson grimly. "He just wants—" He

swung around abruptly, staring at a cabin that, with a belt of trees, masked the eastern approaches to the camp. De Mérac took two steps forward. George barked, "What the devil's that?"

The hidden road beyond the cabin and the trees was suddenly thick with the roar of hoofs. Then out onto the open road poured a wave of blue riders. In the van, a white horse carried lightly a tall figure whose red-lined cape billowed back over a jacket thick with gold braid. De Mérac tried to shout but his voice choked in his throat. The cavalcade swung onto the field and the leader flung up one hand to halt it, the wind ruffling an empty sleeve and the sun glowing on the wild gaiety of a hawklike face.

De Mérac stammered, "General Kearny!"

Kearny dropped nimbly from the saddle. "Hello, de Mérac. Hello, Wilson. Got you at last. The whole lot of you. Where's Pelham?"

De Mérac trembled in quick excitement as he stared at the eyes that burned with a fierce joy. He bit back a question and answered, "General Pelham is down the road, sir."

Kearny wheeled on his staff. "De Peyster. Down the road and tell Pelham to be ready to move at once." He faced de Mérac, mustache and imperial bristling. "Yes, I've got you for my division." He slipped out a map. De Mérac and Wilson caught opposite corners. "Look—here you are now, just west of St. Mary's Church. About five miles north and northwest, Jackson and D. H. Hill are trying to smash us at White Oak Bridge. That's what the guns are about. Farther west, Longstreet and A. P. Hill and Huger are bearing down toward these crossroads— Charles City Road, Long Bridge, and Quaker. I'm about due west of the crossroads—see—beyond the place marked Glendale and Frayser's Farm. About five miles from here. On the left, I join McCall by Long Bridge Road and Slocum on the right by the Charles City. Here are my brigades—Robinson, left, Birney, right, with Berry echeloned on him." He stabbed at the crackling paper. "When I send for you, you're going in on Robinson's left, joining with George Meade's brigade of

McCall's. Your center'll be where the Danforth house is marked."

"What'll our job be, sir?" asked Wilson quietly.

Kearny's chin jutted. "Look at Quaker Road and the little ones back of it. They're stiff with transport moving south. It's Lee's last chance to break through and he'll go at it bald-headed." He thumped his saddle. "You'll hold. You crash in and hold so long as you've got one man able to stand on his feet. Just keep that one thing in mind! Hold! Hold! Hold! If as much as *one company* breaks through to the rear, we're wrecked! You'll have Armistead and Wright and Mahone, you'll have Pryor and Featherston and Ransome roaring down at you." He threw back his head exultantly. "All of them, roaring down hell-for-leather!"

De Mérac bent closer to the map. "I see. We shall not be idle, I gather."

Kearny's fist shot into the air. "Idle? Oh, you'll have fighting, *lovely* fighting." He folded his map deftly, shoved it into his saddlebags, and vaulted into the saddle. "That's all. Except this." He snatched off his kepi, shoved it toward de Mérac and Wilson, one finger tapping on a diamond of scarlet cloth stitched to the top. "That's the mark of your new division—the Third. The Rebs know it already, I can tell you. Got any red cloth you can cut up?"

"I doubt it," said Wilson.

Kearny gathered his reins. "Never mind. I'll do what I can." He stood in his stirrups staring at the Rifles, now drawn into neat lines by Corvisart's orders. "Ha! They look like Martimprey's *chasseurs à pied* waiting to go in at Solferino." He chuckled excitedly. "It won't be the first time that I take French troops into action. I'll say a word to them." The men began to yell, *"Ah! Le vieux kébir!"*

He cantered off toward the blue and yellow files, cape fluttering like a banner. De Mérac and Wilson ran over the slippery grass after him. He pulled his white horse back on its haunches, then swept off his kepi, reins hanging loose on the white neck. His voice cracked out like a bugle blast. "I shall take you into action. You have only one order—to *hold!* Hold where you are so long as you can catch a root in your teeth!" He held out his kepi. "My aides are going to pass out these red diamonds as far as they will go. Sew them on your kepis, pin them on, stick them on with thorns if you have to, but *get them on!* Then your own men and the Rebs will know you for Kearny's men."

He spurred his horse off in a wide tearing circle that brought him thundering past the right of the regiment. He swept his kepi higher and roared in French, *"Hauts, les coeurs, mes Zouaves! En avant!"* He pounded on down the line past DuBosc and Péguy and Hein, to whose men he shouted in German. His mount lengthened its gallop and Kearny caught the loose reins in his teeth. Close behind him two aides, plunging their hands into the saddlebags, threw out handfuls of red diamonds that fluttered down through the hot air. The men began to cheer wildly, surged forward out of ranks to pelt after that one arm that swung wide the kepi with its red patch. Kearny roared again. "Gaily! Go in gaily, boys!" Then he was gone, his escort racing after him.

Wilson blew out his cheeks in a long whistle. "I feel as if we had something solid under our feet, John."

De Mérac smiled grimly. "No doubt we shall be shown many interesting things. Now we shall have inspection at once. We leave our packs here. The men will wear horseshoe rolls of one blanket only." He caught a questioning look in Wilson's eye. "We must march light if we follow him."

The sun had begun its slow drop down the sky. A cooler breeze drifted over the rough fields and the wooded patches through which the Rifles moved steadily toward the west. Far ahead of them, unseen muskets cracked flatly and cannon bayed, singly or in sullen packs. George Force marched near the head of his company through scrub wood where branches slapped viciously at him and briars snagged his ankles. Covertly he watched his men as they plodded on, their eyes staring from white faces and their shoulders hunched. Their eyes looked pale. He could see their free hands twitch and their jaws tense at sudden, close noises. Gray and Martin and Carey and Nicolls and Rafferty and Mladnick, eyes quick under their shiny vizors; Sergeant Parsons, horse-faced and solemn; stubby Corporal Chandler, his thick rump jolting his canteen with each step. Behind them came the rest of the company, the rear brought up by old Bates and Randol. The latter had promoted the elaborate fiction that he had been a butcher in civil life and kept saying loudly that he wished he was back of a good butcher's block, by God, right that minute. The men near him laughed mechanically. Bates's voice snarled up the column." Close up, you doughheads, close up."

George spun the cylinder of his heavy Colt, shoved it back into his holster, drew it again. It seemed to him that all he had learned since the first night at Chambers Street had gone from his mind, hung maddeningly just beyond the reach of his consciousness. His joints felt loose and awkward as though he were wading through shallow water, and the muscles of his cheeks twitched spasmodically. He shook himself nervously. Was this the way men went into action? How could men wave a sword or snatch up fallen colors, as they did in the battle pictures in *Leslie's* or *Harper's*, when their joints melted and their minds were numb? Ahead, the last files of LeNoir's company were thrashing through brambles, very close to him. He called, "Watch the distance, Sergeant Parsons. Don't crowd." He was surprised to find that his voice sounded quite steady, to find that pale-faced men broke into uncertain grins as their eyes met his.

Suddenly he was clear of the undergrowth, heading up a long, gentle slope that was bright with the bayonets of the other companies. Far ahead he could see de Mérac riding Torpille, the hilt of his French sword catching a ray of sun. Behind him trotted Dekdebrun and Castex. Beyond de Mérac the Zouaves, deployed as skirmishers, were bright among the trees of the crest. Up and down the column red patches showed here and there. George felt cool air rushing into his lungs. There was the regiment, there was its commander, and there were the bright patches that marked them all as Kearny's men. He no longer stumbled on, lost and helpless; he moved irresistibly. Things might be bad beyond the crossroads, but wait—just *wait* until the one-armed man threw the Rifles into action. He swelled with a cold rage against the gray swarms that were trying to wreck the Union.

There was a stir at the head of the column. Bright color flared out over the red-dotted kepis. The Union colors, the colors of France and of the State of New York, unfolded to the new breeze. He stretched his throat in a wild shout that was swallowed up in the deep-toned roar of the regiment. Up by Chanel's company Wilson turned in his saddle, waving his cap. In the distant fringe of woods the Zouaves turned, saw the colors, and hoisted their fezzes on bright bayonet points. George swung his fist. "Pick up that step, boys. Kearny wants us."

The firing was much closer now as George led his men down the reverse slope. The whole world was closing in. Right and left, heavy masses of fresh blue troops pressed on parallel to the Rifles. With a roar of wheels and a clank of traces a battery of horse artillery swept past, the drivers lashing their horses and the mounted cannoneers galloping behind the rocking pieces.

Another slope and he was closer yet, began to see things in strange disconnected flashes. A white farmhouse, the Frayser Farm of the map; Pelham standing under a tree with folded arms while Dalbiac waved his hat and shouted; aides about the house who bawled for General Sumner; blue heaps wet with purplish stains lying beyond a shed where a yellow hospital flag fluttered. A pulse beat in his temples, marking out the words, "They're dead. I'm looking at dead men. Our dead men."

Then he was crossing a road where traffic still rolled. It must be the vital Quaker Road that de Mérac had shown him on the map. In a ditch sprawled hundreds of infantrymen in wide straw hats. To panted questions they said they were the 16th New York. They were utterly spent and cursed a place they called Gaines's Mill.

There was quick motion up by the head of the

column, a blur of white, a toss of red, and he heard men yelling fiercely as Kearny reined in by de Mérac. Kearny waved his arm and de Mérac drew the curved Austerlitz saber. Then the general was racing down the column, hand high and reins in his teeth. Up ahead Castex's bugle blasted out, was picked up along the companies— "Left front into line! Double time!"

George obliqued his men to the left, saw LeNoir slant out ahead of him, knew that Bolton and LeVau, behind, were conforming. He yelled, "Guide is *right!* Watch it!" Then Kearny, reins loose on his horse's neck, thundered by the spreading front. He leaned from his saddle. "Hold! Get to the Danforth house and hold! The line's broken! Hold! Hold!" George ran on with the memory of hot, fierce eyes blazing down at him.

The ground rose again and the fearful din ahead rose with it. He vaulted a stone wall, his men after him, and saw the other companies clearing the same wall or driving ahead through an orchard. Hot noises keened through the air and the trees echoed to the rap-rap of spent bullets. A new sound arose, thin and knifelike, a sound that sent cold down his back. It came from somewhere out of sight, a high, human yipping: "Yi-yi-yi-yi!" Rebs! The shock struck him like a clenched fist.

The keening noises were thicker, closer. Just behind George there was a dull smack and Dale went down in a clatter, clutching his throat. George yelled, "Don't stop! Close up!" There were more clattering falls. Then he saw the house off to the right, a pillared flat-chested house with a sweeping drive. He was butting through a rose garden where a few broad-hatted shapes sprawled among light trellises. His men began to bunch and he saw that they were mechanically keeping to the paths. He drove them on across the yielding beds as LeNoir's company floundered through a shallow pool dotted with water lilies.

There was a latticed summerhouse in front of him and he ducked around it, then stopped short, arms waving as though glare ice were under his feet. Ahead was a stretch of lawn, a low, white wall not three feet high, and beyond it, sweeping forward in a yelling wave, thick lines of gray men.

George looked wildly right and left. LeNoir on one side had thrown his men into a shallow sunken lane that ran out from the wall. On the other, Bolton's company was taking cover in a rocky stretch where the garden ended. Suddenly George knew, and knew by cold instinct alone, that if the gray tide reached the wall before he did, the whole line would break. It was like a small, insignificant stone against which a wrestler might brace his foot just enough to avert disaster—a stone insignificant, barely heeded, yet vital.

He heard a yell from the other side of the lawn. "Sixth Virginia! Fo'ward!" and a high-pitched scream, "It's them God-damn redtops again!" His heavy Colt slammed and jumped in his hand as he ran on, the company roaring behind him. Twenty yards from the wall— ten. A tall man, sun shining on long, auburn hair, burst out of the gray welter and sprang to the wall, turned and waved a long sword. "Fo'm on me!" It seemed to George that the whole yelling line surged up with him.

He fired his last round, dropped the Colt, and dove headlong at the Rebel officer. He felt his shoulder crash into the gray thighs and the wide ringing garden whirled about him. He fell on the other side of the wall, trying to pin the thrashing legs, rolled over and over. Something heavy and blunt jarred against his head. He felt grass jammed against his mouth; then a stretch of hot sky above him as he rolled again, a bit of sky across which a blue and yellow figure sailed shouting. Face down again he had a glimpse of broken boots, torn gray trousers, sky-blue trousers piped with yellow. He slackened one arm, tried to swing his fist upward. His wrist was caught in a gnawing grip and a hand fumbled about his eyes. He yelled inarticulately through a blinding flash that sent stinging powder smoke into his nostrils. The gray legs went limp under him and he levered himself to his feet dizzily.

The lawn was covered with gray figures that fell back sullenly. Two or three sagged across the wall, more sprawled on the grass beyond. At George's feet the gray officer lay, his hands clenched above his head and his teeth set in a reddish beard. Dark drops trickled slowly from a neat hole under the right ear. First Sergeant Bates, at George's elbow, was calmly reloading. George turned on him. "What the hell did you shoot him for?"

Bates continued his loading unruffled. "It was him or you. Can't use him. Can use you. The loot'nant want to form along this wall?"

George rubbed his fist across his forehead, panting, as he stared at the ground. There were blue and yellow bodies among the gray—Hildreth and Church and Brown. Big Sharpe lay face up across a gray body, his dirty hands still clutching a crumpled rose. Beyond him—

Bates repeated his question, George focused his attention on stowing his Colt, still dangling from its lanyard, into his holster. He drove out the words, "Yes. Have 'em take cover. You're in charge of the left. Oh, Randol! Take the right, will you? Pull in any wounded and detail three men to look after 'em." Sweat still dripped from his forehead and stung his eyes but his voice gained assurance. The company huddled close to the wall. At the far right, Randol knelt, elbow across knee, and his revolver spinning carelessly by the trigger guard. He was calmly talking to his men, all clowning gone. At the left, Bates sent a steady stream of sarcasm around a bulging wad of tobacco. The men themselves were white but their eyes were bright and steady, their voices rather high and shaky. They had been in action. They hadn't broken or run. The two thoughts intoxicated them. George watched the last gray backs filing away down a gully far beyond the end of the garden. He knelt behind the center of the wall and tried to shut out the sprawl of the blue and yellow bodies, the sounds that came from behind him. "Jesus, Yank, mah guts is spilling." ... "God Almighty, don't touch my head." Then a high, thin sound that might have been hysterical laughter. George set his jaw and called, "All right, boys. You've seen your own dead. You know what to do if the bastards come back."

The rear façade of the Danforth house bulged out in a shallow portico that faced west. De Mérac stepped out onto the uneven brick floor and studied the terrain in front of him through his glasses. He could make out little. The house stood on a slight rise that dipped to a hidden run, but a half mile away higher ground, thickly wooded, commanded it. A few clearings showed here and there but they were empty. Nonetheless he was sure that the dense masses of leaves hid uncounted gray troops, masked sunken roads, gullies, and draws through which men and horses were undoubtedly working. In the unnatural hush he thought he heard the faint clink of metal and the rumble of wheels that might indicate batteries changing position.

The whole line of battle seemed irregular. On a bald hill that he thought to be deep in the enemy lines, his glasses picked up the flutter of Union colors, the blue of waiting infantry.

He surveyed his own position. On the far right the Zouaves, their flank covered by a marsh, were in broken country and well sheltered by a sunken road. From them the line trailed on toward him. DuBosc in fair territory, linking up with Péguy along a high wall, then Shea's Irish and Hein's German across the slope in front of the house, more exposed but with a better field of fire. Chanel joined Hein, and extended the line on through the south garden to LeNoir and George Force. Beyond, George Bolton and LeVau lay in wild tangle, high and rocky, at the foot of which the run curved sharply away to the west.

He shut his glasses and stepped back into the house. The position was tenable, so long as the order to hold remained. Liaison between the companies might be difficult in case of advance or withdrawal. He wondered how the regiment would stand in the event of a heavy attack. He discounted the mad, broken rush they had met and repulsed. That seemed to him to consist of a weak force, stumbling forward at a venture, encouraged by a break farther to the left.

In the ground-floor rooms that faced west, a detail of Shea's Irish were piling furniture against the windows, stacking a hideously carved sofa here and armchairs there. The house at least served as a rallying point in case of disaster. Rapp marched up with a suggestion that the upper windows be garnished with infantry. "For, *mon capitaine*, from there one might shoot the Arabs down like rabbits."

De Mérac vetoed the suggestion, The walls of the house were too thin and two or three cannon shot could wreck the upper story. Besides, he was worried about the length of his line and feared to weaken it by such a withdrawal. He peered out over the top of a shiny sideboard jammed against a window. There was still no life outside save for the immobile blue and yellow lines that marked his own front. The hush seemed to have settled deeper over the whole terrain from far right to far left. Only from the rear came a low, broken rumble as transport rolled south to the James.

The front door banged and Wilson, his face drawn, came down the shallow hall stepping lightly as ever. He said quickly, "John, I'm worried about my position. The 11th Penn's much farther to the left than we thought and I've had to stretch Bolton and LeVau so their men are as much as ten to fifteen feet apart. As it is, we're barely within shouting distance of the 11th."

De Mérac lit a cigarette. "The devil! That could be awkward."

"It won't be if you'll O.K. my pulling Chanel and LeNoir and George out of that garden and putting them to the left of LeVau."

"But then you leave a gap," objected de Mérac.

"No. We can still cover the garden from the left and Corvisart says Shea can look after the right. Besides, Gower's just brought two guns up right back of the gap."

De Mérac looked out the window again. Then he nodded. *"Bien!* That garden could really be a trap for our gray friends. And the rest of your position?"

"There's a movement to the right and left but I can't see a soul in front of me. Looks as if one angle of the Reb line just doesn't meet. I'd like to patrol that funnel but I'm afraid I'd get massacred from the flanks."

De Mérac lowered his glasses. "You would. On no account cross that stream that cuts your front. Our orders are to hold only. Corvisart's in a good position and links closely with Bachia's 87th New York."

Wilson dropped his voice. "No chance of our attacking?"

"Not unless Lee is withdrawing. This hush—I do not understand it."

As he spoke the walls of the house shivered to a roar and the western lands were masked in curling, flame-stabbed smoke. A curving clangor of sound spread over the world. Wilson said grimly, "There's your withdrawal. I better get back." He sprinted from the house.

De Mérac returned to the window. The guns on his immediate front had fallen silent after the first salvo but right and left the frenzy swelled. At de Mérac's feet sat Castex, his little round face white and his eyes staring. Dekdebrun, jaw muscles working, leaned at another window, his rifle ready. Rapp stood in the open doorway, hands behind his back and red beard turned defiantly to the uproar. Other men drifted into the house—a hard-eyed lieutenant of Maryland artillery; an Ohio cavalry captain with bandaged head; four of Berdan's Sharpshooters in green who nosed from window to window, growled, "Not a goddam target!" and slipped off to the north lawn.

The terrain in front erupted without warning. A wild scream high in air was followed by a splintering of boards and glass, a trembling of the walls as a solid-shot crashed into the second story. Plaster sifted down into the room. Rapp pulled on his pipe and remarked, *"Poum! Poum! Ah, ça tombe!"* The house shivered, echoed to crash after crash. De Mérac called, "Take cover, you others. Behind the mattresses!"

Lumps of plaster pattered down. Out on the lawn Shea and Hein knelt behind their prostrate lines. Then four clouds formed in the air, shattered in ruddy flame that sent hot metal spatting down. Four more clouds. De Mérac pushed closer to the upturned sofa and pulled his kepi down tighter in unconscious search for protection. The men on the lawn began to look back longingly at the white walls that must have seemed secure shelter to them.

De Mérac could stand the yearning faces no longer. He shoved away from the sofa with an effort, gripped the hilt of his sword, and went out through a side door.

The sky above him ripped and crashed. He threw himself to the ground, worked along until he found shelter behind a low bank, a mere wrinkle, just behind Péguy. Solid-shot thudded into the ground in a whirl of clods, skidded, bounced, crashed into the house, against trees, or vanished into the unseen rear. Above, shrapnel hissed down. De Mérac raised his head when he dared. The volume of fire was less and seemed to come from a single four-gun battery whose position he could not locate.

He heard voices close by and realized that he was not alone. Castex, without orders, had followed him and hugged the ground a few feet to the left. At the right, one of the sharpshooters said in a quick, tense voice, "See him!" Beside him, Dekdebrun peered intently ahead.

De Mérac edged nearer. "You see the battery?"

The sharpshooter grunted. "Stands out like Ascutney on a clear day."

De Mérac handed over his glasses. "Take these."

The man grunted. "Hell, them's no good. Use 'em yourself if your eyes is ailing. See that naked tree? Two fingers right of it there's a mowing. Folly that down."

De Mérac's lenses moved. The man's eyes must have been phenomenal, for he could see nothing save the clearing and the green below it. Then metal glinted and his glasses framed a slash of fresh earth, two gray kepis, and a black muzzle. He groaned. The gun was hidden from Gower's battery and was a good eight hundred yards away. He said, "In safety they may knock us over like ninepins."

"Think so?" said the sharpshooter calmly. He sighted along his rifle. Dekdebrun watched closely. The rifle cracked. De Mérac saw a spurt of earth close by the muzzle of the gun. Eight hundred yards! A lucky shot.

The green man fired again and again dirt jumped, a third shot and another spurt of brown.

It seemed to de Mérac that the gun was emplaced in a hollow so that the muzzle rested nearly on the lip. The crew would be well sheltered. He said, "You make them uncomfortable at least."

"Think so?" said the sharpshooter. He muttered to Dekdebrun, "Gray feller by the left wheel. Chase him the hell away."

Dekdebrun fired, snarled, "Missed him."

"Think so?"

"By a foot."

"Quit shooting and wait."

De Mérac got his glasses on the gun. Shirt-sleeved arms ran it back, a rammer-staff whirled, the muzzle jutted back into place. "Watch," said the green man.

Smoke and flame gushed from the muzzle in slow, sick spurts, settled over the position. When it cleared, shattered spokes showed a twisted mass of metal. De Mérac stared in amazement. "What did you do?" he asked.

"Kept flipping dirt down the bore of that gun. When I'd flipped enough the durned thing just blew up." He levered himself to his knees. "You can lie easy awhile. The boys from the other guns'll come to pull out the arms and legs. Always happens like that." He slung his rifle across his back. "No more targets here. Guess I'll go down the line. Good-bye, both."

De Mérac got up shakily, ready to dive for cover. Down the lawn, Péguy had shifted his men to the shelter of a ditch. Hein and Shea, farther advanced, seemed to have missed the bulk of the shelling. A few blue and yellow shapes lay scattered on the grass and a coatless figure moved among them. The figure came nearer and de Mérac saw that it was Dr. Wayne, whose bare arms were smeared with blood to the shoulder. "*Ça!*" thought de Mérac. "He will do, that *toubib*."

A voice hailed from the rear and he turned to see Greenbaum, the adjutant, who had been left behind to wait for Brady and the wagons. The Jew's heavy features were pale but expressionless. "Brady got there all right. I told him to load the men's packs onto the wagons and wait."

De Mérac raised his eyebrows. In all correctness, Greenbaum could have stayed behind with Brady. Instead he had puzzled his way overland until he found his regiment. The trip had not been an easy one, to judge from the stains and smears on the uniform. De Mérac said, "Good."

Greenbaum pushed back his kepi. "Got anything for me to do here?"

De Mérac thought of sending further word back to Brady, but something in Greenbaum's manner made him change his mind. "Go to the left and see what you can do for Wilson."

Greenbaum nodded in satisfaction, turned back the flap of his holster, and set off at a brisk run. A horse whinnied and de Mérac saw Torpille's sleek head tossing in the lee of a high bank. The mare had emerged so far unscathed! He felt a glow of pleasure. She had brought him through the worst country, swift and sure-footed. In the mad race for the high ground about the Danforth house, she had been steady through the snarl of flying lead, the crash of explosions, and the roar of voices. She could take her place in the family annals along with Great-uncle Raoul's Voltigeur, who had flown up the face of the great Russian redoubt at Borodino in '12.

He called to Castex and Dekdebrun and started out to find Corvisart. He would inspect the right of the line and then cross over to see Wilson's dispositions for himself. The big Zouave greeted him calmly from his perch on a moss-covered rock. "We go on foot, then?" asked Corvisart.

"The ground is too broken for horses," answered de Mérac.

"*Soit*," said Corvisart, and the four set out. At the far end of the Zouave line, well masked by boulders and gullies, the wiry Basque Bordagaray pointed to a strong picket some fifty yards away. "Bachia's 87th. From this point we run on thus." De Mérac and Corvisart stepped along with the Basque, examining the approaches to the position, noting how well groups of skirmishers had been posted in advance of the main line. Faces turned to look at de Mérac—Sergeant Gerlasch, Corporal Pétion, little des Moulins. He smiled at them, asked "*Ça va?*"

The whole line froze as a fresh battery opened on the right front. It was firing solid-shot which crashed through undergrowth and splashed in swampy patches. De Mérac found it easier to keep on his course with all those eyes turned toward him. He said to sallow Corporal Dendrecourt, "It is no use to duck, *mon ami*. More, it is just what the Rebels want."

Private Sordet, next to the corporal, growled, "Lead us against the *costauds*, and none will duck, *mon capitaine*."

"Ah," muttered Bordagaray. "That is what they do not understand, my little devils. To lie here and do nothing, ah, *c'est embêtant!*"

"Orders," said de Mérac. He tried to keep his shoulders straight and his step even as shrapnel ripped over the scrub trees. It was not very close, but bits of metal gouged the soggy ground about his feet, and branches rattled down.

He left Bordagaray where a brook snuffled its way down to the run and found himself among DuBosc's men. The wizened little Scoarnec, whom he remembered from Chambers Street, winked up at him from a secure shelter between two rocks. Private Freycinet growled to his neighbor that it warmed the heart like *la gnolle* to see the *gros légumes* show their teeth to solid-shot like that which had just ricocheted over his head. Captain DuBosc's brown beard was full of twigs from diving to the ground, but he was nervously alert as a fox terrier. "Twenty yards ahead is Lieutenant Pasquié with a platoon, and Sergeant Rogniat beyond him—"

Two shots echoed from the edge of the run where Rogniat was posted. De Mérac snapped, "*Allons-y!*" and ran through the scrub, jumping old logs and slithering down slopes. Dekdebrun and Castex raced after him, Corvisart bringing up the rear. There were shouts, splashes, but no more shots. De Mérac burst through a group of men close by the edge of the run, had a glimpse of an old plank door banging against the rocks of the shore, a sodden mass of blue and yellow clinging to it. Someone held out the butt of a musket, the man on the extemporized raft caught it and swung himself to the bank in a spatter of spray.

"*Vingt dieux!*" cried de Mérac. The man was Greenbaum, sopping wet and with blood dripping from his left hand and his forehead. He shot water from his eyes, panted, "Where's de Mérac?"

De Mérac caught a drenched sleeve. "Here! What is it?"

The Jew stumbled forward, gave a gasp of relief. "Get over there quick! To Wilson!"

"Did he send you?"

"No. But get there. Dalbiac! He'll murder Force and Bolton and LeVau."

"What's that?" de Mérac's voice shot up. "How did you get here?"

"Rode the current down the front on the old door. It was quicker. Rebs nearly got me where the big bend is. Never mind that. Get there or you'll never see those companies again. Dalbiac is going to send them out—"

De Mérac felt cold horror as he remembered the funnel-like hollow that led so invitingly into the Southern lines. "They're across the run?"

"For God's sake *get* there. Maybe you can do something."

De Mérac whirled on his heel without a word, set out with a long, loping stride. Over his shoulder he called, "Corvisart. I go to Wilson." Then he put his head down and ran harder.

He was panting when he had cleared the rough country and his breath sobbed in his lungs. He raced across the garden, past the corner of the house. He cupped his hands about his mouth and roared, "DuChesne!" The old Chasseur ran up, the mare tossing her head eagerly. De Mérac vaulted into the saddle, shouted, "Stay with the other mounts!" and touched Torpille with his spurs.

The mare lengthened her stride at once, slipped over a low wall, and plunged into the rough country south of the garden. De Mérac gave the course entirely over to her with a grim and utter faith in her sure-footedness and intelligence. His mind formed and reformed hideous pictures of the three companies driven out into exposed country. He must get there in time to halt them. Greenbaum! He had seen the danger and come the quickest route on his own initiative. The danger! George's company would lead! No! It wasn't George—it was three companies that he himself commanded. Torpille skimmed over a tangle of broken rocks. On the right, Chanel called from his position, was left behind. LeNoir yelled from a shattered stump. De Mérac's eyes never turned until he saw, in a grassy clearing, two mounted officers. Wilson, white with fury, was storming at Colonel Dalbiac, who stood in his stirrups, heedless of him, and waved his hat as he shouted down the gentle slope. De Mérac pulled Torpille back on her haunches. "Craig! Greenbaum said—"

Wilson's jaws worked but no words came. He could only point downwards toward the run. De Mérac leaned from his saddle. Beyond the far bank, heading for the cul-de-sac, three blue and yellow companies marched resolutely. The first was thrown out in skirmish order and beyond the most advanced bayonet walked a tall officer, bareheaded.

From head to foot de Mérac froze. He said in a strangled voice, "Did you order that, Colonel Dalbiac?"

Dalbiac swung his hat and the wind stirred the folds of a woman's bright scarf, red and white, knotted through a saddle ring. "Sure I did. Get 'em right there back of the Reb batteries. Not a soul around. Oh, we'll murder them! Wait till I tell Pelham!" He rose in his stirrups and bawled, "Smash 'em, boys, smash 'em."

De Mérac shot a glance at the little column. There was no fire from the immediate right and left, although farther on each side there seemed to be heavy action. For the moment, the Confederates were holding their fire—waiting. He wet his lips. Then he cleared the hilt of the Austerlitz saber, loosened his Colt. "Craig—you command the regiment until I return!"

He sent Torpille shooting down the grade toward the run. Far across, George's skirmishers had reached the higher ground and were moving on cautiously. The other companies followed. De Mérac clenched his reins. "If I can get there in time!" Torpille shied and he looked down at the swift waters of the run. Then the mare swung without guidance, pelted along the bank, squattered through a rocky ford where the water splashed on de Mérac's boots. With a bound she was on the far bank, gathering herself for her full, flowing stride. De Mérac stood in his stirrups and shouted, "George! LeVau! Bolton! Halt!" To his surprise, a clear bugle blast rang behind him. He turned in his saddle. Twenty yards in the rear, little Castex galloped, his bugle to his lips. Beside him rode Dekdebrun, rifle across his forearm. De Mérac waved to Castex, who blasted again.

It was too late. George's men were already out of sight in the funnel-like hollow, and the other two companies were slipping into it. Deep in the hidden funnel, a rippling volley rang out and smoke sifted up lazily.

De Mérac lashed Torpille with his kepi, then drew his Colt. The funnel opened before him. It was hideous with pitching bodies and hot lead that sang and stung from the slopes. Right, center, and lapping toward the left there was gray infantry moving among the trees, forming to fire down into the hollow. De Mérac roared: "Halt! Form on Bolton!" but his words were drowned out. Through smoke he caught a glimpse of George edging left to the higher ground, the skirmishers after him. De Mérac shot by the huge Bolton, whose eyes were like glittering pin points. "To the high ground. Quickly," shouted de Mérac, and swept on to LeVau. "To the left! Out of the hollow!"

The gray infantry was moving closer. LeVau's company began to fray out at the sides, wavered. Men broke in quick panic, threw down their muskets and blanket rolls as though they found safety in disassociating themselves with the war. De Mérac rode among the fugitives, striking down with the flat of his saber. Knots of men staggered about blindly, faced to the front, to the rear, while the fire from the slopes struck them down in writhing heaps. Behind, Bolton was roaring at his men, herding them up the empty left slope where George's men were opening fire on the gray lines.

Suddenly there were yipping men all about de Mérac, swarming down from the right, from the front. Someone bawled, "Surrender, Yank! We got yuh!" De Mérac swung Torpille to meet an onrush headed by a yelling sergeant. He fired once, twice, and the rush melted, swung past him. He drove Torpille back toward Bolton, saw most of his company working up the left slope, facing about. The wreck of LeVau's men followed shakily. De Mérac shouted, "Form on the crest!" and raged among the last stragglers, herding them upward. A yelling man lunged at him with a bayonet and de Mérac squeezed the Colt. The hammer clicked on an empty chamber. Two quick shots smacked by his shoulder. The man went down, another just behind crumpled. He wrenched Torpille around as he crammed his empty Colt into the holster. As he drew his saber again he wondered vaguely when he had fired the other three shots.

Another shot by his shoulder and he realized that Dekdebrun was coldly and methodically covering him. A ripping volley came from the left and two gray men close by pitched to the ground. He gathered Torpille and rode up the slope toward the remnants of the three companies, now firing steadily from fair cover. The ranks opened to let him through and he dropped from the saddle, panting. Force, Bolton, and LeVau ran up. De Mérac held up his hand. "We must get out of here. There is only one way and that is by keeping together. Bolton, you will lead. Then LeVau. George, you will act as rear guard. You comprehend? *Nothing* must pass you."

George, his face powder-blackened, said shortly, "All right. Just want to tell you they're bringing up more men. In our rear and across the hollow."

Scattering shots cracked from the rear, sang viciously among the trees. "Now!" snapped de Mérac. He nodded to Castex, who raised his bugle in a shaky hand. The notes blasted out resolutely. De Mérac remounted as the companies formed and started to move along the shoulder where their position had been. De Mérac paced Torpille behind George's company, his eyes darting right and left to the gray lines that were massing across the hollow, to those that were crashing on through the woods on his right flank. A bugle shrilled out of sight and the enemy spilled down into the hollow.

De Mérac lost count of time and track of events as the gray masses drove and drove at the rear of the column. Now he was driving Torpille through the attacking ranks, sabering right and left while Dekdebrun's repeating rifle cracked steadily by him. Again, he was trapped in a wedge of LeVau's men who huddled back to back against Torpille, their bayonets stabbing outward. A man by the mare's shoulder fell and his bayonet jabbed her. She neighed with fright and broke clear in a tremendous lunge. De Mérac steadied her in time to see a mounted officer in immaculate gray, plumed hat flapping, swing toward him yelling, "Surrender!" His sword waved in awkward circles. De Mérac wheeled Torpille about, parried a clumsy slash, and made a quick riposte. He felt the saber bite, dropped the hilt as he galloped on. There was a tug and the hilt swung back into his hand at the end of the saber knot.

His charge had carried him far too deep. He turned and zigzagged back toward the mouth of the funnel, parrying bayonet thrusts as Torpille swerved and twisted like a rabbit. Through the gathering gloom he saw the flashes of his own muskets where George was making a stand. He roared, "Don't wait for me," and spurred Torpille. She answered with a great burst of speed that suddenly turned into a stumbling run. He gathered the reins, thinking that she must have stumbled on a body. Then he sailed through the air to land with a stunning crash that filled his eyes with red and green flashes. The fall threw him clear and dimly he saw Torpille stretched on the ground, forelegs thrashing and hindquarters dragging limp. He staggered to his feet and she writhed toward him, then collapsed, lifeless. He shouted "Torpille!" and started toward her. Two riders closed in on either side of him, Castex and Dekdebrun reaching down hands to him. He caught the two wrists and ran on.

Another horseman loomed through the smoke, heading

toward him. Dizzy with shock and surprise he loosed his hold and shouted, "Colonel! Colonel Dalbiac! Turn back!"

But Dalbiac thundered on, his Colt blazing wildly. De Mérac shouted again, but the colonel spurred past him. There was a flat, smacking sound. Dalbiac reeled in his saddle, his face a red mask, then pitched backwards to the ground, one foot caught in a stirrup. Farther on, gray men broke their loose ranks. The colonel's bay was lost to sight among them and de Mérac could no longer see that ghastly limp body that dragged and thumped along behind it.

Then de Mérac was among the panting ranks of George's men, trying to bring order into the three companies as they moved out into the flats. The bulk of LeVau's command, together with its captain, seemed to have vanished, and Bolton's men looked pitifully few. He sent a few squads to join George and H Company while he himself, on Dekdebrun's horse, ranged up and down, directing the fire as best he could.

Without warning, pressure on the companies slackened, died away. De Mérac watched the remnant of the command splash over the ford. The men were dim, bobbing shapes in the dusk and he peered at each sagging head half fearfully, half hopefully. Then he saw George, last of the detachment, slither down the bank and splash through the shallow water. He shouted in relief and started up the slope to Wilson and the rest of the left companies.

In the shadowy land above, men began to cheer in great, raw bursts. Wilson rode down the grade and caught de Mérac's shoulders. "Never thought I'd see you again. Look, John, I didn't dare send help. I'd have left a hole in the line."

"And you were right. I'm going back to the center. Keep in touch."

Wilson asked in a low voice, "Dalbiac? He tried to follow you."

"He stayed," said de Mérac dryly as he rode off toward the Danforth house. He was not pleased with himself. A *de facto* regimental commander, he knew, had no right to play knight-errant to three companies. God knew what might have happened in his absence.

Beyond Péguy's men he reined in as Pelham's voice sounded from a half-seen group of horsemen. The brigadier spoke as though the words were dragged from his throat. "You did well to bring your men off, Captain. I thought at first you'd all be casualties."

"The companies brought themselves off, sir."

"I repeat that your handling was good." Then the old, icy tones returned. "Since Wilson still insists that you act in command of the Rifles, you are responsible for them. You will report to me in writing precisely why you attempted an offensive movement without orders. You will further explain why you threw in your American companies while shielding your immigrants. That is all." He was gone in a slow thud of hoofs.

De Mérac shrugged as he gave the borrowed horse back to Dekdebrun and mounted his own spare, Cigale. It would be easy to reply to Pelham, since Dalbiac had given the order and since LeVau's company had suffered more than H and G. He kept on along the lines and found that there had been little change since his departure.

Suddenly men began to stir about him. Someone shouted: *"Ohé! C'est le vieux kébir!"*

De Mérac saw the shimmer of a big white horse, heard the shout taken up louder. He called, *"Nous voici, mon général!"*

Kearny whirled up to him and his tones were quick and tense. "It's going to break right here. Any time. Birney got me some prisoners and they talked a lot. I don't want to know what sort of shape you're in. It doesn't matter. You've got to hold, hold, hold. How close are the Reb skirmishers?"

Bordagaray spoke from a near-by rock. "In the dark, one does not see them."

Kearny peered down into the dusk-cloaked valley. Then he threw back his head and laughed. "Dark, is it? I'll show you where they are." He wheeled his horse about, skirted the right of the Zouaves, and shot along their front at a thudding gallop. De Mérac caught his breath. Near him, Corvisart swore softly. For a while they could only follow the blur of the white mare. Then they lost it. But the old *kébir's* passage was marked by a swelling ripple of musketry that ran quickly from right to left. De Mérac's mouth was dry as the firing died away. Corvisart muttered. "*Mon dieu*, it is over."

"It can't be," de Mérac insisted. Then he was waving his kepi and shouting with hundreds of others. White glimmered off to the left and Kearny swept down on de Mérac, exultant. "There are some targets for you, boys. Blaze away where you saw the flashes. Keep the lines ready, de Mérac. It's coming very soon."

"When?" asked Corvisart. A single gun thudded off to the west.

Kearny swept up his hand. "Now!" he shouted. His laugh rang out. "Oh, we're going to have the devil's own fun, all along the line!" He waved, spurred his horse, and was gone.

In the tense hush that followed the repulse of the last attack, Pelham's voice echoed sharply. "Tell General Kearny, Major," he said, "that I don't have to watch the Rifles. He'll find me with Clay's command. It needs gingering."

De Mérac shrugged at the chance-heard words. Pelham had sat his horse rigidly by the colors all through the blast of the last onslaught. He had made no suggestions, offered no criticism. Nor had he expressed to any of the regiment the slightest approbation as he rode away.

Things had not gone too badly, de Mérac thought, as he leaned on the sword whose blade was oddly dulled. The first lunge against his center and right had been shattered. But over that wrecked attack, other gray men had poured yelling. Twice the center had bulged back to the portico, lapped around the sides of the house. But each time it had sprung back, once through a baretoothed slamming charge of Shea's Irish and once by a stinging flank movement by Bordagaray and the Zouaves. By de Mérac's side, little Castex had crouched, terror-stricken yet always ready to sound a needed call.

Dekdebrun had fired until his rifle became too hot to hold and he had had to go on with a musket. He himself had vague memories of his Colt jarring in his hand, of vicious backhanded cuts with his saber. Once he had fenced with a lithe, dark man who used his blade admirably and who cursed him in Italian as the Austerlitz steel finally bit home. A mounted man had ridden down on him, sword raised. Rapp had glided out, caught the bridle, and thrown the man from the saddle with an old African trick, stunning him.

Another attack was sure to come and de Mérac sent to Wilson and Corvisart for reports on their strength. Then a blackened Zouave ran up, reporting that the enemy had pulled far back on the right. A message from Wilson reported the same on the left. On the heels of this news came an order from Pelham. "Fall in at once on Quaker Road."

There was no time to collect wounded or round up stragglers. The Rifles, with the rest of Kearny's division, tramped wearily on through the night, heading south toward the James and Harrison's Landing, where they had disembarked only the night before.

George stumbled along with his men. He was stunned with the action of the past hours, stunned still further by the move that seemed to him a retreat. Vaguely he tried to reason matters out. Every Rebel attack had been hurled back. The enemy had finally pulled out of range. Damn it, his men weren't beaten! And yet—they had been marched off the ground that they had held.

Then fatigue threw a film over his consciousness. Dimly he saw the shimmer of canvas-topped wagons rolling in long lines through open fields, heard the crash of rails as cannoneers ripped down fences to clear a way for spent gun teams. There were innumerable halts from which he was routed by bugle calls to lurch on again, sometimes for a few scant yards before another maddening stop and fresh start.

Hours later the smell of the river was strong. A fresher sheen glowed in front and George looked through stiff eyelids on the James where low gunboats slipped upstream through false dawn, their smoke black against the sky. Right and left the country opened out, unreal and mist-spotted. To the right a long hill rose in shimmering mystery, probably the same Malvern Hill of which de Mérac had spoken earlier. The column reached the river road, swung left from the hill in whose hollows night lingered sullenly. In the opposite direction endless batteries of artillery moved. George stared at them without comprehension. He swayed as he walked, mechanically lifting one foot, planting it, dragging the other foot, planting it—

He was in a field and the regiment was breaking ranks, the men slumping to the ground. Rest at last. The turf swept up toward him.

De Mérac stood on the edge of the field where the Rifles lay. After two hours' sleep he had shaved and Louvel had brought him coffee and bacon. Now, a fresh mug in his hand, he watched the river road that led left down to Harrison's Landing and right past Malvern Hill and, some twenty miles upstream, to Richmond. Transport and artillery rumbled interminably by. There could be no doubt that McClellan had accomplished an amazing military feat. He had brought his whole army and its trains and herds straight across Lee's front and halted the entire mass intact and unpursued, by the James. More important, it was obvious that communication and staff work had been excellent. Now, a quick lunge upriver could conceivably wreck Lee once for all.

He sipped coffee and kept on staring at the scene before him, a scene such as he had never imagined. Telegraphers laid lines along the tree-fringed banks. Gunboats chugged over the glinting surface of the river. Light guns and heavy guns bumped and rumbled to Malvern Hill and, inland, he could see endless columns of infantry on the move.

Aides galloped past the field but no word came from Pelham. De Mérac turned on his heel as he looked at his watch. Nearly eight o'clock. He ordered DuChesne to saddle Cigale. Greenbaum called hoarsely from a small fire where he and Rapp compared notebooks, "Better get some sleep. You'll be busy enough later."

"Presently. Just now, I go to look for Kearny."

The Jew raised heavy-lidded eyes. "Expect to find him in that mess out there?"

De Mérac answered confidently. "If there is to be action, it will take place around Malvern Hill. That's where I shall find Kearny. Tell Major Wilson, when he wakes, that I shall not be long gone."

Hoofs plopped on the grass. Dekdebrun, astride a bony sorrel, was leading out Cigale. De Mérac said, "There was no need to wake you."

Dekdebrun answered briefly, "Your orders. Go where you go."

De Mérac rode out of the field, followed by Dekdebrun. The sun, striking on the river, threw cool watery patterns up among the trees under which cavalrymen slept in endless rows among tethered horses. In a field to the right, drivers and cannoneers raced about as a sergeant bellowed, "C Battery! Harness and hitch." In the woods beyond, a strong German voice shouted, "Pring up der shack-asses!" and a battery of pack artillery crashed ahead, the men swearing at the mules that carried the dismounted pieces and ammunition.

The road curved inland, was blocked on the first slopes by more halted artillery. De Mérac took to the fields and pushed on until he reached the crest, riding past the arched porch and English brick of the Malvern house. The plateau was crowded with troops through whom horsemen shuttled madly. He recognized Hooker, with his strong, handsome face. There were Birney, senior brigadier of Kearny's division, bearded and weary-eyed, owlish Heintzleman and striking Fitz-John Porter. Off to the left came a burst of cheering and McClellan swept over the hill toward the river. In his suite rode the Comte de Paris and the Duc de Chartres. The young Orléans princes were laughing and waving to the troops. Yes, de Mérac thought, something was going to happen. Every man on the plateau sensed it and was yelling for McClellan, yelling in spite of the memory of the thousands who had fallen before bullets and the thousands who had given up to the deadly fevers of the swamps in the wavering, uncertain maneuvers of the spring.

Beyond the Malvern house, de Mérac reined in, staring in wonder. North, east, and west the mile-wide summit fell away in a tangle of gullies and marshes that slashed through narrow farm lands. Below, dense woods alternated with small clearings through which a few feeble roads twisted. Running almost directly toward him was that same Quaker Road over which he had stumbled the night before. He could even make out a white, steepleless church on whose steps he had rested during a halt. A few more roofs showed in the flatlands, jutting up through trees or slanting to the sun in cultivated fields. South of the hill lay the curving James with the great bulge of Turkey Bend and the dark hulls of the Union gunboats.

He looked to the front again. The hill threw out heavy capes and promontories that framed the approaches in steep amphitheaters, pushed blunt noses ominously out toward swamp, field, and wood of the lowlands. And through all the upland fields, along rail fences, in orchards, among shocks of wheat, in the grounds and gardens of the two small houses just below the crest, lay tier on tier of batteries whose red-piped gunners moved expertly. The hard muzzles commanded every inch of slope, dominated the Quaker Road, the complex tangle of lesser routes that met in a deadly knot just beyond the western meadows. And when he had counted all the batteries he could see, his eye picked up more muzzles, more wheels, or the bright flick of artillery guidons. In the grassy lands between the batteries, along the edges of plowed fields, among the sheds of the two homesteads, thick blue lines of infantry lay, batteries above them, batteries below them. Far down the slope, below the most remote guns, green moved through the fields as Berdan's Sharpshooters wound forward. A bugle sang faintly and the green files melted out of sight in distant woods or took cover behind shocked wheat.

De Mérac blew out his cheeks in wonder at the stupendous massing of artillery. McClellan must have saved nearly every gun he started out with. The concentration of metal was staggering, its sting expert. He studied the tangle of wood, field, and marsh below, desperate country through which to maneuver. So far, it was empty of hostile life.

A scuffle of boots, the clink and rustle of equipment, flowed toward him from the rear. A blue column slogged along in the sun and the men's kepis bore faded red diamonds. De Mérac looked quickly around, hoping to catch sight of a big white horse. Across the plateau trotted bays, roans, sorrels, chestnuts, grays. Then out from behind the sheds of the Malvern house shot an elk-limbed bay, ridden by a tall man whose cape blew out in a flutter of red past an empty sleeve. De Mérac held up his kepi and Kearny swerved toward him, reining in deftly. The lines of his face were deeper than ever, but his chin was set and his eyes snapped eagerly. "I sent an aide to your camp. Forget about Pelham. You'll be under my personal orders for the rest of the day. Mine alone." A wave of keen relief swept over de Mérac as Kearny went on. "What do you think of this position?"

"I should not care to attack it," said de Mérac dryly.

Kearny smacked his hand against his saddle. "And Lee won't attack. He's too good a soldier. Oh, it's a damned shame, but he won't. We'll get no fighting. He'll come and look at us and then sheer off—and we'll just watch him."

"He could be annoyed from here."

Kearny snorted. "We could raise blue hell with him." His voice flattened. "We won't bother him. I've been watching this ever since we hit the Yorktown lines. I've fought so close up that I could look into the kitchen windows in Richmond. What did we do? Slumped off and fought clear across the Peninsula." He glanced at Dekdebrun, who dropped back out of earshot. "I tell you, de Mérac, this war ought to be over right now. But we've poked and we've footled and we've let the Rebs call the turn every time. Why? Because McClellan won't move until he's got everything the textbooks call for and that's something you never get in war. You've got to—here! What are you staring at?"

De Mérac was focusing his glasses on the Quaker Road. "That white church, sir, Willis Church on the maps." He heard Kearny flick out his own glasses. De Mérac's lenses settled on the road by the church. In the center a single blue cavalryman was halted, facing north. Slowly he turned broadside, paused, set off south down the road at a sharp trot. Other blue riders emerged from the woods, fell in behind him.

Kearny barked, "They're coming."

Off to the right more blue troopers swung south across open fields, and far behind them metal winked in the sun. In distant clearings, among clumps of trees, de Mérac made out a screen of gray cavalry working slowly south. After it came clouds of skirmishers on foot. Color broke out on the far reaches of the Quaker Road and the red battle flags of the Confederacy caught the sun.

Kearny said softly, "Ah—our boys have spotted it," and jerked his chin toward the flats. Berdan's green sharpshooters moved swiftly among the trees, probed forward through undergrowth. Nearer, gunners clustered about their pieces like competent, unhurried mechanics. Their short jackets were open and their vizors bent back from their foreheads as they tested handspikes or rewound prolonges.

Kearny stowed away his glasses. "Sir, it's my opinion, from all the crowd that's coming on, that Mr. Lee's going to drop cards on us after all. If he does—oh, then we'll give him some lovely fighting. Better get back to your command."

VIII

Kearny's Men

GEORGE Force had slept through most of the morning. Then he busied himself with Randol rearranging his company, which now numbered forty-seven men, including the survivors of LeVau's command. That done, he repaired his torn uniform as best he could, cleaned and loaded his Colt. There was something in the air, a tang of eager expectancy. He knew that all his men were sure that a quick, new move was in the wind, and he shared their feeling.

Later, he managed to sleep again. Twice he was awakened. Once it was by a rush of bawling newsboys who rode into camp with papers from New York and Wilmington and Richmond and Philadelphia and Newark and even Boston. He bought a *New York Times*, but fell asleep before he had opened it. Later, around two o'clock, he rolled to his knees, alert at once. The ground trembled and from the direction of Malvern Hill artillery thundered and stormed, sent up clouds of smoke that were whipped away by the steady, cool wind. The road past the camp was alive with hurrying regiments, with galloping aides, with reserve caissons, all streaming west toward Malvern. George rubbed his eyes. At the edge of the camp a sentry was leaning on his musket, watching the passing mass. Horses were picketed under a clump of elms. He could not see de Mérac, but close by Cigale, Louvel squatted cross-legged, mending a long rent in a gold-braided jacket. Wilson sat on a fence with Corvisart, smoking calmly. George dropped back onto his blanket and slept again, not realizing that two days before, the din and the movement would have brought him to his feet, staring and wide-awake.

For the third and last time he was roused by a full-throated chorus of bugles. He swept up his blanket and came onto his feet in one movement. DuChesne was leading out the single mounts and de Mérac was calling for Greenbaum and Rapp. All over the field men were rolling their blankets, slinging them like gray horseshoes from shoulder to hip, fumbling with haversacks and cartridge pouches. George rolled up his own blanket, shouting, "Call roll, First Sergeant. Randol, be sure the new men know what they're to do."

The field boiled on as though a hot electric current had shot through it. Bugles blasted "Forward!" and the regiment swung onto the road, turned west toward the bulk of Malvern. Gone was the dull apathy of the night before, gone were fatigue and fright and bewilderment. The torn flags rode high over the column to shouts of: *"En avant! On les aura!"* ... *"Vorwärts! Nach Richmond!"* ... "Yeeaayy! Now we're going! Watch out, Johnny Reb, here come Kearny's men"

George trembled with excitement. He turned and gestured to Randol. "That's it. Bring 'em on." The column thudded along the dirt road, the men slanting forward in eagerness, chins out and eyes curiously bright. The roar from Malvern Hill deepened and throbbed. From the James, flame and smoke spat viciously as a gunboat fired a huge Dahlgren. A man near George shrieked, "Yeeow! Listen to that!" The river guns stunned again and the marching files waved their arms and cheered. Up by the head of the column a mounted man reined in, peered through the dust, and shouted, "This way, de Mérac! The general's up the slope!"

The men roared louder. George called, "Slow down that step. No one ordered double time!" The column was trailing off the road, plunging into the fields that edged the south grade of Malvern Hill. The slope was crawling with men—aides, men with bloody bandages, weaponless white-faced men who ran on, unseeing and trembling. To the left a whole Zouave regiment under the pine-tree flag of Massachusetts kept parallel with the Rifles, waved and shouted to them.

This was different from the blind desperate rush across the fields to the Danforth house. George swung his arms and shouted to his men. Ahead he could see the drive, drive, drive of countless legs as the companies fought up the slope, legs like blue and yellow pistons thudding endlessly. Over the crest a red glow, smeared with black smoke, showed that the sun had dropped far down the horizon. The hard sky line silhouetted de Mérac, Castex, and Dekdebrun, the quick toss of the Zouaves' fezzes.

He was on level ground with a breeze sweeping acrid smoke into his face and the turf shook to the bellow of uncounted guns. He made out a brick house to his left. Far to the front, two other houses showed black against the sunset sky. He jumped like a frightened horse to avoid an abandoned stretcher, blanketed, from which blunt, raw flesh jutted. He jerked his eyes away, fastened them on the houses of the sky line. Wheels and hoofs slammed past and the dust was thickened by a string of caissons rolling on toward the clamoring batteries. He heard wood crash and saw the Zouaves tossing aside a rail fence by the two houses, slipping through the gap.

He was in a sloping, plowed field and the valley below him was masked in a fearful pall of glowing smoke that throbbed and pulsed to the smash of the big guns. There was a banshee scream high in air and shrapnel hurled downward. Twice he stepped quickly to avoid bodies that appeared somehow under his feet. Something whacked against his canteen and stale water gushed to the ground. At the right, a few yards away, a horse writhed in a tangle of slick, steaming intestines and under the ripped belly a single scarlet boot protruded. Round-shot danced up the slope and kicked stinging dirt into his face. He gripped the butt of his Colt tighter and shouted, "Close up! Close up!"

A voice like a bugle cut through the air and he smeared a cuff across his eyes. A tall thin man galloped a bay toward the column. George strained his lungs in a great shout that was swallowed up in a roar from the whole column. "Yeaay! Phil Kearny!" ... *"Le kébir! C'este le vieux kébir!"*

Kearny's arm swept and he dropped his reins. "Bear left, de Mérac! Past the Crewe house. Take them in!"

George saw de Mérac turn and shout, "Where shall we go in?"

Kearny waved in a fierce sweep. "Forward! Forward! Forward! That's all that matters! Watch for the New York 69th and guide on them!"

Up the column a bugle blared and George yelled, "Double time!" as the Rifles broke into a heavy trot. There was musketry ahead, thick and ever nearer. The dusk-filled valley was slashed with quick flame, stabbing from right to left, and bullets tore up the ground. There must have been a bugle call but George only knew that the regiment was changing from column into line, sweeping abreast of a thick blue belt of roaring men who surged on under a green flag.

The Southern yell broke out, high and piercing. There were woods in front, woods that spilled out keening columns of gray infantry who swung into line with amazing speed. George shouted until his throat was raw—exultant, wordless shouts. This was different, sweeping on to meet the advancing gray lines, instead of hugging the ground, fighting for each rock and stump. He roared: "Fire!" and muskets smashed out along his company, echoing the hot blast right and left and in front.

Bullets ripped the ground, ricocheted away off rocks with catlike whines. Cole was down, and West and Porter. George's Colt jolted in his hand and his breath sucked in as he saw a man in gray fall. How had he worked so close?

There were fighting swirls all about him where big, slouch-hatted men stood their ground and fought their lives out, cursing and stabbing. There were sullen groups who fell back under tattered colors. There were men who threw down their muskets and stood gasping with hands held high. Once George found himself with three of his men embedded in the yelling ranks of an Irish company where a sergeant bawled in his ear, "Glory be to God and we're a-drivin' that divil of a Lee, with the Irish in front of all." Next he was far to the right among LeNoir's men where a corporal from Marseilles saved him from tripping over a body and set him on his feet with a husky, *"Doucement, mon bon!"* Then he was with his own men once more, plunging ahead through woods where thin-spaced trees alternated with snagging bushes. He jumped a pool where a gray man lay, making horrible noises as water filled a shattered mouth. A tangle of enemy appeared across a glade and he slipped back to the flank of his company. The Confederates suddenly dropped their muskets and ran forward, hands up. He motioned them roughly to the rear with his Colt, passing them from his knowledge to the roaring dusk behind.

The woods were oddly still but far on either flank fighting raged. Quick fear seized him. He was lost, perhaps hopelessly lost. Somehow, losing touch on both sides, he had bulled his way deep into the Southern lines. He called to Randol, faced the company about, and tried to follow the route by which he had come into the woods. He kept his flankers spread wide and pushed on toward the first glimmer of sky that showed through the trees. Then without warning he was in the open.

Right and left, muskets spurted, and up and down the fading bulk of Malvern Hill, which he now faced, batteries roared and stunned. He took a hasty bearing, called, "By the left flank. March!" and the twenty men who had stayed with him moved along the edge of the woods. He walked cautiously at the head, hoping that he was right. All at once he threw up his hand as a signal to halt. Two riders were moving slowly toward him. The rearmost whipped up a shadowy rifle. George shouted, "Dekdebrun! Hold it! John, where are the Rifles?"

De Mérac loomed huge in the dimness. "George! I was looking for you. We halt here. No one is on our front. Go in through the trees. Report to Wilson."

Puffing with relief, George made his way to the rest of the left companies and reported briefly to Wilson. As he was finishing, a tall figure slipped into the woods and a vibrant voice called, "That you, Wilson? I've seen de Mérac. Halt here till further orders."

George stiffened as Kearny, revolver still clutched in his hand, came up. The general nodded pleasantly to him and went on: "Excellent work, Wilson. Well fought. Now never mind about your wounded. The ambulances are coming right along. Just keep your men in hand, ready to hit out at any instant."

George moved closer, saw LeNoir and Bolton and Chanel edge up. Wilson said, "What may we expect, sir?"

Kearny stuffed his revolver into its holster. "Expect? Why, that we'll smash ahead, right up the river. If McClellan does that, I'll take back everything I ever said about him. Lee's smashed, I tell you. His organization's wrecked. We'll take these boys and hit so hard that he'll be asking for terms before we sight Drewry's Bluff. We'll go right through without stopping for a damn thing."

"We have orders for such a move?" asked Wilson.

Kearny's voice was exultant. "What other orders can there be? Lee's staff's so broken that it takes five hours to get word from one end of his line to the other. We've captured enough of his orders to know that. We've smashed most of his batteries and the others are so jammed in the woods and clearings that he can't shift a piece. Orders for us to attack? They'll come. God damn it, they've *got* to come." He raised his hand to his kepi and slipped off.

Wheels rustled through the grass and George saw a

lantern bobbing at the tail of one of Wayne's ambulances, heard the surgeon's slow tones as he fumbled his way along. "Who's this? That skinny O'Brien boy? Can't do anything there, I guess. You Gerlasch? Turn over and I'll see what's wrong with you. H'm. Flesh wound. Extensor muscle. You can wait. Who's this?" His muttering died away.

Behind the line where the tattered colors had been planted, de Mérac crossed his arms on Cigale's saddle and leaned his head against them. He felt tense and yet light, as though poised on springs. Kearny was sure that orders for a slashing move up the river would come at any instant, and the anticipation of being in the van of a decisive Union triumph drove away fatigue. He shifted his position, lit a cigarette, and inhaled deeply. The bulk of Malvern was shrouded in gloom and heavy clouds blacked out the sky. A drop of rain spatted down, was followed by a steady, hissing deluge. Harder and harder it came. He slipped into his poncho, hunched his shoulders, and waited.

Sometime later, a distant spur of Malvern blazed with gunfire. Through the concussions and the whine of the shells that seemed to be sailing off to the far right, de Mérac heard hoofs coming toward him. A voice called his name and he recognized an aide from Kearny's staff. The aide leaned from the saddle. "Pull out right away. You're back under Pelham. He's where the paths cross by the Malvern house. Bear well to the west going up. Some of Mahone's and Wright's men are still hanging on below the Crewe house."

"Anything else?"

"Only that we're on the move." His hoofbeats died away.

De Mérac sprang into the saddle and called for Castex. Join Pelham on Malvern? That must mean that all Kearny's division would cross the hill and head upriver to hit at Lee's flank. "*Vingt dieux*," he thought, "this may be the end!"

Rain sang against ponchos, beat on cloth-covered

shoulders as the Rifles wound uncertainly back over the flats toward Malvern Hill. There could be no doubt that the whole army was moving. The dark about them was thick with the squelch of boots, the jingle of metal, the thud of hoofs as limbers rolled down to pick up the batteries. By a mired gun an officer declaimed, "Now I want every man to get where he can put two hundred pounds pressure on the wheels." A cannoneer snarled, "If you want the God-damn thing moved, get the hell out of here and don't bother us—sir!" Unseen figures called for Fardella's 105th New York, for Floyd-Jones's 11th Regulars, for Kusserow's battery, for Voegelee's.

George plodded on with his men, sodden boots rasping his heels and rain spilling from his vizor. There could be no doubt of where the Rifles were heading. He could keep his feet going until the last charge shattered Lee's power forever. His company pressed on as he did, heedless of rain and the slick mud that set them skidding and slipping.

Through halts and detours he panted encouragement to them. If only it had not turned hot and sticky despite the drive of the rain. He began to feel suffocated. His eyes ached and his throat was swollen and sore. It was odd, he thought, that his skin was so dry and so hot where the rain couldn't reach it. A pain at the back of his neck bothered him and weird lights shot back of his lids.

At the next halt, his knees buckled and he sat down suddenly. Contact with the ground seemed to clear his eyes and head. He croaked to Bates, "How are the boys doing? So dark I can't see much."

Bates, shoulders hunched to the rain, growled, "Been a few dropping out."

George struggled to his feet. "I'll go back and bring them along. Randol's in command in the meantime." A deeper ache ran through him as he started off. His feet were light and jerked high with each step. His temples pounded. A strange glow shone through the downpour and he no longer saw the company, no longer thought about it.

At the head of the column, de Mérac marched with the Zouaves, Cigale's bridle over his arm. The Rifles were still on Malvern Hill but down the slope lay the river, the ugly gunboats, and the road to Richmond. He ranged up and down the first five companies with Corvisart, trying to catch the temper of the men. Then he heard a Gascon voice in Péguy's company mutter, "Ah, if their Lee should surrender before we have a chance to strike." De Mérac turned back satisfied. So long as a foot could move, the Rifles would press on. At the head of the column he found Dekdebrun straining ahead. Little Castex, whimpering with past fright and present exhaustion, trudged manfully on, leading his pony, Greenbaum's poncho thrown over his head. The dark Jew marched with hunched shoulders, seemingly heedless of the downpour.

Sometime after three in the morning de Mérac forced his eyes open as men ahead shouted. Far below something glowed slick and dull through the rain, and red and green lights wavered. He shouted, "The James!" and without command the cadence of the march increased.

The downslope ended and a lantern flared on a mounted squad. A man shouted, "Turn left, you. Turn left."

De Mérac shouted in protest, but an officer cursed him furiously and waved him east, downstream toward Harrison's Landing. He obeyed in cold, raging frustration as he realized that the whole army was moving in the same direction. The night on all sides was thick with the rumble of wheels and the chewing sound of boots on soggy ground. Each turn of a spoke, each stride of a weary leg, carried the Army of the Potomac farther and farther from Richmond and the hot-fighting gray hordes which it felt it had fairly beaten.

Life went out of the column. There was no more talking in ranks. Men snarled at the incessant "Close up. Close up." Dark figures dropped furtively out. The rest slogged on, sick and sore like strong horses that have been misused. The losses and terrors of the last two days had been in vain and the knowledge bit deep.

Side paths and open fields spilled men from other

units onto the road—lost platoons and companies, stragglers, panting wounded. From dark stretches inland, de Mérac caught furious voices: "I'm through, by Jesus Christ! I had enough." ... "Been shot at all across Virginia for goddam nothing!" ... "I'll follow Joe Hooker anywheres but I'm done assing round after that pimpletailed Mac!" ... "They'll have to send the provost to the Rockies to get me back. God damn it, there goes my gun into the swamp and the hell with it."

De Mérac shut his ears to the angry shouts and to the faint splashes that told of equipment hurled away. He shut them, too, to the bitter oaths of his own men that stung out at wet halts.

As a murky red sun pushed up over the horizon, a muddy hand touched de Mérac's elbow. First Sergeant Bates saluted, saying, "Loot'nant Randol, sir. He want to know is Loot'nant Force with you."

De Mérac started. "With me? But I have not seen him since we left the flats."

Bates's head jerked. "Sure he ain't been with you, sir?"

"Of course."

Bates's old-army shell cracked. "God damn! They ain't none of us laid eyes to him since we begun the climb. He went back to look for stragglers."

De Mérac caught the old Regular's arm. "Since the climb? But he is always with his men."

"Ain't now—sir."

De Mérac felt sudden cold in the pit of his stomach. "And you let him stray off, you and Randol? You will answer for him if—" He stopped. It was plain that old Bates was as shaken by George's disappearance as he himself was. He said quickly, "I know you did what you could. Tell Lieutenant Randol to take five men and go back over the road. He must hunt till he finds him."

"Tried that, sir. Can't no one go back. Cavalry patrols stop 'em."

De Mérac looked down along the column that was unreal in the half-light. He could not leave it. There was nothing that he could do except wait. He rallied himself. "Thank you, First Sergeant. Send me word if you learn anything."

The sun vanished and rain poured down again. He walked on beside Cigale, reasoning with himself. George had left the field unwounded. There had been no firing along the line of march. Therefore he was unhurt. He had gone back to look for stragglers. Very likely he had rounded them up and become embedded in some other unit and been unable to press ahead. Or some fool provost might have stopped him for questioning. No, George had too good a head, could take care of himself too well, for any accident to happen to him. Yet—yet—so much time had passed. "*Mais, vingt dieux*," he muttered, "of course he is safe."

He looked up suddenly as a blasting voice sounded close by the edge of the road. There stood Kearny, his back toward the marching men. He was facing the grave, bearded Birney and two other officers. His fist pounded the air as he trumpeted, "I enter my solemn protest against this retreat, gentlemen. We ought to be clawing at Lee at this instant and you know it. As an old soldier I tell you that an order like this can only be prompted by cowardice and treason."

De Mérac's neck tingled to the words. He heard a snarl of approval from the men within earshot, a ragged cheer as the others recognized the one-armed general. A Zouave croaked, "*A nous, le vieux kébir!*" Kearny wheeled abruptly, raised his hand to his vizor as the Rifles passed him.

There were wheatfields to the left of the road, great stretches where regiments had trodden the grain into a glutinous mass. A staff officer raised his hand, motioned the Rifles through a wide gate. De Mérac stepped back to watch the column begin its left turn. The pace grew slower. Toward the rear of the column, exhausted men hobbled along, trying to overtake their comrades who had outstripped them. Two limping Irishmen supported a bandaged German. A lean Basque used his musket as a crutch and clung to the arm of a swaying New Yorker. In the rear, the yellow hospital flag of Wayne's ambulance floated. Battered and thinned, the Rifles marched into their camp.

De Mérac's eyes were on the slow trickle of stragglers,

searching in vain for George's keen, set face and broad shoulders. Out of the rain galloped Quartermaster Brady, whooping with joy. "So it's home ye've brought the boys, John! An' it's your own tents you're lookin' at an'—"

De Mérac said, "They will want rations. Rations at once."

"Rations, is it?" Brady threw up his hands. "Here's me finding an icehouse that I packed with beef and there's a fine great mountain of coffee for the boys. The best regiment that wasn't all off the old sod. The best—" His voice died in his throat. "Go to God, then! What you done to the boys?" He lurched blindly toward the thin ranks. "Where's little Con Murphy? Mart Sullivan! It's bad you're hurt! Danny Shea!"

A cascade of dogs raced over the field, swept on to break in a wave at the head of the column. A spotted terrier leaped about a Zouave. A bulldog butted against muddy ankles, whining forlornly as he sniffed from man to man. A setter flung himself flat on the ground and howled agonizingly. Something wet and shaggy bumped into de Mérac as Mr. McArdle thumped his paws against him. Then the dog lolloped away toward H Company, yelping expectantly. His voice was suddenly still. Without a whine he scuttled through the rain to sit, patient and alert, at the edge of the road down which stragglers still drifted.

Once the regiment was fed and bedded down, de Mérac threw himself into a mass of paper work with Wilson, Greenbaum, and Rapp. There were casualty reports to be drawn up, requisitions for new equipment. Above all, a clear statement had to be obtained from Wilson on the exact steps by which Dalbiac had thrown the three companies into the funnel.

When the last lines had been written, Wilson looked at de Mérac through reddened eyes. "Don't worry about George. He'll turn up. I'm for some sleep. You better get some yourself, John."

"Presently," de Mérac said.

As soon as Wilson had gone, de Mérac borrowed Brady's mount, to spare Cigale, and trotted off up the river road. He questioned halted units, talked with doctors in hastily established hospitals, but nowhere could he find news of George. He returned, bone-weary and dispirited, to camp, where he saw Mr. McArdle still waiting, his head turning to scan every passing wagon, every squad of soldiers. There must be something else to do besides wait. But there wasn't. He tried to think of the relief of hot water, of the warm embrace of his blankets. He could sleep. He must sleep. On waking, he would surely hear George's voice outside the tent. He sent the mule back to Brady, entered his quarters, where Louvel had spread out his camp bed.

He unbuckled his sword belt and his eye fell on a slip of paper in Rapp's firm handwriting. He picked it up and his head throbbed harder as he read a summary of casualties. He had brought 732 men out of the tents by Fort Corcoran. Now, only 504 would answer rollcall. The rest were killed, wounded, missing—228 men thrown away to no purpose.

He tried to consider the losses impersonally but his mind whirled. More than ever he must sleep. He stepped to the tent flap and looked out through the rain. In B Company street a tent peak swayed, rocked, collapsed. Another followed it, a third. There were tents down in C, in F. The whole north row in the Zouaves' street settled to the mud. The soft soil of the wheatfield had refused to hold the pegs. Men thrashed in sodden canvas, burrowed under the edges, stood in soiled underwear cursing and tugging at guy ropes. De Mérac rebuckled his belt and ran to rouse Castex. "Sound Officers' Call. Sound First Sergeants' Call. Rapp! Turn out the guard!" The men must be put under cover somehow. His blankets were forgotten.

The valley of the James was healthier than the swamps of the Chickahominy but the mists that rose from the wet flats were enough to swell the lines at sick call in every regiment. And there were worse maladies than fever as the army slowly absorbed the shock of its fruitless campaign. Men began to desert in weary discouragement. Every boat that chugged out from the river landings carried officers headed north on the flimsiest pretexts or none at all. They who stayed, whatever their rank, went about their work with little spirit. The air was full of rumors that McClellan would start a great drive upriver, but few believed them.

Yet activity throbbed through the cloud of apathy. Steamers docked, unloaded new batteries, cases of muskets, wagons, and field forges. Chests of clothing were dumped at the camps and the old uniforms with their foreign flavor vanished. The Rifles discarded their blue and yellow and assembled in plain blue anonymity. Their kepis were unadorned blue, save for the Kearny patch, their jackets the same color and their trousers light blue. The change was resented by many, especially the Zouaves, who stormed angrily at having to surrender their baggy red breeches and tasseled fezzes. Alone of the whole army, a few favored Zouave regiments clung to their old garb, and Berdan's Sharpshooters were still in their green.

The river boats brought other cargo, passengers who swept down on the camps a-tingle with excitement. There were shifty-eyed men and hard faced women, obviously unused to their fine clothes and to the shining carriages they brought with them, probably fruits of the sale of shoddy cloth, sanded powder, and flawed steel. Such people seemed to view the army as a gaudy spectacle provided for their amusement and profit. Politicians came down on a hunt for campaign material, for data gleaned from the troops that might help pull down one general, build up another. Bright-cheeked and bright-skirted women and girls appeared, hoping to find entree to the tent of as high an officer as possible. There were frank sightseers, too young or too protected to feel anything beyond delicious awe at the lines of parked batteries, the click and rattle of marching infantry, or the jingling flow of cavalry. Other types, too, stepped ashore—serious-faced men on legitimate business who talked long and late with officers expert in ordnance and supply, then slipped away with notes on how mechanical difficulties, dangerous shortages, might be avoided in the future.

Then there were the ever-present wan couples from as far away as Minnesota or Maine who timidly haunted the hospitals, pathetically eager not to be in the way. Yes, they had had word from the War Department but there could be a mistake, couldn't there? Sometimes, weary eyes alight, they moved carefully up a gangplank with a limping blue figure between them. More often they could be seen seated by the river with empty, white faces, hand in hand and silent. There was no way of visiting a grave in the tangles of White Oak Swamp or the rustling thickets above Savage's Station.

Through all this de Mérac kept as tight a grip on the Rifles as he could. Dominating his every waking hour was the thought of George Force. Personally or by deputy he had combed every hospital along the James, had questioned every available officer and man who might have been on that part of Malvern Hill crossed by the Rifles between the last sight of George and the news of his disappearance. As his efforts proved fruitless, a heavy black cloud began to gather in his mind. Over and over he reasoned that the missing man had been seen long after the last shot had been fired. Therefore, he could not be a casualty. And yet—where was he?

He knew that his temper was growing short and he formed a habit of speaking slowly and seldom. He found it hard to control himself when Péguy and Chanel quarreled over the possession of a mess kit, arranged a duel, and then threw the whole matter back on him when he threatened them with arrest. He had to swallow exasperation when the broad-faced Rohde whispered his hints. Did de Mérac see how LeNoir allowed his men to straggle? Did he know that Dr. Wayne was selling hospital whiskey to the Negroes? And was it wise to have a Jew as adjutant? Back in the days of Fort Corcoran, Rohde had appeared as merely a nuisance. Now de Mérac saw him as a definite source of trouble with his clumsy tattling.

One hot noon de Mérac was invited to lunch at the mess of a Wisconsin regiment, some of whose officers he had met in Milwaukee on his first visit. He thought of declining through sheer uneasiness and depression until he learned that two of them had finished a detail inspecting hospital ships. Hoping as always for news of George, he accepted.

The food was good and normally he would have found the talk stimulating, recalling as it did the deep forests, the hidden lakes, the stretches of open country where quail rose over the sights of shotgun. But there was no news of George and he was anxious only to get away.

When he was at last able to take his leave, his host, a tall Milwaukee lawyer named Hammond, walked through the Wisconsin camp with him. De Mérac tried to follow his comments on recruiting. "You see, we don't form new regiments in our state. We recruit to fill up the old ones. Now take New York for example. It wants credit at Washington for regiments raised. So, if they raise a thousand men and send five hundred to the 55th and the same to the 56th, they get no credit. So they let those two outfits melt away, form a brand-new 57th and holler, 'Hey, Abe! Look! Here's another regiment.' That way, the seasoned outfits never get built up again, never get their losses made good."

De Mérac said absently, "Losses. Yes, they are the devil. In my own ranks I find—*dieu de dieu!* What is that?" He stopped, his preoccupation gone for the moment, to stare at a tethered black mare, a superb, slim-legged animal with short ears and small Arab head. Fine shoulders and chest gave promise of endurance to sustain the speed of the nervous limbs.

Hammond cried, "Watch out, John! She belongs to Major Groves."

"I shall not steal her."

"Groves'd thank you if you did," grunted Hammond.

De Mérac asked quickly, "She is for sale?"

"No one'd buy her. She's got to be shot."

"Impossible!" exclaimed de Mérac.

"She's a heller. Kicks like the devil but biting's her worst trick. Ripped the guts out of an orderly with her teeth. The poor fellow died."

De Mérac leaned on the hilt of his sword, fascinated by the mare. She turned her head slowly, her ears flattened, and her lips rolled back over strong teeth. Hammond jerked him back out of reach as the head shot out with a vicious clack of jaws. "Watch out, man."

De Mérac closed his eyes, trying to recall bits of forgotten stable lore. Then he said, "I'll pay Major Groves one hundred dollars for her."

Hammond hooted in protest. "He'd pay you that to take her away."

De Mérac said, "In your kitchens just now I saw two legs of mutton roasting. One of them was very small. I wish to borrow it. No—I am quite serious. The small one, and it must be brought to me very hot." Hammond tossed up his hands in surrender and sent an orderly for the roast. De Mérac called to DuChesne, who watched two tethered mounts in the shade. "What is your opinion of that horse?" he asked as the old Chasseur came up.

DuChesne's eyes widened. *"Besicles de dieu!* It is the horse of a *maréchal de France."*

The orderly came back grinning. The roast was jammed into a bucket and hot grease still popped and sizzled on its surface. DuChesne cried suddenly, "Ah— now one understands. It is I who should do it, *mon capitaine."*

"The risk is mine," said de Mérac. "That bit of sacking, please DuChesne." He wound the cloth heavily about the bone end of the roast, gripped it firmly, and walked toward the mare murmuring, *"Doucement, doucement, ma belle. Pas de mal."*

The mare's neck rippled, her lips went back, and she struck like a snake. De Mérac sidestepped and thrust out the smoking mutton. The mare snatched at it. Then she screamed. The roast dropped at her feet and she stood trembling, gums still bared. De Mérac glided to her side, slipped an arm about her neck, and began to stroke her. The black head swung toward him. Hammond yelled a warning but de Mérac remained motionless. The lips closed, the muzzle bumped against his hand, nuzzled his open palm.

De Mérac cried, *"Voilà.* Now the white salve from your kit." DuChesne handed him a small tin and he smeared the mixture over lips, tongue, and gums. Then he stepped back. "Your turn, DuChesne, since it is you who must saddle her."

DuChesne picked up the still-hot roast and walked forward. The mare pawed the ground, then stood still. The old Chasseur tossed the mutton away. "*Ca va bien.* And the burns, they are light."

Hammond exhaled deeply. "I'm weak, just watching you. I happened to see the orderly she ripped. Sure she'll be all right now?"

"Watch," said de Mérac. He unfastened the halter shank and vaulted onto the glossy back, guiding her only by the rope. She moved off at a walk, flowing and effortless, broke into a spirited trot. The gaits were faultless. He waved his kepi, touched the mare with his spurs, and headed for an open stretch by the river. She skimmed along through the sticky air, hoofs drumming in perfect rhythm. A low fence lay ahead and he set her at it. She cleared it without visible effort, fell into a smooth, clean stride. Carefree and exhilarated for the moment, he shot her off in a wide circle, wove her through figure eights. Men crowded the open stretch, shouted, and waved their arms. A few scaled broad hats past the mare's nose but she galloped on steadily. The men began to cheer. "Stick to it, Frenchy! Look at the long-legged bastard!"

De Mérac pulled up by Hammond and DuChesne, slid to the ground. "I shall send your major one hundred dollars in gold. What a horse! How shall she be named, DuChesne?"

DuChesne puffed out his cheeks. "*Ca*—she resembles that Lisette which our Bourbaki rode in Africa."

"Lisette it shall be. Good-bye, Harry. Come and dine with us tomorrow night." He mounted Cigale reluctantly and rode back to camp. Behind him cantered DuChesne, bursting with pride as cavalrymen stopped to exclaim over the black mare that trotted beside him.

De Mérac saw Lisette installed on the picket line and walked toward his tent. His elation over the new horse ebbed and he began to wonder if a medical major, to whom he had written about George at a venture, could have had time to reply. As he approached his quarters from the rear he heard a voice say in quick French, "Excellent, Sergeant Major Rapp. They are well ordered."

In front of the tent Rapp, his red beard abristle, was standing before Kearny, glowing with admiration of the *kébir* who spoke French so well and who knew the details of all his regiments, even to the name of one not inconspicuous (one might be allowed to hope) Alsatian sergeant major.

De Mérac saluted and Kearny said in English, "I was just telling Rapp that his reports to Division are models." The old veteran's spine stiffened even more and his scarred cheeks flushed with pleasure.

"We should be lost without Rapp, sir," said de Mérac.

Kearny laughed. "If I weren't at least reasonably honest, I'd steal him from you. Now I'm going to give an order that may puzzle you. I want you to bring up enough men to form a cordon around your tent, and I don't want anyone nearer than thirty feet. I'd like Rapp to be in charge of it."

De Mérac gave Rapp the necessary orders. When the detail had arrived and been spaced to Kearny's satisfaction, the general said, "Shall we go in now?"

Within the tent, Kearny pulled up a camp chair to the light table and drew out some papers. "In the first place, I want to give you these." He handed them to de Mérac, who stared at them. The sheets were his report to Pelham of the Dalbiac fiasco.

He said, "What shall I do with these?"

Kearny's trim imperial bristled. "Do? Frame them. Burn them. Do you think I'd take action on charges like those? Pelham's damned antiforeign ideas aren't going to interfere with any unit that wears the Kearny patch." He waved his hand. "So forget him. I'm taking your regiment away from him. You'll be under my personal orders the way you were at Malvern. He'll have no more to do with you than the Sultan of Morocco."

De Mérac started. "Then we serve directly under you, sir?"

"The Rifles do. Exactly. There are things to talk over. One or two of the captains could be improved upon. Corvisart should go up to major. You need another surgeon to help Wayne." He talked on, showing amazing knowledge of detail. There ought to be a chaplain, an office which, like that of lieutenant colonel, had never been filled. "And for lieutenant colonel," observed Kearny, "Wilson's the logical choice." He paused. "Unless, of course, he goes up to full colonel."

"That would be excellent," said de Mérac. "In that case, I could be truly the adjutant and Greenbaum could go back to a company."

Kearny eyed him keenly. "Is that all you can think of?"

De Mérac looked at the lined face, the high cheekbones, and the burning eyes. "I am thinking at this moment, as I should have thought before, that you did not throw that cordon around the tent merely to tell me that we are free of Pelham."

Kearny's face set in firm lines and his eyes snapped. "Right! There's a lot more. On your word as an officer and gentleman, what I say now will go no further."

"You have my word, sir."

Kearny's left shoulder twitched the cloth of the empty sleeve. He leaned across the table and it seemed to de Mérac that he looked suddenly ten years younger. "McClellan is going out."

De Mérac felt hypnotized by the hawklike eyes. There was more to come, the real reason for the cordon outside in the sun. All at once he knew the reason and the impact of that knowledge shook him. He said huskily, "And you will succeed McClellan!"

One arm swung high and the empty sleeve twitched again as though the general were trying to throw two hands to the sky. "Yes! I can do it. I can beat Lee and he's the best they've got." His voice rose. "I can beat him, beat them all. I'll have to fight Lee, fight our own West Pointers and our politicians, abolitionists who don't think I'm radical enough. This army! It's been frittered away and still it's kept on going. You went in beside Corcoran's Irish at Malvern. They'd been through enough to wreck a Roman Legion and you saw how they charged. Top to bottom it's the same. Poor Ollie Howard—you know, the Maine general—lost his right arm. I saw him after the amputation. He reached out his good arm, tapped my left sleeve, and said, 'Guess you and I better buy our gloves together from now on.' What can you do with a man like that? And he's just one of ninety thousand. Look at Hooker's boys, throwing away their muskets after Malvern—not because they were licked but because they weren't. Now! They'll have their chance to fight and that fight won't stop till Lee's wrecked or backed clear down to the Gulf of Mexico."

De Mérac asked, "When may this happen, sir?"

Kearny dropped his hand to his sword hilt. "I can't say yet. I only knew yesterday. I was asked—I can't tell you by whom—just one question. 'Will you fight?' It's going to take a little time. You know that Pope's been brought out of the west and given command of the Army of Virginia. If Pope wins, I'm to command the whole east. If he doesn't, I get his army and he goes out. Either way—" he threw back his head—"I'm the man Lee's got to beat. And he can't do it."

De Mérac smoothed his mustache thoughtfully. "And in the meantime, I forget all this?"

"Every word. I'm looking about now for the men I'll want when the change comes. I want that French cavalryman, Duffié. I want George Meade as soon as he's over his wounds. I want John Sedgwick. There's young Francis Barlow of the 64th New York, a born soldier if I ever saw one, even if he did go to Harvard. If I possibly can, I'll steal Cump Sherman from Grant." He paused, fingers straying through his imperial. Then he asked abruptly. "Think you could handle a brigade?"

De Mérac gasped. "A brigade? But I have no experience beyond this regiment. Rank? I do not care about it."

Kearny snapped, "No, but there's something else you do care about or you wouldn't be here. It's some idea you've got—the Union or the end of slavery or something. You want to serve where you can do the most good. I'll say where that spot is. Is that understood?"

"*Parfaitement.*"

"Then for the time being you'll go on with the Rifles. Later—" his eyes glittered—"later, there'll be something else. Try and fit yourself for it." He rose quickly, shook hands, and strode out of the tent, calling to Rapp to dismiss the cordon.

Deep in thought de Mérac paced up and down his tent. Every item of Kearny's news had been amazing. Within regimental limits, the permanent freeing of the unit from Pelham seemed the most important thing. But looking at the army as a whole, the appointment of Kearny as virtual commander in chief was possibly the most dynamic move since the President's first call for volunteers. He tried to look into the future, to visualize the Union armies guided by Kearny's blazing impetuosity that was so oddly tempered by cool judgment.

The canvas rustled and Wilson pushed in. "Hello, John. What's the matter with you? I yelled my lungs out and then just tramped in." He looked sharply at de Mérac. "Something's up. Have you found George?"

De Mérac's eyes were suddenly grave. "No. Still no word. But something has happened, Craig. Listen. Kearny was here. He's going to be—" his excitement grew as he recalled the general's words—"he's just—well, you see, he came and—"

Wilson laughed in exasperation. "Go on, go on. He came here. All right. What then?"

De Mérac threw back his head. "He's taking us away from Pelham. For good. We serve under Kearny's personal orders."

"No more Pelham?" Wilson's voice soared in relief. "That's wonderful. It's—h'm—by Jove, hold on a minute. I'll bet you've got something else up your sleeve."

De Mérac smiled to himself. "What single sleeve could hold more than the news that we may forget the good Dudley Pelham?"

As de Mérac shaved the next morning he felt as though he had never known fatigue. Every problem that had perplexed him in the Union Army seemed easy of solution. More, after retreat the night before, twenty-odd stragglers had rejoined the regiment. While they had no news of George they told him that, lost in the dark, they had been seized by other units and thrown out to the rear of the retreat to ward off a possible move by Lee. Now Lee had fallen back from Malvern Hill and they had been released. That was precisely the sort of thing that George would have done, once separated from his company. He would on his own initiative have joined some unit where he might be of immediate use. Any moment now might bring yaps of joy from Mr. McArdle, who waited the days out down by the road.

The orders detaching the Rifles from Pelham's command arrived just before assembly. De Mérac had the bugles blow a flourish before he read them out. He made no attempt to stem the outburst that swept down the whole regiment. Red-topped caps flew into the air. Officers and men roared with joy. Over the din Shea's voice blared, "An' ye'll be notin' the name—*Kearny! Kearn* is soldier in Irish and he's soldier in any talk. Kearny! No bloody Sassenach like Lee and no bloody Scotch sheep stealer like McClellan."

Pride and Clay rode over in full uniform, aides chattering behind them. Pride was flushed and embarrassed, Clay formal and rigidly courteous. Pride swallowed hard and nudged Clay. "Thought we agreed you'd do the parleeing."

Clay inclined his head gravely. "I speak, Captain, for all the New Jersey and Indiana officers, in congratulating you on the order of which we have just heard. I may say further that you will be greatly missed—you and your regiment."

De Mérac found an odd difficulty in replying. He began. "I appreciate your coming here, gentlemen, and—"

Pride growled, "Damn ceremony. Just wanted you to know we all think you had a tough job and did it well." He shook hands and swung his horse about, clearing his throat furiously. Clay raised his hand to his kepi. "Good luck, de Mérac."

"I find that they move me, the two," thought de Mérac as he walked to the orderly tent to go over the day's papers with Greenbaum. "They meant more than they said. They—*ah, ça!* Here is time wasted!"

Across the grass, completely at ease, cool in white linen and spotless panama, strolled Cusler, smiling blandly in the morning sun. He joined de Mérac at the tent and shook his hand warmly. "We've been hearing great things about your boys. You've got a way with them, I guess."

"They are little trouble," said de Mérac and introduced Greenbaum.

Cusler surveyed the adjutant coolly. "Greenbaum? From West 33rd?"

"Yorkville."

Cusler narrowed his eyes. "H'm. Know Sol Lazarus?"

"Know who he is."

"How'd you vote last time?"

"For anyone who'd beat Fernando Wood."

Cusler smiled tolerantly. "Bet I could change your mind."

"You'd lose," said Greenbaum, picking up a pen unconcernedly.

"Don't very often. Well, if you'll excuse us, Captain de Mérac and I want to have a talk."

"Do we?" thought de Mérac, grinning inwardly as Greenbaum wrote on, oblivious of Cusler. He said aloud, "My tent is over there."

Cusler frowned at Greenbaum, then followed de Mérac. "Too bad you got saddled with a Jew like that. They're all damned tricky. I'll get him shifted for you."

De Mérac pushed out a camp chair. "Do not trouble. He is an excellent soldier and a fine adjutant."

Cusler sat down. "You mean you *want* to keep him? Well, that's your worry, if you can stand him." He lit a cigar and surveyed the camp. "Nice place you got here. I've got a few boys after commissions. Guess I'll send them down to you."

"I shall be glad to have them—if they are competent."

"They'll be all right," said Cusler.

"Possibly our standards of judgment may differ."

Cusler smiled. "You know," he remarked to the morning in general, "I've never held any office. Don't want to. But—" he dabbed with his cigar—" but a whole lot of men who do hold office know *me*. Those boys'll be all right."

"I do not follow."

"No? Put it this way. *I* back those boys. What'd Pelham say if I told him that you'd objected to them—especially when I told Pelham who these boys' fathers are?"

De Mérac's hand jerked slightly. Cusler did not know that the Rifles were out of Pelham's reach! The fact astounded him, but it was obvious. He stifled a smile. "No doubt the general would be shocked."

"That's it. You're learning. I'll send 'em along to you."

"And," said de Mérac as blandly as Cusler, "I shall send them back if they do not suit their command. Or I shall set them to grooming Brady's mules."

Something of the smoothness went out of Cusler's manner but he said evenly, "Look here, de Mérac. Personally, I like you."

De Mérac inclined his head. "I am glad to know that."

"But you're going at everything the wrong way. In all friendliness I warn you that you're making a mistake. You're sailing smack into trouble."

De Mérac interposed, "Are you sure you want your protégés with us? This regiment has seen hard service. It is apt to see more."

"And it'll be up to you to keep these boys out of it. They've got some mighty valuable connections."

"If they are competent to march with Bolton and Dan Shea and Bordagaray, I welcome them. If not—" He shrugged.

Cusler rose sighing. "I'll say this for you. You plunk your cards right down on the table where I can see 'em. But you're playing with the wrong deck. I don't need to tell you I'm going to see Pelham about this."

"By all means, see him."

Cusler shook hands. "Remember, there's nothing personal in this. And I'm damn sorry to see you heading the wrong way."

When Cusler had gone, de Mérac sat smiling over a cigarette. Pelham would be helpless. And—if Cusler went to Kearny—*mais alors!* He reveled in the soul-freeing change.

There were other, immediate symptoms of Kearny's order. The chaplaincy, unfilled despite repeated requests, was suddenly taken up by a red-cheeked, black-jowled young priest fresh from the College of the Holy Cross in Worcester. Father Leo Doyle plunged into his new appointment with his black kepi rakishly askew and was instantly adopted by the whole regiment, Protestant as well as Catholic. Almost on arrival he stripped off his black coat and followed Wayne to the regimental hospital, where he took pulses, laughed, told stories, counseled, advised, admonished. He washed fever-wasted bodies, rushed out for stacks of newspapers, wrote letters when asked, and matched Latin tags with a dying young German from Heidelberg.

When Dr. Wayne tersely reported Father Doyle's activities, Wilson said, "There's a damn strong link in our chain, John."

"Ah!" said de Mérac. "I believe you. Our only difficulty will be to persuade Father Doyle that he is a noncombatant."

Through the joy of operating the regiment efficiently and without the chilling clutch of Pelham, fear came back to gnaw at de Mérac. No more stragglers tramped down the river road and Mr. McArdle still sat drooping by the edge of the field.

The question of regimental supply had undergone radical adjustment. Under Pelham, the quartermasters from the other two regiments had been served first, so that Brady had to take the least desirable remains of any issue from underwear to beef. Now the Rifles, as a detached unit, drew directly through Division. De Mérac had Lisette saddled and rode down to the wharves to look at a string of mules that Quarles, the Division quartermaster, had told him were coming in. On the river road de Mérac came face to face with Pelham and his staff. The brigadier's prim mouth tightened and his shaven cheeks flushed. De Mérac saluted. Pelham eyed him coldly, then returned the salute with cutting deliberation that said plainly, "Regulations force me to do this." Clay nodded courteously and Pride rumbled defiantly, "H'are you, John?"

There were many carriages wheeling and turning down by the piers. Colonels were arch and youthful with overdressed girls who tilted parasols in the cush-

196

ioned seats. Junior officers were voluble and learned as they explained aspects of the camp to excited sweethearts, staring sisters, or anxious-eyed mothers. A low barouche swept up toward the road and de Mérac started. Radiant and smiling, Lisa von Horstmar bowed to him. On the seat beside her was a captain from Pelham's staff, a dark young man named Conway. De Mérac swept off his kepi. "Ah, Lisa! How charming you look. Take care that Rebel scouts do not see you for, being gallant men, they would surely carry you off."

She tilted her parasol as the carriage stopped. "Captain Conway guards me well, Jean." The dark man managed an acknowledging smile between deep scowls at de Mérac's intrusion. Lisa went on, "I came down on the Gallwitzes' yacht which lies beyond Westover. For two days, I have it quite to myself. You must call on me."

Conway stirred impatiently. De Mérac bowed from the saddle. "A guard posted by a brigade, dear Lisa, may scarcely be relieved by one from a mere regiment."

She tossed her head and smiled. "Ways can be found around military etiquette, Jean."

De Mérac held his kepi over his heart. "*Chère baronne*, who may doubt it?" He drew Lisette to the side of the road as the carriage started up again. "The very best of luck attend you, Captain Conway," he thought, smiling wryly. "May your conquest outlast the war. *Diable*, I can at least assure him that it will be something he will not soon forget."

He rode on, delighted to see Lisa apparently so absorbed, yet aware of memories of her that were sharpened by the unnatural loneliness of army life. Then he forgot about her as he watched fine, strong-shouldered mules being unloaded at the wharf where Brady greeted them with strange Hibernian whoops. It was a fine shipment and de Mérac could feel assured that the wagons of the Rifles would bowl smoothly along in the wake of the regiment.

At the next pier a Sanitary Commission steamer was being warped in. Its rails were lined with civilians, women's bright skirts making patches of color among the somber browns and grays of the men. A girl cried excitedly. "Look! All those cannons over there." Another wavered, "This can't be the right place. Ralph's regiment has green stripes all over its coats. I can't see a soul."

Half amused, half sympathetic, de Mérac listened. These soft-looking people, men and women, belonged in another world, not his. Suddenly a dark, thin-cheeked girl pressed against the rail crying, "There he is! Charley! Oh—Char-*ley!*" A wan-faced Michigan lieutenant stopped by the end of the wharf, limped forward a few paces, his eyes creased in unbelief. The girl called again in a tight voice, "Charley! You're hurt!" The officer threw out his hands and scrambled awkwardly forward, one leg stiff. "Bess! Bess! Didn't expect you till tomorrow. Not hurt. Feeling tip-top. Wait right there. Oh, my God, this is wonderful." He hauled himself up the gangplank and vanished into the ship.

A cavalry sergeant shouted to a gray-haired woman with a broad, competent face, "Hello, Mother Beale! You back again?" The lined cheeks broke into a smile that de Mérac liked at once. She waved a mitted hand. "If it isn't Sergeant Godfrey. Look—did those dratted staff idiots move my store tent to Westover the way I said?" The sergeant stepped to the edge of the wharf and the two chatted on.

De Mérac tried to shake off a wave of loneliness as people called from ship to shore. It was like coming into his tent on mail day and finding no letters on his gray blankets. Then there was a stir along the deck. Two civilians edged apart and a slim girl in green, her bonnet scarcely reaching their shoulders, wedged in between them. She waved a green parasol frantically. "Baron de Mérac! Baron! Oh, John! Up here."

His throat tightened. Louise Duane, dark eyes dancing, leaned over the rail, waving. He dropped from Lisette, tossed the reins to Castex, and ran toward the gangplank and the clear voice that linked him with the world beyond the camps.

IX

The Hospital

THE big stone house near Georgetown had been turned over by its owner to the army as a hospital, and patients were scattered through its rambling floors. In the wide ballroom crystal chandeliers swayed from a ceiling that was spotted with garlands, dingy cherubs, and discreetly opulent goddesses. Long mirrors set between French windows reflected the rows of cots where men lay still, turned and twisted in fever sleep, or hunched in groups where cards fluttered softly.

George Force stirred on his cot that was set close to a long window. When he shifted his head on the clammy pillow the nearest mirror showed him that he was hollow-cheeked and dull-eyed. Only his straw-colored hair looked healthy and glossy. On one side of him a giant lumberman from Maine moaned in delirium from which he would rouse to know that his left leg was gone at mid-thigh. On the other, a New York lieutenant sat smoking nervously, an empty sleeve pinned across his jacket.

George waited in the afternoon heat for the daily surge of weakness, one symptom of the fever that he had picked up between the James and the Quaker Road. He opened heavy eyes as two doctors, one bearded and wheezing, the other stoop-shouldered with a nose like a crane's bill, paused by him. "All right, boy?" wheezed the first. George nodded weakly. Such questions seemed to make up that doctor's entire theory of treatment. "That's it. Don't let it get any worse." He clumped out.

His bill-nosed colleague clucked in soft admiration. "Jesus! How that feller hates porcupines."

George said weakly, "What?"

"Hates porcupines. Reg'lar God-damn gift. Been hunting with him in the Catskills. Never see anything like it. God, don't he hate 'em."

George's mind fumbled wildly with this unusual distinction. Then he gave it up and dropped into a heavy sleep. When he opened his eyes the New Yorker was awkwardly stowing away a watch. Two more cigar butts lay crushed at his feet. George asked, "About time for her to get here?"

"Any minute. I'm worried sick. Don't know how she'll take this." He touched his empty sleeve. "Coming clear from Alexandria Bay, she is."

George rallied himself. "I wouldn't worry about that, from what you told me about her. So you're from the North Country? Wonderful stretch up there, Raymer."

"It's all right." Raymer stepped on a cigar butt, lit a fresh one. "Hell, my brains'll be nix if I don't quit stewing over this. I was crazy letting her come. Maybe she won't want to get married now." He laughed shortly. "Not that I'd blame her a damn."

There were voices outside. Raymer rocked to his feet, still unused to balancing with only one arm. The broad door creaked open. George knew vaguely that the girl was tall, with masses of brown hair framing a plain, tender face. Soft, eager eyes swept the endless cots. Raymer said defiantly, "Well—here I am." The girl gave a low cry, put out her hands, and skimmed over the nicked floor. "Oh—gosh—darling! This is—this is—" Her voice broke as one blue arm curved about her.

George turned his back on them and the hum of their talk. Fever sleep closed over him, hot and uneasy. Sometime later Raymer's voice woke him. "Force—George Force. Come out of it. Hate to stir you up but—we'll be getting married just as soon as I get out of here. Rose darling, this is George Force."

George managed a grin. Rose was sitting close to Raymer, her face alight. One hand clutched the empty cuff. George said, "Don't need to wish you two luck. You've got it."

She said softly, eyes on the floor, "I know *I* have."

The Maine captain began to whimper. The girl's soft mouth quivered and she edged closer to Raymer. George said, "If you two go out that door between the middle windows, you'll be in a garden. Raymer, ring for an orderly, will you?"

Raymer looked gratefully at him and led Rose out through the door, tugging at a bellpull as he went. An orderly stumped in. George said. "Captain Baxter's drugs are wearing off. Better do something about him." The orderly called an untidy colleague and the two trundled the cot out of the room.

George ran a dry tongue over his lips. He looked out into the sunbaked garden that somehow reminded him of the rose-littered ground of the Danforth house near Frayser's Farm and the Quaker Road. Raymer and the girl were walking slowly up and down. Her head rested on his shoulder and she still clung to the empty sleeve. George felt sicker than ever. Why didn't he get strong again? Why was he so forgotten? He had written, shakily, to Dora, to his family, to John de Mérac. To none of the letters had he had an answer. A depression hard as his bone-deep weariness settled over him.

There was a scurry in the corridor. He thought in feeble disgust, "Nurse O'Neil's seen an officer. Only time she ever hurries." A woman's voice shrieked, "Saints alive! Get that nasty thing out of here. Eeeek! Orderly!" George thought in satisfaction, "Seen a rat. Hope he scares the daylights out of her."

Then his swollen eyes widened. There was a crisp patter of claws, a questioning "Whuff!" The door swept open and a dog with a wild tousled head lunged over

201

the threshold, a long leash trailing behind him. George sat up with a jerk. "My God! Mr. McArdle!"

The dog yelped, shot across the floor, and landed spraddled on the cot, his tail a bush of quivering ecstasy. George clutched the woolly body in unsteady arms and his eyes smarted. He rubbed his face against the dog's neck and quick words broke in his throat. Spurs clicked on the floor beside his cot. A strong hand caught his and de Mérac's voice, oddly pitched, cried, *"Enfin! C'est toi, Georges!"*

The long room whirled about in an opal-tinted mist. The mist cleared slowly. Mr. McArdle was still there, paws dancing on the blankets. De Mérac still held his hand tightly. George whispered, "This is great." He felt steadier and turned his head on the pillow. De Mérac was looking down at him with a deep solicitude. "It's great," whispered George again.

De Mérac released his hand and drew up a battered chair close to the cot. *"Doucement, Georges.* You have been very sick."

George's thin cheeks twitched in a grin. "Never mind that now. I want to hear about—" He broke off, staring at the plain blue uniform with its modest shoulder straps. Alarm filled his voice. "That uniform! You—you haven't got transferred, have you?"

"Pas de chance," said de Mérac, touching the interlocking "RR" on his collar. "This blue we all wear now."

George sank back in relief, suddenly aware of the fear that had haunted him all through his illness, of being assigned to some strange command, of learning that the Rifles had been disbanded and his friends scattered. He said, "Then that part's all right. You're still with them. How did you get here?"

De Mérac spread out his hands. "I was greatly afraid about you, George." Accent and French phrasing slipped away as he talked. "There was news nowhere. Then Louise Duane came to the camps with her father. She told me that she had seen you brought ashore by the Tenth Street wharf. Then naturally I secured Mr. McArdle and came looking. Now you must get well as we need you badly."

George said quickly, "Sure I won't be transferred when I get out of here?"

"I spoke of that to Kearny, who gave me my pass. He arranges your return. There is much news of the regiment for you, but that must wait. George, what *did* happen to you?"

George lay back contently. He rubbed Mr. McArdle's battered ears while the dog curled up tightly back of his knees, crowding him a good deal. George said, frowning, "I can't remember much, John. Honestly. I began to feel damn funny when we started back to Malvern. I remember that I seemed to be walking off in a great circle. I must have gotten into the Reb lines because I'm sure they had me once. Someone shot at me because a bullet hit my ribs and just curved around them. I'm pretty sure about a sergeant in gray sticking a bandage on me and giving me whiskey. I might have been his own brother, he was so damned decent. Then I guess I was in a cart or an ambulance because it was stopped and a Reb surgeon dumped us all out—the others with me were Rebs, too—and said he needed the cart for amputation cases. I'm not kicking."

"Of course not. He was right," said de Mérac. "And then—"

"Mind you, a lot of this is guesswork. I was out of my head a lot of the time. I think the guards they left over me just quit and went back to their outfits. I remember walking a lot and falling down and getting up again. The fever grew worse. Once I came to in a little cabin and an old, snuff-chewing woman was feeding me a thin broth. She and her husband were Rebs all right, but they kept me there and fed me and washed me. One funny thing I do remember. There was a picture of a lion on the wall opposite the bed they gave me. I thought it was real. I could see it getting ready to spring so I jumped out of bed, took a chair, and slammed the lion to shreds. Don't know how I got out of the house. Probably just walked. Like to find the place again and thank those people. Anyhow, the next I knew I was on a stretcher, being carted onto a Sanitary ship somewhere down the James. Then I woke up here. I figure I must have walked right through the Reb lines and back into ours. God, it's been awful here. I wrote Dad and Mother and Dora, soon's I could hold a pen. I wrote you first of all. Bet those damned orderlies threw the letters away and kept the stamp money."

De Mérac whistled softly. "You have been very lucky, George. And so has the regiment. Now this hospital—it does not suit you?"

George nudged Mr. McArdle with his knee. "How about letting me have some of my own bed!" Mr. McArdle whuffed happily and leaned more heavily against him. George gave up and returned to de Mérac. "The hospital? It's a damned shambles. Look at this room. Fever cases, venereal cases, dysentery, amputations, gunshot wounds, plain malingering, all piled in together. We've got two army horse doctors and the rest are contract surgeons, paid so much a head. Just clumsy butchers. Only two or three of the nurses in this ward are any good!"

De Mérac smiled quietly. "I have another paper from Kearny that will get you out of here."

George breathed deeply and for the first time felt cool air flowing into his lungs. "That's all right, then. Now tell me about the regiment. I'd have worried more about H if Randol hadn't done such a job once we got into action."

De Mérac shook his head sadly. "He has, I fear, reverted. He wears his kepi sideways to make the men laugh. When our band gave a concert of German music, our Mr. Randol shrieked that Dubiel had his Bach to the wall."

"I better hurry down there," murmured George. "What else?"

"We have a magnificent young Irishman named Leo Doyle as chaplain. The intense Mr. Rohde has formed the habit of dining at Pelham's mess, an arrangement which I trust they both find satisfactory. Dr. Wayne looks after the sick very well, drinks immense quantities of whiskey with Brady, and has evolved a theory that our fevers come from the bites of mosquitoes. Your Mr. Geranium Jones was thrown in the James by his tentmates and scoured with a grooming kit. Cook Metzger of Hein's is under arrest for trading a hind of beef to a young girl in return for favors unspecified. Chaplain Doyle makes the point that the crime is worse in that the beef was tainted."

George grinned. "Same old regiment."

"Not quite," said de Mérac gravely.

George winced. "Of course not. Sorry. How bad were we hit?"

De Mérac gave him the last figures, corrected by the return of stragglers.

"Lord, that's bad," sighed George.

"It is war, *mon ami,* and hence can only be bad. But there is better news. Listen to this. For all time we are detached from Pelham and serve under the direct orders of General Kearny. Ah! That makes you sit up, *hein?*" He detailed the changes that had taken place already— the better rations, better mules, more easily obtained equipment, instead of drawing the scant leavings of two other regiments as in the days of Pelham. Even the band had benefited, for most regimental music had either been sent home or incorporated in brigade bands. "But we, as we serve under Kearny, keep Dubiel and his men, who, moreover, are permitted to wear the old blue and yellow of Chambers Street and Kearny buys them new instruments out of his own funds."

"Fine, fine," murmured George. The stimulus of excitement was wearing off and his head throbbed so that it seemed to shake his whole body. He felt de Mérac's hand on his forehead, heard concern in his voice. "You must sleep now, *mon ami.*"

He muttered, "Don't go."

"I shall stay and make you worse? No. But first tell me whom I see to arrange that Mr. McArdle stays with you."

George's eyes closed and he whispered heavily, "It's the man who hates porcupines."

De Mérac stared. "Ah! A delirium of the fever." He went quietly out, leaving George asleep. He looked for a nurse. When he had first arrived, DuChesne, now waiting outside with the horses, had loudly announced him by title and nurses had swarmed about to stare and whisper. Now there was not one in sight. He started down the corridor, heading deeper into the building, but found only closed doors with patients' names tacked to them. Then down a passage to the right, he heard a swift click of heels on hardwood, a brisk, assured tread unlike that of the other nurses he had seen. There was something heartening in the sound—click-click-click-click. A slight figure muffled from chin to ankles in a gray coverall swung into sight. He called, "Oh, Nurse!"

She stopped in the dimness of the corridor. The coverall, gathered at the waist, swathed her in a kind of anonymity. Above the white band of the collar de Mérac saw a rebellious mouth and chin, a face that might have been pretty under its mask of fatigue, clear gray eyes, dark-circled. Her head was bound in a towel that pulled her forehead tight and completely hid her hair. He thought suddenly of a kitten with its ears pushed back. She asked, "What may I do for you?" Her voice was pleasant but businesslike.

"I want to see a man about a dog," said de Mérac.

Her mouth tightened. "Please—we're very busy."

"But I am serious. Permission for a patient to keep a dog until his release."

"You'll see Captain Mortimer about that. This way, please."

She clicked on ahead of de Mérac, out onto a strip of lawn. The rhythm of her steps fascinated him as they tapped on broad flagstones. She opened the door of a long wooden shack and pointed to a small room at the right. "Will you wait here, please?"

De Mérac lit a cigarette. "Now she goes to some office where she will hear that in France I am a baron. She will come back to stare like the others. DuChesne *must* omit the title. Ah—here she comes."

The heels were coming back down a long passage. De Mérac sighed. He also settled his collar and twirled the ends of his mustache. The heels were just outside the door. A blur of gray flitted past in the hall. The heels clicked on the outer flagstone, faded away entirely. De Mérac flipped away his cigarette and stared from the window at a slight gray back that was vanishing into the main building. *"Mais enfin!"* he muttered.

A long-nosed man with green shoulder straps came jerkily in. "Nurse said you wanted to see me. What's bothering you?"

De Mérac waved a letter from Kearny, spoke of the general's concern about George, urged the necessity of Mr. McArdle's staying with his master. The doctor yawned. "If Phil Kearny wants all that, I guess it's all right. I'll move your friend and the dog into a little room on the other side. If any big Indians come snooping round, I'll keep the pup myself till they're gone."

De Mérac thanked the doctor. As he walked to the front of the hospital, he unconsciously cocked his ear, listening in vain for a distant click-click.

The next morning George lay on a shady terrace at the west side of the house with Mr. McArdle curled across his knees. He felt steadier, as if the last of the poison were draining from his blood. He fingered a telegram happily. Mr. McArdle lifted his head and whuffed twice. George looked toward the house and saw de Mérac hurrying toward him. "Hello, John. Bet you did this." He waved the telegram. "Dad and Mother are bringing Dora down from New York. What do you think of that?"

De Mérac patted his shoulder. "It would have happened in any event."

"But not so soon. Judas! What's the matter with you? Did you spend the night in a barroom?"

De Mérac pulled up a chair. "But very nearly. I share an omnibus garret room at Willard's with five others. At sunrise one of them bawled for a glass of sherry, drank it, ordered a cherry bounce and ended up with a brandy smash—all in the space of one half hour. There was no sleep after that. As a matter of fact, I got in rather late. I had dined at the Duanes'."

"H'm," said George.

De Mérac added quickly, "Yes. You see it was Louise who told me about you at Harrison's Landing and then I came back on the same boat with her and her father. They asked me to dine, so, of course—"

"Good Lord, no reason why you shouldn't dine there." He looked curiously at de Mérac. "Dining *chez* someone tonight?"

"*Chez* Mrs. Welles. I had cards to them when I first went to Albany."

"I know who they are. Louise going to be there?"

George saw lines form between de Mérac's eyes. "Ah—why, no. I do not think so. In fact, I am assured she will be somewhere else."

George thought, "And you don't like it for a damn, either." He scratched Mr. McArdle's chin. "Well, to get down to trivia, what's happening to the army? Who's this Pope I've read about?"

"Labanieff has been at our camp several times," de Mérac said. "He wears the Tambov uniform topped with a Union steeple-crowned hat whose gold cords hang down the wrong way. At most times, he can tell you every detail of every officer, Union or Southern. Of Pope he only says that as a cadet at West Point he introduced flyfront trousers, which so shocked the commander's wife that she would receive no cadet whose trousers did not button at the sides. Beyond that, he tells us nothing."

George chuckled. "That suggests an inventive temperament, anyway. Seriously, things do look stirring?"

"Ah, they stir. No doubt of that. The city is thick with troops moving into Virginia."

"And we stay anchored down on the James?"

"There are signs that our anchor may be dragging," de Mérac answered quietly. "Hooker dines with Kearny nearly every night and it is not my opinion that they plan charades."

"Don't tell me that McClellan's going to move!"

"No, no. Not that one! Besides, he is nearly powerless. But our old *kébir* advised me, and no doubt others, in all privacy, to study maps of Northern Virginia from Skinker's Neck to Popcastle Creek."

"But that would be in Pope's territory," protested George.

De Mérac held out his hands. "And you think that

Pope would sue for trespass if our whole Corps under Heintzelman appeared there to serve at his orders?"

"Could be. Could be," said George thoughtfully. "Lord, all this talk makes me want to get back."

De Mérac rose. "I return to town now. I must be there in time to send flowers to Louise, who gives a luncheon for some Washington misses. I shall be here again this afternoon."

George watched him walk across the terrace in front of the house. "Damned if I don't think Claire Wilson was right last spring when she said that that Duane snip had made up her mind to be the Baroness de Mérac! Oh Lord!"

The food was excellent, the wines expertly chosen, for the Welleses were famous for their dinners. Yet de Mérac found himself wishing that he had declined. For one thing, he was too aware of the contrast between this cool room and its carefree people and the crowded, baking hospitals and camps. Then, too, he was disappointed in his partner, a sullen-faced girl who answered in monosyllables. The chair on the other side of him was vacant. Mrs. Welles had apologized for it. "It's for my little niece, Gail. She told me she'd be late, if she came at all, but I'm saving the place anyway." That was the most he had to hope for—some bread-and-buttery little girl tongue-tied among elders.

He glowered across the table at a young civilian with a soft face and hard eyes who cried to a fat dowager, "What! You haven't been to *Newport?* Oh, but you must go! I assure you. Your season will be spoiled if you don't. Really, you *must.*"

De Mérac thought angrily, "Ah, *mon beau!* I should like to see you among the mosquitoes of Harrison's Landing." He avoided the man's eyes as the latter tried to draw him into the conversation. The people he wanted most to talk to were too far down the table, like the lean Tennessee major who had raised several troops of cavalry in his own state, or like the pale Boston gunner who was defending the Barbizon School against the attacks of a whiskered classicist.

He tried to rouse himself, knowing that much of his lack of ease came from the fact that Louise Duane had been either unable or unwilling to see him that evening. In the two days of waiting for a boat at Harrison's Landing he had been aware of her appeal as never before. She was delighted with everything he had planned for her, from a review of the regiment to an invitation to a ball held in the gracious charm of the Byrd mansion at Westover, now Fitz-John Porter's headquarters. She had a habit of stepping close to him when he presented other officers to her, a gesture that suggested intimacies linking them secretly. At reviews her elbow brushed his, or her hand rested for an instant on his cuff as she looked up at him. In generous *décolletage* that revealed her firm breasts, she had a way of hitching at the flimsy material while her eyes sought his with a look that might have been unconscious. Twice in chance solitude she had disturbed him so that he had been on the verge of sweeping her into his arms despite the fact that in words, at least, she had never departed from her frank, almost sexless air of companionship. He was glad that he had not yielded. With a young American girl like Louise it would not have done, he was sure.

Diable! He had seen her for a few moments that afternoon on his return from the hospital. It was inconceivable that he should miss her so much now. The soft-faced civilian opposite him chattered on about Newport and the horses that he was shipping up there, how August Belmont was driving about behind a pair for which he had paid twenty-five thousand dollars.

There was a stir at the head of the table and the men rose as a girl all in white came quietly in. De Mérac had a fleeting impression of a clear young face crowned by a simply dressed mass of red-gold hair as she bent to kiss Mrs. Welles. Then she moved down the table and de Mérac's ill-humor vanished. He placed her chair before a hurrying servant could reach it.

She smiled at him, showing small, even teeth between rather full lips as she settled herself in a wide billow of skirts. Her neck and shoulders rose flawless from the simply cut evening gown. She said, "Don't bother about me, Williams, I'll start wherever the others are." She turned to de Mérac. "I can see your place card so I know all about you." De Mérac hurriedly upset it to hide the word "Baron." She went on, "I'm Gail Shortland and Mrs. Welles is my favorite aunt. Are you with General Pope?"

He liked her direct look. It was evident that she was not asking merely to make conversation. He said, "No, not with General Pope. I am with the Rochambeau Rifles under General Kearny. He was good enough to give me special leave."

"Oh—then that was your cap I saw in the hall! The one with the red patch and the gorgeous tortoise-shell vizor! That could be carved beautifully, you know." She made a graceful gesture as though setting a comb in the sweep of her bright hair.

He laughed. "You should have it for knowing so much about our division."

"Oh—it's been in the papers. Now do tell me about yourself. You're French, of course. Had you been here long before the war?" Her manner had something oddly boyish about it, yet was utterly feminine. He found himself telling of his first visit, of his return and the choice that led him to the Rochambeau Rifles.

She said, "I like that."

He looked quickly at her. There was no trace of coquetry or flattery in those three words, just a statement of fact. He said, "But I may take no credit. Perhaps it was feeling, not reason."

She shook her head. "You reasoned that if the Union fell, the whole world would suffer. That's not feeling."

"I am afraid it is merely the expression of a feeling. To have come here, every step guided by cold reason, would have been more logical."

She laughed and dimples flicked across her cheeks. "Does a Frenchman *always* have to be logical?"

"In theory. Yet you see how I fail in practice. It is illogical to talk about me—a subject of interest to few—instead of about yourself. Do you live in Albany, as does Mrs. Welles?"

Somehow he couldn't keep the conversation on her.

211

He gathered that her father had a parish up the Mohawk near Herkimer and that she spent a good deal of the year with him in a stone house that had been built as a fort in Indian days. There was no way of telling whether the farm that went with the house was vast and feudal, like some of the estates he remembered around Casenovia, or a small holding. Often she made her aunt long visits in Albany. Now Mrs. Welles had brought her to Washington, where Mr. Welles acted in some mysterious advisory capacity to the War Department.

"Ha!" thought de Mérac. "Brought her down here to see the war!" Yet the cynical observation did not satisfy him. He wanted to hear more about the Mohawk Valley, but found that he was talking about himself again, trailing on in the wake of her questions and comments. He told of his father's death at Sidi Brahim, of life at Loudéac where the rumble of guns from the Coëtquidan artillery range stirred the air about the old terraces. He spoke of his disgust with Bonaparte, of his troubles with Bonaparte's political police that had brought about his exile. He found that he enjoyed talking, rather than listening, for he could watch the play of expression about her full, mobile mouth, the direct look in her clear gray eyes, and the slight lift of her arched eyebrows.

The scrape of chairs filled him with disappointment. He had hardly time for another word as Mrs. Welles led the women into the drawing room. He smoked cigarette after cigarette over brandy and coffee. The Tennessee major sought him out and talked with keen perception of affairs in that state. He insisted that much of it was as Union as Maine. "A single corps sent there, Captain, would bring every loyal man to the colors. We're losing them through neglect, I tell you. That idiot in the White House can't see beyond capturing Richmond!"

Then he was in the drawing room amid a swish of silks and crinolines and the vague hint of perfumes. He tried to find Gail Shortland and drifted from group to group, hopefully. Then he saw her standing in the hall, hooking the clasp of a light wrap. He crossed quickly to her. "I had hoped that we might talk more," he said.

She smiled pleasantly. "This is late, for me at least."

"Then I suggest that you and Mrs. Welles drive with me tomorrow afternoon."

She shook out a tulle scarf. "I don't go out much." There was no hint of snub in her voice.

"I could show you a great deal. You'd like to see the hospitals, I'm sure."

Her eyes widened as she wound the scarf about her hair. She drew the scarf tighter and he stifled an exclamation. The kitten with its ears pushed back!

He burst out, "Why did you not say something?"

"I saw you didn't recognize me. And what do I have to tell one of Kearny's men?"

"All the more reason for driving. It will do you good. I have tomorrow ahead of me."

"So have I—at the hospital."

"On my next visit, then. I shall write Mrs. Welles."

She dropped her hands to her sides. "My work isn't much. But it's something that I can *do!*"

"You'll be all the better for an afternoon in the open."

Her chin tightened. "Listen. In Ward One yesterday there was a Maine captain who'd lost his leg. He died early this morning." Her chin quivered, tightened again. "I—I sat up with him. Not that I could help, not in any way, only—only he thought I was his mother. He clung to my hand until he died. I had to call an orderly—" she spoke faster, crowding all emotion from her bleak statement of facts—"I had to call the orderly to help pry his fingers loose from mine. I can't sit up there, watching a clock and thinking that in an hour *I'm* free to go out for a nice drive when we've dozens of men like that captain—dozens worse!"

He looked gravely at her. "Please forgive me."

She put out her hand in a boyish gesture. "You understand. Goodbye and good luck, Captain de Mérac." The door closed on a swish of wide skirts.

De Mérac took his leave as soon as he decently could and walked toward Willard's. One of the new horsecars trundled down Pennsylvania Avenue, red lights glowing through its stained-glass windows. People stood in the aisles, clung to the platform. A ragged, under-strength regiment in broad hats stared dumbly at it as it passed.

Outside Willard's the sidewalks were jammed with troops who shouted, "Wallace! Lew Wallace!" German voices bawled, "Ve vant Sigel, Sigel, *Sigel!*" Against a bright window two men appeared, one lean and spare, the other thick-set. De Mérac pushed on, impatient of the cheering. Sigel, ex-Baden regular, had come on with a record of Arkansas victories. Wallace, an Indiana politician, was said to have fought well. But McClellan, too, had come out of the west victorious and men had cheered him. As de Mérac climbed to his omnibus garret room, he thought grimly that before long Kearny would test these new men.

The room was stifling. The man who had started the day with three drinks was calmly shaking out the folds of a well-cut brown coat. On the next bed a cavalry officer, still booted, slept in a thick haze of whiskey. Beyond, a fat man sweated and snored, woke to spit on the floor, snored again. De Mérac flung open the casement and let cool air wash over him. He shook his head in bewilderment as he thought of the dinner.

"*Incroyable!* She goes among patients of every kind. She must have to bathe them and they come to her filthy as *fumiers*. She smells abdominal wounds. She picks up arms and legs that are hacked off!"

As he dropped between rough sheets he realized with a shock that Louise Duane had been out of his thoughts for most of the evening. "*Doucement!* Does the unnatural life of the army fill my mind with each pretty girl that I see?"

Out at the hospital, Gail Shortland got out of her white dress in the little, high room that she shared with Nurse Pender, a plain, stocky, cheerful girl in her late twenties. Pender watched her with frank admiration. "You look just elegant in that dress. Your beau like it?"

Gail smiled. "This was just a dinner at my aunt's. All my beaux are out here."

Pender slipped off a cotton wrapper and stood, squat and bulbous, in her shift. "You know, when I first saw you, I thought you'd bust in two days." She yawned and slid her hand inside her shift, scratching her ribs noisily.

"Got to say you lug your share, though. If you'd had two years at the New York Hospital like I did, you could run a ward by yourself. 'Sakes! You're losing weight, Shortland. Your hip bones stick out like a herring's and I can see your ribs under your breasts."

Gail shook herself hurriedly into a nightgown, pulled on a blue wrapper, "I'm no thinner than the boys they bring here," she said defiantly.

Pender swung her thick legs into bed. "Well, if you're asleep when the rising bell rings tomorrow, I won't wake you. I'll tell Matron you're sick. Will I blow out the candle?"

"Don't bother. I want to brush my hair." Her whole body ached and her feet burned as she stood in front of the cracked mirror, but she brushed on resolutely. She'd been a fool to go to her aunt's. While she had been enjoying herself, a hundred things could have been happening here. In the mirror she saw the corners of her mouth curve in a faint smile. She tried to erase it, but it lingered. She said abruptly, "You know, Pender, I've been thinking about these foreign boys in our army."

Pender stirred wrathfully. "So've I. I had to make out the papers for a sergeant named Piotr Vroblewski—" she spelled the name out in weary cadence—"you know, the one they cut the buttock off of and came from Illinois. Been a citizen ten years, I found out."

"I don't mean like him or like Guido Guidi. I mean those who are still foreigners and so far as you can see haven't a thing to gain by being with us. They just seem to believe in us enough to want to fight with us."

"They'll take up just as much room as a farm boy from Saugerties. And they'll need as many enemas and bedpans. They'll—" Pender sat up suddenly, corners of her mouth drawn down.

In the house below, a bell had begun to ring. Mrs. Guild, the matron, called up the stairs. "Ladies! Hurry up, ladies! Five wagons from the docks. Be here any minute!"

Gail Shortland sat down on the edge of her cot. Revulsion struck her. Her throat tightened and her eyes began to burn. She buried her face against the folds of her white dress. Her mind clamored. "I can't! Not till I've slept. Oh, God make them forget me. Just this once!" There would be reeking, dirt-caked bodies to wash, filthy underclothes swarming with lice to be carried out. There would be bluish-red stumps where maggots crawled lazily or dropped in squirming knots onto blood-soaked bandages. Her fingers wound about the clean hem of her dress.

Pender's hand rested on her shoulder. "You been going too strong. Get into bed. It'll be dark and Matron won't see who's there. Go on, now."

Gail let her head sink lower. Then she forced herself to her feet. "No!" She twisted her hair into a quick knot, bound a towel around it, snatched up her coverall, and scuffed into shoes that she kept for night calls. Pender began, "Well, of all the ninnies—" Then she dropped a heavy arm about Gail's shoulder. "Come on. We'll handle 'em alone if we have to."

Out on the scarred driveway, cool air flowed against Gail's face and for an instant she felt better. Then the fever of fatigue wrapped slowly about her. Lanterns flicked in the dark and wheels creaked. Other nurses, a doctor or two, a handful of orderlies, crunched onto the gravel from the house. Mrs. Guild snapped, "Smart, now! Here they come."

Gail closed her eyes, drew a deep breath, and then moved to the first stretcher that the orderlies lowered from the leading wagon. Light shone on a battered felt hat marked with state letters, hollow temples, and sunken, bristly cheeks. She unslung a canteen from her shoulder, soaked a sponge from it, and passed the wet mass over the wasted face. Her quick eyes took stock of the misshapen bulge about the shoulders which, with the heavy, strangling smell that rose to her, told of amputation bandages.

She stifled a retching cramp. The reddened lids in the shade of the wide hat flickered and a thick voice muttered. "Oh, Christ Almighty!"

Gail forced a smile that she hoped was cheerful. "Hello, Wisconsin! We're going to give you a bath and put you in the best bed you've had since you left home.

Ready, orderly!" As the man was lifted, a clawlike hand reached out for hers, closed around it. She walked on beside the stretcher. The smell rose heavier. There would be maggots to pick out, one by one. She steadied her voice and called, "Careful, orderly! We don't get many Wisconsin boys and we've got to take good care of this one!"

It was surprisingly cool in the Washington station. George Force lay on a wheeled stretcher and stared unbelievingly at Dora Chase. Things had been happening too fast. First Mr. McArdle, now firmly tethered to the stretcher, then de Mérac, then his parents, and now Dora. Her face seemed to hover between him and the high, smoky vault of the train shed, her dark hair touched with light reflected from the yawning entrance, her blue-gray eyes soft with a light that he had never seen before, and her mouth trembling in a smile. He said weakly, "I still don't understand."

She said gently, "You don't have to, George. Claire Wilson and your mother did it—they got me down here."

George turned his head to glance at his parents, who stood a few feet away, watching, with forced intensity, the relief of the provost guard ride up outside the station. His father was erect as ever but his face was drawn and his carefully parted beard was more gray than pepper-and-salt. His mother looked frailer but her chin was proudly set. Dora whispered, "Call them over, George. Your mother has hardly had a word with you yet and she insisted on waiting behind so we'd be alone."

George called huskily, "There's nothing contagious about me. Come on over."

The two moved quickly to him and Mrs. Force touched the girl's hand, smiling warmly at her. The station roared with the din of an incoming train, then echoed to the clump of boots as waves of men in blue tumbled out. George stirred uneasily as he ran an eye over them. Massachusetts troops, and new, to judge by the unstained flags. Very likely by afternoon they'd be across the Potomac, tramping over the red roads that he knew so well. From a farther train, stretchers were being unloaded and ranged on the platform. He felt still more ill at ease, lying on his wheeled pallet while a nurse from the hospital and the man who hated porcupines stood a little distance away like a guard of honor. He drew in his breath sharply. Dora closed her hand about his and said gently, "I understand, George. You'll be back with them."

He smiled up at her. "Don't have to explain much to you, do I, darling? Lord, but I'm lucky!"

"Tired?" asked his mother.

"Of course not. Just feel a little— Hi! Here's John!"

De Mérac was pushing his way through the crowd. "This is a pleasure, Miss Chase!" he called. "Ah—Du-Chesne. *Par ici.*" The old Chasseur clanked up, two great clusters of roses incongruous in his scarred hands. "For you, Mrs. Force, and for Miss Chase," said de Mérac. He fanned himself with his kepi. "I thought I should miss this. They kept me late at the War Department."

George grinned. "I'd have resigned if you'd been too late. You engineered most of this, so—" He saw de Mérac raise his head quickly and turn toward the nurse, heard him cry, "Good morning, Nurse Shortland!"

Her pleasant voice answered, "Good morning, Captain de Mérac! Are you on your way to rejoin General Kearny?"

"*Du tout.* I came here to see my friend safely onto the train—a somewhat needless precaution. You must let me drive you back to the hospital afterwards."

"Thank you. I'll have to go in the ambulance with the stretcher and—" The rest of her words were drowned in the roar of the incoming train. Then George saw her close to the stretcher, directing four grinning Negroes. "This way, boys. Get it like this. Lift so he doesn't tilt." He felt himself raised gently to the car platform where the nurse had skipped nimbly.

De Mérac shrugged. Then he saw Mr. and Mrs. Force and Dora, looking helplessly up the car steps, blocked by the stretcher. He ran to them. "By the front door. Quickly." He guided the two women down the platform, Mr. Force striding on by his elbow. They filed into the car and found that two seats had had their backs slid out and placed in the gap lengthwise to form a broad couch. Mr. Force explained. "I had these seats reserved and—ah! here he comes. This way, boys."

A gray figure slipped past the Negroes and took charge. "Under the shoulders—under the knees—you take the feet." In an instant, George lay stretched out with a light blanket over him. The nurse said, "His head ought to be a little higher."

Dora moved quickly. "I can do that."

Gail Shortland looked keenly at her, then stepped aside. "That's fine." She smiled at Dora. "Give him all the water he wants and let him sleep when he can." She nodded to Mrs. Force and went down the aisle after the stretcher and became entangled with the butting press of incoming passengers.

George caught de Mérac's blue sleeve. "Say, John—when did you know that nurse?"

"I met her," said de Mérac vaguely. "Now, George, I am not going to wait until the train starts. Look after him, Miss Chase. Good luck, George." He shook hands with Mr. Force, spoke with especial warmth to Mrs. Force, who had stood resolutely aside while another woman looked after her son. Then he dropped to the platform, waving his kepi as he passed their window.

The gray figure was just coming down the rear steps, directing the Negroes toward the stretcher. He caught up with her. "Let me trundle that. And I am serious about driving you to Georgetown."

The Negroes came trotting up; she shot the stretcher toward them and dusted her palms briskly. "That's all there is to the trundling, Captain. I'd love to drive out, but it's against rules." She started to move away.

He stepped beside her. "Look—I sail tonight. I shan't see you again. Will you let me write you?"

"I'd like that very much." Her laugh was low and friendly. "Tell me what's happening to the army and to you."

"You'll answer?"

She tucked back a wisp of red-gold hair. "If I can. I have to write letters for boys who can't do it for themselves. Then some who've left the hospital write me—

from home or from the army. I always answer. That takes a lot of time, you see."

"Surely, you could find a moment for me among all the lucky ones?"

"Really, I'd like very much to hear from you—but please don't be offended if I can't answer often." Her hands flew to her cheeks and her eyes widened. "Oh! What *are* they doing to that poor man over there?" She skimmed away across the tracks toward the waiting stretchers, where a clumsily handled patient had been rolled off onto the platform.

De Mérac sighed. "Not only am I a fool. I am also in the way." He hitched his sword belt and passed out into the sun, frowning. "*Diantre!* I am not her brother, nor the son of her mother's sister! Not that I expect her to flirt! No! Decidedly, I should not want that. Still—*vingt dieux!* Once more, I am *not* her brother!"

He went on past the Capitol, where builders still swarmed, and saw a horsecar clanking up the Avenue. He ran for it.

When he reached the Duanes', where he was to lunch, Louise met him, radiant and gay. She had found a little shop on F Street that carried cigarettes and explained delightedly, "Now when you call, you won't have to struggle with those awful cigars of Father's. Light one up quick. I love the smell. It makes me think of Europe!"

He was touched by her thought and by her obvious joy in her discovery. He watched the quick sparkle of her eyes, the play of light on her blond hair and the lithe sway of her gait. She was so charming now. One day she would be fully wakened and be far more charming—to the eternal delight of some lucky suitor.

Yet at lunch, where there were two elderly guests, he kept wishing that she would not say "Baron" so often. But when her brown eyes met his across the table and she smiled her secret smile, he swept away all criticism.

Flights of sea gulls with sun-tipped wings skimmed close to the curling lips of waves that broke on the quiet New Jersey beach. George Force lay back in a long chair on the sands in his patched blue and yellow uniform. His cheeks showed a healthy tinge of color and his lips moved in a smile as he looked at his watch. Dora would soon be coming down from the house that her father had grudgingly rented next to the place that the Forces had taken. He slowly put his watch back and called encouragingly to Mr. McArdle as the dog made wild dashes close to the edge of the surf in fruitless yelping forays after gulls.

Shoes drummed lightly on the steps that led down from the low bluffs to the beach and Dora's voice called, fresh and happy, "Asleep, darling?"

George tried to wrench the chair about to face the bluffs, but she was at his side in an instant, pulling up the light rug that had fallen from his knees. She kissed him and he slid an arm about her shoulders, ruffled her dark curls. "Been missing you, honey."

She rubbed her cheek against his mended jacket. "You're such a solid sort of a dear, George. Really, you are getting solid. I can't find a thing to pinch on your arm." She sank onto a cushion beside his chair, her head level with his.

"Your mother have a good afternoon?" he asked.

Dora's delicate face lightened. "Such a restful nap. She sent her love and hopes she'll be able to see you before dinner. I wish she could be out here with us now. There's always the loveliest purply light on the sea as the sun goes down."

George sighed. "I wish she were, too. She's a wonderful person, Dora. You wait. She'll get your father to say yes about us before long. And another thing—" He tweaked her ear gently. "She'd back me up in my anti-coddling campaign. Between you and Mother I feel like a cocoon that's been stuffed into a lime kiln."

She frowned in mock severity. "You do what we say and please keep that rug at least up to your knees. Didn't I promise John de Mérac you'd be looked after?"

"That didn't mean tying me down when I feel strong enough to beat Hercules's brains out. Good old John. Wonder what he's doing now?"

Dora sniffed. "I hope he isn't galloping around after

that Louise Duane. George, he isn't really serious about her, is he?"

George pursed his lips. "Serious? Lord no. Oh, he likes her all right. He thinks she's pretty and all that. And then she's always playing the frank, gay friend with no demands. She puzzles him too. She'll say something or do something and he'll tell me later, 'Were it a European girl I should be shocked—or alarmed—or delighted—' or whatever it may be—'but your American girls—'" He imitated de Mérac's shrug.

Dora tossed her head. "He may not be serious, but I'll bet a doughnut she is. Frank, gay friend! Fuff!" She flounced on her cushion and paper crackled. "Oh—that's the *Tribune* in my reticule. I brought it down for you. There's a lot about the army. Tell me what it means."

George opened the paper. "H'm. Guess John was right. Something's going to happen in Virginia. The country's stiff with troops."

Her eyes went wide. "Not—not along the James?"

"No. With Pope along the Rappahannock. And they've brought Halleck on from the west to Washington as chief of staff. Old Brains himself. Wonder what he'll do."

"Is he really so clever?"

George looked amused. "He knows everything about every battle that was ever fought—if you don't go later than 1707. He's worse than John's friend Labanieff, Major Dunn says. Why, Halleck'll tell you—"

She laid her fingers on his mouth. "Maybe he will, but you won't. Just tell me—" She swayed forward in sudden alarm as George's expression grew grave. "What is it?"

"Old Brains. He's ordering most of the Army of the Potomac to join Pope."

She said wonderingly, "What does that mean?"

George sat up. "All of us. We'll get out of those blasted fever camps along the James and join Pope." Dora felt a darkening chill settling about her. George's eyes were on the quick dance of the waves. He said slowly, "I can get a boat from New York tomorrow or the day after." He caught Mr. McArdle's collar. "Come on, pup. We've got to see about this."

Dora did not recognize her own voice as she cried, "No!"

George let go of the collar and looked at her in surprise. "But I've got to."

She clutched at his hand, at his sleeve. "Not yet! No! George, you're not well enough."

"This is different. The Rifles were rotting on the James and it didn't matter much where I was. But now—they're on the move. I'm strong as I ever was—or will be pretty quick."

She began to cry quietly. "Is it always going to be like this? I find you and then the army takes you away again." She rested her forehead on her knuckles. "I hate it. I hate it. Nothing's worth all this murder and horror over and over again. You had a nightmare on the train coming north and you moaned about a hollow across a stream and someone being bayoneted and John de Mérac pinned under his horse. I want to love you and care for you and not send you back into places like that again and again until one day you don't come home to me." Her slim shoulders shook and her voice rose. "No! Nothing's worth that."

He put his arm about her and said gently, "The Union is. The Union's worth anything. You know it. Darling, if you could have seen some of the things I've seen. If you could know how much it means to so many people, people you'd hardly expect it to. Pelham said once we ought to take all the foreign-born and make them go to school until they learned what it was to be an American. That was on one of his gentler days. Pelham! I sometimes think we're the ones who ought to go to school under *them* and stop taking for granted the things that mean so much to them. There's that little bugler, Castex, who rides after John. He's always jerky as a flushed rabbit but he tears ahead whimpering to himself wherever John goes. And John's not the most careful person in the world. Castex. He used to sell papers in Union Square. That idiot Rohde asked him why he enlisted and the little tyke drew himself up grave as Dan'l Webster and said, 'One may at least try to pay a debt.'"

She whispered, "But it's you I love."

He went on. "At Frayser's Farm—well, I could keep on citing things like that all day. Can't you see it, dear? All those men, thousands and tens of thousands of them, feel so strongly about what's been built up here that they're willing to go out and get shot at rather than see it knocked to pieces. Oh, I don't mean they're doing all the work, not by a long shot. We'd probably win without them. But there's so much behind their just *being* there."

She said simply, "I love you, George." She dabbed at her eyes. "I'll go to the boat with you. But—oh, my dear, my dear—be careful."

A wind was whipping up Chesapeake Bay, shattering the sun-touched waters into a thousand glinting mirrors. George leaned against the rail and watched the bulk of Fortress Monroe and the sprawling Hygeia Hotel come closer as the tubby *State of Maine* butted its way along. He was one of a line of blue-coated men who stared eagerly or reluctantly at the widening mouth of James. A deck chair scraped behind him and he saw a big, strong-featured colonel with carefully tended mustache and imperial settle himself painfully. Under a new crimson-lined cloak, faded red breeches showed and a red kepi was cocked jauntily above a fever-gnawed face. Something in the set of the gold-banded cap seemed familiar. George left the rail. "Colonel de Trobriand, I think."

Bloodshot eyes surveyed him calmly. "If you always think as correctly, I should welcome you to my staff." He spoke painfully, as though the climb to the deck had been a strain. "Ah—blue and yellow. The Rifles. Yes, I have you now, *justement*. You came to my camp with your de Mérac. You are Georges Force, his friend. You were wounded, perhaps?"

"Mostly fever, Colonel."

"Ah! *Sacrée fièvre!* Myself, I went no farther than Fair Oaks when it took me. At my age, you conceive—" He shrugged as though tolerantly critical of his years.

George eyed the yellowed cheeks, the unsteady hands. "They passed you for duty, sir?"

"*Quasiment comme ça!* I could have enjoyed remaining longer with Madame and with my little Caroline—you may remember the *môme* who rode the fat pony at the Loughboros' beyond Tennallytown? But when I learned of this move I judged it prudent to return. I am away from my red-legged devils too long."

"I saw the 55th at Malvern, sir. They looked in good shape, considering."

De Trobriand's thick eyebrows lifted. "That does not surprise me. Young man, this army is like no other in my knowledge. It has fought three enemies: the first, fevers; the second, Lee; and the third, the worst of all—McClellan. Ah—we must get back, you and I, back to that army." He leaned forward, frowning. "Did it never occur to you, young man, that we could lose this war? The thought alarms you? Ah, we could, I assure you, even with such an army."

"The same thought hit me on the march to Malvern." His jaws tightened. "We're not going to, though."

De Trobriand muttered, "If all the army knows that we might and vows that we shall *not—ah, ça!* Then even McClellan may not beat us!" His eyelids shivered down and he cursed the "*sacrée fièvre*" again, adding, "Your pardon. But one grows sleepy of it, all the same."

George went back to the rail. A gaunt captain of cavalry, adjusting the sling that supported his right arm, remarked, "That colonel looks sick to me."

"He says he isn't." George glanced back at the dozing Breton baron, a mercenary immigrant to Pelham and his kind, who was driving himself without complaint to take his place with the Army of the Potomac.

The paddles churned on, pushing the ship up and up the winding James. George went below, rescued Mr. McArdle from the ignominy of the hold, and took his place on the starboard side. The banks were very close and wreathed with curtains of dust raised by rolling caissons or marching men. There were camps, centering about big, pillared houses, and parks of artillery and long lines of picketed horses.

George leaned farther over the rail, his eyes blurring as they blinked at the stir and movement of blue columns. He suddenly thought of the great base as a magnet that was drawing him and the pounding paddle wheels to its very heart. The world that lay astern no longer existed. Bugles were sounding retreat and the clear notes brought a tightening in his throat. Mr. McArdle whined and thrust his nose into his master's hand. George said thickly, "Getting there, boy, getting there!" Up toward the bow a bearded major shouted, "Look—see those red-tops? Kearny's men. I told you about them!"

George shivered in spite of the level rays of the sun that poured against the ship through a golden haze of dust. There was the tall Harrison house, the jutting lines of the piers where men swarmed and wagons thumped on worn planks. The ship butted against a long wharf and was swiftly moored. Vaguely he saw red diamonds swimming below him, red diamonds on kepis, on broad-brimmed hats. He stumbled down to the wharf, with Mr. McArdle yelping and straining at the leash. Bluecoats swallowed him up. Quartermaster Brady was thumping his back and roaring, "Glory be to God and it's home ye are!" Sergeant Cahusac, in charge of a detail, was saluting smartly, and a dozen men, French, Irish, and American, shouted a welcome that took no account of the tarnished shoulder straps.

Then George was on the seat of a wagon, bowling on along the river road, staring down at a Maine regiment that filed past, red diamonds bright on their caps. More of Kearny's men. Driver Sullivan whooped and bawled at the quick-stepping mules. Off to the right, a band was playing "Hail, Columbia" and colors were fluttering down from a tall pole. A sunset gun thudded. George still shivered and thought it odd that his forehead was sweat-beaded. Mr. McArdle perched beside him and hurled violent objurgations at passing dogs.

The wagon swung off the road and George strained his eyes through drifting dust and the tart smoke from the cookshacks. Columns of men were filing off toward the company streets. By a flagpole a group of officers chatted, their scabbards bright in the sunset. He tried to shout but his voice was dry in his throat. A rigid man with wide white splashes on his sleeves turned as Mr. McArdle raised a frenzy of yelps. Sergeant Major Rapp, red beard glinting, flung both arms in the air shouting, "*Voilà! C'est Monsieur Force qui est revenu!*"

George's knees were unsteady as he dropped to the ground and saw men running from the flagpole. The Rifles closed about him. De Mérac had his hand and Wilson was slapping his shoulder. He saw Greenbaum and knew that the dark Jew was shouting for once. Corvisart called his name. There were the huge Bolton and Dr. Wayne and DuBosc. Bordagaray ran up, and Péguy and Hein and Shea. Randol cut a clog step and whooped. A man in black, bright-eyed and dark-jowled, was introduced to him as Father Doyle.

Then the group broke up as by tacit consent and George and de Mérac walked arm in arm toward H Company Street. De Mérac said, "Ah, this is good, George, good. You come in the nick of time. We are packed to sail—our whole division and Hooker's. Word may come any day now. We wait only—" He paused.

Men were milling about the head of H Street. A deep-toned shout went up, the same resonant cheer that George had heard at Frayser's Farm and Malvern Hill. Arms waved and red-topped caps scaled into the air. De Mérac gave him a gentle shove. "I shall be in the way here, *mon vieux*. Come to my tent for dinner and then we two present ourselves to General Kearny." He slipped away.

George stepped uncertainly forward. Leather-faced First Sergeant Bates held up his hand. An accordion began to wheeze. It was hard to stand there, facing what was left of H Company, hard to keep his eyes on the scrubbed faces and the slicked-down hair. It was harder to listen to the wail of the instrument and the earnest discord of voices that sang:

> Should auld acquaintance be forgot
> And never brought to mind—

Mr. McArdle edged closer to him as the song swelled.

X

Defeat

TEN days later an evil-smelling schooner, towed by a paddle-wheeler, brought the Rifles to Alexandria, to the very dock where they had embarked, a powerful blue and yellow column under a June sun. Now, in late August, they tramped down the gangplank, thinned and battered, their uniforms two somber tones of blue. Their packs, the heavy baggage, Brady and his wagons, were somewhere far down the Potomac, and the companies formed under a thin night rain, a bare five hundred men equipped and supported only by what they carried. Yet even in the wet darkness the column had an air of tough solidity as it filed off through the town to the waiting flatcars on the Orange and Alexandria Railroad. Blankets were slung from shoulder to hip like gray horse collars. Haversacks bulged with cooked rations and pouches were weighted down with forty rounds supplemented by those crammed loosely into blue pockets.

On rough benches, heads ducked to the drizzle, they rode the flatcars as far as Burke's Station and then plunged on into the heart of Northern Virginia. The rain broke with dawn and the column plodded on. Somewhere behind it were Pride and Clay, led by the scowling Pelham. Ahead marched the brigades of Poe and Berry and Birney. Somewhere off in the mystery of the rolling lands, Pope and the Army of Virginia were fumbling ahead to pin Stonewall Jackson before Lee and Longstreet could join him.

Who was ahead and who was behind, where they marched and why, soon became matters of complete indifference to the Rochambeau Rifles. Each morning the sun rose in a brassy sky to hang above them like a heavy red-hot ball. Thick air closed in, hotter and hotter, until each second seemed to mark the pitch beyond which heat could not go. Dust rose higher than their kepis, wrapped them in a dense, murky fog bank in whose heart the blackened men struggled on. Muskets weighed down unendurably and the filled pouches and canteens dragged at aching loins.

George Force panted on with his company. His face streamed with sweat which mixed with the dust to form a grotesque mask. His mouth and nostrils slowly clogged and his lungs worked convulsively. Yet he knew that he was better off than his men who slogged on in the ranks, each heated still more by the very nearness of those to right and left. He watched their sagging mouths and their eyes that stared ahead so fixedly. He tried to make them husband the water in their canteens, saw to it that every man draped a handkerchief, masklike, across his face like the African veterans in LeNoir's company. They passed small houses in clearings and swayed toward stone-curbed wells clutching at empty canteens, only to be blocked by provost guards and big signs, "No trespassing. Per Order John Pope, Maj. Gen., U.S.A." George had to harden himself to shove and butt them back into ranks with Randol's help, shouting, "Not enough for us and we'd dry up the well for the people who live there!" The overheat of the road settled about the men as they stumbled back into ranks, swearing through cracked lips: "God damn John Pope. Bet the Jesus he's cooling his ass on a keg of ice water!" . . . "Yeah! Cooling his brains! Them folks back there was goddamn Rebs. Who the hell cares they got water or not?"

There were halts along baking stretches of the railroad where the rails shimmered in the heat, and halts in wooded stretches where the sun was held off by high foliage but where the dust cloud settled heavier than ever. There were bivouacs in open fields, in mosquito-haunted woodlands, night camps that were broken as the red-hot sun swung up over a heat-fouled horizon and the dust cloud formed again so thick and so heavy that George seemed to march alone with the squads at his right. Head and tail of the company were hidden and LeNoir in front and Bolton in the rear might have been marching on another continent.

Mr. McArdle, his coat damp and matted, labored on close by George, deserting him only when woods parallel to the road allowed the weary dog to pad on through shade, and where muddy pools gave him a chance to gulp and slobber to his heart's content. Through the dust, black-faced devils rode down the column, their horses coughing and wheezing in the heavy air. Through reddened lids George saw the black masks split and recognized de Mérac or Wilson or Greenbaum, who repeated the eternal monotonous command, "Close up! Keep closed up!"

Following the path of the riders, a dismounted man labored incessantly. Father Doyle, his black uniform doughy with moist dust, sweat dripping from his caked eyebrows, managed to appear where the going was worst—in a sunken road where men sobbed for breath and blood pounded fiercely in aching temples, or by a swamp where dank air heightened the agony of clammy uniforms. A half-dozen canteens were slung from his broad shoulders, which had been filled by untold scourings of the country on either side of the line of march. These were passed out to hands that bristled from the dust bank. On the priest's first appearance, a man in George's company growled, "Keep your God-damn water. I ain't no Catholic." Doyle chuckled. "The good God put the well there for every division of His army. Take it or I'll be murdering you." The man drank and pushed on, blinking and muttering.

George lost count of days and miles. He had vague,

heat-twisted memories of wilderness stations on the railroad—Clifton's—Manassas—Bristoe—Catlett's, sometimes standing stark by the right of way, sometimes still smoldering with burned supplies, and off to the right and left blue bodies and gray bodies turning black and swelling in the sun; such wreckage, material and human, marked the swift passage of Jackson's raiders.

Then the column turned sharply north at Warrenton Junction, crossed the railroad, and labored over a burning plain on hazy-with-dust roads. Not a whisper of wind rose to shatter the dust cloud and George gave up any attempt to keep formation. Unconsciously the men fought away from the heat radiated by their neighbors and spread out wider and wider until they straggled in the fields at either side of the road. Other units became mixed with his command. He found men from LeNoir's company, from Hein's, from Bordagaray's, stumbling on with his own. There were broad-hatted men from Poe's Michigan, even Pennsylvanians and Massachusetts men from Reno's corps that was said to be just ahead of the van of Kearny's men.

The march reached Greenwich where the Rifles bivouacked by a swift stream. George lay on the bank and buried his face in the clear water. There were mosquitoes that night in whining droves but most of the company lay naked in the shallow stream, heedless of the hot needle stabs. The men even began to quarrel and grumble, always a sign of sound spirits. But at reveille the next morning the same burnished disk crawled sullenly up the sky and the same stifling cloud formed over the road.

There was gunfire through the morning and into the afternoon, sometimes the patter of distant musketry, sometimes the muttering thud of artillery, but they seemed unimportant compared to the endless sifting of dust and unbroken, chewing sound of hundreds of boots. George knew that he was marching north and east now, almost parallel to the course that had been followed to Warrenton Junction, but in the opposite direction. He was too parched and sodden to wonder at the new course, too exhausted even to speculate on the gunfire that throbbed so impersonally. At each camp he had fallen asleep at once as soon as he had tended to his company. He had rarely seen de Mérac, who was said to be riding much of the time far ahead with Kearny himself. He had been too weary to seek news from Greenbaum or Rapp or his fellow company commanders.

Now, with thick throat and bursting eyes, he was so intent on keeping himself and his company going that he did not notice that strange staff officers were riding past him with the eternal cry, "Close up! Close up!" He was too much absorbed with sheer existence to connect their appearance with the muted explosions so far away.

He was marching now on a fairly good highway and the dust cloud thinned a little. The harder surface was a relief at first, but soon his feet began to burn. Fine grit worked down past the cords about his trousers where they were tucked into his socks, a grit that sifted and rasped his sweat-softened soles, rucked his socks into hard ridges under the balls of his feet. He stepped carefully along. It would never do to break down like a foundered horse, particularly when out of his company of nearly forty men only five had dropped out through the whole march. Keep going—keep closed up. That was the end and aim of all effort. Even news that the head of the division, miles up the road, had engaged a Rebel force and driven it out made no impression.

The highway rose ahead of him over a stone bridge that spanned a sluggish stream. Mr. McArdle yelped with joy and squattered through a shallow ford. The men, boots ringing on the arch, cursed the dog and cursed the welter of dead mules and horses that fouled the water. George stared vaguely at the dull ripples of the current. A hand caught his arm and he looked around at Randol's smeared face. The latter pointed to the stream and croaked, "Bull Run."

"What? What?" asked George through a curtain of fatigue.

"Bull Run. This is the stone bridge you read about in the papers. I retreated over it with the DeWitt Clinton Rangers last year. God, be funny if we fought here all over again."

"Sure. Damn funny," mumbled George. "Better go to the rear and watch the tail of the company." Randol fell back to his place. His words buzzed oddly in George's mind. Fight here? At Bull Run? People didn't fight on battlefields. They made parks out of them and listened to Senators on the Fourth of July.

The sun was suddenly low and he knew that he was directing his company through a gap in high earthworks that lay to the west of a desolate wooden hamlet. There were blue bodies and gray bodies that must have been alive and moving not long ago as their legs had not yet swelled their trousers into sausage-skin tightness and their faces were waxen, not black. Off to the left men began to bark out gasping cheers and George saw Kearny, dust-caked like the humblest private but still somehow blazing through dirt and fatigue. The company filed on quite close to the general where he sat a powerful brown mare listening to a crimson-faced staff officer whose words tumbled out in excited confusion. "Thoroughfare Gap—Jackson and his whole God-damn tribe—Gregg—A. P. Hill—chance of a lifetime to snap 'em up!"

George saw Kearny nod eagerly, then ride off shouting, "Oh, de Mérac! Go find von Steinwehr of Sigel's corps. Arrange about keeping touch if he's on our left. Then report back to me, please."

George squared his shoulders as he looked at his men who were waving their kepis and cheering Kearny in hoarse bursts. Their caked faces were alight with a new life. He called, "Close up. Close up. We'll be showing Jackson the Kearny patch tomorrow."

Then the march was over. Burke's Station, Sideburn Station, Bristoe Station, Catlett's—they had all been passed. Now the Rifles were halted at their destination, a spot that was marked on no map, close to a town called Centerville and near a stream named Bull Run. Thick dusty bushes edged year-old ruts. When the breeze blew strong, the leaves parted to show shattered rib bones, skulls, femurs that were, like the ruts, a year old.

There were live, pleasant smells in the night that shimmered with the promise of dawn—the damp, sedgy scent that the wind brought from Cub Run a half mile to the rear, the tang of wood smoke or the tart reek of dying coals. There were the richness of Wilson's cigar, the aromatic waft from a fresh-broken bale of hay, and the indefinable odor of well-groomed horses. De Mérac breathed deeply as he watched DuChesne carefully sponging Lisette's delicate nostrils.

The gray of coming dawn threw trees and buildings into black relief against the silvering ground, turned them from shapeless masses into the sharp forms that man or nature had created. Wilson's face changed from a whitish blur into discernible features that were intent, cool, and alert—what his wife called his "office face." Corvisart strolled up, sipping at a cup of coffee. "He has not come yet?"

De Mérac answered, "Not yet." He felt the electric wave of anticipation that the very thought of Kearny always provoked and his eyes strained through the wavering light for a sight of the great white horse, Moscow, and the tall, one-armed figure that rode her. He glanced over his shoulder at the fields behind him. Fires were glowing and men were getting stiffly to their feet, yawning, stretching, and scratching.

Wilson cried, "Look—off there!" He pointed down a gentle slope that was slowly unveiling in the half-light. Across a narrow run a white shape jumped easily, darker blurs following it. A clear laugh rang out, gay and exultant. De Mérac held up his kepi as horse and rider swept on, the others swinging off to the left. Kearny's voice echoed, "There you are, de Mérac. Morning, Wilson. Morning, Corvisart." Kearny dropped to the ground. "You've routed your men out? Good. Here, open this map. Bring that lantern, please, DuChesne. Ha! I've been over calling on Stonewall Jackson. See this high ground on the map? Right here? Jackson'll hold *that*. Superb position. This unfinished railway embankment runs all the way along it on the slope toward us. We'll have the devil's own time clawing him out of it."

Wilson asked cautiously, "Is the map accurate?"

Kearny's laugh rang out again. "You've got my word for it. I told you I'd been calling on Jackson. Rode right over there and the first thing I knew I was smack in the middle of the 16th North Carolina, Pender's brigade."

"*Mille vierges!*" muttered Corvisart. "You had trouble?"

"Not I. I just asked them what the devil they were doing there and sent them packing back. You see, in the dark they took me for one of their own officers. Lord, I'd like to see Billy Pender's face when he finds them trooping off in the wrong direction." His mustache and imperial quivered in boyish delight. "Now, about your job. *Our* whole division's going to hit up here, slashing at Jackson's left flank." His jaw snapped. "Gentlemen, I mean to roll that whole flank up like a carpet. A. P. Hill's there and we've got to rip into him and keep on ripping, never give him a chance to get his breath. I'll hit with Birney and Robinson, with Poe and Pelham in reserve. Now for yourselves. See where Sudley Springs Church is marked? You'll wait there one half mile this side of it until you hear from me."

"And that is our role—we wait?" asked de Mérac, disappointed.

Kearny's eyes flashed. "This is the chance of a lifetime. We've got to hit hard and fast, because Longstreet's coming up way over on our left front. There's going to come a time when things'll be swaying back and forth and one regiment, thrown hard at the right place, will tear the whole enemy line apart." He shook his fist. "It can be done, I tell you, but it's got to be done hard and fast and no letup. So keep alert and be ready to jump when I give the word." He mounted, raised his hand to his kepi, and rode off.

De Mérac met the eyes of Wilson and Corvisart, tense, eager, and expectant. He nodded and they ran back to the regiment, where bugles were blasting, drowning out the heavy drums of a Michigan unit in the next field. DuChesne saddled Lisette in the growing light. Castex and Dekdebrun rode up and swung in behind de Mérac as he mounted. The companies were forming rapidly. At one side a thick arc of men knelt about Father Doyle, who held up a crucifix and intoned, *"Domine, in manus tuas—"*

The Rifles headed northwest across rolling pasture land. De Mérac reined in Lisette to watch them. There was promise of relief from the heat of the last few days and the files marched with a fresh, eager swing. With a ripple of color the three tattered flags of the regiment blossomed over the kepis and the men began to cheer. More than the mere promise of cooling winds underlay their springy stride. They had seen Kearny, the old *kébir*, the night before and knew that the end of purposeless marching had come.

De Mérac pulled at his mustache as he studied the free gait and the forward-thrusting faces. Bordagaray shook his fist in the air and shouted, *"On les aura, mes Zouaves!"* Shea swung his arms and shouted to his men to shorten their stride that was carrying them onto the heels of Péguy's files. Hein clanked his scabbard, calling, *"Vorwärts! Vorwärts!"* George strode by the flank of his company, kepi in one hand and Mr. McArdle's leash in the other. Huge Bolton lumbered on, grinning shyly to himself as he always did when there was action in the air.

De Mérac shook his bridle and trotted up the column, satisfied with his command. He wished that he felt more confidence in the whole army that Pope had gathered. Actually, it was a collection of corps and divisions, few of which had worked together before. Last night he had talked with von Steinwehr of Pope's Ist Corps and Abner Doubleday of the IIIrd. They were able, competent men but they had no knowledge of the strengths and weaknesses of any of the commanders under Kearny and Hooker with whom they might have to work the next day. More than that, Pope would be facing an army that had, generally speaking, fought as a unit up and down the Peninsula and across to the James.

The Rifles pressed on through fields where other red-topped companies were forming, through groves where horses stamped and artillery drivers handled traces and saddles with irritable efficiency. The light grew stronger and stronger and long shadows slanted from the column.

Then off to the west a single gun thudded and heads turned toward the sound, heads that nodded in understanding. Sergeant Cahusac twisted his mustache and grunted, *"V'là! Ça boulotte, hein?"* Melchior Rapp, pacing beside him, jerked his red beard toward the dying echo. *"Foutus, les Arabes, quoi!"* Other guns answered the first and the fire thickened to a long, drumming roll that spread from northeast to southwest. De Mérac felt a tingling along his spine, a cold congestion below his breastbone. The fight was on.

At last the stone walls of Sudley Springs Church shimmered silver through a grove of trees. The column swung left, scrambling over threadlike streams that flowed down to Bull Run. George Force ran an appreciative eye over the stretch of meadowland where the leading companies were halting. The turf was soft and a little brook trailed away south toward rising ground that was masked by woods. On the far horizon the Bull Run Mountains showed blue and hazy. This would be a good place to wait and listen to the thudding guns until a one-armed man on a white horse should tear out of those woods with word that there was work up ahead for the Rochambeau Rifles. The column halted and the men sprawled on the lush grass.

Through the bright morning, artillery bayed and thundered but there seemed to be little musketry. George sat on the ground and threw sticks for Mr. McArdle. He wondered if that chance-met cavalryman of the night before would remember to post his hasty note to Dora, wondered if mail would ever catch up with Kearny's rapidly moving division. This was August 29 and he had had just one letter from her way back at Harrison's Landing. He pushed speculation from his mind and lit a frayed cigar that Bolton had given him. All about him men were lying on their backs asleep or buzzing in desultory talk. A few games of poker and seven-up were going on and Hein, Chanel, and Péguy were playing skat. Out of sight the gunfire drummed on, staining the far sky with whitish-yellow smoke. George yawned, stretched out with his kepi over his eyes, and slept while the forgotten cigar smoldered out.

At the crest of the distant rise de Mérac, Wilson, Corvisart, and Greenbaum lay flat on their bellies under rustling sycamores, their glasses to their eyes. Behind them, Castex waited, turning his bugle in his hands and shivering at each blast of the guns. Dekdebrun sat huddled against a tree, nursing his rifle, while his cold eyes were fixed unwavering on the terrain ahead.

De Mérac adjusted his eyepieces, remarking that the position was better than a loge at the *Opéra*. Wilson and Corvisart muttered in agreement. They were looking down a virtually neutral zone between the two armies. On the right, or enemy, side was a low, wooded ridge. From it, smoke and dust welled to meet the down-reaching shrapnel bursts. In a brownish welt, the unfinished railroad, part cutting, part embankment, slanted along just in front of the woods. Down the shallow valley that crept on to the ridge, woody patches alternated with wide clearings, and here and there a roof line shouldered up. To the left, along the Union lines, there was more high ground from which smoke spouted, erupting in sunny fields where blue gunners moved about their pieces, and sifting up from woods that hid muzzles, wheels, and men.

Wilson raised himself on his elbows. "Sure as God made little apples, we're hanging just off the end of the Reb's left flank."

De Mérac said, "That will be A. P. Hill. Kearny thinks that Maxcy Gregg holds the extreme left with his South Carolina Brigade. Make out anything else, Greenbaum?"

The Jew nodded. "Been watching where our shells are dropping. Hill's got his left flank refused. See? Watch that dirt fly. The line bends right back at an angle."

Corvisart muttered, "You have an eye, young man. It is there that Kearny will push us."

De Mérac's glasses ranged along the Southern lines, over the valley where smoke from Sigel's guns, and perhaps McDowell's, rose above the trees. He could make out no troops in the woods of Hill's front and guessed that they were taking cover from the steady beat of the fire. A vague feeling of uneasiness stole over him. Kearny had stressed the need for haste. Why was there no attack from the Union side? Had something gone wrong? The sun slipped down the sky, throwing its rays obliquely into the woods where the party lay. De Mérac pulled out his watch. Past three o'clock. Where was the attack? Wilson gnawed his mustache and Corvisart's fingers drummed against a root.

The hush fell without warning over the immediate front, although Sigel's distant guns roared on. De Mérac stiffened. Then one—two—three cannon snarled in crisp precision from the Union side. A bugle tore the air. Out of the wooded slopes broke a sudden, long line of men in blue, men whose kepis were topped with scarlet. De Mérac whipped up his glasses, counted stand after stand of colors where the flag of the Union rode high with those of New York, Michigan, Indiana, New York again, Pennsylvania, Ohio. A second line surged into sight, a third, tearing waves that moved at a double while mounted officers paced at the flanks. Smoke and flame exploded from Hill's ridge and blue heaps spun to the ground. From the far left flank of the attack raced a big white horse. De Mérac froze as a one-armed man, now capeless, swept down the front, reins in his teeth and kepi waving. A steady, deep-toned roar followed Kearny along the line.

De Mérac snapped to his feet. "Greenbaum! Wait here. As soon as you see one of Kearny's aides coming this way, gallop back to the regiment. Now, you others, we rejoin the Rifles." The group mounted and dashed off toward the waiting companies, Castex blasting assembly.

The Rifles stood to arms as the minutes ticked by. De Mérac, on foot, smoked cigarette after cigarette as the path up to the wooded rise showed no signs of Greenbaum. Hooker and Kearny must have run into savage resistance. A regiment of Poe's brigade which had been in a field to the left moved out, and he caught a glimpse of Pelham's command crossing a stream farther away. The sun slanted low, glared under his tortoise-shell vizor.

Suddenly he mounted. Greenbaum was galloping out of the trees waving his hand. Castex blared out a call and the companies stiffened with a rattle of equipment. George shouted, "Come on, you terriers!" There were other voices. *"Vite, les vieux!" "Schnell, schnell!"* Greenbaum pulled up, followed by a red-topped aide who yelled, "Kearny wants you! Right away!" De Mérac waved his arm and Corvisart led out the regiment. The aide swung his sweat-lathered horse beside de Mérac, panting, "For God's sake hurry!"

"Kearny has broken through?"

"Don't know. Damnedest mess. Longstreet's come up and got between Porter and Sigel. Sigel's pinned and says he's too bust-up to move. We're getting no support—just us and Hooker. Jesus Christ! Everyone's so slow! Porter's barely moved and there's no sign of Franklin and Sumner. Hurry it up!"

The Rifles pushed on and on along a sunken road that seemed to lead to the very heart of the din ahead. The aide pointed to a straggling orchard to the left where apples hung green and hard. De Mérac raised his arm. Castex rapped out a series of sharp notes and the first five companies swung into line, followed by the remaining four. The air under the gnarled trees hummed with drilling sounds and bark flew from the trunks. The crash of volleys and the hysterical ripple of uncontrolled fire sounded nearer and nearer. Lisette shied away from a blue body that sprawled frogwise in the grass, recovered herself, and leapt over a tangle of blue and gray coats.

De Mérac leaned from the saddle, peering ahead under the trees. More and more bodies, a wrecked limber, two dead horses that showed yellow teeth in hideous grins. Excitement gripped him as he read the message of the littered orchard. Kearny was driving Hill back and back. He turned in the saddle, shouted, *"En avant!"* and thrilled to the deep cheer that answered him. Bayonets slanted forward. The torn colors snapped in the air and the brass eagles on the poles seemed to scream down on the kepis below.

He shouted again, drew his sword. Lisette slipped easily across a shallow trench where bodies huddled. A bullet flicked through his kepi, unnoticed in the intoxication of advance. This made up for the defensive agony of Frayser's Farm, for the orders that checked too soon the quick sweep down Malvern Hill.

The orchard ended and there was dim movement to the right and left but only empty land directly ahead. Then out of a copse tore Kearny, his eyes aflame, his uniform ripped by bullets and his scabbard shot away. He swung up his arm. "Rifles! Right oblique! Take them in, de Mérac! Hit anything in your way. Link your right to Pride if you can, but drive, drive, drive. Keep them to it. We'll win this damned battle alone if we have to. Drive, drive, drive!"

The Rifles broke into a double, obliquing sharply. De Mérac shouted approval of the alignment that was kept in the difficult maneuver. Kearny, from the flank, signaled the end of the oblique and galloped off. The regiment drove on into scrubby woods that were thick with smoke and echoing to the fury of fire to the right and left. The woods were left behind and infantry, some in gray, some in drab brown, were retiring across an open field. Fire ripped from the right flank of the Rifles and straggling knots of the enemy broke, tearing to the shelter of another belt of trees.

Someone yelled, "Pride's outfit! Off to the right!" and de Mérac saw a few panting men in broad hats emerge from a crumbly ravine. Hoofs crashed in the undergrowth and Colonel Pride broke into the open, his face blood-smeared and anxious. Then he saw de Mérac and his thick beard split in a welcoming shout. "Jiminy, this is good. Scared my left was in the air, John. Hello, Craig. Going to join onto me?"

Wilson said grimly, "If you keep Pelham off my neck."

"He's way over where I join Clay. By jingo, he can handle a brigade! Ought to have seen the country he brought us over."

"Try and keep him with Clay," said de Mérac. "My orders are to go forward. Nothing else."

"Good," said Pride. "We got the same ones. Let's get going. By God, it's great to have you on my flank." There was a quick handshake and Pride trotted off to the woods.

De Mérac hurried the Rifles on, echeloning Wilson's companies on Corvisart's. He crossed more timber, a plowed field, watching anxiously to the left where Bordagaray's skirmishers were feeling out the terrain. He set his teeth. If—if he could bring the regiment, unshaken and well-linked to Pride, into the rear of Hill, it might serve as a wedge to split the whole Southern line. It could happen. It could! Tense with hope and anticipation he twisted in his saddle, shaking his saber.

A bullet sang past his cheek, hot and vicious. The ragged woods erupted men who fell on the left of his line. He saw Corvisart detach the rest of Bordagaray's men, reinforce them with DuBosc's, and throw them into action. The open field whined with flying lead. De Mérac shouted to Corvisart to neutralize the copse and waved the rest of the regiment on. It must go on. He visualized every move that he would make when he actually struck Hill's rear.

A feverish "Yi-yi-yi-yi-yi—" cut through the air. His head went back as though he had been struck. The fire from the left went on undiminished and off to the right a long grayish line was advancing at the double, under a red and blue battle flag. De Mérac stood in his stirrups, shouted, "A *la baïonnette!*" Feet drummed behind him as Wilson brought his companies into line with the others. A prolongation of fire to the far right told him that Pride had met unexpected opposition. A flame burned inside him. He must smash through that line ahead, must keep on and on to conform with Kearny's orders.

The gray infantry halted, blasted a single volley. De Mérac held Lisette to a gait that kept her between the running men of Hein and Shea. He shouted, "Hit hard! Hit hard." Somewhere to the right Wilson was yelling, "Tear 'em, boys, tear 'em!" The enemy was falling back. The Rifles cheered louder. Then the enemy vanished as though swallowed up by the earth. Shea shouted, "A gully! They're in a gully." The red and blue flag reappeared, a row of heads showed just at ground level, and bullets sang low through the grass. Men went down. Hein's hand dripped blood and Shea showed a raw welt across his forehead.

"At them! Quick! Before they can reload!" de Mérac roared. But the left companies were slowed by woods and rocks, the extreme right waited to dress roughly on them. The chance was gone.

Shrill Southern yells ripped the air. De Mérac shouted in relief as the enemy, instead of waiting to fire from cover, swarmed out of their shelter, formed hastily, and drove at the pursuit. "Now! Now! Through them! Smash through them!" De Mérac dropped to the ground, trusting Castex to catch Lisette's reins. "Clear them out!"

The two lines met in a stunning crash and knots of men swayed and wrestled, lunged with bayonets, swung musket butts. De Mérac ranged up and down, urging his men to keep their formation, but they kept whirling away in raging fights that involved two men, five or twenty men. Then the mêlée became individual for him and he had to shift, give ground, side-step, advance with quick, dancerlike paces as his saber warded off darting bayonets. Once he fought back to back with Sergeant Conneau of Péguy's until his blade slid along the musket of a sharp-faced man and the steel bit deep. To the left he caught a glimpse of George, who had picked up a musket. He saw the weapon smashed from his hands, saw him twist his body, catch the threatening musket by the barrel, wrench it from his opponent's grasp, and shatter the butt against the gray-hatted head. Rapp fought silently with a short Arab dirk. When the blade snapped, the Alsatian dropped to the ground. His heavy boot shot up in the jaw-shattering kick of the *savate* and a Southern sergeant collapsed in a twitching heap.

All at once the gully was wide under de Mérac's feet. The trench-like hollow was full of gray infantry, clawing their way up the other face in sudden flight. De Mérac cried, "Hein! Bolton! Clear out the hollow! Craig! Spread to the right. Pride is coming up." He sprang across the gap, heart pounding with excitement. His men followed and he formed them quickly on the other side, waved them on. The last barrier was crossed!

Then the piercing yell broke from more woods in the front. Some of the fugitives stopped. One of them threw his hands to the sky and yelled, "It's ol' Jube, boys! Jube Early's comin' runnin'."

Fire flashed ahead. A fighting swirl of fresh Southern

infantry ripped into the open. De Mérac saw one, two, three battle flags. Three new regiments on his own narrow front. There was no time to count losses, to attach names to the blue figures that fell right and left. He shouted, "To the gully. Craig! Corvisart. Rally there."

He drew his Colt and backed away, knowing that his feet kicked high each time dirt spouted close to him. He passed bodies that lay in ghastly stillness or writhed away from the lead-filled air. There was no chance to help the wounded. Once in the gully he could rally his men, link tightly with Pride, and resume his forward push. Early's force was coming slowly now, keeping up an irregular fire. It was obvious that they did not know what strength they would meet or what threats the broken country might hold.

De Mérac dropped into the gully, found that Castex had sheltered Lisette in it. He took stock quickly, issued terse orders. Those three regiments were obviously under strength. He would hold his fire until they came closer, then allow one volley, and charge home before Early's men could recover. He sent Greenbaum to tell Pride of his decision. But Greenbaum came tumbling back on the heels of furious fire from the right. Pride was heavily attacked, he reported, and unable to move. De Mérac's jaw snapped. "Very good. We go on alone." Greenbaum nodded coolly and loosened his Colt.

De Mérac leaned on the parapet, watching the approach of the enemy. When the leading files passed a shattered birch, he would give the command to fire.

A hand touched his shoulder and he looked down at Rapp's red beard. The Alsatian pointed silently to the left front. Bushes stirred and small trees swayed. A fourth red and blue flag showed through the leaves.

De Mérac felt a heavy, cold weight settle in his chest as he pounded the dirt with his fist. Then he said in a strangled voice, "Castex. Sound retire by companies."

The horses were dragged out of the long gully. Men spilled over its lip. For an instant they were a disorganized mass. Then they fell into column and started back over the ground across which they had charged earlier. Farther off, Pride's men could be seen retiring.

De Mérac mounted Lisette. Wilson was covering the withdrawal, spreading out Bolton's company and Force's so the column looked like a great letter "T," the crossbar facing toward Early. Hostile fire thickened but the Rifles moved steadily on. The whole maneuver was being smartly carried out but de Mérac took no pride in it. He beat his hand against the saddle, looking for the smallest cover, the least support, that would allow him to reform.

It grew darker as the trees thickened and the slope dropped more and more. He rode on ahead of the column, saw a stone wall that cut across his line of march, and whirled Lisette about. He would send the three color-bearers to it at the double to mark the rallying place. Then he would throw his three best attack companies—Shea, Bordagaray, and George—against the still hesitant gray advance, follow them with the rest of the regiment. Pride would see the action and surely resume his own offensive.

Off to the right, a new gray wave broke, yelling and firing as it came. There was no hesitation about this attack. The companies barely had time to face about, take a volley like men heading into sharp sleet, and fire in return. The onset was checked, brought to a halt. But the fire went on.

Horses crashed through the dusk and three quick shots rang out to the rear. De Mérac braced himself. Cavalry! Then a group of horsemen pounded up and the leading rider held his reins in his teeth while his Colt spat red at stray Rebel infantrymen. Kearny's voice blared like a trumpet. "De Mérac! Beautiful. Superb. Now oblique off to the left. Join on with the 5th Michigan, Poe's brigade. They're coming up fast."

The sweating desperate files heard the clanging tones. Without looking around they began to cheer. Kearny raced close to the rear rank, waving his revolver. "Fine! Fine! *Tirez juste, les Zouaves!*" He drummed away to the left, four aides at his heels. Among them galloped a riderless horse whose stirrups beat against his barrel.

There were Union cheers among the trees in the direction that Kearny had taken. Fire on front and flank died away to spasmodic, snarling flares. The Rifles lurched on, unpursued. De Mérac rode by the colors, his lungs heaving and his mind busy with the next step. Castex bobbed behind him, swaying with fatigue. Greenbaum and Dekdebrun had lost their mounts in the last wild surges and walked on either side of him, each clinging to a stirrup leather.

Soon there were broad-hatted Michigan men all about, edging cautiously through the gloom. All at once Greenbaum said, "It's over." De Mérac listened intently. No batteries jarred the air. Musketry had faded to a dull spattering in the southwest. An aide cantered up, identified the Rifles, and gave orders in Kearny's name to push on to the railroad embankment and rest the men in its shelter.

In the lee of the embankment, men dropped to the ground, exhausted. "What orders now?" asked Greenbaum.

"Be ready to strike again—at any time. Go to the company commanders. Tell them to have their men roll up their right sleeves. The bare arms will show when we move out in the dark again. In the meantime, rest."

A shapeless bulk showed at the top of the bank. Father Doyle called down: "Lend me a hand, boys, will you?"

Two or three privates scrambled to the chaplain and helped him ease a groaning man from his shoulders to the ground. "You were supposed to stay back at the base, Father," de Mérac protested.

Doyle flexed his arms. "I'm supposed to be where the boys need me."

De Mêrac squinted through the dark. The muzzle of a carbine jutted up past Doyle's shoulder. Wilson exclaimed, "Just what were you doing up there?"

From the embankment Péguy spoke. "He took the place of Corporal LeSage, who was killed."

Doyle said defiantly, "All right. I did. Report me if you want to."

"I shall surely report you," said de Mérac. "To General Kearny, who will not, I think, be offended. We need more noncombatants like yourself. Craig, will you see about your losses? And please have the men ready to move at any instant."

Fires began to smolder. Water gurgled into cups and men scraped coffee from the linings of their haversacks. De Mérac sniffed the steam as he listened to random snatches of talk. "*'Cré nom de dieu.* It is as I tell you. The bayonet protruded itself between the shoulders...." "And hell roast the gray divil that done for little Tim. His face I'd know in a million and when we're meetin' with 'em again." ... "*Nu, nu.* It is small but it will make a pretty little wound to show my Nelschen when I go home." A voice said sadly, "*Ach,* but mine I cannot show to Hedwig until we marry." ... "What makes you Dutchmen think you're going to get home, with the butchers that's running us? Christ, I'd rather plug McClellan or Pope than a Reb."

The smell of coffee became stronger. A dark shape crept up and Louvel quavered, "Your coffee, *mon capitaine.*"

De Mérac reached for the cup. A ringing voice said from beyond the last fire, "There is some for me, Louvel?"

De Mérac stepped quickly forward. "Take this, sir. Louvel will make more."

Kearny came into the light, waving away the cup. "I'll wait. But make it strong, Louvel. Let's get out of earshot, de Mérac."

They walked to a heap of stones. "My report will be ready, sir, as soon as I have my total losses. It will, perhaps, explain why I judged it wise to break off my advance."

Kearny perched on the stones. "You did just right. So did Pride. I'm mentioning you both in my report to Heintzelman." He dropped his voice. "I don't need to tell you that such reports will be past history very soon now. Perhaps within a week. Things have gone badly today. Very badly. Sigel let himself get cut up. Porter must have been asleep and Longstreet blocked him off completely. When we attacked up here, we were supposed to meet Sigel's men. As it was, Hooker and Reno and I had to fight Jackson just about alone. We were spread thin, horribly thin. That's why you had one flank in the air." He slapped his hand on his knee. "One more regiment coming up at the right time. Just one more. That's all we needed. As it was, we bent Jackson's flank almost double. Why—*why* didn't Sigel hit hard? What stopped us was the men that Jackson was able to spare from Sigel's front after Longstreet came up. Good God, Pope should have known better than to attack when he did. He should have struck earlier and caught Jackson alone, or he should have waited until Franklin and Sumner came up. But—even so, we should have beaten them today."

"The day isn't over," said de Mérac.

"Good! That's the way to feel. It isn't over." His voice dropped. "But it *is* over—for Pope." He held up a warning hand while Louvel brought more coffee, trotted silently away. "I don't know yet what'll happen. Pope may break off action and fall back to the Potomac. He may try to strike again tomorrow. *If* we strike, I want you right here, ready to move as you did today. If we fall back, I want you, personally, to join me at once."

"And the Rifles?"

"Wilson will command them. As soon as I'm confirmed, he goes to colonel, Corvisart to lieutenant colonel, and Shea to major."

"Then I attach myself to your staff?"

Kearny grinned suddenly. "Don't ask questions about yourself. I've got plans for you. I may have the news we're waiting for at any time, and when it comes I want you where I can lay my hands on you like that—" he snapped his fingers—"and don't be surprised at where I throw you."

De Mérac watched the firelight play over the lined face. "I shall be proud to serve wherever you place me, sir."

Kearny inclined his head. "Thank you. You know, you've done a fine job here—with people, I mean. They all like you. Pride and Clay and Wilson and Dunn of Pelham's staff. They talk to me about you as if you were some fellow American with whom they've grown up. Yet all the time you manage to stay French as *escargots*. Did you ever think of settling here?"

"I have always been content in America. But France is my country."

Kearny sighed. "I can understand that. It's been a sort of second country to me. I hope I can get back there soon." He set down his empty cup. "Many thanks for the coffee. Come and see us after the war in Paris—Avenue Matignon—and I'll return it with interest. If any aides are looking for me, I'll be with General Hooker at the Carter place back there. Now remember—if we attack tomorrow, wait here. If we fall back, turn the command over to Wilson and get to me as fast as God'll let you."

"*Entendu.* And may I hope, sir, that you won't go calling on Jackson again, or riding out in front of the skirmishers?"

Kearny's laugh rang out. "Ho! Don't worry about me. I tell you, they *can't* get me." He strode away through the night.

De Mérac squared his shoulders and walked back to the embankment where Wilson and Corvisart waited ominously, slips of paper in their hands. He said quickly, "*Eh bien,* what have we to go on with?" The news was better than he had feared. Some fifty men were killed or missing, nearly seventy wounded. Of the wounded, forty-three could continue in ranks. He drew a deep breath. "Good. There will be no move tonight. For tomorrow, the same orders and probably the same work as today."

From the dark an unknown voice snarled, "Who says so?" and de Mérac could hear men stirring by the dying fires. He snapped, "General Kearny," and the murmur of protest died abruptly. Wilson and Corvisart returned to their posts and de Mérac settled himself in the lee of a boulder. As he spread his blanket, he saw Dekdebrun perched on the very crest of the bank, staring off toward the Southern lines.

Soon after sunrise an aide led the Rifles near the spot where they waited the day before, but on the east side of Bull Run. They lay in a broad, basinlike hollow that shut off any outlook and de Mérac did not dare seek higher ground where he himself could watch. In any event, when the Rifles were thrown in, they would follow much the same course as that of the first attack. He posted guards and saw to it that the men slept all they could.

The sun beat down hotter and hotter and a heavy calm settled over the whole countryside. Birds flicked from tree to tree. By a brook the single-mounts stood picketed, switching their tails as they grazed contentedly. Sometime after noon a terrific cannonade opened and men who had been sleeping sprang to their feet, muskets ready or Colts drawn. De Mérac ordered the regiment ready for immediate action and stood by Lisette, who continued her calm grazing. Smoke clouds thickened over the trees to the right front, curved away out of sight, and the ground quivered gently to the incessant shocks.

The sun dropped slowly and shadows from the west lengthened, but no aide came from Kearny. A trickle of wounded, infantry and gunners, limped through the fields across Bull Run, but de Mérac knew better than to hope for coherent reports from men who had seen only one torn corner of an action. A few wore the Kearny patch on dusty kepis, showing that some of the brigades had been thrown in, but that in itself meant little.

Clouds began to bank threateningly across the shimmering sky and a sudden wind sprang up. Far to the Union left, firing swelled in muffled fury and there seemed to be fierce action. In the bowl-like field, men stood apart from each other, listening and wondering. By six o'clock, clouds brought premature twilight and big drops of rain spatted sullenly down. On the other side of the Run a single horseman trotted toward the Rifles.

De Mérac mounted Lisette, splashed her through a sandy ford, and rode to meet him. His heart sank. The rider was Major Dunn, of Pelham's staff. De Mérac called, "We are wanted?"

Dunn reined in. "Hello, de Mérac. Don't know anything about you. Have you seen Poe?" The major's face was gray with fatigue and he panted heavily.

"Colonel Poe has not been here," de Mérac answered, "Major, in the name of God, what is happening?"

Dunn made a wild gesture. "Every God-damn thing you can think of. The left's been slow again. Longstreet's got batteries set so he hits every advance we make in the flank—mows us down before we even get started. Like yesterday. We're doing it all alone on the right. You better get ready for about anything. Good luck." He wheeled and trotted off.

De Mérac rode slowly back through the ford under a rain that drilled down more and more heavily. In the gathering dusk, he saw the Rifles waiting patiently, the company commanders standing out ahead of the line. Another horseman slipped out of a grove at the north of the field and whirled up to de Mérac. "You're to head your command straight to Centerville over that cart path that follows the Warrenton Pike. You'll get more orders there."

George Force, standing close by, broke out, "Fall *back?* My God, we haven't even been in, yet!"

De Mérac straightened in his saddle. Orders had come for him as well as for the regiment. He trotted Lisette over to Wilson, who sat his mount, pale but confident, in the swelling rain. He held out his hand. "Take command, Craig. You heard the orders. Good luck, *mon ami,* and look for me at Centerville." He had a word with Corvisart, hand still tingling from Wilson's firm grasp. Then he rode close by H Company where George held a corner of his poncho over Mr. McArdle, ready leashed to hand over to DuChesne in case of action. George cried, "What's the matter? Where are you going?" Raindrops dotted his clear skin and clung to the bright hair that showed beneath the kepi.

"To find Kearny. I may not see you until Centerville. Look to yourself and keep your boys closed up. *Au 'voir,* George." He caught his friend's hand and then galloped off after the aide.

George called, "Wait—wait a second!" But Lisette's drumming gallop faded across the fields.

XI

The Old Kébir

NEARLY forty-eight hours later de Mérac rode close by Kearny, threading an impatient way through the army that was falling back over the Warrenton Pike towards the approaches of the Potomac. Dekdebrun padded on in the rear, his cold eyes playing about the high ground to the left front. Overhead, slaty clouds quivered to blasts of thunder that swallowed up all other sound, died away to reveal the squelch of boots, the grind of wheels, and the vague echoes of distant gunfire, then volleyed again. Rain slashed in tearing slants, its relentless hiss knifelike between the thunderclaps.

Roads and fields were jammed with plodding regiments, with streams of transport. Kearny cursed violently as he found the Pike blocked by a broken-down pontoon train. De Mérac started Lisette for the fields at the left, but swung back as he saw that they were as badly jammed as the roads with straggling men, overturned wagons, and laboring batteries. Kearny turned in his saddle and de Mérac saw the black poncho dance to the touch of the rain. The general's voice cracked as he tried to shout above the din. "Damnation! We can't crawl like this."

De Mérac nodded grimly. Off to the northwest, where Little River Road slanted down to a junction with the Pike, Stonewall Jackson was driving his men in a terrific effort to block Pope's retreat to the Potomac. Without orders, Stevens and the Spaniard Ferrero had thrown their commands on Jackson. Now Kearny, rushing his division to join them, found himself held to a walk in the traffic that worked slowly past the wrecked train. De Mérac stood in his stirrups and stared through the drops that pattered over the vizor of his kepi. In the fields ahead the crowds seemed to be thinner now. He shouted, "To the left, sir," and shot off the road. He swerved past an upturned wagon, broke through a knot of unarmed men, jumped Lisette over a wrecked limber, and raced past a jolting three-inch rifle where an exhausted sergeant slept face down along the barrel, arms and legs dangling on either side. Kearny caught up with him as the rain swept down with increased violence. He shook his gauntleted fist at the sky. "Hold off, damn you! You'll ruin our muskets!" As though in answer the clouds ripped in darting flame. He shook his fist again and trumpeted, "I'll beat you yet, you and the whole damned Reb army. Now's our chance, de Mérac. Gallop!"

De Mérac ducked his head and followed. They were riding in the lee of that same abandoned railway whose extension he had seen beyond Bull Run. Musketry sounded nearer and nearer. Through the rain, wounded worked to the rear with dragging steps. Kearny shouted inarticulately and his face began to glow as the fight drew nearer. Suddenly he flung up his hand and whirled his mount to a halt as four men, a covered stretcher on their shoulders, toiled up. Kearny shouted, "Who's that?"

The nearest bearer turned a woebegone face to him. "General Stevens, sir." His voice was husky and shaken.

Kearny started. "What! General Stevens?"

"It was his son, sir, the loot'nant, 79th Highlanders. He was carrying the colors and the general seen him hit and come forward to pick 'em up. It was just when he'd throwed us in, sir. Reb caught him over the eye, sir."

Kearny swept off his kepi. "And we have to lose a man who knew enough to attack without waiting for orders!" He inclined his head toward the stretcher, then clapped on his kepi and spurred on.

De Mérac touched his vizor and pressed on after Kearny. The general had slithered his horse into the shallow cutting and up the other side to halt in a shower of clods. His face turned toward the firing. Outlined against the livid sky, Kearny seemed to grow taller, to stiffen as though his back had become steel. Lisette shot through the cutting like a cat and danced to a halt. De Mérac drew in his breath sharply.

Beyond the railway, long fields swept north, hedged on three sides by woods. Directly ahead a plain farmhouse hunched its roof to the rain. Right and left of the house, blue infantry was forming. Out of the eastern woods where smoke still oozed, more infantry thrashed, their ranks in bad order. Far north of the farm, cornstalks nodded and dipped as though calling attention to the gray infantry withdrawing into the distant woods.

Kearny's fist swung like the jab of a prize fighter. "We can do it. Those Rebs over there don't know what they're doing. We'll throw men into these fields. Doesn't matter what they are—orderlies, sutlers, anyone. We'll use scarecrows if we have to. Just something for the Rebs to look at. It'll shake 'em, give us time. Then we'll slash forward with everything that's left. God above, we'll hit Jackson with a charge of red-hot hell. Come on."

De Mérac spurred after him toward the men who were straggling out of the woods. Kearny blared, "What outfit?"

A haggard major panted, "21st Massachusetts, sir. Got into an ambush—"

Kearny roared above the thunder, "All right! Get your men out there quick. Form on Stevens's right. Push out ahead of him. Get into that corn. On the double, now!"

The major winced. "Need time to draw our charges, sir. Our locks got soaked in the woods."

Kearny's arm swung. "I can give you anything but time. Damn your locks. Use your bayonets! Use your fists! Use rocks if you have to! God's thunder, man, aren't you *sick* of retreating?"

The major gave orders in a weary voice. De Mérac sympathized with him, for that officer could not see what Kearny had seen. He only knew that he had spent men with useless muskets. De Mérac nodded encouragingly to him as the skeleton regiment moved off with sullen resoluteness. Kearny whipped about and water flew from the coat of his black horse. "We'll take a look ahead. Then you get back as fast as God'll let you. Hurry on the division. Grab any troops you can find. I don't give a damn if they're pontoniers or blacksmiths. Come on, now."

The wind drove vast black clouds over the sky, thickened the twilight to ghastly darkness. The Massachusetts men moved out into the corn, their boots clogged with masses of mud. De Mérac wove on through them, trying to keep the bobbing haunches of Kearny's horse in sight. Behind him he heard Dekdebrun unslinging his rifle. Soon there were only skirmishes ahead and a muddy officer jumped from the cornstalks to clutch at the general's reins. "Better not go farther. Nasty people out there!"

Kearny struck at the man's hand. "They've fallen back! Let go, sir! At once!"

De Mérac saw the officer raise his arms in protest as they rode past him. Kearny shouted over the storm, "When you see Birney, tell him to send skirmishers to the clump on the left. He's got to knock over that rail fence!" De Mérac made quick mental notes while sopping stalks slapped at him. The rail fence. An unexpected hollow. A cart path that cut through the fields just beyond—

Kearny roared without warning, "Ride for it, de Mérac. Get back to Birney and the division." De Mérac's blood turned to ice as gray infantry, yelling, shrilly, broke from the woods at the right. He swung Lisette toward Kearny, but the general bellowed, "I'm clear. Get to Birney. I order it. I'm clear, I tell you!"

De Mérac wheeled Lisette about and tried to cut off in a wide arc to the left. He heard shots behind him and a bullet flicked through the crown of his kepi. He shouted, Dekdebrun! *Nom de dieu!* Fire!" There was no response to his call. He turned in the saddle and looked back. The darkness had lifted a little and he saw men on foot running after him, shouting. There was no sign of Dekdebrun. Suddenly a blast of thunder shattered the air, stunned his ears. Hard on its echoes, long, jagged stabs of red lightning lit up the field. Far to the right a single horseman galloped alone, bathed in bloody flickering light. His reins were in his teeth and his head was turned back toward shadowy pursuers. His single hand lifted and flame spat dull and livid from it, spat sharp and hard as the last hellish glare died quickly in the sky. Faint but ringing Kearny's voice carried through the unnatural gloom: "Ride for it, de Mérac! I'm clear—clear for good!"

De Mérac wrenched himself around in his saddle, his dazzled eyes still carrying the picture of the lone rider, reins in his teeth and revolver blazing. Then a hot wave of relief swept over him as he heard the deep-toned beat of Union cheers from the direction of the Massachusetts line. Kearny must have reached the end of his mad ride.

Lisette swerved and men shouted close by. The clouds had thinned and de Mérac rode in a blackish-silver light, shifting and unreal. There was gray infantry all about him, wavering figures who yelled, "Got yuh, Yank. Surrender!"

De Mérac drew his sword and bent low in the saddle. Lisette swerved and pivoted and he let the reins hang loose on her neck. Tattered arms waved in front of him and Lisette's forefeet shot out viciously, thudded in sickening impact. She recovered, answered the touch of de Mérac's knee, and swerved toward the wood. A line of men formed in front of him and he hurled Lisette straight at them, then, relying on her amazing sureness of foot, cut sharp to the right, slashing down at the nearest man as the mare turned. Branches slapped at his face, stung knees and thighs, but the drive carried him into empty woods. Lisette shot on, took a narrow brook, slipped easily over a low fence. There were shots behind him and bullets whacked against trees. De Mérac laughed exultantly over his shoulder. Out in the open they had not dared fire for fear of hitting each other. Now, when they were free to aim, the trees protected him.

Cautiously he pulled in. There was no sound save for the hiss of the rain that sifted through the branches. He wiped water from his eyes and considered his position. Lisette was fresh as ever and seemed to have carried him into an empty pocket beyond what he took to be a stray body of Rebels. His one task now was to head south toward the railway and the Warrenton Pike, hurry on any of Kearny's men whom he met, as well as any troops who would take orders from him. Then he would race on to rejoin Kearny, who even at the moment must be planning the shattering attack that would carry through the woods and on as far perhaps as Chantilly on the Little River Road.

He sheathed his saber and let Lisette pick her own way south through the woods. He patted her neck. What a horse! On any other mount that he had ever ridden, he knew that he would have been taken. Suddenly a man screamed in pain. Lisette shied and a vague figure shot up from the ground. "Get you' God-damn horse off'n my ass or by Jesus I'll drill yuh, officer or no officer!" The voice rose higher. "Hi! Jesus! It's a Yank! Git up, Slim. A Yank!"

There was no time to draw his sword. Hard hands twitched it from his grasp, dragged him from the saddle, pinned his arms behind him as more men ran up. He struggled, broke loose, snatched for his holster, was pinned again, still struggling. He twisted, writhed, swung his fists when he could, lunged and strained, his teeth set and eyes staring. He must break free, must gallop south to the Pike where long columns of men with red diamonds on their caps marched, not knowing that Kearny needed them at once.

Then steel burned against his ribs and a harsh voice snarled, "Keerful, bub, or you'll git natchly pried open."

Furious, de Mérac was forced to cease his struggles. There was a bayonet at his heart, at his throat, at his back. His mind raged. "But I must get back to Kearny."

An inner voice answered, "Excellent, my friend. Explain that to your captors, who will then release you, no doubt." The thought cleared his head a little. He suddenly recalled the words of an uncle, captured over and over again by Wellington's dragoons in Spain and always escaping. "It is in the half hour *after* one is taken that one escapes, not in the first flush of capture."

He threw back his head and studied the men about him, some of whom were fumbling in his saddlebags, stripping off sword belt and holster, snapping open the case of his fine German glasses. Some of them were barefoot and many wore odd bits of Union equipment. They were dirty and ragged but their muskets were bright and their pouches looked supple with grease. A young corporal smiled at him and said, "Reckon this is what the books call the fo'tunes of war, suh."

"Fortunes may change," answered de Mérac, forcing a smile.

A rat-faced man close by muttered, "Them boots is mine."

In the dimness a sergeant hitched at his belt. "Don't touch them fixin's. That's rules. Take him to the loot and he'll divide up. See can you hit him for a gourd of drinkin' likker."

The others, unheeding, muttered over the gold mountings of the Austerlitz sword, the glasses, crooning. "Major Branch'll maybe give fo' dollars fo' them glasses. Who gits the horse fixin's? By damn, nothin' but 'ho'-house tobacco to the saddlebags. God-damn little paper seegars!"

The sergeant growled. "Drop thet stuff and git him back to the loot. You Mule, Dode, Slim, take him 'long and leave his truck be. Ramble, now."

De Mérac was prodded off along a path that led deeper into the woods. He tried to bend his shoulders to a discouraged slouch while all the time his eyes darted right and left, noting terrain as well as the attitude of his guards. The man Slim, vast and oxlike, led Lisette. Rat-faced Mule and sallow, scowling Dode walked behind de Mérac with ready bayonets. He gathered from their talk that they were Georgia troops of Thomas's command and that Branch's North Carolinians lay to the west. Dode carried de Mérac's saber in his free hand and jabbed the ferrule angrily into the ground at each step. "Plumb sick wearin' out my feet fo' them Virginians. Hear 'em talk you'd think 't wa'n't nobody but them fightin'."

Slim growled, "Ol' Jack's out'n Virginny and I ain't aimin' to hear him made small of."

"Ain't countin' Stonewall. But them others! Jesus, Slim, make thet critter move! Want to git lost in the dark?"

De Mérac watched his guards covertly. The woods were masked in dimness but there was a glow about the treetops that suggested a clearing sky to light up the open fields a little. He slackened his pace so as to fall abreast of Mule and Dode, but the latter snarled, "Run into you slick red-tops afore. Git movin'." Then Dode railed at Slim again. "Goda'mighty what you got there? A cow? Make her move them feet."

Slim grunted, "Doin' the best I know."

"The best you know on! I'll show you!" He moved quickly and his bayonet pricked Lisette's withers. The mare wheeled with a whinny of pain and the whole scene changed with hideous swiftness. De Mérac saw a long black neck shoot out, had a vision of flattened ears and bared teeth. There was a horrible, strangling sound and Dode was a limp gray sack, shaken and tossed while the mare's jaw clamped about his face. Slim screeched. "She's a killin' of him!" Dode's arms and legs struggled in dreadful impotence. De Mérac could only stare in sick horror. Lisette turned and turned, lashing out with her forefeet at the awful mass that dangled from her jaws. The two guards danced about her, bawling, "Git out my way, God damn you. Could a plugged her twicet. Jesus! Don't shoot. I'm plumb agin your muzzle."

De Mérac's mind suddenly cleared, though he was sick with the awful scene before him. He slipped quickly, picked up the fallen saber. The hilt seemed to fly into his hands and he loosed a savage backhander at Mule, who fell coughing and clawing. Slim swung from Lisette gabbling, "God damn, Yank, drop thet sword!"

De Mérac ducked back of a tree to avoid the wavering muzzle. He saw Slim start toward him, saw, as in a hellish background, Lisette toss her dripping muzzle to the sky and then pound sharp hoofs into Dode's ghastly body. Slim croaked, "Got you covered. Git out thar, now or—"

A rifleshot cracked clean and sharp from the left. Slim raised on his toes, swung both arms across his chest, and sagged to the ground. From the undergrowth Dekdebrun darted out, rifle at trail, and pushed de Mérac. "Hurry up if you want to get out of here. Take this path. No one on it."

De Mérac, dizzy with the quick turn of events, stared at him. Then the realization that he was free, free to race back to the Pike and on to Kearny, shot life through him. He sprang into the saddle. Lisette shivered, then stood still. At her feet the body of Dode turned upward a face that glistened hideously in the murk, a face from which lips, nose, cheeks, and lids had been ripped. De Mérac shuddered, caught up the reins, and stepped the mare carefully to the path where Dekdebrun stood alert. He asked shortly, "Where is your mount?"

Dekdebrun snapped, "Turned her loose. Followed you better on foot. Lots of Rebs. Hard to get through. Better hurry." He caught hold of the left stirrup leather and matched Lisette's pace as de Mérac set the mare to a trot.

The trees thinned and at last de Mérac rode out onto a plowed field with woods to the east. It was quite dark now, but the darkness was natural, not the livid, cloud-strangled gloom of the storm. He sensed that men were moving to his right and left but who they were or what their purpose was he could not guess. From the south came the muted grind and scrunch of moving transport and men, the occasional glow of distant fires, as though small units had encamped.

He stared off to the east. There was no sound of firing. The now remote cornfields where he had left Kearny gave off no hint of life. He edged Lisette off the path, thinking that a slanting course northeast would bring him more quickly onto the Warrenton Pike, where the brigades with the red diamonds marched. Dekdebrun pushed at Lisette's neck. "Keep heading this way. Rebs had spread out west."

De Mérac protested, "But I must reach the Pike."

"Want the Rebs to get you again? Head straight."

De Mérac held to the path that wound crazily over the plowed ground. Dekdebrun had seen more of the last Rebel moves than he had, and was probably right in steering the present course. But the silence from the direction of the cornfields maddened him and the path seemed to lead him farther and farther away from his destination. At this rate, he might not reach the Pike until nearly Centerville, past whose earthworks he had ridden with Kearny a few hours earlier. He swore with impatience as he remembered the tangle of traffic on the road. He trotted on, Dekdebrun's strides matching Lisette's pace.

Hoofs sounded beyond a rise ahead. De Mérac checked Lisette and drew his Colt. Dekdebrun slithered away toward some rocks at the right. Then a rider was silhouetted on the crest. He was tall and lean and wore a kepi rakishly. De Mérac lowered his revolver. The rider turned broadside and his cloak-muffled body seemed to lack an arm. De Mérac shouted, "General Kearny! What has happened?" His heart sank as the rider moved forward, one hand holding a raised revolver, the other the reins. A strange voice called, "Who's that? Take it easy or I'll shoot."

De Mérac put away his weapon and rode forward, both hands high. "Captain de Mérac here. From General Kearny."

"I'm Colonel Lloyd, 6th Ohio Cavalry. What are you doing here?"

The two horses halted, head to tail. "I am ordered to bring up men for General Kearny. How far is it to the Pike?"

"Less than a mile."

"Is it safe to go ahead?"

The colonel grunted. "I'm with Pope, so I don't know anything. I've got two squadrons patrolling east of here up ahead. They haven't reported anything. Better trail on with me."

"I must get to the Pike." He shook his bridle. Lisette started forward, stumbled. There was the clank of a loose shoe, then an uneven muffled sound that told him that the shoe was cast. He called to the Ohio colonel, who was just moving off, "Can you lend me a horse from your regiment? Lisette will knock her hoofs to pieces on this ground."

Lloyd said, "Sorry. A third of my men are dismounted, as it is."

"But this is important. Kearny is waiting for me and the rest of his division."

"Can't do a thing for you."

"Where are your field forges?"

"Back at Centerville. Maybe you can grab a mount on the Pike. Von Steinwehr's passing just now and Wratislaw's right behind him. Good luck."

De Mérac dismounted as Dekdebrun joined him and the two pushed on toward the Pike, Lisette stepping daintily after them. The clank and rumble grew louder. The fields were thick with stragglers, with anxious-voiced aides, with empty supply wagons that dared to leave the firm surface of the road. De Mérac led Lisette past the jerking heads of the lead pair of a gun team and scrambled onto the Pike, the sour smell of unwashed infantry strong in his nostrils.

He hailed and German voices answered him. He had struck the 73rd Pennsylvania and fought his way up the road until he found the commander, Colonel Muhleck. Muhleck threw up his hands at his request. In no way could he help. Perhaps Schimmelfennig, just ahead, might, or Cantador. For himself—"*Gott in Himmel!* Not even for the *Christkindlein* could I find a pony."

Soon de Mérac lost track of the regiments that he passed. There were seasoned troops, stripped down to a single blanket, with a skillet or a coffeepot dangling from well-kept muskets, men who swung along at a veteran stride that not even exhaustion could mask. There were new units, weighted down with a welter of equipment, footsore and shaken with the first taste of retreat. He called to majors and to colonels, to the staffs of brigadiers, but nowhere in the whole mud-caked column could he find a remount. He worked on at a pace that kept Lisette breaking from walk to trot and back to a walk again. It was maddening to be foundered far from his destination, leading as fine a horse as there was in the Army of the Potomac, but useless to him now.

By a mudhole where a big Parrott gun lay mired, an aide from Abner Doubleday's staff told him that action toward the Little River Road had been broken off and that Kearny's whole division lay a few miles up the Pike.

De Mérac tugged Lisette off the road without waiting for more details and thrashed his way on. Broken off! Why? Because word had not reached Birney and the rest of the division in time for Kearny's attack. He, de Mérac, had failed the general. There was no use in saying that he had done his best. He had not done Kearny's best and that was what mattered. Somehow, in some way, he could have and should have avoided capture and galloped back to the road. Now there was nothing to do except push on until he found Kearny, state what had happened, and wait for the one-armed man's comments. That Kearny would be fair did not matter. What was important was that he had been disappointed.

Time did not count so much now, so de Mérac kept to the soft fields to spare Lisette's unshod hoof. He began to find pup tents pitched in the better-drained spots, to catch the acrid reek of fires where wood smoke blended with the rich fullness of coffee. Twice he stumbled over guy ropes and wakened men swore at him. Dogs raced out of rude shelters barking, careful to keep clear of Lisette's nervous heels. The eastern sky lightened vaguely as he passed a long line of picketed gun teams with the limbers and pieces neatly aligned behind them. Lisette stretched her head toward the hay bales that tousled cannoneers were breaking up, whinnied as oats were poured into feed bags, but de Mérac kept her to her course.

There could be no doubt of the correctness of the report of Doubleday's aide. Already the junction of the Pike and the Little River Road had been passed, the point at which Jackson had obviously been aiming. The air was dead and still and the half-seen forms in the false dawn were Union troops, either on the road or in hasty bivouacs. Suddenly a dog began to bark. A guard challenged sharply in French. De Mérac held up his hand and headed toward the dim figure, fatigue melting for an instant from shoulders and legs. He called, "*Holà! Les Rochambeau! Scoarnec, c'est vous?*"

Little Scoarnec lowered his bayonet, muttering, "But one thought—*enfin*, I mean to say—" The little Breton's voice sounded flat and desolate. "One heard that—"

Among the tents that showed vaguely beyond Scoarnec a tall figure walked slowly, checked, then burst into a run. "John! For God's sake come here where I can look at you." George Force, kepi askew on his bright hair, raced up to him, disregarding Scoarnec. He caught de Mérac's hand, wrung it excitedly, patted his shoulder, wrung his hand again.

"Ah, this is good to see you, George!" de Mérac laughed. "You are officer of the guard? I must report to Kearny that you keep good watch! *Diable*, it occurs to me that I have missed you and the Rifles enough to split these last days. But you should have slept, *mon vieux*." He peered at George's usually clear eyes, noted a shadow in them, a deep shadow, and deep lines about them and about his mouth. "Now tell me where I find Kearny. I have a report to make."

He saw George's mouth tighten, then widen to a smile. "You don't want to be routing out the old *kébir* from his first sleep, John. Catch your breath here first."

"No. You must send me on to join him. Get some sleep and then I come back to you from Kearny."

George said shortly to Scoarnec, who was staring oddly at de Mérac, "Get Major Wilson. I'll stand your post."

De Mérac said, "No. Let Craig sleep. You all need— Ah, *baste*, he is roused already." Through the dim light Wilson ran with his quick step, his jacket buttoned as trimly as though on parade. He called, "Don't tell me that's John, George. Lord above, John, I'm relieved to see you. We'd heard—but never mind that just now." De

Mérac noticed that his eyes held the same shadows as George's.

George said quickly, "John's all in a sweat to get back to Kearny and report to him."

Wilson's lean jaw snapped shut. "Better wait, John. Have some coffee with us first. And, Lord, look at Lisette's off forefoot. We've got the field forge going and de la Mater'll snap a shoe on while you have your coffee. It'll really save you time. Kearny—well, he's quite a long way from here."

"But I can borrow your mount or Corvisart's."

George shouted, "De la Mater! Take Lisette and fix her up. Damn it, John, you can't find a horse that'll stand on four legs right now." He caught de Mérac's arm as a leather-aproned man led Lisette off. "Dekdebrun'll bring her round to you. Five minutes. That's all you need. Come on."

Wilson took his other arm. "That's it. Five minutes, John."

De Mérac laughed, half exasperated. "You act like conspirators. Very well. Coffee and new slippers for Lisette." He let himself be led away to the far end of the little camp. George steered him past the last row of tents to a fire where a blackened pot smoked under a tulip tree.

"There you are, John. Not as good coffee as Louvel's, but it'll do." George filled three cups. "Now taste that and tell us what's happened to you since you left us by Bull Run." He carefully placed an empty crate by the fire, pushed de Mérac onto it.

De Mérac protested. "But you turn my back to the camp! I see nothing of it. Do you think my brain is so turned by headquarters that I forget the Rifles?"

Wilson sloshed coffee about in his cup. "You'll see it all—later. We want to hear about you. We got word—well, that if you were lucky, you were a prisoner. We were worried."

De Mérac let rich strong coffee burn through him. "And Kearny thinks I'm lost—temporarily or permanently? That's all the more reason that I find him." There was a faint whuff behind him and Mr. McArdle pawed his knee. De Mérac stroked the shaggy head. "I can find a wagon, at least. I can—" He lowered his cup slowly, staring hard ahead of him. "What is that man doing?" he asked in a cold voice.

Ten yards away a grubby-faced bugler was tying a strip of black cloth about his bugle. De Mérac rose stiffly. "Who is it for?" he snapped. "Greenbaum? Corvisart?" George and Wilson looked away. The bugler went on knotting his crepe. Dull hammers beat back of de Mérac's eyes. His voice was harsh to cover a sudden, deadly fear. "Speak up, you two. Not—Kearny?"

The others closed in on either side and their hands fell to his shoulders. George said, "It's true, John. We—we just didn't know how to tell you. Word came from the Reb lines about an hour ago. It's all over the division by now."

De Mérac turned on him fiercely. "It can't be true. Never. I saw him riding free in a flash of lightning and he called, 'I'm clear—clear for good!'"

Wilson said quietly, "And so he is, John."

The hammers were beating intolerably now and shock blurred the dull, growing dawn into an opaque mist. He took two uncertain steps and sat heavily on the crate. There could be no doubt. George and Wilson knew. The sentry Scoarnec had known and the bugler Jeanblanc knew. How—*how* could it have happened? That did not matter. It had happened. His aching brain whirled and a tight band formed about his throat. He saw Kearny standing like a chained eagle in the Fifth Avenue Hotel while a crowd cheered Bob Anderson; saw him again on the steps of St. Paul's in New York, still a civilian, shouting *"En avant!"* to the departing Rifles. He had burst into the camp by Fort Corcoran in a whirl of red-lined cape and offered de Mérac a choice of commands in the New Jersey Brigade. He had sat his horse time and again, watching the Rifles file past on maneuvers while men hailed him as *le vieux kébir*, the old chieftain.

Mechanically de Mérac picked up the cup that he had dropped, let it dangle from inert fingers. Mr. McArdle laid his head on his knee. Kearny had galloped past the Rifles at Frayser's Farm shouting, "Go in gaily, boys!

Gaily!" At Malvern Hill he had swept down the column crying, "Forward! Forward! Forward! That's all that matters!"

At Harrison's Landing he had blazed with rage at the waste of a magnificent army, furious at timid half-measures that had spent men uselessly. And then there had been evenings at Kearny's mess along the James where the man of the world replaced the *kébir* and talk ran on buried African cities and the little white towns dotting the valley of the Marne. Or, effortless, he had drawn out his guests, and men like the Pole Krzyzanowski had told of revolution and exile and the finding of a new country that made that exile something to laugh at.

"Ride for it, de Mérac. I'm clear, I tell you ... I'm clear for good!" The old bugle tones throbbed and rang through de Mérac's head. Had Kearny known that he was lost and given the order to save at least one life?

No. It couldn't *be* that he was lost. Such fire, such vitality, had come through far more scorching places than the sodden cornfields by the woods. De Mérac saw again the erect figure, reins in teeth and revolver blasting back at the pursuit, saw it as he had seen it in the ripping lightning flashes.

Bugles wailed out in the camp, cold and cheerless, but their notes beat against deaf ears. It was so. The old *kébir* had gone in gaily for the last time. De Mérac's brain quivered to the thought. His throat twitched but his eyes were hot and dry.

There were footsteps behind him. George and Wilson, who had moved away, came slowly back. George said, "He thought an awful lot of you, John. He talked to me on the boat to Alexandria." De Mérac heard the words dully. George went on, "You've lost a mighty good friend. So have we all. So has the Union."

De Mérac looked up slowly, read a deep grief for Kearny in the two faces, a greater concern for himself almost masking it. He said, "*C'est ça.* It is the Union which has lost. We do not count—we others."

Wilson, eyes on the ground and fraying a ragged tobacco leaf between his long fingers, said in a low tone, "The boys are pretty badly shaken by the news, John.

Yes, it's hit them mighty hard." He paused. "They're falling in now. Wonder if you'd—well, just say something to them. It would steady them."

De Mérac got slowly to his feet. He said, "Yes," in a tight voice.

George muttered, "Good. I'll join my company." He ran off at a heavy trot.

"Right now, John?" suggested Wilson.

"Now," said de Mérac, and followed him.

The Rifles were drawn up at the east end of the camp. It was the first time that de Mérac had seen them in formation since they had massed near Sudley Springs Church. His chest contracted as his eye took in the thin companies. Péguy was gone and his lieutenant, St. Antoine; DuBosc lay somewhere up in the orchard beyond the abandoned railway. He looked for faces familiar since Chambers Street and Fort Corcoran—Sergeant Sullivan, Lieutenant Ritter, Private Lehagre, Corporal Denslow—

There were too many gaps. He turned his attention to those who remained, to the men who stared like sleepwalkers who still moved in a trance. Shea's hard, long-nosed face was tragic; Hein's mouth twitched behind his blond beard and Bolton had the glassy fixity of an unconscious man. In the rear of the line stood Father Doyle, his eyes on the ground, his lips stirring silently as his fingers played over the rents in his rusty black sleeves.

De Mérac studied the dazed faces. How could he talk to them? Then his eye caught the rows of red patches, faded and stained, that marked each kepi—red patches, Kearny patches. He began to speak. "Rochambeau Rifles! Remember this one thing—wherever you go, you are *still* Kearny's men." He turned on his heel and walked swiftly back to the fire. As he went he heard a quick rustle as though life were returning to the ranks, caught a murmur that spoke far deeper than any cheer.

At the fire, he forced himself to drink more coffee and drove his mind to consider where his next duty lay. "*Enfin,*" he muttered, "I, too, wear the red patch."

Lisette, newly shod, was led up by Dekdebrun, who

alone of the whole camp showed no mark of grief. A man was dead. As that man did not wear gray, he was unimportant. De Mérac turned from Dekdebrun without a word and drew new strength as George and Wilson joined him. George pulled soggy hardtack from his pocket. "Crumble it into your coffee. It's better than nothing. No sign of rations coming up yet."

Wilson asked, "What'll you do, John? Take over command again?"

De Mérac shook his head. "I must call on Birney, who will be in charge of the division now."

George protested, "But Kearny only detached you verbally. Birney won't know anything about that. Stay with us."

"It's a military courtesy, George. Besides—I think that Kearny would have liked it so."

Wilson said quietly, "You know best about such things, John. But get back to us as quick as you can."

As de Mérac rode down the slope, a tight band still about head and chest, he found that the news had spread wide over the fields and along the Pike. Something had gone out of the army and each mud-splashed private knew it. By a hospital, Negroes dug graves, singing plaintively:

> Oh, honey, don' yo' weep don' yo' moan,
> Pharioh's army's gwin carry yo' home.
> Pharioh's army got drownded.
> Oh, honey, don' yo' weep.

Once on the Pike, it was hard to find General Birney. He was said to be along Difficult Run, or at Flint Hill, or beyond Fairfax Courthouse. De Mérac took to the fields, looking for a knot of horses that would indicate a headquarters. Here and there men stood about tattered colors shouting, "Pennsylvania Bucktails, this way!" . . . "Von Puttkammer's Battery, rally here!" . . . "7th Wisconsin! Head for the crossroads!" . . . "Hey, that true? Colonel Webster killed? Old Dan'l Webster's son? Jesus!" . . . "2nd Maryland this way."

There was a hospital tent beyond a parked battery, a

tent whose walls were hideously smeared. Lisette shied at a heap of severed arms and legs and danced close to a figure that stood by the door. A woman's voice called, "Young man, get that animal out of my way. I've enough to do, with all the male nurses drunk."

De Mérac was jarred from his lethargy and stared down at a small, prim-faced woman in a bedraggled brown dress, her sleeves rolled over thin arms nearly to the elbow. She looked past forty, with the nervous mouth of a schoolmarm and brown eyes in which terror fought a drawn battle with white-hot determination. She called past de Mérac, "You get going with that team. Tell General Hancock that Clara Barton wants bread and bandages and morphine and wants them quick!" A light wagon rumbled off.

Her incisive tones that always threatened to break in a quaver, and yet stayed firm, revived him like cold water. Here was one person who knew precisely what she was doing and what she wanted. He took off his kepi and reined in Lisette. "You are busy, Madam, but could you tell me where to find General Birney?"

The prim, tight face turned up and the wide mouth snapped, "Fairfax. The little house in the fields beyond Gorton's store." She started to turn away, then her brown eyes narrowed. "H'm. The red patch. I've heard. Don't feel too badly. He went the way he'd have wanted to go. And he was *good*. Gave me five hundred dollars in gold for my wounded two days ago. They'll miss him." She blinked rapidly. "He always—here, you don't look too chipper yourself. Take a swallow of this!" She handed de Mérac a steaming tin cup and he found himself drinking eagerly. The mixture was strong and rather sweet and thick. Clara Barton watched him firmly. "Finish it. Pounded hardtack and wine and whiskey and brown sugar and water. All we've got. Do you good." Wheels rumbled over the grass and she looked around. "More of the boys. Give me that cup." Before de Mérac could thank her she had taken the cup, snatched up a steaming bucket, and swarmed up the spokes of the rear wheel crying, "All safe now, boys. Take a drink of this. All safe now!"

De Mérac rode away feeling suddenly very humble and almost reverent.

Without realizing it, he was among the houses of Fairfax grouped about the mellow, cupolaed brick of the old Courthouse. The main street was packed with kepis and broad black hats and on every corner men were shouting for regiments of a dozen states. He located the battered front of Gorton's store and dismounted by the little white house in its rear where aides with red-topped kepis slept on the sodden turf.

In a bare hallway that was gritty with the print of muddy boots a puffy-eyed major shook his head curtly. "The general's pretty hard hit. Unless it's orders, you'd better not disturb him in there." He jerked his head toward a splintery door at the right.

"I report from General Kearny. Captain de Mérac. I was with him."

The major stared. "*With* him? Oh, good God." He slid through the door, closed it, then reappeared, still staring. "Go right in."

David Birney, son of a Kentucky abolitionist, was broad-shouldered and rigid behind a battered table. The clear eyes under the high, wide forehead turned toward de Mérac with grave courtesy that masked impatience. "You've got some last order for me from—from the general?"

De Mérac said, "No, sir."

Birney frowned but his voice was still courteous. "Then I hope, Captain de Mérac, that what you have is important. I'm waiting for orders to move and of course this—this news has upset us all."

"I merely report to you for orders, sir."

Birney waved his hand impatiently. "But you'll get them when I do. Just keep on doing whatever you were doing."

"That, sir, is not possible. My last orders were to leave my regiment and follow General Kearny."

Birney smoothed his short beard. "Oh—I see. Of course." He rose and stood by the window, back toward de Mérac. "How did it happen? No. I shouldn't put you through that now." His booted foot tapped the floor.

"You didn't join the division till just before Malvern, did you? I went on leave just after that and I'm afraid I don't know much about you—meaning, of course, the Rochambeau Rifles. The general said something about detaching you from brigade command. That's it. I begin to remember a few things. You commanded the regiment with rank of captain and—of course." He resumed his seat. "Take a chair, Captain. The general was speaking of you just a few nights ago. You and the Rifles. Do you know what his plans were?"

De Mérac said, "I have nothing in writing, sir."

Birney smoothed his beard again, clear eyes on de Mérac. "He thought a lot of you. He had plans for you. Definite plans, but he never told me what they were."

"Nor me," said de Mérac.

"It's a pity," said Birney reflectively.

"Je m'en fous," said de Mérac shortly.

A bleak smile passed over Birney's face. "In English— to hell with them? Good. He had plans for you. He had plans for—a lot of us. Ever notice how he was always planning for others? He—well, anyway, he was satisfied with your work in the Rifles. Suppose you take over again from—Wilson, isn't it? Then we'll see what we can do about regularizing your position a little."

"It is not necessary, sir. You may count upon myself and the Rifles to serve you as we served General Kearny."

Birney inclined his head. "Thank you. You really don't need to assure me of that. There's another thing, though." He turned sideways in his chair and looked into the cold fireplace. "They brought his body in a little while ago. Lee sent it to Hooker. Damn courteous thing, sending it to another real fighter like Joe Hooker. Lee couldn't help it that the body'd been plundered. Guess he feels pretty badly about that. It's the sort of thing that'd hit him hard. Can't say that I blame his men, either. Lee can fight them but he can't seem to feed them or clothe them somehow. I've sent an escort along with the body to Washington. Captain Mindil of Kearny's staff and my son, Captain Fitz Hugh Birney of mine, are in command. I'm going to write a pass for you. I think he'd like to have his French troops represented."

De Mérac said, "You wish *me* to go?"

"Who else? There's an ambulance leaving for Alexandria in five minutes. Take it and catch up with Fitz and Mindil."

De Mérac held out his arms. "But in this *tenue?*"

Birney, writing busily, nodded. "Mud'll dry off your boots and breeches. Your coat's pretty badly torn and you've a hole in your cap. You got all that fighting under Kearny. He wouldn't like you slicked up. My boy and Mindil won't pass as fashion plates, either. There. Show that to any provost who halts you. I'd like to send you right on to Newark for the funeral but I'll need you back here."

De Mérac rose and slipped the pass into his pocket. "As far as the station, then. And where do I find the division on my return?"

Birney shrugged. "Probably we'll fall back to the Potomac Forts. But in any event—" he straightened in his chair and pointed to de Mérac's kepi—"you just have to look for one thing—so long as I command this division, it wears the Kearny patch. I won't wish you *bon voyage* on such a mission. Thank you for reporting."

As de Mérac stepped out of the little house in search of his ambulance and a groom to take Lisette back to the Rifles, a volcano of cheers burst from the streets of Fairfax Courthouse.

Men were running past the house, bawling incoherently, joining a disorganized welter that stormed across the fields. A group of riders swung off the road and started across country at a gallop, a long pennon of racing, cheering men fanning out behind. Hats and kepis skimmed into the air. The press closed about the horsemen, forced them to a walk, to a halt. De Mérac ran over a bridge that spanned a small stream, jostled and hurried by other speeding men. Then he stopped short. The leading rider was waving a small kepi and laughing down at the shouting soldiers who were jamming as close as they could, catching at the man's hands, at his boots, even throwing their arms about his horse's neck.

Deeper and deeper the roar swelled and de Mérac turned pale as he saw veterans of the Peninsula leaping high in air and shouting "Mac! Yeaah! Mac! Little Mac's back in command again! *He'll* look after us! Mac! Mac! Mac!"

De Mérac walked back toward the waiting ambulance with lowered head. Except for a shot in the lightning-stabbed dusk, they would be cheering Phil Kearny. Now disgust with Pope had swept them back to McClellan, who would feed them well, clothe them well, maneuver them expertly in laborious schemes that led to nothing but waste, waste, waste.

Acrid smoke drifted through the Washington station and hung pall-like about the waiting train. Six officers carefully raised a flag-draped coffin and eased it gently through the open doors of the baggage car. Kearny's Negro valet, his face wet with misery, climbed awkwardly after them and dropped a handful of wilted flowers onto the casket. De Mérac swayed as he stood to attention, his saber at the salute. More than smoke blurred his vision, made the forest of naked blades dance before him. The doors of the car slowly closed and a score of sabers flickered in the dimness. There was more smoke and then the train was gone.

De Mérac sheathed his saber and walked down the train shed with sagging shoulders through a crowd of officers who moved off listlessly and in utter silence. Out in the street he straightened himself. Kearny was gone, but the task on which he had spent himself still hung like a cloud over the land. It must be finished. De Mérac walked on up the avenue, stopped at Hammond's to buy field glasses to replace those lost during his brief capture. He saw a neatly lettered card at the jeweler's next door, "Buy our GUARANTEED STERLING SILVERWARE and you'll help save the Union." He turned away, sickened by the tawdry appeal. He wanted someone with whom he could share his burden of sorrow in silent understanding—George or Wilson or Corvisart, or Father Doyle, or Greenbaum. The hurrying people on the sidewalks, soldier or civilian, were cut off from him and he from them. Some looked terrified, for the news of Pope's failure had thrown people into panic and there had been piles of luggage at the station. By Willard's four women drew their skirts aside to avoid de Mérac and he saw Rebel colors at their throats. He raised his kepi with icy courtesy and stepped aside to let a tall woman pass between him and the curb. She spat on the ground and swept on.

He left the sidewalk and threw himself into a carriage that waited by the curb. He jerked out the words "Minnesota Row." The driver started his horses. He hoped Louise Duane would be at home. She had greatly admired Kearny and would understand the weight of the blow, a weight felt by every man who wore the Kearny patch. She was quick in sympathy and would talk sparingly and gently.

A carriage heaped with trunks and bags stood in front of the Duane house and another was drawn up behind it, empty. De Mérac tossed a coin to his driver, sprang to the ground, and ran toward the broad steps. The door opened and Louise Duane, a light cloak over her arm, swept out. De Mérac called in a husky voice, "Louise!"

She poised on the top step, then both her hands went out. "John! Oh—I've heard about it! It's awful! Whatever will we do?"

He caught her hands. "I knew you'd understand. It's *effroyant!*"

Her dark eyes were wide and haunted and her full mouth was drawn down at the corners. "It's in the papers! It's true! Everyone says so! You wouldn't be here if it wasn't. And you came to me first of all!" The shadows in her eyes lightened and her hands held his tighter.

"It's true. I was with him. Just now at the station—"

Bewilderment spread over her face. "*Him?* Who?"

"But General Kearny, of course! *Mon dieu*, he was so—"

Her voice jumped to a higher pitch. "But the Rebels. They'll be in Washington any minute. Kearny! We've got lots of generals but the Rebels'll be here, I tell you. They're coming across the Potomac now. I know it! Oh, it's dreadful. They'll do awful things!" She shifted her grasp to his sleeves while he stared in unbelief. "I'm not going to stay here a minute longer. I'll meet Mother in Baltimore." Her round chin quivered.

De Mérac said gently, "There's no cause for alarm. You're as safe here as in New York. Forget those newspapers. Lee has been stopped."

She threw back her head and the light breeze flicked tendrils of ash-blond hair about her cheeks. "It's no use. We haven't got any soldiers left. Take me to Baltimore, to New York. Now! We'll pick up Mother—" Her dark eyes widened in fright as horses clopped along the street. "Cavalry! Our men are running away." She tugged at his arm. "Come on. We'll be too late."

A squad of horsemen reined in at the door and a young officer with a wreathed "N.H." on his kepi dropped to the curb. "Sorry, Captain. Got to see your papers."

De Mérac shrugged and went down the steps while Louise watched impatiently. He pulled out Birney's pass. The officer shook his head. "Afraid that's no good now. New orders. Everyone back to his regiment."

"What's happened?" asked de Mérac sharply.

The provost remounted. "Hell's bust loose again. Lee's across the river in Maryland, up Harpers Ferry way. McClellan's back in command."

De Mérac dropped his voice. "Could you give me a pass that would let me see this young lady to the cars?"

"Wouldn't do you any good. Lord, heading for the station with all those bags at a time like this? Too damn many have hit north as it is. You'd be grabbed by the first patrol that saw you. No. You go right down Fourteenth Street alone and on foot." He looked at Louise admiringly. "Wish I could do more, but that's how it is." He touched his kepi and clattered off.

Louise ran down the steps. "He's gone? Then get in. Quick."

"But Louise, that is not possible."

She stamped her foot. "You're stupid! No, I don't mean that, John. But we've always been friends and I can't see you going back to that awful business. You belong in New York. Please!" She stood close to him, very feminine, very desirable, suddenly full again of hints of intimacy. "It wouldn't be like deserting. You know so many people. You could go to New York and then tell some of your important friends to fix up leave papers for you. There are dozens of ways."

His mouth tightened. "But Louise, this is sheer panic. Things aren't bad at all. You'll see that—"

"I can see that you're obstinate and pigheaded and—oh, John, please come!" He shook his head. She turned her back on him abruptly and got into the carriage. "The station, driver." The rig bowled off, followed by the luggage.

Irritation struggled in his mind with bewilderment as he made his way down Fourteenth Street where long lines of men rounded up by the Provost were being marched to the wharves. He was stopped several times by hard-eyed guards who looked at his papers and told him to hurry on. The press of men, on foot or mounted, thickened, steaming on toward Long Bridge. Jostled by privates and colonels, de Mérac crossed the malodorous canal to the parklike stretch where the red towers of the Smithsonian lifted high. A fresh stream of traffic, northbound from the bridge, butted against the disordered crowd. Empty supply wagons rocked and jolted, swung off across the turf. Flagged ambulances rolled over the grass, drew up in a growing mass by the stump of the Washington Monument. More wheels, more swaying canvas tops, more cracking whips. A commandeered sutler's cart cut through the crowd, its wheels grazing de Mérac. The cart halted. De Mérac slapped at the mules with his kepi. "Keep on. You block the road."

The civilian driver growled, "Far's I go. Orders. Want a tech of this whip? Then git away from my mules."

De Mérac worked on past the cart. The back curtain flapped and a thickset woman jumped to the ground calling, "Here's where we stop," as she jerked at her rumpled gray coverall. A slighter figure climbed down protesting, "But this can't be right, Pender!"

De Mérac whirled about at the new voice. Pale and drawn, with streaks of blood on her white neck and on her stained gray clothes, stood Gail Shortland, her eyes reddened and troubled but her chin as firmly set as ever. De Mérac cried, "Miss Shortland!" his voice thick with surprise.

Pleasure overcame the fatigue in the gray eyes and she put out her hand. "Captain de Mérac! Oh—I'm so *glad!* I came past your regiment once and didn't see you and I wondered if—oh, if you were still with it."

De Mérac said, "Past the regiment? And you looked for me?"

She nodded but a mask of impersonality settled about her tired face. "Of course. I know what's been happening out there and we need every trained officer. Besides, I did want to say something to you. You see, I'd heard about General Kearny. I think I can understand a little of what he meant to you. What I could have said wouldn't have helped but I did want you to know that I sympathize."

"Thank you," said de Mérac gravely. "He would have liked your speaking of him. He was—*Holà!*" She swayed, slipped sidewise against the side of the cart. He caught her, steadied her gently. "*Tiens,* you are sick." She leaned against his shoulder for an instant and he marveled at how light and frail she seemed. Then she stepped back and shook her head. "Just tired. We haven't had much sleep since we started for Centerville last week."

"Centerville?" His voice rose in surprise. "By Bull Run? But how—"

She tucked back a strand of red-gold hair that had slipped from under her wide straw hat. "They called for volunteers. Most of us from the hospital went. Nothing had been done and nothing was ready. The male nurses drank up all the hospital whiskey. We didn't have many supplies but we did what we could. Then we looked after the men in the woods near Chantilly. That's how I heard about General Kearny."

"But all those days. And so many wounded!"

"And so few of us. I'm afraid we didn't help much."

He stared at her, remembering the drenching rains and the blind surge of the retreat. She had been out there, working in the open. He could only say, "When do you rest?"

"Oh, we've been resting, coming over in the cart. Now Matron's meeting all of us with a wagon and we'll rest more going back to the hospital. Pender's looking for her. Oh—there she is. Over by the broken limber. You should have seen Pender. She's the one over there with the man's cap on her head." Her eyes filled. "She was wonderful. One night she sang 'Kathleen Mavourneen' to an Irish boy while they took off his arm. There. She's waving. I've got to go. Good luck, Captain de Mérac."

He looked keenly at the face that was still pretty under its mask of fatigue. He said, "Good luck to you."

"I need it. Clara Barton's managed to get a cart of her own and she's going to follow the army into Maryland. I want to get permission to go with her."

He said quickly, "But you ought to be at home!"

She smiled up at him. "My home's with the army. Good luck again." She raised a slim hand and threaded her way past a tugging mule team.

A provost tapped de Mérac's shoulder. He sighed and moved on toward Long Bridge. As the plants rang under his feet he looked upstream. On the high shore he could see heavy bodies of troops moving north and west, hurrying toward the fords and crossings into Maryland where Lee's gray columns were pouring. Angry clouds banked heavy against a red sunset. Low on the horizon they split to form a jagged diamond so that there seemed to hang in blazing threat, black bordered, the Kearny patch, vivid and glowing.

The windows of the bishop's office looked out toward the abandoned Seminary and the walls of Fort Albany that formed part of the ever-growing defenses on the Virginia side of the Potomac. General David Birney leaned back in the chair of the absent bishop and smiled sympathetically across the desk at the major who fumbled with stacks of papers. "Hard on you, Brevoort, having this job when you've just joined us. Damn it, though, we've got to get the division into shape."

Henry Brevoort, newly joined assistant adjutant general, tugged at his long mustache. "Worse for you, sir, having me. Never thought of the army until poor Kearny sent for me. I never knew how he happened to think of me."

"De Trobriand suggested you to him. Heard him myself."

"Old Régis? Well, I'll do my best but I hope you won't be cursing him." He shuffled his papers. "Now—that fixes Poe's brigade and he gets the 5th Michigan, too. Oh—had another question to ask you. Here's the—let's see—yes, the Rochambeau Rifles. Phil had detached them but no one seems to know why. What'll I do about them?"

"Where were they before?"

"Pelham had them in his brigade."

Birney tugged at his beard. "Phil never did anything without a reason, but it was always mighty hard to guess in advance what his reason was. The Rifles. They didn't come to us till just before Frayser's Farm, so I don't know as much about them, firsthand, as I do about those we've had right through. What's their strength now?"

Brevoort pulled out a sheet. "Three hundred eighty-eight fit for duty, this says. What sort of an outfit are they?"

"As I say, I've hardly seen them in action. But Phil rated them mighty high as an assault regiment—or any kind of a regiment for that matter. They've got a funny setup. No colonel, and a young Frenchman named John de Mérac commands them, *de facto*, with rank of captain. Damned irregular, but Phil didn't care. Who's Pelham got now?"

"Just Pride and Clay."

"Too damn weak for a brigade. Give him the Rifles. They seem to be a tough outfit, regardless of numbers, and he ought to be glad to get 'em."

Brevoort nodded. "Rochambeau Rifles to Pelham. Right. Now about Robinson's brigade."

XII

Pursuit

THERE was eager, vibrant life in the September air as thick blue columns drove on into Maryland. George Force felt it as he swung along with Mr. McArdle beside the twenty-seven men who composed his company. His men sensed it, too, as did the forty of LeNoir's ahead and the thirty-three of Shea's Irish beyond them. Every file of the Rifles sensed it. George knew that, as the regiment pushed on into the rolling Maryland countryside. He knew that the surging spirit was everywhere, exulted in it as he topped a sun-swept crest and looked over the fat lands on the Monocacy Valley and saw networks of roads, all heading west and all thickly blue with marching men. He caught the far glint of bayonets, the gliding flow of cavalry, the slower rock of batteries, caught it from the right, the front, the left. When he turned to look back at Bolton's command, the lowlands to the rear were crosshatched with blue, with the weaving sway of canvas-topped wagons and the dull sheen of heavy ordnance.

There were fresh, untried regiments, strong and well-equipped, winding through orchards and slipping through neat stone towns. But by thousands and tens of thousands there marched the weary men who had fought and marched and fought from Yorktown to Malvern Hill and on to the stinging hollows at the foot of the Bull Run Mountains. They marched in rags, marched in their drawers, marched with rag-wrapped feet or with bare feet slapping on the hard roads of Maryland. There were sick men in the ranks, slightly wounded men who could have shown blood to a provost and been sent to the rear. But on they rolled into Maryland, aiming at Lee's flank.

George, seeing the tense keenness of every face and every gesture in the endless columns, was reminded of a prize fighter who strains from his corner, strong in his second wind. And here that second wind came from one fact. *McClellan was moving, driving, racing on after Lee!* Gone was the hesitant fumbling of the Peninsula, the self-distrustful, halfhearted measures. He had unleashed his pack and sent it, baying full-throated, after its prey.

Oh, George could catch the grim exultation from passing patrols of cavalry, from intent staff officers seen in Hyattstown, from resting infantry near Urbana, and from watchful engineers at the Monocacy bridges. Ahead lay the bluish lift of the Catoctin Mountains, and beyond them towered South Mountain and the great shaggy spine of the Blue Ridge that sheltered the invasion.

The men of the Rifles did not sing. They rarely talked. New York recruit and African veteran, they gave themselves utterly to this new, intoxicating sweep. They drank sparingly from their canteens and rarely straggled.

There was little for George to do, no need to keep urging, "Close up! Close up!" He had only to march on with the click of equipment, the grind of boots, and the crisp patter of Mr. McArdle's feet in his ears. At the head of the column rode de Mérac in close talk with Pride, who had dropped back to see him. There was the lithe Bordagaray moving with his dancer's step to set the pace of the whole column, a killing pace of which no man complained. There was Wilson. Father Doyle seemed to be murmuring an endless Nunc Dimittis as he strode on by Hein's company, carrying a German musket. At the rear of the column, old Sergeant Major Rapp had lost something of his unshakable calm and clipped along at his veteran's stride, puffing fiercely at his *brûle-gueule*.

Through orchards that smelled richly of apples, through fat fields where the sun hung hot over late crops, over brawling streams littered with brown rocks. George drank in the new tang of the whole army, felt it overpoweringly as he marched with his company through towns where people hung out Union colors and where women rushed to the side of the column with aprons full of fresh bread, of pies, where old men brought out pitchers of beer, where, by a white church, massed children sang shrilly, "The Union forever, hurrah, boys, hurrah!" It was hard to answer the voices, hard to meet the yearning eyes that looked down from windows. George thought, "This is what it's all been for—everything. At last we've got our chance to tear into Lee's flank, rip him up for good and all."

Mrs. Force sat very erect in the green and white drawing room, her chair close to a window that looked out onto Twenty-fourth Street. The chair was not very big but her diminutive daintiness gave it almost the air of a massive throne. The slanting sun touched her white hair and her smooth face as she carefully finished the last stitch on a coarse nightgown and tossed it onto a pile of others that swelled out of a box marked "U. S. Sanitary Commission." She picked up a fresh garment and sent her needle slipping through the heavy weave. As she worked, the muscles at the corners of her mouth flickered lightly.

There was so much she couldn't understand. The paper said that Birney's division was still near Fort Albany, across the Potomac from Washington. Yet the last word she had from George was that the Rifles were moving into Maryland. How could that be? Maryland! The boys last night raced through the streets shouting of action near a place called South Mountain and that was in Maryland. She worked steadily on, unconscious of the flicker about her mouth. Could she go through more days like those when George was missing? More of the awful uncertainty that followed the Bull Run fighting?

She heard the maid go to the door, heard a rustle of voices and then a light step. The drawing-room door flew open and Dora Chase swept in, her cheeks glowing and eyes sparkling. Mrs. Force cried, "Why, Dora! How nice! Have you had a letter?"

Dora's laugh rippled through the room. "I didn't mean to bounce in just like this, but look!" She whipped a folded newspaper from her reticule and handed it to the older woman. "Look! Right there!" She settled herself opposite in a whirl of brown skirts and watched eagerly.

Mrs. Force dropped her work. One hand flew to her throat. "Oh!" Her voice trembled as the bold headlines danced before her. "Great Victory! Lee Routed in Maryland! A Masterpiece of Art!" She whispered, "Oh, thank God, thank God! 'Driven in panic over the river,' it says. 'McClellan harrying him. Huge Rebel losses.'" Her face went white. "But we'll have them, too. Oh, this waiting again, this—"

Dora sprang up. "But Mrs. Force, you're not reading the place I marked. Here, I'll read it to you. It's perfectly nasty, about that Pelham, but I don't care. Listen. 'I can also report to my readers that I visited the headquarters of the gallant and dashing General Dudley Pelham, who surely needs no introduction in these pages. He was martial and commanding as ever, but in his breast there burned a fierce flame of disappointment, a just fire that he manfully strove to conceal. His brigade, detached for the emergency from the command of General Birney, was left behind to guard the approaches to Catoctin Creek. This slight may be attributed entirely to the reassignment to him of an immigrant regiment of known unreliability and'—and, well, that's all. That means George is safe. Oh, this is glorious news. The war must be almost over. I know George'll be sick with disappointment at not being in it and I feel perfectly contemptible exulting like this, but I can't help it. It's over and he's safe. Oh, he *mustn't* feel too badly."

Mrs. Force leaned over and kissed Dora. "He's too

sensible, dear. He doesn't want glory. He's fought and fought well. He won't care, just missing the last battle. The war'll be ended and that's what he went for. We'll manage somehow to set you two up in spite of your father, and that's the first thing George'll think of." She folded her hands in her lap. "My dear, I suddenly feel very weak and humble. I do wish I could see George right now. He'll be so happy."

The camp of Pelham's brigade lay in the bend of Catoctin Creek on the high ground just above the bridge of the Frederick road. The site was well chosen so far as shade and drainage went, but overdriven cavalry had passed that way en route to Antietam, and the slopes of the hill were spotted with bodies of work-killed horses. They lay in ditches, under trees, in the open, their bodies hideously bloated and their four legs sticking skywards in a last, mute protest. The smell of decomposition hung heavy among the tents and clung to grass, wood, and cloth like a palpable fog.

For the moment, swollen carcass and sullen stench were forgotten in the camp of the Rifles. A mail had come in and the rip of envelope and the crackle of paper whispered through the still air. Under a fly that had been rigged in the shade of an apple tree de Mérac suspended work with Greenbaum and Rapp while all three reached eagerly for their letters.

Rapp opened his thin envelope and read in placid approval. Clémence was doing well with the paper shop and reported as a good adjutant should. Through the intercession of their neighbor, Mr. Rafferty, she had been able to sell much fine paper to the State of New York for military commissions, and while it had been necessary to make proper acknowledgment to this good Mr. Rafferty, as one would conceive, the profit had been highly satisfactory. Taxes were high, but what would you? Rapp nodded to himself. *Un bon vieux sabot,* Clémence. That leaped to the eye.

De Mérac glanced through a letter from his guardian, saw that it contained chiefly Breton gossip and military advice based on the grand strategy of 1805, and laid it aside. He laughed over a letter from Venice. His friend Baron Panoff was volubly puzzled by the disregarded list of Cusler's promotions which he had sent him. He frowned as he recognized Louise's hand on the next envelope. In retrospect, it was easy to excuse her panic in Washington, but her urge that he virtually desert disturbed him. She had been in the Capital long enough to know the seriousness of what she said.

The letter was a mixture of frankness and contrition. Surely, she wrote, he knew that an invaded city was no place for a young girl and it did look as though those awful Rebels would be coming right up the Avenue any minute, didn't it, now? She was afraid that she had seemed sharp at his refusal to escort her at least to Baltimore, but really she had been thinking of him all the time. Weren't they old friends enough for her to urge him to get out for his own good? She would come back to Washington quite soon now that that wonderful McClellan had practically won the war and she hoped to have a good, long talk.

"*Ça!*" thought de Mérac. "Yes—one sees that she would like to. I must read this again later. Now at home, such a recalling of a friendship would almost amount to a declaration which no *jeune fille* would permit herself. But over here—" He looked up. "Ready, you others? We must be prepared to move at once, since McClellan is bound to follow Lee into Virginia. I am puzzled that he has not done so already."

Greenbaum carefully tucked away a letter. "One thing more. I want to put in for a furlough the first time they're allowed."

De Mérac laughed. "Furlough? You, who never miss a formation?"

"Want to get married." His heavy, dark features glowed. "You met her at Corcoran. Rachel Talamo. She just said yes."

De Mérac waved. "Inform the pretty Miss Talamo, whom I remember indeed, that at this moment one good adjutant is worth forty husbands. But the furlough, you shall have it. If there is delay, then bring her down here and the Rifles will give you a military ceremony. Now,

Rapp, I want you to see to the issue of those boots we took from the dead cavalrymen and have them—" He broke off as Mr. McArdle rushed into the tent, his tail whacking against the rough table. "*Alors*, what do you want? Come in, George, and—*vingt dieux*, what is the matter?"

George stood in the door, his face white and his eyes blazing. He started to speak, choked in the middle of a word, then drew his sword and slammed it into the turf, where it stuck, quivering. At last he said, "John, I want to resign. I'm going to resign. By God, I can't stand it!"

De Mérac stared, speechless. Greenbaum's jaw dropped. Rapp looked shocked to the depths of his military soul.

De Mérac got up quickly, laid an arm about George's shoulder and drew him into the tent. Then he reached under the table and drew out a bottle of commissary whiskey. "A drink, *mon vieux*." He splashed whiskey into the cup. "There. It marches. Now, wait one little instant until we finish and then you and I shall talk this over."

Force shook his head violently. "What I've got to say I'll say anywhere. Do you know what's happened now? About that bastard McClellan's orders? Well, you'll get 'em. I just saw Marty Callahan from staff and he told me. Know what that God-damn Napoleonic genius of ours has done? Issued orders calling himself a hero for *chasing Lee out of Maryland!* Calls it a masterpiece of art. Chased him out as though he were just a common burglar and that's all. Great victory! He was able to make Lee retreat! God damn it, for just one minute of Phil Kearny!" He stopped for breath and the color came and went in his face.

De Mérac said gently, "But, George, while I agree that the order is something ridiculous, I do not think we are called upon to criticize McClellan's military style."

George dashed his kepi onto the ground. "That's not all. He isn't even moving, isn't even following Lee with patrols. Ten thousand men would end the war. I've talked to some of the Reb prisoners and they think it's over. *They* know, but they don't know Mac. He had a whole corps, Sedgwick's, that he never used over by Antietam, and even so, Lee's in horrible shape. Mac's letting him get away. A victory! Chased him out of Maryland! Was that worth ten thousand or fifteen thousand casualties? Hell, Lee was trying to retreat anyway."

"But there is still time," urged de Mérac.

"With Mac? No damn fear. We're going to sit right here, the whole Army of the Potomac, and refit. He's already yowling that he's got to have fifty thousand fresh men and cursing Lincoln for starving him. God blast him, he could sweep up Lee without touching his reserves, I tell you. He doesn't *want* to win. Look what'll happen now. Lee'll fall back into Virginia and we'll limp after him in a month or two. We'll come right back over the old, old trail led by a bungler. I'm through, I tell you. I'm not going to take what's left of my men over that trail just to get butchered."

De Mérac reached for the bottle. "Have another drink, George. And think of this. This war must be won for the Union, whether our generals fight it well or badly. You and I, we do not count, nor do—"

"I'm not quitting. Oh, don't make any mistake about that. I'm just not passing down orders that'll kill men so some lunk-headed general can write a report on it. I'll take my place in any company you say as a private. But that's all. Damn it, I can't look my men in the eye. They trust me. And when I take them into some place like the old cutting at Bull Run, they think I know what I'm doing. Well, I do know, now. I'm getting them killed for nothing, I tell you. I can't go on with it. I'm through and I mean it. Randol can handle what's left of the company and I'll be high private in the rear rank, starting right now."

De Mérac drew a deep breath. "*Soit*. You will be hard to replace. But let me ask one question, George. Do you remember how you received your commission?"

George kicked the turf with his scuffed boots. "Why—I got elected, of course."

De Mérac spread out his hands. "*Précisément*. Elected to an office which the men wanted you to fill." He leaned forward suddenly. "Is it not right, then, that they have a word to say about your decision? They are intelligent. No doubt they feel much as you do about the wastage. Are they, who trust you, better off when no longer led by you?" He pushed George onto a cracker box. "Listen to me. You go to your men and tell them that you wish to surrender the office to which they elected you. If they agree, then I shall say nothing. True, we no longer elect, but I shall forget that. Only, go to them and see what they make of your wish. After retreat would be a good time. Now take the good Mr. McArdle and walk in the field across the river. Plan carefully what you will say to your men. Then tonight, come and mess with me. I have bacon that is not too moldy."

George stretched out his hand impulsively. "Don't know what I'd do without you, John. Thanks a lot. I've still got to think it over. See you tonight. Come on, Mr. McArdle."

The dog scrambled out from under the table and followed his master. De Mérac pulled at his mustache, frowning. Was there more that he could have said? George's mental torment was obvious and he had felt helpless before it. Rapp coughed apologetically and rustled papers.

Greenbaum said in a heavy voice, "So Lee's got away and the whole thing's to be done over!"

Rapp smoothed his red beard calmly. "So it often happens in war, sir, as I remarked after Bull Run to Sergeant Cahusac, who agreed. But now we have this matter of bayonet scabbards to dispose of."

When they had gone, de Mérac sat silent, drumming his fingers on the table. It would all have to be done over again. George was right. Another advance into Virginia, perhaps a winter campaign, more inconclusive fights. The matter could go on for years, unless one side or the other was worn down. Beyond the hazards of combat, what could happen to him? There was Pelham, whom he had come to look upon more as a symbol than as a person. The brigadier had been bitterly disappointed at the reassignment of the Rifles and made no secret of it. His wrath seemed to be centered on de Mérac, as though Pelham in turn had taken him for a symbol. The foreigner. It was obvious that Pelham would have been glad to dispose of him save for the fact of which de Mérac was coldly aware, that he could not afford to for strictly military reasons. It was so easy, also, to shift the blame for defeat onto the foreign-born. Franz Sigel's corps, weak and overworked, had been badly supported at Bull Run. Now, on all sides, de Mérac heard sneers against "the damned Dutchmen" who formed a large part of that corps—trained German officers like von Schimmelfennig, von Steinwehr, young Dilger, men like the Pole Krzyzanowski. Would they have had credit had Fitz-John Porter come up in time? It was not likely. The XIth Corps would still be rotting in the Washington defenses. Unpleasant things could happen to individuals, when such a trend of thought was running. It was something he himself would do well to think about. Now supposing—

As his mind worked he absently ordered the last papers on the rough table. A small envelope, overlooked before, slipped out. It was soiled and bore several thumbprints.

The sheet inside was unstained and bore a few lines in firm, graceful script. His eyes widened as he read.

Dear Captain de Mérac:

They wouldn't let me go with Miss Barton after all, but there is plenty to do right here. I'm just taking a second to say "good luck" to you and to thank you for your very generous concern for me.

Faithfully yours,
Gail Shortland.

He felt deeply and warmly moved that she should have written in the midst of scenes he could well imagine. He suddenly thought that he would like to have the grave gray eyes on him as he spoke of such problems as Pelham. Sunlight danced across the single heavy gold ring that he wore, lit up the worn crest with its Breton motto, "Flam var mor ha var donar." "Brilliant on land and sea," or the *Flam* could be translated as "Steady," perhaps. "Stay steady" would be her advice. He drew a sheet of paper to him and began "My dear Miss Shortland—"

Across the Catoctin, George sat on a rock and stared moodily over the sunny river valley. Mr. McArdle raced up and down the steep bank flushing imaginary rabbits and squirrels. Tiring of this, he came lolloping back with a stick in his jaws for his master to throw. Something told him that the moment was inopportune so he stretched patiently on the ground, his tousled head resting against George's boots.

There was life and death along the twisting river. Away to the left a band sounded faintly and a long procession filed out of sight over a rise, a flag-draped coffin at its head. Squads and platoons drilled on level spaces, careful to avoid the knots of men who labored with pick and shovel to bury the dead horses, breaking their stiff legs with blows of clubs. George knew that his hands were unsteady, felt that his jaw muscles quivered. Life and death. Death was not terrifying if it meant anything. But what meaning had the dead of Second Bull Run, the dead of Antietam?

He saw himself swinging the company into line, heads down and light blue legs driving into a hail of lead, saw little Chase blink as blood spouted from between his eyes, heard gangling Piper say in a conversational tone, "There goes my leg." He felt his own wrist tingle to the memory of blows with the flat of his sword as he whacked at men who flinched in a moment of panic. What difference had it made? Why had he burned with hard approval when LeNoir coldly shot a man who broke for the rear? What difference had that made?

He could do it no more. Let Randol and Bates take the company. He would march as a private until lead struck him down in some futile charge. Dora would understand. He might see her again or he might not. In his numbed state she seemed to hover beyond his horizon, beloved but unattainable.

There was no point in putting the matter of resignation up to the men. The decision was his and they had no right to demand more of him. He cupped his chin in his hand and scowled at the sun-dappled stream where the wind murmured among gold-branched trees.

A new sound was added to the distant rustle and he mechanically noted a long column of men thumping over the narrow swaying bridge. Subconsciously he took in the wide-brimmed hats marked with the Kearny patch. Pride's Indianians. They crossed the stream and wound up a path that mounted the sloping bank to his right. His seasoned eye told him that the detail, possibly three companies strong, was composed of veterans and recruits. Damn it, those western states always seemed to manage to send out recruits to the old regiments instead of forming new, green outfits as was done in the East.

Why worry about it? It was all part of the same futility. He raised his head dully. The Indiana men were singing, led by a bearded sergeant. The voices pounded out full-throated:

Mine eyes have seen the glory of the coming of the Lord;
He is trampling out the vintage where the grapes of wrath are stored—

He ejaculated, "Hey!" without knowing it and leaned forward. Mr. McArdle pricked up his ears.

The column came on, heads back and arms swinging. The men marched at ease but the fever of the hymn forced their broken boots into a steady drumbeat. George growled. "Mr. McArdle, I'm a God-damn fool!" chests were beating against him. Individual faces stamped themselves hard in his mind—a white-haired Swede, a high-cheeked Yankee, a ruddy English face, a fair-skinned German, steady, determined faces under the broad brims with the red patches. They began another verse:

In the beauty of the lilies Christ was born across the sea,
With a glory in His bosom that transfigures you and me.

Something snapped in George's chest. He was on his feet without conscious volition. His kepi was high above his head and he joined in the organ-rich chorus:

Glory, Glory Hallelujah! His truth is marching on!

The blue files swept their deep melody out of sight. George growled. "Mr. McArdle, I'm a God-damn fool!"

He slithered down the bank toward the bridge, the dog flouncing gaily beside him. Along a path on the west bank a line of Negroes pressed eagerly on. A bent old crone raised her hands to George and quavered, "Jurdan! I's 'cross Jurdan at last!" A cadaverous civilian frolicked about the flank of the line, a Christian Commission agent whom he had seen about the camps, handing out Bibles and tracts. He caught sight of George and caroled, "They're free. Oh, Brother, thank God they're free!" His face was suffused with joy.

"What are you going to do with them?" asked George.

The commissioner flapped damp hands. "Preach to them and pray with them, Brother!"

"Better feed 'em first or they'll be fainting in their tracks," George answered.

The agent looked pained. "You'd rob them of manna for their souls? Brother, the light has not touched you. But it is touching the whole army." He held up his hand. "Listen. Those poor, rough men singing hymns out of their hearts!" He pointed to a score of artillery drivers who sat by the bank, washing and oiling their harness. George muttered, "I'll be damned." The tough-looking drivers were singing a hymn.

The wind shifted and the words came clear. The agent's face was contorted with sudden pain. George threw back his head and laughed. The words were sharp and unmistakable.

> Slowly, slowly, slowly, little Mac the tardy,
> Early every morning, Bob Lee gives thanks for thee!

George clapped the agent on his shoulder. "Don't start your revival meeting too soon. And you feed these people as soon as you halt or I'll put in a charge against you."

He left the weary Negroes and their shocked shepherd and scaled the hill to the camp of the Rifles. Bugles were blowing mess call all up and down the river and he suddenly realized that he was very hungry. Outside the headquarters fly, de Mérac, Wayne, and Greenbaum were perched on upturned boxes while the mouselike Louvel handed about tin plates and mugs. George hailed and de Mérac's voice, suddenly gay, answered, "Hurry, or I eat all but the mold on the bacon."

George seized a box and drew up to the rough table. "Mold's fine for me, if you throw in a few weevils from the hardtack." He caught de Mérac's eye, winked, and felt a warm glow at the light that spread over his friend's face. There was no need for words.

Wayne, stoop-shouldered and gray as ever, spluttered through a mouthful of hardtack. "Can't figure out Touzelier's heel. Clean, but the pus keeps rolling out and the flesh looks like that bacon."

De Mérac looked pained but George laughed. "What's the matter with the bacon, Doc? I'd call it fit for a king."

"Sure," grunted Wayne. "If the king was hungry enough."

"You'll get used to it. Mac's in command for good, and ten years from now you'll be sitting right here and tearing into old shoes as if they were roast beef."

De Mérac, sipping coffee, looked at George and felt deeply content. His friend had rallied from shock and fatigue, rallied completely. He lit a cigarette and looked out over the camp where men were squabbling in raucous amity over their rations. The future, he thought, would not be easy, but it would be met.

The Army of the Potomac lay inert on the north bank of the river. McClellan pushed cautious patrols across but beyond that he did little to interfere with Lee, recuperating some twenty miles inside Virginia. The Rifles broke camp by the Catoctin and moved down to the great river close by Edwards's Ferry, a little below Poolesville with its nexus of roads. There they found Birney's whole division encamped and de Mérac was delighted that Berry's brigade now included Baron de Trobriand and the 55th New York. The Rifles' wagons under Brady, which had been left behind on the Peninsula, rejoined the regiment, together with the twenty men of the baggage guard under command of the whispering Rohde. The latter plunged back into the regiment, buzzing with sibilant hints and rumors as to the unfitness and general malfeasance of all officers save the one to whom he happened to be talking.

De Mérac called on Birney, but the grave, bearded general had no hints of future moves. "Your guess is as good as mine," Birney said wearily. "Look at the latest order from McClellan. Wants fifty thousand more men at least. Why? So he'll be able *to keep Lee from coming back into Maryland!* Keep him from coming back! God in a gig! Was Phil Kearny the *only* fighter we had?"

Nonetheless, de Mérac worked to keep the Rifles ready for a move at the least notice.

There was no notice and no need for one. Morning after morning the sharpening air brightened over the camps, bugles blared for sick call and men sang derisively:

> I'm—*sick!* I'm *sick!*
> Send for the doctor and bring me a nurse.
> I'm—sick! I'm *sick!*
> Hurry up, Doctor, I'm getting worse.
> I'm—sick!

And over the broad valley there reigned a calm as deep as that of the Horse Latitudes.

There was divisional business in Washington in connection with pay rolls. Birney, having heard that de Mérac had formed useful contacts at the War Department, sent him over the road to arrange matters. De Mérac would have preferred to send Craig Wilson, thus giving him a chance to see his family, but Birney was adamant; so he set out with Dekdebrun and little Castex.

The ride to Washington was pleasant, so long as they kept to secondary roads, for the main routes were choked with long, swinging columns of infantry—now giant Maine lumbermen and now long-striding boys from the prairie states. De Mérac, always moved by the sight of the men from far places marching on under the same colors, often reined in at crossroads to watch regiments from Massachusetts and Wisconsin, from Illinois and Maryland and Minnesota and Delaware and Vermont. Sometimes he looked almost in awe at formations of Virginia Unionists, drawn from the Tidewater counties, at lean, rangy Tennesseans, hard-bitten men from Kentucky, all flowing on under the flag of the Union.

He broke his journey at the camp of the Ist Massachusetts Cavalry and was welcomed by young Bostonians whom he had met in civilian days. There was champagne punch, and a buzz of voices that spoke of "Pa'k Street" and "Jordan Ma'sh," of the Porcellian Club, until de Mérac could fairly sniff the east wind blowing past the corner of Boylston and Tremont Streets. The faces were as Boston as the rolling green of the Common. His host was Charles Francis Adams, son of the Minister to the Court of St. James's; and Colonel Paul Revere, who had ridden over from the camp of the 20th Massachusetts Infantry, was there also.

Yet there was a change. There was a fine-drawn look to all of them, a weariness at the backs of their eyes, and an air of hard doggedness that had replaced the *élan* of 1861. There was more elasticity in some cases, a slackening of reserve and a marked sense of adaptability. De Mérac mentioned this to a clerical-faced youth who wore his hair in a ministerial bang.

The laugh was distinctly unclerical. "Ought to see us at home when we get leave. The pillars of King's Chapel shake. I came into the bosom of my adoring family, tripped over a rug and barked out, 'Christ Almighty!' Just like that. I was surprised as hell when they were shocked. And Billy Otis over there beyond Revere—his first morning at home he sang 'The Old Black Bull' in his bath—basso profundo."

Adams chuckled. "Damned if I don't love the army. At home I was a regular Old Betty. Worse than brother Henry, who's over in London with the Governor. Look at me now." He exhibited a ragged cuff, broken boots, and a rusty scabbard. "I'm developing a positive genius for being shiftless and I revel in it. When I was home I burned holes in the rugs, left my things all over the place, and once I came down to breakfast without shaving. Let's drink damnation to formality!"

De Mérac raised his glass. "I drink, Captain Adams, to the day when I see you crossing the Common in your shirtsleeves."

"The Common? In shirtsleeves?" Adams stared. "Oh, well—anyhow we've all changed and we'll change Boston when we get back."

"Profoundly, one may be sure," smiled de Mérac.

When he arrived in Washington the next day, he went at once to the War Department. His business, which dealt with ration returns and pay-roll technicalities, promised to be troublesome, but he looked up a major whom he had dined at the Rifles' mess in early '62 and in an hour's talk settled questions which might otherwise have meant endless correspondence.

Leaving the Department, he rode to the Russian Legation, where Labanieff greeted him effusively and launched into ringing praises of McClellan. "Ah, what a campaign! On this, and on the Peninsula, I write long treatises which I shall deliver at the Imperial Staff School when I return. I compare his moves with the advance of Seydlitz on Gotha in 1757, with Turenne's counter to Montecuculi in 1675, with Tilly at Stadt-Lohn in 1623. Here! Russian tea, Russian cigarettes. Ah—that march to South Mountain. Myself, I rode as observer with Joe Hooker."

"McClellan did move quickly for once in his life," de Mérac answered. "You know why? Because he found an order that Lee had lost and hence knew just what the Rebels were going to do. But how did it all end? In slaughter that leaves us just where we were a year ago."

Labanieff waved his hands. "But his plans! Perfection!"

De Mérac laughed wryly. "*Mon cher,* I agree that it all looks well in a pretty staff-school study, which seems to be all that interests you. When I am killed in a classically perfect and blundering campaign, please set down in your treatise that I fell in the best tradition of Jomini, Clausewitz, and George B. McClellan."

Labanieff pulled at his whiskers with an air of mystery. "That will not take place."

"*Merci.* And why not?"

The Russian sipped his glass of tea. "*Entre nous, eh?* the little McClellan will soon go."

De Mérac slapped his knee in quick joy. "*Bon!* And who will follow?"

"That I have not yet learned. Hancock? I think not. Hooker's Antietam wound still bothers. Not long ago, one heard rumors, eh? But he is gone, *le beau* Kearny. No, I give my tongue to the cats. But a change there will be. And for yourself—you are back with the genial Pelham? Now attend. I know nothing, hear nothing, see nothing in that quarter. But, being a Russian, I am mystic. Tread gently, *mon ami.*"

"The brigadier rarely speaks to me."

Labanieff frowned. "It might be better if he poured verbal acid on you. I am sure that he plans something about you. If there ever came acute unpleasantness, get word to me. I could, perhaps, give myself the pleasure of being of some small service."

De Mérac read concern in his host's prominent eyes. In matters that were not colored by dense, military pedantry, the Russian was often surprisingly right. He tried to shrug off a feeling of uneasiness. "Pelham is a good enough soldier not to interfere with a regimental commander who does his work acceptably."

"No doubt. No doubt," said Labanieff. Then, as though changing the subject, he observed, "The good Craig Wilson makes remarkable progress."

"Excellent," said de Mérac enthusiastically. "He could easily command a regiment, in my opinion."

"That opinion may be shared by others," remarked Labanieff.

Speculating on McClellan's possible successor, de Mérac gave Lisette her head as he started west on the return trip. Then his thoughts switched to his own brigadier. Labanieff's hints could not be dismissed lightly, and the feeling of uneasiness deepened. It was obvious, had been obvious from the start, that the Rifles could never win Pelham's approval. Grudging recognition of work well done only seemed to increase his cold hatred of his foreign-born unit. Yet, since the Rifles were an important part of his command, Pelham, as a soldier, would not injure them militarily, nor would he move against their commander, who was, in part at least, responsible for their competence. Logic gave no other answer. Of course, if the Rifles ever failed badly or he himself were guilty of glaring error, then Pelham, beyond any doubt, would hit viciously. He shrugged. He and the Rifles, so long as efficiency was maintained, had nothing to fear. Dudley Pelham simply could not afford to strike.

At the bridge over Rock Creek, he slowed down to give right of way to a smart carriage. It drew abreast of him and he bit his lip as he saw, reclining gracefully in the back seat, Lisa von Horstmar, her full, blond beauty set off by a russet cape. Beside her was young Conway of Pelham's staff. The sun was in her eyes and she did not recognize him. He found himself wishing vaguely that she had found a lover in another corps than his own and in another brigade than Pelham's.

The road wound on toward Georgetown where signal flags at the high station flapped endlessly against the afternoon sky. Then off to the right de Mérac saw the stone walls and the many windows of the hospital where he had found George. He told himself that the idea was idiotic and, in telling himself, headed Lisette toward the curving drive that led to the house.

He passed clumps of dusty shrubs, a stretch of open lawn. With a quick laugh he whirled Lisette off the drive, sent her flying over the grass, took a low hedge and reined in with a flourish just by the low terrace where George had lain with Mr. McArdle.

A slim girl in an immaculate gray coverall turned quickly, cried out partly in surprise, partly in pleasure. "Why, Captain de Mérac!" Gail Shortland's voice rang clear in his ears and she ran to the edge of the terrace.

He swept off his kepi. "I dared not hope for such luck! Riding past, I just thought—and the results of those thoughts you now behold!" He had never seen her look so pretty, he told himself. Gone were the scars of fatigue that followed her home from Bull Run and Centerville. Her gray eyes danced clear and alive and he noticed for the first time that the iris was ringed with black. Her cheeks had filled out, her skin glowed with health, and her teeth sparkled in a gay smile.

She said, "I'm so glad you thought, then. I was speaking of you to Aunt just yesterday. We'd seen in the papers that the Rifles weren't at Antietam and we were saying how nice it was that you were safe."

De Mérac bowed in the saddle. "I was kept safe in order that I might receive a very thoughtful note from you, who are so busy. I was glad, too, that you were out of Antietam, much as you wanted to go with Clara Barton. Ah, you looked so tired, there by Long Bridge! But today—"

She stood close by the edge of the terrace and the light wind molded the coverall about her. "Tired?" she said. "Nothing that a night's sleep wouldn't fix. And we've been awfully slack here. They're not sending us gunshot cases just now—only fever and that sort of thing. How well your horse looks! She simply flowed over that hedge. I wish Dad could see her. He loves horses."

"You have more leisure now?" De Mérac said quickly.

She nodded energetically, smiling, and de Mérac was reminded of a little girl excused from her catechism. "A lot more. Why, I'm free until tomorrow and I'm contrary enough to revel in it. I've been sitting here in the sun and—oh, just look at all that!" She waved a slim arm west toward the distant shaggy hills where gold and reddish leaves glowed to the touch of the sun, to the blue bar of the Potomac whose muddy waters reflected the deep October sky. "You know, I was here two months before I realized we could see the Potomac at all."

De Mérac flipped his kepi in the air, caught it deftly. "Now I assume command. You are free? *Épatant!* You shall change to street clothes while I find for you a carriage. Together we shall go to your aunt's, claim ration privilege, and bear her off to Ford's Theater. I neither know nor care what the play may be, but we three shall see it. My pass allows me time for that."

He saw joyful answer in her eyes. She clapped her hands. "What fun! Aunt will—" The answer died, though her voice was warm as ever. "Really, I can't, Captain. It *is* slack here now but there may be calls at any second. Don't you see?"

He swallowed disappointment. "I see that you are free. I see that you drive yourself too hard. I'll ride around and speak to the matron."

Distress creased her broad forehead. "No, no! Please. It—it really wouldn't do!"

"Just for the evening," urged de Mérac.

"I can't! Not possibly!"

"Listen then. We shall be idle up the river for a long time. That much is sure. I shall have leave again. I shall write you in advance and we shall make plans—"

She shook her head, eyes on the ground. "Don't. Please don't."

He said in a low tone, "Are you then trying to tell me that you do not wish to see me?"

Her hands flew out impulsively, were checked, knotted themselves at her breast. Her round cheeks flushed and her eyes were suddenly moist and soft. Her air, her expression, startled de Mérac, set his heart racing. Her voice was low and husky. "I *don't* mean that." She seemed to brace herself, to gather herself. In an instant she became once more friendly, serious, impersonal. "Really, I cut myself off from all that till the end of the war. I told you so at Aunt's. It's thoughtful of you, but—" A bell clanged somewhere in the hospital and she drew a deep breath as though in relief. "You see? I'll have to find out what's wanted."

"But you're free!" cried de Mérac.

She smiled down at him. "We're never free in war, are we? I've really got to go. Good-bye, Captain de Mérac." She waved and ran lightly away.

De Mérac stood in his stirrups. "But I shall write!"

Still running, she called over her shoulder, "I'll try and answer." A big door swung open and swallowed her up.

During the rest of his long ride back to Edwards's Ferry, de Mérac was uneasy and depressed. At nightfall he claimed hospitality of Hubert Dilger's Ohio battery.

The young Prussian, immaculate as always in white doeskin breeches, summoned friends from near-by batteries and companies while orderlies reverently chilled deep-throated steins. The lamplight in Dilger's tent fell on the faces of the guests—zu Putlitz, Schantz, Ingenohl, von Meyer, Reifschneider—Union officers singing lieder on the banks of the Potomac. Ordinarily it was a setting into which de Mérac would have thrown himself wholeheartedly, but his restlessness drove him within himself and he felt that he made poor return for Dilger's courtesy to him.

Even Birney's warm praise at the success of the Washington mission left him still moody. As he unbuckled his eagle-crested belt in his tent he thought irritably, *"Cette vache de guerre!* It makes children of grown men. I, past twenty-seven, mope like a boy in a lycée solely because I find Miss Shortland is too full of duty. I disgust myself."

XIII

The Rappahannock

PREMATURELY cold winds cut down the valley of the Potomac as though the grindstones of winter were whirring fast and early. The army lay and shivered. Jeb Stuart swept his hard-bitten gray cavalry in a vast horseshoe clear around McClellan, crossed back into Virginia laden with booty, unmolested. About a roaring fire outside the headquarters tent of the Rifles, Wilson held his fine hands to the blaze. "Damnation! Does Mac send invitations to Stuart to come and steal the doughnuts out of our pantry?"

Corvisart, coughing hollowly despite his caped overcoat, shrugged. "It was a pretty feat. But only a feat—a tour de force. It affects our war no more than does the French garrison that Bonaparte maintains in Vera Cruz."

Greenbaum said disgustedly, "All the same, it's the third time he's done it to Mac."

"Three strikes and out—for Mac," laughed George bitterly. "That's what Abner Doubleday said when he heard about it, they tell me."

Surgeon Wayne knocked the ashes from his pipe. "Can't help feeling there's some kind of jiggery-pokery going at our headquarters. Stuart went round us easy as rinsing a stomach. Guess I'll hang out a shingle and go into private practice here. Nothing else to do."

De Mérac strolled up wearing an elaborately frogged fur-lined pelisse. A long cigarette dangled from his lips. "Then I recommend to you only such patients as may be quickly cured, Wayne," he smiled.

Wilson raised his eyebrows. "Know something, John?"

"What we all know. That Uncle Abe has been to Harpers Ferry to see the Union Fabius. It was some time ago. That the two discussed nice points of theology I permit myself to doubt. Other indications have come to me." He held up an envelope addressed in Labanieff's characteristic script that combined oddly the Cyrillic and the European alphabets.

"Move?" asked Greenbaum.

"So I read it. Of course, I cannot be sure when or in what direction."

Corvisart's racking cough mingled with a hollow laugh. "If McClellan orders it, we may be sure of this. It will be too late and in the wrong direction."

"The wrong one for me," muttered Greenbaum. "Guess I better write Rachel not to look for me right away."

De Mérac nodded. "There can, of course, be no leaves." His eyes met George's, then Wilson's.

George kicked at an ember. "Oh well—damn it, we'll be *doing* something anyway."

The weather turned suddenly warm as October entered its third week. Craig Wilson sat his horse in an almost summery sunset and watched the first four companies of the Rifles cross the Potomac by the ford above Edward's Ferry. The ranks, still under strength despite an unexpected influx of recruits, flowed down the sloping north bank to fray out at the water's edge. The men hurriedly stripped off boots, socks, and breeches and, in some cases, their long drawers. Then they reformed rapidly in column of twos and plunged into the swift water that rose to mid-thigh. It was an odd sight, Wilson thought, the white legs in startling contrast to the dark blue of the jackets. There was something almost machinelike about the whole scene—a writhing knot of blue on the low bluffs of the south bank where men struggled to dress themselves, a connecting link of blue and white figures moving through the water, and another knot on the north bank where others made ready for the ford. In a grove across the river he could see de Mérac on Lisette, with Greenbaum, Dekdebrun, and Castex close by him.

A jingle, bump, and clank behind him brought on two guns of a battery of Ohio horse artillery, the drivers gathering their teams for the descent to the water while the cannoneers sent their single mounts squattering on through the ford in the wake of the red guidon with its crossed gold cannon. Then came the last five companies of the Rifles, headed by Chanel's men. Once they crossed, Wilson would follow.

Light wheels rattled, hoofs plopped, and Wilson squinted toward the bright western sky. A barouche pulled up under gnarled tulip trees, two or three riders reining in beside it. Wilson muttered, "Hell and death! What's *he* up to?" Resignedly he trotted his mount toward the trees where Dudley Pelham, with Major Dunn and two aides, sat his horse rigidly. In the barouche, bland and unruffled, Honest John Cusler smoked a thick cigar.

Wilson drew up before Pelham and saluted. Pelham's eyes barely moved toward him. "Had I required your presence, I should have sent for you," said the brigadier, his thin lips snapping down on the last word.

Wilson saluted in silence and turned his mount. Cusler leaned forward in the carriage and called pleasantly, "So you're still a major, Wilson? Pity. Your old legal enemy, Brackett, 's a full colonel. Got him a post where he can live at home, too."

Wilson said politely, "I hope he is duly grateful to you, Cusler."

Cusler waved blandly. "We have ways of seeing that he does not forget. Good luck, Wilson."

As the major rode back toward the column he heard Pelham's hard voice. "Damned idiocy, sending those foreigners into Virginia. I assure you, Mr. Cusler, we'd have 75 per cent desertions if Lee was able to feed 'em. That's what comes of giving a man like Birney a division. His family's supposed to be abolition, but they're out of a slave state and he never heard of West Point until he saw it on a map."

Wilson lit a cigar as he saw the last caisson of the half-battery tug up the opposite bank while the rest of the Rifles prepared for the ford. He thought, "Got to say this for Pelham. He's always consistent." He chuckled as he drew in the first cloud of smoke. The blast against Birney, he was sure, lay in the fact that Baron de Trobriand was to be given acting command of the brigade of the invalid Berry, a brigade of seven regiments and a full battery, while Pelham, the West Pointer, could only boast of three regiments.

The last of Bolton's company, its rear shepherded by Rohde, had reached the other side. Wilson let his mount pick its way over the stones of the ford and joined de Mérac and Corvisart under the trees. On a lanelike road that stretched south over treeless, undulating land the rest of the column was drawn up, waiting for the last companies. The half-battery stood behind Shea's men, the cannoneers' sabers clanking in the thickening dusk as they tested prolonges, tugged at girths, and fussed with the buckles of the traces.

"All in order, Craig?" asked de Mérac.

Wilson flipped away his cigar butt. "In order. You'll be glad to know that we start off on our expedition with the blessings of one Dudley Pelham. He and Honest John Cusler were watching the last of the column."

De Mérac smiled. "My last worries vanish. There. Bolton falls in. You're clear about everything, Craig? Good. Then, *en avant!*"

Wilson paced his mount by the rear of the column where he would be in position to check any straggling, and the Rifles and their supporting guns trailed away over a countryside that was swiftly veiling itself in a lavender-tinted mist. He was clear enough about the plan, as he had assured de Mérac. Spies had reported that Southern forces of unknown strength and composition had been moving toward the Potomac. To test these rumors the Rifles were marching into Virginia. Somewhere ahead of them two squadrons of Illinois cavalry were sweeping the countryside and the Rifles were to make contact with them at a pin point on the map, a desolate crossroads spot known as Pingree's Store. That much was simple.

What troubled Wilson was the composition of the reconnaissance. If the Confederates were in force, it was too small, far too small; if they were merely feeling out with weak patrols, then it seemed to him that the Illinois troopers could accomplish their mission alone. He felt uneasy about the whole matter. In this sort of No Man's Land the Rifles could be readily snapped up if the Illinois cavalry failed in its role. He had not written Claire before starting out, knowing that between his scrawled lines she would read his anxiety. Would they ever sit on the porch of the old stone house in the Berkshires and watch a summer sunset fade over the hill-tossed stretches that led to the Hudson? He shook himself impatiently. That house and that life belonged to Craig Wilson, member of the New York Bar Association, not to Major Craig Wilson, New York Volunteers.

Near midnight, long chants of "Ha-a-a-lt!" echoed down the column. The men fell out at the right of the road and Wilson trotted on toward a shielded light. He found de Mérac dismounted in front of a gutted wooden building that stood where a half-seen east-west road cut their line of march. Wilson swung to the ground. "Sure this is the place, John?"

De Mérac's cigarette glowed in the dark. "The metropolis of Pingree's Store. Here we wait. You may let your men lie down, but they must lie in formation. Where is that gunner officer?" A vague shape loomed up with a clank of saber and click of spurs. "Mr. Morrison, it will be safe, I think, to loosen girths and slip out bits. Your men should stand to head, however. You will find a little brook behind the store. You must water by bucket."

"Don't want me to unlimber? I can feel high ground off to the right."

"Not yet. We wait on Illinois."

Morrison clumped off toward his teams. "Now, John?" asked Wilson.

"We now take up the true occupation of the soldier. We wait."

Wilson scuffed about the rickety porch of the store. Both armies had passed that way since the last sale had been made over the scarred counter inside. He picked up a rotted belt with a buckle marked "C.S.A." and kicked aside a Union holster. Scraps of paper littered porch and floor. He gathered a handful and took them to the shielded lantern. Accounts, bills, receipts, hastily scrawled notes. "Please deliver to the slave Nicodemus ten sacks of flour and oblige..." "Have duly credited yr. acct. with five cartloads of cabbages, which..." "Kindly give my maid, Eula, three bottles of the remedy for Miss Patty Lou's complaint." Soiled, trampled records of the life of a peaceful, easygoing countryside. Wilson's orderly lawyer's mind revolted at this man-made waste. "Who ever took the *mule* as the symbol of stupidity?" he thought bitterly.

The night was very still. He could hear the horses of the gun teams snuffling and shifting, could catch the clink of a trace chain. Off in the fields to the south, Corvisart coughed rackingly as he inspected the patrols that de Mérac had thrown out. A night bird called, repeating two rusty notes over and over.

The night bird was suddenly still. It seemed to Wilson that the whole dark world was all at once listening in intent suspicion. He strained his ears, could hear only the throbbing of his own pulses. Then he caught the sound. Far to the south hoofs churned on the soft road, their br-r-*rup*, b-r-*rup*, b-r-*rup* coming closer and closer. The darkness stirred and a voice distant and brittle snapped, "*Qui vive?*" The hoofs slapped to a halt and Wilson ran down the steps into the road where two of Bordagaray's men were leading a blowing horse. Its rider walked by its head calling, "Where's the commanding officer? I want to see the commanding officer."

De Mérac materialized out of the dark. "What outfit?" and Wilson smiled to himself as the slang word rolled easily from the Frenchman's lips.

"Lieutenant Grayle. Captain Ransford's command."

"Bon!" The word boomed explosively. "Greenbaum! All company commanders and Mr. Morrison here at once. Commands by word of mouth only. No bugles. Ready, Craig? Where is Corvisart? Oh, there you are, Xavier. You company commanders. Come close. Now, Mr. Grayle?"

The young Illinoisan spoke tersely. "Rebs. Maybe four squadrons. No infantry. No guns that we could make out. We tangled with 'em. Captain Ransford's bringing 'em on here."

"Such a meeting—it will charm us," said Corvisart dryly.

"What he thought," said Grayle with equal dryness. "Tell me what you're going to do and I'll get back to Ransford."

"Our plans are simple," said de Mérac. "Now attend."

South of the wrecked store the land rolled on in low waves that finally died away in a level plain. The men of the Rifles, moving on through the dark fields, could feel the undulations beneath their feet. Veterans like Rapp and Cahusac and Bates could deduce the lower plain by the wind that sifted across their faces, could know that the crests of the troughlike hollows right and left of the road that were swallowing up the companies dominated the southern stretches while masking what lay in them. At last the scuff of boots, the clink of traces, the slap of hoofs, died away. The Rifles and the two Napoleon guns lay hidden and waiting.

By the off-wheel of the right piece, Raoul Marot lay, cradling his Springfield in his arms. Like him, the rest of his company huddled close to the ground, guarding the two pieces. Five yards behind him he knew that his terrible captain, LeNoir, crouched, watching for the first false move that a *bleu* like himself might make. Marot had joined the company as a recruit at Edwards's Ferry, and now for the first time he took the field. He rolled the phrase on his tongue and it pleased him vaguely. "Took the field."

He tilted his kepi onto the back of his head to give his

eyes the maximum light. He thought that day was coming on slowly, for he could see, off to the left, a whitish streak that must be the road. It was not far away—say as far away as were the ends of the Palais des Papes in Avignon, one from the other. Ah! Life was not so bad! One had a cloak of rubber as fine as those of *méssieurs les officers, quoi!* And the good cloth of the uniform and the socks of veritable wool! Aegide, the little brother, must be brought to this new country, for was he not past seventeen? Aegide, too, could wear a cape of rubber and a uniform fit for the Gardes Impériales. And each month thirteen American dollars! He hugged his musket closer. Ah, the fierce Captain LeNoir should see how a man of Avignon who had nineteen years could fight!

At the right of the line Sergeant Major Rapp ruffled his red beard. So they were coming, *les Arabes, hein?* That was nothing to disturb an old *sous-off* whose papers were always in order and who had been spoken to *en camarade* by the *vieux kébir*, Kearny. Ah, had the *kébir* but lived. Still, it was all part of a soldier's life. As to *les Arabes*, one had met them before, one would meet them again, and that was the whole of the matter. Five hundred dollars. That was nearly twenty-five hundred francs and should suffice Clémence until the end of the year when the creditors should settle. And she had thought to order, in plenty of time, the fine nougat of Montélimar which the good mothers of Fifth Avenue bought for their *mômes* at Christmas. *Ça marche. Ça marche.*

It certainly was growing lighter, though not light enough yet to be dangerous, de Mérac decided, as he stood on the crest with the gunner Morrison. Bushes began to detach themselves from pools of blackness. Trees stood out, vague but definable, and the road actually seemed to lead somewhere instead of melting into the night a few yards away. Off to his right he could make out the figure of Corvisart, matching that of Wilson on the extreme left. The rest of the regiment, the two guns, were masked in the rolling ground and the limbers were well hidden fifty yards in the rear. The whole line of battle was invisible from where he stood but he knew that it curved in an arc, spread thin as he dared, and that the Napoleons were so sited that they would fire diagonally across the wide, saucerlike depression that lay between his crest and the lower one to the south.

"Don't like this for a damn," said Morrison, sweeping his field glasses toward the silvery shimmer that was creeping over the fields. "Something gone wrong with Ransford? Jesus, we're left out here without any cover if he's stubbed his toe."

De Mérac shook his head impatiently. He was beginning to experience that sweaty queasiness that for six months past had seized him before possible action. It was the same feeling that he remembered from childhood when he had eaten too many bonbons.

He crouched suddenly. Off to the south carbines cracked flatly and distant hoofs rustled. Night melted rapidly and he saw the low hills that Grayle had described the night before. His queasiness vanished as he raised his glasses. He could make out flicks of light at the foot of the hills, flicks that might be carbine flashes or even the wink of metal. He blew a whistle, held up both arms, and threw himself flat on the ground.

Down the road a solid column of blue troopers rode at a sharp trot. Through his glasses de Mérac could see men on the flank and in the rear turn in their saddles to shoot. Automatically he estimated eight troops—Ransford's two squadrons. By his elbow, Morrison's breath went in sharply. "There's the bastards!" he hissed.

A quarter mile in the rear of the last troop poured the gray cavalry at the same sharp gait and firing from the saddle as they came. The gap seemed to close slowly. Then a bugle sang, faint and eerie, among the bluecoats, a single rider swept to the front, stabbing upward with his hand. The eight troops broke into a sharp gallop. "Done it!" The words seemed jolted from Morrison.

De Mérac slipped down the bank, vaulted into Lisette's saddle. In the half-light the sheltering hollow teemed with sudden life. Men were getting to their knees, patting their pouches, nervously tugging at their vizors. The gunners hooked long prolonges onto their pieces and stood braced against the bank, waiting.

De Mérac edged Lisette cautiously up the slope until his head just cleared the crest. Ransford's troopers were pelting faster and faster. In their wake the Rebel yell keened up as the gray horsemen spurred their mounts. The Union squadrons were a hundred yards away, fifty—then they split at full gallop, two squadrons circling to the right and two to the left, hidden from the road by the rolling ground.

De Mérac, gnawing his lip, nodded to Castex. The bugler blared out his notes. As one man the Rifles swarmed up the crest, formed in two ranks, the forward one kneeling, the rear standing. Morrison's red-piped gunners tugged and strained at the prolonges. The Napoleons rocked up the slope, their trails smacked to the ground, and the Number Ones jerked the lanyards.

De Mérac jumped Lisette full onto the crest behind the pieces. Through the smoke he saw pitching gray wreckage. A riderless horse bulleted madly toward him, vanished in the rear. The gunners calmly swung their swabs and rammers, reloaded. Morrison called steadily, "First piece—*fire!*" Then his voice was drowned by the slam of the gun and by the steady blasts of musketry that blazed along the curving front of the Rifles. Something stabbed at de Mérac's ear and he saw Dekdebrun lowering his muzzle, a cold tight smile on his lips.

A high voice yelled, "Here they come!" and gray troopers in a long, yelling line swept on toward the guns. Heads of frantic horses looked through the smoke. Wide-brimmed hats sailed madly through the air. When the smoke cleared, the line of the Rifles stood firm. Out of musket-shot the gray squadrons wheeled, re-formed, heedless of the figures along the slope who writhed or lay still, heedless of the lunging horses.

They came on again, working cleverly to avoid the Napoleons, trying to strike the left flank of the line and roll it up. George Force watched the sea of tossing manes, the dull glitter of raised sabers, watched a tall bearded man who rode in the van handling a superb bay with amazing skill. He felt frozen with rank terror. Never before had he faced cavalry thundering down on him. He croaked, "Steady!" and dropped to one knee.

Out of the corner of his eye he could see the tattered colors bright through the smoke where the center companies guarded them.

Then the charge was on him, striking full along the left wing. The Colt spat and spat. He saw a blade high above his head, a blade that seemed to melt from his consciousness. First Sergeant Bates knelt close by him, bayonet slanting upwards and the butt of his musket braced against the ground. A single rider smashed through the center of the company, was shot down.

George rose shakily. In a whirling cloud of smoke and dust the gray cavalry was milling out of range again. At George's feet, almost touching the body of one of the Rifles' dead, lay the bearded officer who had ridden the big bay so magnificently. His bloody hand still clutched a broken saber. Bates panted, "Looky. Goin' to try the other flank." A white-faced private panted over and over, "Who'n hell said a horse wouldn't go against a bay'net? Who'n hell said a horse wouldn't go against a bay'net!"

Wilson trotted his mare along the rear of his companies. "Good work, boys. Good work. It's not over yet." He hoped his voice was firm. The onrushing torrent of horseflesh had shaken him as it had George. He wondered if he could hold himself steady in the face of another charge. Still, it must be nearly time—he stood in his stirrups and stared at the distant gray cavalry.

Sergeant Major Rapp watched Bordagaray with deep approval as the Basque steadied his men against the coming charge. He himself judged that the attack might be formidable, but what would you? In the first rush a pistol bullet had clipped his sleeve and another had drilled through his haversack. But so far it had not been warm enough to make him miss a puff at his pipe. This might be different.

De Mérac saw the gray cavalry form, saw them start off toward the right where Corvisart commanded, cleverly making use of cover to shield themselves from the fire of the Napoleons. He nodded to Morrison. "That is good. They start in column. Soon they will swing into line—if permitted." He jerked erect in the saddle. From the right and left, out of hidden ground, poured Ransford's troopers, a solid blue battering-ram that struck the Southern column fairly in the flanks, shattered its formation, tore its separate troops into gray shreds. The blind impact swung the direction of the charge inward, brought it within reach of Morrison's guns that slammed out instantly.

That was the end. Through smoke and dust de Mérac could see the remnants of the four gray squadrons withdrawing sullenly south, leaving a field littered with shattered horses and torn men. Ransford's troopers, too few to follow, re-formed and jogged slowly toward the rise where the Rifles lay. Closely guarded, some twenty gray prisoners limped dejectedly. A Union officer with sunburn deep on his bony face left the column and trotted up to de Mérac. "Told you it'd work!" he panted.

"You are Captain Ransford? Yes, it worked. But they had no business charging unshaken infantry supported by two guns, even once they had no business. It was madness."

Ransford grinned. "'Course it was. But when I found out Stuart Davis was in command of those Rebs I could tell what'd happen. I was with him at the Point. He's a hotheaded devil and I knew he'd keep snapping at you till I could get around the two flanks. Well, we can tell Birney that the Rebs aren't in force in this part of the world. But you better get moving. Davis may be going back to get a bigger gang and come at us again. There's enough around here for him to do that, and it'd be just like the damn fool. I'll cover your flank and rear." Ransford raised his hand and rode off.

The prisoners were halted close by the road and the men of the Rifles stared curiously at them and at their panting guards. Morrison clumped up to de Mérac. "All right to give the boys 'Limber rear'? About time they—" He stopped, stared at a tall, middle-aged officer in stained gray with major's insignia on his collar. "Well, for God's sake, Uncle Harry!"

The major stiffened. Then a smile crinkled his eyes. "Damned if it isn't Arnold's boy, Ed! How's Arnold anyway these days?"

"Fine. Rheumatics are bothering him a little, though."

"Well, he's the age for it. Say, I see they caught your cousin Art. He's over there, filling his canteen."

"Art? Where? By God, I'll go see him."

"I wouldn't, Ed. Art took it mighty hard that you went against the Old North State. Says your father moving to Ohio don't make any difference. No—I'd kind of steer clear of Art."

The regiment was re-forming for its march back to the Ferry and the ford. Wilson heard reports from his company commanders and was relieved to know that his loss was only five killed and six wounded, none of the latter seriously. He said to LeNoir, "Take charge. I've got to meet Lieutenant Grayle, who's going to cover this flank. Captain de Mérac knows."

He rode away toward the woody stretch where it had been arranged that he meet the cavalryman. The woods were seamed and scored with paths that twisted deceptively. Far to the right through the trees he saw blue move and headed his mount in that direction. Twice he had to leave the path and work on through undergrowth to keep on the proper course. A horse neighed close by. Wilson called, "Is that you, Mr. Grayle?"

Bushes crashed and a tense voice snapped, "Got one of them, anyway."

Wilson snatched at his holster. Then his hand dropped as he saw a good-looking young Rebel officer covering him with a heavy Colt. Behind him half a dozen troopers fingered their carbines. Too stunned for thought, Wilson raised his hands. The officer rode quickly to him, took his revolver and saber. "Sorry, Major. We want to be gentle with you but if you kick up a racket we just won't be able to be. Take his bridle, Anderson. Hurry him along that path. Ridge, you keep him covered. Trot, now. Too damn many Yanks around here. At least we'll have him to show as an excuse for our getting lost. Don't bother to keep your arms up, Major. Just ride easy as you can." The horses trotted away at a quick, clean gait. Wilson, still stunned, was conscious of only one thought—"Claire. How can I get word to Claire?"

The Rifles began their march back to the river, Morrison's guns clanking once more in the center of the column. Ahead and on either flank, blue troopers scoured the country. De Mérac rode slowly, chin on his chest, as he mentally composed his report of the affair for Birney. He looked up annoyed as Rohde's irritating voice hissed up to him. "Sir! Oh, sir. They're giving *trouble*. The *contrabands*."

"Contrabands?" said de Mérac frowning.

"The *niggers* that came *in* after the *cavalry*. They're getting *stubborn*."

De Mérac turned Lisette wearily and rode to the rear. In view of the expected Emancipation Proclamation and its political repercussions, escaped slaves had to be handled with the greatest care. Beyond Bolton's company he found a dozen Negroes, men and women, trudging along with bundles slung on sticks. They grinned up at him. "Hya', *hah!* Cunnel, we's Freedombóun' at last."

"I see no trouble here, Rohde," said de Mérac impatiently.

"It's *this* man, *here*." Rohde pointed to an intelligent-looking middle-aged Negro. "He won't come *along*. I've had to *make him!*"

The Negro stepped out of the line and looked up at de Mérac. He had a fine, determined face and carried himself well. De Mérac said, "Have you any complaints?"

The Negro threw back his head. "I don' b'long here, suh. This officer, he keeps pokin' that li'l gun in my ribs. I don' b'long here."

De Mérac was puzzled. "Not belong here? You do not want to come with us?"

The black head shook vigorously. "No, *suh*. I jes' standin' by the road watchin' and soon's I c'd wink, li'l gun come in my ribs and officer say, 'You contraband. Git in line.' I ain't contraband. Belong to the Carter place three-fo' mile yonder. Always treated good. Got my own smithy. Got my own house. *My* house. Got a credit to the sto'. Got my woman waitin' fo' me 'long of my two boys. Me, I want home."

316

De Mérac nodded to him. "Go home, then. No one will disturb you. Let him alone, Rohde," he added as the latter snatched at the Negro's arm. The Negro stepped clear, made a quick little bow to de Mérac, and ran, loose-jointed, across the fields.

Rohde sputtered, "But it's against the *law*, sir. Slaves are *contraband* of *war*."

"The intent of the law was not to break up a Negro family and take its head from the place where they live, contented."

He left Rohde and took his place toward the head of the column. The report—it would be easy. Even including the successful ambush and the bag of prisoners, there was little to mark it out from any other small-scale patrol. In a week's time it would probably be buried deep in his mind and forgotten.

When de Mérac reported to David Birney at the pleasant stone house overlooking the brown drift of the Potomac, he found the air acrid with burning papers, saw orderlies packing feverishly and grooms busily cleaning harness out by the stables. In the division office Birney was abstracted but gravely courteous as ever. "Sorry your patrol was useless, de Mérac. If I'd even had a hint we were going to move I shouldn't have sent you. Yes, the whole army's starting south. You've written your report? Leave it with me. I'd like to look at it if I ever get time."

De Mérac laid his papers on a bare table. "And because headquarters delayed to let you know, I lose Craig Wilson," he said with slow bitterness. "The details I cannot learn. I only know that he did not return with us."

Birney's level eyebrows jumped. "You haven't heard? Then I'm damn glad you brought the papers in person. We had a flag of truce up by Point of Rocks. Wilson's unwounded and a prisoner. I've had Brevoort write Washington to arrange his exchange. It shouldn't take too long. You're ready to move, aren't you?"

"When you say," cried de Mérac, his eyes dancing. Wilson unwounded and a prisoner! The major might return in a matter of weeks.

"Good! I'm sending out data on the routes to all brigades and the timetables'll follow." He nodded pleasantly and de Mérac left the room. In the hall he met Henry Brevoort, who halted him. "Look here, de Mérac. This is none of my business, but that report you brought Big Dave—you sent a copy to Pelham, I hope."

De Mérac smiled. "No—the original to Pelham, who commands my brigade. A copy for General Birney."

Brevoort blew out his cheeks. "Wise boy! Damn that Pelham! He was so nasty to de Trobriand the other day—you know his style, remarks about fake titles and foreign mercenaries—well, if I'd been old Régis, I'd have called him out."

De Mérac shrugged. "We Bretons are said to be like peat. We take fire slowly but when we burst out we shrivel the hoofs of the devil himself. The war will not last long enough for Pelham to ignite de Trobriand."

Brevoort pulled at his mustache. "He's giving himself a lot of rope, is Pelham. You know, I suppose, that you were to go up to colonel and Wilson to lieutenant colonel and Corvisart to major, and so on? Well, the papers went through all right but they were killed in Washington. I'll tell you another thing—" he dropped his voice—"Big Dave shifted you to Robinson's brigade to get you away from little Dudley, and Stoneman, who's taken the corps over from Heintzelman, said O.K. Then a word came from Washington not to disturb the organization and Stoneman didn't think it important enough to fight interference with his command. You better develop eyes like a horsefly, de Mérac. I'll pass on anything that I can."

"Thank you. I shall appreciate that."

"Don't forget that Pelham was furious when poor old Phil took your regiment that's largely foreign and made a sort of *corps d'élite* out of it. Another thing. You know Dunn of Pelham's, of course. You can trust him. *Au 'voir.*"

"*Au 'voir,*" said de Mérac, catching up his scabbard and swinging out of the door. He pushed aside the thought of Pelham—who was troublesome, but whom he did not hold dangerous so long as the Rifles and their *de facto* commander were suitable militarily—and rubbed his hands at the news of Wilson. He would write a reassuring letter to Claire, who knew him, de Mérac, well enough to realize that nothing was glossed over. A good little soldier, Claire.

In a blue wave the Army of the Potomac swept over the brown river by ford and by ferry, moving from Harpers Ferry in the west clear down to the barrier forts that ringed Washington. Infantry, cavalry, artillery, engineers, signal corps, it numbered over one hundred and fifteen thousand men. With it marched telegraphers—semi-civilian, semi-military—correspondents, sutlers. On the hardening roads men stared at mysterious, hooded carts marked with the name of Matt Brady, the photographer. They cheered the light wagon where Clara Barton rode, prim, tight-lipped, always terrified and always indomitable. And, because they were moving once more, they cheered stumpy, broad-shouldered George McClellan as he rode past followed by a swarm of aides, like Napoleon at the head of the Marshals of France.

A drop in the great blue tide, the Rifles slogged south and west in the van of Birney's division. They crossed Goose Creek at Oatlands and struck deeper into Virginia. Past Aldie and Middleburg they went with the rolling mass of the Bull Run Mountains looming in the east. Then their frosty camps were pitched in the trough that slanted on still south and east until it was blocked by the wooded reaches of the Watery Mountains and the Pig Nut Mountains.

The weather turned cold and colder as though a ghostly hand had stolen a leaf from the calendar. De Mérac hooked his fur-trimmed pelisse tighter as he rode at the head of the column. Looking back he could find no fault with his companies. A year ago, they would have disgusted him, for dress was no longer uniform, the men had their precious coffeepots and their skillets slung to the muskets, and nearly all had adopted the old French custom of carrying their bread ration skewered to their bayonets. But their stride was veteran, they did not straggle, and, at the briefest camp, they dug their latrines and burned their trash without orders.

At Salem they swung west and in the rugged shadow of Big Cobbler were joined by Labanieff, who clattered down the column shouting joyously at having overtaken them. De Mérac laughed aloud at the sight of the whiskered, stocky Russian. He had discarded his wide-brimmed hat for the plumed steeple-crowned hat of the old Regular Army, its acorns and gunner's badge facing the rear. From some Union officer who had served on the plains he had secured a buffalo coat and a gigantic pair of fringed gauntlets which showed oddly above the raspberry breeches and gold-tasseled boots of the Tambov Hussars. He shouted in glee, "Behold me, the veritable Yankee, Jean!" He waved gaily to Corvisart and Shea who rode with de Mérac. "Corvisart, that cough! You must wrap a raw bearskin, flesh side in, about your chest. Ah, we in Russia understand such things. Captain Dan-Shea"—Labanieff was always uncertain about non-Continental names—"I am very damn-glad to see you safe. See, Jean, I bring my own supplies. You three will mess with me!" He pointed down the column where a light *fourgon* bumped along, a grinning Negro and a tight-buttoned Russian orderly sharing the seat and chattering in happy disregard of their bilingual barrier.

De Mérac handed his cigarette case to Labanieff. "Excellent, *mon ami*. We shall breakfast on vodka and caviare then?"

Labanieff protested as he lit up. "No, no, no, Jean. I have the American whiskey and scrapple from Philadelphia and salt fish to make Boston fish balls. I have canned pigeon from the Maryland and Virginia hams. Ah! That Easton-Summers, my British colleague. No American food will he eat. He says it would 'encourage the bloody natives.' But I! When I pour maple syrup from the Vermont on my scrapple, I pity him! Jean, I fear that I was wrong when I wrote you from Washington."

"In the matter of McClellan?"

"*Précisément!* Now he unfolds his grandest plan which

I come to study in your company. This he must have disclosed to the President."

"Devil a word to us," said Shea, rubbing his long nose. "I might be marching from Ballybunion to Listowel for all I know."

Labanieff wagged his head wisely. "Ah, but I have sources." The three edged their horses closer, knowing that the Russian still maintained the reputation of being the best informed man in Washington. Labanieff waved his cigarette. "Now, McClellan could have moved down the Shenandoah and struck Jackson, whom he would outnumber, you conceive. Ah, but instead he slides east of the Blue Ridge, leaving Mansfield's XIIth Corps to hold at Harpers Ferry while he himself, with the rest of the army, moves on toward Warrenton. Thus he places himself *between* Lee, who is at Culpepper, and the good Jackson who is still several days' march from Thornton's Gap. Thus he may fall first on Lee and then turn on Jackson. In a large way, it somewhat resembles the action at Janikau in 1645 with which I am sure you are familiar."

"*Bien sûr! Bien sûr!*" said de Mérac hastily.

"And supply! His roads to the Potomac are open! More, he has Acquia Creek—"

"Acquia Creek!" croaked Corvisart. "But that finds itself at the mouth of the Rappahannock."

Labanieff puffed out his cheeks. "As you shall soon find yourselves on its banks. Gentlemen, I commend to you the study of the great bend of Skinker's Neck. Even more do I commend consideration of the pretty town of Fredericksburg, higher on its banks."

Shea clucked to himself. "You mean we'll be crossing of a river with those devils of gray boys on the other side? 'Tis a Donnybrook Fair in hell ye'll be looking at, Colonel."

Labanieff threw out his arms. "You miss the genius, friend Dan-Shea. Lee cannot dare to move until it is too late, for McClellan may hop like a flea on a skillet, and should Lee commit himself too soon in *any* direction— ah, then the Southrons will run like Austrians!"

De Mérac rode along in silence. He was sure that

McClellan's plans would be sound. But the execution? If the campaign along the Rappahannock depended on speed—he shivered.

The column of which the Rifles formed a small part was winding on toward the valley of Thumb Creek. On either side hills rose, sharp on the right, gentle and rolling on the left. Tags of bright leaves still clung to the branches here and there but the early gales had stripped most of the trees and the bare branches far ahead were a gray-brown mist, thickening and deepening. It seemed to de Mérac that the Army of the Potomac was marching into a land of cold shadows, ghostly and menacing.

A blinding snowstorm, terrifying in its intensity and untimeliness, for it was only the second week in November, swept over northern Virginia and engulfed the camp of the Rifles near Waterloo, high up the Rappahannock. Old Rapp muttered that Waterloo was a name of ill-omen for any Frenchman and set details cobbling rude shovels out of the boards from an abandoned sawmill. Movement was impossible the next day and de Mérac, after seeing to the comfort of his men, sat drinking hot whiskey with Birney in the tidy little farmhouse that sheltered division headquarters. De Mérac had come to feel respect and real affection for the serious, bearded man, so slow-spoken and thoughtful. True, he did not have the military flair of Kearny but there was no questioning his utter competence and sincerity. Whether he spoke of American politics, of American history, or of the affairs of the division he was always worth listening to. From the white-piled outer world the handsome iron-gray de Trobriand stepped, snow glittering on his trim imperial. With him was Labanieff, who had attached himself to Birney as observer. At the Russian's opening query, Birney shook his head, smiling. "This snow changes everything, Colonel. I'm just waiting for orders from Stoneman."

He looked up as Major Brevoort slammed through the door, eyes wide with suppressed excitement.

Breevort whipped a paper from his overcoat pocket. "Seen this, sir?" He handed it to Birney.

Birney stared at the sheet, and his lower lip crept upward. "Well, I'm damned. I'm—I'm—" He passed it to Labanieff. De Mérac and de Trobriand leaned forward eagerly. The Russian flushed and glanced at Brevoort. "It is official, this?"

"The paper is not. The news is. A friend of mine from Stoneman's sent it on to me."

"Read it aloud," said Birney quietly.

Labanieff tilted the paper toward the light and read slowly. "'Just a tip for you'—ah—of course—as in racing—'a tip for you. Mac is out and out for good.'" He rubbed his forehead. "But it cannot be. In the middle of a campaign, my friend, one does not change."

"Read the rest of it," said Brevoort, rocking back and forth on his heels.

Labanieff cleared his throat. "It says, 'Now grab the sides of the cart and hear the next verse. He is succeeded by Ambrose Burnside.'" He dropped the paper and stared, open-mouthed, at Brevoort.

De Mérac hurled a half-smoked cigarette into the fire and de Trobriand growled, "*Mais enfin!*"

Birney sighed. "Well, gentlemen, there you have it. We'll get confirmation from Stoneman of course. For the moment, I'll be glad if the news is kept between these walls."

De Mérac hastily lit another cigarette and scowled at his broken fingernails. De Trobriand muttered, "But Burnside! A charming man whom I have met. A gentleman. A commander of division, yes—of a resoluteness unshakable. To command the whole army, *tout entier?* No. No!"

Labanieff shook his head. "Burnside? He was offered command after Kearny died. Again, after Antietam was it offered him—"

De Mérac, still frowning, thought of the self-distrustful Burnside and the crossings of the Rappahannock over which he might have to take the Rifles. At least, there would be rest now. The Army of the Potomac would go into winter quarters, for Burnside would never mount a campaign of his own in the brief fighting weather that remained.

The Rifles went into camp on the high ground between Fall Run and the Richmond, Fredericksburg, and Potomac Railroad. The little town of Falmouth lay about a mile away on the banks of the Rappahannock and, diagonally across the river from it, the brick houses, the wood houses, of Fredericksburg sat tight and compact on the west bank. Downstream, on the east side, bluffs, some of them open and others crowned with clean, well-tended woods, sloped down to meet the cold waters that slipped on to the Potomac. Here and there fine brick houses stood proudly, the Lacy house, the Phillips house, the Lee house, high-perched seats that reminded George Force of the manors of the Hudson.

All along the east bank hung an air of uneasy expectancy. Puzzled, like so many other commanders of lower units, as to what he might expect, de Mérac took counsel with himself. He remembered how old Colonel Blondlat, a frequent visitor at Loudéac, had once said that when a unit, however small, halted for more than a few hours, it ought to settle itself as though it were to be there for eternity. This and his increasing conviction that the year 1862 would see no more action guided his course. To Rapp he said, "The men must be helped to build their little *gourbis*. If truly we go into winter quarters, no doubt we shall have lumber by the railway from Acquia Creek." Soon the camp sprouted ingenious huts of branches, scrap boards, flattened tin cans, and tarred canvas.

One afternoon de Mérac road along the bluffs past the Lacy house with Labanieff, Corvisart, and Shea. The Russian sighed. "Never—never will a battle be fought here. It is too perfect for the student. One man, on either bank, would be able to see the utmost flick of the ear of the most distant enemy horse. No. Instead, they will fight in swamps and thickets where one must guess, one must speculate. See, my dear Dan-Shea." And he waved his arm at the west bank.

The flat plain where the spires of Fredericksburg rose reached far right and left of the town, an infinity of meadows cut by little runs. A mile or more from the river rose high bluffs that matched those from which de

Mérac leveled his glasses. The two banks formed a great amphitheater cut through by the broad Rappahannock. As the Russian had said, it formed an observer's paradise. With his map de Mérac identified the landmarks across the stream: the Plank Road running from the town and vanishing over the bluffs; Telegraph Road curving in from the south to join it just outside the town; the railroad to the Potomac, ending at a wrecked bridge whose stone piers stuck up from the river like broken teeth; Marye's Heights, a section of the bluffs behind the town and the white-pillared façade of the brick Marye house; a narrow canal that ran between Marye's and the last roofs of the town. Professionally, the terrain presented many interesting features, he thought. If Burnside could move quickly enough, he might do well to seize the other bank.

The new commander began to make daily tours of the camps and the men commented favorably on him. He was big and ruddy. De Mérac thought he would have been handsome save for the odd whiskers that gave him the look of a Saint Bernard dog, heavy-jowled. There were other moves beside the inspections. The old formations were broken up and a system of what the new commander called "Grand Divisions" was instituted—Sumner's the Right Grand Division, Hooker's the Center, and Franklin's the Left. In the new shuffle the Rifles, with the rest of Stoneman's corps, found themselves under Hooker's command. *"Le vieux kébir,"* observed Bordagaray, "spoke well of Hooker. Under him, action may come quickly!" *"Paperasse!"* growled Claudel, his lieutenant. "Such moves are to keep the clerks at headquarters occupied. Winter quarters, *mon vieux*. *Enfin*, have not civilian visitors begun to arrive from Acquia Creek?"

A cold wind blew from the north and whistled through the chinks of the little hut that the men of the company had built for George Force. Wrapped in his overcoat, he laid down his pen, blowing on his numbed fingers as he read over the first page of a letter to Dora. It was difficult, writing her. There was so much that he wanted to say, but that "much" was for her eyes alone and he knew that her father would carefully read any letter for her and doubtless withhold it if he thought the contents were unsuitable. So far he had only been able to describe the camp and to report on the health of Mr. McArdle, who lay curled in a tight ball at his feet. He rumpled his light hair. When was his next leave? So many men he knew in other units had had leaves. He remembered wryly Randol's latest dubious *mot*. "We're the Pine-Tree Brigade. See why? No leaves!" He picked up his pen again and stirred the thick ink. The feeble joke would do to send along.

A shadow fell across the door. A choked voice said, "George—*darling!*"

He shot to his feet. Eyes shining and pretty face framed in furs, Dora Chase held her arms and stumbled toward him. He said, "Oh, my *God!*" thickly. Then the coolness of her cheek lay against his, her breath was quick in his ear, and her whole body quivered against him. He could only murmer, "Oh—my God. *Dora!*" over and over while her broken whispers sounded low. "I can't believe it's happened. I'm here! I'm here! I've dreamed of this, George—coming into this other life of yours. Now it's part of us. I've seen it. It won't ever be between us." She staggered as Mr. McArdle uncoiled from under the table and whacked his paws against her side. She laughed happily. "You too, old soldier!" she cried and reached down an arm to the woolly neck.

"Keep that blasted dog out of this," said George. "He upset my table at breakfast, chewed a hole in my one best blanket, and now he tries to claw you away from me. He's in disgrace!"

An explosive cough sounded outside. They stepped quickly apart, flushing. Sergeant Major Rapp walked rapidly away from them. His beard was turned to the high sky and his eyes were intent on the clouds that floated far above Marye's Heights. Dora's hands flew to her cheeks. "How awful of us! But darling, I just forgot there could be anyone else around!"

He said unevenly, "That's the effect I ought to have on you." He caught her hands again.

"Dearest, how—how—*how* did you ever get here?"

She rubbed her cheek against a button of his jacket. "I

wrote. But I suppose it never did catch up with you. Claire Wilson—she wrote Mother to see if I could come and stay with her in Washington—you know, after Major Wilson was captured, and—and Mother got after Father and the very day I came to Washington, the papers said civilians were going to Acquia Creek and Claire had me on a boat before I knew what was happening. George, she's perfectly wonderful. I know she's worried sick about her husband but she never shows a thing. You'd have thought she didn't have a care in the world beyond getting me where you were."

"She is wonderful. I always said so. But I haven't got time to admire other women, darling."

"You've got to have. Come and thank Claire."

"But you'll be going back! We're wasting—"

"We're at a place they call a hotel at Acquia—for officers' wives and things, and we're going to stay at least a week and Claire's got a pass for us on the railroad. Come along now!"

"Where is she?" asked George dubiously.

She shook him gently. "Right over there. That old hack by the pines. You'd walk right into it in three steps."

Claire Wilson's gentle face showed at the lowered window of the shabby hack. He waved his kepi. "Hello, duenna," he called.

She laughed as George bowed over her hand. "Duenna! If one hundred thousand men aren't chaperon enough for Mrs. Grundy, one frail woman certainly isn't. Oh, George, it's so good to see the Kearny patch again. Dora and I nearly fell out of the cars when we saw some men, Robinson's I guess they were, marching beside the tracks. And when we drove up here, there was dear old Rapp and Cahusac and Captain Shea and Bigourdin and McCarthy and Joesting and—oh, I'll remember them all to write Craig." Her mouth tightened a little. "They tell me he'll get exchanged soon. Loretta Scott's husband got out right away after Antietam. Now I'm going to drive back to headquarters. I want to see John de Mérac. I suppose you two'd rather walk."

Dora's eyes flicked toward Claire. "Going to tell John about—" She left the sentence unfinished.

"Here!" cried George. "What's all this? Plots?"

Dora's firm chin hitched. "That little—*fmf*—dratted Louise Duane's heading this way. The Sanitary Commission's landing supplies at Acquia and she's so dying to know all about dear papa's work that she has to come along and see."

George walked on, his head swimming. Dora's arm was under his, a faint trace of scent was in his nostrils, and her soft voice was ringing in his ears. Dora tried to match her step to his and clasped both hands about his elbow. "A week, darling. Think of that!"

"I can't think of anything else. I haven't even asked about your mother."

"They say she's better." Dora's voice was low. "I don't know, George, she's *so* frail and she's the only one who can manage Father the least bit. He was so upset by Claire's asking me that he smashed his pet stick against one of the sparrow houses in Madison Square. Of course, it's only at times like that, because I hardly see anyone—any boys, I mean—but he fusses about you and about your letters and my letters to you. He really is as sweet as he can be—he's a darling but—it's dreadful to say. I honestly think he'd object to anyone. He'd like to keep me just to himself forever, like the Pruyn girls who've been going to the theater with their father and no one else for forty years."

"Leave him to me. *I* can handle him because I understand him."

She patted his arm. "You do?"

"Sure. Don't I want to keep you for myself? Look, Dora, I've been wondering about one thing. I'd like to get John's idea on it. Is it really safe for you to be here? There've been Rebs across the river. Maybe a whole brigade, maybe more. You know what I mean. I want you here. I wish you could march with us. But—"

She squeezed his arm. "You're a dear, George. But of course it's safe. People are beginning to flock down here. Oh! If you could have seen some of the passengers on the boat." She dropped her voice. "There were two women with paint on their faces! Really! Like people you read about!"

He checked her pace suddenly and snapped, "Look!" They had topped a treeless rise behind Falmouth. Beyond the last scattered houses lay the Rappahannock and the bulge of the west bank below Beck's Island. Her lips parted in surprise and her eyes turned to him. "What? What is it? George, you've got the funniest expression."

He said, "Look!" again, and pointed. Drab little figures moved cautiously toward the river. "Rebs. Patrolling their side of the river. In broad daylight."

Dora turned pale. "Rebels?" she said in a low voice.

"Having a look at us. About two platoons. Their officer's letting them bunch up too much. Hey! What's that?"

Smoke mushroomed fatly among the drab men and a faint report rattled along the bluffs. Dora flinched and buried her face against George's sleeve. He patted her shoulder, eyes still on the far bank. We're way out of range." Dora closed her eyes and shivered. George cried, "Berdan's Sharpshooters. On our side of the river! Watch 'em, Dora. Oh, oh, oh! Reb! For God's sake fan your men out. You'll get 'em slaughtered. See what he's up to?"

She whispered, "I can't look. I simply can't." She started nervously as a Napoleon slammed on the Union side and white puffballs opened over the patrol.

George said, "Roemer's battery. There go the Rebs. Into cover and out of range. That officer ought to get a court-martial for letting his men bunch up like that. You just can't—Oh, I'm sorry, darling. Didn't have an idea we'd see anything like that."

She said unsteadily, "Men were trying to kill each other."

"Take it easy, dear. But you see what I meant about being safe here?"

She straightened her shoulders. "But you have to go down into places like that." She said almost to herself, "All the same, I know a little now. And I'm glad I know."

He patted her hand as he led her slowly back toward the camp.

It seemed as though the whole regiment and the friends of the regiment conspired to make Dora's visit as easy as possible. Randol insisted on taking over H Company for the time being, insisted so earnestly that George almost forgave his closing remark, "It's time I did a little work. I've been loafing so much I'll end up in a bakery!" A detail laid a plank floor in the big headquarters tent and ran up a cat-and-clay fireplace so that Dora and Claire Wilson could warm themselves at the end of their ten-mile trip from Acquia Creek. Labanieff turned over to George and Dora his light carriage and an odd, slant-eyed driver who had come from the tablelands of Central Asia to the banks of the Rappahannock.

It was past mid-November and the carriage was halted in a pine grove overlooking the approaches to Falmouth along which were pouring the thick blue columns of Couch's IInd Corps of Sumner's Grand Division. The Tartar-faced driver stood at the edge of the grove, impassively watching a squadron of Rush's 6th Pennsylvania Lancers winding off through a shallow defile, their red pennons fluttering in the wind that had turned soft with Dora's arrival. On the other side of the grove, batteries of heavy artillery flowed toward the river in a ponderous, clanking stream. In the back seat of the carriage, Dora clung to George, her eyes wet and her lips tremulous. She whispered, "It just sometimes seems as though I couldn't stand it. I want to be with you—always and forever!"

He smoothed her brown hair. "You haven't got a chance of being anywhere else, dearest."

"But this goes on and on and on. I'm scared—scared you'll change and I won't be able to understand the change. When Claire made me go to the hut to find you— I was such a little coward I wanted her to go—I didn't dare speak for a second. Then when you jumped up I knew everything was all right."

"So why worry? It always will be."

She hooked a finger under his tarnished shoulder strap. "Will it? You might change without knowing it.

Like—oh, don't misunderstand me—like yesterday when we saw the Rebs across the river and they were shooting back and forth. The expression on your face! You almost looked like that awful man, Dekdebrun, with the rifle who follows John around, the one with the eyes like a stuffed lynx."

He laughed. "I was momentarily absorbed by professional matters."

"But you didn't know you had that expression, George. I'm sure you didn't. Suppose it gets etched into you? It's a look that belongs here and nowhere else. What if you bring it back with you? You won't know you have it. But it'll stand for the way you feel and think. Oh, I know this sounds awful, *awful*. I don't mean it to be awful at all. It's you I'm worrying about, not me."

"I know you are," he said softly. "And I love you for understanding and trying to make me see it. I didn't know I looked any different. I'll try not to, but you see—"

"Oh, I can see why you do—a little. I mean, just that glimpse across the river yesterday. All of that's utterly foreign to you and you must have to batter and batter at yourself to stand it."

He said lightly, "Oh, it's not so bad. It's—" His expression darkened. He burst out, "Damn the war! Damn all war! Sorry, dearest, but—oh, getting into a scrap's not so bad if you can only think of yourself and no one else. What's hellish is the stuff that looks so simple on paper. You know, 'G and H Companies moved across the run at half-past three and in the face of a brisk fire succeeded in securing a footing on the ridge.' There's the killing part. I have to take men and see to it that they secure that footing. I have to make myself think that the *securing's* the important thing, not the fact that some of my men, because *I* give them the order, will be ripped and torn. Then I have to say, 'Good work, boys!' to the fellows who are left. It's like—"

She suddenly clung tighter. "Go on, darling, go on if it helps. Talk it out." She thought fiercely, "It isn't fair. No man should be put through this."

His voice was flat. "The night before Second Bull Run, St. Antoine of Péguy's company got hold of a bottle of whiskey and brought it to me and Kelleher. We drank it—the three of us. The next day I saw them both killed within ten feet of me. That's another thing you've got to march with. Every time you go into action, some man you've liked a great deal, or just someone you've known pleasantly, isn't going to come out. You know that. I like John de Mérac as well as any man I ever knew. Liked him from the start. I've sometimes been useless, worse than useless, with sheer terror at seeing some of the shaves he's had. He doesn't get reckless but when he sees something that he knows ought to be done, he smashes in. God! The things I've seen him do! I saw Craig Wilson go down under his horse with the Rebs coming on; one leg pinned under his horse and his Colt going steady as if he was on a target range. Stuff like that's grand and thrilling when you read about it in the papers. But it's damned ghastly and sickening when it's someone you know and admire, like Craig. I suppose that that's where the professional soldier's got the advantage, if that's what it is, over us volunteers. He's been bred up to it, bred to live with the knowledge that he's going to see his closest friends wiped out. I guess that's about the most important thing to learn when you're fighting, but it comes damned hard."

She thought wildly, "But it's *you* I love. Oh, dear Lord in Heaven, *he* doesn't know it, but John de Mérac could be saying the same thing and meaning him—meaning George." She steadied her voice. "Oh, my dearest, I don't see how you do it."

He shook himself. "I've been talking too much. Damned theatrical twaddle. This is a job, just like any other."

She rubbed her cheek against his shoulder. "No such thing. Do let me borrow your handkerchief and—oh!—look at the sun! We've got to be getting back."

"The devil! Well, there's tomorrow coming." He hailed the driver, who stumped over to the carriage. Mr. McArdle galloped out of some bushes and thumped down across Dora's feet. George motioned the driver to head back to camp.

By the tents they left the carriage and strolled toward headquarters. As they entered, Father Doyle sprang to his feet, stifling a sigh. There was much that a priest gave up, he thought with fleeting sadness. He recalled the look on Claire Wilson's face not five minutes before when Bordagaray had rushed in to tell her that a telegram was coming in for her over the military wire and might hold good news about her husband.

Claire's voice called from outside, "George! Oh, George! Can Dora spare you for a second?"

Doyle pushed up a board seat for Dora as George went out. So the pair had been to see the IInd Corps come in? Ah, a fine, grand sight that must have been! And had she heard about the new field altar that John de Mérac had bought out of his own pocket for the regiment?

She smiled at him. "Isn't that fine? George wrote me that you wanted one. You know, Father Doyle, he tells me, too, that the Protestant boys go to you, just as much as the Catholics."

Doyle's dark face softened. "And it's humble it makes me. Never a bit do I preach to them. It's man to man between us. I like to think maybe it's helping them, though it's a different way they go."

"Doesn't it almost seem that creeds and sects don't matter in times like these? The way you handle those Protestant boys, for example."

Doyle shook his head slowly. "It's not myself that counts. It's the strength that the true Church gives me." He got to his feet. "And here's your lucky young man looking for you."

George said, "Dora, I'm afraid you've got to start back for Acquia a little earlier today."

"What? Why earlier?" She rose slowly, took two steps toward him, the brightness of her face fading. "What is it? You're going to move? Tell me. No—it's not that! Look at me." Her voice was low in her throat. "Is it Mother?"

He swallowed hard. "Came over the wire, care of

Claire. Don't know how they got the message through."
He put his arms about her tenderly. "My darling, I'd have given anything to spare you this. She was such a wonderful person."

She stepped back and turned from the two men, hands to her cheeks. Father Doyle started to leave, but George checked him. Dora faced them, very erect and her arms close to her sides. "I'm not going to cry. Not George checked him. Dora faced them, very erect and her arms close to her sides. "I'm not going to cry. Not now. George—I'm going home. I think—I think I'd like Father Doyle to drive to the train with us." She threw back her head, took George's arm, and stepped out of the tent. The priest picked up his rusty black kepi and followed. Claire Wilson stood by the carriage. Dora said, "Thank you, Claire, for letting it be George." The older woman waved her gently to her seat and motioned to George to sit beside her. Dora clutched George's hand.

Father Doyle took his place beside Claire. He crossed himself and thought, "Let me give her strength. Holy Mary, help her. And the other too, who must have been thinking that the telegram was good news about the major."

The gray, lagoonlike stretch of Acquia Creek tossed in an endless ruffle of hard, slapping waves that broke against the sides of paddlewheelers, scows, schooners, and tugs. Off the flats of Brent's Point on the north and beyond the fistlike Marlboro Point to the south, more craft hung in the current, waiting their turn to edge up to the clumsy wharves or anchor where lighters could reach them. A hundred yards from the steep shore a crane picked up mules from a vessel, slung them out over the water, dropped them to swim ashore where yielding Negroes caught them.

De Mérac, forearm across his knee, rested a foot on a crude bollard and ran an appraising eye over the flotilla as he whistled tunelessly under his breath. By now it was common knowledge that Burnside was about to throw his whole force across the Rappahannock. It was equally known that lack of pontoon trains delayed him.

The days were slipping by and with the days, Burnside's best chance. Already "Dutch" Longstreet's corps was hovering about Fredericksburg. Soon the bulk of Lee's strength would pack the wicked heights behind the town, and it was even said that Stonewall Jackson was past Winchester, driving his steel-legged men on to join Lee. Perhaps there was still time for Burnside—if he only had pontoons to span the river. But where were they? De Mérac was sure that none of the vessels in the creek carried them. Did some man, some clique in Washington, want the new general to fail?

He turned away from the stream, deeply worried. Lesser cares crept into his mind, adding their weight to the major one. Where were the new boots for his men? Then Corvisart, with his shattering cough, was a sick man. Who could replace him if necessary? Hein? LeNoir? Bolton? He shook his head and shouted for Castex, who held Lisette on the other side of a great park of waiting wagons.

A twangy voice said, "That the feller?" and a cavalry sergeant pushed toward him past a team of mules. The sergeant saluted, shifted a quid of tobacco. "Provost guard, sir. Someone's hollering to see you."

"To see me?"

"Yes, sir. This way, sir." De Mérac shrugged and followed, stepping over packing cases and edging around high-piled bales. Then in a clear space, a slim girl, in a gray cape slashed with cherry, broke from between two troopers and ran to him. "John! Make them let me go! I came all the way—and—oh, send them away!" De Mérac stood motionless, stunned by surprise. Louise Duane held his arms tightly and pressed her bonneted head against his chest. "Help me, help me, John. Don't let them send me away!"

De Mérac freed an arm gently and laid it about her shoulder. He said angrily to the sergeant, "The meaning of this? At once!"

The sergeant looked sheepish. "Orders, sir. Just come. All civilians out of the area. No exceptions."

"Whose orders?" De Mérac patted Louise's shoulder protectively and she wriggled like a rescued kitten.

"General Burnside's, sir. Far's I'm concerned, they're Colonel Sparhawk's, commanding provost. I ain't aiming to lose my stripes and he flicks 'em off like swatting skeeters."

Louise whispered, "Send them away. Please, please, I can't go back. I only just came."

De Mérac nodded to the sergeant. "I make myself responsible that all orders are complied with."

The sergeant shook his head in sullen obstinacy. "You ain't no provost, sir. And you ain't talking to me. You're talking to Colonel Sparhawk. If I miss on even one civilian, he'll likely send me to Dry Tortugas. He's done it before."

"I order you to leave Miss Duane. If there's trouble, I'll settle with your colonel."

"And he'll settle with me. Ample. All right. You're a captain and you order me. But I'm going to be where I can see that pink hat, and if it don't go up the gangplank of that Sanitary boat pretty quick, I got authority to make it." He saluted and clanked away.

Louise drew a deep breath. "Oh—I knew you'd do it, John." She looked up at him and her underlip quivered. "Now make them let me stay."

She was so vividly alive as she stood there, her eyes wide, her breasts swelling against the soft material of her dress, her hand white and fragile on his sleeve. He passed a hand over his forehead. "Ah—but I cannot do that, Louise. If I could, then you should see—"

"But you always manage to do everything, fix everything, John. I don't want to go back." Her voice was low and pleading. "If you knew the trouble I had getting down here. I had to persuade Father to let me come and we just poked along, and when I got ashore those nasty provost men said they'd never heard of you. Then—"

He smiled down at her, happy in this brief propinquity. "But after the campaign, Louise—then you may come and go as you wish."

She shivered. "This wind! Can't we get out of it?" She dropped her hands and slipped into an angle of the great buttress of wooden cases that towered high above their heads. Then she turned to him again, lips parted and smooth forehead puckered. "But don't you see, John? It's *now* that I want to be here. Do fix it." She clasped her hands and her dark eyes were full of appeal.

Her utter trust in his powers and his authority melted him. "But the campaign—it may begin any day. There would be no place."

She stood very close to him, eyes on his and her fingers working. "They stopped me as soon as I got off the boat." Her eyelids fluttered and she went on slowly, "I thought everything would be all right as soon as I found you, John." She turned her head away and the collar of her cape fell back to show the smooth column of her neck.

De Mérac caught her hands. "But things *are* right, my dear. I myself will see you on board and—"

She tugged her hands free and turned her back on him. "I might as well not have come," she said dully. "I didn't think it would be like this."

He put his hands on her shoulders. "Oh, *ma chère*—"

She went on brokenly, "I came to see you. I'm a fool to tell you, but I did. I missed you. I just couldn't stand it." She began to cry softly. "And you're sending me away." She raised a hand to her face. The wind ruffled her cape, fanned it out gently to show the slimness of her waist, the generous rounding of a breast.

He cried, "Ah—*la pauvre!*" and all the loneliness, all the yearning of the unnatural, womanless months spoke through his tones. "I have been stupid. I have been cruel. The words have always been in my heart and I have been too imbecile to say them. Louise—"

She said, "No!" in a tight voice and tried to glide past him. Her foot slipped in the loose dirt and his arms, half protecting, half demanding, went about her. Her hands drummed against his chest, then flew about his neck where they clung tightly.

His brain whirled as he felt the soft fur trimming of her bonnet brush his face, saw her parted lips turn upward toward his. *Vingt dieux!* Why had he not spoken before! Her arms were warm about his neck, her soft body pressed against his. She murmured something broken and undistinguishable in his ear, then clung closer, the hoops of her skirt cutting into his leg. He whispered, "Ah, *ma chérisette*, how blind I have been. How blind!"

She laid a slim hand on his cheek. "You've been so wonderful, always, John darling. I admire you so. Wherever I see you, you seem just to fill up everything. The way you wear your kepi, the way your mustache curls ever so little. The way you hold your head when you're watching your men. You're so big. You're so strong I'm almost afraid of you."

"Not of me, *bien-aimée*. It is I who have been in awe of you, a Venus de Milo in Dresdenware. The glint of your eyes and the wave of your wonderful hair. Your smile. Ah—there is so much—I have always wanted to kiss that hollow at the base of your throat—" She laughed softly and tilted her chin back with a happy shudder.

A little later she said breathlessly, "And we'll live in your lovely château at Loudéc?"

"Where you like, *chérie*. That may be our headquarters."

Her laugh rippled in his ear. "And we'll tell everyone right away? Of course we will. Oh, darling, I don't mind going back so much now. And you'll come to me whenever you can, just as soon as ever you can?"

"With the permission of Burnside and Lee, *mon cœur*. I must go to Hammond's and find a ring for you. One to wear until Aunt Frédégonde shall send over the diamond that my father gave my mother. And in the meantime—" he slipped off the heavy ring with its worn device and the motto *Flam var mor ha var donar*—"this would slide from your slim fingers but you must have it as hostage against something more fitting. *Sang de dieu*—" he released her quickly—"here comes the obstinate sergeant."

Her hands flew to her hair and she laughed up at him, color bright in her cheeks and her eyes moist and soft. "I don't care—so much—now. Oh dear, but it seems so soon. Give me your arm, John, and we'll go back to the boat."

More than ever she seemed utterly feminine and utterly desirable as she stepped along beside him with her swaying, gliding gait. Eyes followed her, frankly curious, speculative, leering, melancholy. Louise laughed softly. "They all think I'm a prisoner, John."

"Ah, and it is they who are wrong. I, not you, am the prisoner."

"You're such fun. Here's the boat and, oh, gracious, the whistle's screeching and look at the sailors at the gangplank. Hurry, dearest, and you'll have time for a word with Father. Up we go."

When the ship finally backed into the stream, Louise leaned from the railing, waving and blowing kisses. De Mérac flung both hands into the air in a wild gesture. Parting was a wrench, but a day would come soon when that laughing, sparkling girl would be his. Beside him, the cavalry sergeant stared soulfully up at Louise. He sighed deeply and remarked to the world in general, "Yuh. She kind of got that light—that see-same in her eye."

De Mérac rode gaily back along the road that edged the railway. He swung his feet and whistled, *"Rien N'est Sacré à un Sapeur!"* How dense he had been! But now this delicious, this adorable girl would be his forever at the end of the campaign. Or perhaps the pontoons would never come and that would mean winter quarters and an early wedding. Such a helpless little morsel she was, but how quick! And how much she combined in her slim person.

He spurred Lisette. Here was news for the camp. He would buy barrels of good red wine for the regiment, not forgetting beer for Hein's Germans. Champagne, of course, at the mess. He could beg a dozen or so bottles from Labanieff, since he himself was traveling light. Ah, this America! It should be well toasted along with Louise, *la bien-aimée!* Now in Europe—he grimaced. The mysterious conversations, the flood of letters. The visit of the solicitor of the family. The summons from the head of the family. "It has been arranged, Jean—or Claude—or Onésime—that you marry the elder daughter of the *de la Quelque-chose*. She is in perfect health. The dowry and settlement are satisfactory and her Uncle Hubert possesses notable connections. You will present yourself to Mademoiselle—ah—yes—to Mademoiselle Ernestine on Thursday to make her acquaintance." ... "*Oui, mon père.*"

He flung himself from the saddle and stormed into headquarters, sending Castex to Labanieff to borrow champagne. "Greenbaum, *mon ami*, Father Doyle, there is news. Louvel, fetch Lieutenant Force, fetch Lieutenant Bordagaray, every officer you may see, even including Lieutenant Rohde."

The chaplain stared at him. "I'd think it was the Shannon you'd been looking at, not Acquia Creek. And what might the news be?"

Officers came streaming into the tent. Labanieff's *fourgon* rattled up, escorted by the Russian himself, and champagne was unloaded in eager haste. The reception of the news lifted de Mérac still higher. Men slapped his back, shouted, drank with him. Mr. McArdle yelped and whacked his tail against legs and scabbards and tables. De Mérac cried, "But you, George, you say nothing. You do not comprehend?"

George rallied himself. "You've been in too much of a buzz to know what *anyone* said. I told you—you're getting a damn pretty girl—damn pretty. Here's hoping that you'll be as happy as Dora and I are going to be. Here's to you and Louise!"

XIV

The Stone Wall

BULGING, silvery clouds rolled across northern Virginia, flattened to a thick, unwholesome blanket, and snow beat down unmercifully on the two armies that watched each other. The woods about the camp of Birney's division were smothered in the wet, heavy flakes. The pines bent over to frame long, arched vistas like endless colonnades lined with deep jade. Sentries stood huddled at their posts, caked and plastered with snow like statue warriors at the grave of a dead king. The horses turned their tails to the blast and patiently waited out the storm, dreaming perhaps of the fat Maryland meadows of the autumn where the sun beat strong and where flies were too lazy to be worth the flick of a tail. Maine lumbermen felled trees for firewood with negligent skill, marking the great trunks so that their crashes in the close-packed camps brushed not a single tent or stand of arms.

De Mérac plowed happily about through the drifts, wrapped in a warm glow that insulated him against cold and wet. Louise had written twice since her return to Washington, letters shining with a warm, eager affection. "Ah," he thought, "a *jeune fille* of my own country, she would not dream of writing this! *Triple-sot* I, who might even now think of her installed in our snug Washington home had I spoken earlier. *Bigre!* Were George's problems but resolved and Craig released by the Rebels!"

The snow ended and intense cold set in. In the headquarters tent Dr. Wayne huddled by the fireplace and drank hot whiskey. "Winter quarters sure as shooting fish," he observed. "Only December 7 and I got five frostbite cases already."

Corvisart shivered. His cough was gone but bright spots showed on his cheeks and his big-shouldered frame looked shrunken. "One may wish, Doctor. But it is a week that the pontoons are here, hidden by the banks."

"Tell you another thing," said Greenbaum. "November elections went heavy against the administration. We'll attack and we'll be hitting the Copperheads as well as Lee." He looked impassively into the fire.

"Just the same," said Wayne, turning his mug in his hands, "I'll bet a busted scalpel against a barrel of whiskey that we stay here. The Maine and the Michigan boys have built huts like they did last year at Corcoran and Rohde says Dud Pelham's had two cases of books sent down to him."

"Hell," said Greenbaum, "if Rohde says we stay, then we're right across the river now and don't know it."

The concentration of artillery was terrifying. From the extreme Union right by Beck's Island to the far left opposite the hamlet of Smithfield, along the riverbank and sited deep on the rising ground, muzzles flashed and smoke rolled out over the Rappahannock. The sharp *gam-gam!* of the light pieces blurred into the heavy, slow *thup* of the big guns. Benjamin's battery, Roemer's, Hazard's, Kusserow's, Waterman's, Diederich's, Voegelee's, McCarthy's, Leppien's, Ricketts's, Taft's—they sent their hot metal arching across the river to fall on the open flats and on the brick town of Fredericksburg.

De Mérac stood with a group of officers on the high ground back of the Lacy house and slowly turned the eyepieces of his glasses. There was little to see beyond the flash of the Union guns. A thin but all-enveloping mist rose from the valley to blend with the volcano blasts that welled out from the east bank. Well above the wrecked railroad trestle, a half-finished pontoon bridge jutted out into the stream. On its far end, a single blue figure lay. Even at that distance de Mérac could see the pale sun wink on the engineer emblem of the dead man's hat.

George lay beside de Mérac and pounded the hard ground with his fist. "Why in hell didn't they turn the guns loose on the town at the start? Shoving those poor devils of engineers into the river with no cover and the houses jammed with Rebs picking them off! Jesus! Been at it since one. How many times did they try, John?"

Labanieff, beyond de Mérac, answered, "Nine, to my count. And why not? The movement follows closely Mouton's bridging of the Danube by the island of Lobau in 1809."

Pride pulled at his beard. "Maybe—but this ain't the Danube and we're fighting Americans, not Austrians."

Colonel Duffié, cape open over his short cavalry jacket, pushed out his hand as though to drive the mist away and his medals glittered softly. "Ah—those houses! Those ridges behind! The place smells of murder. Me, I have been as far as Popcastle Run opposite Skinker's Neck with my little devils. There we might have crossed in a waltz for my patrols found nothing but a weak force of D. H. Hill's."

His voice echoed strangely in a sudden hush. The artillery was mute. George rose to his knees with a jerk and Mr. McArdle, close by him, sat up abruptly. De Mérac cried, *"Vingt dieux!"* Duffié tugged at his imperial and Pride nervously chafed his hands together.

From the Union bank, hidden from de Mérac by the steep rise, a string of pontoons pushed slowly into the stream—ten—fifteen—twenty light boats packed with blue freight. Here and there furled colors rose above the bristle of bayonets. A strange officer who had joined the group muttered, "7th Michigan, 19th and 20th Massachusetts. Jesus. My brother's with the 7th."

De Mérac tried to hold his glasses steady. Musketry broke out from the shattered and burning houses of the town and the pontoons poled and paddled steadily into a billowing curtain that slowly wrapped them. There was confusion among the blue masses. Twice he was sure that he saw men slip overboard into the icy stream. Then the pontoons were hidden and he could only stare into the mist and smoke. Daylight was fading fast and dull yellow flecks winked and winked along the opposite bank as though the Rebel muzzles were spewing out fireflies.

Pride barked, "Done it!" The flecks were winking farther and farther inland. "Chasing Barksdale's Mississippi boys back to the hills!" Other pontoons poled out from the shore, swung in toward the half-finished bridge, were lashed into place, anchored bow and stern.

Someone shouted, "Downstream! Look-a there! Downstream." Darkness was falling swiftly but the air had cleared. A mile below Fredericksburg, two bridges swayed in the current, the light board plankings faint but distinguishable. Then the planks vanished under a living tide and the dull pounding of boots and hoofs drifted to the watchers back of the Lacy house. Infantry on the farther bridge, cavalry and artillery on the nearer, an endless rope of men flowed to the opposite shore. Franklin's Left Grand Division was crossing the Rappahannock. Soon Sumner's men would pound over the bridge at their feet.

George slanted his watch to catch the last light. "Five o'clock! And Franklin's bridges were finished twelve hours ago! God, they've been empty all day."

Labanieff rubbed his hands. "Ah! You noted that? You will find a parallel in the state of the Berezina bridges in 1812. Tomorrow I shall plant a chair in this exact spot, for there will be much to watch now that the move has truly begun."

George muttered, "I wish it hadn't!"

Duffié sighed. "My young friend, I fear that I agree. Over there we now find Lee in full strength. We must strike him with an army that does not strain like a greyhound. It is puzzled by changes and delays. It is hesitant and who may blame it?"

"Ah, but we are strong," said de Mérac. Somehow he felt no longer appalled at the thought of attacking over those flat plains toward the steel-crowned highlands. Why, *parbleu*, a flanking movement could pinch Lee off the crests and back onto the plain in his rear. As the group walked back over ground sodden with melting snow, he thought of little vignettes of the day which he could put on paper for Louise: lancers' red pennons sharp against a snowy slope; men of a Zouave unit, still in its old glory of fez and red breeches, chasing rabbits over a white plain; an English observer in pillbox cap, red jacket, and plaid trews, putting a fine hunter over a fence; Professor Lowe's balloons, in their first appearance since the Peninsula, hanging like high golden domes in the sky; the lurid murk that hung over Fredericksburg and its smoldering houses. As for the campaign, Lee might well withdraw as he was outnumbered nearly two to one. Or he might well be overwhelmed. Or, if the campaign proved inconclusive, there would be winter quarters and business of the most official to take him to Washington.

The day following the first crossing was exhausted in regrouping the masses of troops who had poured over the rocking bridges, in a welter of orders and counterorders. Now, on the thirteenth of December, under a noon sun that glowed pale through the everpresent mist, the Rochambeau Rifles hugged the ground on the railroad embankment that skirted the high ground where Stonewall Jackson's men lay half hidden by the crown of ragged woods. Other units of Birney's division, detached from Hooker to support Franklin's attack on the Rebel right, were spaced along the same shelter or echeloned back toward the Richmond road. On the right of the Rifles, the remnants of the 55th New York, the old La-Fayette Guards, clung stubbornly.

De Mérac crept on hands and knees behind his own line. When he came to the color guard, holding their eagle-topped poles below the level of the rails, he had to glide over the body of Sergeant Cahusac, the neck horribly torn by a Minié ball. Beyond Cahusac, out in exposed ground, Captain Chanel lay stiffly across a dead, red-piped gunner from Walcott's battery, now withdrawn nearly to the Richmond road. Farther on, Wayne and Father Doyle unhurriedly bandaged the shoulder of a bearded private who rocked back and forth, hissing through his teeth with each motion. There were other bodies, whose kepis bore the Kearny patch, strewn over the ground between the railroad and the Richmond road, but the pattering fire from the high woods made investigation dangerous. Besides, identity was not important at the moment.

De Mérac crawled on. Here was LeNoir, scowling and biting his nails. Then George Force helping Randol put a rude tourniquet on Corporal Mladnick's wrist. De Mérac cautioned, "Keep your head low!"

"I'm apt to." George jerked his chin upward at the random bullets that whined overhead or clanged against the rails. "Where are you going? To your old watchtower?"

De Mérac nodded and worked on toward a stone culvert where George's company joined Bolton's. Then he carefully wriggled up the bank until his head cleared it. The curb of the culvert afforded some protection and his head, just filling the angle, made an inconspicuous target. Somewhere up above, a musket cracked and a ball sang a few feet away. He disregarded it. This was his third trip to the culvert and he had learned that the particular marksman covering it was aiming high and to the right. He drew a deep breath and studied the terrain in front.

The rough, shaggy ground rose quite sharply from the other side of the right of way. The mist of the last days hung thin and filmy, but high up among the trees of the crest there was continuous, shifting movement, an occasional glint of color as a Southern battle flag caught a whiff of light wind. Archer's men and Gregg's of A. P. Hill's division. Beyond them he counted once more the fourteen-gun battery that covered the Southern right flank where the hill trailed away to the plain. Archer and Gregg, Pender and Lane and Thomas, Brockenbrough's artillery—enemy names, slowly imprinted on his mind from past battles, were becoming more and more familiar, almost welcome. Recognition changed the anonymous threat of those men moving among the trees, identified them as human beings of known commands and known states. And those same men had shouted shrilly when the Rifles debouched from the Richmond road, "Jesus! It's them redtops again!"

A gun of Brockenbrough's battery slammed and a shot wailed over his head to burst somewhere in the flatland below, perhaps among Pride's men and Clay's, sheltering in the twisting course of a run. He let his eye follow down the contour of the hill. Isolated posts, marked by quick flashes and gouts of smoke, were firing at some target he couldn't see. In the brush, doubled over roots of trees, sprawled over rocks, lay bodies in blue or gray. They lay thicker in the open, blue heaped on gray, gray on blue, marking the path of Meade's Pennsylvanians who had smashed through between Lane and Pender, only to be dislodged by a quick counterattack. Then the gray tide had come on too far, had been struck front and flank and driven back in a rout, the Rifles striking in the van.

It was no use counting the red patches in the grass out there—papery grass that had been sheltered from the snow and dried by the steady winds. The broad back at the foot of the rock was Hein. The single hand that jutted up from a hollow belonged to Bates, first sergeant of George's company. De Mérac remembered seeing him fall just there in the move back to the railroad. Pinned to a tree by a bayonet the little Breton Scoarnec hung lifeless. De Mérac thought mechanically that he must call Wayne's attention to the body, the surgeon having said earlier that he had never seen a bayonet wound.

The hidden marksman fired again, closer this time, and sand stung de Mérac's cheek. He settled closer against the culvert, sure that he was in a dead space, to judge from the angle at which the bullet had struck. Firing was brisker now from the high ground. Far off to the right, Southern batteries grouped on Marye's Hill sprang into a frenzy of fire. He could just make out the pieces, but the low ground between the heights and the river was hidden by a spur of land that shut out everything save two spires in Fredericksburg that seemed to hang in the soft air. The embankment against which he lay shook and quivered to the distant concussions.

Someone scrabbled up the bank beside him, careful to keep below the sky line. It was Greenbaum. He jerked his head to the right as de Mérac looked down at him. "That's the fourth time we've been after Marye's. Must be hell to pay over there. Reb guns sound as if they hadn't moved a foot. Say, lot of wounded out in front of us."

"A pity. Neither side will let the other go to them." He glanced down the track. Two of Berdans' green sharpshooters were sprawled on the rails, blind eyes to the sky. Beyond them lay Dekdebrun, cunningly sheltered. As de Merac looked, the cold-eyed man fired, passed his own rifle back to unseen hands, took a freshly loaded one from the same source. He was using the rifles of the dead sharpshooters to insure an endless chain of loaded weapons. From time to time, other red-topped kepis bobbed into sight, fired, vanished. From the hill, the gnawing crackle continued.

"Have to wait till dark," said the Jew. "Damn, doesn't that smoke sting your eyes! It's—" he sniffed again— "wood smoke. The Rebs firing their rations up there?" He heaved himself up beside de Mérac.

De Mérac tried to thrust him back. "Fool. There is shelter only for one. Get down!"

Greenbaum's dark face turned to parchment and his thick lips hung open. He made horrible clucking sounds in his throat as he pointed. The smoke rolled heavier, acrid. Greenbaum croaked, "Burning. The grass! And—"

De Mérac's stomach chilled. Twenty yards away on the other side of the tracks, a wide patch, ignited by gun wadding or the flash of a shell, burned with a searing crackle. Something stirred in the smoke cloud. A gray figure staggered to its feet, turned toward the railroad. Yellow tongues of flame licked about the ragged uniform, ran through the long beard and uncut hair, seared over a face that was half bloody eyesocket. Then the figure fell.

Greenbaum whinnied incoherently. Then he sprang to the tracks and two bullets whacked about his feet. He unbuckled his belt, let his sword and holster clatter to the tracks, and plunged into the smoke.

De Mérac wrenched himself to his knees, blind with the horror of the scene. Then he found himself rolling down the other side of the embankment, scrambling to his feet. He had lost Greenbaum in the eddying smoke and butted ahead. Someone was screaming in a high-pitched voice to the left and de Mérac veered toward the sound. An officer in gray, blood-soaked from the waist down, was propped on his arms, staring in horror at the flames that shot over the grass, licked up through tangles of dried branches. De Mérac tried to beat out the closest flames shouting, "Where are you hit?"

"Mah laigs. Both's bruk. Jesus, Yank, fire's gittin' closer!"

De Mérac dropped the bough with which he had been thrashing, caught the officer under the arms, and dragged him up the slope. The wounded man yelled with pain, then set his teeth and ground out, "Don't mind me. Just git me out'n thet fire!" De Mérac felt soggy ground under his boots, found he was on a jutting rock covered with wet, dead leaves. "This will be safe. For the moment." He unbuckled his canteen. "If the smoke is too thick, wet your coat with this and wrap your head in it." Then he plunged into the low, dry ground again.

Men were shrieking everywhere in high thin tones that sounded almost like hysterical laughter. He stumbled over a heavy fallen branch, shell-covered, saw that a big Pennsylvanian was wedged under it beating out with futile hands at the racing flames. Beyond, a dim shape loomed. He tugged at the branch shouting, "Greenbaum! Moe! *C'est vous?* Pull, *'cré nom de dieu!*"

Out of the smoke emerged a broad-hatted man, musket slung over his back. "Take tother end, Yank. Thar she goes. Kin yuh crawl, bub? Then hit fer the high ground." He turned to de Mérac. "Git a branch like this an' start whuppin', Yank."

De Mérac thrashed his way on, his eyes streaming. He saw a charred hand through the smoke, pulled at it. The skin peeled off in his palm and the weight at the other end was inert. He helped two butternut-shirted men carry a Union major to safety, returned to find the smoke pall alive with kepis and wide, shapeless hats. He bumped into Father Doyle, into Wayne, heard George calling huskily to Randol, saw Bordagaray and Shea and Rapp keeping a space clear around a Southern sergeant too badly wounded to be moved. Then a tall man in a gray frock coat with a bright "CSA" on his hat called to de Mérac. "Reckon the blaze is about done, sir, and the wounded are all moved." He panted and his thin, pleasant face was smoke-blackened. "Got to admit you people gave us the lead."

De Mérac inclined his head. "Yours were on the ground as soon as were ours."

"You are very fair, sir. I am Captain Comer of the 5th Alabama, Archer's brigade. I have authority to give you ten minutes' grace to get your men under cover. May I ask your name and unit?" De Mérac gave the information. Comer saluted. "I assure you that any of your men taken prisoner will meet with every consideration. I shall report the matter to General Archer." He saluted and vanished into the still smoky woods.

De Mérac saw Castex close by, ordered him to sound the recall. In twos and threes and tens and twenties, the men of the Rifles straggled into the shelter of the embankment. Only Dekdebrun remained in his original position, rifle resting on the rails, like a billiard player who waits patiently for the marker to brush the green cloth clean.

De Mérac cautioned his men to keep low, pending the resumption of fire. Ten minutes passed. A single shot cracked up among the trees. In the flats to the rear Hall's battery and then Seelye's erupted in quick salvos. De Mérac sat with his back against the embankment and wondered what the rest of the day would bring. Off by Marye's Heights there was a fresh fury of fire, but on his own front neither side seemed ready to act. Toward the river the commands of Doubleday and Meade and

Sickles and Howe stood to their arms but showed no signs of movement. Light was beginning to fade. De Mérac shook his head. He did not like the position of the whole Union left. It was cut off from the center by the unfordable course of Deep Run and its only line of retreat lay over two shaky bridges—if it came to a question of retreat. He thought that unlikely, although action off at Marye's seemed to have been as inconclusive as that by the wooded hills. Still, fresh troops could easily be brought up and a new attack hurled at Jackson. Like his men, who huddled silent against the embankment, he was too shaken by the rush into the blazing grass to feel anything more than acceptance toward any decision which might be made. He rallied himself enough to make a note of Greenbaum's act for transmission to headquarters. Pelham, of course, would disregard it, but a copy could be sent to Birney.

He stowed away notebook and pencil and looked up, startled. At the far end of the regiment, his men were cheering, the sound was spreading and spreading. Then he saw a trim, sparely built man moving with a light quick step, half running, half crouching, just in the rear of the line.

De Mérac got to his feet cautiously and stared. Then he shouted, "Craig! *Nom de dieu de nom de dieu!*"

Wilson caught de Mérac's hand. "Thought I'd never get here, John. Lord, it's good to be back. What do you want me to do?"

De Mérac felt strengthened by the reappearance of his friend. "Keep your head down, Craig. For the moment, that is all. But to see you here! Have you been home? And how were you exchanged so quickly?"

Wilson sighed. "To see Claire? No. God, I wanted to but when I heard what was happening here—well, I just lit out. Sorry I couldn't join you sooner but it was hard getting up from Fortress Monroe. Oh—about the exchange. I was just lucky. Seems there was some Reb major who was also a Reb Congressman and they wanted him back. I was at hand—hadn't even been sent to prison camp—so, here I am. What's happening?"

"What you see, *justement*. We wait. Ah—and I must

tell you. Claire was at our camp and brought pretty Dora Chase, whose mother died while she visited. Yes, it was sad but I may tell you that Claire looks very well." A shell screeched overhead, to burst with a hollow cough far away toward the river. "There is no need to duck. We sit in a dead space. But the greatest news, Craig—I, whom you see before you, am to be married at the end of the campaign."

Wilson's thin face lit up. "My dear John! I'm delighted. I may ask?"

"But to Louise Duane! Who else? My thick brain at last comprehended her and to my amazement she consented!"

"Louise *Duane?* Lord Almighty. Why—John, that's—delightful of course. Congratulations! You've told Claire? She'll certainly be interested—delighted. Yes. We all are. Now about the regiment. I'd like to take over my command at once. Then give me some idea of what may happen to us."

"But surely." He paused. Off to the right he saw a blue kepi working up the slanting gully that afforded the only safe approach to the railroad. "Here's an aide. I may answer you better after I have his message. Wait here." He crept along the bank toward the gully, cocking his head at the whine of stray bullets that passed about him. The aide, grimy and panting, shoved an envelope at him. "Sign please, sir. From General Birney. General Pelham knows about it, he says." De Mérac signed, and crouched low to read the firm writing on the sheet. When he had finished he still crouched, scuffing a boot on the ground and worrying at his mustache. Then he slid along back toward Wilson, who was talking to George, Corvisart, and other bent figures. He called, "Craig. One moment, please."

Wilson worked over to him. "What's up, John?"

De Mérac patted his shoulder. "Got to get rid of you for about an hour. No. I am serious. Birney is across the river with Burnside. You will find him by the railroad just back of Kusserow's battery. He wishes an immediate report on our situation. Assure him that he can hold here indefinitely so long as the rear batteries are not withdrawn. Say to him that we have ample ammuntion."

Wilson frowned. "Can't you send someone else? I've only just come."

"He wishes that an officer report, Craig. To send another, I must take one from the companies. Ah, *mon vieux*, you will miss nothing. Hurry over and hurry back. I shall be waiting."

"Well, if you say so, John."

"I think it better. Just keep in that gully. You know it?"

"Ought to. It's the way I came."

"Then go on past the gutted brick house—Mansfield, they call it—and make for the pontoons."

Wilson dropped reluctantly into the gully. De Mérac leaned back against the embankment and looked at his watch. Four o'clock. In another hour it would be nearly dark. He called, "Greenbaum!"

The Jew, his face still blackened from the grass fires, crept up. "Say, did I hear you tell Wilson he'd find Birney across the river? Why, Birney's just over by the Richmond road near Smithfield," he said.

"Then I have misled him. He may hunt for several hours on the wrong bank."

Greenbaum said slowly, "So that's it. When do we move?"

"In twenty minutes. The whole brigade. Send the company commanders and Castex to me."

Greenbaum looked steadily at him. "Marye's?" he asked. De Mérac nodded. The Jew whistled softly. "Hell to pay," he said and edged away.

De Mérac shrugged and fumbled out a cigarette. "And why not? Shea holds the command since Craig's capture. He has given orders, made arrangements with his companies that may not be changed in an instant— particularly in the instant before an attack. So if Craig went with us, he would go as supernumerary, with no command and no duties. We move on Marye's for a purpose and that purpose Craig's presence would in no way further. Moreover—he is fresh from prison, comes new to the action—and his wife and child. *Diantre!* Could I only find pretexts to send to the rear George and Castex and the sick Corvisart and Greenbaum and—and—*enfin*, the whole regiment, save Dekdebrun and myself." He flicked away his cigarette as he saw the company commanders, now mainly lieutenants and sergeants, creeping carefully toward him.

Dusk piled thicker and thicker in the narrow streets of Fredericksburg. The air was rank with river damp, wood smoke, the tang of burnt powder, the smell of wounds, and the cloying reek of chloroform. Dead men lay in the gutters. Wounded were everywhere, hobbling close to the walls or sitting on the low curbs, their heads resting on their knees. In a lane by the long brick warehouse sprawled the body of a cavalryman. His horse stood over him, occasionally stretching out its neck to nose inquiringly at the stiffening chest of its master. De Mérac halted the Rifles in a narrow way that ran parallel to the river, trying to give his men as much shelter as he could from the artillery fire that had broken out again along Marye's Heights. He turned command over to Corvisart, who leaned against a house, vomiting from time to time and gasping for breath. Then he started for Hanover Street, the broad thoroughfare that ran inland toward Telegraph Road and Marye's Heights.

From open windows he heard surgeons swearing wearily over amputation cases, heard men gasping, "*Ah*-ah-ah-ah! *Ah*-ah-ah-ah-ah!" in an endless litany of suffering. From a shattered doorway an old woman, tangle-haired and daft-eyed, stared at him unseeing while she held a short pipe in clawlike hands. A solid shot smashed into a shed near by with a hideous clanging of boards. The eyes still stared into the dusk, unseeing, oblivious to more distant explosions and to the lighted fuses of shells, high, whizzing sparks, that crisscrossed against the dim sky.

De Mérac turned into Hanover Street and entered the bulletpocked brick house that the guide had pointed out to him earlier. In the first room a candle burned dimly beside a chair where a big man with colonel's eagles sat rigid. De Mérac said, "General Pelham, sir?" The colonel did not stir. The candle flickered on a gaping wound just under the chin from which drying blood hung in greasy clots. He was dead.

From the next room a voice snapped, "And where is Colonel Clay?" Someone answered, "Wounded, sir. I'm Major Gaylord, now in command."

Pelham said coldly, "I shall require a certified report from the brigade surgeon that his wound was of such a nature as to oblige him to quit the field."

De Mérac stepped through the door. Pelham stood by a dead fireplace, his hands behind his back. There was a bullet hole through his high-crowned hat but he was tight-buttoned, clean-shaven, and cold as ever. He raised his eyes to de Mérac's, ostentatiously drew out his watch, glanced at it, replaced it in his fob. "You will account to me later for your delay in reporting. Now your attention, gentlemen."

Pride nodded gravely to de Mérac. Pelham began, "Our problem, gentlemen, is a simple one of attack against entrenched infantry." He rocked back on his heels and de Mérac was strangely reminded of the brigadier's first lecture in the old house near Georgetown. The precise voice went on. "The brigade will move out along Hanover Street. Between the end of the town and Marye's Heights are several features of importance. Small houses are found, scattered here and there. One fifth of a mile from the edge of the town, there is a canal which your commands must cross on the stringers of destroyed bridges. Beyond it there is a shallow ravine. In this you will form in line of battle. A member of my staff will send up a single red rocket. On seeing this, you will move out at once in column of regiments, making sure that you keep in touch with Donohoe's 10th New Hampshire, Getty's division. In that clear?"

De Mérac, Pride, and Gaylord nodded in silence.

"Very good. The Rochambeau Rifles, in line, will head the column. Colonel Pride, you follow and Gaylord brings up the rear. You will instruct your men, Colonel Pride, that they are to shoot down any men of the Rifles who attempt to run." He held up his hand as Pride stuttered a protest. "There is no comment needed."

Gaylord flushed. "Are my men supposed to watch Colonel Pride's the same way, sir?"

"Had you been included in those orders, I should have mentioned the fact. They concern Colonel Pride only. That, then, is the order of attack. Your objective is, of course, Marye's Heights. You will find at the base of these heights a long, sunken road. On the town side it is masked by a stone wall which shelters the defending infantry perfectly. In this sunken road they are formed four deep. By passing loaded muskets from rear to front, they are able to sustain a well-nourished fire which is supported, until the attacking force is quite close, by the artillery on the heights. Since noon, seven attacks have been mounted against that sunken road. They have all failed." He tightened his thin lips but his voice did not change. "This one will *not!* You will form in Hanover Street in ten minutes in the prescribed order. I presume that you have no comments."

De Mérac said, "I request permission, sir, to order one officer to the rear. He is too sick to exercise command."

Pelham raised his eyebrows. "And that officer is yourself?"

De Mérac tightened his chin and answered, "Captain Corvisart, sir. Dr. Wayne thinks him consumptive."

Pelham said clearly: "Captain Corvisart as a mercenary is now receiving more money than he ever dreamed of. Let him earn it. He will march with you unless he can show blood—not self-induced. That is all."

The three left the building. Shells were still arching their sparks high overhead but the Rebel gunners had lifted their ranges to feel out the banks by the pontoons and the town was quiet for a moment. Pride dropped a heavy arm over de Mérac's shoulder. "Don't worry about me being behind you, John. God damn it, when the war's over I'm going into politics and I'm going to clean all the Pelhams out of this army. Not just him. One man don't count—but what he stands for."

De Mérac shrugged. "*Au fond,* the Pelhams kill themselves with the knives they prepare for others. And now good luck. Good luck to you, Gaylord."

The Rifles were squatting against the sides of the

buildings in the narrow street. When they saw de Mérac moving through the dimming light, they stirred restlessly. De Mérac called the other officers to him, drew them apart, and repeated as closely as possible Pelham's instructions. He ended, "On seizing the sunken road we then move on up to the batteries on the crest. All officers, on forming line, will take their places in front of their commands, not on the flank or rear. Now fall in your companies. We shall move out at right-shoulder shift."

There was no talking as the officer moved away. George squeezed de Mérac's arm and raised a hand in silence. Greenbaum stood with his feet apart, carefully spinning the chamber of his Colt. Then with a slap and shuffle of boots the Rifles formed and filed out into Hanover Street. De Mérac, marching at the head, fixed his mind on the terrain in front of the heights, trying to recapture every detail as he had seen it from the high ground of the other bank. Seven attacks had failed. And now Pelham proposed to herald his part in the eighth with a red rocket. "But the sunken road," thought de Mérac. "It will not show itself from the opposite shore. We march at it blindly." He shivered.

Other regiments, other brigades, had debouched from the town before them and crossed the stringers over the ditchlike canal. There was a light film of snow on level and hollow, a whitish sheet glimmering in the twilight and spotted darkly with bodies. There they lay, wreckage of the earlier attacks—the men of Kimball and Palmer, Zook and Caldwell, the Irish of Meagher's brigade, the files of Whipple and Griffin and Humphreys. From the shelter of the ravine where Pelham's brigade waited, hidden, in line of battle, de Mérac looked ahead to Marye's Heights. On the crest, strung out right and left from the dimly seen Marye house, batteries blasted in spasmodic orange stabs. The slopes were silent, fading in ominous gloom.

Then he made out the sunken road and the stone wall that sheltered it, running close at the very base of the heights. The gray blocks of the wall showed sullen against the white approaches but no sound, no flicker, told of life behind them. The whole stretch might have been chilled by the same plague touch that had swept over the foreground. Halfway between the ravine and the wall the hard outlines of a brick house showed and the ground about was rough with a motionless dark litter, part of the thinning flotsam of the tide that had flowed out from the town toward the wall and sunken road, flowed, checked, and stopped.

The last light was fading. De Mérac still stared ahead, frozen by past disaster and future threat. Mist grew heavier, swirled in from the river, rose sluggishly about Marye's Heights, writhed and twisted, assumed weird forms before his smarting eyes until the gray masses seemed to take the shape of a single gigantic gray figure, slouch-hatted, a figure that loomed over the waiting brigade, musket slowly lifting.

He jumped like a cat at a sudden, sharp hissing and faced to the rear. A red thread climbed high into the blurred sky, hovered, burst in pinkish clouds.

He yelled, *"En avant!"* raised his sword, and sprang to the lip of the ravine. Commands rattled behind him, boots scraped, and the line of the Rifles topped the crest. He shot a quick look back over his shoulder. At the right, Corvisart staggered along, supported by two men. At the left, Shea bellowed and slashed the air with his sword. In front of the companies, officers were walking backwards, waving their arms, shouting to their men not to bunch. He faced the front again. The only possible order had been given—*"En avant."* Once spoken, the only thing was to keep going—keep going.

The stone wall looked no nearer than it had from the ravine. It was still silent, waiting. De Mérac heard the quick crunch of Dekdebrun's steps just behind him, caught the rolling thud of the companies still coming on. Now it was hardly possible to move without stepping on dead bodies that made a pattern of ghastly lace against the white. There were living, too. Men who moaned in semicoma. Untouched men who sheltered behind heaps of corpses or against the bloating bellies of dead horses. A hand reached up, caught his ankle. He kicked free and went mechanically on—one foot high over a headless man, the next swinging wide past an outstretched leg.

A red-orange snake darted from one end of the wall to the other, darted in a terrific roar while the air about de Mérac snarled and hissed. Back the snake darted, broke into fragments, re-formed, shot along the wall again. He ducked his head, hunched his shoulders, and kept going. Dekdebrun's rifle began to crack with steady, spaced shots. But for that sound de Mérac might have been staggering on alone toward the vast gray figure that his mind had conjured up from the rising mists of Marye's Heights.

Doux Jésus! But the dead of the seven attacks were thick here! Piled to the snowy lip of that little hollow! Spread in a long windrow beyond the shed roof that lay so oddly in the middle of a field! Funneled out into dark arrowheads whose point was the man who had gone farthest in a charge forgotten in its failure!

He turned to wave the Zouave company toward the right. There was no Zouave company, just a stumbling fringe of men at the right of his line. Corvisart and his two supporters were gone. The center of the regiment was crumpling, the left bending back. The colors, three stark poles against the stark sky, swayed, pitched, vanished, reappeared.

He halted. Fifty yards away, the wall flamed and crashed like a foundry. A bullet burned his leg. Another rasped across his throat. His vizor cracked and the kepi spun on his head. He raised both arms, old saber and Colt high. *"Pas de charge! En avant!"* His voice blasted even above the ripping blaze from the wall. He faced the wall, knew that his men had broken into the double. He began to run, his Colt slamming futilely at targets he could not see. He tripped over a body, rolled to his feet. The front rank was on him. A man screamed, fell against him, went limp across his feet. A pole whacked against his shoulders, bounced off, and skidded ahead into the clear. A voice that was Greenbaum's yelled, "No. No!" A shape that was Greenbaum's darted ahead, raised the tatters of the national colors, and plunged on. His "Follow me!" split high above the din.

Yellow and red light, red light tinged with black, exploded inside de Mérac. He felt snow against his face but no snow could cool the fire that blazed in his chest. Red lights burst and burst inside him. The red lights were swallowed up by their black borders. He no longer felt the snow on his face, could not feel the shock as a hard body fell across him. His ears were deaf to the last crescendo of fury from the wall, deaf to the throbbing silence that followed it, deaf to the drums of hell that still pounded up on Marye's Heights.

Deep in de Mérac's consciousness vague awareness flickered. His eyes were tight shut, his ears deaf, his limbs powerless. But the fact of cold crept into his brain. Cold, intense cold, and a feeling of being jolted, jarred. He drew a long, quivering breath and his awareness stretched to include pain—a raw band in the inside of his throat, a stabbing ache about his chest. The jolting continued. His eyelids stirred. He blinked up at a white pall that melted and full consciousness flooded slowly over him. A ragged, bearded, leanjawed Southerner stood over him, a pile of blue clothes in his arms. Another tugged and hauled at de Mérac's left boot. De Mérac shouted hoarsely. The man sprang back, dropped his foot heavily, "Chris-a'mighty. He ain't dead!"

The second man growled, "Hell with it. Git them boots."

De Mérac saw the other look cautiously around as he said, "Gawddamn li'l ol' loot's a-playin' sneaky-peeky. Cain't tech only the daid. Come he finds us like this, he raise hell."

"Yeah! 'At bastard'll raise hell 'long of you winnin' them boots and he gits fixin's from home reg'lar as I gits the trots. Son of a bitch! Soon's we finish lickin' them damn Yanks, I'm gittin' me fo'-five boys an' some guns an' whup out the plantation folks like you'd whup dogs out'n a meat house. Ain't no one lookin'. Git them boots."

"Ain't dast to. 'Sides, they shot through top the ankle. I'll git me better ones. Right smart of daid Yanks, and I'll git better off'n 'em."

The two moved out of sight. De Mérac stirred cautiously. It was close to dawn, so far as he could tell, and bitterly cold. For a second he could not recall where he was. Then his eyes fell on the stone wall, some thirty yards away. Men in gray moved about it, laden with armloads of blue clothing, boots, ponchos. His eyes went higher, climbed Marye's Heights. There was the white-fronted house, the massed batteries. From a high pole the red flag, blue-barred, snapped derisively in the keen wind.

Failure! Realization brought no shock to him. He knew that he had tasted its bitterness hours before by the flat-chested houses off Hanover Street. He moved his legs, his arms. They responded. Cautiously he felt himself from head to foot. There was a spot on his left side many times as sore as a raw blister, a spot that ached far worse than any bruise. But he could find no blood, no other seat of pain beyond a few burns and abrasions.

He raised himself on his elbows and his chest seemed to fly apart in a fit of coughing that brought sweat to his face. His throat filled. He spat and there was a dark blotch on the snow. Clotted blood, produced by whatever shock had struck his ribs. Nothing serious, he was sure. His head ached viciously, the raw band still clung to the inside of his throat, and breathing was an agony. But he was alive. A few hours would heal him, fit him for the field again.

The Rifles! He propped himself higher. Right, left, and to the rear, bodies sprawled, naked or half-naked, and ragged gray men were still prowling among them. A few feet ahead of him a completely naked body lay like a great cross. It lay flat, head thrown back, arms flung wide and heels together. Hands, feet, and side were bloody. In a gesture that he had rarely used since childhood, de Mérac crossed himself. It was the Jew, Greenbaum.

He rallied himself to crawl toward the stiff figure. Then running feet swept toward him and he fell back quickly. Scuds of gray men carrying bits of Union equipment raced back toward the stone wall. He lay stiffly as he could. If they thought him dead, they might plunder him, leave him to freeze. Alive, he would be taken prisoner. But the men stopped for nothing. They laughed excitedly, shouted to each other, "Yanks back thar goin' to start shootin'. Light for thet wall, Clubby. Jesus—looky thet monkey-hat. Red-top. Must a been Phil Kearny's ol' boys hit us las' night!"

A few scattering shots came from the direction of Fredericksburg. The last of the Southerners dove for shelter. De Mérac lay still and thought. He wished that he could get near enough at least to cover Greenbaum's face. However, his first duty was to return to the Rifles, wherever they might be. Painfully he sat up, gathered himself, and started to rise.

A musket cracked and snow spurted close to his hand. Someone yelled, "Lay easy, Yank. You ain't goin' nowhars!"

He sank back, shivering. Then out of the corner of his eye he saw a hummock a few yards to the rear. With infinite pain that started him sweating through the bitter cold again, he gathered himself, braced arms and legs, lunged toward the hummock, rolled when he hit the ground. Two shots echoed. The pain from his movement was so knifelike that he thought at least one bullet had struck him. He looked around. He lay in a miniature of the sunken road, a path, beaten by generations of feet and dipping behind the hummock. Here he was hidden from the sight of the Rebels, and partially sheltered from the wind.

Carefully he sat up, secure, and stripped off sopping jacket and shirt. On his left ribs a huge, shiny raw spot showed. Its center was pinkish, but the edges and the flesh around it were turning livid. He couldn't understand it. A broken strap tumbled from his shoulder and a strange mass of leather, metal, and glass dropped to the ground—his field glasses and their case. His injury was suddenly clear. A spent ball of some light-caliber field piece had crushed case and instrument against his side hard enough to produce prolonged coma. It might have cracked a rib or two. Wayne could tell him at a glance Or—could Wayne? Was the graying doctor one of the stripped bodies on the white plain? At any rate the case had probably saved his life. It had been saved again when the foraging Southerner had handled him roughly, trying to get at his boots. The bumping and jolting had probably set circulation in motion again to end the unconsciousness that would have been followed by freezing. Had they had time to take anything? By some miracle his Colt still hung from its lanyard. The Austerlitz sword, its leather scabbard scored and furrowed, lay against his thigh.

Nothing remained now but to get back. He tried to work along the path, hoping to see cover that would lead him at right angles to it. But the path petered out and the sight of his head brought shots whistling uncomfortably close to him. He wriggled painfully back to the hummock. He was pinned there until dark.

Vingt dieux! If Lee should counterattack, a move which he surely would be justified in making! He huddled closer, listening for the warning cannonade, the sudden drum of boots, that would send the gray legions sweeping across the path. A fever crept over him and he began to doze. During the endless, dragging cold hours, musketry broke out on both sides. Artillery joined in. Then the firing died away, to be resumed in short-lived, nervous outbursts.

When the early darkness fell, the fever had gone. He felt weak and empty, every motion racked him, but his head was clear. He knew that he had to move and move quickly, for the end of light would bring another swarm of foraging Rebels down from the heights. His body bent to the left to ease the strain on that side, he crept away toward the stir of Fredericksburg and the Rappahannock. Lanterns began to flick over the ground and he heard the voices of surgeons, the creak of ambulance wheels.

When he felt that he was nearing the ravine from which the Rifles had launched their attack he slowed his pace even more. He knew the danger of startling a nervous sentry. He tumbled into a hollow where his boots clacked against the sabers of three dead gunners. Cautiously he looked out. He could just make out a kneeling figure, musket resting across a tense forearm. He gathered his breath, cried, "What outfit?" His tones rang strangely in his ears. He feared that shock, fatigue, and exposure had increased his accent and made of the phrase "Wad oudt-feed?" At least, it wouldn't sound Alabama or Georgia.

The figure stiffened, flattened to the ground. A voice called, "Who the hell you?"

"Commanding officer, Rochambeau Rifles. Wounded. Returning."

"Get over here with your hands where I c'n see 'em."

De Mérac advanced warily, saw the blur of a face studying him. "O.K. Red-top, huh? I mean, *sir*. Picket of C Company, 3rd U.S. Regular. Head straight back. Keep hollering for Sergeant Connor, C of the 3rd."

De Mérac limped on through a thick network composed largely of Sykes's division of Regular Army troops. When he struck into the outer reaches of Hanover Street, his side burned so he had to stop and rest, his right hand pressing against the crude pad that he had rigged back by the hummock. The hand increased the pressure on the raw spot but also took some of the strain off the muscles of that side. He kept on down the street, passed the first houses. No lights showed; the only smell was the familiar one of river damp, stale wood smoke, stale powder smoke, the stench of wounds, and the cloying reek of chloroform. A colony of the dead. Men slipped past him furtively in twos and threes. Small columns slouched by. Horsemen loomed in the darkness. The few men who stopped at his repeated questions mumbled unintelligibly and pushed on.

By a side street he caught a sudden fresh smell, a familiar smell, the sharp, lively whiff of Algerian tobacco. In a darkened doorway stood a solid, erect figure, feet apart and shoulders back. The glow of a pipe lit up a bristling beard. De Mérac pulled himself up and his voice shook. "Sergeant Major Rapp!"

The figure jerked backward and with the motion Rapp's shell of discipline cracked. Scarred hands caught de Mérac's and the old soldier babbled, *"Mais c'est vous, c'est vous!* I, myself, who speak to you now, saw—ah, *qu'on est content!* Ah—you are not one to be killed. Thus did I observe to the Sergeant Goriot, who agreed."

"And you, Rapp—they could not dent your iron, old soldier?"

Rapp made a hoarse noise in his throat. "*Les sales Arabes!* No—they ruffle my beard, they curry my back with their *sacré feu d'enfer*. More they could not do."

"And the regiment?"

Discipline threw its clamps back about Melchior Rapp, Sergeant Major of New York Volunteers. "*Parfaitement, mon capitaine!* It finds itself down this little *boyau, tout droit.*" He saluted and stepped back.

De Mérac leaned against the building to ease his side. "*Un moment.* Who commands?"

"Le Capitaine Shea."

"Captain Corvisart, then?"

"*Mort sur le champ d'honneur*—that sick one who must borrow legs to walk and who would not stay behind."

"The commanders of companies?"

"Lieutenant Bordagaray lives. Of the old companies, the Sergeant Cormier commands DuBosc's, the Corporal St. Anselme that of Péguy. Among the Germans, Lieutenant Haffner; for the Irish, the Sergeant O'Callahan. Private Regnier leads those left of Chanel's, the Capitaine LeNoir gives orders to five men and a bugler. The Capitaine Bolton, that big one, is gone, a fact which troubles me, for now the Lieutenant Rohde commands what is left."

De Mérac felt a sudden stab, deeper than the burn of his side. He caught Rapp's arm. "Sergeant Major! You say nothing of H Company."

Rapp's tone was aggrieved. "Eh, *mon capitaine!* Had accidents arrived, would I not have mentioned *ce bon vieux* Lieutenant Georges the first? *Ah, baste!* No. He lives and will, no doubt, soon greet his Monsieur McArdle."

De Mérac said, "Ah!" Then he asked about others. Dr. Wayne was safe and tending wounded in a near-by cellar. And Father Doyle?

Rapp shook his head sadly. "He will live say the *tou-*

bibs. But the bullet, it lodged itself in his throat and they fear that it may arrive that *ce bon père* will not speak again. A fact," Rapp went on seriously, "which may be grave for a *curé* who, while he has little to do, has much to say."

De Mérac felt his throat tighten. "*Foi d'honneur.* Doctors shall be brought from New York. Father Doyle has made himself like a flag to Catholic, Protestant, and atheist."

"*Parfaitement, mon capitaine*," rumbled Rapp.

De Mérac felt his way down the street. In the darkness he sensed that there were men about him, many men. Then he saw a sliver of light and made his way toward it. His eyes suddenly blurred. George Force sat on the curbstone, the center of a thick knot of men. A beam from the dark lantern fell on his hands that held a pair of shears and a cardboard diamond. Across his knees was spread a red artillery saddle blanket. As the shears cut the pattern he was saying, "Cold camp tonight. No fires, because the Rebs'll shell the town if they see too much light. Never mind that. Every man grab a Kearny patch. Rip off your old one and get the new one right on. Remember after Second Bull Run the old man said we were still Phil Kearny's men? Well, that still goes. Stuff extra ones in your pockets for the boys who'll straggle in later. We may look like tramps from the neck down when we fall in tomorrow, but by God from the vizors up we'll be the same crowd that Kearny took in at Malvern."

De Mérac said, "You have a patch for the 'old man,' *mon vieux?*" Then he thought that the look on George's face was worth every physical suffering which he had undergone in the last twenty-four hours. His friend shot out of the light of the lantern, became a blur in the dark, a blur that muttered again and again: "I knew it! I knew you'd make it. I—I—oh, but God, I wasn't sure. You got nicked? Here—take my arm. I know where Wayne is."

"I can wait. You are safe, George?"

Relief drove the air from George's lungs. "Lucky as a pair of loaded dice. Barked in a couple of places. That's all." He became serious again. "Look, John, I haven't seen Moe Greenbaum."

"No," said de Mérac, and told him of the crosslike figure in the snow.

George hunched his shoulders. "Hell, I never actually knew a Jew before. He was real. Too damn real to be smashed against a stone wall." His voice rose. "I've been trying to get the whole damn picture out of my mind. All those poor devils that had tried it before. We walked over them. And, oh God Almighty—all that Goddamned brainless slaughter and we're just where we started from! What's it all for? Why does a man like Burnside have the power to massacre a man like Corvisart or Bolton? Look at Father Doyle—the first priest I ever really knew. Hear who brought him in? The atheist LePage and Burton, who used to sell Methodist tracts. Now Doyle's in that house over there, suffering like hell but holding up his crucifix and making signs to any boy that wants to confess to him, making signs because if he talks his throat'll rip open again. Burnside! Halleck! Know what I'd like to do?"

De Mérac painfully raised his hand and laid it on Force's shoulder. "Yes—to help me find out the state of the regiment."

George picked up the dark lantern. Its slice of light cut in a wide arc, lit up men in the street, on the curb, lying in doorways. De Mérac tried to form a quick estimate of the strength in this street. Seventy—eighty—perhaps one hundred and ten or even one hundred and twenty. "And where are the other companies?" he asked.

George said bitterly, "You're looking at every sound man left in the Rochambeau Rifles!"

De Mérac threw back his head. "George, they are still the Rochambeau Rifles and they are still the same men for whom you were cutting the Kearny patch. Ah, *mon ami*, blunders do not change the value of what we fight for. You knew that when you stole the artillery blanket to revive the flame in our men. Finish your cutting and tell me where I find Wayne."

In the flare of a smoky lamp, de Mérac lay on a heap

of straw in a cellar while Wayne deftly dressed the deep contusion. De Mérac closed his eyes. There could be no more fighting for a while. Lee's only chance to counter-attack had passed. There would be rest. He would have George and Craig Wilson with him. He would build up the Rifles somehow. Then—then there would be leave. Pain ebbed as a deep glow spread through him. Washington! He and Louise...

Wayne touched his shoulder. "You're all fixed, Cap. See me tomorrow." De Mérac sat up. His eyes fell on a blue figure crouching in a corner by the lamp, a blue figure that carefully drew an oiled wick through the bore of a rifle. The light shone down into intent eyes, but gave them no light. Dekdebrun knew that the war went on.

XV

Lettre de Cachet

A LOG city sprang up along the Rappahannock, spreading deep inland from Falmouth and Stafford Heights. Smoke drifted from tarbarrel chimneys, from cat-and-clay chimneys, from huts and cookhouses, eddied over the sullen river and spread to the farther shore where Lee's army lay, coldly watchful. An odd mood hovered over both forces. Pickets blazed away at each other across the current. But at dusk and dawn, boats poled furtively out, met in midstream or passed each other with a wave. Yankee coffee was traded for Rebel tobacco, New York papers for those of Richmond. Captain Shea of the Rifles, muffled in a gray cloak, paddled himself across, a case of whiskey at his feet, and spent a day with the officers of Company I, 8th Alabama, who called themselves the Emerald Guards. De Mérac dropped in at the mess of the 20th Massachusetts where a crowd of young officers drank punch and roared out, "We Don't Serve Bread with One Fish-Ball!" Two lieutenants wearing ill-fitting Union overcoats rose at de Mérac's entrance. Captain Codman introduced them as Claiborne Howell, Class of '58, and Ransford Gaines, '56. "Gaines roomed below me in Hollis senior year," explained Codman. "He's the man whose bull pup bit the dean the night we took him into Pudding." Nothing was said about military matters, nor did de Mérac hear any pledge given by the young Southerners not to take advantage of what they might see or hear. He was sure that no such promise was necessary, just as Shea had talked only of personalities after his visit to the Emerald Guards across the river. Yet during daylight hours it was not safe to expose oneself close by the Rappahannock.

De Mérac spent a deliriously happy Christmas with the Duanes. It was agreed that no date be set for the wedding until the military probabilities of the next months were clearer. It would be held, however, in Trinity Church in New York, and Louise showed him clever sketches of her trousseau, flicking her left hand happily to display the winking diamond from Hammond's.

At a tea at the Russian Legation, while Louise was getting her wraps, de Mérac caught sight of a mass of red-gold hair. He felt an odd pang as he recognized Gail Shortland looking as though her whole life had been spent in an atmosphere of brittle teacups and brittler cakes. He checked an impulse to go and speak to her, but as he moved away she turned and her eyes met his. They were clear and gray as ever, but a sudden shadow fell over them. She smiled mechanically and her hands clenched into tight little fists. She took a step backward, but a line of guests, moving toward one of the long tables, cut off her retreat, forced her slowly toward de Mérac.

Her eyelids flickered and the tip of her tongue ran over her lips. Her smile was even stiffer as she said, "I really did mean to write you about your engagement, Captain de Mérac. The papers were full of it."

He bowed. "Of your good wishes I was sure."

"Of course. Ah—I saw you earlier here. Was—was that Miss Duane with you? She's really very pretty. I hope you will both be very happy." A tall officer stepped up beside her. "Oh—this is Major Cruise of the Oneida Rangers. Captain de Mérac. Now Ralph, we must hurry.

Really, I've got to be going. Come along. Good-bye and good luck, Captain de Mérac."

He watched her vanish in the crowd, his eyes grave and a little resentful, as though he were questioning himself. "Ah—she is *épatante*. But, *bigre!* She permits this species of Cruise to escort her to a tea and yet would never so much as drive with me. In what way is that *sacré* major more acceptable than I?" Then he saw Louise, bewitching in soft furs that framed her piquant face, and all shadows fled from his eyes.

When he returned to camp, he found that twenty-two recruits had been sent down from New York. This new acquisition, together with returned wounded and stragglers, raised the strength of the Rifles to nearly one hundred and sixty. He did not like the looks of the men. To promote recruiting, cities and counties and states, even individuals, were offering bounties for enlistments and some men could collect as much as four hundred dollars on taking the oath. The older volunteers shared his misgivings and sang derisively:

> I'm a raw recruit with a brand-new suit
> Five hundred dollars bounty,
> And I've come down from Darbytown
> To fight for Oxford County!

Rapp licked his lips as he watched the new men file in and soon the camp echoed to screams of "*Sacré*-damn, *bleu!* Do you then imagine—"

George Force took over the duties of adjutant and plodded through his work resignedly. There was no leave for him, since Jonas Chase had spirited Dora away to off-season Saratoga on the pretext that her health demanded the change. George shrugged. He had become used to waiting in his army months. Waiting for pay, waiting for rations, waiting for mail, waiting for orders, waiting to attack, waiting to be relieved. He could wait, probably would have to wait a long time for Dora. It was all part of the same pattern.

Past mid-January, in a thaw that swept in on driving rain clouds, the army suddenly moved, aiming for a crossing higher up the Rappahannock. George saw mules drown in mud, saw men drown in mud. He saw great pontoon trains bogged over their wheels, saw light batteries whose muzzles rested flush with the mud while drivers cursed and struggled to save their floundering horses. Men drowned, men died of exhaustion. The army turned back without crossing and crept away to its log city about Falmouth. A few days later, a thousand orderly rooms received word that Burnside no longer commanded and that orders in future would be signed by Joseph Hooker of Hadley, in Massachusetts. "What do you think of that, John?" asked Wilson, frowning over the order.

De Mérac sighed. "Of him, Kearny always spoke well—as a fighter. But even Marshal Ney scarcely shone as a commander." He turned back to his letter, then looked up. "Louise wishes to present her respects to you, Craig, and wonders if we may have enough officers at the wedding so that she may leave the church under an arch of swords as at British army weddings."

"Respectfully referred to Dudley Pelham," said Wilson. He thought that Cossacks and lances would be his choice. You always saw pictures of them escorting people to Siberia.

There was a light powdering of snow outside in which the steps of the sentries posted at the door of the orderly room crunched crisply. George sat close by the stove, his fet resting on Mr. McArdle, and chewed a pencil thoughtfully. On the other side of the stove, Bordagaray protested, "But, *mon bon*, as adjutant, you need think only of one regiment. And—as we are now, of little more than a full-strength company."

George ruffled papers and shoved his kepi back on his head. "Sure. But I want to see what the whole thing looks like. When we first start drilling, back in '61, I tried to see how the company tied onto a regiment and the regiment onto a brigade and so on. The whole damn thing's much clearer if you do that."

"One may not say no," observed Bordagaray, gently

touching the Fredericksburg scar that showed livid on his chin.

George poised his pencil. "Then look here. A Union soldier eats three pounds of rations each day. That's Q.M. figures. Add Q.M. supplies and ordnance stuff and that makes four pounds to be carried each day for each man. Now each horse or mule eats twenty-five pounds a day and *that* has to be toted to him. Our six-mule hitch can lug two thousand pounds or enough for five hundred men for one day, *if* the hitch can make the round trip— depot to troops—in one day. If they need two days for the trip, then four wagons for each five hundred men, eight for a thousand, or eight hundred for a hundred thousand."

Bordagaray said banteringly, "Our regimental Archimedes! The figures form in your brain, then?"

"I'm primarily a businessman," grinned George. "Now let's get on. Take an army of fifty thousand men with eight thousand cavalry and artillery horses and mules."

"Where will you find such an army, save in the French military books that our General Halleck translates at three cents the page?" asked the Basque.

"This is my army. Anyhow, your mules themselves eat twenty-five pounds a day, not counting preserve cans and my spare socks, so you've got to have extra wagons for *their* rations. After that—"

The door snapped open and Wilson came in with his light, quick step. His high-boned face looked worried and he breathed as though he had been hurrying. "Look here, you two, know anything about John?"

George stuck his pencil behind his ear. "Only that he's probably enjoying the smiles of la Duane. Why?"

"Look at that," Wilson dropped a telegraph form on the table. George picked it up and Bordagaray peered over his shoulder. They read, "Terribly alarmed. No sign of John. Has anything happened? Please, please answer." It was signed by Louise Duane.

George stared. "Hell, he left for Washington four days ago. Maybe some smart girl's kidnaped him, someone like that pretty nurse at the hospital."

Wilson threw himself into a flimsy chair. "Wish I

373

could feel that way about it." He took off his kepi and ruffled his graying hair. "Look here—just among us. None of us saw John the day he left. It was hours before reveille—that is, unless you did, Lucien." He looked at the Basque.

"I? Not at all. At that moment I was dreaming that I stood by the stage door of the Théâtre Français in New York, a bouquet of roses in my hand and thoughts in my head—what thoughts!"

Wilson hitched closer. "Then listen to this. When I got the telegram, I called Louvel. He didn't know anything, so we went into John's hut." He beat out the slow words with his hands. "His saber's there. His holster. Nearly all his kit's there. Louvel thinks there's some shaving stuff, toothbrush, and so on missing, but he can't be sure. John had such a lot of that sort of stuff. *And*—that new uniform's still hanging behind the sacking curtain at the head of his bunk."

"*Bordel de dieu!*" muttered Bordagaray while George sat silent, his face emptied of expression by surprise.

"Any ideas?" asked Wilson.

"Oh, the devil!" cried George. "There's *some* explanation."

"For example?" put in Bordagaray.

Wilson rested his forehead on his fist. "I've thought of a million and each is worse than the one before."

"Oh, Lord," cried George. "There *must* be a right one. Look—supposing he'd lost his pass—"

"That is not the way of our Jean," murmured the Basque.

"Or, it was stolen then. The provost held him up. They've been tough as hell since Joe Hooker took over."

"That is so," said Wilson slowly. "Damned unlikely, though."

"What *isn't* unlikely? Tell me that," growled George.

Wilson stretched out his legs and jammed his hands into his pockets. "It's only a few hours from Acquia to Washington. He'd have gone straight to the Duanes. So, if he was picked up, it would have been right away. And, through routine, Corps, Division, and Brigade would

374

have been notified by telegraph. Word would have come to us from Brigade."

"You feel, Major, that our exquisite friend and admirer, Dudley Pelham, would have galloped, *ventre à terre*, to notify us?" said Bordagaray.

Wilson smiled bitterly. "No doubt. Just the same, George, you've got the first idea that gives us something to work on." He got up quickly. "I'll go to Brigade right away."

George shook his head. "I wouldn't, Craig. Dunn's the only friend we've got there and he's on sick leave. Brevoort thinks that Pelham wants to get rid of him."

Wilson nodded. "Guess you're right. I'll get to Brevoort at Division. Maybe I'll be able to see Birney himself. You'll keep this to yourselves, of course. Try and think of likely leads, both of you. I'll be back as soon as I can!" He left the hut quickly.

Bordagaray threw out his hands. *"Mais c'est tout à fait ridicule! C'est incroyable! Enfin, c'est goddam bouleversant!"*

George sprang to his feet and paced up and down. "Damn, damn, *damn!* He can't have been picked up anyway. Look at the truck he left behind! It's—it's—oh, *hell!* How long do you think it'll take Craig to get back here?"

Craig Wilson returned in half an hour, his face graver than ever. He shook his head slowly in answer to the questioning looks that met him. "Division doesn't know a damn thing. Birney's in Washington but Brevoort told me that so far's they know, everything's all right. Brevoort'll keep quiet, of course, and he'll send word the instant he finds out anything."

George kicked a chair. "And in the meantime we just wait? God damn it, someone knows."

"For example?" said Wilson. "Anyway, we three and Brevoort are the only ones who know there's anything wrong."

People began to guess, however. In the camp of the Rifles, men looked inquiringly at each other, speculated in low tones. A rumor spread that de Mérac had deserted and was now in command of a Southern regiment in Fredericksburg. Brady, roaring with rage, tracked the rumor down to the whispering Rohde and publicly dumped him in the mules' watering trough. Colonel Pride, looking like a bewildered child despite his heavy beard, tramped over from the Indiana camp and talked long and low with Wilson and George. He chafed his big hands. "It just ain't so, Craig. I've known John since the brigade was formed."

"Of course it isn't," snapped George. "But *where* the hell *is* he? We get telegrams from Louise Duane and her father about every day."

Pride said slowly, "When they opened up Indiana, it was pretty wild country. Folks used to get lost or caught by Indians. But there was always some old-timer who knew the country like a book and he'd start out and pretty soon he'd pick up the feller's trace."

Wilson frowned. "Wish we could find a scout like that now."

"Just an idea I had," said Pride. "I was thinking the feller that knows more'n anyone else about our army's that Russian friend of John's—Labanieff. Kind of a book-soldier, but he gets to hear a lot."

Wilson sprang to his feet. "You've got it! By God, you have. I'll write the whole story as far as we know it. Someone's got to take it by hand to Labanieff. I'll see Brevoort about a pass for someone."

George ran his fingers wearily through his hair. "I've got a crazy idea it may be better if it's someone outside of Brigade, Division, or even Corps that takes it. Tell you what, I'll go over to the 2nd Mass. Cavalry. John knows a Captain Adams there—you know, his old man's Minister to England."

"Think he's safe?" asked Pride.

George laughed shortly. "Safe? He's so damned New England he won't order à la carte at a restaurant for fear he'll be telling the waiter what he likes. He'll help us find someone to go."

Wilson moved to the table. "I'll scratch out a letter and you better be getting ready to go over there. We can't waste time. God above, what *can* have happened?"

The Army of the Potomac, dazed, battered, straggling, suddenly felt the touch of a skilled hand. The men cheered handsome Joe Hooker while he guided the disjointed mass into a single, pulling whole, as an expert mule driver gathers a wayward hitch and sets the strong shoulders leaning against collars and breast straps. There were inspections, reviews. Discipline was tightened. New clothing was issued and food flowed more plentifully. In every camp, forges roared while armorers and smiths toiled at musket locks or clanged their hammers against glowing horseshoes.

General Butterfield, Hooker's chief of staff, rode through the army and noticed how the men who wore the Kearny patch carried themselves—proudly and a little aloof from the rest. He decreed that all corps should wear some distinctive insignia and soon the banks of the Rappahannock were thick with kepis and slouch hats that bore the circle of the 1st Corps, the cloverleaf of the IInd, the Maltese Cross of the Vth, the Greek Cross of the VIth, the Crescent of the XIth. The IIIrd retained the Kearny patch. For distinction within all corps, the Ist Division wore a red badge, the second, white and the third, blue. Thus, Birney's division became the first of the IIIrd Corps, now commanded by Dan Sickles, and hence had the right to cling to the original red diamond—the Kearny patch.

George and Wilson went through their duties mechanically, their minds obsessed with the mystery of de Mérac, on which no ray of light fell. Then after anxious days, Wilson received a cryptic telegram from Labanieff and went at once to George's hut. "He's coming here tonight. His telegram sounds pretty foggy but it looks as if he had news."

George sprang to his feet. "About time! We'll use the headquarters hut and put a guard around it. Who else ought to be there?"

Wilson pulled at his mustache. "Besides us? I'd say Bordagaray. He's senior captain. Shea, of course. Now there's Colonel Pride. He thinks a lot of John and, as a matter of fact, he thought of using Labanieff. I'll send him a note."

"Right! When does Labanieff get here?"

"Seven o'clock train from Acquia."

George drummed impatiently on the wall. "Not till then? Good God, it's only five-thirty now!"

Candlelight shone down on Labanieff's green and gold, for he had thought that the occasion called for the full dress of the Tambov Hussars. Near him, at the long table, was Wilson, outwardly composed, but with lips and fists closed tightly. Beyond Wilson, George shifted and fidgeted as he scowled at the guttering candles. Colonel Pride hunched silent in a corner, his eyes on the Russian and his fingers busy with his beard. Shea was flushed to the tip of his long nose and his eyes were smoldering as he tilted back and forth in his chair. Bordagaray sat close by George, his mouth compressed.

Labanieff, his hands on the table in front of him, inclined his head toward Wilson, the senior officer present. "As I said in my telegram, dear Craig-Wilson, I come with full intelligence." A dead hush fell over the room and five intent faces turned toward him. He savored the increased attention and went on. "The affair—ah, it is odd!"

Pride sputtered impatiently. "Hell, we know that. What we're after is—where is he?"

Labanieff drew a deep breath and looked about in triumph. "That I may tell you. He is in a cell in Fort LaFayette in New York Harbor."

George shouted "Christ!" and sprang to his feet. Pride clumped forward. "He can't be!" Shea exploded in a thick brogue, "Shpawn of a thousand divils! Who's after putting him there?"

Wilson brightened a little. "A question of law? Well, there's a chance for me to do something. I'd better go right up and see him."

"No," said Labanieff. "He is what you call 'held solitary.' We say 'incommunicado.' One may neither see nor communicate with him."

"Good God," cried Wilson. "On what charges?"

"None. He is merely held."

"But they can't do that," stormed George. "The Articles of War say that charges must be preferred at once or they have to let him go."

"Exactly," said Wilson. "You must have made a mistake, Colonel."

"I could wish that I had."

Bordagaray said quietly, "And there is more to your story, Colonel?"

Labanieff's face grew grave. "Much more, my friends. Craig-Wilson, you spoke of charges. There are none, as I remarked. But if there were, they might run thus: at the affair at Frayser's Farm, he sacrificed his American companies to shield the foreign-born by sending the former to butchery in a cul-de-sac."

Wilson and George shot to their feet. The major shouted, "No! No! By God, no! Dalbiac did that. I was there. Five companies went in—three French and two American. And John went after them."

George pounded the table. "And John brought us back. I was in that column. I can prove—I'm ready to swear—"

The Russian shook his head sadly. "And Dalbiac is dead. No order of his in writing exists. As I say, there are no charges, but were there such, ill-disposed ones would argue that of course you support your friend while slandering a dead man."

"What else?" snarled Shea, his eyes blazing.

"There was your very pretty little affair at Pingree's Store where the Rebel cavalry was so neatly ambushed. Returning from Pingree's, fugitive blacks followed you. One or more of these, our Jean permitted to return to their masters."

There was a tap at the door and a voice whispered, "May I come in?" Colonel Pride lifted the latch and Father Doyle limped in, leaning on a stick and with his throat heavily bandaged. "It's no real right I have here. But he was a friend," he said.

George shoved up a chair for him. "We ought to have thought of you in the first place, Chaplain. Colonel, will you sum up for him?"

Labanieff spoke rapidly, checking off the points on his thick fingers. When he had finished, Father Doyle whispered, "Letting the blacks go? It's what any humane man, Christian or pagan, would have done. What sin are they finding there?"

"Yes," urged Shea. "What's in it? Where's the harm, letting the poor black gossoons go home?"

Wilson said wearily, "I can answer that. Since slaves are legally held to be Rebel property, they are contraband of war, like foundry supplies or mules or cotton bales. I've never agreed with the interpretation."

"No doubt," said Labanieff. "Now—back of all this is, of course, General Pelham. His part in it puzzles me. One knew, of course, that he disliked Jean. But this passes the bounds of ordinary dislike."

Wilson ran his hand wearily over his forehead. "I can give you the answer there, Colonel. Pelham belongs to a group, and I regret to state that it's not a small one, which lives on the hatred of foreigners. People like him were even numerous enough to start a political party—the Know-Nothings. Von Stoeckl can probably tell you a lot about them. Any man with an odd-sounding name, any creed other than a rather primitive Protestantism, set them off into a sort of diseased fury."

Labanieff nodded. "Ah! One begins to understand. Now, Pelham would like to have destroyed Jean long ago. The question remained, however, who should command the Rifles. At last he feels that you, *mon cher* Craig-Wilson, are competent."

"He's crazy as a spring rabbit," snapped Wilson. "This stuff comes naturally to John. It doesn't to me."

"Pelham is not of that opinion!"

Pride growled, "But how did all this stuff, that'd been lying around like spilled oats, get swept up?"

Labanieff fluffed out his beard. "Me, I compare the heap to snow, rather than oats. Several pairs of hands have shaped it into a ball like little boys along the Neva."

George crouched in his chair. "Whose hands?" he asked.

Labanieff cocked his head. "One pair was very pretty. It belonged to Baroness Lisa von Horstmar."

"That won't go," cried George. "John wouldn't have anything to do with her."

"She helped *because* he would have nothing to do with her. But in the past, there had been *une affaire passionelle*. She wished to revive it. Jean would only bury it. So she made semblance of forgetting, all the while seething within."

Pride rubbed his hands nervously. "I've seen her around camp. I don't know much about women like that but I guess—well, I guess she'd be quite an experience."

Wilson smiled wryly. "Why, Colonel Pride! You shock me. Go on, Colonel. What did she do?"

"First, she acquired a *bel-ami* of Pelham's staff, a young man named Conway. This was not difficult, as Colonel Pride suggests. She played on his jealousy, I am told, always comparing him to Jean and hinting that soon her old love will supplant the new. Hence, Conway comes to hate Jean more than he hates the worst Rebel. The Baroness, by no means a stupid woman, plies him with tales of Jean's past and present, tales which can be viewed, if one wishes, in a doubtful light, to pass on to Pelham. The question of the Negroes at Pingree's Store reached him through that channel."

Shea muttered, "But there's nothing in that to put John in a cell."

"True, my dear Dan-Shea. So another pair of hands comes into the picture, the hands of a man of politics. His name is Cusler and my Minister, von Stoeckl, assures me that Cusler was offended, as Jean was not willing to use the Rifles to further his political plots. He shows von Horstmar and Pelham how the affair of the blacks may be used to avenge the slight to one and to crush the hated foreigner for the other."

"And Cusler?" asked Bordagaray, eyes on the Russian.

"To the Radicals of Congress he goes. Ah, it leaps to the eye, that move. For they are in terror, so von Stoeckl informs me, owing to the recent elections which went badly for them. To these zealots he says in effect, 'Here one finds a Union officer who hurls the poor African back into slavery, denies him the sacred freedom which you and all true patriots wish to hold out to him, which our great President has promised.'"

Pride rocked back and forth on his heels. "*Now* the cows are coming into the pasture! Go on."

Labanieff spread out his hands. "There was anger among those Radicals, who, in turn, infected the Moderates. To fan this anger, Cusler expanded his tale. 'Such a man, you have kept in high command through your criminal negligence. Have you not heard that native-born troops were slaughtered by this man's order which also caused the death of that hero-foe of slavery, Colonel Dalbiac? But first, foremost, eternally, reflect on his action of denying the blessings of freedom to our black brethren, of deliberately thwarting the aims that you voice on behalf of our great sovereign people.'" He paused and looked along the table.

Wilson's hands worked. "It could be done," he muttered. "Not the least doubt in the world."

George sprang to his feet, slamming his fist on the table. "Let's get started on this. By God, we're not going to sit around while they play tricks like that on John!"

"*Doucement*," said Labanieff. "This may all lead into quarters where none of us can reach."

"What! Are you trying to tell us we *can't* help John?"

"You recall, perhaps, the case—no, no, I do not hark back to Clausewitz or Jomini—of your own General Stone—Charles Stone—in the fall of '61? No? Then let me give you the merest facts. After the affair of Ball's Bluff, in which he was little concerned, the general disappears. There are no charges, you conceive. But he is held—as is our Jean held at this moment. After many months he is released. Still there are no charges. He can learn nothing. No apology or explanation is made to him. He has no command. Indeed, I happen to know that Hooker wishes him for his Chief of Staff. But, being out of favor with the politicians, Stone is still idle."

"Yes!" cried George. "I begin to remember about Stone. He wasn't radical enough to suit people like Zach Chandler, so they just shelved him. But John! Good God, he just did his work and to hell with politics."

"I do not say," observed Labanieff, "but I point out

that while he may not concern himself with politicians, politicians may concern themselves with *him*."

Shea pounded the arm of his chair. "High or low, the hell-born devils that did this have got me to answer to."

Father Doyle whispered, "We'll best do nothing to prejudice John's case."

"You got any ideas of what we *can* do, Chaplain?" asked Pride.

"Only a first step to suggest. The story must be told in the right place. And I'm thinking there's only *one* right place."

Pride stared at him. "You mean—take it right to the big wigwam?"

Doyle leaned forward. "Tell the President the story of what's being done to one of his boys. He'll not be caring if the boy was born in Sangamon County or County Meath or in France. He'll only see it's a black story and a damnable story and blacker and more damnable for the doing of it's mostly in the hands of blinded men who think they're doing right. Yes. Go to the President."

Labanieff sighed. "I refer again to the case of General Stone. Again and again this has been brought to the eyes of the President. He finds himself powerless, as I am assured in the best of quarters."

"Damn!" said Wilson. "If that can happen to a Massachusetts West Pointer—well, I just don't know. The political situation's touch and go right now. These damned elections and the Copperhead strength might tie the President's hands. Yes, Colonel, letting those Negroes go gave Cusler his trump card. The rest just trails along. I'm in favor of following Father Doyle's advice. If it's agreeable to the rest of you, George and I will try to get to the White House. But I'm not hiding the fact that I'm not very sanguine."

George rocked forward in his chair. "At least, we'll be *doing* something." He crashed his elbow onto the table. "Good God, have any of you dared think what John must be going through?"

Louise Duane sat rigidly on the drawing room sofa and stared at Craig Wilson. Her hands were tight-locked in her lap and her lips, still vivid, in a face from which all other color had been drained, worked nervously. She said sharply, "I don't believe it." Then she cried louder, "I don't believe it."

"I'm afraid you'll have to, Louise," he said gently. "I've told it to you just as we had it from Colonel Labanieff ten days ago."

Her white neck quivered and she shut her eyes tightly. "Lord," thought Wilson. "Now it's coming. Wish I'd let George do this." But Louise's dark lashes flew back and they were dry. "Why doesn't someone *do* something?" she asked, her words sounding brittle. "All you've got to do is to *say* none of it's true! Why doesn't he tell them himself?"

Wilson fingered the worn vizor of his kepi. "Didn't I explain, Louise, that, the way he's held, there's no one he can tell *anything*. He won't be allowed to write. That's the main thing for *you* to think about. We've all got plenty to worry about, but you mustn't be upset at not hearing from him. That's really what I wanted to say most of all to you."

She sat up straighter than ever. "But I've *got* to. Got to hear from him. He's my fiancé. Isn't *any*one doing *any*thing?"

Wilson sighed. "I'm trying to get to the President. I'm trying to find the right people to see up on the Hill. We're all doing what we can."

Color flooded her face and she seemed to lose control of herself as though the initial shock had finally lost its power to numb. "It's not enough! If no one else can get anywhere, *I'll* go to the President. I'll go to General Halleck. I'll go to the police." Her eyes widened. "Hasn't anyone thought of going to Monsieur Mercier, the French Minister? Well, *I'll* go to him and at least we'll have *him* doing something."

Wilson said gently, "I know it's hard, Louise. But everything that can be done is being done." He got up from his chair. "Let us handle this—for the moment anyway. I'm going by the White House now to see about an appointment. Don't worry. We'll have him out." Then he added with a sigh, "Lord knows what he'll do then. I wouldn't blame him if he quit the army. Good-bye, my dear. We'll see this through."

Her face cleared suddenly and she held out a small hand. "I hope I didn't sound too upset, Major Wilson, but I've been so worried. And thanks for coming to see me. It's a wonderful relief just to know something. You'll get him out. I know you will."

George Force came out of the converted ballroom where, in the summer of 1862, he had lain helpless with fever. He felt listless and dejected. A classmate, now a captain in the 1st New York Cavalry, whom he had called to see, had sat dazed and blinking in a chair, his jaw muscles working and his hands frantically clutching the arms at any unexpected sound. A heavy shell had burst directly under his horse, shattering the animal. The rider was seemingly untouched but had been left with a stunned mind and vague, almost helpless limbs, a state which struck George as being worse than the horrible mutilations which he had seen. Heavy on his mind was the realization that his brief leave was running out and that he and Wilson seemed to be floundering helplessly in de Mérac's case. He stepped into the broad corridor with its smell of chloroform and medicines and fever, with its nurses who waddled or scurried or teetered in gossiping groups. Sounds and odors deepened his depression. He cheered himself a little with the thought that Dora, steadfast as ever, was back in New York and wrote him whenever possible. Damn it though, waiting was hard.

Down the corridor behind him came a brisk, assured step. A girl called softly. "Lieutenant Force! Oh—Lieutenant Force!"

George turned in surprise. Then he smiled at a slim nurse whose figure the anonymity of the gray coverall could hardly hide, whose hair showed in delicate tendrils under the close-bound towel. "Of course! Nurse Shortland! You put me on the train last year. John de Mérac and I used to speak of you!"

Her gray eyes lit for an instant, then concern darkened them. "I saw your patch as I was coming down the corridor. Then I recognized you." She dropped her voice. "What *is* the truth of that dreadful story?"

George's chin set. "It's not true. You know it."

She dropped her eyes for an instant, raised them quickly. "I—I don't know him well. But I *do* know whatever it is, isn't true. Will you tell me what happened?"

George said slowly, "He likes you. He admires you a lot. I guess he'd want you to know." As though he were repeating an old lesson he told her as much as the regiment knew.

Gail Shortland turned her head away and seemed to listen almost abstractedly, her eyes on the grounds outside where the pale February sun shone. Her face was impassive. Her fingers pleated and unpleated a starched towel that hung at her belt.

When George finished, there was a silence, broken only by the muted stir of the hospital. Her eyes were still on the outer glow. Then she squared her shoulders and her chin lifted. "There's no use in saying how horrible this is. What are you doing about it?"

"Everything we can."

"I'm sure of that." She pinched her lower lip reflectively. "You've probably thought of everything. I was just wondering, though—there's Carl Schurz—the President thinks a lot of him. Why don't you send Captain Hein to General Schurz—you know, German to German."

He said, "We lost Hein—by the tracks by Fredericksburg."

She murmured, "Always they're gone." Then in a more natural tone, "The Duanes are helping, of course."

George shrugged. "I sneaked off and let Craig Wilson see about them."

She glanced quickly at him out of the corner of her eye, started to ask a question, then apparently changed her mind. "We've got to do something, you know."

He said grimly, "Damn it, I guess so. We're all trying. We've been chasing ideas and plans like mules through woods. But Lord, Craig and I had a devil of a time getting away and it's not for long, either. Joe Hooker's got a mighty big kettle to shove onto the fire. Then what can we do?"

"You'll hit on something. And when you do, let me know. I can get leave and I'll stay with my aunt in town. I'll write letters for you, see people for you, do anything you suggest."

George held out his hand. She took it simply. He said, "You can help us a lot. Did you ever meet Colonel Labanieff? I'll tell him about you, although of course he'll take the field as observer as soon as Hooker moves. I'll get him to come out here and see you right away. Another thing—John'd like it if you wrote him."

"But you said he was incommunicado."

"We only guess that, because we don't get answers from him and that's not like John. But we keep on writing, Craig and I and the others. It'd be a good idea if you made two copies and sent one to the Rifles and one to Ford LaFayette."

She nodded quickly. "I'll write tonight. Now I've got to run. Send me word the instant I can help."

George watched her sway gracefully down the corridor until she was out of sight. He slid his kepi over his hair and sighed. "Jesus—why couldn't *she* have been Louise?"

Gail Shortland hurried on, unaware that she held her fingers tight against her temples. "Why didn't I go driving with him—just once? Or to the theater with him—just once? It couldn't have done any harm."

Every morning, as soon as the grudging gap of window detached itself from the surrounding blackness and slowly stood out as a silvery square in the thick stone wall, de Mérac threw off his blankets and braced himself for the shock of the cold floor against his feet. Then he put himself briskly through bayonet drill, using his flimsy chair for a weapon. He lunged, stamped, parried, thrust, swung with simulated butt until he managed to sweat in the dank, chill air of the converted casement that was his cell. It was dangerous to pause for breath, for then his mind began to whirl and spin through a maze of questions as gray and hard and cold as the old stone walls that shut him in. It was better to go on until his knees shook and wrists and elbows turned to water, to vary the bayonet drill with the shadow-boxing he had learned in England.

When he felt sufficiently tired, he stripped, braced himself again, and splashed cold water about, feeling its sting on neck, abdomen, and thighs. By that time, it was light enough to shave, a rite which he performed meticulously. The cracked mirror, wedged into an angle of the bricked-up embrasure which held the window, was enough to guide his razor. Shaving had to be carefully drawn out. If too long a pause followed it, the anesthesia of fatigue wore off. Throat and stomach burned with a forewarning of nausea. Skin turned hot and sore. Nerves of neck, shoulders, and back tightened and tightened until they all seemed drawn into a central knot on the spine, produced a maddening tension that led, if not watched, to a continuous nervous shrugging. With threatened nausea and tension came memories:

Blustering Colonel LaFayette Baker and his armed guards slipping into the hut long before sunrise; the shuttered carriage rolling away toward Acquia Creek, the clop-clop of the troopers' horses, the rigid intentness of the armed guards who sat on the opposite seat, revolvers drawn; "Don't talk; don't ask questions; you'll find out soon enough; you'll find out where you're going when you get there; don't talk"; a sealed cabin and more guards who shook their heads coldly to all questions; the feeling of almost amused exasperation; the inward assurance that, in a few hours, release and apologies would come, leaving only a good story to be told at mess; drawn blinds of a railway carriage; a government launch and the final clang of a heavy cell door; days slipping by; inspections by hard-faced officers (there seemed no other species); the tramp of sentries in the flagged corridor outside; demands for explanation, release, court-martial, legal counsel; "Got no orders about you, except to hold you. No. Forbidden to send or receive mail. No. No newspapers allowed. Books? Nothing about them, I guess, long as you pay for 'em. Your money belt's to the orderly room. No, I told you *twicet*. No charges here yet."

Books, which were first carefully scrutinized down in the orderly room. Chateaubriand's *René*. Hugo's *Les Misérables*. Théophile Gautier's *Émaux et Camées*. Nat Willis's *Paul Fane*. Henry Longfellow's *The Seaside and the Fireside*.

Bald fiction or romantic, essays, poems—each form of the printed word had to be bent and hammered into a sharp hook on which the mind might be fixed for an hour or so, halted in its hot race round and round, the race which it followed like a horse in the riding ring at Saumur, being groomed for the paces of the *haute école*.

It was better, sometimes, to stare out of the misted barred window that looked across The Narrows to Staten Island and the low bastions of Fort Tompkins, to time the sweep of the tide about the riprap that lined the stony base of Fort LaFayette, to hold a watch and observe how many minutes would elapse before that jagged rock with its clusters of dark blue-black mussels and wreaths of seaweed would be submerged or bared.

Foggy days were best with the ships' dark blotches in The Narrows. When the sun rose clear and sharp, the roads over on Staten Island showed far too plainly. One could follow the slow progress of a cart as it toiled from the shore up to the high crests to vanish into some vast, unknown world. One could even see little figures walking along the shore or rowboats slipping out from shaky piers. Clearly, far too clearly, one could see people *moving* untrammeled.

Why? Why? Why? Where were his friends? What were George and Craig Wilson thinking and doing? What had they been thinking and doing while winter died and the snow shoulders of Staten Island, which the old embrasure framed, became mottled black and white and now gave off a hint of green through the brown? Louise? What had she been told? What would she believe? It was better to think of George and Craig. What would they find out and, finding out, do? Days and weeks and now a new season, and never a word.

Three times a day there were meals, good meals. At

first they were welcome but soon the sight and smell of food pricked on the feeling of nausea. Nevertheless, the meals must be eaten—not only to keep up strength but for the very effect of the act of eating on the unseen eyes that watched him through the slit in the heavy door.

Footsteps along the corridor, footsteps in the early morning, at noon, in the late afternoon. *This* might be the day when the cell door would open in wide freedom or onto a fair field where one could battle against unknown charges leveled by unknown minds. This might be—until the corridor is silent again.

XVI

Civis Americanus Sum

THE March sun that slanted into the old casemate of Fort LaFayette was bright with a promise of warmth to strengthen the weak radiation of the smoky fireplace. De Mérac stopped in his endless morning pacing as he heard a rattle of equipment that told of a new guard-relief out in the corridor. The old regular, Dunphy, would be taking up his beat. De Mérac rapped on the sliding panel of the door. It grated back and a pair of close-set eyes peered in. "Any news for me, Dunphy?" asked de Mérac.

The eyes shifted oddly in a negative shake. "Same's ever, sir. Reckon we'd a heard it to the guardroom if they'd been anything 'bout you."

De Mérac shrugged. Another twenty-four hours, forty-eight, seventy-two hours, a week, a month, six months more to wait. At least, he could pass away a little time talking to Dunphy, who alone of all the guards was willing to chat, one ear cocked for the saber clank of an approaching officer. He had seen Dunphy often when food was brought to the cell or when orderlies swept the floor during the scant two hours' exercise in the paved court below. But in his mind Dunphy always materialized as two furtive close-set eyes peering through the slide, a voice that seemed to come out of the corner of an unseen mouth.

Now he retailed the gossip of the prison fort. "Them two blockade runners was let out last night—them as had No. 6 down the corridor. Limey bastards. Get five hundred dollars a run—sometimes five hundred *pounds* a run—just for sailing from Bermuda to Wilmington." There was a pause while Mr. Dunphy dealt noisily with his quid. "Thumper Joyce let 'em out an' one of them Limeys looks at his pack—guards are under full equipment to the sallyport—and hollers, 'Eh, laddie, wot ye got on yer back?' An' Thumper he hollers right back, 'Bunker Hill, you son of a bitch. Want to climb it?' Jeez, it was cute, 'cept the Limey, not bein' educated, didn't know what Bunker Hill meant."

De Mérac forced a laugh to keep Mr. Dunphy in a good humor. Then he said abruptly, "You've been long in the army, Dunphy?"

"Twelve year, sir."

"You have heard of officers held like myself perhaps?"

A ragged forefinger dabbed through the grill. "You can't be held, sir. It's all clear. Now, first thing I done when I 'listed was to get them Articles of War by heart. Know 'em front and back and upside down, I do. No, sir. They *can't* hold you, 'thout charges bein' brought."

"I know that," said de Mérac impatiently. "But—"

"Just hold to them Articles, sir. Now take me. I was with the old Fifth, on the march to Utah in '57. Mormons burnt us out and the temp'ture hit down close to forty-five below. We was like to starve, I tell you. Well, the Fifth got orders to hit down to Fort Taos in New Mexico for supplies. Now, 'cause I knew the Articles I knew what I was entitled to every God-damn day—rations and such. I knew when the law says I got to get leave. Under the Articles I wasn't gettin' my rations, wasn't gettin' my leave, nor my pay like Articles says I ought. I set down an' quit. See? *They couldn't do it to me.* Jesus, was Capt'n Marcy mad. At Taos I lost my stripes and got shoved in the brig, but by God, I proved my point, see? That's what *you* got to remember, sir. Maybe they'll keep you here. Maybe you'll see Dry Tortugas. Maybe a cold bastard of a fort on the Great Lakes. But you ain't got nothing to worry about. 'Cause why? 'Cause whatever they do to you, they *can't do it!*"

De Mérac said dryly, "You tell me, then, that I am not here?"

Dunphy dealt with his quid again. "Legally, sir, under the Articles, you *ain't*. Hey! Officers comin'."

The slide clicked back in place. A familiar clank of scabbard rings sounded down the corridor. De Mérac stepped away from the door. The steps were quicker, more assured than those to which he had become accustomed. Some new officer, perhaps a convalescent, assigned to the LaFayette post. He lounged to the barred window and watched a string of scows waddling up the Narrows, a fussy tug at the head.

A key rasped in the door. He shrugged. The new officer must inspect the prisoners, of course. Then he swung about as a voice rang out, a voice that swept his memory from a smelly hall in Chambers Street on to a narrow alley in Fredericksburg. He reeled as though struck. His hands reached behind him and clutched the low mantel of the fireplace.

George Force and Craig Wilson stood in the doorway. A lightning flash snapped across his mind. Prisoners, too? Then his swimming vision took in the fact of sabers and holsters, worn only by free men.

George burst across the threshold, flung an arm about his shoulder while Wilson followed a little more soberly. "John! John! You're out! Out! D'you hear? Oh, my God, I never thought I'd see this day!" George's fist thumped de Mérac's back. "You're clear! Every damn thing's smashed. Tell him, Craig!"

Wilson's voice sounded through the haze that slowly crept up about de Mérac. "Quashed, John. Broken to smithereens." Paper crackled in de Mérac's ear. "Signed by the President! Immediate release. Immediate restoration of everything. The regiment'll go crazy. We wired Birney. John, believe me, this should never have happened. But it's over now."

De Mérac still clung unsteadily to the mantel. Dunphy now clumped into the room. There was the glint of black leather, brass, and gold. De Mérac felt a buckle snap about his waist, knew that the scarred scabbard of his sword rubbed against his knee, that his Colt weighted his right hip.

He tried to speak but his voice was only a hoarse whisper. "And Louise?"

"Fine! Fine!" said George. "She's stood by you like a brick wall. Crazy to see you."

De Mérac's breath went out in a long, slow "Ah!" Then he walked uncertainly to his cot and sat down. George plumped down beside him, an arm about his shoulders. Finally de Mérac said dully, *"Eh bien? Et l'histoire? Qu'est-ce que c'est que s'est agit?"*

Wilson drew up a chair. "John, it's so damned grotesque that it's—well, I'll make it short." He tried to keep his eyes off de Mérac's listless face, tried not to notice the sagging shoulders. John de Mérac was a client whose hard case had been won. That was the way to go at it. A terse summation. It was as well, too, not to take heed of the growing look of concern in George Force's eyes, of the bewilderment that creased his forehead. "To begin with, John—" He went over the old story that was so deep-furrowed in his brain that words formed almost without volition. De Mérac nodded from time to time. Once or twice he muttered, "Ah, *ça!*" without lifting his gaze from the floor. When Wilson had finished, a hush fell over the cell. The faint *tsss—ahhhh* of the waters of The Narrows lapping about the riprap drifted through the open window.

De Mérac drew a deep breath and raised his head. "Ah—when one has such friends as you. Friends who believe *jusqu'à l'outrance!*" He reached out a hand to Wilson, let his arm fall across George's shoulder. "I, a lucky one, had you two—and Louise."

George's face lit up at the slight return of animation. "Us? Of course you had us. But you had hundreds of others. Shea and Labanieff and young Adams and Pride and Birney and Louvel and DuChesne. Oh—wait till you see Lisette! DuChesne's polished her like a mirror. And

394

Dad and Mr. Duane. And people you never heard of, too. George Strong—he's treasurer of the Sanitary Commission. An Iowa captain named Ingham from Berdan's Sharpshooters—he went at things as if you'd been his brother, soon's he heard the story. Oh, there were lots more."

De Mérac said, "And you mobilized them all, you two."

Wilson shifted uncomfortably. "As a matter of fact, John, we floundered and fumbled damnably. George hasn't mentioned our most effective ally. A young lady named Gail Shortland."

For the first time de Mérac's voice rose to its old pitch. "*Qui, donc?*"

George nodded vigorously. "You know—the nurse. She got leave from the hospital and went to work. We'd been trying all sorts of stealthy approaches to the President. You know—through proper channels. Well, Miss Shortland just went ahead and used common sense. She learned all she could about old Abe. She found out that he was apt to walk late at night, across the White House grounds to the War Department. Walked alone."

"*Sapristi!*" muttered de Mérac. "And one of you waited for him?"

"Not us," said Wilson. "We were held at Falmouth. Leaves are damned scarce under Joe Hooker. It was Gail Shortland who waited, night after night, by the bushes where the path curves toward the War Department."

De Mérac sat up. "And you permitted that? A young girl—there—at night? In a city like Washington?"

"She wasn't alone," put in George. "We gave her a bodyguard you'd approve of—Dekdebrun. Well, she collared Abe—about the fifth night, wasn't it, Craig? She won't say much about what went on, but so far as we can piece it together, it was something like this. She said, 'Mr. President, what do you think of a man who gives up everything in his own country and fights for our Union just because he believes in it?' I guess Abe was a little surprised, but he took off his hat and said, 'Madam, thank God we've got thousands like that.' So she cut right in, 'What would you say if you knew that one of those men was being falsely held, without a chance to defend himself, held incommunicado in a New York fort?' Abe's voice got a little queer then, she says, and the most she could make out of it was, 'Reckon I'd ask any young lady who knew about it to keep right on talking.' Then he steered her to a room in the Department and she showed him copies of the papers we'd given her."

"I still do not understand," muttered de Mérac.

"You don't have to," said Wilson. "Anyway, when she was done showing him the stuff and talking, Abe blew up. He shot into the air looking about a mile high and his eyes were hot as burning fuses. He yelled to an aide, 'Go to Mr. Stanton's house and tell him the President wants him here and wants him quick.' Then he smiled down at her and she says the smile about finished her—sad and glad, she called it. 'You've done a fine night's work, young lady. I'm sending you home in a carriage. If you've got the story straight, I'll clear that officer and send his friends right down to LaFayette to pull him out.' And the last she saw of him he was sitting with his face in his hands staring at the floor and waiting for the Secretary of War to come in." He opened his palms. "That's the way it went. Here we are. You're free. We've got a carriage that'll take us to the ferry."

De Mérac walked slowly to the window. There was a buzzing in his head that he could not shake off. "It comes so suddenly," he said. "This first step into the world."

George joined him. "Take your time, John. Craig and I have been talking a lot about this. I guess in your place we'd feel like telling the army to go hell. But . . ."

"Something has gone out of me," de Mérac said slowly. "Not to be with you others—ah, that revolts me. But always to be looking over one's shoulder, thinking that another Pelham, another Cusler, may be drawing a net about a soldier who does his best—Yes, something goes out of one. When men truly believe in an idea as vast as your Union, then one has the right to expect that human nature develop at least a little to match that idea. But when nature shrivels to such vindictiveness as Pelham's—ah, *ça*—then the idea shrivels, too."

George worried at the knot of his sword hilt. "I'd figure exactly that way in your place, John. Guess anyone trying his best to play clean would. Probably it'd explain one or two retirements that have had us guessing."

Wilson, leaning back with his chin in his hand, watched de Mérac carefully. His friend was leaning listlessly against the wall. "Look here, John. I don't need to say that this must have been one hell of a shock. Here's the way you are now. You're clear—absolutely clear. You are not reassigned to active duty and won't be until *you* say the word. If you do, you go about where you please. Berdan's raising another regiment of sharpshooters and he'd like you to command it. General Hunt of the artillery'd give you a battery of your own—and your St. Cyr training'd make that a mighty easy job. It'd lead damn quick to a group of batteries and then—who knows? That Iowa lad, Ingham, told us his state is raising some new cavalry outfits and you could get command of one of them easy as picking an apple off a tree. You'd serve with Grant and Sherman on the Mississippi and I tell you they and their Western boys are making us in the East look damned silly. Of course, if you *do* come back—why, I don't need to tell you we all hope you'll head straight for the Rifles."

"But we're not urging anything, John," broke in George. "Whatever you decide, Craig and I are cheering right now. What we want you to do is to take a little time off. Get out of uniform. Remember, you've got an indefinite leave that no one but yourself can terminate. We'll keep the Rifles going. Craig's doing a wonderful job. You get a perspective on things and then decide."

De Mérac lit a cigarette, coughed over the first tang of the tobacco. Then he said, "Perspective. Yes. To push myself out of my mind. To sum up correctly this long column of figures. But that must wait."

George and Wilson exchanged quick glances. "For what?" asked the Major.

"Here, I do not see newspapers. But I do see something spread out before me which cannot lie." He pointed across to Staten Island. "I have watched carts mired in deep mud. Now, they roll easily. The ground is drying here. It will dry even faster in northern Virginia. A campaign will open. I must go back to the Rifles. Then when the campaign ends itself, I shall claim my leave."

Wilson cried, "No! You're asking too much of yourself."

"I ask nothing of myself, Craig. But I can't hide in a village on the Hudson while you and the Rifles take the field again."

"I've really got you between my sights now, John." Wilson rose from his chair. "All right—there will be a campaign opening. But—you've been away. "I've got the regiment running—just the way Shea had my companies running when I came back at Fredericksburg and you sent me away. I was mad as hell at you when I found out what you'd done, but I had to admit that you were right. *Now*—I've turned the tables on you. Before you got the feel of command again, we'd be in action. You'd be supernumerary—just the way I was at Fredericksburg. You stay out of this."

George shouted, "Right, Craig, right!"

De Mérac said quietly, "What would you have done, Craig, had you known of the purpose of your errand at Fredericksburg?"

"Done? With the warmest feelings toward you, I'd have raised holy hell."

"Such will I do now. You deny me a command, and yet that would be the clearest sign of confidence in me. Very well, I see the President. I see Villard of the *Tribune*. Injustice! Falsely accused foreign officer denied chance to clear himself. No, Craig, *mon ami*, it is you who are in *my* sights."

Wilson sighed, "John, by God, I wish you'd do what we suggested."

George pleaded, "You've *got* to!"

De Mérac's chin set in all its old firmness. "Were a campaign just concluded—ah—that would be different. But it is about to open and there is no more to be said."

"Look at yourself, John," Wilson urged. "You've been through three tough campaigns and then had this damnable business to top it all off. No doctor in his senses would pass you as fit."

"Then I must find a mad one, Craig. Now tell me about the regiment."

Wilson sat on the cot, scabbard across his knees. "The Rifles are about the same. Recruits have brought us up to almost two hundred. Dan Sickles commands the corps instead of Stoneman. Father Doyle's back on duty, but talking's hell for him."

"And you still expect me to—but go on."

"Well, a few things happened fast. LaFayette Baker ran von Horstmar out of the District and her minister, von Gerolt, is raising hell. Mr. Conway is on his way to Illinois where he'll spend his time guarding Reb prisoners at Rock Island. Now, as to Pelham—well, Pelham's going to be transferred to a frontier command where he'll do nothing but watch Indians."

"Going to be?" asked de Mérac.

"Department raised a row at transferring an active brigadier when a campaign was going to start pretty soon. You can see their point. You've said yourself that Pelham fights."

"In all directions," agreed de Mérac dryly. "And Cusler? I ask not in vengeance but in curiosity."

George grimaced. "He's taken up the cudgels for you. He's getting speeches made about you in Congress. As soon as you're out he wants to give a testimonial dinner for you in New York and have Governor Morgan come down from Albany to make the main speech."

Something of de Mérac's old smile returned. "How profound are my regrets that a *subsequent* engagement with General Lee prevents my acceptance."

"Let's clear out of here, John," said Wilson.

De Mérac sat on the edge of his cot beside the major. "Clear out? One may truly walk out? *Sang de dieu*. How hard the idea is to grasp."

An orderly came in to pack up de Mérac's few belongings. At the commandant's office, while de Mérac privately thanked Dunphy, Wilson reluctantly surrendered the precious paper with its bold "A. Lincoln." A shabby guard detail turned out, presented arms, and de Mérac, between his two friends, walked out of the sallyport. George slapped de Mérac's back. "Out! Oh, you old rapscallion! God, but it's good to be with you again. Dinner at the Fifth Avenue and then the ferry to Jersey!"

"Give him time to look at his mail, George. We brought up a lot from camp and there are about five bundles that were being held at the post office. You'll find them in the room we got for you, John. We figured you'd want a bath and a change."

Dizziness and a strange, hot, disjointed feeling crept over de Mérac as he climbed into the carriage. He clung tight to a broad strap and said thickly, "Should telegraph Louise. Right away."

"That's easy," agreed George. "We'll stop at the telegraph office."

Five minutes after de Mérac had sent his telegram to Louise and crossed the lobby of the Fifth Avenue Hotel, he was stretched on a bed in the room reserved for him, while Wilson and George sent messengers for a doctor. They nervously laid cold cloths on his flushed forehead, rang for more ice, and made futile dashes into the corridor in hope of seeing the doctor heading toward them.

When he did come, at the end of an hour, they disliked and distrusted him at once. He was a small, heavily bearded man with sniffles and a nervous trot. He examined the unconscious de Mérac, questioned the two friends with a running undercurrent of petulant mutterings interspersed with sniffs. He prodded uncertainly at de Mérac. Suddenly he brightened up. "Your friend ever had a shock of any kind? Bad news or something? Excessive strain?"

George burst out, "No! His life's been a lovely bed of roses, especially the last two years. Damn it, look at his uniform, for one thing. Shock! We told you his name. Don't you read the New York papers? They've been full of him."

The doctor looked helpless. "Never knew many foreigners. But I can tell you his life wa'n't as easy as you seem to think."

Wilson turned on the pathetic little man. "God damn

it, tell us something! How long'll he be laid up? Is it serious?"

"You're so impatient!" The indecision on the man's face was so deep that Wilson's patience returned.

"He's a very dear friend of ours and a most valuable officer. Naturally we're worried. George, sit down and he'll tell us what it is. Go ahead, Doctor. Make it as simple as you can."

A maze of words drifted up from the heavy beard, words that were retracted as soon as they were spoken, corrected, and the corrections corrected. George fidgeted and shuffled, bit his lip to keep from bursting out. Wilson finally cut in. "I'm sure that a colleague of yours would admire your marshaling of the facts. Even I, a layman, can appreciate such a summing up." The little doctor beamed and scuffed his hands together. Wilson went on, "I shall have to wire his fianceé at once. Shall I be correct in saying that your diagnosis is—ah—"

"My dear Colonel. Precisely. Brain fever. Following unhealthy living and prolonged strain."

"Dangerous?" asked George, out of his chair in one movement.

Again the doctor wrapped himself in sniffs and circumlocutions. They finally gathered the attack need not be serious if a proper regimen was pursued. Then he picked up his battered bag. "Someone must stay with him. Quiet! He must be very quiet and never permitted to worry. He'll come out of that coma pretty quickly, but his mind won't be clear. Keep the ice on him—head and feet. Cooling drinks if he'll take them. I'll look in again in the evening. There's my card. Send word to my office of any change for better or worse. If you wish other opinion to compare with mine, by all means call in another doctor. Most happy. Most happy. Good day, gentlemen!"

George and Wilson stared at each other. "Brain fever!" George said dully. "Didn't John have enough without adding this?" His eyes began to smart and he gulped. "Craig, how the poor old boy must have suffered! It'd take an awful lot to crack him, but those bastards, those sons of bitches—they've done it! The President's got to know about this! We'll run Pelham out of the army. We'll land that stinking Cusler in Sing Sing." He caught up de Mérac's left wrist and felt the pulse running quick and hot. "Feel that, Craig!"

Wilson gently pushed George into a chair by the window. "We've got to move fast, George. Our leave's up—*and*—he can't be left alone."

"But what can we *do*?"

"First of all, we turn the case over to Billy Bull. He and Valentine Mott are the best in New York—I know Bull better. Then we mobilize your family. I'll send a note to Bull and you run across the Square and rout out your mother. She'll stand by. I'll telegraph Claire to come up from Washington and I guess she'd better bring Louise and her mother."

"Guess so," said George glumly.

"So get going. I'll ring for a messenger and wait here till Bull comes. Hurry, now, we may have to ride a cowcatcher back to Washington if we miss the last passenger train. And do you know, George—this'll be a tough thing for John to get over but in a way it's a blessing."

George stared. "A blessing?"

Wilson nodded. "He could never have stood a long campaign and I think that's what's ahead."

George found that his mother was calling at a house on East Eighth Street and stormed into a cab. As he rolled down Broadway, unconsciously rocking back and forth on the seat, his eye caught bright gold letters on a second-floor window below Sixteenth Street. They were repeated on the next window, the next, the next, "John Cusler." George made a strangled noise in his throat, managed to shout, "Stop!" whipped onto the sidewalk and up broad, well-swept stairs that had shiny brass treads. He had no clear idea of what he wanted to do. But back of the slick gold letters sat one of the men who had brought John de Mèrac to his present state. There was a general office with a heavy mahogany railing, a door marked "Mr. Cusler. Private." A scared-looking clerk rose like a flushed partridge and tried to bar the way. George brushed him aside and flung open the lettered door.

Honest John Cusler was no longer ruddy and dapper. He turned a streaked, mottled face as the door creaked. Tears rolled from his full eyes and his loose mouth quivered and puckered. His plump hands held a telegram. George was not sure that Cusler recognized him, knew him for anything more than a vaguely seen officer. The telegram fluttered to the desk. A sob same from the fat throat. "Billy. Along the Yazoo. Wouldn't stay East where I could watch him. Billy's—Billy's *gone.*"

George suddenly held out his hand, silent. Cusler took it weakly and George somehow had the feeling that he was shaking hands with the son, not the father, with the son who had fled from the supervised safety of an Eastern berth to go with Grant and Sherman and their hard-fighting Westerners. Then he saluted, left the office, leaving the powerful boss blindly turning and turning the telegram as though he hoped to find somewhere a magic sentence that would tell him the news was false.

"God above," muttered Force as he jumped back into the carriage. "The poor bastard. He's lived by sham so damn long that he's just a baby when something real hits him. Poor bastard."

De Mérac hung in a hot, whirling world that was sometimes lighted from without, sometimes pitch-dark, as the sun swung across the sky, vanished, swung back again. The little doctor had said shock. He should have said shocks. Shock and strain in camp as he struggled to whip a regiment into shape with the contempt of Pelham always beating about his shoulders. Shock at Frayser's Farm when his men were a part of the thin line that kept Lee from rolling McClellan into the James; shock at Malvern Hill and the bitter disillusionment of the retreat of an unbeaten army; shock again to the east of the Bull Run Mountains, in the woods near Chantilly where a one-armed man shouted in a lightning flash, "I'm clear—clear for good! Ride for it!"; shock by the railroad of Fredericksburg and in the roaring hell that burst from the stone wall below Marye's Heights; shock in the camp at Falmouth and at Fort LaFayette.

Sometimes the fever shadows lifted and he stared

weakly into a real world, his thoughts creeping out timidly and pressing their soft footprints into his brain. Strong body and strong mind fought against shock bruise. One day he took in a figure that sat quietly by the window and managed to smile and mutter, "But it is *you*, Mrs. Force! I must have fallen asleep." It might have been a matter of hours or days that he saw the heavy-set, gentle-voiced Dr. Bull with his square chin and fighter's eyes, heard him say in easy, tripping French, "*Ca va àmerveille, mon ami. C'est on ne peut mieux.* Yes, Mrs. Force, he's on the mend. I'll send a telegram to Craig Wilson and George."

Again—days or hours later—Mrs. Force, with her snowy hair and young, delicate face, bent over him. "We've bags and bags of mail for you, John. Dr. Bull says I can read to you if you like. But you mustn't use your own eyes yet."

De Mérac said, "Louise!"

Ella Force held out a thick packet. "I'll put these under your pillow and you can dream on them. You'll want to read those to yourself."

He nodded weakly. "Where is she?"

"Just down on Fourteenth Street, John. She's been here every day. Poor little chick. She's so young. She felt dreadful when you didn't know her. She'll be in today and she'll be so happy when she sees you like this. Shall I begin to read now? And you're to tell me the instant you feel too tired."

"I have been here long?"

"Over three weeks."

"And you?"

"Oh, George brought me up the first day and I took the room next to you."

"All this time? *Mais c'est déjà quelque chose!*"

"A godsend, John. I—I don't have a lot to do with George away, you know. Now—for the first letter." Letters from Loudéac, from Paris, from Venice and Rome and Boston and New York and Milwaukee and Chicago and Washington. He listened dreamily. Most of them were pleasant, friendly, inconsequential, often written long before his arrest. They seemed to echo to him from across a chasm. He was vaguely pleased by them.

Mrs. Force began a new letter. After the first few lines he turned his head. "And the writer of that?"

She flipped the pages over. "It's—it's—oh—that nurse—Miss Shortland. Craig says she's wonderful. Here's another in the same writing. More. Why, there's quite a stack. Perhaps you want to read those yourself."

"I should like to hear you read them."

There was little in those letters, one would have said at a first glance. But through each line there shone a spirit that was unmistakable. A spirit that was cheerful simply in understanding, by undertone and implication, hopeful by the very thought that inspired the writing, quietly amusing in the very way that the writer's mind reached out to the reader's in unspoken comradeship. No newspaper would ever have published them under the caption, "Letters to the Boys in Blue." No "Boy in Blue" as he existed in an editorial mind could have comprehended more than the delicately formed words. But a man of the Army of the Potomac would have savored each line, found each phrase expanding into fresh thoughts and the fresh thoughts leaping on to others, speaking to him in his own tongue.

Mrs. Force's rich voice began to blur in his ears and heat waves crept like armies of ants over him. He murmured, "Thank you. There are more?"

She said, "Oh, yes, several."

Much later the scorching heat ebbed and ebbed. He felt, emerging from the hot depths, a fresh presence in the hotel room. His nostrils brought a quick familiar scent to him. He cried "Louise!" and his eyes swept the vision of her delicate face.

Her murmured "Darling!" was low and broken. She slipped to her knees and her arms were gentle about his neck and her cheek cool against his. She chanted softly, "My darling. You're better! You're better. Oh, my own. It was so dreadful! You looked at me and didn't know me. I couldn't bear it!"

He lay with his eyes closed, content with her nearness, her fragrance, and her voice in his ear. "That is all past, *ma chérissette.* Every day now I shall see you and grow stronger and stronger with the sight. And I have all your letters and shall live through each one. Ah—what a time it was for you! I, at least, knew what had happened. You could only guess and wonder." He made a gesture of protest as she drew her arms away.

She laid her cheek closer against his. "But I can't stay long, darling. I don't *want* to go—ever, ever. But Dr. Bull says it's better if you don't see me for too long at a time." She gave a low, intimate laugh. "He says it would be bad for you. Isn't he sweet! Now my time's up." She kissed him quickly and for the first time he realized that Mrs. Force had been standing in the open door. Louise touched his cheek, gave a twitch to the sheet and a pat to the pillow, and glided out.

In the corridor Mrs. Force said, "He's looking so much better."

Louise nodded vigorously. "He'll be up long before Dr. Bull said he would be. *I'll* get him up! Good-bye, Mrs. Force."

As Mrs. Force came back into the room, de Mérac said, "But she is more radiant than even I remembered her."

"She's a very lovely-looking girl, John." But her mind was saying, "Sick as you are, I'd like to *shake* you! Lord, why *isn't* it decent to tell you that she's just after your title?"

Dr. Bull fluffed out the tufts of hair over his temples and looked severely at de Mérac. "You're on your feet all right. But you're fifteen pounds underweight. Your heart flutters like a canary if you walk upstairs. You're going to need more rest, young man."

There was a flash of petulance across Louise's face. "Well, don't make it too long," she cried crisply.

Her mother broke in, "Louise, *dear!* Dr. Bull knows best."

Dr. Bull's fingers strayed toward his watch. "Big people sometimes need more care and rest than smaller ones. You've found that out, haven't you, Captain?"

"You invite me to coddle myself," laughed de Mèrac.

"It's true, though. In '61 I was dazzled by the big lumbermen in the Maine regiments. But de Trobriand tells me—"

"That's *Baron* de Trobriand, Doctor," said Louise, nodding in deep satisfaction. "He's coming to our wedding."

"*Bien, sûr*," said de Mérac. "As I say, de Trobriand tells me that the big Maine men in his brigade broke down very quick. It is the small, spare man who is the last to drop out on a long march."

Dr. Bull chuckled. "You seem to know a good deal about our history but I wonder if you ever heard of Colonel Dan Morgan and his Riflemen in the Revolution. Old Dan always said that his best men were lean Pennsylvania Dutchmen, because they *starved* better than his big Irish. Now, Captain, I'm giving you my last prescription."

Louise clapped her hands. "A sea voyage right after the wedding!"

"That comes later, my dear. Captain, I want you to go into the country—say for three or four weeks. Less, if you pick up fast, more if you don't."

"*Compris*," said de Mérac.

Louise cried, "But John! It isn't the *season* for the country and it would take me days and days to get the right clothes. Don't shake your head like that, Mother."

Dr. Bull ruffled his tufts again. "My prescription may seem severe, but it's better for him to go alone."

"You're quite right, Doctor," said Mrs. Duane. "Louise dear, it may be only two weeks. That won't be long."

De Mérac said slowly, "I think it wise to follow Dr. Bull in this matter."

Louise cried, "John!"

"Right. Dead right," rumbled Dr. Bull. "He's got to build himself up, to wear off the effects of cumulative strain. I want him in new surroundings, away from cities and camps and uniforms. I want him to go where he won't see a familiar face or hear a familiar sound."

Louise perched on the arm of de Mérac's chair. "I don't think it's fair to me," she pouted. "Do you *have* to go alone, John?" she asked.

He took her hand and looked gravely up at her. "I think so. And there is one more thing for me to settle."

"Settle?" Her voice was sharp.

"Yes. Do I return to the army or do I not?"

Dr. Bull's eyes narrowed in quick understanding. "The rest will help you make up your mind."

Louise beamed suddenly on the doctor. "Oh, of course. I understand now. Somewhere upriver where people won't always be talking about brigades and cannons and things." Her eyes sparkled. Up there, out of reach of the people who wanted to drag him back into the service, he'd come to the right decision. Her letters would help. No more army for *him*. He'd get well fast and they could be married just as soon as he came back to town. That was it. And then—*she* would be Baroness de Mérac. Perhaps she and her mother might even go to Loudéac and wait for him; the wedding could be in France. Her smile deepened. "You're so wise, Dr. Bull," she said softly.

"Sensible girl" said the doctor, getting to his feet. "Now, Captain, know the White Mountains?"

"I have been to Mt. Washington."

"The hotels will, of course, be closed, but a colleague of mine has a camp just south of Franconia Notch. I've arranged things with him. An old couple keep the place open for him and they'll look after you. Go up there as soon as you feel like it. Come back when you feel like it."

Louise urged, "John—say you'll go. It sounds perfectly heavenly. And perhaps we'll go there together sometime after we're married." She suddenly felt very happy. John would be in an ideal spot—and there would be no one there, no wives or daughters or sisters.

It was cold for the second of May and George Force, in his sleep, gathered his blankets tighter about him. The chill bit deeper and he woke, grunting in discomfort. He lay just ahead of the short regimental line that was sited in what seemed to be an endless tangle of scrub wood, unhealthy looking, weedy, and impenetrable. He saw a small fire going and stumbled toward it, sniffing the full, rich scent of coffee. A dark figure huddled over the fire revealed itself as Randol. "Have some, George?" asked Randol.

George filled a blackened tin cup from the pot and drank, his hand shaking with cold and the coffee slopping over the rim. He blinked and tried to orient himself. Just ahead a track, hardly more than a path, led away to Catherine Furnace, trailing like a scar through the prickly bristle of the scrub. Behind him and to the left the dull gray that told of coming dawn was stained orange by innumerable fires that burned about the big half-house, half-tavern, of Chancellorsville. On the right flank of the Rifles' position ran a broad scratchy road hacked through the wilderness. West, it led on past Dowdall's Tavern, Wilderness Tavern, and at last to Germanna Ford on the upper Rappahannock. East, it drove straight on to Salem Church and the battered streets of Fredericksburg, nearly twenty miles away.

George muttered, "Been round the pickets?"

Randol nodded. "Went on past where we join onto von Steinwehr of the XIth. Dilger's got his battery covering the Orange Plank Road. Then come Krzyzanowski and Devens. Schurz is on the road to Ely's Ford. De Trobriand's right back of us and the rest of our corps's stretched out beyond him."

"All quiet?"

"Hell of a sight quieter than this." He jerked his chin toward the lines of the Rifles, where men were shaking themselves out of their blankets, moving about stiffly and talking in dull, shivery undertones.

"Don't like the feel of it," said George. "We got across the Rappahannock slick as grease and now we're just waiting. Sedgwick can't have hit Fredericksburg yet or we'd hear the racket." He started suddenly. "What the hell's that?"

Randol made a quick dive at a rabbit that shot past "Come to Daddy, ol' Lucky-foot. Pot's all waiting for you. Jesus! Missed him. Hey. There's another. Shy a rock at him. Damn it, don't be so slow. If you don't want to eat, *I* do."

George was on one knee, staring at the thick undergrowth ahead. Saplings tossed and swayed, rustling their budding tops. Branches and twigs crackled all through the dimness. All along the line of the Rifles, faces were turning toward the woods.

Randol yelled, "Look at 'em all. For Christ's sake get busy!"

Rabbits, dozens of them, scurried madly toward the wakening lines, checked, doubled, raced frantically about. Game birds broke into the open in screeching scurries, took off, rocketed high to the rear. There were louder crashes. A magnificent buck burst out of a thick clump, stood trembling for a second, shot away in soaring, graceful bounds. Randol picked up a musket. "Hello, banquet!" he yelled. "Get going, George. Haven't you ever seen a wild deer before?"

George pried himself slowly upright, his hands working along his trouser seams. "Scared! *But what the hell scared them?*" He wrenched himself about. "Sergeant Wadsworth! Find Major Wilson. Tell him—"

There was nothing to tell which the major couldn't hear. Off to the right, hard on the heels of the terrified game, a ripping smash of musketry sounded, the high-pitched knifing of the Rebel yell. Artillery slammed in sudden, vicious barks. Bugles brayed through the scrub. The Rifles formed. Someone screeched, "It's Stonewall, Stonewall Jackson. God damn it, he's got clear 'round our right."

The scrub turned into a blazing, staggering hell into which the Rifles moved and, moving, left time and space behind them. There were gray men everywhere up ahead. There were men in blue. Down the plank road fugitives poured. Gunners cut loose their teams and lashed on through the flying rack. Supply wagons rocked and pitched, the drivers cutting their whips at anyone who tried to check them. From a clearing, George saw the one-armed General Howard, the staff of a flag tucked under his stump, lashing out with the flat of his sword at the sweaty-eyed men who poured past him. Then the torrent caught by the Rifles, swept them back while Wilson and Shea struggled to form a new line, a line that wavered, shifted, finally hardened. Later the thin companies came up to support Dilger's battery and the men cheered the young German who stood behind his guns in white shirt and doeskin breeches, directing the fire by a series of handclaps that carried better than any voice.

Yelling gray waves smashed and drove about the guns, swept the Rifles back until they enclosed the battery in a shallow V. George fought with a musket, loading and firing as quickly as he could. Then the V was straightened out and he crouched between Rapp and Bordagaray behind natural abatis of fallen limbs. A horse writhed and kicked a few yards away, his hoofs crashing against a blue and gray heap that was repeated again and again over the torn ground. But the attack was broken. Fresh troops were filing up in long blue coils through the paths and the firing had died away to sullen, sporadic exchanges. The Union Army was not wrecked. But its plans, its promises that had begun so brightly with Hooker's quick, aggressive move up and across the Rappahannock, were shattered beyond all hope of repair. George smeared his cuff over his powder-blackened lips and listened to the pounding of his heart. He looked groggily about, then rallied. "There's Major Wilson over there, Sergeant Major. Better go tell him we're about out of ammunition here. And tell him LeNoir's dead. God, I'm glad John didn't have to see this. Can't we do *anything* right?"

In the White Mountains spring settled in fitful patches. There were days when the ground sighed gently to the drying touch of the sun and pockets of air lay warm and pine-fragrant in the hollows. Then regiments and brigades of clouds rolled down from the vast stretches to the northwest and high winds drove scurries of snow that seemed to have been gale-gathered in the high reaches of Ontario and the eternal snows beyond. De Mérac came to know the piny scent of a still noon as he worked his way up the shaggy sides of the Flume or scrambled up the towering ridge to the west to face a knifelike wind under the Old Man of the Mountains. He struck farther afield and stood warm in his cape in a blinding snowstorm by Crawford Notch, while to the south and east, range on range of mountains surged toward him like white-tipped surf. Through the gaps, between rocky shoulders, he could see on the far plains below church spires shimmering in the sunlight that driving clouds slowly darkened, muffled, then buried under a woolly mass.

The tonic of mountain air, the smell of balsam, and the sharp reek of streams tearing past black, ice-coated rocks began to do their work, and each day he was able to push his expeditions deeper and deeper into the wild ridges, returning ravenously hungry to the big log-cabin camp. The silent elderly couple who lived in a smaller building close by fed him lavishly. His table in front of the arched, field-stone fireplace was rich with stacks of pancakes and maple syrup, with haunches of venison and even bear steak, pots of beans baked long and carefully in an ember-banked pit, fine strong coffee. There were partridge and grouse in pies, on slabs of toasted homemade bread; fresh-ground cornmeal mush with heavy cream and brown sugar poured over it, and crisp, hollow popovers that could be stuffed with butter.

The old people rarely spoke to him and thus formed a barrier against the outer world as steep and rugged as Twin Mountain, Mt. Hancock or Indian Head, as impassable as the gushing course of the Ammonoosuc to the north or the Pemigewasset to the south. They were childless and the war seemed not to have touched them. From sparing words de Mérac gathered that the man—or perhaps his father before him—had held lands in Vermont under a New York grant and claimed to have been ruined by the final settling of the boundary and the extinguishing of old titles. Resentment, bitter and deep, had subordinated all life to the memory of the lost acres.

While his body gained steadily in strength, de Mérac found that his mind was far slower to answer. Thoughts of war, of the army, seemed to start waves of heat in his brain, to shrivel him with hot nausea and to rob his limbs momentarily of power. But he could recall with warmth George and Craig Wilson as he could recall countless other friends of less degree now somewhere along the Rappahannock, could recall them so long as they strayed through his mind as individuals.

Each night he slept heavily for a while, then awoke, restless and tossing, to worry again and again at his problems. He tried to shut it from his mind by plunging back to the memories of his childhood. Step by step he guided himself through the old château at Loudéac, winding along each passage and broad corridor; he retraced his youth through the passes of the Vosges and the Jura, picturing the French Alps and the Pyrenees, trying from memory to plot the best ascents of the Dent du Midi and the Cime de Canigou. When his thoughts became calmer and clearer he tried to bring logic to bear on his next steps, struggling to batter back the personal element. Emotion said, *"This* was done to *me!"* Logic replied, *"Tu n'est plus rien.* You yourself no longer count!" But could one annihilate oneself, could one truly say, "That it was done to *me* does not matter?" Sometimes he lay uneasily while his mind raced. Sometimes he muffled himself in a heavy cape and stared out into the growing warmth of spring nights while from hidden brooks and ponds a chorus of spring frogs, the "pinkletinks," made the air vibrant.

The unease of his mind set him wondering if Dr. Bull had been right in sending him to the mountains, wrapping him in a sort of echoing, disembodied world among the age-old peaks. At times he ached with loneliness for old contacts, but particularly for Louise. *Ce sacré* Bull! There had been nothing gained by going so far from her. If the looming contours of Franconia Notch were unsuitable for her, there were other spots in the Union where she and her mother could have come. Or there could have been a hurried marriage. "*Va,*" he thought. "The army has turned me into an old soldier as obedient to authority as a pensioned *sous-off* at the Invalides! There would have been nothing impossible in saying to him, 'I regret that I do not agree.'"

News of Chancellorsville drifted slowly up to the mountains in the first week of May. The hideous reverse threw de Mérac into a turmoil that was in no way lessened by the knowledge that in any event he could

413

not have participated in it. He picked up a walking stick, slung on a haversack stuffed with sandwiches, and hooked a rolled-up cape about his shoulders. Then he struck out along a pine-roofed ridge that led west and south.

Had Hooker's disaster taken the need of decision from him? Would Lee gather every available man and throw himself on the army that had Fredericksburg and Chancellorsville behind it? It was hard to see how Hooker could rally to meet such a lightning blow. And yet—after Second Bull Run, after Fredericksburg, the Southern leader had not followed up his defensive victories. Thus there might again be stalemate and the usual interminable maneuverings about northern Virginia. In which case, his own decision would still remain to be made.

The sun was warm along the ridge where granite outcroppings were barred by light which filtered down through the branches. Squirrels scolded in the trees and jays swept by in clamoring flashes of blue. De Mérac kept on through the morning that was rich with the sharpness of pine and the heavier, peaty smell of bogs. He was heading for a favorite spot on the flank of North Kinsman Mountain where thronelike rocks on a shoulder commanded a sweeping view south down the valley toward Woodstock and Thornton. The sunny peace of the unending prospect might give him calmness and balance. He worked up the rocks of a watercourse that trailed away to empty into the Basin or even into Echo Lake. At last he saw above him the treeless contours and the high-piled granite of his objective. Then he heard a man's cough.

A head was silhouetted against the sky among the rocks not more than a dozen yards away. It was a striking head, the features cut with cameo clarity, the face clean-shaven and the complexion amazingly clear. The head turned as de Mérac, coming closer, sent a big stone rattling down the slope behind him, and eyes as clear as the cheeks looked at him.

The man laughed a little ruefully. "Are you the one who found my private haunt?" he called. "Some one left burnt matches and cigarette stubs here. Yours? I should have put up a No Trespassing sign. It's the finest view on North Kinsman. You might as well come up now that you're here."

De Mérac stopped. "But I would not disturb you," he said hesitantly.

"Plenty of room for both of us. Come up past those blueberry bushes."

De Mérac shrugged. "Then, with your permission—" He liked the direct look of the clear eyes, the jut of the chin. The pitch of the voice matched the firm-cut mouth. He thrashed through the bushes, circled a boulder, and swung into the rocky amphitheater where the other waited courteously.

It was hard not to show amazement. De Mérac, flushing, hoped that he had managed to mask the least start. The magnificent head was set deep in broad shoulders, one of which slanted high while the other sloped sharply down. The rest of the body was spiderlike, long, thin arms that ended in finely formed hands, sticklike legs that kicked and spraddled out grotesquely with the slightest movement. Well-cut greenish-brown tweed covered but did not mask a warped, twisted chest.

The cripple smiled and de Mérac thought that he had never seen such deep-seated warmth. "Don't think I was barking at you like a watchdog. You must love this place as much as I do if you jam yourself up that gully to get here. *I* use this path that comes up from the west. You could wheel a baby carriage along it. In fact, my own baby carriage is waiting down there." A long, threadlike arm pointed to a straggly road not far below where a horse's head tossed from time to time.

"You chose well," said de Mérac, settling himself against a rock. The sun, high and full in the sky, bathed the great green-yellow expanse far below in a shimmering light, touched with mellow emphasis the yellow houses, the white houses, and the inevitable red barns.

The other looked curiously at him. "You're a foreigner, aren't you?" he asked. "You've picked the best time for a tour, even if it is an odd time."

"Today, all times seem odd," said de Mérac.

"Except when you're up here. I can feel the hill winds blow over me and watch thunderstorms chase each other across the lowlands. The sun puts on a wonderful show for me every dusk. I can see it begin to drop down over the flats to the west where the Connecticut swings away and then it hits all the windows down there in the lowlands until every house seems to be on fire. And you ought to come here in the autumn—scarlets and crimsons and golds and lemon-yellow as far as you can see. No—when you're up here—I don't know, you sort of get the feeling—almost the *knowledge*—that everything's all right."

De Mérac hurriedly lit a cigarette, thinking, "*Vingt dieux, mon pauvre*, I could wish to settle you here forever in sight of that knowledge. Ah, *ça*. There is courage under that warped chest."

The cripple brushed away hair that the wind blew across his forehead. "I found this place three years ago and I've grown to think of it as my own. There are lots of places that I can't get to, but this one's easy." There was no appeal for sympathy in the words—a mere statement of fact such as any man might make. "By the way, my name's Elliot Manning. My people live across the Massachusetts line in Winchendon. Just now I'm staying at a farm down below in the valley."

De Mérac hesitated. Then he said, "My name is de Mérac—Jean de Mérac."

Manning drew his level brows together. "Not *Captain* Jean de Mérac? The deuce! I won't pretend I haven't heard about you. There was something in *Leslie's* not so long ago. Well, I should think you'd be on the deck of a steam packet instead of in the White Mountains."

"It is partly to make up my mind concerning that packet that I am here." The clear eyes turned full on him and he felt a sudden impulse to talk the whole matter out, for the glance held no trace of inquiry, no probing, but a deep sympathy, a wish to understand. De Mérac went on, "My question is, of course, whether or not to go back to the army. There are many aspects. For example, is one justified as a *man*, in returning to a milieu that may again turn suspicious of his best efforts? The point may appear trivial in such times—"

Manning coiled his long arms about his knees and shook his head vigorously. "No! No! It's something you've got to consider. You offered yourself. It seems to me that we've destroyed every single claim that you gave us to your allegiance." He looked keenly at de Mérac. "Sure you don't mind talking about this? It's none of my business and you've got a perfect right to tell me so."

"Not at all. I'd like to have your opinion."

"My opinion? On what *you* should do?" For the first time a shadow fell across the handsome face. "How can I say anything about that when I can't possibly—"

"I repeat," said de Mérac quickly, "that I should value your opinion."

Manning again tossed back the long hair from his forehead. "All right," he said flushing. "But I'll have to ask questions. I don't know anything except what I saw in the papers. Why did you come to us in the first place?"

De Mérac, speaking slowly, sketched out his early interest in the Union, reviving much the same thoughts that Kearny had brought out at the Fifth Avenue Hotel, dwelling on his own plan of bringing de Tocqueville's writing on the United States up to date.

Manning nodded in approval. "That was a great idea. I tell you, we need it just as much as Europe does. What then?"

Still slowly, de Mérac told of his meeting with Kearny and how the one-armed man had shown him that the very fact of the Union touched every living person who believed in the dignity of man. "Clear he made it—to me, at least—that the failure of the idea of the Union went far beyond your coasts. It would mean that the last liberal hopes of Europe would die. The sixteenth century would triumph over the nineteenth—triumph over your Revolution and ours."

Manning scrabbled with a stick in a dirt pocket. "The papers say you've got a title. *Leslie's* ran a picture of your château with sketched-in Crusaders riding out from the gates. Doesn't liberalism rather go against the whole existence of your kind?"

"That existence is based on privilege. Now, such privilege may have been fairly earned in another age. It may have been important, even necessary, five hundred years ago. But no longer. I'd gladly surrender the last trace of it if Bonaparte should fall and France have a republic again."

"H'm," said Manning. "So you came to us out of sheer conviction—out of a belief in what the Union stood for, not just here but all over the world. And then our Union played a damned, dirty trick on you. Lord, it's a hard decision for you to make. You know, it never occurred to me that the Union could hit an outsider like that. I've always thought of it as something belonging to us. You've seen it a whole lot clearer than many people I know. And you've put a great deal of my own feeling into words for me. The Union! I've only been able to watch. If I only could—" his voice tightened—"if I could do one thing, the least thing for it. If only—"

De Mérac quickly put out his hand. "Ah—*mon ami*—"

Manning shook his head impatiently and his voice cleared as though by some powerful inner volition. "Individuals don't count—unless they use what they have to help. Let's get back to the point. You came to us of your own free will. You've been shamefully handled. But—" he slapped his hand against a rock—"but the *idea* is still there, strong as ever. If the idea's any good at all, then it's far too big for those mongrels who set on you to spoil."

"Nonetheless, they are there and they have power."

"If they have power to drive you away from your beliefs, even though you are released and cleared, *then* they've beaten you—beaten you infinitely more than exiling you to the Dry Tortugas."

"But that they should have been able—" began de Mérac.

Manning painfully uncoiled his long legs, sat with his chin in his hand staring out at the panorama below him. "When I was taken sick, an ignorant doctor got hold of me. It was an emergency. Due to him I'm the way I am

418

today. A better doctor could have helped me a little—not much—but how just that little would have helped! Am I justified, on account of that ignorant hack, in damning the whole medical profession? Of course I'm not. So, you can—" He let his ropelike arms dangle in sudden depression. "But I can't draw parallels for you. *I'm* in no position to say that because the ideal that brought you here is still valid you ought to go back to Virginia. *I'm* not the one who'll be going back. I can't even picture what you'd be going back to, so how can I—"

De Mérac got up abruptly. "But you have," he said and a great weight was suddenly lifted from him. "You are right. The idea, it does not die. My arrest? What was that compared to what other men with whom I have marched have given—a leg or an arm or their eyes or their life?"

Manning said sharply, "I'm not telling *you* what to do!"

"Yesterday," said de Mérac, "there was a jam in the Flume. The water was choked off and only a thin trickle ran down. I pulled out one small stick, hardly big enough to throw at a squirrel. But it was the right stick and as soon as I'd pulled it clear, the water flowed again. You have found the right stick in my mind."

"You're beginning to see ahead?" asked Manning eagerly.

"*J'en suis sûr.* I got back to New York. I marry—"

"Ho! You didn't tell me about *that*. Fine! Fine!"

"And then—why, I go back to the Rifles, to the men who wear the Kearny patch. Ah, *mon ami*, I wish you might have known our old *kébir*."

Manning cleared his throat diffidently. "Couldn't you add one more step? I'd like it awfully if you'd come down by way of Winchendon and stay over with us. You can go on to Worcester from there and get your New York train."

"I should be very glad to."

"Great! I've been thinking how much Dad and Mother'd like to meet you. You've got your mind all made up and you can just sit back with us and get your breath."

"Yes," said de Mérac thoughtfully. "My mind—it is made up. And yet—" He paused.

Manning said, "If you've got any reservations, don't take a single step until you've thrashed them out with yourself."

"There are no reservations. I go back to the Rifles. But there is something else, I think. Partially, at least, I have identified myself with the Union."

"Good Lord, how *could* you identify yourself more than by fighting for it?"

"The North may lose. I do not think it likely. But it may. Don't you see that in such a case, my identification ends? The winners may do what they please with losers like Craig Wilson or George Force. But they can't touch me—a French citizen."

Manning stared at him. Then he said slowly, "You mean you feel that you ought to become a citizen? But—but—why, that's nothing you *have* to do."

"Ah—but it is."

"It's quite a step—giving up your nationality."

"No more so than becoming a Union soldier. Of course, in Bonaparte's eyes, I should have dual nationality. But not in mine."

"And for the Union, you'd give up being a Frenchman," said Manning thoughtfully.

"If you could walk with me through the Union Army you'd think less of the old idea of nationality. I could show you American citizens like my sergeant major, Melchior Rapp. You would see citizen Bordagaray, citizen Shea. And there are others—Alfred Duffié, Krzyzanowski, de Trobriand, von Gilsa, Turchanineff, Meagher, Ferrero. I ought to have seen all this at the start. It wasn't enough to have joined the army. I should have joined the nation."

"That's a brave step," said Manning.

"*Du tout.* It's logical and hence most simple."

Manning got up, arms and legs waving erratically. "Now you've *got* to come to Winchendon. Dad knows lots of people and he'll help you with your papers. It will be easy for you now, since that act Congress passed last year. Mind giving me your arm? Usually I have to shout for the driver to come up from the carriage, but this'll save him the trip." They walked carefully down a winding trail together. "Now you'll want to get right off, I guess. Meet me here tomorrow, if that's not too soon, with all your kit packed. We'll drive down the valley and get the Winchendon stage."

De Mérac walked on, filled with deep contentment. It was almost certain that American citizenship would cost him any claim to Loudéac, and with that property went a good portion of his income. It wasn't worth thinking about. Like hundreds and thousands of others he would stand on his own feet and make a new life. Others had started with far less. There would remain enough at least to assure comfort for Louise and himself. Already a most respectable balance had accumulated in his name at the Chemical Bank in New York. He said aloud, "I'll say nothing about this in my telegram to Louise. I'll surprise her with it."

That night he wrote at length to Craig Wilson and to George. Then, as though clarifying the matter in his own mind, he wrote a long letter to Gail Shortland.

XVII

The Turn of the Tide

It was intoxicating to see Louise again. How had he been able to stay away so long! The sun, in the bright drawing room in East Fourteenth Street, shone down on her hair into which gold dust had been brushed, intensified the sparkle of her dark eyes. She looked so exquisite, poised momentarily in the doorway, her slim arms wide in invitation and her full breasts accentuated by the tight green bodice. He drew in his breath sharply at her swift grace.

At first he could think only of the soft, rounded body tight in his arms, the little hands that clung so eagerly. Her quick, broken words were low in his ear, almost indistinguishable from his own hurried whispers. When her tenseness slackened he looked down at her, her head thrown back against his shoulder, her eyes closed and her lips parted. Her eyelids fluttered and her mouth curved in a smile. "Your telegram, darling. It was such a wonderful surprise."

He kissed the white column of her throat. "And there is another for you, *chérissete*."

Her eyes widened eagerly. "What is it?"

He laughed softly. 'A gentleman—I trust—whom you must meet."

She looked bewildered. "Oh—a man? Is he nice?"

"It is my hope that he wins your eternal approval." He stepped back, bowed. "May I present to you Mr. John de Mérac—American citizen?"

She laughed. "You're so funny, John."

"But I am serious!"

"What on earth are you talking about?"

"I tell you, I have taken the logical step. I have become an American citizen, with the help of my friends, the Mannings."

She drew herself up and her eyes narrowed. "A citizen! You're fooling. You *couldn't!*" She put her hand to her throat. "You—you mean you aren't a Frenchman any more? You're just an American?"

"Just an American, *ma chère*. A fellow countryman of your own."

She turned white. "American! My God. Loudéac! What about Loudéac?"

He tried to take her hands but she snatched them away. He stammered in amazement. "Louise—think only an instant—"

She moved quickly from him. "Think? *Think?* What's there to think about? Stop pawing the air and tell me about Loudéac."

"*Doucement*. The property is my uncle's until his death in any event and—"

She rapped out, "And when he's dead?"

"Then, since under the old deed it may not go to one who has become a subject of a foreign power, it will very likely pass to my cousin Alceste. I wish him joy of it. It is not, I assure you, a cheerful place to live unless one brings with one the habits and customs of the sixteenth century."

Her eyes snapped. "And you—*you* let it go, just to be an American! And another thing! What about your title?"

"Ah—as to that, it is something which I have not used here, so—"

Her fingers flew to her hair and he saw his diamond

winking among the bright tresses. "My God, what a fool I've been. The talking I've done! I'll never be able to hold up my head again. Never!"

He stood, staring and dumbfounded. "Louise! One moment! You don't understand!"

"I certainly *do* understand. You get those citizenship papers and you tear them up and—"

He caught her, tried to draw her closer. "*I* have not changed. I am still the fiancé who loves and adores—"

She wrenched loose and turned on him across a long table. Her voice was shrill with anger. "You fool! Who do you think *you* are? You conceited idiot, take your title and things away from you and not even a trollop would look at you twice, and I don't care if it *is* a bad word. I chose you because I was fool enough to think—" Her fists drummed on the table. "What are you now? Just another Yankee captain. Oh! I thought I was being so smart. Go ahead! Gloat over me. It makes me sick to think of the way I had to let you paw me." She slammed her hands on the table again and her gold bracelet clanked against the wood. She lifted her wrist, glared at the gold band, and then with surprising strength her fingers ripped the old crested ring from the links that held it. She hurled it onto the table. It bounced, struck against a lamp, and rolled at de Mérac's feet. "That's what I think of that piece of brass! And this!" She stripped the diamond from her finger and sent it spinning. "I don't ever want to see you again. I don't ever want to hear of you."

De Mérac snapped out, "Louise!"

"Didn't you hear me? And don't shout at me as if I was one of your nasty hired soldiers. You've humiliated me and tricked me. Now get out!" She spun in a whirl of wide skirts and ran to the door. Over her shoulder she called, "Don't hang round here hoping I'll come down again, because I won't and that's flat, *Mr.* de Mérac!" Her shoes drummed up and up the stairs.

He stood staring after her. Then he mechanically picked up the two rings and slipped them into his pocket. As mechanically, he walked from the room, picked up his tall hat in the hall, and let himself out onto Fourteenth Street.

In his room at the Fifth Avenue Hotel he sat in a stiff chair by the window, turning the rings over and over in his hands. At last he sighed. "The poor little *môme*. She had built so much on so little." He jingled the rings together as amazement, surprise, and disillusionment rolled through his mind. "She might at least have heard me speak. But she gave me no chance. I could not tell her that while I may renounce Loudéac, the pretty little title of Baron is not affected—in France at least. *Ça*—that hurts, that she would not hear me."

He got up slowly and strolled to his dresser to look through the pile of letters that had come for him. With surprise he saw a note from Claire Wilson. She had written the hastiest of lines. "Can you possibly be at the Cortlandt Street ferry tomorrow morning? I'm taking the 10.10 for Washington from Jersey City and want very much to see you."

He drew a long breath as he got into his worn old uniform. Not only could he be at the ferry, he could take the very same train with Claire.

The next day, well before ferry time, he stood in the echoing shed, looking out from its dimness to the bright North River and the purplish heights of Hoboken. There was a touch at his elbow and Claire Wilson smiled up at him. "This was good of you, John. I hated to take you away from Louise when you've just come back."

He raised his eyebrows. "You are always thoughtful, Claire. But the taking away has been done—as Craig would say—in perpetuity."

She gasped. "Oh, *John!* I *am* sorry. You've had enough hurts without *that*. Do you want to tell me about it?"

He shrugged. "What little there is to tell, Claire, you'll hear on the cars. I'm going to Washington with you."

She looked keenly at him, then nodded. "I see. I'm so glad we'll go down together. Now listen. I'm breaking all sorts of laws."

"*Épatant*, my dear Claire. I have always dreamed of a life of law defiance."

"See that girl over there on the bench?"

425

He craned his neck. "It is—why, it's Dora Chase!"

"I'm abducting her. That idiot father of hers has done about everything except shut her up in a nunnery, and he'd do that if the nuns were broad-minded enough to let him in, too. He's out of town now. I'm taking her to Washington and George is there waiting. Here I am acting like a corrupt duenna out of Molière."

"It is mad! It's ridiculous! It's superb!"

Claire tossed her flowered bonnet. "I don't feel the least bit sorry for Jonas Chase. But he can't do anything. New York law doesn't hold in the District of Columbia, a fact which Craig calmly announced to me after I'd been fretting for months trying to find a way out for those children. Jonas can cut off her money for the present but when she's twenty-one he'll have to give her what's hers. I do wish I could have got word to Willett and Ella Force, but they're up the Hudson somewhere. Anyway I know I've got carte blanche from them." She threw back her cape and waved. "Dora! Dora! Here he is."

Dora slipped through the crowd, her face alight. "I was afraid I'd be going down there without being able to tell George I'd seen you, John."

"He will see me, for I appoint myself military escort for you."

"Then you'll be at the wedding! I'm so happy and I can tell you George will be, too. Major Wilson can't come. She was suddenly grave. "John, am I doing something dreadful? I can't feel that I am. And yet—poor Father!"

"The dreadful thing would be to stay in New York. Now here comes our ferry."

It was a wonderful sight, de Mérac thought, as George and Dora came up the steps of St. John's Church through the clear June sunlight. Dora was slim and lovely in much-ruffled dark blue and smiled up at her fiancé over a great sheaf of yellow roses. George threw back his head exultantly as he waved his kepi. Just behind them, Claire Wilson looked quietly radiant. George called, "Hi, fellow citizen! I've been trying to tell Claire, all the way up from the docks, what a wonderful thing all of you have done and I made a fearful mess of it." He held out his free hand and caught de Mérac's. "Honestly, all I can say is just 'Gosh.'"

"Never mind, George," Claire laughed. "You looked a lot more than that."

De Mérac chuckled delightedly as he watched the two, standing close together and their eyes always seeking each other's. "But I did nothing more than applaud the wisdom of Dora and Claire. No, no, *mon vieux*, I can't claim credit." He patted George's shoulder. "Not that I shall not try to and—*mais enfin*—what is this?" He stared at the new shoulder straps with their double bars of silver.

Dora said proudly, "I was wondering how soon you'd notice them. I'm going to be Mrs. Captain, John."

De Mérac clapped his hands. "But I find this marvelous."

George grinned. "Happened just before I left. I got these bars from a sutler at Acquia. Oh—but the biggest thing—Claire—you haven't even hinted at that. Listen, John—Craig's gone up to lieutenant colonel! What do you think of that? Oh, there've been some big changes in the Rifles. Tell you about them later.—Oh, sorry— Dora told me about you and Louise."

De Mérac cried, "Ah, it is no doubt for the best. Claire, I am happy about Craig, but all this must wait for the biggest change of all and for that the curate stands by the chancel. I have brought a witness—an old friend."

From the dimness of the nave burst Labanieff, magnificent in green and gold. He flung his arms wide. "Out of sight I wait until you greet your oldest of friends. Now, Mademoiselle Dora—" he bowed over her hand— "and George Force! Not for the governorship of the Crimea would I have missed this. The Legation gardens are not at their best, but they contributed a few blossoms to add to those of our dear Mrs. Craig Wilson and of *notre vieux* Jean." He fluffed out his beard, tucked his low fur busby more securely under his arm, and bowed again. "As senior in all ways, I represent the family of the bride. Mademoiselle Dora, you will take my arm and we shall proceed to the chancel. Dear Mrs. Craig Wilson, you will follow us at precisely three paces distance. Jean, you and my friend George Force bring up the rear, exactly six paces behind her. The step you will all take from me." He crooked an arm, offered it to Dora.

She slipped her hand under his elbow. "I'm so glad you could be with us, Colonel," she said softly.

Labanieff beamed. "But it is I who am happy as a young boyar. Now—if you please—the steps from me. It is most important." He threw back his head, kicked out his gold-tasseled boots, his bearing combining that of a high prince of the Church with that of royalty about to give over a daughter to another reigning house.

The end of the ceremony was quiet, blissfully free of the high-pitched, gushing good wishes of a formal wedding. George gripped de Mérac's hand and Dora kissed him gently. De Mérac said, "Now everything is what Rapp would call *klim-bim*. The wedding breakfast is arranged by Claire and myself. At one o'clock."

Labanieff sighed. "I must drink your healths *in absentia*. There was little notice and I was hard put to be here at all. I must go back to my duties." He raised his hand as George and Dora started to protest. "It wrings my heart that I must now make my farewells—" he sighed again—"especially as the breakfast is to be at Cruchet's."

When he had gone in a flurry of bows and good wishes, George whistled. "Cruchet's? How'll I ever go back to beans and bacon after that? Now listen, John, Dora and Claire and I are going out to Meridian Hill to see the house Claire found for us—all furnished and everything. You've got business of your own, Claire told me. Your worry is to get through that and be at Cruchet's at one."

"Then *en avant!*" said de Mérac. Arm in arm George and Dora went down the aisle. De Mérac and Claire followed. He suddenly felt a wave of loneliness, of vague melancholy, as he watched the two figures, their heads bent in low, happy whispers. So he himself might have walked, had not—he tried to shrug off the feeling. Louise no longer stood for a deep hurt in his mind, but still the sense of loneliness persisted.

The wedding breakfast was bright and sparkling as the sunny private room at Cruchet's where scented air flooded lazily in through open windows. De Mérac, a little late, burst in upon the party. George called, "Two days on regimental fatigue for you. This is the army, sir. Can't have unpunctuality."

Dora cried, "George! His coat. Look at his coat!"

"Coat? Coat? Well—I'll be—"

It was new and glossy. Cut in cavalry style, it fitted closely and ended at the hips. Its double-breasted front showed two rows of seven buttons each. Claire exclaimed, "And the shoulder straps! Eagles!"

De Mérac bowed. "Did you ever see birds with such kindly expressions? Note the right one especially. Oh, you shall hear all about it! Now waiter—bring on the sherry with the soup and on no account allow the chef to hurry the *soufflé* which comes later. It must be brought in as light as our hearts." He smiled as the party took its seats. Gone was the feeling of depression which he had experienced earlier. Instead, he was filled with a deep happiness that increased while the talk, as carefree as talk could be in the early summer of 1863, flowed about the table.

Claire looked up from the famous planked shad that followed the soup. "I haven't forgotten that we haven't heard the story of that lovely jacket, John. Not to mention the eagles that we drank to. Did they all come from the War Department?"

De Mérac laid down his fork and his face became grave. "No—in fact the business about which I was so mysterious didn't take me there."

"Don't tell me you've been nosing around Senators." George sounded shocked.

"Not at all. I was taken to the White House."

"To the *Pres*ident?" Dora's soft voice was hushed.

De Mérac spread out his hands. "I wish you could have seen him. He is weary. So weary. Yet he found simply because he felt that injustice had been done. time to concern himself with a mere captain of infantry,

And, as it had been done, he felt that he must right it as best he could." He paused.

"What did he say?" asked Claire eagerly.

De Mérac hesitated. There was much the President had said about the loyalty and the steadfastness of the foreign-born troops, of the debt the Union owed those who fought from sheer conviction. He could still hear the slow, grave words. But they must not be repeated, unless by one born in the Union. He sipped his wine. "What he said, Claire? Why, he talked of reparations, in which I was not interested. Then he said that since I was now a fellow citizen, I must be aware that he was Commander in Chief of all the armed forces. As such, he said, he was responsible for their well-being. I must serve in the place and with the rank that he thought best. Reparation to me was by his order and was not my decision. The entire country, he felt, was involved in all that might be considered unpleasant. So, in the name of the country, he commissioned me captain in the Regular Army. As I had enlisted in New York, that state was giving me a brevet as colonel. By his wish, as well as my own, I return to the Rifles. Ah, I cannot give you all this in his words. I cannot make you see his expression as he talked. That is impossible. I can only say that I came away prouder than ever to be citizen of the country of which he is President."

"Yes," said George slowly. "Old Abe hits you that way. Well, then you came right on here?"

"Oh, there were papers at the War Department after that, of course. Then I came by my tailor's and found that he had this shell jacket all made up, complete with eagles. It fitted me, so I walked out in it. And that is how I spent my morning. Now, for a moment, tell me something about the Rifles as you promised."

George threw back his head. "Oh, Lord. There's so much that I'll only try to sketch it. You see, when they began looking into your business, they found a whole lot more stuff that Pelham and his friends had done or been induced to do. Rotten, undercover stuff. They managed to get even Kearny's recommendations for promotion killed, let alone Stoneman's and Birney's. It's all fixed now. You know about Craig and me. Shea goes up to major. Bordagaray's a captain. Sergeant Rohleder's a first lieutenant commanding the Germans. They wanted to commission Rapp but he said 'Nix,' or words to that effect."

De Mérac grinned. "More like *'ta gueule'* or something less delicate."

Dora touched George's sleeve. "And tell him about Pelham."

George laughed. "Oh, you ought to see him now. He's stripped down to what's left of Pride's outfit and Clay's. We're under de Trobriand. Birney liked his work so much that he's made him acting head of the 3rd Brigade. It's us and the 17th Maine, 3rd and 5th Michigan, 40th New York—that includes what's left of de Trobriand's old LaFayette Guards—and the 110th Penn."

De Mérac's mind went back to the weary man in the White House. How that worn face would light up at the thought of men from four states, east and west, led into action by a citizen-colonel from Brittany! For himself, he felt quite indifferent to Pelham's reduced command. The cold-mouthed brigadier could no longer touch him or any other man for reasons of birth, or creed.

When *fine champagne* and *marc de Bourgogne* came on with the coffee he asked permission to smoke and lit a cigarette. He listened while George and the two women talked on about the new-found house. There were roses over one whole end of it and a little garden in front. It was high enough to be out of the valley heat and there would probably be few mosquitoes. In the fall—

De Mérac repressed a sigh. The fall was a long way off. George's brief wedding leave was nearly up and the next morning he would have to kiss Dora good-bye at the wharf. For himself, there were more papers to sign at the Department, a new kit to be bought. Colonel Townsend had recommended a stay of another three or four days, possibly more if the exigencies of the service permitted. He sipped his *marc*, fixed his mind on the immediate present and on the happiness of his friends.

De Mérac walked thoughtfully toward LaFayette Park with the June sun warm on his shoulders. He had completed the assembly of his kit, even to drawing spare ammunition for his Colt. The new uniforms, finished by his tailor at top speed, were of fine, light cloth, but almost severely plain. Save for the small eagles on his shoulder straps, and the double rows of buttons on the cavalry-style jacket that he had adopted, he could have passed for the most junior second lieutenant. He had ruled out the addition of thick loops and whorls of gold braid on his sleeves, decorations that the men disrespectfully termed "chicken guts." Of his original uniform, only the French-style kepi remained, a rakish kepi with its mended tortoise-shell vizor and brand-knew Kearny patch in the sunken crown. By his side clanked the open-hilted Austerlitz sword.

He kept on in deep thought, pulled at his mustache as he reviewed the interview that he had just had with the French minister, Mercier. The courteous summons to call at the Chancery had been unexpected and rather unwelcome. It was possible that Bonaparte's government had enacted penalizing laws for Frenchmen who surrendered their nationality, laws that might well strike back at any kin remaining in France.

To his surprise, Mercier was the model of suave urbanity. The name of Jean de Mérac, along with many others, had been removed from the displeasure, official or unofficial, of the Emperor. Every port in France was open, without let or hindrance.

"And more," Mercier had said, "through my dispatches, His Imperial Majesty has followed with interest the career of yourself, as well as those of Colonel Duffié and Baron de Trobriand. His interest has been highly benevolent, let me assure you. Despite your new citizenship, which in no way offends at the Tuileries, I hope one day to call upon you at your inheritance at Loudéac."

"But," de Mérac had objected, "under the old deeds, I renounce Loudéac in assuming this citizenship."

Mercier's amazement had been genuine. There could be no doubt about that. And there could be no doubt about his facts, he who was a renowned antiquarian. The deeds to which de Mérac referred were abolished by the Revolution. Mercier cited acts, supporting acts, confirmatory acts, until de Mérac's mind whirled and he left the Chancery rather dizzily.

As he kept on along H Street, he thought, "But by my great gesture, I renounced nothing. Nonetheless, the gesture was honest. I believed I spoke the truth when I told Louise that I could never hold Loudéac—and its revenues."

What if he had seen Mercier before Louise! He might still be held to his word, for it was the loss of Loudéac as well as the loss of title that produced her violent explosion. He was aware, in retrospect, that the scene had been a severe shock to him, but the sort of shock which a man experiences when he sees a crevasse open before him, sees it in the last safe moment.

Gardeners were working hopefully along the paths and over the new grass that hid the scars of earlier camps in LaFayette Park. Children raced along the graveled ways and Clark Mills's bronze Andrew Jackson bared its head to the sun in complete disregard of equitation. De Mérac slackened his pace. The peace of the scene, contrasted with what he would soon return to, soothed him and yet somehow rendered him uneasy.

On a bench under an elm, a slim girl in sprigged muslin read a copy of *Leslie's Weekly*. At the sound of his boots on the gravel she raised her eyes from the magazine. He started as a clear voice said, "Captain—oh, Captain de Mérac." In astonishment he looked down into the gray eyes of Gail Shortland.

He lifted his kepi. "But this is delightful."

She made room for him. "Can you sit down for a minute? Do smoke if you want to." She folded the magazine and turned toward him, the sun glinting down onto her red-gold hair. "I've tried to write you about your letter from Franconia. I wanted you to know what it meant to me. But it was hard to get onto paper and then—well, I don't imagine that girls who are engaged like to have other girls write to their fiancés. Of course it was different when you were at Fort LaFayette."

De Mérac said, "But my letter only thanked you for those you wrote while I was at Fort LaFayette."

She shook her head. "Don't you remember? You told me about that Mr. Manning and your talk with him. And you made me see so clearly what you felt you ought to do—and why you felt that way."

"Ah—yes. I knew somehow that you would understand Elliot Manning."

She clasped her hands in her lap and leaned forward, the light sifting down into the smooth roundness of her neck. "There was that. But what helped me most was your saying that you were coming back to the army. You see, your letter came when I'd about made up my mind to quit the hospital. I was so tired that I felt I'd done enough and we had a new matron who seemed nasty beyond belief. Then—I hope this doesn't sound funny—then I tried to imagine myself up on your rocks talking it all over with your Mr. Manning. I stayed."

"But that decision, if it were the right one, you would have come to by yourself," protested de Mérac.

She twisted the strings of the bonnet that lay beside her, eyes absorbed in the slow play of her fingers. De Mérac looked at the curve of her cheek, the firm set of her chin, the fine lines of her figure. Ah, but she was lovely, utterly feminine despite the businesslike mask that her work and her determination had given her. She raised her eyes quickly, glanced away as she found his gaze on her. Then she looked back at him and her eyes widened. "I didn't see them before. You're so tall, and then when you sat down—Your eagles! Oh, I do congratulate you."

De Mérac said gently, "I find that I do not like them, since I feel they interrupted something else you were going to say."

"Oh—it wasn't—" She suddenly seemed to him much younger, even more appealing, less self-assured. It was hard to imagine her directing the unloading of an ambulance. She went on hurriedly. "It was just—well, sometimes you form a very quick opinion of a person and then you go right on reading everything that that person

434

does or says in the light of that opinion—always twisting things to fit that first idea."

De Mérac nodded. "Ah—I believe you that one does."

Eyes still on her bonnet string, she said, "It's natural, I suppose." Then she looked up with her old friendly smile, friendly and impersonal. "Now don't let me keep you any longer if you were headed for the Department. Really, I wouldn't have stopped you except I wanted to thank you for that letter. Congratulations on the eagles again, Colonel de Mérac, and my best wishes for yourself and Miss Duane."

De Mérac said, "For the eagles, I accept your congratulations in their name—both the right and the left. But I ought to tell you that Miss Duane and I are no longer engaged. We part as friends, you understand."

Gail Shortland's hand flew to her throat. "Oh—but I didn't *know*. I—I can't have you think—"

"Think what?"

"I mean—I shouldn't have said that—about getting your opinions of people all wrong. I don't want you to think—" She broke off, rose quickly.

De Mérac stood beside her. "Think what?" he urged. He made an impatient gesture as voices clamored off on the Avenue. The voices came nearer. Newsboys tore through the Park, squalling at the tops of their lungs. At first the words were indistinguishable, then came louder and sharper. "Lee moving! Reb army on the march! Extra! Extra! Lee moving."

Gail turned to him, wide-eyed and alert. "Invasion?"

"I am afraid so. I must go to the Department. Can I find you here when I come back? I won't be long."

"But they'll be needing everyone at the hospital. I've got to go."

"Still, I want to ask—"

"Another time—I'll get that carriage over on H Street. No—please don't come with me. They may want you right away. Good luck." She fluttered a hand to him and hurried off over the gravel.

He watched her climb gracefully into the carriage, saw it bowl away. "*Diantre*—it almost seemed possible that I was about to learn why she always fends me off.

For an instant I thought—but all that must wait." He settled his kepi and walked quickly to the Department.

There he found messengers choking the corridors, anxious-eyed officers racing to the telegraph room. He managed to reach Colonel Townsend's office, where a harassed aide threw up his hands. "God knows what's happening. *I* don't. Gregg and Duffié hit Stuart's cavalry off by Brandy Station on the ninth. Oh—Lee's moving, all right. He's pulled everyone but Hood away from Fredericksburg. Looks to me as if Ewell's heading for the Blue Ridge gaps."

"The Blue Ridge?" snapped de Mérac. "No! He can't try the old Antietam move again. It is not possible. Lee is too clever."

The aide waved his arms again. "I don't *know!* I don't *know!* I don't *know.* Christ, Lee may be just regrouping or planning a strawberry festival. Read the papers if you want omniscience." He rubbed reddened eyes. "Hell! Sorry, sir. Didn't see the eagles. Been figuring out garbled telegrams all night."

"No harm done," said de Mérac. "Where do I find my regiment?"

"Can't tell yet. Hooker's moved your corps west—to watch Longstreet, I guess. Come in tomorrow. We ought to have better intelligence for you by then."

De Mérac left the War Department, spent hot hours buying a jaded horse at a ruinous price, and made ready for the next day. That night in his room at Willard's he pored over each extra that came out. While waiting for fresh editions he reread, slowly and thoughtfully, the letters that Gail Shortland had sent to Fort LaFayette.

The next morning at the Department, he found the same aide holding a cup of black coffee in an unsteady hand. "Guess it's invasion, all right, sir. Longstreet's at the Blue Ridge now and Ewell's swung up toward the Potomac. Stuff's coming in so fast the wires are smoking but it all points the same way. Hooker's got orders to cover Washington no matter what happens, so it's pretty sure he'll parallel Lee. Now your outfit—let's see—3rd Brigade, 3rd Division. IIIrd Corps—Centerville."

De Mérac hitched his belt. "So it is made easy for me, eh? I cross to Arlington and go on to Fairfax Courthouse." He smiled grimly. "Nonetheless, I dislike the omen of Centerville."

"Too close to Bull Run? Don't let that worry you. The corps'll probably have moved before you get there. Besides, we've had reports that the country's thick with guerrillas and you'd run a damn good chance of getting snapped up. This bank of the river's clear as far as Point of Rocks, so the office is sending anyone trying to pick up his outfit on the move to Edwards's Ferry to wait for it. You can bet your bottom dollar there won't be any action south of the river."

"The Ferry? Near Poolesville?" said de Mérac doubtfully. "It seems a long way around."

The aide shrugged. "When you try to hit a duck on the wing, you aim ahead of him and let him run into your shot. The way the IIIrd's been moving, you've got a good chance of picking them right at the fords. Got your travel papers all right? Well, good-bye and good luck, Colonel."

De Mérac came out of the Department into a sun that was beginning to blaze with premature summer heat. He gave a coin to the little Negro who held his recently acquired horse and carefully went over his equipment. The girth fitted just snugly enough, the stirrups were adjusted to the length. Two new Colts rested in the saddle holsters and oats for three days were neatly sacked on the pommel. To the cantle were strapped poncho, light overcoat, and two blankets. He tested the headstall absently. "This was not my doing, this route to Poolesville," he muttered. "And since I have plenty of time—for a corps cannot move as fast as that weary young man in there appears to think—and since my road leads out through Georgetown—" He left his thought uncompleted and vaulted into the saddle.

The road west trailed on through checkered stretches of shade and sun. When de Mérac saw the high slate roof that he sought glaring above a belt of deep green, he swung his mount along a side road until he came to the curving drive that led up to the gray bulk of the hospital. He halted at the gates, stood in his stirrups, and looked eagerly over the broad lawns. Care had been expended on the place since that day, nearly a year ago, when he had found George Force in the scarred ballroom. Now the grass was trim and smooth and there were roses everywhere—soft-glowing arbors of deep red, climbing masses of sulphur yellow, banks and banks of pink and crimson and cardinal. By a pool, iris showed deep purple and yellow. Hydrangeas lined a path, holding out their clusters of white blossoms. A thick hedge of lilac, higher than the head of a mounted man, rolled its rich perfume out to the sun.

The transformation de Mérac took in unconsciously while his eyes strayed slowly along wall and terrace. There were a few hurrying nurses in gray coveralls, a line of convalescents in long chairs, men in patched blue who limped through soft earth, tying up swaying rosebushes or spading languidly.

He shook his head. He had hoped that luck would grant him the sight of a slim figure moving within intercepting range. Now, inside the great pile, anyone wishing anonymity could easily secure it. *"Allons!"* he said to his unlovely horse.

The woman who met him just inside the door was an unmistakable matron—tall, angular, with a bony, rather masculine face, wideset competent eyes, and a small mouth shaped to give terse, uncompromising orders. Her patients she would view as impersonal objects to be dealt with firmly, but they would, if it were humanly possible, recover quickly and efficiently. Now she rapidly filed de Mérac in her mind—not a patient, nonmedical and hence unwelcome, someone to be disposed of quickly, regardless of rank. She said with a dry briskness, "Yes, Colonel?"

He took off his kepi. "I wish to speak with one of your nurses. Miss Gail Shortland."

"I am sorry. It is against the rules. All nurses within the limits of the hospital are considered to be on duty."

"The matter is important."

"Unless it concerns the administration of the hospital, our rules do not consider anything important."

"It does not exactly concern, perhaps—"

"Then may I suggest that you communicate with Nurse Shortland by letter. You'll excuse me, I hope. I am very busy. And we do not encourage visitors." She stepped back, obviously expecting him to leave.

He bit his lip, then said quickly, "There are higher administrations even than that of a hospital, Matron. You may recall that Miss Shorland gave evidence to the President on behalf of a Captain de Mérac." He emphasized the title. "The matter was thought to be of some importance and the President concerned himself directly with it. You may have read of the affair in the press."

"The papers do not interest me. They either say that we coddle malingerers or butcher heroes," she said dryly, but he could see that she was growing uncertain of her position.

He pressed his advantage. "I call in connection with that affair."

She frowned. "Then the case isn't settled?"

"All but one point—and it is felt that Miss Shortland alone can provide the answer to it. It is one of vital importance to the officer in question. As I say, the President took an interest in the case and it was thought better to see Miss Shortland in person rather than summon her to the White House, a measure which might take much of her time."

The matron shook her head. "I don't like to do this. Besides, I ordered her to take a rest this morning."

De Mérac raised his hand. "Ah, my dear Matron, I have every hope that what I tell Miss Shortland, added to what she tells me, will produce a tonic effect."

Her mouth tightened. "I suppose, Colonel, you could make trouble if I refuse. All right. Go out that side door and follow the path right to the little summerhouse and remember that this does not constitute a precedent."

"*Dieu de dieu,*" thought de Mérac as he walked on past a welter of lilac, "I do not dare let myself think that it does not." The path topped the western slope of the grounds and then dipped to a ledgelike grassy platform that looked out toward the river. He quickened his pace as he caught sight of the roof of a little latticed summerhouse. He checked himself. *"Doucement!* By all rules of chivalry I may not approach a fortress without first sending out a herald." He cupped his hands about his mouth and called, "Gail! *Ohé!* Gail!"

There was a brisk scramble inside the summerhouse, and Gail Shortland, in immaculate gray, stood in the rose-draped doorway, her hair bright in the sun. Her eyes were wide with surprise. She waited, silent, until he came close. Then she said, "You—you called me 'Gail'!"

He took off his kepi. "To warn you of my coming. If I'd used your last name you might have thought me a patient or even your lovely matron. In that case you would merely have answered, 'Yes?' instead of coming to the door."

She rested her hands on the latticework and said in a low voice, "You shouldn't have come. Matron will—"

"Matron is charmingly impressed with my credentials." His eyes were on her lithe rounded figure, framed by the roses.

She looked away. "You can't stay long, you know."

"That is the decision of Lee, not of the Matron. He's moving fast and the Department won't let me join the Rifles by the most direct route. I know that our time is short. Listen—we did not finish our talk in the Park."

"I shouldn't have begun it."

"We must discuss that, too." He moved closer. She stepped back quickly. He smiled and entered the summerhouse. There was one chair on the stone floor and a broad seat ran along three sides. He said, "Do sit down," and moved the chair forward. She sank into it, eyes still uncertain and fingers straying over the chair arms. He went on. "Yesterday you began to tell me that you had been under a misapprehension about me."

She said in a low voice, "You don't have to remind me."

"But when you learned that I was no longer engaged, you seemed to regret having spoken." He sat on the broad seat facing her and leaned forward. "In all fairness, don't you think you ought to go on?"

She whispered, "I don't know. It's—" She got up

slowly and walked to the far end of the house where she stood, one knee resting on the bench and her eyes on the blue-brown glint of the Potomac. She seemed to gather herself and went on. "Yes. I did think all sorts of things about you—"

"*Tiens!*" cried de Mérac. "Then you *did* at times—"

Without turning she raised a slim hand. "Please let me go on. I'd never known any foreigners before. And you seemed always so gay and always dashing about in Washington. And then, you *were* French and it seemed so sure that you'd be going home after the war. You had no roots here—no roots that touched mine. Then you were always with people with lots of money. And there was your title. It was just another thing that set you apart."

"But I do not use it here," he protested.

"No—but you had it. Don't you see? I know it was stupid of me but I began to form such a clear picture of you. Foreign, irresponsible, always amusing yourself, working hard at your regiment because it interested you, pleasant to meet but someone who would come lightly and go lightly."

"Ah, no!" said de Mérac quickly. "Not all that. We talked, you and I, at your aunt's dinner. I do not think that I made light of why I was here."

"There's where I was wrong again. You see—I came to think of that as some speech you'd thought up for such occasions. I snubbed you badly lots of times and you didn't deserve it. I knew that as soon as I read your letter from Franconia. When I saw you in the Park, I thought I'd make sort of an apology. I owed it to you." She faced him, hands behind her.

He said slowly, "I needed no proof of your fairness."

A trailing breeze, heavy with rose and lilac, drifted through the summerhouse. A sheet of paper rustled in Gail's chair, stirred, sailed to the floor. De Mérac snatched it up as he recognized his own handwriting. She took a quick step forward. "Oh, I thought I'd put that away. Please give it to me." She caught one edge of the sheet.

He looked steadily at her. "So—you read this—*my* letter—as you looked out over the Potomac?"

"No. I—I just had it with me. I was going to put it away." She sat on the bench at arm's length, still holding the sheet.

He said, "Gail—look at me." She turned her head away. "Very well," he went on. "You can't turn your ears away. You must hear this and you must answer this. Will you marry me? I hope I need make no more declaration than that. Ah—believe me, Gail, this is no—what is your word—'rebound'—for while I have not reread your letters as recently as you have mine, the difference is only a matter of hours."

She said in a low voice, "You mean that if I hadn't snubbed you so often—"

"I thought to myself just yesterday that you had always held me off like a Breton sailor with a boat hook. For that holding off, I don't blame you, whose chief thought was for the sick and the wounded."

She bit her lip, head still turned away. "You're not being fair!"

"Not fair? But you cannot say that—"

"You're not." She twisted suddenly toward him. You're making me say that you—well—I mean—the very first time I saw you and—" Her gold hair fell across one of the new eagles and the letter, suddenly released, fluttered lazily to the floor. At last Gail said shakily, "It's true—and I was afraid of so many things. I didn't dare let myself think of you most of the time. I was afraid of you for being French and afraid of your being a baron. I'm still afraid that you may be rich. People say you are but then everyone over here thinks that a title means being a nabob. Why didn't I see that that was all surface? Why didn't I see that really we were both going the same way, believed in the same things?"

"But how could you have? Much that I did must have seemed like confirmation to you. And why did I not know—not guess how you felt? Ah—had I, you would have needed far more than a Breton boat hook. Do turn your head and look up at me again like that. So!"

She said in a muffled voice, "But I *can't* look at you

442

when you're so close. Ouch! My hair's caught on your eagle."

"Don't move and you will not know it, my dearest Mrs. de Mérac. Now—as to one of your fears—some would call me rich, some poor, some comfortable."

"Oh—I'm still frightened of that. We're poor as church mice. You don't mind, do you? Dad's a darling old saint but he's refused call after call to bigger places because the people along the Mohawk do depend on him so."

"Through you I see him, Gail. Ah—could he have seen you as I saw you after Second Bull Run when you'd been out in the field—"

A voice snapped, "Well—really!"

De Mérac jumped to his feet. The matron, grim and forbidding, stood in the doorway. Her jaw quivered with surprise. "In all my years of work—impudence—brazen, double-faced-gall—I—I shall most certainly report you at once to the War Department, and as for you, Shortland—"

De Mérac said evenly, "The news I brought was tonic to us both, Matron." He put an arm about Gail, who had defiantly straightened up at his side. "As to Miss Shortland, may I suggest that your remarks be tempered by the knowledge that as soon as possible she will become Mrs. de Mérac."

The matron looked as though she would have been glad to doubt him, but at last her eyes wavered and she took refuge in sarcasm. "So I suppose we'll have to let her go with a campaign just starting and nurses so hard to get."

Gail's chin lifted. "We have married nurses and nurses that are engaged here. Of course I'll stay. The war isn't over." She leaned against de Mérac. "Colonel de Mérac and I both have our work to do."

The matron snorted. "Well—all *I've* got to say is—" She wheeled abruptly and tramped off up the path.

"What a beautiful sentiment," murmured de Mérac. "Gail, my love, this is forever—between us."

She said, "Of course, John."

"Plans we must leave for the moment—but they are a detail. The great thing is that we find each other on the same road." He sighed. "And now I must reclaim my lamentable horse and ride for Edwards's Ferry."

They walked arm in arm up the path to the front of the house. There, in full view of all the doors and windows, he kissed her good-bye.

She watched him ride down the drive, her hands to her cheeks. She whispered, "I won't—I won't call after him and tell him to be careful. But oh—I can't lose him now." She turned and ran into the building. "Why did I go to Centerville? I only saw a little—so little—but I know *something* of what he's going into and I wish I didn't."

De Mérac rode west, letting his horse choose its own pace. He felt very sober and oddly humble, as though from a high mountain a vision of great and quiet beauty had opened before him.

The red-eyed aide at the Department had vastly overestimated the speed of the marching armies, as de Mérac found when he rode down from the high ground about Poolesville toward the Potomac. Looking across the river to the rise where the village of Mahala marked the road to Leesburg, he could see no wink of steel, no stir of blue, no dust cloud lifting into the clear, hot air.

There was nothing to do but to follow the Department's instructions and wait, irksome as the prospect was. He found a room in a farmhouse between Poolesville and the river and spent his days studying the opposite shore. In the evenings while cowbells clanked through the still nights and mosquitoes whined against the muslin screens of his windows, he wrote long pages to Gail projecting their life together. Each noon he clattered into the Poolesville Post Office to find sometimes as many as three envelopes addressed in her graceful script. There might be a single sheet filled in a spare moment, or a pack of closely written pages. He read them all with a feeling of solemn joy, seated under a big oak not far from the river, and every line told him of a life fulfillment such as few men dare hope for or even dream of.

XVIII

Gettysburg

WHILE he waited, Lee's swift columns were sweeping up through the vast shovel scoop to the west of the Blue Ridge Mountains that ran from deep Virginia on through Maryland, across Pennsylvania, even to the low banks of the Susquehanna. By the seventeenth of June, Rodes, with Jenkins's cavalry, had passed Hagerstown and was circling about Chambersburg in Pennsylvania. Then Longstreet and Ewell were at Hagerstown, pouring north and east through the tree-shrouded funnel.

To the east of the gray surge, the Union blue flowed cautiously, hampered by the orders that made the defense of Washington the first charge on Hooker, but following a course roughly paralleling Lee's. To the east again, the bulk of the Southern cavalry was starting on a wide-flung raid that would pace Stuart and Hampton and "Rooney" Lee between Hooker and Washington, would finally carry in a great arc to Columbia on the Susquehanna and to the very gates of Harrisburg, the Pennsylvania capital. So the blue tide rolled slowly on between two distant banks of gray.

De Mérac found old maps in a brick schoolhouse that

was closed for the summer, and tried to visualize Lee's aim. The grave, calm Virginian seemed to be following step for step his strategy of Antietam, and as that move had seemed to de Mérac to have been a vague, fumbling raid-in-force, the parallel afforded him little light. What could Lee *do*? Was it possible that the move had been forced on him by Richmond as moves had been forced on Union leaders by Washington? Was it a gesture of desperation, a stroke simply for the sake of striking, with no clear aim as its result? De Mérac smoked innumerable cigarettes, drank endless cups of coffee as he pored over the colored maps which gave forth no answer. "I give my tongue to the cats," he wrote to Gail. "Does he mean to sweep north and then come down on Washington? No. He can hardly do that for then he will have stretched his lines so far that he will have Hooker on his right flank and rear. No, *ma mie*, the very vagueness of all this alarms me. There will be blasting times ahead. You will be equal to them and I must try to be."

The next night, the twentieth of June, he scrawled a hurried note to her. "I can wait no longer, *très chère*. Despite orders, wherever the IIIrd is, I go to meet it. *Rassure-toi*. All is quiet and I shall write soon."

Before dawn the next morning he crossed the Potomac, followed the course of Goose Creek a mile or so, and then struck off down the road toward Gum Springs. The sun was a molten spot in a murky sky, promising heat despite the lazy breeze that rippled through the fine oaks and dawdled past whitewashed cabin walls. To the south the horizon looked sticky with its bank of haze. Haze?

The haze was yellowish and stirred with a life of its own. Troops on the march, trailing dust-cloud banners endlessly. De Mérac laughed with a high gaiety and sent his horse trotting down a side road toward a thinner plume of dust where the traffic would be less dense. Suddenly he was among free-striding infantry whose kepis were marked with the red crescent of the 1st Division, XIth Corps. Regiment by regiment they strode past him—von Einsiedel's 41st New York, Kovacs's 54th, Gottholf Bourry's 68th, and Frueauff's 153rd Pennsylvania.

De Mérac shouted questions, received a variety of answers. The IIIrd Corps was "somewhere back there, I guess" or *"bei der* Gum Springs, *ja"* . . . "Keep off the main road. Von Steinwehr's on it and Carl Schurz is right behind him." Then in a gap between von Gilsa's brigade and that of Adelbert Ames he saw dust sifting through an orchard, noted the rutted brown of another lanelike road, and shot toward it.

The road was jammed with quick-stepping men in green and he hailed the Swiss, Casper Trepp. Colonel Trepp shouted over the grind of boots that the 3rd Brigade was *"Là-bas*—already marching *sacs à dos."*

Là-bas! He was closer and closer to his friends and his regiment! Horsemen beat down the road toward him and Colonel de Trobriand shouted to him in bas-Breton, embracing him with both arms. Yes, yes, the Rifles were not a mile away and pushing on strongly. *Vas-y, mon ami,* and take command from Wilson at once.

Less than a mile. De Mérac spurred on, road and trees blurring until a thick rope of blue just ahead tore the air with a frenzied, spontaneous cheer and broke ranks to sweep about him as he slid from the saddle. There was George, there was Craig Wilson. Then Shea and Rapp and Sergeant Gallifet and Private Holtzer and Private Mulcahey and Private Adams. Sleeves reached out toward him from the pressing welter, sleeves with frayed *galons*, with the broad V's of sergeants and corporals, plain, worn sleeves. There was Castex, DuChesne leading Lisette with her fine, black head and sensitive ears. His wrists aching with repeated handclasps, his shoulders stinging with hearty slaps, de Mérac thought shakily, "Oh, no, no! Never could I have stayed away. *This* is where I belong!"

The pace of the march quickened, became surer as they crossed the Potomac at Edwards's Ferry and swung west toward the Monocacy and Point of Rocks. By the twenty-sixth they had plunged deeper inland pointing north toward Jefferson, Middletown, and Frederick. In a way it was like the march to Antietam. There was the same eager, reaching stride in the columns that wound on through Maryland, the same straining. Yet there was a difference. The year before the dominant hope was to catch Lee in the flank as he fell back from his strangely planned raid. But now Lee was far into the north, fanning out and out. His men were reported simultaneously about York, Carlisle, Gettysburg, Chambersburg, Greenwood. Where would they appear next? In the hills above Philadelphia? Along the Delaware? Already they had engulfed the homes of thousands who marched up the valley of the Monocacy with the Catoctin Mountains towering on the left. Yes, it was different now; something new, something grim, cold, and hard underlay the drive and the plunge of the blue columns.

Through trim Maryland towns de Mérac led the Rifles and saw the citizens pour out of their houses to cheer as they had cheered a year before. Again women ran down the column with loaves of bread and pitchers of milk. Old men hobbled into the street to quaver hopefully as they caught at passing hands. From open windows, flowers pelted down. Yet these people were different as the marching men were different, and in their eyes there was a dark, unspoken question. Before Antietam the gray tide had been way, way off beyond the mountains and their steep gaps. Now it hung above the little towns, hung just over a state line to the north and east.

At each camp de Mérac rode Lisette to division headquarters for news, fearful each time that intelligence might show the whole gray mass curving down toward Washington. On the night of the twenty-eighth of June he returned from his quest and found Wilson, George, and Father Doyle sitting in a garden beyond Harmony Grove, a still, scented spot in front of a gray stone house with Tuscarora Creek whispering beyond the last bed of phlox. Wilson asked sharply, "What's up, John?"

De Mérac perched on a stump and lit a cigarette. "Brevoort showed me the disposition of corps. The Ist, XIth, and XIIth cover South Mountain as far as Turner's Gap. The IInd, Vth, and VIth are close behind us. We may move to any point of the compass to counter Lee, so I think that *that* danger is over."

"And what danger might *not* be over, Colonel?" whispered Father Doyle.

"One that now begins."

"*Begins?* What other danger *is* there?" asked Force. "We can cover Washington, and Lee can't move without our hitting him—our seventy thousand against his."

De Mérac said quietly, "Hooker has just resigned since he feels that Halleck, safe in the War Department, ties his hands."

"Saints above!" said Father Doyle. "And the army sure to have action within the fortnight. It's little time the new man'll be having to get ready."

Wilson flicked his cigar butt into the creek. "Don't tell me they've given the job back to Burnside!"

"No, Craig. To Meade."

"*Meade?*" cried George.

Doyle said, "I'm not knowing the man."

"No reason why you should," said Wilson. "Lord, the man's drab as a Quaker's bonnet. The only thing I remember about him is that he's a Pennsylvanian—oh yes, and his men call him a 'God-damn goggle-eyed old snapping turtle'!"

De Mérac laughed shortly. "Men have been appointed to high command on far odder qualifications. Nonetheless, Father Doyle, Meade will not have even a fortnight in which to prepare. Lee is massing his whole strength, aiming, I think, for some spot close to the south border of Pennsylvania. On our very roof, one may say."

Wilson slapped his kepi against his knee. "Good Lord, and Meade's got to face all that before he's got his saddle warm! Oh, there's something wrong there. It's a job that even Phil Kearny couldn't do."

De Mérac rose from the stump. "Nonetheless, it is one that Meade *must* do—Meade and ourselves."

"Hell," said George. "Makes me feel all empty inside. What's Meade doing?"

"He accepts the job, and with it, Lee's challenge."

"How?" asked Wilson.

A bugle blared in the night, close by the garden.

"Thus," said de Mérac. "The Ist and XIth will be at Emmitsburg tomorrow. And that pretty tune which Castex plays tells us that we leave at once for Pipe Creek just south of Taneytown. *Mes amis*, I think there will be some very hard fighting ahead—and that before the week is out."

They marched on through soft darkness and felt in their faces the damp air of Pipe Creek, brought by the stirring winds that crept down through the hill gaps to the east of Westminster and Manchester. George found that it was increasingly difficult to keep his files closed up. Fierce eagerness still held the whole column, as it held every column on the move through the Maryland night. But the hard highways gnawed at feet softened by miles and miles of the yielding red and brown Virginia roads. Men stumbled on, walking on their heels, walking on the sides of their feet, swinging their ankles rigidly, leaning on sticks, shuffling crablike to ease burning blister or aching callus. Sometimes they fell out, sobbing with fatigue and pain, then hobbled on again muttering broken curses.

George felt the sting and beat with the rest, for he spared himself nothing that his men had to face. At halts he flashed a bull's-eye lantern on the faces of the resting files, curtly ordered two or three to fall out and join the company later as best they could, knowing that the effort to keep up would lead to collapse. To one man he gave a note authorizing him to ride in one of Quartermaster Brady's wagons, now following in the wake of the brigade.

But there was one marcher for whom he could do nothing. Mr. McArdle, almost alone of the dogs of the regiment, still wallowed along with George, now dropping back, now lashing himself into a whimpering trot that brought him to the head of the company and his master again. By a swift brook, George urged him into the water, then examined his feet by the light of the lantern. Rough, unyielding surfaces had cracked the pads that oozed slow, dark drops

"Christ Almighty, what am I going to do?" thought George as the march started once more. He tried walking through the fields that edged the road, but they were covered with a sharp stubble that brought shrill yelps from the dog and sent him lurching back to the road.

Sergeant Hooks watched the dark shape toiling along the column. "Hey, fellers, the pup's in trouble. Fix him up. He joined up in Chambers Street!"

Before George could take in the plan, the men had rigged a crude stretcher of poles and coats, tumbled Mr. McArdle onto it and lifted him shoulder-high. But the dog was restless, raising and lowering himself on his front legs, jamming his head over the side as though to jump. The men, exhausted and footsore, labored silently under their added burden.

George said, "Sorry, boys, it won't do."

"What you want, Captain?" growled Hooks. "Going to leave him to get run over by a mule team like Kling's dog?"

George tilted his kepi onto the back of his head. What *was* there to do? Then he saw a light shining across the fields. He held up his arms. "Let me have him. I'll catch up."

The dog was heavy and awkward to carry. He thrashed his four legs about, wriggled, tried to lick George's cheek. At last George knocked on the blistered door of the farmhouse.

A thick-bearded face showed in the lamplight as the door opened. A voice growled, "Ain't got nothing for Yanks here. Make tracks."

"Damn your politics," snapped George. "It's my dog. He's broken down." He set Mr. McArdle on the splintery floor, one hand tight on his collar. "I just want to leave him with you till his feet heal."

The small eyes above the beard brightened. "Feet ought to be wore clear through if our boys been chasing him along of you." He patted Mr. McArdle gently. "'Bout tuckered, boy, huh? Sure, I'll look after him. I'm the only real loyalist in these parts and I'll learn him to sing 'The Bonnie Blue Flag' afore sunup."

"Teach him the Black Mass if you want to." George laid a dollar on the scoured table. "This'll pay for his keep till I can get back here."

The man waved contemptuously. "Put it away. Bob Lee'll have you scooting past here so fast that your vest pockets'll be scooping sand and your pup won't have time to eat a dime's worth. Now you jump out that door quick so he can't duck after you. I'll tie him up."

Back on the road with the column, George pushed stubbornly on, trying to close his ears to the sharp barking that cut through the night.

It was the morning of July first, a hot clear morning. Holiday weather, the sort of day to sit on a sunny beach and mock the endless industry of the surf, to eat sandwiches in a pine grove while creels and rods stood idle against a tree close by. Orioles flashed through the bright fields where the Rifles lay encamped close to Emmitsburg, dragonflies were metallic darts over the pools where horses and mules gulped eagerly. Locusts sailed toward the green shimmer of the oaks with a rending *yeeeeee*. The air was hushed and gentle.

De Mérac smoked in the shade of an elm and watched the five companies of the Rifles falling in for inspection —five companies that averaged less than forty men each. Yet it seemed to him that in fighting value those five were worth double the ten full companies that he had taken in action over the low ridges about Frayser's Farm barely a year ago.

Wilson rode onto the field and dismounted by de Mérac. "Division doesn't know a thing, John. Plenty of rumors, though. They say Buford's cavalry's run into the Rebs beyond Gettysburg—I think that's the name of the town—and the Ist and XIth are moving up to support them. But that's only talk, so far's I know."

"There were no signs to tell you more?" asked de Mérac.

Wilson laughed. "Two, perhaps. Four of Matt Brady's 'Whatzit' photograph wagons were pulling out of Bridgeport heading north and I saw Labanieff heading the same way. He's worried. Says so far as he can gather. Lee's moving down pretty compact and we're still scattered badly. I left him drawing parallels from Marathon to Waterloo."

"But you heard no sounds—nothing like firing?"

"Quiet as Central Park. Guess that means nothing's on."

De Mérac frowned. "Perhaps. But sound plays odd tricks. For instance, I have read that the firing at the battle of Bennington was not heard two miles distant." He snapped his fingers. "An old trick which I forget." He sent Castex to the neighboring 40th New York—which now included the remnants of de Trobriand's original LaFayette Guards—to borrow a drum. This he placed on the ground and then pressed his ear to its taut top.

George strolled up, reasonably at peace with the world. He had managed to find time to write Dora, and a man whom he had sent back on a borrowed horse to the farm of the Rebel sympathizer had reported that while Mr. McArdle still yelped, the farmer had cunningly bandaged his paws after smearing them with healing ointments. George called. "What are you doing, John? Taking the pulse of the world?"

De Mérac got up and gave the drum back to Castex. "Sometimes it happens, on certain kinds of ground, that drumheads will give off a vibration from gunfire that is out of earshot."

"Well?" asked Wilson.

De Mérac shrugged. "Either the ground is not right or there is no gunfire." He looked about the pleasant rolling valley where the Rifles lay. The view to the north was blocked by higher ground. "Napoleon always longed for some magic that would let him see what was happening behind the next hill. I sympathize with him." He slapped his hands together. "Ah! Why didn't I see that before?" He pointed off toward Emmitsburg where a high white cupola, topped by a gilded cross, hung in the bland sunlight. "There is my magic. Father Doyle!"

The chaplain, drawn and haggard, limped up. "You're needing me?"

"As ambassador. You can ride? Then take my spare horse and come with me. Castex! Dekdebrun!"

As the four rode off down the shady road de Mérac called the chaplain's attention to the cross against the soft blue of the sky. Father Doyle started. "And it's there you're going? Mother of God! 'Tis the Convent of St. Joseph!"

"To me—at least for the moment—it can only be a building with a high cupola. Father, I *must* climb it."

Doyle said resignedly, "I'll explain to the Mother Superior. More I cannot do. The permission must be hers, you'll understand."

"*Parfaitement*," said de Mérac.

They trotted on past fields thick with troops, past batteries unlimbered at crossroads. Then they turned in a long drive, clattered up to the wide brick front of the convent. A startled, elderly lay sister, evidently the doorkeeper, stammered in amazement. De Mérac disregarded her as he saw the robed figure that stood in the opening. She was tall and her face, framed by the tight coif, was unlined and glowed with a sure, inner calm. Her hands, which were folded before her, were white and tapering. De Mérac whipped off his kepi as Father Doyle dismounted and said a few, rapid words in an undertone.

The Mother Superior listened quietly. Then she looked at de Mérac and nodded. "The convent chaplain will show you the way," she said in a low, rich voice. "The nuns are all in their cells at this hour so you may go freely." She inclined her head and stepped aside.

The chaplain, a bent old Italian, pattered ahead of de Mérac and Father Doyle through long, echoing corridors. De Mérac's spurs and scabbard clanked in startling incongruity as he strode by framed prints of saints and martyrs, past closed rooms where, doubtless, nuns knelt in prayer. The Old Italian finally opened a door on the top story and motioned de Mérac up a flight of narrow, dusty steps.

He started up quickly, aware of a stir and murmur above him. Then he breathed "*Vingt dieux!*" as his head emerged through the trap.

Pressed to the windows of the cupola were the eager faces of a dozen young nuns, utterly absorbed in the spectacle below them, staring at galloping aides, at a battery on the march with its red guidon proud at its head, at lines of stacked muskets, at sentries walking their posts, at every detail of this vibrant, startling, undreamed-of world that lay at their feet.

Then one of them turned, squeaked like a mouse, and de Mérac looked into twelve startled faces. Some of the nuns gaped in a daze, others covered their eyes with their fingers. There was no retreat for them, since de Mérac blocked it. They fluttered back against the wide windows like birds beating against the bars of a cage.

Then Father Doyle stood beside de Mérac and an infectious grin played about his strong mouth. "Ah, the sin of curiosity's a very venial one I'm thinking, sisters, and no doubt Father Sant' Ilario'll give absolution therefor."

The sisters still looked terrified. Then one of them put her fingers to her lips and giggled, pushed her neighbor playfully, and turned her back on the men. Tension broke and the girls, novices by their robes, scurried down the narrow stairs, in a cloud of whispers and stifled, half-shocked laughter. A muffled voice drifted up, "Isn't he *hand*some?" "Which one?" "Both, you goose. Oooh. Don't pinch me!"

De Mérac and Father Doyle exchanged glances. The latter said, "Ah, and it's no harm they'll be taking."

"They'll take none in this house under that Mother Superior," said de Mérac gravely. The deep calm of the convent, its detachment from the wrenching world outside, had impressed him profoundly. Then he turned to the windows and at once forgot convent and inmates.

The cupola dominated the whole countryside, looked far to the tree-masked hills of the north. De Mérac got out map and glasses, took a reading from his compass. Gettysburg. That was the name of the town he had been hearing more and more the past few days, a sleepy little town where ten roads met, ten roads that could pour men onto the ridges that shut it in. Oriented, he raised his glasses.

He could hope to see no detail at ten miles' distance, but under his lenses the trees that must look down into little Gettysburg stood infinitely small, yet clear. Among the trees he could make out yellow-brown patches that were the open fields. He shook his head. Unless metal glinted to betray it, an entire army might lie on that far, high ground.

He raked the sky for telltale dust but could hope for little from the hard Pennsylvania roads. He only saw the endlesss blue of the sky, the sky and fat, woolly clouds, the clouds of fair weather, drifting across it. Clouds and— He exclaimed under his breath.

Just above the crest of an oak grove, a new cloud formed under his very eyes, a pin point of a cloud whose center winked hotly. Another formed just beyond it, tore itself into shreds that mingled with a third cloud, a fourth, a fifth, a sixth. Wind swept them out of his consciousness but six more formed in their place, still another six.

Father Doyle said, "You're seeing something, Colonel?"

De Mérac stepped back, handed the glasses to the chaplain. He needed no further evidence. "Look for yourself. Focus two fingers to the left of that bald hill." Doyle squinted, then whistled. "And it's shrapnel as I'm a sinful mortal. Does it tell you more?"

De Mérac said tersely, "A six-gun battery. Whitworth rifles, from the angle of the burst. English guns and hence Rebel."

The chaplain handed the glasses back to de Mérac. "So it's begun."

"It is well under way, Father. The Rifles must be ready to move at any minute."

Doyle nodded. "I'd be glad to be leaving at once. Some of the boys'll be wanting to confess that they've got drunk or stolen rations from another outfit or maybe looked at a girl longer than they should have and they'll be craving absolution. I'm thinking that men who go through what they do carry their own absolution with them and it's little help they need from me. After you, Colonel."

At the door they thanked the matron, who inclined her head gently in unconquerable calm, although she crossed herself when her eyes met those of Dekdebrun.

Back at camp, de Mérac held the Rifles under a rigid alert and waited for news and orders. In the late afternoon, thick clouds rolled slowly from the east, poured drenching showers over the camps and over the oak ridges to the north where de Mérac had seen white puffballs forming above the trees. He remembered Fredericksburg and was grateful for the rain which would extinguish the blazing grasses where the wounded lay. By nightfall he had a distinct sense that the darkness was filled with moving troops, but no orders came to him. After a hurried mess he sat, still waiting, with Wilson and Shea. All three were nervous and impatient. De Mérac lit one cigarette after another. Wilson paced restlessly up and down, brushing the back of his hand across his mustache, and Shea sat hunched on a log, pulling at his long nose and muttering under his breath.

Suddenly de Mérac hurled away his latest cigarette. Hoofs were coming toward them through the dripping night. Shea and Wilson froze at once. Colonel de Trobriand called through the darkness. *"Les Rochambeau! Hold! Les Rochambeau!"*

De Mérac felt his voice crack as he answered, *"Ici! Tout droit!"*

Then the acting brigadier dismounted and strode up to them. His tone was calm but there was an undercurrent of excitement in it. *"Bon soir, messieurs.* Sickles moves our corps to Gettysburg. We—"

"Then there's been fighting already!" cried Shea.

"I believe you, Major, there has been fighting. Sickles leaves his brigade and Burling's New Jersey men here."

"A fight and us not in it?" protested Shea.

"We may have more than we wish, *mon ami,*" said de Trobriand. "We guard the approaches to Emmitsburg since it is down that road that Lee will pursue—if he pursues."

"Things going badly?" asked Wilson quickly.

"No. Nor well. It is too soon. Neither army appears in full strength yet." The Breton spoke calmly. "But both sides fight like ten thousand devils. Buford's cavalry, dismounted, held off the first Rebel rush northwest of the town. More Rebels appeared. Also parts of our Ist and XIth came presently. Ah, it was hot, you conceive. My poor friend, General Reynolds, was killed. The Rebel

Archer and most of his brigade are taken and now march under guard down the Baltimore Pike. Our Schimmelfennig is missing."

"We still are northwest of the town?" asked de Mérac.

De Trobriand shook his handsome head. "We fell back. No—let us be frank and say that we were driven back by numbers far too heavy. We hold a ridge to the south and east. You will see it on your maps. At the north end is a cemetery, at the south two rocky wooded hills, and the Emmitsburg road runs at its base. *Alors*—hold yourselves in readiness for anything. My aide, Lieutenant Houghton, will bring you all that there may be of news. *Bon soir et bonne chance.*"

Wilson drew a long breath. "Well, I guess the big stakes are on the table at last."

"And Lee and Meade looking at their cards," said Shea. "We stand by same as ever, John?"

De Mérac nodded. "As ever. But each of you—see that every man cooks his rations before he sleeps. See that fire's burn to assure hot coffee when our orders come. George Force is in command of the guard. Be sure that that guard is as small as possible. Every man who can must sleep."

Wilson and Shea walked off through the gloom. De Mérac spread his poncho on the wet grass under a wide-branched tree and slid off his boots. The rain had stopped and he could see stars thinly veiled by scudding, ragged clouds. He wondered what Gail might be doing at that moment, what news was drifting down to the hospital above the Potomac. "Yes," he thought, "the stakes are on the table and they were never bigger. *Sang de dieu!* The fighting must *not* sweep south. It must not—for us. It must not—for the Union in which we believe and which a victory for Lee might shatter. *Dors-toi bien, Gail, ma bien-aimée.*"

Some hours later he sat bolt upright, his senses abnormally alert. The camp about him was still. Red fire eyes glowed among the sleeping ranks of the Rifles. Behind him he could hear the soft "crop-crop" as Lisette grazed contentedly at the end of her long tether. Off in the woods a bird chittered drowsily. De Mérac muttered,

"But it was *some*thing! I do not wake like this without—"

In the fields off to the right a lantern flashed. Leather lungs bellowed, "A Battery! Harness and hitch! Cannoneers! In the rear of your pieces—*fall in!*"

De Mérac bounded up, stamping his feet into his long boots. "Castex! *Lève-toi!* Sound the general!" On the echo of his words, hoofs thundered along the road, beat to a halt. Young Houghton of de Trobriand's staff leaned from his saddle as de Mérac ran to him. "The brigadier's compliments, sir. Rifles to fall in by the stone mill on the Emmitsburg road in half an hour from now, ready for instant action!"

De Mérac snapped, "*Entendu!* Inform the brigadier that the Rifles will be there—and on time!"

Houghton shouted, "Right, sir. The 40th's straight ahead, isn't it? Thanks." His hoofs beat off through the darkness.

To the blare of Castex's bugle, which was answered by the peals of the five other trumpeters of the regiment, the men of the Rifles shook themselves to their feet, adjusted clothing and equipment, crowded about the fires that sprang into new life, rattling coffeepots and tin cups. George handed a cup to de Mérac, who took it gratefully. "Guess this is the real big thing, John."

"Nothing more real, nothing more big, George. If we fail now, there will be no getting ready for the next time. There will be no next time."

"No use blinking facts, John. Look—if anything happens to me, I'd like Dora to hear about it from you. All right?"

"But certainly. And for my part, it is you who will see Gail? I do not feel that there will be need for either of us, but we have both seen too much to know that it cannot happen."

Randol clumped up, sniffing eagerly. "Got some coffee for me? Thanks. Say, is it true that Georgie Meade's hollering for us?" He groaned at George's terse assent. "Well, it's been a grand world, all full of wonderful liquor and red-headed women. Jesus, I'm going to miss it! Been a real pleasure to know you, gentlemen, at times. Company's all in order. In order to what? I'll think up the answer to that one and come back and tell it to you!"

"Write it to me," said George wearily. "Care of the American Consul at Macao. Hold till called for!" Randol tramped off, chuckling to himself. George said: "Damned queer what lack of sleep'll do to you. It gets me so lightheaded I almost start to think that that baboon's funny."

"I have never reached that state of fatigue," said de Mérac dryly. "But he makes the men laugh and they will need a lot of laughter between here and Gettysburg." Two mounted figures rode toward de Mérac. "Ah, Craig, you are ready? And you, Dan? *Bon!* DuChesne! Bring up Lisette! Castex! The command is forward!"

The roads were heavy with the late rain. The bad footing, added to frequent, exasperating halts, slowed the pace of de Trobriand's brigade to little better than a mile an hour. The sun broke over the hills behind the column, swung up the sky as the Rifles, leading the brigade, struggled on. Sometime after eight o'clock de Mérac checked Lisette. He pointed and cried, "Craig! You see that?"

Wilson got out his glasses and focused them on the rounded woody hills to the north, rising just to the right of the Emmitsburg Pike, swung them to the ridge that swept up on the left in generous contours. Then he lowered his lenses. "No mistake, John. Little Round Top and Big Round Top on the right. Seminary Ridge on the left."

De Mérac studied the western rise, slowly adjusting his eyepieces. "Two—three Rebel batteries moving along that ridge, Craig. There! Below them. The battle flag. A regiment. At the double."

Wilson bit his mustache. "And more just coming into sight. See—beyond that big white house in the grove. Yes, *sir*, we're riding right down a funnel between the two armies. Good Lord, if we'd been half an hour later we'd have walked right into them!"

Boots clumped up from the rear and de Mérac looked down at Rapp's red beard, the inevitable short pipe jutting from it. The pipe vanished as though by magic and Rapp saluted. "*Mon colonel*—no doubt it has been noted. But—*les Arabes—hein?*"

"They cannot reach us in time, Sergeant Major."

"Not those on the high ground, *mon colonel*, but those nearer among he rocks and trees—*ah, les méchants*—they make different case, those ones!"

De Mérac stood in his stirrups, staring off to the left. Past a plowed field, past an abandoned shed, long lines of gray skirmishers were moving swiftly. Smoke stabbed the still air and de Mérac stiffened as the old, high-pitched Rebel yell swept toward him. He spun his horse about. "Castex! Sound double time. Craig, please take the head of the column. You turn off the Pike beyond the peach orchard and halt by the house marked 'Trostle's' on the map. I wait for the rear!"

In a jangle of equipment the five companies broke into a heavy trot. De Mérac turned his back on the hurrying gray skirmishers and tried to hold himself steady as his men went by. He nodded to Bordagaray, to Rohleder of the Germans, to Gilhooley who commanded the Irish and the remains of the dead LeNoir's men, to George and to Randol, shepherding Bolton's old company. He hoped that he looked easy and confident, for such bearing would have a calming effect on the men. He only knew that the skin between his shoulders itched excruciatingly as his mind insisted on the presence of the gray skirmishers.

At last he saw the tail of Randol's company turning off the Emmitsburg Pike beyond the peach orchard and making for the Trostle house and the wheat field in front of it where the green of Berdan's Sharpshooters showed. Then he looked over his shoulder. The skirmishers were closer than ever, though not yet in dangerous range. They shouted to each other and the soft air carried their words clearly. "Hey! Go easy! Them ain't milishy! Ain't you seen them goddam red-tops to their caps? Christ, they're out'n Kearny's!"

The gray lines checked, came on more slowly. Men fired from time to time but the range was too great and the bullets hummed wide. An officer on a beautiful roan shot out of cover and headed toward de Mérac, obviously trying to cut him off. De Mérac took a quick glance down the road. The rest of the brigade, duly warned, had turned off and he could see the Kearny patches moving up over the rough ground just short of the Round Tops. He gathered Lisette, shot a look at the galloping officer on the roan, and started off toward the peach orchard at a smart trot.

The Rebel officer yipped like a fox hunter and the roan stretched out in a magnificent stride. De Mérac measured it, gauged the point at which his foe would strike his course, and gave Lisette her head. Her dainty hoofs seemed to flick along the Pike. His pursuer lashed the roan with his hat, coaxing the last burst of speed from her and driving toward a point where a board fence ran along the road on the right. His sword was out, but his pistols were still in their holsters. Men high on the ridge at the right, men in the fields to the left, began to cheer. The roan came on faster and de Mérac saw that the officer was young, with a fine blond beard that streamed in the wind. When he was twenty yards away, de Mérac swerved Lisette, put her at the fence. The mare gathered herself, sprang, shot over the rough boards in a tremendous leap, landed cleanly on firm turf on the other side. De Mérac slowed her down in a wide circle, looked back toward the Pike. The Southern officer's horse had balked the jump and he had been forced to turn her back into the fields. Blond beard glinting in the sun, he swept off his broad hat and waved to de Mérac. De Mérac laughed aloud, returned the gallant salute, and cantered on up the slope whose crest was thick with men in blue. Then he saw another horseman trotting down toward the road, a horseman who stared intently ahead, checked his mount, and raised a rifle. De Mérac shouted: "Dekdebrun! You will *not* fire!" The rifle still poised. De Mérac whipped out his Colt, sent a shot snapping into the ground just ahead of the horse, yelling: "Next time I will not miss. Put up your rifle and follow me!" Dekdebrun sullenly dropped his rifle into its boot and swung his horse toward de Mérac, eyes cold with resentment.

De Mérac skirted the south edge of the wheat field, crossed a rise where a hideous tangle of misshapen boulders loomed on his right. Directly ahead of him was more rough ground, thick woods, and the bald rocks of Little Round Top. He heard laughter among the trees, saw men waving to him. George ran to the edge of the woods and slapped his thigh. "What a steeplechase! How'd you know you could beat that Reb?"

"By comparing the stride of his mount with Lisette's," he answered. "And I saw from the roan's haunches it was not a good jumper." He dismounted and gave his reins to Castex, who had followed George out of the woods. Under the rough branches, the Rifles were shouting and cheering as though the race had been staged for their own benefit. Wilson jumped down from a rock, laughing in exasperation. "Pretty, John. Damned pretty. But what the hell did you do it for?"

"There was logic, I assure you. I wished to see if his men broke out when he did. They did not. Hence I judged that they were not anxious to show their weakness in numbers. I should say that there were only two or three small companies, wandering at a venture and unsupported by cavalry. A good run with Lisette was a small price to pay for the knowledge. No. I assure you that I was not playing *beau sabreur*. Any orders?"

"Birney's gone to look for Sickles. Geary's division of the XIIth just pulled out of here. I heard von Hammerstein of the 78th New York say that the whole lot's going on to a place they call Culp's Hill. It's to the east of some sort of a cemetery along this ridge." He rubbed his hands nervously. "I can't seem to get the hang of this terrain. Let's go up to the Little Round Top crest. Ought to be a good view from there."

"Excellent," said de Mérac. He called to Shea, who was deep in talk with Rohleder and Gilhooley. "Take command, Dan, unless you want to join us. If you do, leave Bordagaray in charge."

Shea shook his head. "I've been up there already. Besides, I'm telling these boys the story of Strong Man Clancy of Ireland that it's a shame that a man with the fine name of Gilhooley's not heard before."

De Mérac swung himself over the huge gray rocks with George and Wilson following him. Wilson panted, "Looks as if the devil had gone crazy up here." He pointed to boulder piled on boulder, to lichened mouths that led away into unfathomable blackness and tortured, twisting passages.

"It is like Les Baux in France where Dante got the idea for his *Inferno*," said de Mérac.

George grunted. "He ought to have signed up with the Army of the Potomac if he really wanted to know what hell was like. Let's have a look at the map, John."

De Mérac deftly unfolded the stiff sheet. "Will you hold the other corner, Craig? Thanks." He took a quick look at the far-spreading panorama. "Now we orient ourselves. Ça! This is simple as Fredericksburg. Two ridges form an amphitheater about the valley."

Wilson pushed back his kepi. "Spot out the points. Here we are on Little Round Top. How does it tie in with the rest of the business?"

"Look at it this way. The Round Tops form the left end of Cemetery Ridge which runs generally north and south. Start at the north, which we cannot actually see due to bends and curves. Here is Culp's Hill which runs north and then rounds in to join Cemetery Hill with its graves and great gates. Ah—these are fine maps they give us these days. But I feel that *our* interest in that fishhook end is academic."

"Good to know, though," said George. "Funny—the ridge is pretty much bare until we come right down here. Woods begin at—what's the name of that house? George Weikert's. Then they run east and west like a saddle right on to the end of the Round Tops. How about this stuff to our right front?" He waved a blue arm toward the rolling fields where neat roofs shone up through little groves of shade trees and corn and wheat rippled to the morning winds.

Wilson lowered his glasses. "Guess you're right, John. This is the part where our hunting licenses will be good. What's this road that runs up toward the crest just beyond the trees?"

De Mérac's eyes went from brown road to wavy-lined

map. "It's marked 'wheat-field road.' It must run over the crest and join the Taneytown road behind us. Now what else?"

There was much else as their eyes flicked from the map to the valley below them. A peach orchard. Sherfy's farm, Trostle's and Codori's and Roger's. The Emmitsburg Pike cutting up the valley toward hidden Gettysburg. There was Plum Run that flowed past Trostle's, and on until it was lost to sight in the rough ground at their feet.

Then they turned questioning glances across to the tree-masked bulk of Seminary Ridge where the woods, in places, came down almost to the Pike. Somewhere beyond its crest, Pitzer's Run flowed into Willoughby's Run. It was all rich country—good timberland, good farm land, peaceful in the morning sun. De Mérac could detect no movement now, no flash of bright bunting, no glint of metal across in the quiet land that was enemy territory, and that quiet suddenly filled him with sinister foreboding. He fingered his mustache and muttered, "Over there, under those trees beyond the crest, Lee may be massing a whole army. I do not like it."

Wilson grunted. "Damned convenient for Lee. He's completely masked—at least on our front—by those ridge woods. And look at us! Except for the Round Tops and a few other patches, we're squatting under a microscope in the open. Lee can count the number of buttons on Meade's coat."

George burst out, "Why the hell are *we* always in the open or in the flats while Lee's always covered by high ground? The only time I ever looked down on the Rebs was at Malvern Hill and then McClellan just said, 'My mistake,' and skedaddled for Harrison's Landing as if someone had slapped turpentine on his tail! I'm sick of it. Come on. We've seen enough!"

De Mérac led the way back to the Rifles. It seemed to him that Meade was gambling on bringing a strong force to the Gettysburg ridges in time to strike before Lee could gather his whole strength. Otherwise, he reasoned, it would have been better for Meade to have waited with all his troops in hand along the high ground by Pipe Creek in Maryland. In that case, Lee would have had to come to him in a position of Meade's choosing.

The men of the Rifles were sprawled in the woods north of Little Round Top, sleeping, mending clothes, and arguing in desultory tones. There Germans played skat on a flack rock and Castex rolled dice on a drumhead with a Rhode Island drummer who had somehow drifted into the woods. There was sporadic firing from the north, probably about the Cemetery at the far end of the ridge or at Culp's Hill, which the map showed bent back south and east like a long hook. Somehow the distant explosions only intensified the summer calm. De Mérac stepped to the edge of the woods and looked down the road which dropped to the valley and the Emmitsburg Pike. Wheat field, peach orchard, and farm in the golden haze seemed an almost artificially pastoral setting for a bad canvas to be called "Summer Fields." Off to the right front, bluecoats moved by the Pike and green-coated sharpshooters crossed Trostle's barnyard, but distance robbed them of any intent and turned them into casual strollers. Beyond the Pike there was no life at all. The troops whom he had seen in his one glimpse of open country on Seminary Ridge had vanished, as had the skirmishers who had fired on the Rifles in the lower reaches. He looked at his watch. It was nearly eleven. It was odd that he had had no word from de Trobriand or Birney. He suddenly felt the deep unease of his schooldays, the unease that followed his discovery that he sat idle while his fellows worked. He called to Wilson, who was scribbling a note, using an upturned knapsack for a desk. "Something is wrong. I am going to look for de Trobriand."

He left the woods and crossed the road that led down toward the Pike. As shadow gave way to sunlight, a sudden transformation swept over the whole ridge and the valley. Bugles blasted and long blue lines moved with a glint of steel and the flutter of colors, halted where the crest began to slope west. There were the diamonds of the IIIrd Corps on the kepis nearest him, clover leaves on those that stretched away north to be lost in the ridge curves.

He looked down the east slope and saw endless masses of artillery moving on that side of Cemetery Ridge. Batteries were rolling up the wide road from Taneytown, flowing west along a crossroad that led from the Baltimore Pike toward the ridge. They were parked in an open field, halted in groves, while drivers led their hitches out to water in the streams that spilled into Rock Creek. "*Ça!*" thought de Mérac. "Meade may yet win his gamble. Now where—where is the brigadier?"

He saw tethered horses near a steep-roofed building which the map called the house of George Weikert. A group of officers stood by its south end, staring west through their glasses. Four who faced him were bearded. The two others had their backs toward him. The larger of the two threw up his head. De Mérac recognized the flat top of a French kepi and began to run. The bearded men showed clearer. One was Birney with his long, straight legs in dragoon boots. The next was foxy-eyed Sickles, New York politician turned corps commander. Suddenly de Mérac recognized the third—a plain, tired-looking man with a straggling beard and a sad, schoolmaster's face. He had flat, lead-colored pouches under his eyes and steel spectacles dangled from one ear to make way for his field glasses. General George Meade, the new commander of the Army of the Potomac, had come up from Taneytown. The last bearded man, stocky with a brigadier's star on red gunner's epaulettes, he did not know, but there was no mistaking the green of Colonel Berdan's coat as he stood beside de Trobriand.

De Trobriand looked around at the sound of running feet. "*Voilà!*" he cried. "This man I was about to suggest. General Meade, this is Colonel de Mérac."

At the name, Meade, the unknown brigadier, and Sickles looked up sharply as though thinking, "Oh—so *that's* the man, is it?" Meade smiled pleasantly. "Thought you'd look older, somehow. Hunt, you haven't met de Mérac? Colonel, this is General Hunt, my Chief of Artillery. And of course, General Sickles." De Mérac acknowledged the introductions, was greeted cordially by Birney and Berdan, appraisingly by Sickles.

Meade raised his glasses again while de Mérac wondered how he could remain so calm after being pitchforked into command of the whole army with no notice and in the presence of the enemy. His steady tones showed nothing of the anxiety behind the gray-pouched eyes, as he watched the steady deployment of the IInd and IIIrd Corps. "That's it, Birney. You must hold from here to the Round Tops. Humphreys joins you well above Trostle's. Mustn't push too far out toward the Pike, de Trobriand. We're going to be stretched thin, mighty thin, as it is."

Hunt lifted his glasses to his heavy-boned eyes and snapped, "There! Now you've got it, by God." There was sudden color and dull metal at the near edge of the woods across on Seminary Ridge. A single gray rider galloped out into the open, a bright guidon snapping above him. Out of the trees in purposeful column rolled three batteries. They unlimbered with an expertness that brought a grunt of approval from Hunt. "Cabell and Alexander—if that's really Longstreet over there."

Meade murmured, "Very pretty. What have you got to show *them*, Birney?"

Birney smiled. "Seven batteries—all in position."

The gray batteries across the valley flashed in quick salvos and shrapnel opened in woolly puffs that sent rattling echoes through the hot air. "Two more. Over to the left," said Hunt. There was another salvo. "At least three that I can't see."

Sickles rasped, "I'd like to shove out farther—get right down to the wheat field and the orchard and the road south of it."

Meade tapped his boot on the ground. "We don't know enough, yet. We don't know enough. If Longstreet's really going to hit here—well, he could make us quite a lot of trouble. Yes, a lot. If he got round our flank and rolled right up along this ridge. Or if he should bust through between the Round Tops and the orchard it'd do the same thing."

De Trobriand laid a hand on de Mérac's shoulder.

"When this young man came up, I was about to make a suggestion that he take the Rifles across the valley. Then we should know what Longstreet intends."

Meade turned grave eyes on de Mérac. "Your strength?"

"One hundred ninety-five, sir."

Meade shook his head. "Too few."

Berdan spoke quickly, his thick mustache bristling with eagerness. "I'll send four of my companies with him. They'll give another hundred."

"Still mighty weak—if you do hit anything," said Hunt.

Berdan laughed shortly. "Don't forget that each of my sharpshooters has eight rounds in his magazine!"

Meade ran his fingers through his ragged beard. "H'm—can you spare anyone else, Birney?"

"I'm pretty thin down there but—well, I'll throw in Lakeman's 3rd Maine. He's got over two hundred."

Meade no longer hesitated. "Go ahead. Berdan, you better take command. My idea is to strike the peach orchard and then slant northwest right up the ridge. We haven't seen any Rebs there and the contours'll protect you from those batteries. Remember, Berdan, you're primarily after information, but if you see a chance to do damage, use your own judgment." He inclined his head courteously and left them.

Birney struck his palms together. "Better get going. I'll send word to Lakeman. Assemble where Plum Run crosses the wheat-field road. Good Luck."

As the Rifles waited in the noon glare, de Mérac called his officers together. "Berdan will march in line of skirmishers. I assure you that *anything* may happen so we must be ready to move quickly in support. George, the first concern of your company will be to bring back prisoners. Now to your posts, please. Here come the others."

Lakeman's men tramped over from the northern fields. Berdan's green men wove deftly onto the road—four companies under Casper Trepp, D of New York, E of New Hampshire, F of Vermont, and I of Michigan. They were barely one hundred all told, but the fire power of their Sharpe rifles was terrific. George stepped into the long grass to let the Michigan men pass. His foot struck against something that clanked and liquid gushed over his boot. He cried: "Christ bite it! What was that?" He had overturned an abandoned bucket whose oily contents gave out a pungent tarry reek. He shrugged. No harm done. The oily stuff might even soften the leather. He moved back onto the road and the little command started. He saw de Mérac canter up to the head of the column to join Berdan and Trepp beyond the green kepis of D Company. Berdan stared thoughtfully ahead while Trepp stretched his ruddy cheeks in a grin and twirled his reddish mustache. They rode on past staring infantry, past gunners who looked up in surprise as they unshipped limber chests.

"Damned funny," said Berdan. "I keep getting the feeling that we're recruits out for a practice march."

"Perhaps it is the Rebels who will make practice," said Trepp amiably.

De Mérac shook himself. The thunder of the rebel batteries on Seminary Ridge was fainter as the contours of the ground began to blanket it. The sullen bursts from Culp's Hill seemed meaningless, impersonal. The march did not lack reality but that reality was wrapped in a false calm. The air from the big orchard as they passed it was still and sleepy. De Mérac looked up and down the broad Pike and it stretched away empty, north and south, as though it lazily waited to receive a string of Sunday carriages, church bound.

Then they crossed the Pike and Berdan raised his arm. De Mérac twisted in the saddle to watch the green column flow into a double line, the men spacing deftly some ten feet apart. For ordinary troops the interval might have seemed dangerous, but the sharpshooters patted the magazines of their rifles and pushed on alertly. On their left rear the Rifles' column jutted back like a dark prop, was matched by Lakeman's men on the other flank. De Mérac waved and Dekdebrun and Castex galloped up to join him.

The field over which they marched sloped smoothly up toward that same belt of trees which de Mérac had studied from the rocks of Cemetery Ridge. Berdan leaned forward in the saddle. "The crest's low here. I can see light through those damned trees." His voice sounded loud in the stillness of the field and de Mérac looked about, startled, as though the echoes must bring some threat out of the sunlit trees. But nothing moved save for a single crow which shot cawing from a dead oak ahead.

Trepp puffed out his mustache. "From the crest, Colonel, one must look down the west slope. It would be enough, perhaps?"

Berdan nodded. "Get back there. Bring the boys onto the edge of the woods and have 'em lie down. No bugles. No talking. Then wait for me." Trepp nodded and trotted back toward the advancing men. Berdan gathered his reins. "Ye-e-es—guess that's the only thing to do." He glanced at de Mérac: "Want to come with me?"

De Mérac stifled an impulse to get out of the uncanny hush of the woods and back to the reassuring solidity of his companies. He said, "I'll come with you."

The trees were quite widely spaced and the floor cleared of undergrowth. Lisette stepped nimbly along, giving catlike hops every now and then as the slope increased unexpectedly. At last leap and the trees ended.

De Mérac and Berdan reined in abruptly and drew their mounts back among the trunks. There, slanting to the southwest, flowed the quick waters of Pitzer's Run. Two hundred yards away, stepping down the near bank, came a column of gray infantry. Berdan snapped in a low tone, "Count the colors!"

De Mérac, frozen with alarm and excitement, stammered, "Three—which means three full regiments. *Vingt dieux!* A brigade flag tops the rise beyond." He jerked his head to stare across Pitzer's Run. The country was open and rolling. More infantry pushed on at a quick, light step and beyond two more regimental flags a battery of twelve-pounders jolted unconcernedly.

Berdan whispered, "Forming to hit Meade's left. Can't mistake that."

De Mérac shook his head. "They have been badly

471

delayed by *something*. But, *'cré nom de Dieu*, they come now!"

Berdan muttered tensely, "It'll be quite a report for Meade." Then his eyes sought de Mérac's. "What do you think?"

De Mérac whistled under his breath. Then he brought his fist down on his knee. "It is worth it. Yes. I agree."

Berdan turned to Castex, who hung deeper in the woods. "You saw the lieutenant colonel who was riding with us? The one with the red mustache?"

Castex blinked. *"Oui, Monsieur le colonel*. I saw him."

"Go back to him. Tell him to bring the whole crowd up here quick. Got that?"

Castex nodded and trotted off. De Mérac suddenly remembered Dekdebrun and turned in alarm, fearing a premature shot, but the cold-eyed man had dismounted and stood licking his lips. He could afford to wait. De Mérac looked back at the open fields. The column on the near bank was following the course of the run, which slanted their line of march diagonally away from the woods. Then he looked back over his shoulder. The green line was slipping up through the trees, moving rapidly but cautiously. Off to the right, he could make out Wilson, dismounted, fanning out the Rifles to prolong the line of Berdan's men. On the far flank, Rapp darted on, crouching and limber-kneed.

Berdan shook his fists in tight circles and whispered to himself, "Steady, boys, steady." Then he shot both arms out level with his shoulders, dropped them. De Mérac saw company commanders repeat the gesture and the sharpshooters broke into a gliding run.

The colonel turned to de Mérac. "Done it. If we lose every man we've got, it'll be worth it."

"Double," said de Mérac gravely. "We buy time for Meade."

Suddenly green bodies were diving to the ground all about him, hugging close to the edge of the woods. Berdan roared, "Fire!"

De Mérac had seen the sharpshooters in action before, but only in small squads or platoons on a skirmish line, and he was unprepared for the terrific burst of fire that followed. His ears sang until he could make out no one noise—just a blending series of shocks overlapping each other. Smoke rose thick and under it he saw rifles passed back for reloading, saw fresh weapons shoved to the front. By Pitzer's Run, the gray columns reeled and shook. There were sunny patches between the smoke clouds and in those patches men whirled to the ground, stumbled over each other, ran blindly from the torn ranks to fall across other bodies while still others pitched across them.

He recovered himself, spun Lisette behind the last green rank, and galloped for the Rifles. He leaped to the ground back of Gilhooley's company and shouted: "Faster! Fire faster! *Vite! Vite!* That is the only order!" He ran down the line of prostrate men. "Keep them at it, George. Randol! Look to the left. Fresh troops come up there. Faster, faster, faster!"

Wilson, white-faced and staring, caught his arm. "My God, whose idea was this?"

"Berdan's! I agreed at once. Do you?"

"To the hilt. We're raising hell. Lord above! Look at 'em coming up on the left. I'll have to bend my line back at an angle to cover that!"

"Bend it in a circle if you must. Nothing counts but time. You know that the whole VIth Corps is still on the march—miles away. Bordagaray! *En garde!* To your right!"

Between the Rifles and Lakeman, the sharpshooters still blazed away in a rate of fire that dazed de Mérac. But the Southern troops recovering from their first shock had turned with the fighting surge that every man in the Army of the Potomac knew so well. They clawed their way forward to the woods, falling in rows only to uncover fresh rows driving on while their shrill yell shot high over the blue-crossed banners. Only the eight-shot magazines of the Sharpe rifles held them off, while on the flanks the Rifles and the 3rd Maine battled desperately with their clumsy muskets.

Time and again, yelling men lapped around de Mérac's left flank, wavered, fell back, rushed again. He could distinguish little in the smoky gloom of the woods—vague figures loomed, vanished. Once George bumped into him on the ebb of a gray rush, yelled in a high voice, "It's crazy! God-damn crazy. Five hundred men against Jesus knows how many—a brigade—two brigades! Hold it, boys! Here they come again."

There had been five hundred men. Now, in front of de Mérac, prone figures lay still. A few crept to the rear, clutching bleeding wrists or knees. To the right many of Berdan's men lay on their backs or hunched forward, their heads doubled at odd angles. The trees shivered to hollow raps as bullets thwacked against them and leaves and branches pattered down in a thick shower. In an oak just above de Mérac a sharpshooter perched with a pair of glasses, shouting in a strange code to a fellow who fired slowly from a jutting branch beyond him. "Eight hundred. You're right! You're left! Eight fifty. Now you're on it. Hold it. All right. Lead driver. Swing driver. Wheel driver. You cleaned the hitch. Get the one beyond. Try nine hundred twenty-five. You're short—"

Then a new rush on his own front narrowed de Mérac's world to the dim figures that rushed through the smoke. This time they were almost into his line when a savage burst from the sharpshooters swept most of them away as a hose smashes away rubbish. There was still yelling on his left and he ran to the aid of Rapp, who, with his face a mass of blood, fought against two men with a clubbed musket. De Mérac fired two rounds from his Colt and Rapp staggered back, recovered himself, and calmly reloaded. A voice off in the woods yelled, "Don't shoot! Don't shoot! John! John! I've got your prisoners."

In the momentary lull, George, at the head of a file of men, butted his way through to the rear, panting. "Caught them off by the rocks there. Five! One officer! What'll I do with them?"

De Mérac slapped his shoulder. "Take them right to our lines."

George's jaw dropped. "And leave you here?"

"They will not go by themselves and Meade will want to talk to them. Hurry, now."

"But—"

"Those prisoners are worth more just now than any of us. Back with them."

George motioned his men guarding the dazed prisoners to herd them to the rear and followed sullenly.

A brittle hush lay over the woods. There was artillery fire to the south of Seminary Ridge, more about Culp's Hill, but the air under the trees was so still that de Mérac could hear a sullen drip-drip-drip that might have been water—had there been water about. Somewhere a man was groaning: "Aaaaah-*uh!* Aaaaah-*uh!*"

He felt a tug at his sleeve and looked into Trepp's powder-blackened face. The Swiss croaked, "We leave. More and more come up on the right, as I saw from a tree. Soon they find out how few we are—for up to now they must think us three regiments at least. I do not wish to be here when they discover their error."

"That is Colonel Berdan's order?"

"His order. Lakeman leaves first. Then you. We reload now and cover you."

De Mérac found Lisette unhurt at the far edge of the woods and sent her back to the Pike at a gallop under Castex's care. Dekdebrun dropped from a tree, his face set in steel-hard satisfaction. One by one the companies withdrew. Wilson was safe, Shea was safe. Bordagaray thrust a red-swathed hand into the front of his coat. Rohleder, unconscious from a blow of a musket butt, was carried by his men, breathing heavily. Seven bodies, three of them sergeants, had to be left under the trees. Rapp calmly held a handkerchief to a cut on his cheekbone and waved Father Doyle and Wayne on to a German whose neck bled freely.

The 3rd Maine, looking little damaged, was moving down toward the Pike at the double. Berdan waved to de Mérac. "Keep them stepping. Don't worry about us. That's an order."

De Mérac followed his last company over the rich grass. Wilson walked dizzily beside him. "I've got the shakes, now that it's over," he panted. "Those rifles are sheer murder! Even so I don't see how we got out of it."

"Berdan's judgment," said de Mérac. "Ah, *mon ami*, it is hard to believe that we have seen what we have seen.

Sapristi! I am weak as a lamb of the Côte d'Or." He wheeled about as ripping fire echoed from the woods. One by one the four green companies, their rifles spitting, broke into the open, each turning to cover its neighbor, breaking into a run, turning again.

"Safe!" said Wilson.

"And just in time," said de Mérac, pointing south along Seminary Ridge. Out of distant woods gray infantry appeared, heading on toward the blue and green men who hurried down the last of the hostile slope. Somewhere along the shaggy sides of the Round Tops a Union battery opened up on the new target. Wilson swung his arms with the gesture of a man who has been bent over a desk all day. "Safe enough now. You know, I keep thinking of that column we hit. Suppose *we'd* been hit that way when we came up at Second Bull Run with Kearny waiting for us."

De Mérac nodded. "That is the point, Craig. The losses were heavy. But what is more important, it will take hours to correct the confusion we caused and those hours were bought very cheaply for Meade. And in next in value—" He pointed ahead to a distant file of gray figures closely guarded, resignedly climbing the slope beyond the wheat field. "George's prisoners. You and I might wrongly report the strength and identity of what we saw. But headquarters will know how to question them."

They crossed the Pike at the bold knoll where the peach orchard basked in the sunshine. Berdan overtook de Mérac and Wilson. "I'm going ahead to report to Birney and he can forward the stuff to Meade."

"You have a lot to tell him," said de Mérac.

Berdan smoothed his heavy mustache, frowning. "I've got a hell of a lot more, but the War Department won't listen. Know how long we were in action?"

"An hour," ventured Wilson.

"Forty-five minutes," said de Mérac.

Berdan grinned. "Exactly twenty, from the opening round to the last. And in that time, my outfit—this doesn't include yours or Lakeman's—fired an average of ninety-five rounds per man. I've been checking each company."

"*Sang de dieu*," cried de Mérac. "Then those poor devils of Rebels took nearly ten thousand rounds from you alone! Incredible!"

Berdan shrugged. "Go back and count what's left in the pouches." He swung his fist. "That's what the Department can't *see!* They dribble out my companies in twos and threes. Good God, can you figure what we could have done if I'd been allowed to take the *entire* 1st and 2nd Sharpshooters with their repeaters? Say there'd be seven hundred and fifty men all told, firing at one target at that rate."

"I can't take it in," said Wilson. "Over seventy thousand rounds. Lord, human flesh couldn't stand it. It'd be the end of all wars!"

Berdan laughed bitterly. "Maybe that's why the Department boys don't like rifles. Scared they'd be out of a job. I had to carry my fight right up to the President to get my first outfit accepted. They told me that the *musket* was the American soldier's true weapon and always would be. They wanted to kill my rifles the same way they've killed Lowe's ballons. How'd you like to see the *Columbia* hanging over our ridge? We'd be able to see so far west that Lee'd have to detour his men fifteen or twenty miles to keep out of our sight. Lord, why do you suppose we found the Rebs clear over on the west slope? It's a lot farther than using the cover of the trees on the crest or the east slope, isn't it? Well, that's because we've got signal stations on the Round Tops and they'd probably be seen. But with Lowe's balloons, we'd increase our visibility ten times and more. But balloons aren't military! It's nice to know we'll be killed in accordance with the regulations of 1812. Anyway, the Rebs are as bad as we are, if not worse, and that evens things up. Thanks for your help. I'll make sure that Birney gets the whole story." He trotted off up the growing slope of Cemetery Ridge.

"*Experientia docet*," observed Wilson. "That's the biggest lie in human history. If experience did teach we wouldn't be messing up a lovely valley like this with a war. Or if we missed out on that point, we'd use our brains more in fighting."

"At the moment, this is not too bad, so long as one looks at the right places," said de Mérac. He sniffed the hot, summery scents of the wheat-field road where butterflies, black and yellow, danced out of the low bushes. Off to the left the Trostle house with its deep double galleries sat peacefully behind its white picket fence. Then he let his eyes climb the heights ahead of him and saw the thick ranks of the IInd and IIIrd Corps hanging like a blue cloud along the ridge, laced with the glitter of bayonets and the sleek menace of fieldpieces. "However," he concluded, "it must be admitted that those right places are few. *Allons-y!*"

He found de Trobriand's brigade not far from Little Round Top and reported his return. The brigadier, using a broken-treed saddle for a chair, waved genially. "Ah, it is Meade who will be pleased, Jean. Your gray guests must be enjoying his hospitality now. You amused yourself well *là-haut?*"

"*Assez bien,*" answered de Mérac. He described the effect of Berdan's fire on the chance-met column. De Trobriand listened thoughtfully, then said, "*C'est bien.* There will be many strings for Longstreet to unravel. The first sergeant who came with the prisoners has already returned. He tells me that they think at least three regiments struck them. They are, he says, from Anderson's of A. P. Hill."

"First Sergeant Hooks? You did not see Captain Force?"

De Trobriand shook his head. "No doubt he remains for further questioning. Now as to yourself—Berdan's *coup de main* undoubtedly gives us time. It must. I shall hold you in reserve. Echelon yourself between my left and Ward's brigade. That will bring you to the east slope and you will be sheltered if that *sacré* artillery over there searches the Round Tops again."

De Mérac saw his men stretched out among the rocks and long grasses of a field that trailed east to the Taneytown road and the dark masses of parked batteries. Then he walked down to H Company where First Sergeant Hooks sat with one foot bare, drawing a thin cord across a piece of cobblers' wax. De Mérac said, "At ease, First Sergeant. Go on with your work. I only want to ask if Captain Force remained at headquarters."

Hooks dropped the awl that dangled from the waxed thread and stared. "At *head*quarters? Jesus—sir—I thought he was with you."

"You mean he looked for me when he returned?"

Hooks slowly picked up his boot and fitted a patch over a gaping hole. "Hell, no. I mean down to the Pike. We run into a provost patrol that was lost and gave 'em the Rebs. He made us go along to be sure they didn't say *they* captured 'em. Then he started back to you. You was still in the woods."

Another man raised on his elbow. "That's so, sir. I heard him say, 'This is just as good as taking 'em up the ridge.' He started back to you. Looked like he was heading too far right so I hollered at him but he ain't heard, I guess."

De Mérac stared blankly at the bright awl that slid through the leather. Then he said, "Thank you," and walked slowly away. George was all right, of course. He could not very well have reached the woods before the firing ceased. He might have crossed the Emmitsburg Pike farther north, say by the Codori house, owing to his mistaken bearing. He might have found friends in a patrol on the lower slopes of Cemetery Ridge and stopped to talk with them. He might— He looked at his watch. Nearly two o'clock. Too early to worry. A slight detour could have easily delayed him this long.

Down in the fields beyond the Taneytown road, along the tree-girt banks of Rock Creek, thin bugles sang and tinny voices drifted up to de Mérac. There was a sudden stir through all the great artillery park. Already batteries were on the move, lurching at a walk over grassy stretches and heading for the road that led up over Cemetery Ridge and down past the wheat field on the west slope.

Wilson jumped over a rock and stood beside de Mérac. "Know any reason for that?" He pointed to the weaving pattern of blue and red below.

"No. But I shall find out." Castex, without orders, had untethered Lisette and trotted her to de Mérac. He mounted, picked his way through the men who were sitting up and staring down into the valley. When he reached the crest he galloped toward the Weikert house. He saw de Trobriand and Birney talking earnestly under a tree at the south side. The brigadier was obviously excited and kept cutting his hand across his chest as though in protest. Then he shrugged, turned away. De Mérac halted Lisette and dismounted. "There are orders, sir?"

De Trobriand looked both grave and angry. "Ah, there are orders you conceive. Sickles moves the whole corps where Meade forbade. You heard this morning, *hein?* Sickles spoke of wheat field and orchard to Meade, who refused. Now Meade is far off at the Cemetery and Sickles moves. So it is we must cover from the Round Tops through field and orchard to the Pike."

De Mérac was stunned. "But we are too few. How shall you do it?"

De Trobriand shrugged. *"Je te dis franchement, je ne sais pas."*

Ten minutes later the Rifles marched wearily in the rear of the brigade, crossed the crest, and began the western descent. Already Ward's brigade was massing in a long slant from the Round Tops. Off to the right, beyond the wheat field, Graham's men were edging through Trostle's land toward the orchard and the Pike. Batteries rattled and clanked down the wheat-field road.

De Mérac halted the Rifles in the deep cleft of Plum Run just above the wheat field and told them to lie down in ranks against the steep bank. Then he called to Wilson and Shea. "Better study the terrain. We shall not be in reserve forever." They joined him on the upper lip of the run. The line of the division, marked by bobbing red-topped kepis, followed an insane course. While it looked generally southwest towards the Pike and the sloping end of Seminary Ridge, the great distance and the contours forced the brigade commanders to conform to a series of angles and spurs which spaced their men at fearful intervals.

A single six-gun battery had unlimbered along the

wheat-field road, its muzzles covering to the southwest while its limbers took shelter behind the Trostle house.

Shea muttered: "I'd not be choosing this place."

De Mérac lowered his glasses and felt cold creep across his shoulders. "Look to your left rear and then to your right flank," he said tersely. Wilson and Shea looked and turned pale. To the left, above Ward's, the Round Tops showed high and empty, save for three signalers who whipped their flags frantically. The whole left of the Union line was dominated by this high unoccupied ground. To the right, the IInd Corps still held its position on the crest, leaving a gaping, glaring avenue between its left and the distant right of Humphreys far below on the Pike.

"God's teeth," muttered Wilson. "What a mess! What a perfectly, ghastly, God-damned awful mess!"

"And there's himself admiring it, hell roast him," snarled Shea. Close by Trostle's, Sickles sat his horse while aides galloped up to him, saluted, galloped away.

The first Southern guns opened with a startling crash and shrapnel puffs were touched by the sun high over the orchard, the wheat field, and the Round Tops. Shells tore into the ground, throwing up brown geysers of earth. The guns were everywhere—in the flatlands to the south about the Rose house on the Pike; bristling just inside the woods of Seminary Ridge; out in the full glare of the afternoon with bare-chested gunners firing, dodging the recoil, running the pieces back into position. From the right of Humphreys by the Pike to the left of Ward by the Round Tops the earth quivered and shook; the soft blue of the sky was stippled with shrapnel.

De Mérac looked at his watch. Just past three. Wilson caught his eye. "One of the prisoners said Longstreet was supposed to attack at one. Guess our walk this noon helped a little."

De Mérac nodded abstractedly. His thoughts still went back to George, who might have become inextricably tangled up in Sickles' unauthorized move. Then he said, "Ah!" sharply while Shea swore under his breath.

Out of the same woods through which the Rifles had fought that morning slipped a long line of skirmishers.

481

They advanced cautiously, feeling their way down toward the Pike and the orchard. Batteries began to slam on the Union side, but the wide-spaced gray men came on. After them, in thick ranks, appeared solid regiments. Union and Southern shrapnel crossed in mid-air, flowered down through the heat. Gray skirmishers and gray regiments halted, threw themselves flat on the ground, lay motionless. It seemed to de Mérac, from the way heads turned to the south, that the newcomers had expected to find other troops in support on their right, were shaken and disconcerted at their absence. The time purchased in the morning was still working for Meade and the Union.

The Rebel gunners were lifting their ranges and shrapnel hissed down through the trees about de Mérac, dug up the ground, sent showers of bark and leaves flying about him. Solid shot wailed above him, sent heavy branches smashing to earth. Above the din he shouted, "Craig—Dan—better get down!" and the three slithered to greater safety. A horrible bellowing and roaring broke out on the left, died, broke out once more. De Mérac saw Lisette toss her head nervously and snatched the bridle from Castex. There was a dry course that branched deeper from the bed of Plum Run. He led the mare down it.

Then he ducked back quickly. A steer, its neck and flank bloody, bellowed agonizingly and charged him, horns lowered. A cow, its bowels dragging and udder ripped, staggered across the steer's path and the two went down in a dun, kicking heap. De Mérac turned Lisette's head back to the run, slapped her gently to send her along to Castex, and jumped on a rock. The dry course opened out into a broad glade where dozens of cattle milled, rushing first to one opening, then to another, turning back at the blocking rocks, rushing again. Broken-legged cows were overthrown, slashed by sharp hoofs, calves were crushed against boulders. And all the time shrapnel sang blindly down among them, striking into the sleek bodies that had been hidden here for safety by the Codoris or the Trostles or the Sherfys.

He ran back to the Rifles, shouting a warning to keep

clear of the fear maddened beasts. He saw Wilson, up on the bank once more, sheltering himself behind a tree and pointing out something to Shea. He waited for the next burst, then sprang up beside them. Down to the south about the Rose house, heavy masses of Southern infantry were shifting and maneuvering. Mounted aides galloped between them and the units that still lay in the open west of the peach orchard. To the north, along the wheat-field road, three more Union batteries swept at a gallop, unlimbered, and went into position facing south. Shea looked back to the Rose house. "The gray boys aren't knowing what to do. D'ye think maybe Mr. Lee forgot to wind his watch?"

"Something has gone wrong with them," said de Mérac.

"We did," said Wilson grimly. "I've counted five brigades around Rose's and four near the orchard. Wonder who they are."

A young voice said diffidently, "Hood's division by Rose's. McLaws's is near the orchard. That's Barksdale's brigade north of the road."

De Mérac turned with a start. An apple-cheeked corporal in Berdan's green was taking expert cover at the next trunk. Wilson said, "How do you know?"

The boy said simply, "I was over there this morning. E Company, 1st U.S.S.S. Know where they are, sir?"

"Some company's by Trostle's house," said Wilson. "Wait a minute. How can you know what troops those are? We were there, too, and I couldn't tell."

"I know you were, sir. Guess I was there longer. Just came back now. I heard 'em talking and saw 'em go by. Wilcox and Wright of Anderson's division'll be coming in beyond Barksdale pretty soon."

De Mérac looked at the boy closely. He did not seem more than seventeen and certainly those round, high-colored cheeks had never been touched with a razor. The shrapnel had stopped for a moment and de Mérac relaxed. "This is, perhaps, your first action?"

The boy flushed. No, sir. I've been out since '61. Haven't missed a trick since Yorktown. Got my third stripe last week, but I haven't had time to put it on. Now I want to find E."

"You got lost over there?" asked Wilson.

The boy nodded sheepishly. "Got cut off, trying for a last shot. I hid for a while. Then I found two more of our outfit and a Maine sergeant and one of your officers."

De Mérac snapped, "One of ours? What was his name?"

"I meant to get it because we were talking about Columbia and Dartmouth. I was in my junior year when I enlisted. But I forgot. He was a captain and had hair like a straw pile and—"

De Mérac caught his arm. "And you left him over there? Where is he now?"

The corporal shook his head. "I came by myself. He tried to stop me but I knew I could get out. Sure, I can show you where he is all right, unless he's been fool enough to move and I don't think he is. Got your glasses? Well—look over to Seminary. See that big gray rock sticking up by a clump of pines? Well, go two fingers right of that. There's a kind of ravine running down the face of the ridge. Your captain's in a cave just at the head."

"How did you get out?" asked Wilson sharply.

"Followed the ravine or old brook or whatever it is, right down to the road, and then I ducked across. You see, that ravine is where McLaws and Anderson join. Now, I saw that the ground slopes away both sides of it and I knew if troops moved down, the slope'd split 'em, make 'em edge farther and farther apart. It always does. Colonel Berdan makes us learn things like that. So I figured if I came right down it, I'd be in a dead space and no one'd see me. I was right."

De Mérac cried eagerly, "Then I could get word to him, over there in the Rebel lines?"

The corporal shook his head. "You'd get spotted moving *toward* it. But he'll be all right if he sticks where he is. They're too busy to do much scouting. You say some of my outfit's near Trostle's. I'll find 'em. Thank you, sir." He saluted and slipped away.

De Mérac cried, "*Vingt dieux!* There is George almost in sight and no way to reach him!"

"Ah, and he's a bright lad, is George," said Shea. "He'll—whisht! The guns are still!"

De Mérac looked at his watch again. "Quarter to four." By the orchard, by the Rose house, the gray lines still waited. Higher, the guns were silent and mounted officers galloped toward them, hands held high. De Mérac said: "Craig, Colonel Berdan was right. If we'd all been casualties, this delay would have been worth it." If only the Round Tops were manned, if only the gap between Humphreys and the IInd Corps were closed! If only there were some way of getting word to George."

There was a scrambling behind him and Father Doyle and Rapp climbed up, with an air of conspiratorial mystery. Doyle whispered: "I heard you talking to the corporal. It's Rapp and myself that'll show you how to get word to George."

De Mérac shook his head. "Your cloth's no armor against bullets."

"Oh, it's not that. The boys'll be needing me. There's another way."

"*Parfaitement*," said Rapp. "It is a *truc* which I myself have practiced in Africa. This I explained to Father Doyle, who agreed."

The Southern sergeant who had blundered into the cave had been deftly bayoneted by Wesley, the Maine sergeant, and now lay stiffening outside the grotesquely heaped rocks. George Force, bareheaded, cautiously lifted his chin above a sheltering boulder and peered across toward Cemetery Ridge. There was still movement in the woods about him but it seemed to divide mysteriously right and left of the rocky scar that ran down from his hiding place. The fearful pounding roar that had broken out at four o'clock raged unabated, but owing to curves and dips of the ground he could see only odd patches of the valley floor with its knolls and low spines. Higher up, he could mark the flashes of the Union guns to the right of a big clump of trees. South of the trees, the ridge puzzled him. The IInd Corps was still in position on the crest, but Sickles's IIIrd seemed to have been withdrawn, for the sky line showed bare. He tried to reason out the direction of the attack from the smoke that rose heavier and thicker. It seemed to come from the direction of the peach orchard and the Round Tops. He could only deduce that fresh troops must have come up, allowing the IIIrd to be pushed far out by the wheat field. The Round Tops themselves showed hard and empty against the sky. Suddenly life stirred on them. He could just make out the jut of barrels and the flick of turning spokes as the sun struck them. Then the peaks were masked in smoke as at least a full battery went into action. He said over his shoulder in a low tone, "Got guns on the Round Tops! How the hell'd they ever do it?"

Cole, one of Berdan's men, said, "Had to, I guess. Can do an awful lot that way."

George went back to his limited outlook. The main attack was falling on the Union left. The very presence of the new batteries proved that. He thought, "It'll hit right on us and I'm chained up here. God damn it, why didn't I take a chance and go with that corporal?"

Wesley began to whistle shrilly. George hissed: "Shut up!" and dropped back into the cave. "Want to have the Rebs call on us?"

"Jesus. Plumb forgot. I started to whistle 'cause I heard—" There was a sudden whuff outside. A shaggy head blocked the opening, Mr. McArdle scrambled in and threw himself on George in a crescendo of shrill yelps.

George shouted, "Oh my God! How in hell—" Retz, the other sharpshooter, kicked his shin and he remembered the need for silence. He firmly clamped the dog's muzzle shut and whispered, "How in *hell*—no, boy—got to keep quiet—easy now—good God, I left him near Pipe Creek."

Retz said incredulously, "Mean that's your dog?"

"Sure. He and I were high privates in the rear rank together."

Cole caught one of Mr. McArdle's paws. "Holy jumping mackerel. God-damn pup's got shoes on!"

"Shoes?" George knelt beside the wriggling dog. The Maryland farmer had contrived soft leather pads to protect the sore paws, had cunningly bound them on with rawhide.

Wesley wagged his head admiringly. "That's a smart pup, Cap'n. Most would have set down and scrup them leathers off with his teeth."

"Beats me how he *got* here," said George. The hushed voices made a soft rustling in the cave.

"If he's smart enough to leave them shoe-pacs alone, he's smart enough to trail you from Machias to Bath. Hey—looks like he was wondering 'bout *your* boots, Cap'n." He slapped his knee and sniffed. "By Crinus, that's it. You step' in something? Got it now. Oil of tar or something like that. There's been a smell hanging round here that minded me of a farm or a shipyard or the like."

George stared. "You've hit it. I tipped over a bucket of some damn stuff in the wheat-field road. Stunk like sheep-dip."

"Scent like that'll last a hell of a time," said Cole. "I've used the stuff on fence posts."

"But I still don't see—" began George.

Retz stretched out his hand quickly. "Lemme see that collar. Hi! Got paper tied to it."

George twisted the shaggy head about. Inside the broad collar a cylinder of paper was carefully fastened. He ripped the tough cords that bound it on, opened it with shaky fingers. He swayed toward the light, blinking in unbelief at the wrinkled sheet that was covered with de Mérac's firm, square script. Sergeant Wesley asked impatiently, "What's in it?"

George stammered, "Corporal Ricker got through. By God, he did. He told John where we were and— Look, they took an old boot from the pack I left up there and dipped it in the tar stuff. Then they gave it to Mr. McArdle to sniff. Wait a minute—yes—we can get back to our own lines now."

Wesley scratched his long chin. "Hell, *I* know the way we come. What you expect me to do? Sniff the dog's pacs and trail *him* back through the Rebs?"

"Stay here till the Rebs pick you up and ship you to Andersonville if you want," snapped Force. "Now listen to this." He summarized quickly what de Mérac had written about the high-sided hollow that slanted down the Seminary Ridge.

When he had finished, Retz scuffed the back of his hand over his clipped head. "Could be. Don't take much of a slope to set troops veering right or left. God damn me; that little college boy seen the whole thing and I cussed him for a 'tarnal fool."

George said, "Who is the best scout here?"

"Cole—he's done a lot," said Retz.

"Want to go out and take a look, Cole?" asked George.

"Don't mind if I do," said Cole calmly. He took off his green kepi. "I'll borry that Reb's hat outside. May want to stick my head up."

He slithered out of the cave. The others sat waiting in the dimness, George whistling under his breath and rubbing Mr. McArdle's ears. In ten minutes, Cole was back. "It's like Ricker said. Kind of as if someone had made a big crease down the ridge and then dug it out. Sides slope away like a roof and it's hollow inside."

"Good cover?" asked Wesley.

"Good as we'll get. All hell busting in the valley, though. Sounds like the boys was playing marbles for keeps. But far as I could see, there's 'bout fifty yards clear on the right and near a hundred on the left down by the Pike and the Rebs ain't crossed it yet—not where I looked. Want to go?"

There was a silence. George said, "It's go, with a chance of getting through, or stay, with Andersonville a sure thing."

There was a murmur of assent. Cole tossed a length of cord to George. "The Reb's belt. You'll have to leash the pup on the way down. Ready?" He crawled out of the cave, the others creeping behind him.

It was half-past four and the sun slanted down on their backs as they took their first steps down the old watercourse. The route was as Cole had described it. The bottom was rough with eroded stones but the sides were grassy and climbed higher than George's head.

Like the others he walked bent over to guard against some unexpected dip in the banks. Mr. McArdle, close-leashed, scuttled contentedly at his side. Ahead of him Cole's cropped head bobbed and dipped. From time to time he held up his hand and George signaled to Retz and Wesley in the rear. Then Cole put on the battered gray-brown felt that he had picked up and cautiously peered over the edge, dropped back again, reporting no change.

The air shook and hummed to the blast of guns. Musketry rattled like angry drums. Right and left, fieldpieces stunned and jarred. High overhead Union shells yelled derisively, burst with smacking reports that sent trickles of earth running down the sheltering sides.

When they had gone about one hundred yards, heavy concussions beat at George's ears and acrid smoke rolled over the natural trench. Cole looked back. "Bunch of Reb batteries either side here. Hope they keep blasting. Smoke makes good cover for us." His words were drowned in a hideous banshee scream as a Federal shell with a loose rotating band shot through the sky. An instant later, George was thrown against the wall by a fearful explosion and hot air beat across his face. That shell, or one of its fellows, had struck a Confederate caisson near by and blown it up with its precious ammunition. He rubbed dust from his eyes and hunched along.

Cole yelled, "Down!" and threw himself flat on his face. George clutched Mr. McArdle and dropped. Through the uproar an odd *drum-drum-drum* sounded, racing closer and closer. The quick beat seemed to break at the very edge of the shelter and George, looking up involuntarily, had a glimpse of a horse's legs stretched for the leap, a black belly cut with a girth, a gray rider who flogged his mount with his hat, a swish of floating tail. Then the air above was empty again and the drumming died and died.

The four men resumed their course. Cole looked back. "Getting close to where we can make a break." He clapped on his battered hat and peered cautiously out. Then he dropped back, head hanging dejectedly.

"Blocked, by God! Stumped, by Jesus! They moved!"

"What?" snapped George. "Moved?"

Cole nodded wearily. "Thicker'n bull pouts where I was lotting to cross."

"Give me that hat!" George snatched it from him, clapped it on his head, and levered himself just above the grassy edge.

He was much farther north than he had thought. To his left front the Codori house and its clustering barns shimmered back of thinning smoke. He could see the Emmitsburg Pike nearly midway between himself and the farm. There were lines and lines of blue figures in yards and fields, lines and lines of gray on the west side of the road, but there seemed to be little more than desultory, long-range firing between the two bodies. Directly in front, the rocky funnel petered out a few yards from the Pike and Southern infantry massed and shifted on either side of the mouth and directly across it. "Oh, Christ!" said George between his teeth. It was obvious that had the shuffling troops been just a little to the right or left of the steep parapet of the shelter, his group could have worked down close to the Pike and then made a run for it to the slopes of Cemetery Ridge where Union troops waited under arms.

To the south, then? He shifted his position. To the south the slamming and crashing rode on a high level of fury. Smoke rolled in dense sluggish banks out of which the treetops of the peach orchard showed like a drowned forest. The pall was thicker and thicker toward the wheat field, curled in slow wreaths about the Round Tops. The southerly crest of Cemetery Ridge looked fearfully bare, save for a few hurrying clouds of men on the sky line. The batteries that he could see were obviously laid on that angle that ran from the peach orchard up to the bare peaks. He could learn little save that escape in that direction was utterly hopeless.

He ducked quickly. A horseman was galloping somewhere off to the left, heading for the Pike. His thin voice slashed the air. "Captain Branch! Who the hell tol' you to put yo' people theah?" Voice and hoofs died away. George raised himself again. The infantry that had been strung out in front of him were moving off to the right flank led by an immensely tall bearded man who carried cased colors on his shoulder like a pitchfork.

George dropped back to the others. "Clear for at least forty yards each way. We'll run for it. Make for the Codori place. That's where the lines are farthest apart."

Wesley ran his thumb along his chin. "Suppose we get plugged by our own boys?"

"Got to take that chance." He ripped off his jacket, pulled his shirt over his head, and tossed it to Cole. "You'll go first," he said. "That shirt was white two days ago. Wave it like hell and maybe they'll think we're Rebs deserting. Happens often enough." He refastened his jacket. "Sling your guns over your backs. That's it. On your feet, Mr. McArdle. Ready?" He crouched. *"Go!"*

Clear of the protecting funnel, the thundering world struck him like a great fist. His long shadow danced ahead of him, flicking over Cole's back, glancing off to the waving grasses. He felt terrifyingly naked, a helpless magnet to draw every hostile eye and muzzle. The wind freshened and a merciful belt of smoke drifted from the south, changing the fugitives into four running men without identity, purpose, or direction.

The ground sloped away, rose again to meet the Pike. Mr. McArdle coughed and snuffled in the acrid tang, picking the softest spots so far as the short leash allowed him. In the rear, Retz and Wesley pounded.

There was a ditch at the edge of the Pike. Cole cleared it in a single leap and began waving the dingy shirt that George had given him. A tattered gray man shot up from the grass at the edge of the road, his jaw sagging. Without slackening his stride, George clawed a clublike stick from the ground, whacked at a dusty ear that stuck out from uncut hair. The club splintered but the man went down with a sobbing yelp. Other gray figures, wide-spaced, stuck up their heads—a line of skirmishers unseen and unsuspected.

For an instant they seemed to stare, paralyzed at the sudden apparitions. Then one of them yelled, "Yanks, by Jesus!" George was across the Pike, skating down the bank on the far side, when the first bullet sang over his head. He looked back hurriedly. Wesley dove safely but Retz, leaving the crown of the Pike, threw up his hands and dove through the air. George knew from the boneless lurch that there was no use going back for him. It was hard, getting hit like that on the edge of safety.

He ran faster. Two shots cracked out in front and dirt spurted off to the left. Cole waved his shirt, yelling frantically. There was a fence in front. Its worn brown rails jarred against George's chest before he could check himself. He ducked through, hauled Mr. McArdle after him, and stood panting in the reek of a barnyard. The Codori buildings loomed unexpectedly about him as though they had suddenly materialized from the smoke-blurred air. His feet squelched in sour-smelling muck.

Men in blue were crowding up. A goat-faced lieutenant whined over and over, "What you got to say for yourself? What you got to say for yourself?"

George looked at the red clover leaf on the man's cap. "IInd Corps? What outfit?"

"Fifteenth Mass., and I ought to put you under arrest."

"And an officer of the 15th Mass. ought to have more sense than to talk like that. Where's your colonel?"

"Oh—he's—he's up there on the ridge. I wouldn't want to bother *him*. Hell, no. Just looked funny, your running out the Reb lines."

"Never heard of people getting cut off? Well, forget it. What's beyond here?"

"Three companies, New York 82nd. Just four companies of us. Got orders to haul back if they start anything over there." He pointed to long lines of Southern infantry standing to arms more than six hundred yards away.

George looked at the west slope. The gray troops over there seemed alert but in no way ready to move. "All right, I'm going to find my outfit. Sergeant, you and Cole can do what you want."

Cole saw green coats back of a wall two fields away and loped off to join them. Wesley clung to George, who started away on a long slant to the southeast, making a gradual ascent of the ridge. As they jumped the upper reaches of Plum Run, the sergeant panted: "Can you see what's going on?"

George shook his head. There was far too much smoke down by the peach orchard and wheat-field angle to make out a great deal. The lines seemed to be in about the same position as they had been when he had first seen them from the west ridge. But he could not understand the disposition of the Union troops. All the IIIrd Corps seemed to be jammed in the smoky angle. But the IInd had not moved down from the crest, barring the weak detachments about Codori's. He and Wesley were moving along a great diagonal gap between the two corps. If the Rebels once drove in that advanced left flank or rolled on up the slanting corridor—he shook his head. The whole picture looked fatal.

The sun was dropping fast. Probably not more than three quarters of an hour of daylight left, George thought. Then a breeze that foretold darkness rolled down the valley, shook the mask of smoke that hung from the peach orchard up to the Round Tops, began to shift it up the ridge.

Wesley yelped in surprise. Down by the Pike, stretching north from the orchard, ragged blue lines were falling back sullenly, breaking, rallying, turning to fire, fraying out, gathering again. Up Trostle's Lane and up the wheat-field road, batteries of artillery galloped in retreat. Some had four horses to a hitch, some only two. Very few cannoneers ran by the jarring wheels.

The immediate foreground was swept quite clear now. From the soggy banks of Plum Run down to the Trostle house blue figures sprawled. Some seemed to be snatching a nap in the midst of action. Others were fearfully torn. Mr. McArdle whined and jumped away from a boot that seemed stuffed with raw beef. Wesley kicked at a pinkish root and swore in high-pitched hysteria as a long coil of intestine slapped about his ankles. Under a fence a head, its kepi still rakishly cocked, grinned as though the jagged flesh of its neck were some obscene joke. Horses, some of them already beginning to swell, turned their stiff legs to the sky.

Wounded trickled back from the fighting along the Pike, their heads sagging and the powder marks about their mouths intensified by their ashen faces. One of them shouted, "Hey! Dan Sickles got hit down by Trostle's. Smashed the hell out of his leg." Another answered: "Wish to Jesus it'd been his God-damn head, sendin' us down there with no support. Son of a bitch! And they made him a major general."

"God damn it," muttered George. "I don't like this. What the hell am I getting into, keeping on? Mr. McArdle! Stick down there in the run. Lot of lead drifting up this way. Hey—I'll be damned." He stopped, gaping in amazement. A few feet away from him, musket slung across his shoulders, an unmistakable Chinese walked calmly toward Trostle's. George shouted, "Hey! John Chinaman! Go where?"

The Chinese turned his slant eyes toward George, grinned widely. "My savvy, master. Go make all ploper!" He vanished into a clump of bushes.

George blinked after him. "A Chink. In the Excelsior Brigade. I'll be damned!"

The wind was now a steady current flowing down the valley, piling the smoke higher and higher toward the Round Tops. George yelled, "My God, there's none of our infantry down there!" The smoking peach orchard swarmed with Southern infantry, with yelling men who rushed on down the knoll and moved diagonally astride the wheat-field road.

Wesley gasped, "Better get where we're going. Humphreys's boys is falling back fast from the Pike."

George started running, holding his leash at arm's length so the dog could keep in the cover of the stream. A single horseman bore down on him, a lieutenant colonel of artillery. Riding to meet him swept a captain from the Trostle field. The senior officer shouted, "Sorry, Bigelow, you'll have to stay there."

The captain, swinging his horse around, panted, "Hell, I won't have a man or a horse left in five minutes if I don't get out."

"Can't be helped. There's not a damn thing in the gap between us and the IInd. I'm trying to rush up enough batteries to hold them off. You've got to plug the gap until we're ready."

Captain Bigelow's handsome face set like a metal

mask and his eyes were unwavering. He nodded curtly. "We won't let you down, Colonel McGilvery." Then he turned and raced back to his guns shouting, "Battery—*halt!*"

George felt cold creep over him. The battery was to be a sacrifice for that whole part of the field! He said abruptly to Wesley, "I can't watch that."

"Me neither."

"Come on," said George. He hauled Mr. McArdle out of the run and sprinted for the Trostle house fifty yards away. Some change for the worse had taken place off to the right and bullets hummed and snarled past him, sent leaves fluttering down in slow spirals. There were many bodies close to the house. By the back door lay the Chinese, still grinning, with a bluish hole in his forehead. George hurried past the dead, unheeding, found an outside vegetable cellar, shoved the dog into it, and banged the door.

When he came out into Trostle's field that looked toward the orchard and waving wheat, three of the six guns were still slamming. The horses of two of the pieces were stretched motionless on the ground, and red-piped breeches showed in the tangle. He ran to the nearest piece where a sergeant, short jacket open on a hairy chest, bent over an ammunition case. George shouted, "For Christ's sake, show me what to do."

The sergeant blinked pale eyes at him. Then he handed him a sleezy, foot-long cylinder. "Jam that down the muzzle. Rip her here first. Careful." George ran to the muzzle, ripped the cartridge, jammed it home with a bloodstained rammer. The sergeant snapped: "Now get back and haul the lanyard when I holler." As he spoke he shoved an open-sided metal case into the muzzle. By the breech, George caught the dangling lanyard, saw Wesley helping at the muzzle. The gunner sergeant shouted: "Stand clear and yank! Clear of the wheel!"

George tugged the lanyard and in the act was aware for the first time since his arrival of gray infantry scrambling over the farther wall of Trostle's field. Several had their legs across, others were gripping the crest. It seemed an eternity between the tug on the lanyard and the final, answering roar from the bronze piece. Smoke blotted out field and wall. The piece shot back past him in recoil, checked and stopped. The gunner and Wesley grabbed the spokes, rolled the gun back into position. There were more bursts down the line. Smoke thinned and the wall showed clear, save for three or four torn bodies that hung over it. The gunner suddenly screamed, "God damn it, are you helping or aren't you? Heave that trail left. Look at the bastards on that side!"

George caught the handspike, swung the trail until the gunner dropped his hand, and struggled with the next charge. Muskets began to crack right and left. Out of the corner of his eye George saw a gray man spring to a limber chest and wave a Southern flag. Two bullets rapped on the trail close by the handspike. He jumped forward at the gunner's signal, tugged at the lanyard again. But the splintering world was packed with men who rushed forward, front and flank.

Then high overhead, over the peach orchard, over the rushing attack, Union shrapnel flashed. Hoofs beat behind George as he dodged the recoil of the last round. Captain Bigelow loomed above him, shouting, "Abandon pieces! Fall back to the crest!"

The gunner shouted, "No!" as he and Wesley rammed home a fresh charge. Bigelow shouted again: "It's an order. You've done your job. To the crest!"

There was a single crash from the left, another. Men began pelting past, scrambling over the wall by Trostle's Lane. Bigelow coolly paced his horse after them. George looked about in a sudden daze. The hitches of the five pieces beyond him were down and Southern infantry swarmed about the trails and over the dead cannoneers. Someone screeched, "Twenty-first Mississip'! Git fo'ward!"

The gunner sergeant yelled to George, "I promised the loot when he got hit we wouldn't lose the gun. I'm stayin'." George shook himself. The piece was still attached to the limber by the limp prolonge. Lead and swing horses were down and three drivers lay in the grass near them. But the wheel pair stood unharmed, tossing their heads and switching their tails. He cried:

"Wesley! Unhitch the traces," and swung onto the high saddle.

Wesley ran to the dead horses, wrenched the traces free. George kicked his heels against the big wheeler. The pair strained, leaned into their collars, and started off. There was a joyous shout from the piece. The gunner sergeant roared, "Make 'em move! Here's the last for them." The wheels rolled and rolled, picking up speed with each step of the powerful horses. The piece crashed out and the sergeant whooped above its echoes. Then George saw him, trotting on the other side of the off horse with Wesley. From the narrow gate in the stone wall Bigelow called: "Well done!" A boy whose face was disfigured by a bleeding gash trotted a small black toward Bigelow, a red guidon fluttering above his head. Bullets spattered about the moving piece. Bigelow's horse reared, recovered, reared again. The captain slipped from the saddle. Wesley and the gunner sergeant ran to him, picked him up, half carried, half dragged him up the lane.

More and more shrapnel was breaking overhead. George turned the team east up the ridge, and a sudden shout burst from him. The higher slope was wreathed in smoke and a seemingly endless line of Union batteries blazed and thundered. McGilvery had closed the gap. The wounded Bigelow freed an arm from Wesley and waved to the guns on the crest. Just ahead of George the bleeding boy rode and the wind caught the torn guidon, stretching it wide to show the crossed golden guns with a gold "9" in the upper angle and a gold "Mass." in the lower. George unconsciously raised his hand to his vizor.

He looked over his shoulder. In Trostle's field, men were kneeling to fire but the light was failing and the range increasing. Then he bent in the saddle. Four Southern infantrymen broke from bushes to his right, their muskets raised. Oddly, it never occurred to George to throw up his hands. He stared down at a sallow, blackened, bearded face barely a dozen yards away, at the leveled barrel of the nearest enemy. Suddenly the eyes narrowed and the barrel dropped. The infantryman waved the muzzle up the hill in a slow arc. "Go on,

Yank. Reckon you earned that-a-one." He and his companions ducked back into the undergrowth.

"I'll be damned," George thought. "Could have winged me like a partridge." He waved in acknowledgment, hoping that the little group might be watching him. They were still a good distance from the Trostle house and must have come up from the peach orchard. Trostle's!

He looked wildly about. A red-piped jacket showed a few yards ahead of him. He shouted, "Gunner! Hi! Gunner. Take this hitch the rest of the way."

He slid from the saddle, doubled back toward Trostle's. A thin drift of exhausted men in blue wove toward him. Someone croaked, "Don't go that way. Reb's coming hell-bending."

George shouted, "Wounded man from my own outfit back there. Got to get him." He dodged past bushes, clung to sheds, took cover where he could. Ahead of him Southern voices shouted. He saw the vegetable cellar close by, wrenched open the door and caught the leash as Mr. McArdle burst out in a storm of protesting yelps. "Think I'd leave you? Get going now, boy. We've got to run!"

It was quite dark in the shaggy woods between the Round Tops and the wheat field. De Mérac held the cloth of his trousers away from his right leg to keep the deep bullet gouge on his thigh from chafing as he led the Rifles along the path up the hill. Path and woods were littered with heaps that should have been anonymous in the gloom but too many of them he knew. That was Wayne, curled in a tight knot by the root of an oak. Rohleder lay just beyond the six dark patches that were Confederates. Sergeant Hooks and Sergeant Gallifet and four privates had all gone down under a single shell. Even in good light, it would have been difficult to recognize Randol with his blood-blackened face as he hung head down over a rocky ledge.

Three times the Rifles had been thrown into the seesaw fight, that ranged from the wheat field up toward the peaks. They had seen Ward's wreckage beating off the driving attacks of Hood's Texans, had seen relief come to the whole brigade when Caldwell's division of the IInd Corps rushed to the thin lines. They had been thrown in again as Zook's brigade had slowly melted under heavy fire, and they had seen General Zook fall. All this and more the Rifles had seen and de Mérac had seen it with them.

He clung for sure comfort to the knowledge that despite savage attacks and thin defenses, the lines now stood almost as they had stood when the first bewildering move to the wheat field had been made at Sickles's order. The Union left still held and the losses of the Rochambeau Rifles formed a part of the price paid for that holding.

He slackened his pace until the stretcher behind him caught up. "It is still not too bad, Craig?" he asked.

Wilson's voice sounded weak but assured from the dimness. "Not too bad. I can't feel much from the waist down, but that surgeon says it's shock. He's sure they'll be able to save the right one with a good chance for the left." A cigar end glowed from the stretcher.

"You don't want to stop for a rest?"

Wilson gave the ghost of a chuckle. "Don't baby me. Wait till the shock wears off and then I'll yell enough to keep you awake all night."

De Mérac laid a flask on the stretcher. "There is more whiskey when you need it. I must go ahead to find de Trobriand. Carry him gently, boys."

He lengthened his stride painfully. There was no need to seek out the brigadier, but Wilson's cheery voice that seemed to deny shell-smashed legs seemed more than his taut nerves and racked body could stand at the moment. And Dan Shea! Surely he could not live with his whole abdomen opened by a bullet. And George. Where could George be? Had it been foolish to send the dog across the valley to him? Perhaps the dog had never reached him. Perhaps he had reached him, lured him out to sure capture and death. He thought: *"Je n'en peux plus! Je n'en peux plus.* Ah, Gail, you could scarcely be proud of me now—if ever."

The woods toward the crest were suddenly loud with

new life as heavy, fresh columns of the VIth Corps, strongest in the army, began to deploy along the ridge. In the dark pit of the valley, muskets whacked with sullen sporadic bursts. Far off by the Cemetery, snarling, querulous fighting seemed to have broken out between the Rebel Ewell and the exhausted ranks of von Steinwehr and von Gilsa and Krzyzanowski and von Amberg. Swift sparks shot across the northern sky and shrapnel burst in tiny, lurid flashes. The men of the veteran VIth took stock of the sounds and called to the thin units that they were relieving: "Hey—what's it like down there?" Voices snapped dully back at them. "Stick your Goddamn nose over the rocks above the wheat field and you'll find out." An officer whose shaded lantern shone on gold major's leaves said to de Mérac: "Rebs tough as ever, are they?" De Mérac answered: "They are still the Southern infantry." The major nodded in grim understanding and passed on.

The brigade finally halted in the same sloping eastern field where it had lain in reserve prior to Sickles's nearly fatal move. De Mérac watched the men collapse in their places, not even bothering to strip off their blanket rolls. He stepped among them. "You know what you did today. To that knowledge, I can add nothing. I am proud to have been on the same field with you."

The feeble, almost wordless response gave him a kind of sad cheer, a response that was summed up by a whisper from the few men grouped about Bordagaray. "We were there together, *mon colonel.*"

Then de Mérac was aware of a statuelike figure at his elbow. The indestructible Melchior Rapp, sergeant major and now acting adjutant, waited patiently for his colonel's attention. De Mérac said, "Yes, Sergeant Major?"

Rapp saluted. "The casualty returns, *mon colonel.*" He spoke as calmly as though submitting a summary of a regimental morning-reports at Fort Corcoran. "Of killed—there are twenty-two. Of wounded and missing, seventy-four. Total under arms at this moment, ninety-nine officers and men."

De Mérac nodded and sat down under a bush that

was covered with sweet-smelling white flowers. The scent did something to smother the heavy cloying reek that was beginning to waft up over the ridge from the western slopes. Nothing could dull the sounds, the high-pitched wails, the slow, racking moans that began to fill the night as the anesthesia of excitement and shock wore off. Wilson had already been carried down to the hospitals by Rock Creek. But there had seemed little point in moving Shea. He was now stretched under a tree a few yards away with his abdomen a mass of bloody rags and his lungs swelling and contracting as they drew in waves of hot agony. Father Doyle knelt between him and a Maine private who lay unconscious, mercifully spared, for the time at least, the knowledge that his left arm and shoulder were a vealy tangle of bone and cartilage.

De Mérac knew that he ought to try to sleep but the instant he closed his eyes, his nerves began to tauten and jump. Even with his eyes open, he started at sudden sounds like the clank of a bayonet against a canteen, the continual shuffle of boots and hoofs along the path just above him. He heard his name called and jerked to his feet. He couldn't place the voice, yet it seemed vaguely familiar. A huddle of horsemen came along the path and his name was repeated.

He limped toward the riders, answering in a dull, flat tone. The leading rider spoke. "That you, Colonel? I'm General Hunt. Met you this morning with Birney and Sickles."

This morning? All meaning had been ripped away from time in the woods across on Seminary Ridge, in the blasting tangles above the wheat field. Hunt? Of course. The chief of artillery. Hunt went on, "Have you got an officer who answers this description? Very fair-haired, about six feet tall?"

De Mérac started. George! Yet there must be hundreds of officers in the army whom that would fit. He said as much to General Hunt. "But they don't all wear a belt with 'R.R.' on it," said the general.

De Mérac, not daring to hope, stammered, "He could be Captain George Force. He was missing after the raid with Berdan."

Hunt called over his shoulder, "Be sure you get that name straight, Danforth. I want to send it right on to General Meade." He said to de Mérac, "A captain answering that description joined Bigelow's 9th Mass. down by Trostle's. He served a piece as a volunteer and then drove it out of the field just ahead of the Rebs. Both McGilvery and Bigelow told me about it. Is he here now?"

"He has not returned," said de Mérac huskily.

"I'm sorry. I heard he went back to look for wounded and the battery lost track of him. By God, I want to salute him, living, captured, or dead. Magnificent work. Over and above any call of duty, mind you."

"Yes," said de Mérac.

Hunt clucked to his mount. "I'd be glad if you'd let me know when he comes back, Colonel. Good night."

De Mérac slumped back to his tree. It was too early to give up hope of George's return. Still, the quickly aroused hope and its equally quick dashing lay like a heavy cloud over him. He wished that he dared move his command farther down the east slope. The constant coming and going along the upper path drummed against his aching brain. Boots and hoofs, hoofs and boots. Men calling. Hoofs closer and closer. An aide shouting: "No, sir, not there. There's the Rochambeau Rifles." Then a voice that brought de Mérac to his feet. "Of course. You'd be sure to find those damned immigrants skulking in the rear. Heard they ran like rabbits when the first shells came over. Thank God, I'm not responsible for them any more."

De Mérac in blind rage ran toward the dim figures. "General Pelham! I demand—"

Another group of figures loomed on the path and sharp tones, slicing like a saber, cut the air. "General Pelham!"

Pelham disregarded de Mérac. "My apologies, General Birney." His voice was icy. "I didn't recognize you. I am more familiar with the generals who were my contemporaries at West Point. Those from civil life—"

"Those from civil life in many cases rank you, Pelham." Birney and his staff were now distinct against the summer sky. "Your West Point training will no doubt assure of the correctness of *this* order: you will consider yourself under arrest. You will report yourself at once to the provost."

Pelham grew rigid. "Very good, sir. I am entitled under the Articles of War, to inquire concerning the charge against me."

Birney said pointedly. "In *this* case, Pelham, the prisoner will be informed at once. He will know the full extent of the charge and will *not* be held incommunicado. The charge is conduct unbecoming an officer and a gentleman. It should have been brought before because of your utterly contemptible attitude toward our foreign-born regiments."

Pelham's close-buttoned torso was a stiff, black silhouette. "I shall report myself under arrest at once, sir." He saluted and trotted away through the darkness.

Then Birney called down the slope. "You there, de Mérac?"

"At your orders, sir."

"Just one for you and your men—rest. Good night and my thanks for an excellent day's work."

"Good night, sir."

De Mérac sat down again, his ears filled with the excited comment of his men, who had heard the dialogue between the two generals. He found it impossible to regret in any way Pelham's disgrace before the uncounted numbers within earshot. Yet he had grudgingly to pay homage to the unshaken voice of Pelham and to the rigid, tight-buttoned figure that had melted away against the sky.

Then an exultant laugh echoed through the woods. "Hi! John! Where are you?"

De Mérac's voice cracked in sudden answer. George Force came running down the slope through the gloom, Mr. McArdle trailing bravely after him. George shook de Mérac's shoulders. "God, the things I've heard! You were cut to pieces! You were wiped out! Then I struck de Trobriand and he told me. And I came in just when Birney was removing Deadly Pelham's hide." He laughed again. "I had to clamp the pup's jaws and my own to keep from yelling 'Encore.' Look—d'you suppose they'll call me as a witness? I could tell 'em enough to send him to Dry Tortugas for ten lifetimes."

De Mérac sighed. "I shall be as well pleased if he is merely set to chasing Indians. Ah, George—you come back to very few of your friends." He gave George the figures, cited names.

George nodded gravely. "It's about what I expected. Hell, I'm sorry I wasn't with you. When we got back to this side I stopped to watch some of our batteries and by the time I got up here it was all over."

De Mérac found himself laughing and some of the strain went from him. "*Watching* some batteries, George? But I heard of that. Your truancy so impressed General Hunt that he came here seeking your name."

George whistled. "Did I do anything wrong?"

"You will find Hunt most lenient. In fact you will doubtless receive a letter from General Meade himself. Now I truly think I shall sleep and you had better, too. Remember—" his voice grew very serious—"today we only held Lee back. Tomorrow must come his great effort or else—"

"Or else what?"

"We shall see Dora and Gail very soon, *mon ami*, as we shall also if his effort fails. We gain nothing by considering the possibility of his success."

De Trobriand's brigade was moved before dawn farther down the reverse slope of the ridge and closer to the center of the Union line. Through the hot morning the Rifles had slept and eaten and slept again, lying in ranks in the lush grass. Around noon, a beaming Labanieff scaled up from the banks of Rock Creek to drink coffee with de Mérac and George. He was in high spirits. "On the first of July, I rode with Custer's brigade from the Michigan about Two Taverns. Yesterday, the second, I watch your fight from General Meade's headquarters. This day I shall return to General Meade." He gestured toward the crest. "Ah, a storm gathers, friends. You have been up there? But you should. Lee moves batteries, masses troops. It will be interesting to watch when that storm breaks."

"We'll see it, all right," observed George. "Storms get made just to bust over us."

Labanieff waved the fringed sleeve of a new jacket which the young General Custer had given him. "You miss the point, *mon cher*. There is uncertainty over there. The men fight as ever, but the generals—ah, I can scent it like an old hound—their moves are not sure. They do not seem to know what to do. In my kit I have three beautifully drawn plans of what Lee might have done on the first two days. In each of the three, he is given a sweeping victory, and each of the three will be worth a full lecture at our Staff College."

"Had you been in the wheat field, you would have found no quarrel with Lee's sureness," said de Mérac dryly.

"But that was the *men!*" urged Labanieff. "It is not good warfare when men correct the mistakes of the generals. So I told my friend Craig Wilson as I saw him placed in an ambulance just now. Ah—he is cheered by the news that both legs will heal."

"Both? Good!" said de Mérac.

"Well supposing Lee makes more errors when he hits us today and the men correct them all, what's the result going to be?" asked George.

Labanieff looked very grave. "I, like my minister, have always favored the Union cause. I tremble for it if Lee is able to take this ridge. Yes—my friends, just that rocky strip of ground suddenly possesses precisely that significance."

"And if he fails?" asked de Mérac.

"That is different. Meade is new in command and—" The hush that brooded over the sunny hill was broken by a single shrapnel burst that flamed low in the sky. Its echoes rattled away through rocky glens and over broad fields on the west slope. On their last dying note a full-throated blast sounded from the hidden Southern lines. "Ah—" said Labanieff—"soon speculation is replaced by knowledge. It begins."

The crest of Cemetery Ridge began to smoke and

fume. The three lay flat on the grass, pressed against turf that shook and quivered as though some great monster were struggling under it. The intensity of the firing was incredible. Then a wall of smoke was reared against the sky, solid as the granite of the ridge itself, as the Union batteries answered, in lighter volume.

George felt his teeth chattering to the repeated concussions. The minutes crept by unmarked and still the blasting went on. Men began to burst through the smoke wall, stagger down to shelter. A Union caisson blew up; another, and solid wheels whirled through the air; dark ragged chunks that suggested living origin sailed with them. Horses plunged screaming out of the yellow-white world and galloped madly down the slope.

"Holy hell!" shouted George. "How much longer can this last?"

Labanieff raised himself suddenly. "I forget that which brings me here. I go to the crest."

De Mérac caught his arm. "*Vingt dieux!* Not into that furnace!"

"One must observe, regardless of conditions," came the calm answer. "*Le métier veut ça!*" He picked up a bulging haversack stamped with the crossed sabers of the 7th Michigan and trudged up toward the rocky ridges where the massed guns of the Confederacy rained shell, shrapnel, and solid shot.

"Ah—he does not lack courage—that one," said de Mérac.

"God," said George. "I wouldn't go up there unless Abe Lincoln ordered me in person." Then side by side they braced themselves against the endless smashing roar that filled the hot afternoon.

It was impossible to guess what was going on along the crest or down the west slope. Like the thousands of other blue figures lying on the east slope, de Mérac and George could only wonder and hope. They stiffened in sudden fright as seven batteries emerged from the crest and started down the hill. Three—four—eight—followed them and de Mérac called his resting men to attention. But the batteries turned parallel to the ridge and halted. It was some rearrangement of Hunt's, not a retreat.

By half past two, there was an ominous slackening of the Union fire, and a more ominous crescendo from the western ridge. De Mérac drummed his fingers against his scabbard and George chewed blade after blade of grass, snatching up the green shoots automatically, biting hard on the pulpy stems.

At three o'clock a great hush fell. De Mérac found himself on his knees, staring ahead. Out of the swirling fogs of the crest galloped an aide who pelted down the hill toward the last of the reserve artillery. As he thundered by de Mérac he called to a red-faced engineer major: "Christ, they're coming! Ought to see it. Lee's chucking in every God-damn thing he's got."

De Mérac knew that he was trembling. His senses seemed blurred. He did not feel the rough ground under his knee. George's tones, oddly thin and metallic beside him, he recognized but did not understand. He shook when the Union batteries opened, one by one; stared when the guns that sheltered under the crest rolled forward, swung up into the crashing fog again; stared once more at other batteries that swept up from the lowlands, the drivers leaning forward in their saddles, the cannoneers clinging to limber chests or sprinting beside their pieces.

He was on his feet. There was musketry from the ridge, musketry in two belts of sound—one faint but swelling, the other louder and unchanging. George's voice broke as he yelled: "Look—more reserves!" and pointed to the 2nd Pennsylvania that had been lying fifty yards above them, pointed to the broad, cloverleafed hats that ducked, behind a bristle of bayonets, into the clanging welter beyond. Musketry closer and closer; more and more wounded, more and more stragglers streaming down past the Rifles; the high, keening sound of the Rebel yell, clear above the pounding and slamming.

A single rider broke out from the right. De Mérac's brain cleared as though a wet sponge had been passed over it. He shouted: "Castex—sound attention." He mounted Lisette and saw Dekdebrun trot up from the rear. Leaning from a black, sweat-spattered horse, Régis de Trobriand shouted *"En avant!"*, wheeled and led the way on a slant to the left.

The Rifles led the brigade and de Trobraind bent far from the saddle to call to de Mérac, "If I am hit, it is you who lead. Lee has thrown fifteen thousand men at our center. We drive at his flank. That is all. At his flank, until you can go no farther or there is no flank!"

The way led up over the ridge through a blasted world. De Mérac jumped a shattered limber pole and Lisette shied at the six bay bodies dead in their harness, shied again as her hoof struck the iron rim of a wheel, dismounted by some terrific blast. A gun, its trail smashed, lifted its bronze throat like a drowning animal.

Castex's bugle clamored and the Rifles swung into line. There was a stone wall ahead of them where blackened men sheltered and stared up at them through glassy, expressionless eyes. The smoke was thinning as the Rifles scrambled over the wall. They were far to the left of the attack and de Mérac kept his eyes on de Trobriand, who looked back over his shoulder. Then the brigadier raised one arm, swept it to the right, and the whole command wheeled, swinging north along the slope toward the flank of Lee's desperate drive.

De Mérac shouted in surprise as de Trobriand's arm again shot into the air, stayed there. In amazement de Mérac repeated the signal and the brigade halted. He ran Lisette to the brigadier, who pointed along the slope.

From the stone walls at the top, clear to the Emmitsburg road at the bottom, a disorderly mass was flying, racing for the shelter of its own lines while Union shell and shrapnel flogged it along. Striking from the south, heavy masses of Union troops a few hundred yards ahead of de Mérac, smashed like a battering-ram into the wrecked attack. Far away toward the bulge of Cemetery Hill, men were throwing down their arms, running with upraised hands toward the lines of bayonets that swooped down from the crest. Bright Southern battle flags bobbed and dipped, went down, reappeared, were swallowed up for good. Close by de Mérac, thin files of

Berdan's green men hurried a solid, weaponless column of Confederates up the slope.

De Trobriand said, *"C'est tout,"* in an odd, strained voice. De Mérac could only gulp and stare. His men crowded about him, staring like their colonel, swabbing their foreheads, leaning on their muskets. George stepped up beside de Mérac and clung weakly to a stirrup leather.

So the wreck of Lee's last cast was watched by the Rifles—barely ninety men who, with the rest of de Trobriand's command, could add nothing more to the weight that was battering the flying fragments of the gray brigades.

Then a white-haired major by the stone wall yelled that at the Cemetery and Culp's Hill, the Rebel attacks had utterly broken down, that Stuart's cavalry had been shattered by Kilpatrick and Gregg and Custer and Duffié.

De Mérac echoed de Trobriand. *"C'est tout.* That's all," he said. Around him his men threw back their shoulders, sank to the ground like troops shedding heavy packs at the end of a long, long march.

Two days later the Rifles took the road again but this time they were heading south. Lee was falling back and back across the Maryland line, surging over South Mountain. Outside Emmitsburg de Mérac took advantage of a halt to have Father Doyle put a fresh bandage over the gutter that the bullet had scooped out of his right leg. With a ripple of fringed shirt and a torrent of mixed Russian, French, and English Labanieff swept down on him, vaulted from the saddle. "Ah—*mon cher*—it is over!"

De Mérac jumped and Father Doyle dropped the old, blood-stained wrappings. They both cried, "Over?"

"It can be nothing less. Grant has taken Vicksburg on the Mississippi. Ah, Mr. Jeff Davis will see at once. It leaps to the eye. He is of West Point, that one, and will of course compare his position to that of Archduke Charles after Wagram in 1809 when he found that Napoleon controlled the Danube. With pen, paper, and five minutes I can prove to you that without the great river—which the Union now controls—the Confederacy cannot live."

Father Doyle grinned wryly. "It's not myself that would argue with you, Colonel. I'm convinced by your words alone. But there's others you'll be longer in persuading."

Labanieff looked hurt. "It is you, Jean, who are stubborn? Ah—but only consider—"

De Mérac carefully flexed the muscles of his legs and smiled at the chaplain. *"Du tout, mon ami.* If I may interpret Father Doyle's thought, he means that those who must truly be convinced and those who will be most obstinate are our friends the infantry of the South. No—to show them the military truth you will need more than pen, paper, and five minutes—you will need long months, you will need the Army of the Potomac and all the western troops, backed by the Union Navy. And even then, I assure you that they will remain obdurate. Ah—the bandage suits to a marvel, Father. I am your debtor. Ride with me, Colonel, and expound to me the glories of General Grant. In all seriousness, this is tremendous news."

The march went on, south and south again. Somewhere beyond the bluish lift of the Maryland hills, Gail waited, and the thought filled de Mérac with a solemn joy. He could visualize her standing in the summer sun before the stone house, the morning bright on her redgold hair, her level gray eyes watching the road from Washington over which the newsboys would ride with great tidings, whether good or evil, her soft mouth set in firm courage and her chin high. Then one day he himself would ride up that same road and up the gravel drive. The war would go on, but they would face it side by side, indissoluble; they would face whatever the distant, misty end of the war might bring. *"Dieu de dieu!"* he thought. "I must make myself worthy of her and of the life that is before us. Ah—this country. It has given me George and Craig. It has given me the deep fellowship of the Rifles. Now it gives me Gail. It is a great deal, all that, for one country to give to one man. And perhaps the greatest of all, this country gives me itself, as I try to give myself to it."

From the saddle he looked back at the little river of scarlet-topped kepis. In his mind the river seemed suddenly to lengthen, as though unsummoned men had stepped into the ranks, as though the men who had fallen on the Peninsula, at Second Bull Run, at Fredericksburg, at Chancellorsville, and in the ghastly sway of the wheat field, had joined their living comrades as the long march to final victory began. Ghosts of fallen men, men killed in action, ghosts of men dead of fever, now tramped that winding Maryland road—LeVau and Péguy and Hein and LeNoir, Bolton and Wayne and Shea—men from the Black Forest and the Rhine valleys, from the Limousin, the Côte d'Or, the Landes, from Picardy plains and the ringing Breton coast, from County Kerry and County Meath and County Clare, from the boroughs of New York and the shallow beaches of Staten Island and Long Island. They were all there—they *must* be there to march with the others and to know that the shattering threat to the Union for which they had died had been parried and smashed.

Then from the hills of the receding north, a wind stirred, gathered strength, swept on down the road, overtook the column and the memories that marched with it. Out of the rush of air, out of the quick rustle of leaves, a clear, strong voice seemed to ring, a voice that was vibrant with high triumph—"Go in gaily, boys, gaily!" In the ranks, living men shivered a little, looked over their shoulders and thought of the old *kébir*.

EPILOGUE

Washington—May 23, 1865

THE house stood at the intersection of New York and Pennsylvania Avenues and the bay window of the rented room looked down Pennsylvania as it ran past the State and Treasury Departments just before vanishing in its great swing southeast to the Capitol. To the right, the farthest section of the bay showed a glimpse of the trees of LaFayette Park and a hint of the flag-draped reviewing stand that masked the smooth green of the White House lawns. It was still early but the sidewalks below the house were dense with a swaying mass of bright bonnets, beavers, and the slouch hats and kepis of the army. Hawkers sidled along the fringes of the crowds selling flags, wreaths, and bright garlands of flowers. Children scurried yelling across the street, scrambled up lampposts or led harassed parents on frantic chases through the press.

In the bay window Craig Wilson, back in uniform for the day, looked out into the flawless morning. He was still drawn and pale and when he shifted in his chair his legs moved awkwardly. But his back was straight and the colonel's eagles, awarded him on his final discharge, rested on square, unbowed shoulders. He hitched himself closer to the open window and glanced at the three heads beside him that looked eagerly down into the Avenue. Claire, graying but gentle and clear-featured as ever; Dora Force, her face alight in its frame of dark ringlets; Gail de Mérac, her fine figure set off by a pale green dress and the sun bringing out hidden lights in her red-gold hair. On the floor between Dora and Gail sat Mr. McArdle, a blue blanket marked with the Kearny patch about his shaggy shoulders.

Claire caught her husband's eye and smiled up at him, laying her hand on his. He returned the pressure of her fingers and wondered if she or the others could catch a new, strange silence that underlay the hum and clatter drifting up from below. It was a deep, uneasy silence that brought back vividly to him other hushes that he remembered in the days when his knees bent easily and his lithe muscles carried him smoothly along behind the waiting ranks of the Rifles. After the hush would come the sudden ripping of the Rebel yell or the deep-toned cheers of his own men. His body grew tense, as though awaiting a signal.

Gail leaned back in her chair and tried to hold her hands quiet in her lap. "Craig," she said, "isn't it about time?"

He nodded. "Getting close. Lord, I wish we could find out something about the Rifles."

Dora adjusted Mr. McArdle's blanket. "I've been through and through the order of march in the papers. They just aren't there."

"I can't stand it if they're not in it," said Claire. "If anyone deserves to be here today those boys do. The papers said something about 'mixed brigades.' They might be in one of those."

Wilson pulled at his mustache. "Just can't tell in the army. They may have been grabbed for provost duty at the last minute. Plenty of other outfits have been. Lord, if Dudley Pelham weren't west of the Mississippi, I'd suspect his hand in this. We—" He started and Mr. McArdle gave a sharp yelp.

Far off by the Capitol, a single cannon slammed, sent

rattling echoes through the air, like the single shot that had heralded so many actions in the past. Out of sight, down beyond the bend of the Avenue, voices beat into the air, swelled to a roar that swept nearer and nearer. Gail swayed forward, rested her hands on the sill. Claire half rose and Dora drummed her hands on her knees crying, "What is it? What *is* it? O—those wretched buildings down there. They shut off everything." Then her breath went out in a broken sigh.

A single rider in Union blue swung into sight, turned up the Avenue. After him clattered a staff, a cluster of bright flags, the winking sabers of a cavalry escort. The leading rider came nearer. He was gaunt and thin with a schoolmaster's stoop accentuated by a thin beard and the glint of spectacles. His free arm held a sheaf of flowers, red and white and blue. The crowd roared louder. By the Treasury a woman broke from the curb and looped a wreath about the neck of the sleek horse.

Wilson muttered, "There he is. Old George Meade."

Dora tried to answer, but she could only nod as she thought of all that the stooping man, now just below her, represented. Behind him were the roaring ridges of Gettysburg, the desperate, dogged drive and slash and drive through the tangles of Virginia, and at last the day when he and his men saw the tall gray figure of Lee come slowly down the steps of a farmhouse near Appomattox, superb in defeat as he had been magnificent in stalemate or victory. Bright flags and escort blurred before her. She sat back and glanced at Gail, who was wiping her eyes unashamedly. Dora smiled shakily at her.

"I know," said Gail. "Oh, Dora, can you really believe it? I don't think I ever quite grasped that it was all over at Appomattox. But now—oh—something else is coming!"

Over the din of the crowd came a steady unbroken rattle and clatter welling up from the hidden reaches of the Avenue. More horsemen, more colors swung into view. Wilson straightened. "Here they are—Merritt's Cavalry Corps!"

Gail twisted her handkerchief between her fingers as she thought, "The first combat troops of the day." There was brass at the turn of the Avenue and a mounted band blared out "Garry Owen," while Custer, commanding the first division, made his horse rear and buck to the screaming delight of the crowd.

On they came, the cavalry of the Army of the Potomac. They came on twenty abreast, the troopers erect in their saddles, their sabers at the carry and their carbines creaking in the leather buckets. Blue and blue and blue they rode by with the silver of their blades and the crimson of the scarves about their necks.

Gail watched the flow of men and horses, the six yellow-flagged ambulances that followed each brigade. When she looked west along the line of march toward the hidden reviewing stand, the clusters of battle flags made bright patches to mark the regiments. Just below her, when the ranks wheeled left with the turn of the Avenue, the colors fluttered out. Each oncoming squadron brought a tightness to her throat, a mistiness to her eyes as she read their battle honors on the outblown streamers—Brandy Station—Trevilian Station—Aldie—Cedar Mountain—Five Forks—milestones that measured the black gap beween Bull Run and Appomattox. And with them rode the state flags—New York and West Virginia and Connecticut, Ohio and Massachusetts and Michigan, more and more states of the Union as Davies's division and Devin's succeeded Custer's. Then battery after battery of horse artillery, the red-piped cannoneers pacing their mounts beside piece or caisson.

The last clanking section was gone and for an instant the Avenue, as far as she could see, was clear. Dora clenched her fists and whispered, "Now—now—the infantry."

Gail closed her eyes. "Dear God, let John be with them. He belongs with them, he and the Rifles."

When she looked out again, the crowd was swaying and surging. General Parke was bringing on the colors of the IXth Corps. She made a quick gesture as though brushing away staff and escort, as though clearing a path for the foot soldiers. In her hospital days she had seen them so often tramping past the big stone house in

515

endless files, bound for northern Virginia, bound for Antietam, for Gettysburg, for the ringing thickets of the Wilderness and the dank rifle pits about Petersburg. In their narrow cots she had seen them suffer, seen them carried out to the sheds where the coffins were stacked, seen them limp away lacking arm or leg. Now, still more her heart reached out toward them since somewhere in their ranks her husband rode.

They marched straight toward her, twenty abreast, and her breath caught in her throat as she saw the thin ranks, saw how regiments were compressed into companies to give the prescribed frontage of the march, how brigades shrank to regiments. And the flags! Sometimes they were new, bright silk. But most were blackened shreds clinging to bullet-chipped poles—or they were bare poles topped by battered eagles.

Banners and bayonets came on toward her in waves, kepis and slouch hats marked with the crossed cannon and anchor of the IXth Corps. They came with the blare of bands, the piercing screech of fifes. "Oh, the men will cheer and the boys will shout and the ladies they will all turn out *and* we'll *all* feel *gay* when *Johnny* comes *march*ing *home!*" The drummers twirled their sticks and banged out the infectious rhythm.

Wisconsin gave way to Michigan and Michigan to New York. More bands, Maine men singing, "The Union forever! Hurrah boys, hurrah!" Gail was trembling. "It's *over!* They'll never have to go back to it again!" She leaned toward Dora, who caught her hand. "Oh, Gail, it's so wonderful and it's so awful. Look—that's the 24th Iowa. We saw them at City Point that time. Now there aren't a hundred of them left."

Wreaths and garlands were scaling out from the crowd, falling under worn boots or settling over pack-galled shoulders. A white-haired woman in a little black bonnet hobbled to the very flank of the march and caught at passing hands. Gail could see her lips move in endless question, could see kepied heads shake gently, turn to look after her. Slowly the bent black figure worked down the line of march and was lost to sight.

Griffin and the Maltese crosses of the Vth Corps. A

girl in red by a lamppost crying, "Joe! Joe! There he is! I see him! Joe!" Maryland and Delaware and the endless lift of bayonets and the drum of boots. New York and Michigan and Massachusetts and Iowa and Maine. Glittering brass and the whirl of fat drumsticks and the toss of a ribboned baton. "He has sounded forth the trumpet that shall never call retreat." A thin company of Berdan's Sharpshooters, gliding on in their worn green. Rumbling batteries bringing up the rear of each brigade. Fifes and drums. "*And* we'll *all* feel *gay* when *Johnny* comes *march*ing *home!*"

There was a long wait between the disappearance of the Vth Corps and the leading ranks of the IInd. Craig Wilson brought out sandwiches, and Madeira.

Then tall, handsome Humphreys was leading the clover leaf of the IInd Corps into view and the four turned back to the windows. Mr. McArdle, replete with sandwiches and beginning to be a little bored, stretched out on the floor with one ear languidly cocked to the bands.

At last Wilson said slowly, "I don't see how there can be much more to this. That's Frank Barlow down there with his outfit."

Dora cried, "But there's got to be more! The Rifles!"

Wilson shrugged resignedly. "Barlow's got the 2nd Division. There isn't any 3rd."

Gail felt disappointment, biting cold, settle over her. Down in the street the crowds were cheering young Barlow, cheering two of his famous regiments, the 19th Massachusetts and the 1st Minnesota. She tried to join in the clapping but her hands beat limply together.

Wilson said, "Damnation!" under his breath. Woodell's, the last brigade of Barlow's division, had completed its turn and crowds far down the Avenue were closing in behind it.

Gail sighed. "The poor boys. I know from John's last letter how he and George and the rest were looking forward to this." She got up slowly. The others sat, staring out into the sunlit world. Then Gail said, "Wait! I think—yes—something else *is* coming. Oh, we've still got a chance!"

People were shuffling back onto the sidewalks. An erect figure on a big gray horse rode into sight at the head of a small staff. Dora jumped to her feet. "I know who that is! Look! I'm sure of it. It's General de Trobriand! Oh, Craig, couldn't you call to him when he goes by? He may know something."

A single, clear bugle note blared out of sight. Mr. McArdle sprang to his feet and hooked his forepaws across the sill. A hush fell over the room.

Then around the bend ten buglers wheeled in perfect alignment, a sergeant bugler leading them. They carried long trumpets with the flares resting against their hips and the tops of their kepis showed red. The sergeant raised his instrument. In perfect unison, eleven bugles glittered high above the kepis, spun dizzily, were brought down in a single gesture and a quickstep echoed up the Avenue. Mr. McArdle broke into frenzied yelps. Gail's voice broke as she tried to cry, "Here they are!"

The Avenue swam before her. Claire and Dora were hugging her and Wilson was on his feet shouting, "The Rifles! The Rifles!" Down below the crowd was growing wild as the buglers broke off their march, twirled their bugles, and blasted out again.

Gail brushed her hand over her eyes, tried to clear her vision. It was true. There was de Trobriand looking up at the window and laughing as he pointed down the Avenue with his sword. And there—there—at the bend by the Treasury, a small, Arab head coming into sight, a sleek neck from which long garlands hung. She cried, "Lisette!" Then she forgot the mount as she saw its rider, saw the tall, broad-shouldered man. Sun caught the vizor of his kepi, made it glint with the reddish sheen of tortoise shell. Sun flashed on the broad curved blade of his saber. Her whole world settled on man and horse.

There was another rider close behind de Mérac and Dora was hugging her and calling, "It's George! George! It's the first time I've seen him as lieutenant colonel!" A third horseman. "Good for Bordagaray!" shouted Wilson. "Out of the hospital and a major."

518

"Go on. Mr. McArdle! Howl your head off," cried Claire. "Here are the rest of them. Craig! The Rifles!"

In three thin ranks, the Rifles turned up toward them and Gail felt her breath coming faster. She dropped to her knees and beat her palms on the sill. The buglers were just below, blaring out an old French quickstep, and she could look down on the scarlet patches on their kepis.

Then she forgot the musicians as the three riders came close. Wilson shouted. "There—there—now! Wave something! Get his eye!"

There was no need to wave. De Mérac, lean and tanned, looked up and gave a great joyous shout that struck deep to Gail's heart. "Ah—I knew it. Wait there! Wait, all of you! We break up soon." There was a flick of the sword as Lisette carried him out of earshot.

Beside Gail, Dora called wildly to George and the sun touched his bright hair as he whipped off his kepi. His shouts were drowned in the frantic, struggling howls of Mr. McArdle, who seemed bent on hurling himself through space to his master. Then George was gone and Bordagaray, his swarthiness softened by hospital pallor, bowed from the saddle.

Now Gail looked down at the three ranks of the Rifles, marching at the quick, French step—barely sixty men and a handful of officers. In the center of the front rank, three battered poles lifted shreds of silk to the wind—the flags of France, of New York, and of the Union. On came the Rifles. Their uniforms were worn and faded, but the scarlet patch that the old *kébir* had bestowed on them in Virginia fields nearly three years ago still shone bright from their kepis.

The beat-beat-beat of their step seemed to strike against Gail's heart. She cried suddenly, "But I don't know any of them. Why, at City Point last year—"

Then faces looked up from the ranks and some of them she knew. There was Father Doyle in rusty black marching bravely along with the aid of a blackthorn stick. That gaunt, hollow-cheeked sergeant on the near flank was little Castex, grown suddenly into serious manhood. There was Sergeant Flaherty with the New York colors, there was Lieutenant Schoch, last survivor of Hein's old company. One by one she picked them out—privates who had joined after Spottsylvania, a sergeant whose record went back to Malvern Hill in far-off '62. And there was the old Chasseur, DuChesne, stepping out with his cavalryman's roll. And Reichert and Mike Boyle, Tufveson and Mauhin and Pratt. Didier was first sergeant over a dozen men and Croiset led a squad.

Gail whispered to Claire, "I just can't look at them. So many, many gone in the last year."

Claire said softly, "I know. It was the same in every year. Oh, Gail—I don't—I don't see our old—"

Then from right flank a voice snapped, "*Bleu!* Your guide, *'cré nom de dieu!*"

Claire gave a gasp of relief. In solemn majesty, his red beard touched by the sun, marched Melchior Rapp. On he strode, head high and back as rigid as ever it had been at Chambers Street.

A limping man in black joined Rapp, said something to him. The pair shaded their eyes against the sun that was striking on the broad panes. Then Rapp whipped off his kepi and bellowed, "*À la fenétre, les vieux. C'est notre commandant!*" Doyle called huskily, "A cheer for the major, then!"

Gail saw the lines waver, saw Castex swinging his kepi about his head, saw ragged vizors lifted high on bayonet points, heard steady cheers thunder up as though six hundred throats had been shouting. At the far window Wilson stood like a statue, his hand raised in salute and his face pale and working. In the street, Father Doyle was shaking his stick while Rapp flailed the air with his fist. The crowd caught the infection, pointed to the stiff figure in the window and joined in the cheers of the Rifles.

Wilson dropped his hand quickly and stepped back out of sight. As one man the three ranks froze into rigid alignment, picked up the step flawlessly. Someone began to sing, "*Le caporal est un légume, Il baise, il boit, il chique, il fume . . .*"

Claire moved quickly to her husband's side. Gail and Dora leaned from the window to see the last of the

520

Rifles. Far ahead Gail caught a flash of brass as the bugles went whirling through the old French drill. There was her husband looming over the bayonets on Lisette. George and Bordagaray were close behind him, framed by the three bare poles of the colors. Sun played along the triple rows of steel and the Rochambeau Rifles were lost to sight.

Gail sat down quietly. More troops were going by but she could not watch them. A band thundered on, "I have seen Him in the watchfires of a hundred circling camps—"

But camps were done with. They were being trodden out by the steady beat of boots on the pavement. Camps by Mine Run, camps by lost stores and taverns in the Wilderness, by the James, before Petersburg—they and their watch fires were gone forever. After four years of agony, the Union stood unchallenged, and about its colors men from Massachusetts stood guard with men from Pomerania, Iowa watched with Brittany and County Meath with Maine. The names drummed in Gail's ears—Illinois and Catalonia—Breslau and Detroit—Providence and Arles. In the same uniform and under the same flag, men from the farthest reaches had become kin through the idea and the ideal for which flag and uniform stood.

Addenda

WHILE it is not possible to append sketches of all the foreign-born officers who have appeared in or been mentioned in the course of this book, a few brief biographies are presented below. Carl Schurz is omitted for the simple reason that he alone seems to remain in the public mind; to summarize his career would be to repeat what is generally known.

BARON, LATER COUNT, RÉGIS DE TROBRIAND commanded a division in the last years of the war. After Appomattox he returned to France with his wife (daughter of Isaac Jones, President of the Chemical Bank of New York) and there wrote, for European consumption, *Quatre Ans de Campagnes à l'Armée du Potomac*. While so engaged he was tendered a commission in the Regular Army by General Grant. This was a distinct tribute, since the whole trend in the United States was toward reducing the military establishment. De Trobriand was then fifty years old, but he seems to have looked upon this tender as another call from his adopted country. He accepted and soon was stationed at Fort Stevenson in the Dakotas. He fought Indians, pacified the

Mormons, brought peace to New Orleans, and wrote *La Vie Militaire dans les Dakotas*. Retiring as full major general of United States Regulars, he died at Bayport, Long Island, July 15, 1897.

ALFRED DUFFIÉ ended the war as a brigadier general of cavalry, his last principal service being the training of the cavalry brigades which formed the nucleus of Sheridan's forces in 1864-1865. Married to a girl from Staten Island, he left the army and was sent as United States Consul to Spain, where he died not long after his arrival, probably as a result of his war years here, added to severe wounds received in the French service in the Crimea and in Italy. He is buried in Providence, Rhode Island.

WLADIMIR KRZYZANOWSKI, called "Old Kriz" by his brother officers; like Duffié ended his career a brigadier general after long and distinguished service. After the war he resumed his profession of civil engineer, for which he had trained in Poland prior to the insurrections of 1846. In 1854 he, too, married an American girl, niece of General Burnett, U.S.A.

JOSEPH KARGE is claimed by both Germans and Poles, having been born, like Krzyzanowski, in what was then Prussian Poland. He finally reached the rank of brigadier. He served in the Regular Army until 1870 when he was given the chair of Continental Languages and Literature at Princeton University, a post which he held until 1892.

FREDERICK CAVADA, a Cuban, rose from captain to colonel. After the war he served as U.S. Consul at Cienfuegos, Cuba. He does not seem to have become a citizen as the Spanish government executed him as a dangerous rebel. American friends petitioned Washington to intervene in his behalf and the list of his sponsors from the old Army of the Potomac is an impressive one. There was no time to act, however, and Cavada was shot.

The Italian COUNT DI CESNOLA not only served

through the war but received the Congressional Medal of Honor. After 1865 he was appointed U.S. Consul at Cyprus, where his archaeological researches won him world-wide fame. From 1879 to 1904 he served as Director of the Metropolitan Museum of Art, New York City.

In this very brief listing of names drawn largely at random, I have not included the Comte de Paris, the Duc de Chartres, or the Prince de Joinville, who served with McClellan, nor the Prince de Penthièvre, who was identified with the Union Navy. They were strong Union sympathizers but took part rather as observers and did not identify themselves with the Union cause. Nor does Prince Salm-Salm with his Vermont wife, although he keeps bobbing up in the Northern armies, deserve to rank in the same class with men like Schurz and de Trobriand and Krzyzanowski.

There are many others, however, who may not here be given the attention that they merit. There was Sir Percy Wyndham, Colonel of the 1st New Jersey Cavalry. And how can one omit the Swiss, Emil Frey, who went from private to colonel in an Ohio regiment, served in Washington in the '70s as Swiss Minister and ended as President of the Swiss Confederation? No artilleryman can fail to be roused by the story of the Prussian, Hubert Dilger, commander of an Ohio battery. He was said to be the best gunner in the Union armies, which was high praise, and directed fire by a series of handclaps, although his voice was strong and his English excellent. He always went into action in a white shirt and white doeskin breeches.

And there were Magnicki and Ferrero and Sokalski and von Schimmelfennig and de Montheil and Bonnafon and O'Neil and Callahan. Whatever their origins, they may be marked with one common title—Soldier of the Union.

Brimming with the passion, intrigue, and excitement of America's great history is The Scarlet Patch, *the first of four books of Bruce Lancaster's brilliant historical romances set in the Civil War. As in the author's novels of the Revolutionary War, the Bicentennial Classics Series, which includes* Phantom Fortress, The Secret Road, Trumpet to Arms, *and* The Guns of Burgoyne, *this novel boldly portrays the people and events that altered the course of our great nation.* The Scarlet Patch *gives a compelling and authentic panorama of unforgettable people, thundering events, and families and lovers torn apart by their dedication to a cause. Watch for* No Bugles Tonight, *Pinnacle's second book in this series, coming in July, to be followed by* Night March *and* Roll Shenandoah.

In the tumultuous, romantic tradition of
Rosemary Rogers, Jennifer Wilde, and
Kathleen Woodiwiss

Love's Avenging Heart
Patricia Matthews

P987 $1.95

The stormy saga of Hannah McCambridge, whose fiery red hair, voluptuous body, and beautiful face made her irresistible to men...Silas Quint, her brutal stepfather, sold her as an indentured servant...Amos Stritch, the lascivious tavernkeeper, bought her and forced her to submit to his lecherous desires...Malcolm Verner, the wealthy master of Malvern Plantation, rescued her from a life of poverty and shame. But for Hannah, her new life at Malvern was just the beginning. She still had to find the man of her dreams—the man who could unleash the smouldering passions burning inside her and free her questing heart.

You've read other historical romances, now _live_ one!

If you can't find this book at your local bookstore, simply send the cover price, plus 25¢ for postage and handling to:

Pinnacle Books
275 Madison Avenue
New York, N.Y. 10016